CW00960119

THE
BEAST
IN THE
LABYRINTH

THE
BEAST
IN THE
LABYRINTH

TOBY ROBERTS

The Book Guild Ltd

First published in Great Britain in 2023 by
The Book Guild Ltd
Unit E2 Airfield Business Park,
Harrison Road, Market Harborough,
Leicestershire. LE16 7UL
Tel: 0116 2792299
www.bookguild.co.uk
Email: info@bookguild.co.uk
Twitter: @bookguild

Typeset in 11pt Adobe Garamond Pro

Printed on FSC accredited paper
Printed and bound in Great Britain by 4edge Limited

ISBN 978 1915603 135

British Library Cataloguing in Publication Data.
A catalogue record for this book is available from the British Library.

For Alex, Georgie and Oliver.

ACKNOWLEDGEMENTS

My gratitude is due first to the late, wondrous Clare Dunkel, who wrote her own splendidly violent novels under the pen name Mo Hayder. Without her encouragement and guidance, this volume would not have been completed. I picture her ghost laughing through eternity with a glass of champagne. Laugh on, darling, laugh on.

I am indebted to Professors John Yardley and Dexter Hoyos for their generous help with my research. Any remaining howlers are mine alone.

Several friends doggedly ploughed through earlier drafts and provided invaluable advice: Paul Leighton, Keith Norton, John-Andrew Ovenstone, Dave Carson, John Wallis, Sam Jordison and, perhaps above all, the brilliant literary critic Ian Watson. My heartfelt thanks to all of them.

For Sharon, my ever-loved and long-suffering wife, no words of appreciation would appear sufficient.

DRAMATIS PERSONAE

Italicised characters are historical.

Agatha: a slave woman of Korinna's.
Agathocles: a former tyrant of Syracuse.
Agbal: a young slave belonging to Dion.
Ajax: a sergeant in the City Guard.
Alexander (1): "the Great", King of Macedonia, founder of the Greek empire.
Alexander (2): a boy, a refugee from Pachynus.
Alpha: a Numidian slave belonging to Dion.
Andranodoros: a son-in-law of King Hieron, married to his younger daughter.
Apollonius: the brother-in-law of King Hieron, captain of the City Guard.
Archimedes: mathematician, cousin of King Hieron, great uncle of Dion. See historical notes at the end.
Aristarchus: an astronomer, credited as having been the first to demonstrate that the earth and planets revolve around the sun.
Aristo: an actor.

Castor: the adjutant of the City Guard.
Cerberus: an elderly slave, the porter at Dion's villa.

Chrysanthe: Archimedes' wife.
Cleopatra: a prostitute.

Delia: High Priestess of Athena, great aunt of Dion.
Demosthenes: an Athenian orator, famous for his denunciations of Philip of Macedonia.
Dinomenes: a soldier in the Royal Watch, a bodyguard of Prince Gelon.
Diogenes: a Cynic philosopher, said to have lived in a barrel. When Alexander the Great visited him, and offered him anything he wanted, Diogenes told Alexander just to stand out of his sunlight.
Dion ("The Bull of Syracuse"): the principal narrator.
Dionysia: Dion's sister.
Dionysius (1): a criminal.
Dionysius (2): Dion's father.
Dionysius **(3)**: the name of two former kings of Syracuse, ancestors of Dion's.

Eryx: an army captain, commander of the Yellow Shield division.
"Etna" (Jason): a former army boxing champion.
Eulus: the commander of the Syracusian cavalry.

Felix: a Roman officer, son of Senator Torquatus.

Gelon **(1)**: Prince of Syracuse, heir of King Hieron.
Gelon **(2)**: a former king of Syracuse, ancestor of Theodotus.

Hannibal: general of the Carthaginian army.
Hannon: an African slave in the royal household.
Harmonia: daughter of Prince Gelon, wife of Themistos ("Woodpecker").
Heraclia: elder daughter of King Hieron, wife of Zoippos, sister of Gelon.
Hieron: King of Syracuse.

Hieronymus: son of Prince Gelon, grandson of King Hieron.

Ision: a Royal Councillor, responsible for the slave population.

Kallikrates: a minor mathematician.
Kleitos: a soldier in the Royal Watch, bodyguard of Archimedes.
Kleoxenos: a former Olympic boxing champion.
Korinna: Dion's mother, niece of Archimedes.

Leander: a young officer in the City Guard.
"Leatherskin" (Polyaenus): a Royal Councillor, Speaker of the Senate, father-in-law of Theodotus.
Leon: a sergeant in the City Guard.
Lepides: late general of Syracuse.
Linus: Dion's lawyer and business manager.

Maia: mother of Thraso, paternal aunt of Dion, priestess of Athena.
Malmeides: an officer in the City Guard.
Marcellus: a Roman general. One of only two men ever to win the *spolia opima*, an honour reserved for commanders who killed the enemy leader in single combat.
Medon: a soldier in the Royal Watch, one of Korinna's bodyguards.

Nebit: an Egyptian eunuch, a secretary of King Hieron's.
Needle: a soldier in the City Guard.
Nereis: wife of Prince Gelon, mother of Hieronymus and Harmonia.
Nico: an army lieutenant of Carthaginian descent.

Omega: a Numidian slave belonging to Dion.
Otacilius: the commander of Rome's Sicilian fleet, half-bother of Marcellus.

Pelion: a distant relative by marriage of Dion's.
Perdix: a stable boy, a child slave of Dion's.
Phidias: a soldier in the Royal Watch, one of Korinna's bodyguards.

Philistis: late wife of King Hieron, sister of Apollonius.

Philocrates: an elderly secretary of King Hieron's.

Phylas: a soldier in the City Guard.

Piso: a young soldier, son of Dinomenes.

Polybius: Greek historian. The earliest source for the events described here, although parts of his account have been lost. Livy, who relied on Polybius, provides a more complete record.

Ptolemy: the hereditary name of a line of Egyptian kings of Greek descent. Cleopatra and her son Ptolemy XV were the last of the dynasty.

Seema: wife of Senator Torquatus, mother of Vita, niece of King Hieron.

Sophia: a distant relative of Dion's, wife of Pelion.

Sosis: adjutant and subsequently captain of the Gold Shield division.

Tabnit: priest of Ba'al, leader of the Carthaginian community in Syracuse.

Theodotos: captain of the White Shield division, Dion's best friend.

Thraso: a Royal Councillor, cousin of Dion.

Torquatus: a leading Roman senator, father of Dion's bride Vita.

Vita: Dion's bride, daughter of Torquatus and Seema.

"Woodpecker" (Themistos): husband of Gelon's daughter Harmonia.

Xeno: a one-handed veteran officer in the City Guard.

Zoippos: elder son-in-law of King Hieron, husband of Heraclia.

Zopyros of Syracuse: an Olympic sprint champion.

CHARACTERS REFERENCED
FROM GREEK LEGENDS

Achilles: hero of the Trojan War. Dipped in the River Styx as an infant, the only vulnerable part of his body was the heel by which his mother had held him.

Hercules (properly, Herakles): the son of Zeus and a mortal woman, celebrated for his supernatural strength. Having killed his own sons in a fit of madness, he undertook the Twelve Labours in atonement.

Icarus: Icarus's father Daedalus made two pairs of wings, to enable them to flee the island of Crete. Despite his father's warnings, Icarus flew too close to the sun. The wax holding the feathers to his wings melted, and he fell to his death.

Jason: captain of the Argonauts, who led them in the quest for the Golden Fleece.

The Minotaur: for a summary of the myth and its significance, see the historical notes at the end.

Odysseus: the protagonist of Homer's *Odyssey*, the story of his ten-year voyage home after the Trojan War.

PROLOGUE

THE FIRST FRAGMENT

I, Archimedes the mathematician, son of Phidias the astronomer, prostrate myself before the goddess of wisdom. May Athena restore our people to her favour and see us through the descending storm.

In the preceding volumes of this confidential history, I described how my cousin Hieron assumed the vacant throne of Syracuse, though he had no very obvious right to it.

I also explained how he turned the twenty-year war between the empires of Rome and Carthage to his own advantage.

At the point at which I left off, matters stood as follows: that war had at last stuttered to a close, with Rome having got the better of it. Chief among the territories that she had forced the Carthaginians to cede was the province of Greater Sicily, which abutted our kingdom on the east of the island. Shrewdly, Hieron had chosen to side with the Romans, so at least our new neighbours looked on us as friends, in much the same way as a crocodile might regard the bird perched on its head as a friend.

In any event, by then, both barbarian empires were so utterly exhausted that neither appeared capable of menacing Syracuse for several generations – which had of course been the object of my cousin's policy from the outset. The fact that he had anonymously passed the Carthaginians helpful information on many occasions, in order to bleed his allies as thoroughly as his enemies, was a secret of which Rome naturally remained ignorant. It says much for Hieron's masterful handling of affairs that our own lands had emerged from the carnage largely untouched by it and significantly expanded.

In this volume, I turn to the years of peace that ensued, and I must begin my account of them by introducing another branch of my singularly gifted if somewhat reptilian family.

My great-nephew was first forced upon my attention when the number of my years was ten times his own and was also twice the square of his. I had been informed of his birth five years earlier, and had rather casually assumed that he had continued to draw breath ever since. At any rate, I could not recall anyone having told me otherwise. But apart from his name, that was all I knew of the boy.

My wife, Chrysanthe, and I were both at our desks, working away in pleasurable silence, when a slave girl entered the study to hand me my niece's letter. I examined the seal uncomfortably, in two minds as to whether even to open it.

It would be a redundancy to describe the interruption as unwelcome. Although the war had been over for a year, Hieron was still making considerable demands on my time, and such spare hours as I enjoyed I wished to devote to my own studies. I had recently embarked upon an analysis of the stable equilibrium positions of certain floating paraboloids, which promised to result in a treatise of exceptional interest, and desired no more of humanity than that it might desist from bothering me.

After a few moments, I sighed and broke the seal. I couldn't help grunting in relief as I scanned the contents. Nothing that could not readily be ignored.

I tossed the note onto the pile of correspondence that lay on the floor to the left of my chair. Those were the letters in which I had no interest, mainly from people begging my help with something or other. I used to receive a surprising number asking if I could bring dead children back to life. I left it to my two secretaries in the room next door to deal with that pile. The letters that I might get round to answering myself at some point lay in a heap to my right. Enquiries from fellow mathematicians made up most of those. Only messages from the king were ever accorded the honour of an immediate place on my desk, although his own correspondence was more usually addressed to Chrysanthe.

I suppose this is the currency of fame, I told myself gloomily, as I surveyed the papyrus scrolls clustered accusingly around my chair. There were days when I almost regretted my own brilliance.

I returned to my work, only to find my concentration disrupted by an annoying tug of guilt. Of my many relations, I had been closest to my sister and her daughter was all that now remained of her. After some minutes, I reluctantly bent over to retrieve my niece's letter, and dropped it onto the pile to the right of my feet instead.

Chrysanthe noticed me do so.

"So, who's that one from, Husband?" she asked in amusement. "Another merchant wanting you to build him a flying machine?"

I chuckled.

"No, my love. It seems Korinna would like me to tutor her boy. Do you know, I can't remember ever setting eyes on him."

"I trust you are going to accept. You need the distraction: you've been terribly grumpy these last few months. You do so enjoy teaching clever children and he's bound to be clever if he's her son."

She picked up a small silver bell from her desk and rang it to summon one of her own assistants. She had six of them toiling away further down the corridor, and a most curious menagerie of characters they were too; but then, her work was of a very different nature to my own.

"Do you really think I should?" I said.

"Oh yes, most definitely. You see far too little of your family. You really ought to make more of an effort to descend from Mount

Olympus occasionally, dear. And it would be a pleasant change for me not to have to listen to you grunting and snuffling all day long."

✳

And so it was that, a week later, I found myself responding to Korinna's invitation to call on her at the preposterously large town house of her husband. Happily, he was overseas at the time. If I remember rightly, Hieron had packed him off on a goodwill visit to the city of Corinth, presumably with a view to sharing the burden of the man's existence with someone else. I still regard it as something of a miracle that the Corinthians did not sever all relations in protest. Why my niece, no cheerful sufferer of fools, should have been so devoted to her swaggering husband is a mystery that even I cannot fathom.

The gates of the house were opened to my knock, and after being left to kick my heels for a few minutes in the colonnade of the main courtyard, a slave appeared and led me through to the garden at the side of the compound.

Korinna, then in her early twenties, was sitting in the shade of a canopy of vines. When she saw me approaching, she put the scroll in her hand aside and stood in greeting. Like me, she was tall and thin, but had been spared my own protuberant ears and beak of a nose. It was certainly not to my side of her family that she owed her beauty.

"Uncle," she said coolly as we embraced, "you look well."

"As do you, Korinna. It has been too long."

She beckoned forward one of the two slave girls who were standing in attendance behind her.

"Pour Archimedes a cup of water, would you, and then go and find Dion."

Korinna gathered her dress and returned to her chair, flicking back her long blonde hair, while I settled myself on a stool opposite. Neither of us had ever had much appetite for small talk, and to my relief she went straight to the point.

"Thank you for coming, Archimedes. I'm afraid I can't tell you much about the child, except that he strikes me as a blockhead. Do what you can with him. I do not expect dazzling results; it will be sufficient if he is eventually able to understand the estate accounts… For pity's sake, Uncle, must you chew on your beard like that? It really is a most repulsive habit… Thank you… Anyway, the boy's governess tells me that he has mastered his twice tables but cannot yet multiply by three. As to his character, he seems to veer between extreme obstinacy and a puppyish desire to please. Feel free to beat him, or if you prefer, have the governess beat him for you. If there is anything else you need to know about him, she will no doubt be able to answer you better than I. Would you like me to send for her?"

This is what comes from opening letters, I thought. I should have known better. What a waste of a morning.

"No, that won't be necessary… Look, forgive me for being blunt, my dear. I'm afraid I'm going to have to disappoint you. I assumed your son was clever enough for you to think he might be of interest to me. But from what you say…" I snorted lightly. "Well, this just isn't going to work. I'm already extremely busy, and it would hardly appear to be a good use of my time. I'm sorry, but there it is."

Korinna gazed at me thoughtfully for a moment, as if trying to match her wits against my own. I confess I was mildly amused by her presumption.

"Uncle," she replied eventually, "Dion is the heir to a great fortune and an even greater name. He descends in an unbroken male line from the most revered of our ancient kings. And given that the boy also happens to be a close relative of yours, surely it would look rather odd for anyone else to tutor him? Naturally, he will have a separate tutor for his other subjects: you need only try to teach him some mathematics. That hardly seems too much to ask of you, does it?" She paused briefly to examine the red paint on her fingernails. "Of course, should you decline, I suppose I could always engage Kallikrates instead…"

I stared at her.

"Kallikrates…? *Kallikrates?*" I spluttered.

She looked up at me in apparent surprise.

"Oh, you do not approve of him, then?"

"Surely you can't be serious, Korinna? The fool can barely count his own toes."

"Well, if you say so, Uncle. But he *is* highly recommended…" She smiled coldly. "Of course, you and I would both know that he was only my second choice, although that is not necessarily what the world would think, is it? I dare say Kallikrates would waste no time in telling everyone that your own niece preferred him to you."

She folded her hands placidly in her lap, leaving me to gurgle indignantly. Kallikrates, indeed! (A man whose treatise on polyhedra had contained no fewer than six errors, and who had thanked me for listing them all, during a dinner party we had both attended, by throwing his water in my face.)

"Well, I do hope you will reconsider…" Korinna resumed. "Ah, here's the boy now."

A child had emerged from the house holding the hand of the slave girl who had been sent to fetch him. A little wooden sword dangled from his belt and he was wearing a helmet that someone must have glued together for him out of old scraps of papyrus. Apart from the two eye slits, his face was entirely hidden behind a haphazard patchwork of paragraphs.

"Dion, take off that absurd thing," his mother snapped. "Can't you even make an appearance without embarrassing me?"

"I'm sorry, Mother," the boy replied, and carefully removed the fragile helmet.

They say the gods sometimes father earthly sons. Perhaps it's true. Dion's curly golden hair reached down to his shoulders; his eyes were large and sapphire blue and his lips full. Even then, he had a square, firm arrangement of features that seemed to speak to his future character. I have never had the slightest physical interest in children, but I dare say he was the most entrancing child I had ever seen.

"Take that helmet away from him," Korinna said irritably to the slave girl.

Dion meekly handed it over.

"I want you to go and throw it in the kitchen fire," my niece continued. "I never wish to see him wearing it again."

The boy's eyes widened in a desperate plea.

"One squeak out of you, Dion, and you'll feel a willow switch on your backside for good measure. Now, pay attention. This is your Great Uncle Archimedes. He is a very famous man and, apparently, also a busy one, but I am hoping he will agree to teach you some mathematics. Greet him, answer any questions he may have of you, and then leave us."

The child's chin quivered and he gulped as he struggled to choke back his tears. I tried to smile reassuringly at him. He managed a quick bow in my general direction, then turned and scampered back into the house, clearly not trusting himself to speak. The flustered slave girl hurried after him, cradling the condemned helmet.

Korinna sighed.

"I apologise for Dion's manners, Uncle," she said. "I'll deal with him later."

In the event, I only tutored my great-nephew for slightly over a year, seeing him every other day for two hours or so. In that time, I grew very fond of him. He was open and willing, and I do not recall ever having had occasion to reprimand him. I heard from his other tutor that he was proving reasonably adept at languages; sadly, mathematics remained to Dion an impenetrable fog, through which he could do no more than stumble bravely but blindly. On those rare occasions that he chanced to trip over a correct answer, he had no idea how it came to be lying there and nor could he retrace his footsteps. The best he could usually manage was to smile sweetly and shrug; and yet I hope he was able to derive some small enjoyment from my lessons, even if he profited little from them.

It was ultimately a regret to me that our arrangement proved so short-lived, and all the more so for the memorably unpleasant way in which it was brought to an end.

I had arrived at the house at the appointed time, to find Dion and his governess waiting for me as usual under the archway of the main entrance gate.

"You can only have the boy for an hour today, sir," the slave woman announced with obvious satisfaction, crossing her arms over her breasts, which seemed to merge with her belly to form a single amorphous pulp. "His father wants him after that. I'll come and collect him from you."

I waved my hand dismissively at her. She sneered back and turned to waddle off in the direction of the slaves' yard.

"So, Dion," I remarked casually as we crossed the courtyard, "perhaps when you grow up, you'll be a great soldier like your father. I hear he has recently started teaching you to ride. Is that the reason we must cut our time short?"

The child looked up at me. I can only describe his expression as something close to terror.

It took me a minute or two to get it out of him, but what he had to say struck me as so distasteful that I found I could not put it out of my mind for the duration of the lesson. We sat side by side in the villa's schoolroom, an airless chamber in the attics that was scarcely larger than a cupboard.

"Now," I said, when I judged that the greater part of our hour had been expended, "I think that's quite enough of triangles for one day. Perhaps it's time I taught you a little about the arrangement of the sun and planets instead. Would you like that?"

Dion grinned and nodded. Mind you, he would probably have grinned and nodded at any suggestion that spared him from further Pythagorean torments.

"Good," I said. "But maybe it would be better to do this outdoors. Tell me, is there a quiet corner of the garden where we won't be disturbed?"

Dion thought about it for a moment.

"Well, there's the herb garden, Great-uncle. Would that do?"

"It sounds like it might do very well. Why don't you show me? And bring some wax tablets with you."

The herb garden proved perfect for my stratagem, being concealed behind a high hedge. We sat on the small central patch of grass, while I drew diagrams on the wax tablets. Dion nodded attentively but I am not sure how much he managed to absorb.

I had decided to teach the boy the theory of Aristarchus, which holds that the sun is the immobile hub, around which the earth and planets revolve, while the stars are sewn like sequins into the periphery of the cosmos. Old Aristarchus had only died the year before, still pathetically grateful to me for having endorsed his ideas in a treatise of my own. That was the celebrated paper in which I estimated how many grains of sand it might take to fill the universe. Of course, the only purpose of the exercise had been to demonstrate my methods for expressing and manipulating immense numbers. No mathematician before me had ever attempted a calculation on such a scale, for the simple reason that the means to do so did not exist, till I invented them. Still, I was pleased to have done Aristarchus a favour along the way. I am not a man who needs be jealous of the modest achievements of others.

But to resume: it soon became apparent that each successive diagram was merely compounding Dion's bafflement, and so in the end I resolved on a more practical approach.

"Dion, imagine that I am the sun," I said, rising to my feet. "I shall stand here, in the middle of the lawn. Now, imagine that you are the earth. I want you to walk slowly around me in a circle, spinning as you go… Go on… Yes, that's it… Well done… Now, let's pretend that your nose is the kingdom of Syracuse. You will find that sometimes it is pointing towards me, and sometimes it is pointing away from me. You see? And that's the reason we have days and nights."

"But, Great-uncle, I don't understand," he said, stopping in his tracks. "The sun comes up over there and goes down over there, behind the slaves' yard. So it doesn't stand still, does it? It moves over the house and then it goes down under the earth and comes up over there again."

"Ah, but that's just an illusion, Dion. Imagine that you are standing on a boat, sailing along the coast. It may seem as though the coast is moving, but in fact, you are the one who is moving."

"So you mean, the earth is a boat?"

I beamed at him.

"Yes, that's it, Dion. Well done! You've got it!"

He scratched his head.

"So, when the sun goes down under the earth, does that mean we've capsized?"

"Well, yes, I suppose so, in a way."

"So why don't we fall out?"

It was at this moment that we were interrupted by the governess, who stomped into the herb garden in a foul mood that she made no effort to hide.

"Ah, I thought I heard your voices," she grunted breathlessly. "I've been running all over looking for you two. You really had no business bringing him out here, sir: I told you I'd need to fetch him. Anyway, come along now, Dion, that's quite enough of this nonsense. You're late already."

"Stay exactly where you are, Dion, " I snapped.

The governess glared at me.

"But sir, the master said he wants Dion with him…"

"Oh, go away, you silly woman! Can't you see I'm trying to teach the boy something important?" I flapped my hand at her. "Well, what's keeping you? Go on: clear off!"

"But sir, the master's waiting…"

"Go away!"

She seemed inclined to argue the point further, but then thought better of it and muttered something under her breath instead. She turned and sullenly lumbered back towards the house, no doubt to consult my niece.

The boy looked at me gratefully.

I resumed our lesson, but with a stone in my heart. It was obvious there was no hope of getting Dion out of it now. I had merely repelled the scouting party; the main body of the enemy had yet to fall upon us.

Sure enough, before long, I heard Korinna's voice, shouting angrily from an upstairs window. I turned to look up at her.

"What on earth are you doing down there, Archimedes? Why aren't you in the schoolroom? You're supposed to be teaching the child, not playing with him! I've had half the household searching for you. Dion, stay there. Don't you dare move. I'm sending Alpha to fetch you."

"I am explaining the universe to him," I yelled back indignantly. "What's the point of getting me to tutor him, if you're going to keep interrupting us?"

She slammed the shutter closed without bothering to reply, and a few minutes later, a lanky Numidian slave came running to find us.

He bowed politely to me.

"I am very sorry, sir," he said sadly, "but I am afraid I really must take him."

I sighed and nodded in defeat. There was always a certain satisfaction to be had in vexing the governess, but I had no wish to get this young fellow into any trouble.

Alpha squatted and held out his long black arms.

"Come to me, Dion. It's alright," he said with a smile.

The child looked from one to the other of us with an expression of despair. I shrugged, pursed my lips and beckoned him over. For a moment he stood still and then he ran across the grass to fling his arms around the slave's neck.

As Alpha lifted him up, the child took in a few sharp gasps and I saw a tear drip onto the slave's shoulder blade and trickle down his back.

The boy sniffled.

"I don't want to watch, Alpha," I heard him say. "Can't you hide me?"

"No, I'm sorry, Dion. Your father has said he wants you there. So you must try to be my brave little soldier. But don't worry, it won't last very long. And I'll be there too. Then afterwards, we can go and find a treat for you in the kitchens. Alright?"

He stroked the child's hair and squatted again to set him back down.

"Alright?" he asked a second time, wiping the boy's cheek with his finger. "What a good, brave little man you are. Come on then, let's get this over with."

Alpha straightened up and took the boy's hand. I noticed the slave clench his jaw.

It was time to go home. It seemed there was nothing further I could do, and I certainly had no desire to join Dion at his father's repugnant spectacle.

I followed the pair of them across the garden and down the passageway that led to the villa's main courtyard. We made our way in silence around the colonnade to a small gate on the far side.

"Well, I shall leave you here, Dion," I said. "By next week, I expect you to know your twelve times table. Alright?"

"Yes, Great-uncle. I'll try."

I patted his head clumsily and sighed. I might as well have asked him to fly to the moon as to master his times tables.

Alpha nodded to me grimly, then opened the gate and led the boy by the hand into the slaves' yard. As they walked away, I stepped forward to lean against the edge of the gateway for a moment.

In the yard, a thickly bearded giant of a man was waiting beside a table in the sun, his legs apart and his hands on his hips.

"About time!" he bellowed.

"I'm sorry, Master," Alpha replied, bowing timidly. "I'm afraid there must have been some confusion over your instructions."

The man glared at his slave and then he looked across to glare at me instead. I scowled back at him.

"If I find you had any part in this, Alpha, you'll be next... Now, come here, Dion. Stand by me."

The slave let go of the boy's hand and propelled him gently forwards. The child lowered his head and walked slowly over to his father, dragging his feet across the dust.

"Go and join the others, Alpha," the big man said curtly, nodding towards the two lines of slaves who had assembled in the shade by the stable block. There must have been over forty of them altogether, men and women of different races and various ages, with nothing obviously in common, apart from their expressions of fear.

The big man took a deep breath and slowly exhaled again.

"Go on, Dion, look at him," he said, a little more quietly.

The child forced himself to glance over at the slave who stood alone in a corner of the yard. A piece of rag had been stuffed into his mouth and his wrists had been bound together with a leather thong and tied to a wooden post. He stared back at the boy, silently twisting and pulling at the bindings, his eyes wide.

The man looked down at his son and rested a hand on his shoulder. He smiled, in what I imagine was meant to be an encouraging manner.

"I know this is going to be hard for you to watch, Dion, but there's something I need to explain to you… Are you listening to me? Good. But look at me when I'm talking to you… Now, we've cared for this fellow his whole life. We've fed him and given him clothes and somewhere safe to live and a bed to sleep on at night. But he still stole from me. There are rules in this world, son. Without those rules, we would just run around like wild animals, killing each other and stealing whatever we want. You wouldn't like that, would you?"

The boy shook his head meekly.

"No, I should think not. But rules only work, Dion, if men like you and me are willing to punish the people who break them. That is our duty. It is the price we pay for being born into a great family. So that is why I need to make an example of this man. I don't particularly want to do it, but I must. Do you understand?"

The boy looked down miserably and nodded, although I doubt he understood at all.

"Good lad," said the giant. "Don't let me down, now. Remember who you are."

He turned and picked up the whip that lay on the table beside him, allowing the end to drop to the ground to uncoil it.

As he gave it a loud crack in the air to loosen his arm, Dion winced and cringed, and began to cry again.

His father frowned at him, apparently uncertain what to do. He narrowed his eyes and tapped his thigh a few times with the handle of the whip.

"Stop that," he barked.

But Dion couldn't stop.

The giant bristled; his nostrils flared. He hesitated for a moment, and then he raised his free hand and slapped the boy sharply across the face, spinning him round and leaving him sprawling in the dirt.

"I warned you," he said awkwardly. He stared down at his son and bit his lip. He seemed as much confused as angry. "Now, get up. And for pity's sake, stop snivelling."

The first lash landed on the slave's back as Dion was still coming to his feet. It split open the skin across the man's shoulders and threw up a misty red spray. The slave's head jerked sharply backwards and his whole body went taut, his muscles straining in silent paroxysm.

As Dion's father drew back his arm again, I turned away in disgust and started walking around the colonnade to the entrance gate. To make a child watch that... It was a relief to be escaping into the jostling and noisy world outside.

I was not entirely surprised to receive a note from Korinna the following afternoon, thanking me for my efforts, but informing me that she would trouble me no further. Given how little progress Dion seemed to be making, she had decided that she may as well engage Kallikrates after all. Better that his time should be wasted, she wrote, than mine.

As I have already explained, I have chosen to arrange these recollections chronologically rather than thematically, which is why I have recorded my earliest encounters with Dion at this point in my narrative. I shall of course be returning to him in later chapters, but I must now move on to explaining the system of agricultural tithes that Hieron introduced at this time. Just before I do so, however, I shall indulge in a modest digression.

There are many among my acquaintance who maintain that my great-nephew is the creation of circumstances; that is to say, that Dion might well have passed unnoticed from history, had the Carthaginians not recovered far more rapidly than anyone expected, to the point that they were able to launch their terrible war of revenge on Rome a mere twenty-three years after their debilitating defeat. I do not agree with this opinion of my friends, for it is a peculiarity of my family that our gifts are as exceptional as they are diverse. Hieron's genius for power would have raised him to prominence in any circumstances, just as my own facility for mathematics was certain to bring me to the world's attention, no matter the era in which I happened to be born. And though he gave no indication of it as a child, it is now all too apparent that my great-nephew is possessed of an equally pronounced talent, which ensured that he too was always destined to leave his mark.

Naturally, I kept my eye on Dion as he grew to manhood, although I did so from a discreet distance. At first, I was obliged to request reports of him from others; but later, as his reputation grew, I found news of him coming my way without my having to ask for it. It is only recently, almost quarter of a century after he ceased to be my pupil, and with the world again in flames, that I have once more had close dealings with him. There are no mathematics to unravel the human soul, so I do not pretend to understand how my great-nephew became the man that he is. There are moments when I can still glimpse the sweet-natured child in him; but for the most part, I now regard him with much the same dread that he inspires in everybody else. To what ends he will ultimately choose to put his genius for violence, I cannot say.

I

SHADOWS OF THE DEAD

"If I never have to see this piss puddle of a place again, I won't regret it," Sosis muttered, as we strode out through the gates of the little city. "Is this what we joined the fucking army for?"

"It's their own fault," I replied. "The stupid bastards should have known better."

"Maybe. But you can't really blame them, Dion. They were just hungry."

"Well, at least it's done with now. That's five weeks of our lives we won't be getting back. I can certainly blame them for that... By the way, well done. You did a good job back there."

"Thank you," he said, smiling sadly.

Behind us, I could hear the rhythmic tramping of my men following us out. I'd only brought five hundred of them with me, but I had known it would be more than enough.

Kamarina lay in a remote corner of the kingdom, and the road ahead was stony and uneven. It would take us a week to get back to the army base at Plymmerium. I didn't mind; at least every day's hard marching would see us further from this miserable place.

We passed between the two short rows of crosses that lined the way immediately outside the gates. The twenty men hanging from them had all been dead for nearly a fortnight. I knew that smell well enough, but it still made me wince. Dense black clouds of flies swirled around each of the corpses, half-obscuring their contorted faces.

I rolled my tongue around my cheek, tracing the inside edge of the scar that gives my lip its curl. What idiots, I thought. What had they expected to happen? Had they seriously imagined that our king was the sort of man who might just do nothing, while a mob went on the rampage in one of his cities?

Food prices had been rising for months, as we watched our grain sailing over the horizon to feed our desperate allies. I suppose there was always likely to be trouble eventually, and no doubt Kamarina had always been the most likely place for any trouble to start. The Carthaginians had massacred the entire population two centuries earlier, down to the last infant. We had resettled it, of course, but the city had never really managed to recover; it still lay partly ruined, its public spaces uncared for, its trade hopelessly diminished. The inhabitants had the air of whipped dogs, uncertain whether to cringe or bite.

The nauseating smell gradually receded behind me. Twenty wasted lives, I thought, just to remind them why cringing was wiser. But at least there should be no more bother from Kamarina.

We followed the road back towards Syracuse as it twisted wildly around our jagged shoreline. I led the column myself, as I liked to set the pace and preferred not to eat other men's dust. Sosis marched beside me. After a while I slowed down, to ease the strain on his short legs.

Not for the first time, I congratulated myself on having had the foresight to bring him along. While I had set about persuading the inhabitants of Kamarina to behave, my clever adjutant had organised a rationing system for them. So perhaps things might be a little easier for the people now, I thought, though I doubted any improvement would last very long… Well, better an occasional empty belly, than that the Carthaginians should ever visit them again.

There was hardly a town or village through which we passed that did not have its own dismal memories, handed down from generation to generation like some hereditary deformity. Wherever we stopped to refill our flasks or rest for the night, we found only silent market squares and shuttered-up houses. The sight of approaching men in armour, even their own, still sent our villagers scuttling off into the hills and woods.

Fuck it, I thought, as I kicked in the door of a fisherman's cottage. A little gratitude would not have been unwelcome.

Inside, I unslung my shield and unbuckled my breastplate, relieved to be free of the weight. It was our third night on the march and it seemed I would be sharing a dirt floor with the mice again. Whoever owned the place might have done better to stay behind; perhaps they could have earned themselves a silver coin. The whores and rent boys of Kamarina had been too scrawny and diseased to tempt me, and I was starving for some cunt or arse.

The night proved restless and uncomfortable and when I rose at daybreak, I felt even stiffer than when I had lain down. I walked out into the first weak glints of sunshine, still in my undergarment, and began stretching and touching my toes to try to relieve the tension in my muscles.

The reveille drum had not yet been beaten, but several dozen men were awake and sitting on their haunches on the rocky beach, shaving each other or eating. Others were standing around listlessly in small groups. From their scratching, it looked like quite a few of them had already become lousy.

Agbal, my new camp slave, was perched cross-legged on a low ledge a few paces away, staring out to sea. When he noticed me approaching, he hurriedly jumped down and bowed. He was about fifteen or sixteen, I guessed, and still rather nervous in my company. I had only recently won the boy in a drunken game of dice, and had brought him along to get the measure of him before deciding on his future. It crossed my mind that perhaps I should give him to Sosis, as a token of appreciation.

On the rock beside him, Agbal had set out a bowl of water, a leather flask and some food wrapped in a piece of cloth. I grunted appreciatively. I washed my hands and face, then leant against the ledge and unwrapped my breakfast. It was just a hunk of barley bread and some dried fruit: Agbal already knew that I ate the same food as my men. I took a sip of water from the flask, rinsed my mouth and spat.

"Master, may I ask you a question?" he said, as he emptied out the washbowl and squatted down to rinse it in a rock pool. His hair was black and his skin swarthy, but he had blue eyes. He had probably been whelped on some Carthaginian slave girl by her Greek master. Or perhaps the other way round. I wasn't interested enough to ask.

I put some bread in my mouth and nodded reluctantly. I could guess what was coming.

"Are the stories about you true, Master? About all the men you've killed?"

"What stories?" I replied sourly, as I chewed on the bread. "Do you mean, like the one about how I once cut out and ate the tongue of a slave who talked too much?"

He laughed.

"I hadn't heard that one, Master." He had a wide, rather engaging smile. "No, I mean, like... well... like the one about how you were once attacked by three thieves with knives in an alleyway. And that you were unarmed and as drunk as a Gaul, but that you killed them all anyway and walked away without a scratch... Is that really true?"

It was one of the stories my regulars liked to tell the trainees.

"Soldiers exaggerate, Agbal. Now shut up and let me eat."

He smiled happily again, apparently taking my words as confirmation.

But soldiers do exaggerate. It so happened I had nearly died on that particular night. I had taken a nasty cut on the thigh, and another on my forearm, and had ended up in bandages for over a fortnight. And I had only killed two of them. The third I had left with a broken back, for the magistrates to crucify in their own good time, if they thought it worth the trouble.

✳

Later, while the sergeants reformed the column, my officers and I inspected the other buildings in the hamlet. Apart from their splintered door catches, they were tidy enough. On the way to Kamarina, I had made a man march naked for a day for having used a peasant's hovel as a latrine; they all seemed to have got the message after that.

We moved out in silence. Sosis and I had already run out of conversation and by then neither of us felt much like talking anyway.

We had been on the road for maybe two hours when I saw a solitary rider rounding a bend ahead of us. His breastplate glinted in the sun. I brought the column to a halt and walked forward to greet him alone. He drew up, dismounted and saluted, clearly somewhat intimidated. Like most men, he stood a head shorter than me.

I gestured irritably for him to speak.

"Sir, Captain Theodotus sent me to find you. There's news from the camp. He thought you would want to hear it before you got back."

"So, what is it then?"

What he had to say was hardly a surprise, but it still fell on my ears like a slamming door. Our general was dead, at last.

The old man had been writhing in his cot for weeks, intermittently delirious but stubbornly protracting his own ordeal for as long as he could drag it out. It was from his sickbed that Lepides had ordered me to Kamarina through gritted teeth.

I swore under my breath. For years, I had dreaded the sight of that neatly pointed beard suddenly appearing as if from nowhere, always bringing with it the promise of some new petty cruelty. I should have felt relieved to be free of him, but Lepides had commanded the army for so long that the news only aggravated my already unsettled mood.

"So who's to be our new general?" I asked after a moment or two. "Has it been announced yet?"

"Yes, sir," the messenger replied, nodding excitedly. "That's what I've come to tell you. It's Prince Gelon himself. He's already at Plymmerium."

Now, that at least was a surprise. I frowned as I tried to work out what it meant. I was the captain of the Gold Shields, one of the army's three infantry divisions; my two fellow captains were both a few years older than me and I'd expected one or the other of them to get the appointment.

"Very well," I said. "Is there anything else?"

"Only this, sir. Apparently the general sent it over for you the day before he died. Your slaves asked me to bring it to you."

He fumbled around in his satchel and finally produced a wax tablet. There was a single sentence scratched on it in a hand I didn't recognise. Lepides must have already been too weak to write it out himself. *'Perhaps you will restore your family's good name one day. L.'* That was all it said.

I had no idea whether it was intended as a compliment or a final taunt.

"Do you have any message you want me to take back to camp for you, sir?"

"No. We'll be there ourselves soon enough."

I dismissed the messenger and beckoned the column forward. As he approached, Sosis raised his eyebrows in enquiry.

"Lepides?" he asked.

I pursed my lips and nodded.

I found I was still holding the wax tablet. I didn't really know what to do with it. After a moment's thought, I drew back my arm and hurled it as far out to sea as I could.

A few days later, we finally marched back into the camp at Plymmerium, tired and covered in dust. In the wide exercise yard, the trainees of the White Shield division were practising how to manoeuvre in a phalanx, the densely packed block of men that was our standard battle formation. Going directly forwards in a phalanx is easy enough; moving in any other direction is another matter. The young conscripts were struggling with their sarissas, the huge two-handed spears with which the front ranks are armed. My men and I watched in amusement as one of them inadvertently lifted the tip of his spear, allowing the butt to drop and tripping up the man behind him. The effects quickly rippled out, till maybe thirty men lay sprawling in a heap. The whole formation began to dissolve, with some men being brought to a halt while others continued to advance.

Theodotus, the White Shield captain, was my best friend. He gave me a wave across the yard and shrugged his shoulders in good-humoured despair, while his lieutenants and sergeants bellowed at the trainees to try to restore order.

I formed up my men, congratulated them on their performance and dismissed them. I was dirty and unshaved, so I gave Agbal my shield and helmet and told him to meet me at the bathhouse with a clean tunic. I would see the officers I had left in charge of the remainder of the division once I had washed the filth of Kamarina off my skin.

I headed straight to the bathhouse, but before I reached it, an African slave whom I didn't recognise came running up to me.

"Excuse me, Master," he said, in a thick accent, "but are you Captain Dion?" He was nearly as tall as me, with wide-set bulging eyes that gave him something of the appearance of a mantis. It was impossible to judge his age.

I nodded.

"In that case, Master, the prince sends his compliments and requests that you join him at his villa."

I exhaled heavily.

"Very well. When does the prince want me to come over?"

"Now, Master."

"Alright. I'll be there as soon as I've cleaned myself up."

"Master, if I may say so, Prince Gelon is not a man who minds the sight of a little dust. But he may mind being kept waiting unnecessarily. I was told to bring you to him as soon as you returned."

I couldn't help smiling. I turned and wearily headed off towards the general's villa at the far end of the camp but, to my surprise, the slave immediately overtook me and started running ahead at a brisk clip. The hint was clear enough.

I picked up the pace and ten minutes later we arrived at the porch. Half a dozen tough-looking sentries stood around the house. Their black-plumed helmets marked them out as members of the Royal Watch, the small unit of chosen men who acted as bodyguards for the royal family. One of them had previously served under me as a sergeant. I grinned and nodded to him as I recovered my breath.

"It's good to see you again, Dinomenes," I said. "Your boy's doing well."

It was the truth. His son was coming to the end of the military training that all our freeborn citizens were required to undertake and I was hoping he would sign on as a regular. Dinomenes beamed with pride.

"Thank you, sir. Just send the little sod over to me if he gives you any trouble. I'll be happy to put him straight for you. Anyway, best not keep the prince waiting, sir… He's round the back."

The slave led me round the side of the house to the garden behind. Beneath my breastplate, my tunic was now drenched as well as dirty. There seemed to be no sweat at all on the slave.

The villa itself was modest. We all lived as bachelors here: the camp was no place for families. The villa's garden, however, was large and had a spectacular view. It faced directly across the mouth of the great bay, towards the cream white city of Syracuse. The island of Ortygia, our capital's oldest district, lay less than a mile away. Beyond Ortygia, and connected to it by an isthmus, the greater part of the city sprawled out in the sunshine. Disappearing into the haze, its massive walls stretched inland for miles, like the edges of a dagger.

My new general was sitting on a stool behind a camp table, reading some documents in the mean shade of a stunted olive tree. He wore a soldier's simple white tunic.

The heir to our throne may have been a little less feared than his father, but perhaps he was also a little more loved. As a young man, Gelon had done his military training just like everybody else, hauling on the oar of a warship for a year and then being marched around the exercise yard for another, shoulder to shoulder with simple fishermen and ruffians from the slums. He was in his late forties now and his short-cropped hair was already turning grey. I stood to attention and waited, uncomfortably conscious of the strange African slave standing behind me.

The prince put aside his papers and eyed me up and down without comment, as though I were a farm animal he was thinking of buying.

We had only been alone together once before. A few weeks after my father's execution, Gelon had turned up at our door unexpectedly. As far as I can recall, he was our first visitor since that terrible day. Even our slaves had been reluctant to leave the house, for fear of the treatment they might receive on the streets.

I had been running around the garden with my sisters when the prince arrived. He had brought with him a small wooden shield, as a present for me. He took me out onto the street, where he and his bodyguards played and laughed with me for a little while before leaving again. It was a message to all Syracuse: we were under the king's protection. My father's disgrace was not ours.

Although, even now, it still didn't feel that way to me. Some stains seem indelible.

Gelon broke into a grin, stood up and strode over. He clapped my shoulders in his hands and gave me a friendly shake. His smile hadn't changed.

"You know, Captain, I think I'd struggle to carry you on my back these days," he chuckled.

By the look of him, I reckoned he might still manage it. He was not as tall or broad as me, but he was as lean and sharp as a mountain cat.

"I didn't think you would remember, sir," I said.

"Of course I do, Dion, of course I do. Dark times... Anyway, come and sit down. You've been on the march: you must be tired." He gestured to the slave behind me. "Hannon, fetch us some olives and wine."

I waited for him to sit, then placed myself on the stool opposite. I wiped my forehead and felt the grime on my hand. Gelon stared at me silently for a few moments.

"You and Sosis did a good job in Kamarina," he said eventually, in a matter-of-fact way. I wondered how on earth he already knew; we had only just returned. My surprise must have shown.

"Oh, don't be so naïve, Dion. A mouse doesn't steal a crumb in this kingdom without my father and me hearing of it. Did you really imagine we weren't keeping an eye on things?"

"The men performed well, sir," I replied carefully. "I was pleased with the trainees. There were no complaints of theft or rape or anything like that."

"I'm glad to hear it," Gelon said. "The army is here to protect the people, not to pillage them. By the way, when he has a moment, I want you to get Sosis to write up that rationing system of his and have it sent over to me."

"Yes, sir, of course... So you think there's going to be more trouble? Like we had at Kamarina?"

"Oh yes, I fear so... Ah, here's the wine."

We made a libation to the gods and drank each other's health. The wine had been diluted, as was the custom, but I couldn't help noticing that it was far more watered down than was usual.

"You look unhappy, Dion. Perhaps you don't like the wine? I'm afraid I only drink the cheap stuff."

"No, sir, the wine is good, thank you," I lied.

"Feel free to speak your mind, Captain."

"Then, if I may, sir... I have to say, things looked pretty grim in the countryside. So I suppose I just don't understand why we're still sending so much grain to Rome. We're only feeding dead men."

"The Romans aren't dead yet, Dion. And so long as they're still fighting, we'll keep feeding them. Better that Hannibal is killing Romans, than that he's killing us."

"Yes, sir, of course. But it's just that when he's done killing Romans, he's bound to turn on us anyway, isn't he? It's only a matter of time, I'd have thought. So isn't it our own granaries we should be stocking?"

I shouldn't have pressed the point. Gelon's expression hardened.

"My father knows what he's doing, Captain. And if I were you, I'd keep those sorts of thoughts to yourself. The king wouldn't be too pleased to hear that one of his senior officers is openly questioning his policies."

"But sir, I didn't mean… I mean, I was just…"

Gelon took a sip of wine as he watched me squirm.

"That's alright, Dion," he said eventually. "No one doubts your own loyalty. But if you'll take my advice, when it comes to politics, it's wiser to say nothing at all, than to say too much. Especially given your unfortunate family history."

"Yes, sir, of course. I'm sorry."

He smiled again.

"Nothing to apologise for, Captain. In any event, I didn't ask you over to talk about sacks of corn and barley. I'll come straight to the point, although it's more politics, I'm afraid. We're going to have to do something about Lieutenant Nico."

"Nico, sir?"

"Yes. He's caused far too many problems. He has to go."

I felt myself bridle. Not this again, I thought.

"I'm sorry, sir, but what has he done?"

"Oh, he hasn't done anything, poor fellow. In fact, he seems rather a capable officer… No, it's not what he's done: it's what he is."

"He can't help his ancestry, sir."

"Indeed he can't. Who can…? I agree it's most unfair. But my father himself has ordered that Nico should be cashiered, so there's an end to the matter. Sorry, Dion. I can do nothing to help. You can tell Nico yourself, or I will, if you want."

"Well, fuck it," I muttered quietly. Gelon narrowed his eyes and gazed at me but said nothing.

Politics, Gelon had called it. I could think of other words. Ours was a Greek kingdom, and Nico's sin was to have been born of Carthaginian descent. That in itself was nothing unusual in Syracuse: when his people and mine weren't trying to kill each other, we were perfectly happy to trade. There had been a Carthaginian ghetto in the city for centuries, which was protected for the sake of the silver it brought us. Some of their wealthier families had even been granted citizenship, becoming eligible for military service. We always had one or two swarthy faces passing unhappily through our ranks. What made Nico unusual was that, having completed his training, he was the first of his race ever to have been given an officer's commission.

And I was the one who had given it to him.

I met Gelon's gaze.

"Well, sir, the king may refuse to see me, but I shall write to him all the same."

"No, Captain, you won't. I've told you already, the matter is settled."

"With respect, sir, every officer has the right to petition the king."

"But not to argue with him… If he wants, Nico can petition the king on his own behalf, but you will not do it for him. You will do as I tell you. Is that clear?"

I clenched my jaw, but said nothing.

I couldn't explain exactly why I had chosen to take Nico under my wing. It was hardly as though I would have called him a friend. Maybe it was because I had glimpsed a blurred reflection of my own circumstances in his. But however you cut it, I had saddled myself with an obligation to the man.

"Is that clear, Captain?"

General Lepides had sneered when I had sponsored Nico for a lieutenancy, and had sarcastically asked if I wished to make any other imaginative additions to my officer corps. A crossbreed dog, perhaps, or maybe a mule? But he had not vetoed the appointment. He would humour me, he said; it might teach me a lesson. I should have realised then and there that I had done Nico no favours. My own men were too scared of me to cause him any trouble, but there was little I could do to protect him from the spitefulness of officers not directly under my command, while Lepides had watched on in amusement.

There had to be a way round this, I told myself. Perhaps Sosis could think of something.

Gelon folded his arms and stretched out his legs.

"I am not inclined to having my orders debated, Captain, but nor do I wish to get off on the wrong foot with you. So, on this occasion, I shall overlook your obvious defiance and explain why you must do as I tell you. But I shall never indulge you in this manner again. Do we understand each other?"

"Yes, sir. Thank you. I would certainly appreciate that."

"Very well, then. When my father first heard about Nico, he chose not to interfere, for Lepides' sake. But now that Lepides is dead, he wants the mistake corrected. As he puts it, you do not improve the wine by adding lemons. If Hannibal turns on Sicily next, who knows where Nico's loyalties may lie? And the reason I am forbidding you to intercede on his behalf, Captain, is because it would merely bring to my father's attention that it was only thanks to you that the fellow was made an officer in the first place. It is you I am trying to protect, you idiot. So you will now shut up and do as you are told. I want Nico out of Plymmerium by next week. Is that understood?"

I took a deep breath. Was Nico worth that much to me? I knew he wasn't. There were plenty of men for whom I might have fallen on my sword, but when all was said and done, Nico simply wasn't one of them. He could never really be one of us. And King Hieron was hardly known as a forbearing man... Well, fuck it. Fuck it all... What choice did I have? An order is an order, I told myself weakly.

I nodded reluctantly.

"Thank you for explaining that, sir. And I'm sorry if I offended you..." I bit my lip. "I'll deal with it."

"Good," Gelon said. "Your loyalty to your comrades is commendable, Dion, but in this case ill-judged. Anyway, no doubt you'd like to have a bath now: thank you for coming by. Last time we were alone together, you were a little boy with a wooden sword. It's a pleasure to see what a soldier you've become... Hannon will show you out."

I broke the news to Nico an hour later. We sat on the porch of my officer's cottage drinking better wine than Gelon had served. He was one of my more junior lieutenants; he had probably been surprised and flattered to be summoned to my private quarters.

Nico was a smooth talker with an easy grin and a quick wit. I suppose it was his way of trying to deal with the hostility he routinely encountered. But for once the man seemed at a loss. He merely drew his bushy black eyebrows together in shock. I stumbled through some clumsy words of comfort.

"Well, Nico, I'm sorry about all this. I wish you well for the future. Be sure to stay in touch, won't you? If I can ever do anything for you, don't hesitate to ask."

"I appreciate it, sir," he replied after a moment or two, forcing a smile. "And I must thank you for everything you've already tried to do for me. I want you to know I'm in your debt."

I forced a smile in return. It seemed unlikely we would ever meet again: outside the army, we moved in very different circles. I cannot pretend I felt particularly anxious to maintain the acquaintance.

And that was that. Nico left my cottage with a straight back, clenching his fists. I followed him a few minutes later, and headed straight to the officers' brothel.

I remember someone once telling me that every landslide begins with the dislodgment of a single stone. Of course, at the time, I had no inkling of the catastrophe that Nico's dismissal would eventually bring down on all our heads.

Lepides had already been buried by the time I returned from Kamarina, so at least I didn't have to attend his funeral, although I dare say it was a rather more cheerful occasion than most such events. As he had no family, they had put him in the cemetery at Plymmerium. There was a rite that had to be observed on the ninth day after his death, and Gelon instructed me to see to it. Agbal found me a goat, and I dutifully slit its throat over the grave, while a pair of priests blathered away beside me.

As I watched the animal twist and twitch and die, it struck me that Lepides would probably have preferred me to cut my own throat.

"But don't get fat-headed about it," he had snarled at me from behind his desk three years earlier. "By the time he was your age, Alexander had already conquered half the world! You're nothing special."

That was the manner in which he had promoted me to the captaincy of the Gold Shields. I had only just turned twenty-six, and even my father had not been given his own division until the age of thirty.

I stood silently by Lepides' little grave, feeling all my old resentments welling up once more. My father had been the kingdom's general, until his downfall. It was certainly not out of any feelings of sympathy that Lepides had awarded me my captaincy almost two decades later. There was no kindness in the act. Rather, in the years that followed, I came to believe that Lepides was quietly hoping I would fail, so that in some roundabout way he could take his own revenge on my father. That, I felt certain, was why he always rode me harder than my brother captains and seemed to relish giving me the ugliest assignments.

I didn't mind; in fact, I welcomed it. My men had nicknamed me 'the Bull', but it was not merely on account of my unusual strength and size that they had done so. I had a rage in me that craved release. Over time, the army taught me how to control my beast, and when to let it loose. As I stood by his grave, towelling the blood from my hands, I realised I probably had Lepides to thank for that, at least.

✳

Perhaps I had dealt with Kamarina too mildly, because over the next few months, the food riots spread to several other towns. They were not especially serious in themselves, but they were like molehills: the army would stamp on one, only to find two more erupting elsewhere. Gelon used the other two divisions to deal with them, but my brother captains were hard-pressed. Eventually, the prince had to divide the kingdom between them. Theodotus and his White Shields took responsibility for the north; Eryx, the captain of the Yellow Shields, was given the south. Before long, both divisions had been fully deployed, and found themselves uncomfortably dispersed.

I heard from my well-connected mother that there was quite a lot of chatter among the nobles as to whether Hieron had made a mistake in allying the kingdom so closely to Rome: better to keep our grain for ourselves, they said, than to back the losing side. Before the war, the agricultural tithe had been fixed at a tenth; but with Hannibal making it ever more difficult for the Romans to feed themselves, Hieron had raised the rate twice already, and it now stood at a third. "A third!" the nobles wailed. It was becoming almost impossible to squeeze any profits from their country estates. Some voices were even suggesting that it might be time to switch our allegiance to Carthage. I half agreed, but took Gelon's advice and kept my opinions to myself.

While Eryx and Theodotus marched their men around the countryside, in search of hungry citizens to crucify, the Gold Shields stayed at Plymmerium, following our usual camp routine. When we weren't exercising, we drilled. The prince often came to watch, but usually ended up joining in the phalanx formations himself, taking a position in the centre of the front row with a sarissa and shouting encouragement to everyone. He had soon learnt the names of all my junior officers, and even the names of some of the sergeants.

After Lepides, Gelon was an easy man to love.

II

THE FIRST KILLING

One afternoon, as I was taking some drills, the slave Hannon came to find me with a message from his master. The prince and his senior officers were invited to a dinner at the royal palace the following month. We were to be guests of the City Guard.

I groaned inwardly.

The Guards were widely despised by the hard men at Plymmerium. Their only purpose was to garrison the capital and keep order on its streets. All the dirty peacetime chores fell to the regular army: when we weren't training, it was always the Shield divisions who were required to hunt down bandits among the remote hills and mountains of the kingdom, or to man the quinqueremes to chase off pirates. The Guards remained comfortably quartered behind the city walls, with all the pleasures of Syracuse to hand.

Despite our lingering shame, my family was an old one and, as its head, I used to receive regular invitations to the Guards' famous social dinners. I snatched at any excuse to decline. I remained a bachelor, my father having been sent to his grave before arranging a match for me. I knew I would probably end up being cornered by some preening drip or other, anxious to tell me all about his little sister's incomparable charms. After all, I still had my wealth and royal ancestry to commend me, and I had made something of a name for myself as an athlete. It seemed enough for my peers to forgive my parentage, if not quite to forget it.

In a rather offhand way, I told Hannon that I already had a commitment on the night in question and would have to send my apologies.

"The prince warned me there might be some confusion over dates, Master," Hannon replied in a neutral voice. "So he instructed me to make clear that he requires you to attend. May I tell him that you will be pleased to do so?"

It appeared there was no getting out of it.

My brother captains returned to Plymmerium a few weeks later. Gelon had to attend a meeting of the Royal Council the following day and wanted to be briefed about the situation in the countryside. The three of us were to join him at the palace afterwards, for the dinner with the City Guard. Theodotus and Eryx were as unenthusiastic about going as I was.

Naturally, when the time came, we obediently scrubbed up and met at Plymmerium's small jetty, to take the officers' barge across the bay. Eulus, the commander of our little cavalry division, didn't come with us. He was the duty officer that week, which seemed a sufficient excuse to stay behind.

The bay was calm and the crossing easy. The eight slaves who spent their lives silently rowing the barge back and forth barely broke into a sweat. The three of us sat on benches under a canopy at the stern. Eryx was in an even blacker mood than me.

"What a waste of an evening," he grumbled, and spat over the side.

I grunted in agreement.

"Now, you two aren't going to start a fight tonight, are you?" Theodotus said with a laugh. "Remember, we are the poor country cousins. It's a great honour for us to be dining with such fine folk."

Although they were no longer wealthy, Theodotus came from an even older family than mine. There were kings in his lineage, too. I looked from one to the other. Eryx was scowling and absentmindedly stroking his thick blonde beard; Theodotus sprawled lazily on the bench with his legs crossed and his arms stretched out along the gunwale. The breeze was on my face and, as the barge rocked gently backwards and forwards, I felt a moment of intense happiness in our companionship. Eryx and Theodotus were both in their mid-thirties, but despite the difference in age, they had embraced me like a brother on my promotion. It was the army way.

We would normally have berthed at the South Citadel, a fortress on the southernmost tip of the island of Ortygia, at the closest point to Plymmerium. The bay itself was over two miles wide, but Ortygia lay directly across its mouth, half closing it and turning its northern end into a natural shelter that we called the Great Harbour. The South Citadel and Plymmerium were the nearly clenched teeth, between which any ships entering the bay had to pass.

Instead of stopping at the citadel, we rowed on into the Great Harbour, skirting along the landward-facing shore of Ortygia. The island's thick walls rose directly out of the water, concealing most of the buildings behind them.

There must have been well over a hundred merchant ships at anchor in the Great Harbour. More were berthed along the docks, loading or offloading their cargos. The docks extended all the way along the isthmus that connected Ortygia to the mainland. The royal palace loomed up directly behind them, sprawling across the isthmus like a slumbering stone monster.

I sighed as I contemplated the evening ahead.

It was not so much the men of the City Guard whom I despised, as their officers.

In the past, captains had enjoyed the discretion to sell commissions to whomever they chose and to grant exemptions from the standard military training to those who bought them. Lepides had ended the practice in the army, but things were very different in the Guards, over which Lepides had never had authority.

Their own captain was an amiable old gentleman called Apollonius. Apollonius was to Lepides as honey is to salt. He had little interest in military affairs: his chief concern was the quality of his cooks. Being someone who hated to say 'no', Apollonius had allowed his officer corps to swell to an absurd size with the sons of his many friends, to all of whom he sympathetically granted exemptions from the unpleasant business of learning one end of an oar from the other. And once they had bought their commissions, the only obligation their gentle commander seemed to impose on them was attendance at his dinner parties.

Preening drips and little sisters… Well, at least the food should be good, I told myself glumly.

We wove our way between the merchant ships and eventually found a berth. The docks had been built to serve taller vessels than our barge, so we had to climb up a set of rusty and slimy iron rungs that had been set into the stonework. It was late in the day, but the long, cobbled wharf still bustled with fishermen and traders and sailors. Milky-skinned men with red hair mingled with long-legged Africans, while their slaves struggled with a variety of crates and sacks and barrels. A row of customs officers sat behind their desks in the lengthening shadows, collecting duties and issuing merchants with permits to take their goods into the city.

An exposed stretch of road ran alongside the wharf, directly beneath the palace walls. At one end, a large gate tower provided access to the mainland and the greater part of the city; at the other end, there was a gateway onto Ortygia. Between them, directly in front of us, a dozen bored soldiers of the City Guard loitered outside a third gate leading into the palace itself. The sentries seemed to be expecting us. One of them, I imagine the most senior, nodded perfunctorily as we approached. Eryx scowled at him but the man met his gaze insolently. We had no standing here.

A slave belonging to Apollonius was waiting to greet us. He bowed and introduced himself. We followed him through the gateway and onto a bridge, which connected to a gate tower set in a second defensive wall. Beneath us, a steady flow of people and carts passed under the arch of the bridge, following the gloomy, claustrophobic channel between the palace's inner and perimeter walls. The cobbled channel and the road along the wharf were the only two ways on or off Ortygia by land.

We followed the slave across the bridge in silence. There were four more sentries at the far end, squatting on their haunches and playing dice. Their spears were leaning against the wall behind them. The slave nodded to them but they were too engrossed in their game to pay us any attention.

We emerged into a corner of the great colonnaded courtyard.

"Useless," I said under my breath, so the slave wouldn't hear.

"Blame the fucking officers," Eryx growled, rather more loudly. "Bunch of girly arsewipes." He spat.

"Shush," said Theodotus in amusement.

"Arsewipes," Eryx muttered again, a little more quietly. "Fucked if I know why the old man puts up with it."

But all Syracuse knew why our king put up with it. Apollonius was the younger brother of Philistis, Hieron's late queen. In life, Hieron was said to have doted on Philistis, and now that she was dead, some crumb of sentimentality seemed to sustain the king's indulgence of his brother-in-law.

The slave led us around two sides of the colonnade to a large open door and gestured to us to enter. Dinomenes and another royal bodyguard were standing to attention in full armour on either side of the entrance. At least they knew their business, I thought. Dinomenes kept his eyes forward as I walked past, but he couldn't resist a slight, sardonic smile.

As the number of Apollonius's superfluous lieutenants had expanded, so their old mess room in the palace's barracks yard had grown increasingly inadequate. In what was probably the only well-executed manoeuvre of his long military career, Apollonius had managed to secure one of the palace's grand staterooms for his officers' exclusive use. It was frescoed from floor to ceiling and overlooked the open sea.

I saw Prince Gelon a little way down the room, surrounded by a group of fawning young men. I had expected this to be another society event, but the only other people present all seemed to be Guards officers. There were about eighty of them. Castor, their adjutant, stood alone in a corner, looking lost and uncomfortable. I heaved a sigh of relief when I saw him. He, at least, was someone with whom I could have a decent conversation. There were no women present, of course. Rather like our slaves, our womenfolk led their own parallel and largely invisible lives.

Apollonius was chatting merrily to half a dozen men near the door. When he saw us enter a smile lit up his face. He must have been in his mid-sixties, but he still enjoyed something of the good looks for which he had apparently been known in his youth. Detaching himself, he came over to greet us.

"My dear friends," he said, opening his arms in welcome, "I'm so pleased you've come... Dion, you seem to grow larger every time I see you. You really have become a second Hercules."

I laughed politely. Our host gave me a sly glance.

"Tell me," he asked, "how is your dear family?"

The question threw me. I looked at Apollonius in surprise as I tried to work out what he meant by it. Both my sisters were married, so belonged to other men's families now. That only left my mother. It would have been an insult to use her name to my face – well-bred men would never claim familiarity with each other's women – but even the oblique reference was odd. I wondered what on earth my mother had been getting up to now. She seemed to rise effortlessly above the rules by which respectable women were supposed to live. It crossed my mind that the well-informed Apollonius might be trying to pass on some sort of subtle hint. Perhaps it was time to rein my mother in.

"My family is in good health, thank you, sir," I replied politely.

Although we nominally held the same rank, and Apollonius commanded fewer men than me, he enjoyed seniority over everyone except Gelon in the military hierarchy. His captaincy of the Guards brought with it membership of the Royal Council and the right to wear the blue tunic that was otherwise reserved for Hieron's immediate family. Gelon was the only other man in the room dressed in royal blue. The rest of us all wore the purple of the nobility or some other bright colour.

"I'm so pleased to hear it," Apollonius replied cheerfully. "I do hope you won't find our company too dull tonight, Dion. I wanted to organise this little get-together to celebrate my nephew's appointment as your new general. Give him a chance to get to know some of my own fellows better. We thought it best to keep it to comrades-in-arms, so I'm afraid no civilians this evening."

Apollonius looked around the room.

"Well, I think we can get started on the food now," he said. "We've calf's liver to begin, you know, in a rather special sauce. The prince especially requested it. It's a great favourite of his, so I hope you'll enjoy it too, Dion. I've put you next to Castor, by the way. I know how much you two like to talk about swords and spears and things."

When well-to-do men gathered for dinner, we usually ate on couches, but this was clearly impractical with so many people to accommodate. A long row of tables had been set up on one side of the room instead. A line of slaves stood in attendance along the wall. I noticed Gelon's African slave Hannon was among them.

Apollonius made a signal and a bell was rung for silence.

"Gentlemen, would you go to your places, please," Apollonius announced happily.

By custom, we were positioned according to rank. At the centre of the table on the far side, there was a high-backed chair for the most senior officer; the rest of us had stools. The more junior you were, the further from the centre you sat. Castor, the adjutant, came over and escorted the three of us to our seats; the Guards officers already seemed to know how to arrange themselves. Eryx was placed directly opposite the high chair, with Theodotus to his right and me to his left. Having shown us to our stools, Castor fell in beside me. I grinned at him and he rolled his eyes and smiled. It was an open secret that it was only thanks to him that the City Guard still managed to perform any of its duties at all.

We all remained standing, waiting for the senior officer to sit first. Apollonius escorted Gelon down the opposite side of the table. A slave pulled out the chair and Apollonius naturally gestured for Gelon to take it. Even if he hadn't been the heir to the kingdom, Gelon would have enjoyed precedence as the General of the Army. But to everyone's surprise, Gelon refused.

"My dear uncle," he said, affectionately putting his arm round Apollonius's shoulders, "I am your guest. There are no princes or generals here tonight, only friends and family. As our host, you must preside. I insist on it."

It was typical of Gelon's easy charm. The two men were clearly the best of friends. Apollonius laughed and tried to decline, but the prince simply stepped behind the neighbouring stool where Apollonius should have sat and, with a smile, nodded to his uncle to take the chair. Some officers started clapping and cheering in approval at Gelon's generous gesture and soon everyone else was clapping and smiling too. Apollonius blushed and waved his arm in defeat. He positioned himself and, as the slave pushed the chair in for him, sat down.

No sooner had he done so, than he gave a little yelp and jumped up again, shoving the chair back violently. He turned to look down at the seat and cautiously picked up its cushion. He narrowed his eyes and scrutinised it, but could apparently see nothing.

"There's something sharp in this," he said, "a pin or something." He rubbed his backside and handed the cushion to a slave. He seemed awkward rather than angry. "Take it away, would you?"

There was a shocked silence, which only embarrassed the poor man more.

"I am so sorry, nephew," he said. He looked around and spread his arms apologetically. "Please gentlemen, let's eat." He sat himself down again with a wince, and we all did the same.

It was Gelon who broke the silence. We only had water at the table, as the wine would not be served till after the meal, but the prince stood up again with his cup in his hand.

"See how my gallant uncle bleeds for our kingdom! A toast to the brave Apollonius!"

Everyone started laughing and clapping again. We stood and drank the health of the kindly captain. And then Gelon offered up a mock prayer to Ares, the god of war, to heal his uncle's grievous battle wounds. The laughing intensified. Apollonius beamed. His dinner party had been saved.

The first course was brought out by a procession of slaves. Hannon led them, carrying the plates for the prince and Apollonius. Liver is not my favourite food, but it was served in a rich, thick sauce that was really rather good. The conversation was now flowing easily. Gelon was seated directly opposite me and was talking politely to the officer on his right, an empty-headed oaf with whom I had been made to play as a child. I started chatting to Castor about various innovations that the prince was thinking of introducing to some of the army's battle formations.

After a few minutes, I noticed I had lost the adjutant's attention. He was staring at Apollonius.

I stopped talking and looked over at our host. Apollonius had turned white. He was dripping sweat. Gelon must have sensed something was amiss and turned round to gaze at his uncle too.

"I'm afraid I don't feel very well, nephew," Apollonius said weakly. He began shuddering. His hands seemed to be trembling uncontrollably. He swallowed hard and made as if to belch. And then he started heaving violently, throwing up across the table and into his own lap.

He gripped the arms of his chair and stared at Gelon with bulging eyes. A lumpy thread of vomit dangled from his lower lip. Still twitching, Apollonius slumped forward onto his plate.

We all looked on in shock. An instant later, the prince sprang to his feet. Hannon was already behind him.

"Everyone is to remain seated," Gelon barked. "Dion, Eryx, Theodotus, to me. Now!"

Theodotus was the first to understand. He kicked back his stool and vaulted onto the table. Eryx and I were a moment behind. My former childhood playmate looked up at me stupidly. I took a stride across the table and kicked him in the face, sending him sprawling safely out of the way. The three of us jumped down to form a cordon round the prince. We were only wearing our ceremonial captain's daggers, but we drew them anyway. Out of the corner of my eye, I saw Dinomenes and the other royal bodyguard running into the room, their spears levelled. They hurriedly joined our little group. Dinomenes drew his sword and handed it to me.

"You," snapped Gelon, pointing to the nearest slave, "fetch a doctor. Castor, I want the palace sealed. No one is to leave it. If you think any of these idiots might be of any use, take them with you. Go."

Castor stood and pointed.

"You, you and you. With me, now." He sprinted from the room. The three officers he had chosen stood and ran after him. Everyone else sat frozen and speechless.

Gelon looked round the table.

"You are all to remain in this room until you receive word from me that you may leave. On pain of death."

The man I had kicked lay groaning on the floor, his nose bleeding. Gelon stepped around him without a glance. We walked out, with Eryx, Theodotus and the two bodyguards in front of the prince, and Hannon and me close behind him.

Outside, the commotion had already started. Castor stood in the centre of the courtyard shouting orders. A few sentries were running to take positions. I saw the main gates being swung closed as, out of sight, someone began to ring the palace bell.

Gelon directed us round the colonnade to a small but heavy-looking wooden gate. He banged his fist on it and a shutter slid back. A moment later it was swung open from the inside by a soldier in a black-plumed helmet. The gate led into a narrow passageway, maybe thirty-foot long, at the far end of which I caught a glimpse of a garden. It was not an area of the palace I had ever visited.

The prince turned to us.

"I'm safe here. These are my father's apartments. I'm afraid you are all going to have a busy night."

He slipped off his ring and handed it to Eryx.

"I'm putting the three of you in charge," Gelon said calmly. "The whole palace is to be searched. Castor should have a list of everyone who is meant to be here. I want to know if anyone is missing. And if there are any people here who shouldn't be, you are to arrest them. I'll interrogate them myself in the morning... And find that cushion... Report back here when you've something to tell me."

He turned his back on us and strode down the passageway. Hannon and the two bodyguards followed him. The gate closed behind them.

We worked with Castor through the night. The City Guard was roused for a roll call in the exercise yard. Twenty men were absent on leave, but to Castor's evident embarrassment, about a dozen others were also missing. The duty officer was found asleep in his room.

The household slaves were ordered to gather in the main courtyard. There were nearly two hundred of them, but only three were unaccounted for. Over seventy secretaries and officials had rooms in the palace, some of whom were slaves and some free men. Several were absent, but they had all left their names at the gates in the normal way.

We divided the palace garrison into small parties and swept the palace. Eryx led the searches of the barracks. He found a number of prostitutes and rent boys hiding in the officers' rooms or under the men's cots. Further prostitutes of both sexes were discovered in the slaves' quarters and the secretaries' rooms. They were all thrown into the palace cells.

During the course of the night, most of the missing soldiers and secretaries drifted back. They were arrested and also put in the cells. We sent men to search the city taverns and brothels to find those who remained unaccounted for.

The cushion was retrieved. I cut it open myself, with great care. There were four pins concealed inside it, among the down. Their tips were coated in a black, sticky substance, like tar, which smelt faintly of fish. They had been inserted into a small, neatly cut cube of sponge, so as to keep them pointing upwards.

Officers, guards and slaves had been wandering in and out of the room all day, as it was being prepared for the dinner. Anyone could have put the cushion on the chair.

Dawn was breaking when the three of us finally returned to the little gate to make our report to Gelon. We were admitted and waited in the garden while he was fetched. The garden was enclosed on all four sides by high buildings, with a low colonnade running around its perimeter. The passageway seemed to be the only entrance from the main body of the palace and I noticed that the building under which it passed had no windows on the garden side. Pairs of guards from the Royal Watch stood in each corner of the colonnade but I didn't recognise any of them. They were in full armour and wore their distinctive, black-plumed helmets. I guessed the Royal Watch had its own quarters somewhere in this part of the palace.

After a few minutes, Gelon emerged into the garden. He looked fresh; he, at least, had apparently enjoyed an untroubled night's sleep. We stood to attention.

"So, what have you to tell me?" he asked without ceremony.

Eryx handed the prince back his ring and gave him the list of suspects we had drawn up. Gelon said he wanted to start the interrogations immediately. We all left together, accompanied by Dinomenes and three further bodyguards.

The prince sent me to let the Guards officers out of their dining room. To my amusement, it now stank of urine and worse. Apollonius' body had been moved to a corner and covered with a sheet, around which dozens of flies were crawling and buzzing excitedly. I walked over and pulled the sheet back. The captain's eyes were still open and there was some food and vomit stuck to the side of his white face. He had voided his bowels as he died.

I told the Guards officers they could leave but were confined to their quarters until further notice. They would only get in the way.

I headed back to the palace cells, which ran underneath one of the wings of the exercise yard. Although I had never seen them before that night, by now I was becoming quite familiar with them. They were little used any more, and their extensiveness was due to the fact that they were a remnant of a much older fortress, erected by the most famous of my own ancestors, King Dionysius. When my family was ousted, his citadel had been demolished in a silly democratic gesture. Hieron had been obliged to rebuild the whole palace from scratch.

Two men of the City Guards stood nervously by the heavy door to the dungeons, which opened directly onto a steeply descending flight of steps. At their foot, past another door, a single line of torches in wall brackets illuminated a long, damp corridor. Opposite the torches, there ran a row of windowless cells of varying sizes, into which we had bundled all those we had arrested. They sat on the stone floor in the gloom, whimpering forlornly as the palace rats scuttled around their ankles.

The corridor terminated at its distant end in a small and ancient wooden door. It appeared plain enough, but in my ancestor's day, it had acquired sufficient notoriety to be given a name, which the people of Syracuse still remembered. "Unless you behave," parents used to warn their naughty children, "the king will send you through the Hell Gate." I had no idea what lay on the other side of that door, and I had no particular desire to see.

By the time I returned, Gelon had already started the interrogations. He used one of the ordinary cells: on that occasion, at least, the Hell Gate remained shut. The secretaries and officials were questioned first, but they all had good explanations for their absence the previous evening. Men were sent into the city to check their stories and, one by one, we released them. They had suffered no worse than a cramped night on a dirty floor. We were not so gentle with the prostitutes and rent boys.

Sometime in the early afternoon, word reached us that the body of one of the three missing household slaves had been discovered floating in the harbour. We already knew the man had been involved in setting up the tables for the dinner. His naked corpse, washed clean by the sea, was brought back to the palace. There was a small, almost invisible cut in his neck, no more than an inch or so long, across the carotid artery. It was elegant work, I thought to myself, acknowledging the hand of a fellow professional. The other two missing slaves were never found.

By now, we had ruled out the involvement of almost everybody else. Shocked, bloody and bruised, the prostitutes were unceremoniously thrown out into the street. I doubted that they would want to come back. All the absconding guardsmen had either returned or been found, most of them still drunk. Gelon had them flogged that same evening and expelled from the Guards.

When there was nothing more that could usefully be done, he finally allowed Theodotus, Eryx and me to return to Plymmerium. We took the barge back. All three of us fell asleep during the crossing.

Under Gelon's orders, Theodotus and Eryx left the camp the following day to return to their divisions in the countryside. Gelon stayed at the palace and continued his investigation for several days, leaving me in charge at Plymmerium. News of his findings began to leak out. Courtiers, officials, soldiers and slaves enthusiastically relayed the palace gossip to the city beyond. It was transmitted at exclusive society functions and spread through temples and taverns. Wherever men or women gathered, the talk was of little else.

A phial containing an unidentified poison had been found, concealed in the bedding of the dead slave... The slave had a brother who was owned by a prominent Carthaginian family... On the afternoon of the officers' dinner, this family had boarded one of their own ships; it was assumed they had sailed to Carthage, where they had relations… The brother of the dead slave had been found in one of the family's warehouses, also with his throat cut.

It was clear that Gelon had been the intended victim of some sinister Carthaginian plot. Soon everyone in the city knew. Anti-Carthaginian sentiment began to build. Castor posted several hundred men at the entrances to the Carthaginian quarter to prevent trouble. One evening, he had to face down an angry mob intent on getting through, but they backed off when he drew his sword. Even so, any Carthaginians who ventured out of their own district were liable to be pelted with horse dung or beaten up. In a population of blonde-haired, blue-eyed Greeks, their swarthy complexions made them easy enough to spot. One man was killed, but he turned out to have been a Jewish mathematician from Alexandria. He had only just stepped off the boat and was trying to find his way to my Great Uncle Archimedes' house. The Carthaginians and the Jews look very similar, which was apparently sufficient justification for the mob that kicked the poor fellow to death.

From Syracuse, sailors took the news of the assassination attempt up and down our coast. Merchants and officials travelling between towns and villages spread the story inland. Word travelled faster than a plague. A month after Apollonius's death, the kingdom was united in outrage at the attempt on the prince's life.

We Greeks are a strange people. A few weeks earlier, we had been complaining bitterly about the Romans taking our grain. We told each other they were a crude and uncivilised race, for all their haughty ways, and we secretly gloated that they were getting a taste of the bitter Carthaginian medicine that we had been swallowing for five hundred years. But as news of the plot against Gelon spread, they were mysteriously transformed in our collective imagination into the plucky Romans, a solid, down-to-earth people, locked in a heroic struggle with murderous barbarians. Syracuse must do what it could to help them rid the world of the Carthaginian pestilence. Going hungry became a sacrifice to be made with pride, a perverse way of avenging ourselves on our ancient enemy.

The food riots soon fizzled out. There was no more talk at polite dinner parties of switching sides in the war. Syracuse is a kingdom of iron, we told ourselves. We do not abandon our allies just because we must go a little short of grain.

III

HOME

Seven days after the death of Apollonius, I received a message from Gelon that he would be returning to Plymmerium. I was to join him at his villa in the early evening.

I drilled my conscripts as usual. Two of them fainted: it was an unusually hot day, with the sort of smothering, pervasive heat from which there is no escape, even in the shade. I took care to leave in time to wash and change into a clean tunic.

When I arrived at the villa, Dinomenes was again one of the guards on duty. He greeted me with a grin.

"Good evening, sir," he said. "The prince is expecting you. Hope you haven't been getting yourself into trouble again." He winked at me cheekily.

I grinned back at him.

When I was still a junior lieutenant, Hieron had sent the Gold Shields to the aid of Corinth, in one of the shrill, fratricidal squabbles that routinely erupted between our petty Greek kingdoms. Dinomenes and I had ended up fighting back-to-back in the messy victory against the Spartans at Sellasia, where I received the ugly gash that distorts my face. My sword had broken and I had to snap the neck of the man who cut me with my hands. It was Dinomenes who had sewn me up that evening, by the light of a campfire. Few men of his rank or class would have dared to be familiar with me, but as far as I was concerned, Dinomenes could wink at me all he liked.

He knocked on the door, which after a few moments was opened from inside by Hannon. The slave led me through the entrance vestibule and across a small colonnade to the main living room, where Gelon lay on a couch, reading a document. He greeted me with a smile, put down his work and stood up.

"Ah, there you are. Hot, isn't it? Let's cool down in the bath. Hannon, bring us some wine, would you? Follow me, Dion."

He led the way around the side of the colonnade to a modest bathroom. We stripped off and lowered ourselves into the tiled pool. The cold water made me gasp, but I plunged down without hesitation, submerging myself completely for a few moments before coming up for air. Within a few minutes, my body had started to adjust. Hannon brought the wine, which was over-diluted again.

We talked facing each other, with the water up to our chests. I brought Gelon up to date on what had been happening at the camp during his absence. There wasn't much to tell. One of my regulars had absconded. He had received a message that his wife had died and, without thinking, had run off to his home in the slums to make arrangements for his two small boys. At least he had the good sense to come back three days later and face his punishment. I had him flogged and discharged. Gelon nodded his approval but clearly wasn't interested, so I didn't bother telling him I had also arranged for the man and his boys to be resettled on one of my estates.

Gelon began questioning me about administrative details. Exactly how much food remained in our storerooms? Had the camp blacksmiths received their scheduled delivery of ingots? Did we have sufficient coin to meet the upcoming payroll?

He was testing me, of course. I'd guessed that Gelon would expect me to get on top of the administrative trivia of camp life while he was away, and I also had little doubt he already knew the answers to his own questions. I hadn't joined the army to fret about iron ingots and sacks of grain like some common merchant, but I had wanted to prove myself worthy of the prince's trust. Dull as it was, I had dutifully spent time every day with the quartermasters and had even conducted snap inspections of the storerooms a couple of times – although I had no idea what I was supposed to be looking for. Fortunately, Sosis seemed able to discern the secret meanings in the long columns of numbers with which the quartermasters presented me, and had explained their significance to me in private. Although I fumbled my answers to Gelon a little, it was clear I had been making an effort.

"You're coming on, Dion," he said with a smile. "I know you believe such things are unimportant, and perhaps beneath you, but understand this: it is quartermasters who win or lose battles, as much as generals; and it is clerks, as much as kings, who win or lose wars."

I must have looked unconvinced, but Gelon just laughed.

"I see you disagree with me," he said. There was a brief silence as he eyed me coolly across the water.

"No matter. You will learn to appreciate the work of clerks and quartermasters." He was still smiling, but his voice was hard.

I nodded obediently. He continued staring at me in silence, as if weighing me up.

"Anyway," he said eventually, "you seem to have done a pretty good job here while I've been away. Well done... So, enough about Plymmerium. What are we going to do about the City Guard?"

"How do you mean, sir?" I asked.

"Don't be dim, Dion. We have to find a new captain for them. Whom would you recommend?"

"Castor is a good man, sir," I replied without hesitation. "In truth, he was pretty much running things anyway, as your uncle's adjutant. I hope your father will consider him."

"Yes, Castor is certainly a good man. My poor uncle never really appreciated him. But my father believes the Guards are in need of someone a little more... forceful. Any ideas?"

It struck me that the king must be considering transferring Eryx. He was certainly forceful. And as our longest-serving captain, he was also the obvious candidate for promotion.

"Sir, if you are thinking of Eryx, no one deserves the honour more."

"But perhaps the Guards are not exactly his sort of people?" asked Gelon archly. It was a fair point. The effete young blue-bloods of Syracuse would look down their noses at Eryx, whose father had made his fortune in the slave trade.

"'Girly arsewipes' I believe is the term he prefers, sir."

"A good summary of the problem," Gelon chuckled. "But, no, Dion, my father is not going to offer the post to Eryx. He thinks a commoner would find it too difficult. When their pampered life comes to an end, the girly arsewipes will all go crying to their daddies, and unfortunately it is on those daddies that Eryx's family depends for its livelihood."

"So, who then, sir?" Even as I asked the question, I felt my heart start pounding.

"Why, you, Dion, of course. You. My father has decided to offer you the captaincy. My warmest congratulations. I couldn't be happier for you."

I looked at Gelon in confusion. He smiled and raised his eyebrows.

"Would you like to take a moment to think about it?" he asked. His eyes twinkled. "You are of course free to refuse… That is, if you think refusing your king's favour is a sensible thing to do?"

"I don't know quite what to say, sir," I mumbled. "It's a great honour. But, well, the army is my home… This is my family."

"We all have to grow up and leave home eventually, Dion."

Within three or four years of my father's death, I had found I could no longer recall his face. So one day, when I was about twelve, I had walked through the long sequence of rooms in our house in Syracuse, carefully examining all the frescoes. Eventually, I found a face I could borrow for him. Its owner was just an anonymous background character, a sailor of some sort, but he looked gentle and wise. As a child, I used to summon that face at night, to comfort me in whispers. I had never blamed the king for my father's death: one might as well blame the sea for the death of a man who jumps overboard. But I wondered what that face would whisper to me now.

"Would I be able to take Sosis with me, sir?" I asked after a few moments.

"No, I'm afraid not," Gelon replied. "If you accept, Sosis will replace you as captain of the Gold Shields. I appreciate administration isn't your greatest strength, but my father has said he'll lend you one of his own secretaries to help with that side of things."

I ran my hand through my hair.

"I'm sorry if I seemed at all ungrateful, sir," I said. "It's just rather a surprise. Thank you for your confidence in me."

I hesitated for an instant, but of course the lure was too strong.

"I'll do my best not to let the king down."

Gelon beamed at me.

"My father will be delighted to hear of your acceptance. It will be no easy task to get those men into shape. Crack a few skulls if you must, Dion: the king will support you. He's worried about this war. If it reaches our shores, he wants to know the City Guard will be ready to play its part."

He lifted his cup and tilted it in my direction. We both drank and I tried to smile. Because of the scar on my cheek, my smiles and grimaces tend to look much the same.

"Now," Gelon continued happily, "that leaves just one last matter to discuss. Your marriage."

I stared at him.

"I'm sorry, sir?"

"Are you deaf, Dion? Your marriage. You are single, are you not? And free of any commitments?"

"Well, yes sir, but… I'm afraid I don't understand."

"Dion," Gelon said with a hint of exasperation, "as captain of the City Guard, you will have a seat on the Royal Council. My father likes his councillors to be members of the family. Now, I realise you are already distantly related to us in some way, but then so is half Syracuse, as far as I can make out. So the king has decided you should strengthen your ties to our house. It's in your own best interests, really. How should I put this? Let us just say that your family and mine have not always been on the best of terms. A marriage will help heal all those old wounds, once and for all."

My head was spinning.

"But who on earth does the king want me to marry, sir?"

"Well," Gelon replied, "as luck would have it, my father seems to have accumulated quite an abundance of great nieces. I think there are about half a dozen of marriageable age at the moment. I gather one has already been chosen for you. I'm afraid I can't remember her name offhand, but I'm sure she'll do: the women of my family seem quite a fecund lot. Shall we aim for an autumn ceremony? That should be long enough to work out the details. I'll ask the priests to find a propitious date."

He stood up and climbed out of the bath. I woodenly followed him. Naked and suddenly shivering, I stood staring at the puddle gathering around my feet, trying to take everything in.

Gelon walked over and stood directly in front of me. He put his hands on my cheeks and tilted my face down towards his.

"All will be well, Dion," he said quietly. "I promise."

I met his gaze and, as he kissed me, I chose to believe him, like the fool that I was.

My transfer to the Guards was announced in the camp the following afternoon. Sosis was named as my replacement at the same time. I told Sosis I could think of no one better. I meant it: he was a shrewd, cool-headed man. It struck me that he would probably make a better infantry captain in Gelon's eyes than I had been. After all, Sosis was a thinker; I was just a killer.

A week later, the officers of the Gold Shields gave me a farewell dinner. My fellow captains Eryx and Theodotus rode back to Plymmerium to join us. When the hard drinking started, Eryx stood up and gave a very sentimental speech about me. Then Theodotus stood up and gave a very funny one. I remember little more of the evening.

At daybreak, I was woken by a thunderous noise. On and on it went. I threw on a tunic and stumbled out of my bedroom onto the porch. The men of the Gold Shields, all two thousand of them, were gathered in the exercise yard in front of the cottage, beating their shields with their swords and stamping the ground. As I appeared, they began cheering. I stood there mutely, trying to control my emotions. Sosis stepped up and embraced me, then led me by the arm into the throng. Men whose lives I had held in my palm pressed forward to clasp my hand or clap me on the back. Divisions of rank evaporated. A balding sergeant who had once taken a wound that should have been mine stepped in front of me. We hugged like brothers.

Eventually, two men hoisted me onto their shoulders and carried me through the cheering crowd to the officers' podium. Prince Gelon appeared from somewhere and climbed up next to me. He smiled and nodded to me, and then turned to my men and held up his hand. They immediately fell silent.

"Men of the Gold Shields!" Gelon barked. "Form company lines!"

It was an exercise we had repeated countless times. Each company was required to arrange itself as a block, five ranks deep and twenty men wide. The companies had to assemble in two rows, one behind the other, with ten companies in each row. Every company had a fixed position in its designated line, and every man had a fixed position in his own company.

In response to Gelon's command, the master sergeant blew a shrill horn and held up the divisional banner. His place was on the extreme right of the front rank, providing an anchor for the whole formation. Within two or three minutes, a shapeless mass of men was able to transform itself into two parallel lines of equal rectangles.

Sosis stepped forward half a dozen paces. He drew his sword and lifted it in the air in a formal salute to the podium. Then he silently bowed to me.

Behind him, all my men bowed too.

The only sound was the shrieking of the gulls. I swallowed hard.

After a few moments, Sosis lifted his head again. He looked up at me.

"It has been an honour to serve under you, sir. May the gods protect you," he said.

Then he grinned at me.

"Now, fuck off, you ugly bastard," he said.

And with that, he sheathed his sword and turned his back on me. He shouted an order and the company sergeants began marching my men off.

Except they were no longer my men.

Gelon clasped my shoulder and nodded wordlessly. He stepped off the podium and headed away at a brisk pace towards his own villa. I was left alone in the early morning sun, watching the dust settle behind the Gold Shields as they cleared the exercise yard.

Later that morning, Sosis accompanied me down to the officers' barge to wave me off. Agbal walked behind us, carrying a sack over his shoulder that contained a few of my personal possessions and, I guessed, all of his. The rest of my baggage had already been sent ahead by road to my new quarters in the palace, and my other two camp slaves had gone with the cart to prepare for my arrival. I still hadn't got round to deciding what to do with Agbal, lazily allowing the matter to drift. Perhaps my mother could find a use for him.

As we crossed the exercise yard, I saw Gelon and Eryx in the distance, riding at a trot towards the gates. Half a dozen royal bodyguards rode behind them. I stopped and waved and the prince and Eryx waved back but they didn't break their pace or change direction.

"I wonder where they're going," I said. It was just a casual comment. I wasn't expecting Sosis to know the answer.

"The prince wants to see for himself what's happening in the countryside," Sosis replied. "He thinks it'll help to calm things down if he shows his face. Let everyone know he's fine."

It stung to discover my former adjutant was already a party to briefings from which I had obviously been excluded. I felt a little humiliated. I bit my lip and said nothing, but my expression must have told its own story. Sosis raised his eyebrows and scanned me closely. It only took him a moment to understand.

"Oh!" he said in surprise.

I just shrugged and gave him one of my grimace smiles.

"I'm sorry," he said. "That wasn't very tactful of me, was it?"

I clapped him on the back and we continued down to the jetty in embarrassed silence. Agbal climbed on board the barge and stowed the sack under the bench, while Sosis and I embraced and wished each other luck. Sosis stayed long enough to watch the slaves untie and pull away; then, with a final wave, he turned and set off back up the hill.

The barge took Agbal and me across to the South Citadel. As we approached its small jetty, the barge master signalled to a lookout on the wall, who beckoned us on. The citadel was an irregular shape, occupying a rocky point at the tip of Ortygia on which the walls of the island converged. It was one of several city strongholds for which I was now responsible. There was always a company of City Guards quartered here, although the citadel could accommodate a much larger force if necessary.

We tied up and Agbal and I stepped off the barge. A guard on the inside opened the small gate at the foot of the wall for us. He stood to attention as I walked past him. We passed through a dank and slimy tunnel that led to the inner courtyard. As I stepped back out into the sunlight, I found the commander of the garrison and his deputy waiting to greet me. They saluted smartly.

"Good morning, Xeno," I said, nodding to the senior man. All the officers at Plymmerium knew him well, as we regularly passed through the citadel on our way to or from the city. He was a tough veteran who had served in the Yellow Shields, until he lost his right hand to a pirate's sword. Eryx, his captain, had arranged for him to transfer to the Guards as a kindness. Unlike the army, the Guards did not require their officers to be able to lead from the front.

"Good morning, sir," Xeno replied. "And welcome to the Guards. It will be an honour to serve under you." He grinned. "That is, if you have any use for a miserable, one-handed old bugger like me. I believe you already know my junior lieutenant, Leander?"

He gestured with his left hand to a tall and strikingly handsome young man, whom I vaguely recognised. He was related to one of my brothers-in-law in some way, but I couldn't remember exactly how. I nodded to him.

"We weren't expecting you today, sir," Leander said, "but would you care to inspect the men?"

I was rather surprised by his evident eagerness. He seemed a far cry from most of the spoilt young aristocrats whom Apollonius had taken in. I hadn't planned to stop at the citadel, but decided I might as well make the most of it. I smiled at him.

"Very well, Lieutenant. Let's take a look at them."

Leander saluted again, turned and ran off. Xeno chuckled.

"I know he looks like a rent boy, sir, but he's alright. He's keen to learn. Wants to be a proper soldier."

"What's he doing in the Guards then, Xeno?"

"He's an only child, sir. His father insisted. Wouldn't let him do the training, said it was too dangerous. The lad had his heart set on joining the Gold Shields, apparently, on account of you being known as a fighting captain. So I suppose things have turned out quite nicely for him in the end."

In the event, I stayed at the South Citadel for over an hour. I didn't give the garrison a speech, because I am no good at speeches, but after the inspection, I chatted informally to the men. All of them had trained in the army, before applying to the Guards for the better pay and easier life. I recognised several who had passed through my hands in the Gold Shields. Every man in the City Guards must have known my reputation, which could hardly have been more different to that of their previous captain; and yet to my surprise, the garrison seemed to welcome my transfer. With the war threatening to engulf the kingdom, maybe they found it reassuring that the command should have been given to someone like me. Or perhaps they had simply had enough of serving in a division that was widely regarded as a joke. I have always believed that most men can be content without wealth; they can even be content without love; but no man can be content without respect.

I ended up challenging the garrison to a competition. I offered a prize of a silver coin to any men who could swim across to Plymmerium faster than me. Anyone slower would have to give me a bronze coin. I gave them two months to train.

Agbal and I left by the uneven path at the back of the citadel. The short spit of land that led into the city was rocky and jagged and had never been developed, apart from a few storage sheds and a small temple. But two hundred paces behind the citadel, the path widened into a narrow street, which immediately split and split again, fanning out into a web of crowded, airless lanes that smelt of rotten food and sweat. People jostled and elbowed each other to get past. They stepped aside for me – I tend to have that effect – but it still felt as though I were pushing my way through a pile of refuse. Agbal followed in my wake. One cocky young man seemed inclined to try to make me walk around him, but his older companion hurriedly pulled him aside by the arm.

"That's the Lady Korinna's son, you idiot," I heard the older man hiss as I marched past them.

Here in the city, it seemed my mother was more to be feared than I was.

It was a relief when we eventually emerged into a large, sunny square and saw in front of us the Temple of Athena, the goddess of war and wisdom. Artemis was supposed to be the patron goddess of Syracuse, but somehow Athena had managed to elbow her half-sister aside and now claimed our city as her own. Her temple's fat columns and impossibly heavy pediment seemed to erupt from the ground like a blunt spear, stabbing angrily at the naked underbelly of the sky. A giant gilded shield was mounted in the centre of the pediment. In the morning sun, the flashing shield was visible from far out to sea, a warning to any approaching ships that we were under the goddess's protection. The temple was a building that had been designed to intimidate rather than to inspire, and its High Priestess was the only woman in the city whose pronouncements men were expected to heed. Unfortunately, the present High Priestess was senile and had pronounced nothing very intelligible to anyone for years. She was an ancient aunt of my father's: hers was a hereditary office, reserved for the women of my family as a result of some obscure horse-trading among the nobility centuries earlier. My mother had been waiting hungrily to succeed to the position for as long as I could remember.

My family home stood just beyond the square in the Avenue of Athena, which ran from the temple to the royal palace about half a mile away. I had sent word ahead the previous day to expect me. An elderly slave, whom my family had owned since before my birth, opened the heavy gate of our villa at my knock. He had probably been bred in our household. He beamed with pleasure and bowed to me. Behind him, another slave was already scampering off to announce my arrival to my mother.

"It's so very good to see you, Master," the old man said happily as he stood aside to let us into the entrance archway.

"Thank you, Cerberus," I replied, using the nickname by which he had always been known. I couldn't even remember his real name any more. Cerberus is the ferocious three-headed dog that guards the entrance to the underworld, although it would have been hard to imagine anyone less ferocious than our porter. He closed the gate behind us. I gestured towards Agbal.

"See that this boy is fed, would you? Now, where can I find my mother?"

"I believe the Lady Korinna is in the garden, Master," Cerberus replied.

The archway opened directly into the great courtyard, the legacy of a distant past when we had first established ourselves as the preeminent family in Syracuse. The blank, anonymous wall facing the avenue concealed the true size of the villa behind. In truth, it was more of a palace. I owned several estates in the countryside as well, but this had always been our principal family home.

I walked round the colonnade. A large, stern-faced statue of Athena stood in the middle of the courtyard, a reminder of my family's particular relationship with the goddess. My mother had acquired it from somewhere soon after she was widowed. She was not a devout woman: the statue was less a statement of piety than a social proclamation. It had been her way of letting the city know that she would be coming out fighting.

I took the passageway into the densely planted garden at the side of the compound. The smell of lavender obliterated the odours of the streets outside. My mother was sitting on a bench by the fishpond, under the shade of a purple awning. She was staring at the water, immersed in her own thoughts, with her hands folded in her lap. I was struck by how still she seemed. As always, she wore a blonde wig; I no longer knew what her own hair looked like. As I drew close, she turned to look up at me. She smiled thinly and stood to offer me an embrace. She was a tall and straight-backed woman, but all the same, I had to bend down some way to kiss her cheek. It was several months since I had last visited her.

"You look more like your father every time I see you, Dion," she said in her controlled, deliberate way. Everything she did was controlled and deliberate. Even those first words were a perfectly judged rebuke, the implication that I had been neglectful of her being clear enough to needle me, and yet subtle enough to be deniable.

"And you look not a day older, Mother," I replied, choosing not to rise to the bait. It was true enough. She had a long face with high cheekbones and a thin, aristocratic nose. Although nearly fifty, she remained a woman to be admired, in the same way one might admire a finely worked piece of silver. "Are you keeping busy?"

"Yes, busy enough," she replied casually. "We've done rather well out of olive oil this year. I've had the shipyard lay down two more hulls for us."

By law, our women could neither inherit property nor administer it, but my mother had her own ideas about that. After my father's execution, the king had named my great-uncle Archimedes head of our family. It was an unusual provision, as he was a relative of hers, rather than my father's, but he was also a cousin of the king's, and I suppose Hieron wanted someone he trusted in charge of us. Archimedes was meant to manage our affairs until I turned eighteen. My great-uncle couldn't have cared less about our affairs and my mother had had no difficulty in persuading him to appoint our household steward to act as his agent. Archimedes returned to his dodecahedrons and gave us no more thought.

Of course, our steward had always deferred to my mother and, in the absence of any instructions from Archimedes, continued to do so. She took control of everything. When I came of age, the steward simply became my agent instead, with a duplicate of my signet ring. His only task was to trundle off to the public notary's office at the end of the day, to affix my seal to whatever contracts my mother had agreed. I was perfectly content for the arrangement to continue. I had no interest in our family's commercial dealings and, in any event, by then my mother had already proved that she was far more astute with money than any man I knew.

It should have been a public scandal, of course, but somehow she managed to carry it off. She was Archimedes' niece, after all. It was said my great-uncle had once run naked through the streets, whooping like a lunatic in his excitement at solving a problem. Some splinter of the divine lightning that zigzagged through his brain seemed also to zigzag through hers, and it was apparently sufficient to excuse her disregard for convention. In time, it even proved sufficient to excuse her marriage. She was viewed as a minor phenomenon. Instead of censoring her, men came to delight in telling stories of how she had outwitted this hard-nosed trader or that cocksure lawyer. 'She's no Korinna' became the standard lament of those who found their wives dull-witted.

The world seemed to assume that I was blessed in my mother, at least.

I remained standing as the minor phenomenon sat back down on the garden bench. She composed herself, folded her hands in her lap again and eyed me dispassionately. She had never been an affectionate woman and already knew that my visit meant I wanted something. Whatever passed between us would be just another of the day's negotiations to her. She had no intention of being the first to speak.

A slave appeared with a silver bowl of scented water. He held it for me as I rinsed my hands and splashed my face. I nodded and he bowed and took the bowl away again.

"So, how many ships do we have now?" I asked, trying to make small talk.

"Thirty-six," my mother replied flatly.

A wealthy merchant might own four or five.

"And you've ordered another two?" I said. "How many more do you want?" It was intended as a gentle tease. I smiled to show I was joking.

She stared at me in her condescending way.

"Have you only come home to torment me with your stupidity, Dion?" she said. "Listen to me: our landholdings are all well and good, but ships give our family more than wealth. They give us power. What is Syracuse without ships? Nothing. It is cargo ships that pay for Hieron to build his quinqueremes and feed his army and maintain the city walls. It is cargo ships that keep the nobles in their silver and slaves. You ask how many more I want? I'll tell you: I want them all. Now, do you need to use the latrine before we eat?"

"No, thank you," I said, taking a deep breath and biting back on my irritation. She seemed to be in one of her more difficult moods.

My mother stood again and silently led the way over to a shaded terrace, where two couches had been positioned facing each other. Our food had already been set out on side tables: fish, bread, olives, tomatoes, some dried meat. It was perfectly sufficient, but hardly a great celebration of my homecoming. My mother dismissed the two slave girls who were standing in attendance. We settled ourselves and began picking at the food.

"So, Dion," she said coolly, "I hear you're to wear a blue tunic and be married. Should I congratulate you, do you think?"

I sighed. Just for once, I thought, she might have expressed some pride in me. I put up with it only because I knew she was the one person on earth who would never lie to me. Perhaps, in the absence of love, she felt that she at least owed me her honesty. Or maybe, in her eyes, I just wasn't worth the bother of a lie.

"I had hoped you might be more pleased, Mother," I said quietly. "To be a Royal Councillor is no small thing."

"You may find it is no great thing either," she replied offhandedly. "Hieron has ruled here for over fifty years. Do you really think he needs the benefit of your advice, my little Royal Councillor? And as to wearing a blue tunic, well, Dion, it's just a tunic, isn't it? You are the heir of King Dionysius. I don't see how the colour of your clothes adds to your dignity."

"It isn't 'just' a tunic, as you know perfectly well," I replied sharply. "It shows our king values me, even if my own mother doesn't. In fact, it seems he values me enough to marry me into his family. You've made us richer than Midas, Mother, but I'm the one who's winning us back our name. You might at least acknowledge that."

"I wasn't aware that our name had ever been changed. Our family is what it has always been. Your father lost a gamble; that is all. And it was a gamble that only great men are prepared to take. Your shame is your own invention."

"And your pride makes you blind," I muttered.

She eyed me shrewdly.

"Do you even know who your wife is to be?" she asked after a moment. "No, I see you don't… So it's information you've come for, is it? I had thought you might be here to tell me you will be needing this house back for yourself and your bride."

She took a sip of water, waiting for me to respond.

"I've no intention of moving back," I replied carefully. "I'll have my own rooms in the palace. You are welcome to stay on here for the time being. As to my future wife, I was thinking of installing her at Acrae. Perhaps you could arrange for things to be made ready for her there? Make sure she's happy and taken care of?"

My mother put a small piece of meat in her mouth and started chewing it. After a moment, she nodded. Our negotiation had been settled to her satisfaction. She would continue to rule the roost in Syracuse; in return, she would share her information and ensure my new wife was no bother to me. The villa at Acrae had been our summer holiday home. It lay a day's journey outside the city, high up in the breezy hills, overlooking a wooded valley. I had always enjoyed the place as a child, but the house had been shut up since my father's death. The estate itself was of little value. There were a few acres of terraced vineyards and some meadows, but most of the land surrounding the rather grand villa had been given over to pleasure gardens.

She picked up an olive, examined it, dropped it on the ground and selected another.

"I gather you are to be married to Vita of the Manlii," she said in a neutral voice.

I shrugged my shoulders indifferently. The name meant nothing to me.

"Can you tell me anything about her?" I asked.

My mother had her own sources of information. In every house, quiet women watched and listened to their men, and told other women what they heard. Some men even confided in their wives and, with little else to do, their wives naturally confided in each other. My mother was like a black well, through which all these subterranean rivulets of gossip flowed. It was to her door that the important ladies of Syracuse hurried first with their news, to be flattered by her intimacy and rewarded with some carefully chosen nugget of reciprocal information: 'As dear Korinna was telling me only yesterday...' It was no wonder my mother had been getting the better of her oblivious business competitors for years. I sometimes wondered if she was Athena's subtle instrument of revenge, for all the overlooked and powerless women of Syracuse who daily prayed to the goddess for relief.

"I see the significance of this match is entirely lost on you," my mother said. "I'll spell it out for you, then. Hieron had three younger sisters. They're all dead now, of course, but one of them had a daughter called Seema. Thirty years ago, during the last war with Carthage, Hieron was anxious to make as many powerful friends in Rome as possible, so he arranged for Seema to marry Titus Manlius Torquatus. I take it you have heard of him, at least?"

I nodded. It was one of those names most people of my class would probably recognise, without knowing anything much about the man. All I knew of Torquatus was that he was a leading Roman senator.

"I'm pleased to hear it," my mother continued. "Anyway, Seema and Torquatus have three children, of whom your future wife Vita is the youngest. She must be fifteen or sixteen by now. The man she was supposed to marry was killed fighting Hannibal. She has lived all her life in Rome. I hear she speaks no Greek and knows nothing of our ways, despite being the great niece of the King of Syracuse. Her parents apparently dote on her, and with the war on Rome's doorstep, of course they are anxious to get the child out of harm's way. Torquatus wrote to Hieron a few months ago, to see if Hieron could find a suitable husband for her here… Are you beginning to understand now, Dion?"

"No, not exactly. Spit it out, Mother."

"Very well, then. Torquatus would have settled for any young noble with money. But the king has gone further. He wants to show Torquatus how highly he values their connection, and so he's marrying the girl to his new Royal Councillor, no less. Now she'll get to wear the royal blue as well. This marriage isn't about honouring you, you numbskull; it's about flattering Torquatus, and putting him in Hieron's debt."

I dug my nails into my palms and took a breath.

"So if I'm such a numbskull, why choose me to be captain of the City Guard then, Mother?" I managed to keep my voice low. "There were other men he could have picked. But the king chose *me*, didn't he? And if all Hieron wants is to dress this girl in blue, he could have given her to some other councillor. But he chose *me* again."

My mother pursed her lips and nibbled on the olive.

"Yes. You've got to admire the way the old man's mind works. He can't be long for this world, but he's still thinking years ahead. Never underestimate him, Dion."

"You haven't answered me, Mother. Why choose me? You can't give me the credit for anything, can you? Is it really so difficult for you to admit that I might just be the best man for the job?"

She snorted.

"That all depends on what the job is, doesn't it, Dion? Your great virtue, my darling, is that you are a brute, and in dangerous times, I dare say brutes have their uses. If this war comes to Syracuse, Hieron will need someone to help him keep his foot on the city's throat. I certainly agree that you are probably the best man for that particular job, given that you seem to think nothing of jumping over a table to break a fellow noble's nose."

"Oh, you heard about that, did you?" I gave her one of my grimace smiles.

"Of course I did," she snapped back. "It was quite unnecessary. We do business with that family. The boy's mother has been a dear friend of mine for nearly thirty years. I had to sit and listen to her squawking and snivelling about it for over half an hour."

"Next time the prince's life is in danger, I'll try not to cause you any inconvenience, Mother."

She stared at me icily.

"You still don't understand, do you, Dion?" she said. "You should never have agreed to this marriage. Why didn't you speak to me before you accepted? You have allowed Hieron to back us into a corner. And now you come here and expect me to shower you with kisses and congratulate you for it?"

"What the fuck are you talking about now? How on earth have we been backed into a corner?"

I don't know if I expected the obscenity to shock her, but it had about as much effect as throwing a pebble at a warship.

"Do you happen to know who is going to win this war?" she scoffed. "Because I certainly don't. War brings opportunities as well as risks for a family like ours. I have been very careful to keep our options open. But our king has thrown in his lot with the Romans, and by marrying you to this girl, Hieron is binding you to the Romans too. Where will that leave us if Carthage wins? Hieron flatters Torquatus and fetters you, in a single move. And who knows? Perhaps Vita takes after her father, and then you can breed yourself a family of nice little Roman monkeys, with black hair and brown eyes, for everyone in Syracuse to laugh at… And there's another thing, by the way: I imagine it won't be long before the old man starts trying to manipulate our affairs through you. Mark my words. He'll be eyeing my ships soon enough."

I waved my hand irritably, as if trying to swat her away.

"You're a fantasist, Mother. You see schemes and plots everywhere. Besides," I added, a little pompously, "I believe they are actually *my* ships."

"See how long you keep them without me," she sneered.

I looked into her bitter blue eyes. She was the blight that coveted the vine: the further she spread, the greater her frustration. I thought of Prince Gelon, and the pleasure he had seemed to take in my promotion. Later, with my head resting on my arms, I had lain on the bed beside him and watched him sleeping, as dawn slowly broke around his villa. Between simple illusions and complex truths, most of us clutch at simple illusions, but nothing is completely pure. At best, it seemed Gelon had not told me everything.

The anger with which I had been struggling ever since I arrived subsided and drained away. In its place, within me and around me, I felt only a vast, inhuman emptiness.

"What have I ever done, that you must always be so cruel?" I asked with a sigh.

She thought about it for a moment. When she replied, her voice was flat. She might as well have been discussing the weather.

"My friends all seem to love their children and to resent their husbands," she said. "For me, it was always the other way round. That is my misfortune. I suppose it is yours too... In any event, I wish you well at the palace. Maybe we will see more of each other in the future. Now, I am afraid I am expecting some important visitors: you will have to excuse me. Feel free to stay for as long as you like. After all, it is *your* house."

She left me on the terrace. I didn't look at her or stand up to say goodbye and we parted in silence. I drank a cup of water, sipping it slowly, trying to clear my head of her venom. It didn't work. Every time I saw her, I ended up wondering whether it was time to let someone else have the pleasure of dealing with her. She should have been married off to another member of my father's family when she was widowed, but they all had wives already, and so she had become Archimedes' ward instead. Now she was mine to dispose of as I saw fit. She was well past childbearing age, of course, but there must be some old aristocrat, I told myself, who would be willing to take her on for a large enough dowry. When I'd finished my drink, I clapped my hands and one of the slave girls came running from the house.

"I'm leaving soon," I told her. "Go and find my boy. His name's Agbal. He's probably in the kitchens. Tell him to meet me at the gate and he'd better not keep me waiting."

I took my time finishing my lunch, and then strolled back through the main courtyard. Agbal was already there, with his sack by his feet.

"Did they feed you?" I asked as I walked up to him. I wasn't particularly interested in the answer.

"Oh yes, Master," he said happily. He picked up the sack and fell in behind me as I walked past him.

"If I may say so, Master," he chirruped, "the gods favour you greatly. What a wonderful person your lady mother is. She must be the kindest woman in Syracuse."

I stopped in my tracks and turned to stare at him. I was in no mood to be mocked by a slave. His smile disappeared when he saw my expression and his eyes widened in fear.

"And what do you mean by that?" I snarled.

"I only meant, Master, what she does for all those poor women... I didn't mean... I didn't..." His voice trailed off.

"What?"

"I only meant... those poor women... I mean, she's so kind to them..."

"What? What fucking women?"

"The ones in the stables, Master."

"Women in the stables? What on earth are you babbling about, Agbal?"

"The poor women in the stables, Master. The ones your mother takes in."

I was stupefied.

"Agbal, are you telling me there are women living in my stables?"

He nodded meekly. He kept his eyes on the ground.

"If this is a joke, Agbal, I'll flay you alive."

"It's not a joke, Master. I thought you must already know."

"Show me," I said.

He bowed quickly and put his sack down again.

"Of course, Master."

We walked back into the courtyard. Agbal scuttled in front of me like a mouse. We followed the colonnade round to a wooden gate, which led to the adjoining slaves' yard. I had not visited this part of the compound since I was a child. It looked smaller than I remembered. The stable block filled the far end of the yard. In my father's day, we had kept twenty horses here. In the autumn, almost the entire household used to decamp to our principal estate at Leontini for the grape harvest; with our cavalcade of baggage carts, we must have looked like a small army on the march.

I crossed the yard. The door into the central section of the stables was ajar. Before I had even entered, I realised the smell was quite wrong.

It was cool inside. The interior was ventilated by rows of high, small openings that ran along the two longer walls and also provided some dim light. There must have been about sixty or seventy women inside the block, all dressed in coarse brown gowns. They sat alone on bales of hay in the central aisle between the stalls, or huddled together in groups of twos and threes. I walked slowly down the aisle, my astonishment intensifying, with Agbal following behind me. As I approached, the women fell silent and nervously backed away, as if trying to make themselves invisible. It was like a gallery of grotesques. They were mostly old and frail, or in some way deformed. Some were hunched; some twisted. One woman was missing half an arm.

I stopped and swung open the gate to one of the stalls. There were three palettes of straw on the floor, which obviously served as beds. A shapeless form lay on one of them, under a blanket. On another, an old crone sat facing me, with her back to the wall. A thread of drool hung from the corner of her mouth. Her eyes were milky white: she must have been completely blind.

I turned to Agbal in bewilderment.

"Who on earth are these people? Do you know?"

"They are former slaves, Master." Agbal spoke in a whisper, as though he were in a temple. "When they could no longer work, they were freed and thrown out onto the street. These women were not lucky enough to belong to rich families like yours, Master, or to have families of their own to go to."

"But what are they doing here?"

"Your blessed mother takes them in. She gives them these clothes. The cooks told me they are fed every day and she asks nothing in return. She expects them only to help each other to wash and dress, and those who are still well enough must go to the temple in the morning and pray to Athena, but that is all. Many do not have long to live by the time they come here. Some die in the winter, and then others are admitted. But at least they do not die of hunger in the streets."

I was horrified.

"Has my mother gone quite mad?" I exploded. "What on earth possessed her to bring all this disease into my home?"

We had our own household to think of: it was intolerable to expose our slaves to such a risk. The cost could be enormous. I noticed the misshapen creatures nearest to me were cringing in fear at my outburst. One of them began to whimper.

"But Master," Agbal replied meekly, "there is no disease here, only old age and injury. Your mother does not take in the sick."

I was too incensed to listen. To open up my house to the flotsam of Syracuse without my permission… The veins in my neck began to throb.

"How long has this been going on?" I bellowed.

"I don't know exactly, Master. Some time, I think."

"Wait for me at the gate," I snapped. I turned and strode back down the aisle and out into the yard.

Agbal ran after me.

"Master, please wait. Please!"

I ignored him.

I was halfway across the yard when he overtook me. As he did so, he spun on his heel to face me, walking backwards as fast as he could to try to match my pace. He held up the palms of his hands.

"Please, Master, please."

I took a few more steps, but he was awkwardly in my way, slowing me down. I stopped and narrowed my eyes, ready to knock him aside.

"Master, is this not a good thing your mother is doing?" Agbal's voice was imploring. "All the slaves of Syracuse know of it. We even heard about it at Plymmerium. She is loved for it. Please have mercy."

"What's it to you?" I demanded. My nostrils flared.

Agbal was plainly terrified, but he met my gaze all the same.

"My mother is a slave, Master. I don't even know where she is now. But I pray to all the gods that someone will care for her like this."

My fists were clenched. I glowered at him. He flinched and looked down, clearly expecting a blow, perhaps worse.

"You're an impertinent little turd, aren't you?" I snarled. He kept his head bowed, but he didn't move out of my way.

I inhaled deeply, then slowly let my breath out.

The complete absurdity of his courage flummoxed me. I didn't know how to respond to it. He was just a slave. Even my noble friends would never have dared to stand in my path when my blood was up. And Agbal was only a little fellow. And yet to have hurt him would have seemed – I don't know quite what – but at any rate, wrong, like smashing a child's toy.

I felt my anger begin to dissolve. I unclenched my fists and snorted. Finally, after a few moments, I frowned, and nodded curtly.

"But you've certainly got balls."

I took another long breath. Nothing my mother did was ever straightforward. I didn't believe for a moment that she had suddenly succumbed to a generous impulse. Ever since my father's death, she had taken to handing out coins at the temple once a year to our poorest citizens, but that was obviously just politics. Even our most humble citizen still had a voice, after all. But I couldn't see what on earth she stood to gain by patronising useless former slaves. And yet perhaps Agbal had a point… Maybe I was over-reacting… Maybe there was no real harm in it either. It dawned on me that I would hardly be doing my own reputation any favours, if I were the one seen to be throwing the women back out.

I scratched my cheek.

"Very well," I said sourly. "I'll think about it. The hags can stay for now."

"Oh, Master…" Agbal wiped his forehead with the back of his hand. He was shaking.

"But it would be wise never to stand in my way again," I said.

"No, Master, I don't think I will."

I looked into his young, open face. One couldn't help liking him. I snorted again. I gave him a grim smile and suddenly, out of the blue, I found myself chuckling. I was the notorious Bull of Syracuse, a nightmare made flesh, by all accounts. Agbal had probably never tussled with anything more dangerous than a chicken before. And yet this low-born boy had faced me down. One had to see the funny side of it. I decided in that instant that I would keep him.

He looked at me anxiously, not quite sure whether he was safe yet.

"Come on, Agbal," I said with a sigh, clapping my arm round his shoulders. "It's been a long morning. Let's get out of this fucking place."

"Yes, Master."

We headed back to the main porch, where Agbal retrieved his sack. The old porter smiled and bowed and opened the gate for us. I gave him a coin, then stepped out into the wide avenue and turned towards Hieron's palace and my new life. Agbal respectfully kept a few paces behind, and for once stayed silent. As the river of anonymous faces parted to make way for me, I tried to work out what on earth my mother was expecting to obtain by her ostentatious charity. After a while, I decided I simply didn't care.

IV

THE EUNUCH

My old governess, a fat and malodorous slave woman, whose liberality of spirit found its chief outlet in spankings, used to tell me a story.

In the very centre of the Greek homelands, there is a remote and mountainous region called Arcadia. Men live there now, but long before men arrived with their axes and spades, the nymph Arethusa ran freely through Arcadia's forests. She was an innocent creature, and devoted to Artemis, goddess of the hunt and of all things wild and feminine.

One hot day, Arethusa was walking through a glade when she came across a mountain stream. She was a Nereid, a water spirit, and the clear, cool brook was irresistible to her. She undressed and stepped into the water. She did not know that the stream was really the river god Alpheus, who was making his way from Arcadia to the sea. As soon as he touched her, Alpheus was enchanted, and rose up to embrace her. Horrified, Arethusa fled, but Alpheus pursued her. He chased her relentlessly, until eventually he trapped her in a gully. In desperation, Arethusa prayed to Artemis for protection, and the goddess heard her devotee's prayer. Angered by Alpheus's presumption, Artemis hid Arethusa in a cloud. Even there, however, the river god hunted the nymph out. As he closed on her, she began to sweat in fear, and was transformed into a stream herself. Artemis tore the ground open for her, and Arethusa disappeared beneath the earth.

For many days, Arethusa travelled under the seabed, through black caves and channels, until finally she arrived at the little island of Ortygia, hard by the coast of Sicily. Believing herself safe at last, she rose to the surface as a freshwater spring. But Alpheus was still tormented by his desire, and would not relent. He flowed through the sea to reach her, and in a little rocky pool on the shore of the island, Alpheus's salt water finally mingled with the cascade of Arethusa's spring. Theirs has been a long embrace: their waters merge in that rock pool to this day.

In time, travellers from Corinth came to Ortygia. Like all travellers before and since, they had taken to the sea in the hope that it would wash away their old lives and deliver them, cleansed, into new ones. Their leader was called Archias, who had been responsible for the death of a boy with whom he had fallen in love. Before sailing, Archias sacrificed his own son to Poseidon, the patron god of Corinth. The sea god was satisfied, and sent four of his dolphins to guide Archias and his followers to Ortygia. There, the travellers found Arethusa's sweet drinking water. They gave thanks, and sent word back to Corinth for others to join them. And so it was that Syracuse came into being.

I cannot say how much of this story is true: my fat old governess used to lie all the time. But it is certainly a fact that most of the trade routes that criss-cross the Mediterranean from east to west and north to south run past Sicily. As the centuries passed, Syracuse prospered and grew. A causeway, straddled by towers, was built to connect Ortygia to the mainland. Before long, the population spread beyond the causeway, and the new districts on the mainland eventually came to dwarf the settlement on Ortygia. We began founding colonies of our own along the coast, and we absorbed many of the colonies founded by other Greek states. Our coins, engraved with the head of Arethusa encircled by four dolphins, were prized across the Mediterranean.

Whatever dreams those first settlers from Corinth may have had, it is not within the power of men to create a different world for themselves: we can do no more than replicate the same old one in different places. Sometimes, the men of Syracuse fought the native tribes; we often fought our fellow Greeks, and we routinely fought the Carthaginians, who had colonised the other side of the island. The people submitted to a series of tyrants, who proved adept at slaughtering our enemies, but who had a tendency also to slaughter the people. There were periods of democracy, too. I suppose the gods are merciful: at least I have never had to live through one of those. In any event, they never lasted very long. The strong men were always welcomed back by the people eventually, to rescue them from the weak ones.

Every now and again, Syracuse was lucky enough to find itself ruled by a great king. A great king is one who slaughters his people's enemies, but who is relatively discriminating in his domestic bloodletting. Hieron was one such. In fact, by the time I arrived at his court, it had been so long since he had last culled his subjects that he had acquired a reputation for mildness. I imagine this amused him. The truth was that his dry old scales were coiled so tightly around the city that no one had dared challenge him in years.

Agbal and I made our way down the Avenue of Athena as briskly as the crowds would allow. It was the grandest street in Syracuse, lined with the villas of the city's oldest and wealthiest families. As the centuries rolled on, we had quarrelled with each other and intermarried and then quarrelled again. The great nobles lived their lives in a briar patch of rivalries and alliances that grew more tangled with each new generation.

We finally arrived at the canal that marked the end of the avenue and the limit of the island of Ortygia. On the far side, the walls of the palace rose up sheer from the water. A long bridge stretched out over the canal, like a lizard tongue protruding from the mouth of the gates. The only visible remnant of my ancestor's former stronghold was an adjoining series of heavily fortified sea walls, facing the open Mediterranean, which provided a marina for our warships. We called this the Little Harbour. The canal served as both a moat and a back door from the Little Harbour into the Great Harbour and the bay on the other side of the isthmus.

I pushed my way across the bridge, which as usual was a crush of people and mules and carts moving in both directions. Once through the gate, the road turned a corner, following the channel between the perimeter and inner walls that eventually gave access to the mainland districts of the city. Instead of taking the road, I led Agbal up a broad flight of steps directly in front of us, to another gate tower in the middle of the inner wall. At the top, three Guardsmen were leaning on their spears chatting idly; a fourth dozed on a stool. I wore a commonplace white tunic that gave no indication of my rank, and I had deliberately arrived a day earlier than I was expected. One of the sentries looked down carelessly at me as I climbed the steps. I glowered back at him. I could see him registering my size. He scanned the scar on my face and his expression turned, first to puzzlement, then to surprise, and finally to something close to panic.

"Fuck! It's *him*," he whispered, as he elbowed one of the others in the ribs.

"Whoopsy daisy," I heard Agbal chuckle behind me.

I reached the top of the steps. The three of them immediately made way, shrinking from me and clutching their spears; they didn't even have the wit to come to attention. Behind them, the fourth man was still slumbering. I walked on in grim silence, kicking the stool from under him as I passed.

We entered the vast colonnaded courtyard, and Agbal whistled in amazement. He had clearly never been inside the palace before. It dwarfed even my own villa.

I pointed to an archway on the opposite side.

"Agbal, the barracks are through there. Find Lieutenant Castor and tell him I'd like to see him, if he has a moment. I'll be in my rooms; he knows where they are. Come back with him."

Agbal nodded and sprinted off eagerly across the courtyard, trying to weave his way through the dense huddles of palace attendants and hangers-on. He had not got twenty paces before he collided into the back of a powerfully built, dark-haired man in a toga. The man turned and swore. He was about my age, but maybe half a head shorter. I watched as he slapped Agbal hard across the face. Agbal immediately fell to his knees and prostrated himself in apology.

The man was still swearing and cuffing Agbal as I stepped up behind him.

A small group of spectators had gathered round the scene, grinning and laughing. They stopped when they saw me approach. A few of them seemed to know me and sheepishly tried to edge away. The man must have sensed my presence, because he laid off Agbal and turned round to square up to me.

"Is he yours?" he demanded, speaking Greek with a thick Roman accent. He looked at my plain white tunic and sneered. "Just what the fuck do you think you're doing, farmer boy, letting your slave run round like a wild animal?"

I sighed. The day was going from bad to worse. I looked down at Agbal. His lip was split and there was a thin trickle of blood on his chin. I saw tears of shame on his face.

"I'm sorry, Master," he said to me, swallowing. I turned and looked the Roman hard in the eyes. Another young man in a toga stepped forwards to stand just behind him and crossed his arms menacingly. They had a military bearing; I guessed both were officers of some sort. I had hoped my stare would be sufficient to warn the Roman off, but unfortunately the presence of his friend seemed only to embolden him.

"How dare you look at me like that, you fucking peasant?" the Roman barked, jabbing his finger at my chest. "Do you know who I am? I'm…"

I caught his hand in mine, snatching it out of the air like a fly, and snapped it back hard. He squealed, bending his knees and staggering forwards to try to relieve the pressure on his wrist. I twisted his hand back further, forcing him down, until he dropped to the ground in front of me. He looked up, snarling at me in pain and impotent rage.

"I don't care who you are," I said calmly.

His companion stared at me dumbly, trying to take in what he was seeing. I looked complacently at him and raised my eyebrows in invitation.

"Let him go, you fucking lunatic," he shouted nervously.

I shrugged and gave Do-you-know-who-I-am's hand a squeeze, making him yelp. I smiled at his friend in my disfigured way, raised my free hand and crooked a finger at him, beckoning him forward. The man bit his lip. He shot a guilty glance at his helpless companion, and wisely stayed where he was.

I noticed Do-you-know-who-I-am was wearing a heavy gold signet ring on his trapped hand. He squealed again as I twisted his wrist around to examine it. The ring was engraved with the emblem of an axe. I looked down at the Roman.

"That's my property that you've damaged, my friend," I said, tilting my head in Agbal's direction. "And now you'll have to compensate me."

"Fuck you," he hissed through his teeth.

I squeezed a little harder, crunching his knuckles together and distorting his fingers. He screamed.

I began working the ring off his index finger. He screamed again, this time in outrage, and tried to stop me, flailing at me like a girl with his other arm. I bent his wrist back further and squeezed harder still. The Roman shrieked and writhed for a couple of moments and then began patting me frantically in submission.

I pulled the ring off and let him go. He groaned and fell sideways onto his elbow, cradling his injured hand against his chest. It looked a little mangled; it may already have started to swell and turn blue. I'd probably overdone it with the squeezing.

I tossed the ring over to Agbal.

"That's for you," I said. "Now, get up and go and find Castor."

I turned and started to walk away. The whole courtyard had fallen silent.

"You fucking Greek turd," the Roman screamed defiantly after me from the ground. "You're in for it now, farmer boy."

I swung around and took two threatening strides back towards him. His eyes widened. He started paddling backwards with his elbows and kicking out frantically, trying to push himself away from me.

I felt I had made my point.

I stopped and gave him a formal little bow.

"My name is Dion, of the House of Dionysius," I said politely. "I am not a hard man to find, should you wish to talk with me again."

The Roman looked at me in horror. He had clearly heard of me: it seemed I wasn't a peasant after all. Before he could say anything, I turned my back on him once more and strode off.

I knew where to find my rooms. They had been allocated to Apollonius before me, although he had only ever used them for small, informal dinner parties, one or two of which I had begrudgingly attended.

I walked over to an archway that opened directly onto a wide marble staircase, and ran up to the first floor. My apartment lay at the end of a long corridor. The ornately carved door was ajar so I pushed it open and stepped into a large, high-ceilinged room, decorated from end to end with frescoes of mythological scenes. A row of windows on one side overlooked the Little Harbour and the open sea beyond. Apart from a few packing cases and some tatty pieces of furniture that had been brought over from my cottage at Plymmerium, the room was bare.

My two other camp slaves were bustling about unpacking. They were tall and willowy Numidians, as black as the night and just as beautiful. When we were children, my older sister had nicknamed them Alpha and Omega, and the names had stuck.

Alpha was carrying a stack of clay plates in his arms. Omega was fussing around with a broom, sweeping up some broken crockery. As usual, they were arguing.

"You clumsy hippopotamus," Omega wailed.

"Clumsy yourself," Alpha snapped back. "If you hadn't walked into me…"

"Hello," I said.

They turned in surprise and their faces lit up with pleasure. Although they were in their late thirties now, they were still extremely valuable, being an almost perfectly matched pair. At first sight, they might have been mistaken for twins, although if they did happen to be related, no one knew in what way. I had taken them with me to Plymmerium when I first became an officer. I had been trying to show off, I suppose, in the way young men do. My mother had been horrified that I had should have used them as camp slaves, but I had been careful with them and they remained quite undamaged.

"Don't you bow to your master any more?" I demanded.

"Forgive me, Master," said Alpha, bowing as best he could with the armful of plates.

He straightened and looked me up and down. He raised an eyebrow and the corner of his mouth turned down in distaste.

"But I'm afraid I just didn't recognise you in that nasty little tunic," he added.

"It doesn't even fit properly," Omega chipped in sadly. "Please get yourself some decent clothes, Master. It's an embarrassment to be seen out with you." He bowed as an afterthought.

"At least let me fetch you something clean to put on," said Alpha. "That looks quite… filthy." He wrinkled his nose.

"For pity's sake," I growled, "I've had to spend the whole morning listening to my mother. Do I really have to spend the afternoon listening to you two?"

They exchanged mutually reproachful looks.

"I'm sorry, Master," Alpha said soothingly.

"You must have had a difficult day," said Omega. "May I fetch you some wine perhaps?"

"We weren't expecting you till tomorrow, Master," Alpha added. He looked around the room mournfully. "I'm afraid we haven't had time to prepare properly for you."

"Don't worry, I know," I said. "All I'll need tonight is a bed. Have you got one for me?"

"Yes, Master," Omega replied, brightening up. "Would you like to see your room?"

He put down his broom and showed me through a high door into an empty anteroom, which in turn opened into a large bedroom. At its centre, two simple wooden stools faced each other across a square table. They had put my army cot against the back wall. A circlet of dried-out twigs hung from a nail above it, the brittle remains of the olive leaf crown that I had brought back from Olympia four years previously. Three old clothes chests, one with a warped lid, were lined along one of the adjacent walls. The largest had been decorated with a crude little painting of a minotaur and contained my outsized bronze armour. A bundle of spears of various types stood in a corner and, under the window, my collection of swords and knives had been neatly laid out across a long, narrow table.

Along with my armour and the olive crown, my weapons were the only things in the room that mattered to me. I dare say they were also the only evidence that I wasn't entirely destitute.

I walked over to the window. One of our family heirlooms, the rusting sword of King Dionysius, had been given pride of place in the middle of the table. It was a crude weapon: there was more of the butcher's yard than the palace about it. Dionysius would probably have scoffed at his descendants for treating it with reverence.

My own battle sword lay alongside. It had been forged out of Seric iron, a metal of far greater strength than anything produced around the Mediterranean. The iron was smelted, so people said, by magicians in the vast and mysterious kingdoms of India, which bordered the most remote fragments of Alexander of Macedon's shattered empire. The captain of one of my ships had managed to acquire a few precious, hand-sized ingots for me in Egypt. I had entrusted them to a swordsmith in Crete, reputed to be the most gifted in the world. The leaf-shaped blade that he eventually sent back shimmered with dense natural whorls and curlicues that made it seem a wild, living thing. You could travel a lifetime, and never see another weapon like it. As I had requested, the blade was a hand longer than usual and more thickly ribbed, and its two cutting edges were as sharp as an obsidian razor. Most men would have found it too heavy, but I could make the beauty dance well enough. My army sword was a twig of a weapon in comparison.

"Is there anything you would like rearranged, Master?" Omega asked. I turned and noticed they had put some sprigs of lavender in a small jar by my bed. I craved simplicity, but Alpha and Omega had been trained as household slaves and continued to wage their relentless war of domestication on me.

"No, you've both done well, Omega," I said. "Leave everything just as it is. But perhaps you were right about getting some new furniture for the other room. The old stuff from Plymmerium does look a bit out of place."

Omega pouted with pleasure. The pair of them had been grumbling about my furniture for years. They had been mortified when I had insisted on bringing it with me. I suppose I had been hoping to cling to the straightforwardness of my old army life, but in these opulent new surroundings, I realised I was merely making myself look ridiculous.

"How very wise, Master," Omega said, with a triumphant bow. He and Alpha had been unable to conceal their excitement about moving to the palace. No doubt they would soon be strutting around the courtyard like a pair of graceful black egrets, competing with the other palace slaves to see who could hold their noses highest in the air. They clearly had no intention of letting me spoil it for them.

I sighed.

"Very well. Go to my mother this afternoon and have her send over whatever you think we need. She's keeping some old slave women in the stables. Don't ask why. They can have the old furniture."

"The gods are merciful. But what should I do, Master, if the old slave women don't want your furniture?"

"Get out, you cheeky bastard," I said.

"Yes, Master." Omega glided happily away, hand on hip.

"And bring me a bowl of water," I shouted after him. But Alpha had already anticipated the request, and came in carrying a large bronze bowl a moment after Omega had walked out. He set it down on the table in the middle of the room.

"Agbal is back," he said, "and there is an officer here for you. Agbal is preparing some wine." He frowned at me reproachfully. "The poor boy looks like he's been in the wars. Whatever have you been doing with him?"

"It wasn't me. Alright?" I growled.

"I didn't think it was, Master. You've never hit a slave in your life. But you should take better care of him."

"Don't provoke me, Alpha, or I might make a start with you. Now, sod off."

He raised his eyebrows.

"Well, I never," he muttered huffily, and turned on his heels and left.

I told myself I only kept the pair of them around because they amused me. But I had been just a small boy when Alpha and Omega had joined our household. They had belonged to a Carthaginian general, who had used them for his own colourful purposes, until my father had taken them as war booty. They had doted on me from the first, playing with me whenever they could and stealing treats for me from the kitchens. I knew I would never sell them, despite the frequent offers I still received. They were the closest approximation to parents that I had.

I quickly washed my face and hands and changed my tunic. I walked into the anteroom at the same moment as Agbal, who emerged from a small door in the corner that I hadn't noticed before. He was carrying a tray with a clay pitcher and two cups. The door presumably led to a kitchen where my three slaves would have their beds.

Agbal kept his head lowered.

"Look at me," I demanded.

He looked up. His lip was swollen and his eye had blackened. He seemed ashamed.

"Thank you, Master, for what you did," he said meekly.

"Listen to me, Agbal," I said, not bothering to hide my irritation. "I never want to see you grovelling to another man again. If someone knocks you down, you will get back up. And if he knocks you down again, you will get back up again and take another blow. And you will keep standing up until he kills you. I will not be shamed by seeing my property lying at another man's feet. You will uphold the dignity of my household or you will be leaving it for the quarries. Do you understand?"

He nodded silently.

I stared at him. The fool probably thought I'd given him the ring because I felt sorry for him. But I had only wanted to humiliate the Roman, and tossing his family ring to Agbal had seemed as good a way as any. The Roman should have known better than to hit someone else's slave: it was appallingly rude.

There were tears on Agbal's cheeks now. I thought about it for a moment and decided there was probably no point punishing him further.

"Alright. We will put this behind us," I continued more gently. "You're a good lad, Agbal. You'll do fine, I'm sure. When you've served the wine, get Alpha to take care of your face."

I strode into the grand reception room. Agbal followed me forlornly with the tray.

Castor was sitting on one of my threadbare couches. Alpha and Omega stood smartly in attendance on either side of the entrance door. For all the freedom I allowed them in private, they knew what was expected of them when I had visitors. They had been trained under my mother's eye, after all. They could stand by my door for hours, like a pair of onyx urns, without so much as a twitch.

Castor jumped up as I entered and saluted me.

"Welcome to the palace, sir," he said formally.

I smiled at him.

"That's enough of that nonsense," I said, and turned to the slaves. "Alpha, take Agbal into the kitchen, would you, and clean him up."

I walked over to the packing case and poured out two cups of wine.

"My friend, can we get something out of the way?" I said, as I handed Castor a cup. "Hieron should probably have given you the captaincy. You certainly deserved it. I can't imagine what a pigfuck this place would have been without you. So I need to know, do you have a problem about him giving it to me instead?"

His eyes widened. He was maybe ten years older than me and as skinny and tough as twine, with a short beard that he kept meticulously trimmed.

"Shit, no, Dion," he said. "I certainly couldn't do it. You're the answer to my prayers."

"Well, that's a relief. Because I'm going to rely on that cool head of yours," I said.

We performed the usual ceremonies and settled ourselves on the couches. Castor looked at the simple clay cup, then cast an eye over the packing cases and furniture.

"I see you've spared no expense," he said.

"Piss off," I replied. "Now, what do I need to know about the Guards?"

We talked for about an hour. There were twelve Guards companies, Castor explained, of about a hundred and twenty men apiece. All the men were regulars, unlike the army, a third of whose numbers were trainees. Eight Guards companies were needed to garrison the various fortresses around the city walls and four were quartered in the palace. The companies rotated their postings every four months.

Each company required just two officers, but Apollonius had blithely handed out nearly ninety commissions to his friends' sons.

Castor had done the best he could with this mess. There were about a dozen older lieutenants like the one-handed Xeno, who had transferred to the Guards from the army for one reason or another. Castor had put each company under the command of one of these men, and had selected the best of the younger officers to act as their junior lieutenants. The rest of Apollonius's high-living dilettantes were all based permanently at the palace, where Castor had entrusted them with as few responsibilities as possible.

It was far from ideal, of course, as the palace officers had a corrupting influence on the entire division. Even some of the senior lieutenants had ceased to care greatly about their duties. I had known before I arrived that I would have to take a scythe to my officers. But my problem was that once a man had been allowed to buy himself a commission, it became his property, and I didn't have the power to withdraw it. Only the king could do that. Castor suggested I raise the matter at the Royal Council, but almost every councillor had some young relative or other in my officer corps, so that seemed unlikely to work.

We were still discussing the problem of how best to approach the king, when we were interrupted by a knock at the door. I nodded to Omega, who opened it and showed in a strange-looking little man. He was round and white and hairless, and wore some sort of rouge on his lips. His fingernails were painted gold. His unusual, heavily pleated cream robe was too long and trailed behind him on the floor. As the door closed, I caught a glimpse of a second man loitering nervously outside in the corridor.

My visitor ignored Castor but gave me a perfunctory bow.

"I take it I am addressing Captain Dion?" he asked in a high-pitched voice. It seemed he was a eunuch. I nodded in acknowledgement from the couch.

"I have been sent to you by His Majesty, who has asked me to convey his compliments. My name is Secretary Nebit and I am instructed to provide you with whatever assistance you may require for the duration of your captaincy. I am Egyptian by birth but speak eight languages and am highly proficient at mathematics. I understand that this is not a field in which you are yourself greatly interested, Captain, despite your connection to the illustrious Archimedes. It has therefore been suggested that I may be of service with the divisional supplies and accounts. My requirements are modest. I shall need only an office in the barracks yard and access to all divisional records."

Nebit may have been Egyptian, but his Greek was flawless. I guessed he was a freedman, who had been born a slave. I scratched my cheek and looked at Castor, who raised his eyebrows.

"Thank you, Secretary Nebit, that's most generous of His Majesty," I replied warily.

"You will perhaps be reassured to learn, Captain," he continued, "that I am also something of an expert on military matters, which may be why His Majesty has honoured me with this particular assignment."

"Are you, now?" I said.

"Indeed I am, Captain," Nebit replied. "I have read all the standard texts on strategy, tactics and organisation. I am familiar with the campaigns of Alexander and I have studied in detail the last war between Rome and Carthage. I also made a significant contribution to an analysis of their present war, which His Majesty instructed the secretariat to prepare for him last year."

"And what exactly was this contribution of yours?" I asked.

"I provided an assessment of the agricultural resources available to Carthage, Captain, including their timber production," he replied proudly.

"And what did you conclude from your assessment?" I asked, trying not to laugh. I covered my mouth and pretended to cough.

"That is confidential, I am afraid," he replied haughtily.

I glanced at Castor, who was staring up at the ceiling.

"You seem to have rather a high opinion of yourself, Nebit," I said evenly.

His eyes flashed. What was it I saw in his expression? Not exactly anger, but something else I couldn't immediately identify. Pain, perhaps.

"I have served two kings of Egypt and now I serve the King of Syracuse," he replied coldly. "I believe my own opinion of myself is not entirely inconsistent with the opinion that others have formed of me. You have your reputation, Captain, and I have mine. And I would rather have mine than yours."

I put my tongue in my cheek and rolled it round the inside of my scar. It was something I had taught myself to do when I needed to check myself. Hieron was known to have a small army of secretaries. For the most part, they toiled out of sight. I couldn't recall even having met one of them before, but then I had always avoided the court. My friend Theodotus had warned me about them before I left Plymmerium. "Apparently they run everything, Dion," he had said. "Be careful."

I stood up and walked over to within a few feet of the Egyptian, towering over him and forcing him to tilt his head back uncomfortably to meet my gaze. I narrowed my eyes.

"If you expect to work for me, Nebit, I think you had better learn to call me 'sir'," I said quietly.

Most men would have been cowed, but Nebit didn't even blink. In fact, he seemed amused by my crude attempt to intimidate him. If I had been in any doubt before, I knew then that this jellyfish was poisonous enough to feel quite invulnerable to me.

"I fear I may not have made myself entirely clear, Captain," he said, as if talking to a child. "I am here to assist you, but I do not report to you. I answer only to His Majesty."

Sometimes you advance, and sometimes you retreat. The man was clearly Hieron's spy, but I could hardly send him packing. I bit my lip.

"Very well," I said. I stared at the secretary for a moment longer, drew a breath and forced a smile. "Welcome to the City Guards, Nebit. I am sure you will be… invaluable. Why don't you sit down and join us? Let's decide where you're going to fit in. Do you want some wine?"

"Thank you, Captain, but no wine for me," he replied. He looked at the nearest stool doubtfully, then gathered up his gown and settled himself on it with a little wrinkle of his nose. I went back to the couch.

"Nebit, have you met Castor, my adjutant?"

"I regret I have never had that honour," replied the Egyptian, "although I believe we have seen each other occasionally from a distance." The two men exchanged a polite nod.

"Castor is responsible for administration," I said. "I suggest you deal with him on a day-to-day basis. He'll sort out an office for you. Alright?"

Nebit looked at me shrewdly. He obviously realised I was hoping to use Castor to keep him at arm's length.

"It would greatly facilitate my work if I could attend all your officer briefings, Captain," he replied.

I pursed my lips, then nodded. Nebit nodded back.

"Good," he said. "That's settled then. Now, if you will forgive me for bringing up a rather awkward topic, I am afraid there is another matter to discuss, Captain. I gather you had an unfortunate encounter with one of His Majesty's great-nephews in the courtyard a little while ago… Something about a family ring?"

I looked at him in puzzlement.

"I had an encounter with a Roman. He certainly wasn't Greek."

"No Captain, he isn't Greek, but he is the king's great-nephew all the same. He is an officer with the Roman garrison here in Sicily. His name is Felix Manlius Torquatus, and his mother, Seema, is one of His Majesty's favourite nieces."

I closed my eyes.

"Fuck," I said.

The longer I thought about it, the worse it got.

"Fuck," I said again, more emphatically.

"Fuck indeed, Captain," said Nebit, "fuck indeed. But happily, I have been able to arrange an unfuck for you."

"What do you mean?"

"I have smoothed things out."

I looked at him suspiciously.

"You have? How?"

He smiled in a superior way.

"It was no trouble, really. His Majesty decided to be unavailable when young Felix came running over a little while ago with his arm in a sling, and so I met with him instead. He was making all sorts of silly threats and demands. But I pointed out what his father's likely reaction would be, should certain arrangements fail to proceed as planned. I allude to arrangements that Felix has been entrusted to negotiate on his father's behalf, and of which I gather you are yourself aware, Captain, though they are not yet in the public domain. I also suggested that Senator Torquatus might not be best pleased to hear how his son had allowed a family ring to be taken from him in such a humiliating manner. Finally, I reminded poor Felix of why their family emblem is an executioner's axe… Do you happen to know the story, Captain?"

I shrugged my shoulders and shook my head.

"Ah, it is really most fortuitous." Nebit smiled, clearly very pleased with himself. "It so happens the original Manlius Torquatus, who was Dictator of Rome a hundred years or so ago, is celebrated chiefly for having condemned his own son to death. The son had fought heroically in some battle or other, but in the process had disobeyed an order. Hence the emblem. The present Senator Torquatus is apparently forged from much the same metal as his great ancestor. I am sure he would not have gone quite so far in this instance, but even so, I think young Felix would rather be locked in a cage with you than incur his father's displeasure. And so we were able to come to an arrangement. You will return Felix's ring and send him a letter of apology. I have his slave waiting outside to take the ring back. Furthermore, as you may know, Captain, you were yourself to have played a part in the negotiations that Felix is here to conduct, but under the circumstances, you will now be represented by others."

"That's it?" I asked.

"More or less, Captain. Although His Majesty did also ask me to mention that he would be most grateful if, in future, you might be so kind as to refrain from assaulting his relatives."

There was a long silence. I hated to acknowledge Nebit's ascendancy, but it seemed I had no choice but to put myself in his hands. I swallowed my pride.

"Tell me, Nebit, how angry with me is the king? Should I go and apologise to him?"

"A further letter will be sufficient," Nebit replied smoothly. "I shall compose both letters for you this evening. You have been most fortunate, Captain. His Majesty does not much care for Felix. And he is in the process of negotiating a new grain contract with the Roman ambassador. It rather suited him for the Romans to be given a reminder that the citizens of Syracuse are not to be trifled with. But on any other day... Well, Captain, things might have turned out very differently for you."

I gazed at the strange secretary, and wondered what on earth I should make of him.

"Nebit," I said eventually, "I don't know whether I like you, but I find I am already in your debt. Thank you. At this rate, I might even end up sharing your own opinion of yourself."

To my surprise, he laughed. I had thought him humourless.

"Nobody much likes me, Captain. But I get things done. Work with me, and you will find yourself swimming with the tide. Now, if you will kindly remember to give the ring to the man outside, I must be getting along."

We both stood up.

"You will forgive me if I don't offer you my hand," Nebit added. "I'm afraid I still need the use of it."

Omega let him out. When he'd gone, I told Omega to fetch the ring from Agbal, and sat down again. I ran my fingers through my hair.

"What do you think, Castor?" I asked. He hadn't said a word since the Egyptian had arrived.

"Your slave told me on the way over here what you did to that Roman," he replied thoughtfully. "By now, half Syracuse is probably laughing about it and drinking your health. I imagine that's the real reason Hieron isn't punishing you. He likes to work with the grain. But that temper of yours will be your undoing one day, my friend."

"That may be true, but it's not what I meant," I said. "What do you think of Nebit?"

Castor looked at me and shrugged.

"He's dangerous. Let's just hope he's really here to help."

Agbal woke me before dawn with my breakfast, which he put on the table in the centre of the room. He tried his best to appear eager but his eyes were red and puffy. It looked like he'd been crying all night. Until he had been made to give it back, he had probably been clinging to the ring as some sort of reassurance of his value to me. That's the trouble with childish illusions: they don't bend; they just shatter.

I dismissed him, then washed and dressed in my full suit of armour. I had more important things to deal with, but Agbal's bruised face kept intruding on my thoughts. I realised I had made a mistake: if I didn't put matters right, I knew I would risk turning a promising slave into a bad one.

I shouted for him and he came running in a moment later.

"Yes Master?" he said, doing his best to smile through his swollen lip.

I walked over to the large table.

"Come over here, Agbal," I said.

"It seems the palace is a dangerous place," I continued. "You know the last captain of the Guards was murdered, don't you?"

He nodded.

"Well, I have no wish to be murdered as well. So, I am putting you in charge of the security of these rooms. Every night, it will be your responsibility to ensure the doors are properly bolted. And I want you to sleep in the anteroom. You will be my first line of defence if anyone tries to get into my room. Now, you'll need to arm yourself…"

I scrutinised the weapons on the table, and finally picked up a pair of throwing knives with ivory handles. The blades were quite long and thin but were perfectly weighted and tapered to a vicious point. I had acquired them after seeing a Parthian hit a man in the throat at over a dozen paces with a similar weapon. Men the world over have expended a great deal of thought on how best to kill each other, and one should always be open-minded to new methods.

"These are for throwing, Agbal," I explained. I took one out of its scabbard. "You hold them like this... You stand like this, facing your target sideways on, with your front foot pointing at him, and you turn your shoulders into the throw like this..." I demonstrated in slow motion. "Got it?"

He nodded, although he looked bewildered.

"I want you to practise your throw for an hour every day. You will have to find somewhere quiet to do it, where no one can see you. I'm not supposed to let you have a weapon. The hayloft over the barracks stables might be a good place... Now, listen to me: these knives are very valuable. They're worth half a dozen gold rings, so take good care of them." I handed them to him. "When you can hit a shield every time at fifteen paces, they will be my gift to you. Alright, off you go."

He started choking and mumbling something incoherent, but I cut him off and brusquely dismissed him. He would probably see through the lie soon enough: I hardly needed poor little Agbal to protect me. But it wouldn't matter. The truth beneath the lie, that he had a secure place with me, would cheer him up just as much as the lie itself.

Alpha and Omega were already up, gleefully repacking the crates that they had unpacked the day before. Alpha opened the door for me and I headed out, with my heavy round shield slung over my back.

I walked around the colonnade in the gloom of the early dawn and through the archway that led into a large exercise yard. The palace barracks occupied the two long sides stretching away from me; at the far end stood a central gate tower, with stable blocks either side of it. Castor was already waiting for me. He had done as I had asked him: apart from those on sentry duty, the entire garrison was lined up in single file around two sides of the yard. Like me, they were all in full armour. The sun wasn't even fully up yet, but the officers were already fidgeting uncomfortably with their breastplates and helmets. I chuckled to myself. I nodded to Castor, who grinned back at me. He had been waiting for this moment for a long time.

"Attention!" he barked.

I faced the men.

"You know who I am," I said in my parade-ground voice. "We are going to run fifty circuits of the yard. I will set the pace. Most of you will not be able to complete this exercise, and so we will repeat it every morning, until everybody can complete it. I understand yesterday's sentries were drawn from Third Company. I was not impressed. Third Company officers and men will run an additional fifty circuits this afternoon. Now, face left!"

And so my captaincy of the City Guard began.

V

THE MALMEIDES AFFAIR

Within a week, I nearly contrived to bring my captaincy to an end.

It was my own fault, I suppose. Two days after taking up my new duties, I made a spot inspection of the palace in the middle of the night and found that five sentries were missing from their posts. I stormed into the duty officer's room, only to discover him drunk in bed with one of them. The other four had doubtless taken advantage of the situation to abscond to a tavern or brothel. The duty officer's name was Malmeides.

The next afternoon, still in a cold rage, I had all the men and officers of the palace garrison assemble on parade. The five guards were brought out, already gagged, and tied to a row of posts. I stripped naked and, one by one, flogged them myself. When I had finished with the first, he was untied and carried to the infirmary on a stretcher, face down and still quivering. And so it went on. I had to use my left arm on the last man, but as I'm ambidextrous, I doubt it made much difference to him.

After he had also been carried away, I walked silently up and down the lines of men and officers, naked and spattered in blood, with my whip coiled in my hand. It was an image I wished them to remember.

Finally, I had Malmeides brought out. He had also been gagged. I remember how he twisted his head to stare at me desperately as he was dragged to the post. I ran my hand through my hair, which was sticky with blood and sweat, and spat. His eyes widened with fear. When he had been tied up, I gave the whip a loud crack in the air. Anticipation is half the punishment, after all. Malmeides started wriggling and jerking frantically against the ropes.

I set to work on him. He went limp after about a dozen lashes, but I kept going.

I had set the beast loose. It hadn't had a good outing for a long time.

After a while – I don't know how long exactly, but two or three minutes, probably – Castor broke from his place in the lines and ran over. He stepped in front of me to obstruct me and put his hand on my shoulder.

"No, Dion," he said quietly. "No more. Stop now. You must stop."

I remember how shocked he looked.

I realised I had done enough. By now, I was quite tired. I nodded to Castor silently, and dropped my whip hand to my side.

Castor waved and two men hurried over. One of them cut Malmeides down as the second caught him and lowered him gently to the ground. He looked like a piece of raw steak. Two more men ran across with a stretcher. The four of them lifted him onto the stretcher, but oddly, they didn't pick it up. Instead, one of them knelt to look at Malmeides more closely, as the other three huddled round nervously.

Castor put his hand on my back and turned me to try to walk me away. I shook him off irritably and gazed at the ranks of men. A couple of the officers had fainted; several had been sick. Some five hundred men were staring at me in horror.

I sneered back at them contemptuously.

One of the stretcher-bearers started walking over towards us, white as a virgin's tit. I dismissed him with a wave of my hand before he could say anything. I had already realised Malmeides must be dead; I didn't need to be told. His puny heart had probably given way.

I couldn't have cared less.

Few men have ever understood the nature of my rage. Lepides, my old general, was one who did, perhaps. Like many people, I have a short temper, but the beast is something else. When I release him, he does not make me irrational. He merely frees me from any fear or pity or shame. It is not that I lose control; rather, I am able to throw off all the controls that limit a man's capacity to act. That is why I am so very dangerous.

I picked up my tunic and undergarment and started walking towards the archway that led to the bathhouse. Behind me, I heard Castor dismiss the men. They dispersed in silence.

A face in one of the first-floor windows caught my eye. It was the eunuch Nebit. He had obviously watched the whole spectacle. He inclined his head towards me politely, as if we were passing on the street, and I raised my hand in acknowledgement. He seemed to be the only man there as indifferent as I was to the sight of a little blood.

The doctor came to see me an hour later and told me that the men I had flogged would have to remain in the infirmary for several weeks. I sent a message over to Nebit to stop their pay until they returned to duty. Poverty is a great healer.

As a courtesy, I had Malmeides' body delivered to his parents the same day, so they could perform the customary funeral rites.

Castor had warned me not to flog Malmeides. We had argued about it. I told him Malmeides had been the worst offender and it would be unjust for him to escape the same punishment as the others. He told me he didn't think anyone had ever flogged an officer before. He may have been right, but that only makes sense if you want the officer to retain the respect of his men. I didn't. I had wanted to shame Malmeides into resigning his commission. I would have been content for him to leave the Guards on his feet, but it mattered not a jot to me that he had ended up leaving on the remnants of his back instead.

Unfortunately, it turned out that, through his mother, Malmeides was the nephew of the Royal Treasurer, a man called Zoippos.

Zoippos was a middle-aged bore with a high opinion of himself, to which he heroically clung in the teeth of all evidence. He owed his position to his wife, who was one of Hieron's daughters, and he owed his wife to his father, who had helped arrange the coup that brought Hieron to power. Zoippos insisted on making a dreadful fuss about Malmeides' death, telling anyone who would listen that I was no better than a common murderer and must be held to account.

I wasn't particularly worried: it was entirely a military affair, so the courts couldn't touch me. The only man to whom I was answerable was the king, and before he had become a king, Hieron had been a general. I was sure he understood the realities of army life. Commanding officers have always had a great deal of discretion when it comes to disciplinary matters: Lepides had barely let a month go by without hanging or crucifying someone. I was fairly certain Hieron would just ignore the whole business and that it would all soon blow over.

It didn't work out that way. Zoippos was like a dog with a bone. Although I couldn't be prosecuted in the courts, he arranged for a petition to be drawn up and sent to the king, demanding justice for Malmeides. Over fifty of my own useless lieutenants added their names to it. That put the matter on a formal footing. I received a note, bearing the king's own seal, informing me that I was not to leave the city until he had ruled on the petition.

Gelon was the king's only son, but he also had two daughters. The other one, the younger, was married to a smooth character called Andranodoros, whom I had known since childhood, but with whom I had never got on. Although Zoippos and Andranodoros were rivals for Hieron's favour and disliked each other, they must have disliked me even more, because before long they had formed a little anti-Dion alliance. Naturally, they were too frightened of the king to beard him directly, so instead they enlisted their hatchet-faced wives to nag away at the old man.

I still wasn't troubled. Gelon was required to come over from Plymmerium once a week or so, and whenever he did, we tried to steal a night together, discreetly making use of a vacant apartment in the palace. I was confident our intimacy made me invulnerable, despite the best efforts of his sisters. Besides, he had promised that his father would protect me.

One afternoon, maybe three weeks after Malmeides' death, I was working at the table in my bedroom when Agbal interrupted me to announce that I had visitors. Alpha and Omega were out buying food. I followed Agbal into the larger room, which now looked like an Egyptian brothel. It was cluttered from end to end with gilded couches and stools and ornamental display stands, on which huge painted vases balanced precariously. An invading army of marble busts seemed to have gained possession of every available table and ledge, and glared at me defiantly from all angles as I walked down the room.

A frail and elderly man sat wheezing on a stool. An equally ancient and exhausted-looking slave stood beside him. There was a small cedar casket on the floor between them. Agbal, who had taken his new duties as my domestic bodyguard to heart, carefully posted himself against a wall close by. He eyed the old gentleman suspiciously, ready to spring into action at the first sign of trouble.

"Ah, Captain Dion," the old man said. "Please forgive me for not standing. My legs aren't what they were. I am Secretary Philocrates. His Majesty has asked me to bring you this."

He nodded to the slave, who bent down and painfully lifted the casket with both hands. The slave staggered over and, with a wince, handed it to me. He wiped his forehead in relief. The casket probably weighed less than my battle sword.

"Go on, open it," wheezed Philocrates, with a smile.

Inside were a dozen blue tunics. I looked at the old man in surprise.

"As you may know, Captain," he said, "we usually hold a little investiture ceremony for new members of the Royal Council. His

Majesty regrets that he cannot make the time on this occasion, but he looks forward to seeing you when the council next meets. That will be in seventeen days' time. The council always sits on the first day of the new moon."

"Thank you for bringing me these, Secretary Philocrates," I said politely. "Please tell His Majesty I am greatly honoured. May I offer you some wine?"

"Oh no, I'm afraid I can't drink wine these days. Thank you for the thought, but I must be skipping along. I've heard a great deal about you, Captain; it has been a pleasure meeting you at last."

He beckoned to the slave, who went to his master's side and held his elbow to help him up. It seemed to take a long time. When he was finally standing, Philocrates and I exchanged a little bow and my two visitors shuffled off unsteadily, arm in arm. Agbal hurriedly closed the door behind them in evident relief.

I was anything but relieved. It so happened that one of my cousins had been appointed to the Royal Council a few months earlier, and I knew he had been invested in a ceremony attended by all the other Royal Councillors. The message was clear enough: I was in disgrace. It seemed Zoippos's poison was spreading through the veins of the palace.

Alpha and Omega returned a short while later carrying two bulging sacks of shopping, to find me sitting with my chin on my hands, staring at the casket. They cooed with pleasure when they saw the tunics and immediately began nagging me to try one on. I grunted, shrugged in resignation, and decided I might as well.

"It fits!" squealed Alpha, clapping his hands.

"And such fine cotton!" added Omega, pawing at me. "It must be Egyptian, Master."

I brushed him away irritably and quickly took it off again. Agbal was standing behind a couch, trying not to giggle. I put my plain soldier's smock back on over my undergarment. It felt a great deal more comfortable.

"Alright, the entertainment's over," I growled. "You can all get back to your work now."

"Of course, Master," said Alpha, ignoring me. "But you won't believe what they're saying about you in the city."

"You're quite the hero, Master," added Omega.

"What do you mean?"

"Well, Master," replied Alpha, "they say you're just like your famous ancestor, the king. 'Hard as marble, the Bull is, but you can't say he's not fair' were the fishmonger's words, and everyone in the shop agreed. First you put that Roman in his place, and then just a few days later, you give some noble a good whipping. Treated him just the same as anybody else. No one could remember anything like it. A second Dionysius, the fishmonger called you."

"Shit," I said. The snub from the king had already unsettled me, but this was worse. "Listen to me, all three of you. If people ask you about me, you are never to compare me to King Dionysius. Do you understand? I mean it. Never!"

They looked at me in perplexity. But with a man like Hieron on the throne, that sort of chatter was the last thing I wanted.

On the eve of my first council meeting, Nebit came to see me in my office. It had been suggested to him, he said, that it might be diplomatic for me to send my excuses. Feelings were running high over Malmeides and my presence at the table could be a little awkward. He had already drafted a brief note for me, if I would care to attach my seal to it.

It was clearly less of a suggestion than a royal command, so I reluctantly did as he said. Gelon told me later that Zoippos attempted to raise Malmeides' death during the meeting, but that Hieron cut him short. The king promised to rule on the petition, as soon as he could find the time; until then, there was no point discussing it. If Zoippos was frustrated by this answer, then when I heard of it, so too was I. Hieron could simply have declared that I had acted within my authority and that would have been the end of it. But instead, it seemed he had chosen to leave my future hanging in the air.

There was a story that people used to tell about another ancestor of mine, the second King Dionysius, son of the first. A fawning courtier had once suggested that the king must have been an exceptionally happy man. The next day, this Dionysius invited the courtier to try sitting on his throne, to see how he liked it. The courtier, whose name was Damocles, eagerly did so, but when he looked up, he saw a sword suspended over his head by a single horsehair. I knew how my ancestor felt.

If the common people saw me as some sort of hero, the higher classes certainly didn't, thanks to Zoippos and his friends. I regularly used to receive dinner invitations from people whom I barely knew, presumably desperate to obtain some advantage in their dealings with my mother, or perhaps hoping to thrust a daughter upon me. I never went, of course, but after Malmeides' death, the invitations quickly dried up. It seemed I had become as fashionable as leprosy.

One of Zoippos's cronies was another Royal Councillor known as Leatherskin, who foolishly tried to organise a boycott of my family's shipping business.

Leatherskin's father had belonged to a new generation of nobles, created by Hieron in the early years of his reign to dilute the power of the old families. Like all wealthy men of obscure origins, Leatherskin, whose real name was Polyaenus, yearned above all else for social acceptance, and he might even have been welcomed by polite society, had he only been a little less eager to elbow his way into it. Most members of my class were content to mock him behind his back, the nickname being as much an allusion to his coarse rural ancestry as to his pockmarked face. My mother, as usual, was the exception to the rule: she would never waste a knife on someone's back when there was a throat available. At some aristocratic gathering or other, she had once asked Leatherskin's wife if her husband still milked his own cows, sending the poor woman fleeing from the room in tears. Although I had no particular quarrel with the man, it was perhaps unsurprising that he had one with me. And I suppose matters weren't helped by the fact that his wife, the woman whom my mother had humiliated, was one of Malmeides' aunts. Lady Leatherskin – her real name eludes me now – and Malmeides' father were siblings, while Zoippos was his uncle on the other side. But then, in some distant and long-forgotten way, I was probably related to Malmeides too. Syracuse was like that.

My mother crushed Leatherskin's challenge easily enough, by the simple expedient of threatening to boycott the boycotters. She disdainfully let it be known that my family would never do business again with anyone who joined in his scheme. Rather sensibly, the merchants and nobles decided that her capacity for vindictiveness was considerably greater than Leatherskin's own. Besides, they all set more store by silver than by principles, and so the Leatherskins were humiliated once more and were left nurturing an even greater grievance against my family than formerly.

I was largely indifferent to all the buzzing of the wasps in the city; my own life revolved around the palace barracks and the other garrisons. Castor and I drilled the men hard and they seemed to respond well. I exercised alongside them. Every week, I would offer a silver piece to any man who could best me with a sword or in a wrestling match. Quite a few tried their luck with a sword, but only one, a long-legged rogue called Ajax, ever dared to take me on at wrestling. As the Guards' champion, he told me he felt honour-bound to have a go, and in the event he did pretty well, at one point catching me off balance and nearly managing to throw me. By the time we had finished, he had taken something of a bruising, but he smiled happily all the same and politely thanked me for the lesson. I have always liked a gracious loser, so I clapped him warmly on the back and gave him a silver coin anyway.

Later, I discovered that Ajax had already collected a bronze coin from every man in the garrison, as the price he had demanded for agreeing to provide them with their little spectacle, a sum equivalent to four or five silver coins. I dare say Lepides would have had him flogged, but when I found out, I was so amused I made him a sergeant for good measure.

I returned to the South Citadel for my swimming competition. The men of Syracuse are all half-fish but I am not particularly fast in the water – I have the wrong sort of build – and so it proved expensive. I ended up trading twelve silver coins for just over a hundred bronze ones. But I was pleased to find that Leander, the eager young lieutenant, was among those who had beaten me. I gave the bronze coins I'd collected to Xeno, the crusty one-handed commander of the garrison, and told him to buy his men a couple of piglets as a treat.

Soldiers are what they are, of course, and I had to order several punishment details, but the offences were all relatively trivial. My whip stayed on its hook in my office.

If the men were coming along well, the palace officers were a different matter. There were three or four who had decided to make a go of it and were trying to shape up; the rest were a stone around my neck. I had asked to see the king privately, in the hope he would agree to cashier them, but word came back that he was too busy to meet me.

I was stymied. Apart from making my useless officers drill and exercise a couple of times a day, there seemed little I could do to encourage them to leave. Until I could put the Malmeides affair behind me, caution demanded that I tread softly: I didn't want to give my enemies anything more to use against me. Castor agreed.

If I was wary, so were my idle officers. They did the minimum they could get away with, and they did it poorly, but they took care to do it. They clearly believed that Hieron would eventually be persuaded to break me over Malmeides, and they were waiting it out. At society dinners in Syracuse, they schemed behind my back and gleefully anticipated my imminent downfall. I think what they resented most, more than my flaying of their friend, more even than the early morning runs, was that I was starting to win the loyalty of the men. I was exacting, where they had been indulgent, and they couldn't understand it. The idiots had thought they were loved.

✳

One afternoon, Castor and I were standing in the exercise yard, watching the weapons training.

"He looks useful," I said, nodding towards a small man who was part of a group practising their sword work. What the fellow lacked in reach, he more than made up for in speed and ferocity.

"Yes, he's a proper little killer. Everyone calls him Needle. He came to us from the Yellow Shields... Oh, fuck." Castor was staring over my shoulder. I turned to see what had caught his attention.

Two soldiers wearing black-plumed helmets were marching towards us across the yard. Four slaves followed behind them, carrying an awning on poles. A blonde boy of about fourteen sauntered along in its shade, dressed in a flowing blue gown.

"It's Hieronymus," Castor said quietly. "He's an evil little turd. For pity's sake, don't let him provoke you, Dion."

I grunted. The rumour was that Prince Gelon, always preoccupied with work, neglected his son and allowed his wife to spoil the boy appallingly. At least, that's what my mother had told me. But then, my mother's definition of spoiling a child was an unusually wide one and seemed to encompass any small kindness or gesture of affection.

The little procession stopped about forty feet short of where Castor and I were standing.

"I think he expects us to go to him," whispered Castor. "Best to humour him."

"You stay here," I replied. "I'll speak to him."

I walked up to the awning and bowed politely. Hieronymus ignored me. He was watching the men, most of whom had already stopped practising to stare back at him.

"Hello. You must be Hieronymus," I said amiably. "I'm Captain Dion. How can I help you?"

There was a long silence. I noticed his blue robe was embroidered with little golden stars.

"You can begin by learning some manners," the prince said eventually. "You do not speak to me unless I speak to you first, and then you will address me as 'Your Royal Highness'. And another thing: your men should bow when they see me."

He had his father's lean frame and hooked nose, but his hair was greasy and his face covered in acne. His voice hadn't fully broken yet, with the unfortunate result that his speech was punctuated by intermittent squeaks.

I raised my eyebrows.

"I shall overlook your behaviour on this occasion, however," Hieronymus continued, "and attribute it to ignorance. My uncle Zoippos warned me that you are a wild animal and that my grandfather has not yet broken you in properly. But you would do well to remember this lesson in future." The prince tilted back his head and stared at me contemptuously.

I burst out laughing.

The two bodyguards turned to look at me warily. I didn't recognise them but I could tell they were serious men. I met their gaze and shook my head slightly. They took my meaning and turned back round; I fancied I saw one of them smiling as he did so.

"And I shall overlook your behaviour on this occasion, lad," I said evenly. "But if you ever talk to me like that again, I'll put you over my knee and give that royal arse of yours a good spanking. Now, you'd better run along, before your mother starts worrying where you've got to."

His jaw dropped open. I turned away from him and started back towards Castor.

"Come back here. Come back here this instant!" the prince squawked after me. I raised my arm and gave him a backhanded wave over my shoulder without looking round or breaking my stride.

"Get back to your drills!" I bellowed at the men as I drew up alongside my adjutant.

Behind me, I could hear Hieronymus screaming at his slaves. "That seemed to go well," said Castor.

*

I was still keeping Nebit at as great a distance as possible, although I had to admit, he fully lived up to his own opinion of himself. About a month after he started work, he came to tell me that he had completed a projection of the Guards' likely deficit for the year. Hieron's treasury made a contribution to all the military divisions, but it was never enough, and the captains were expected to make good the shortfall. Few men could afford the rank. I had given the matter almost no thought on my transfer from the Gold Shields, beyond a vague and pleasant reflection that my new obligation should be roughly three quarters of the sum I had been spending at Plymmerium, as I now had only three quarters as many men.

"What?" I asked incredulously, when Nebit told me how much my new captaincy would be likely to cost. It was more than double the amount I had been contributing to the Gold Shields, an annoying sum, even for me. "Are you sure?"

"Oh yes, quite sure, Captain. The illustrious and greatly lamented Apollonius appears to have established an unusually liberal regime for the benefit of his officers. There are a great many of them, as you know, and they are rather expensive pets to maintain."

"I never realised Apollonius was such a rich man."

"I suspect, Captain, that your predecessor came to depend on the sale of commissions to keep the City Guard going. Your young comrades were apparently prepared to pay a very considerable price to avoid the usual military training."

"Fuck," I said.

"Fuck indeed, Captain, fuck indeed. There are of course one or two economies I could make, but I am afraid the only real unfuck in this instance would be to dispense with your surplus officers."

"I'm trying, Nebit, I'm trying," I sighed. "Well, do what you can to cut the costs."

"You give me a free hand, Captain?"

"Yes, of course. But don't do anything that would affect the men."

He pouted smugly.

"Leave it to me," he said.

Within an hour, Nebit had posted a notice in my name, announcing the closure of the officers' dining room. From now on, it stated, all officers would either have to eat with their men in the common mess hall, or make their own arrangements. The key to their stateroom was returned to the palace steward, and Apollonius's cooks were consigned to auction.

Nebit's second great economy was a masterstroke.

The young nobles had all brought fine stallions with them to the palace, which were formally assigned to military use and then stabled at the division's expense. Nebit had discovered that these horses were technically the property of the Guards, until such time as their original owners withdrew them from service again.

Two days later, my officers awoke to find the stables almost empty. Nebit had sold most of the horses to a dealer, who had removed them in the night. The only ones that remained, apart from my own, were those belonging to Castor and the three or four palace lieutenants whom I wanted to retain. The rather princely proceeds of the transaction were paid into the division's coffers. Naturally, the officers had all brought grooms with them; it turned out the legal status of the grooms was identical to that of horses, so Nebit sold them too, although they were worth much less.

I was still chuckling about it when Castor came to my rooms that evening. We had taken to eating alone together most nights: neither of us enjoyed the sullen and resentful company of the junior officers.

"I wonder if I misjudged our little jellyfish," I said.

"He's certainly a clever sod," Castor replied. "He can do things in five minutes that used to take me an hour. I'm planning to spend three days at Euryalus next week. I'd never have had the time to do that without him."

I had given Castor responsibility for all the garrisons in the mainland districts of the city. The citadel of Euryalus was easily the most important.

"But can we trust him, do you think?" I asked.

Castor chewed his lip thoughtfully.

"He's a hard man to like, Dion, but given how many enemies you seem to be making, perhaps you should try to embrace him. What have you to lose?"

Alpha and Omega were busy preparing the meal, so Agbal was on duty at the door.

"Agbal," I said on an impulse, "go and find Secretary Nebit. He'll probably still be in his office. Ask him if he'd like to join us for dinner."

Castor and I continued chatting until Agbal returned to say Nebit would be honoured to join us.

The Egyptian arrived a short while later. He had changed into another one of his outsized gowns. This one was red and green. He had rouged his lips and exaggerated his eyebrows in charcoal and, most peculiar of all, he was wearing a small black wig. I was careful to keep a straight face.

I showed him to a couch and we exchanged a few empty pleasantries while Agbal gave him a cup of water. The earthenware was gone; we used silver now. Nebit examined the cup admiringly, which was rather gauche of him. I wondered what sort of social life he led.

"It's very kind of you to invite me over, Captain," he said. "And may I say how beautifully you have furnished your apartment. But I must admit, I am a little curious to know why I am here."

Castor and I exchanged a look.

"I think maybe I've been unfair to you, Nebit," I replied awkwardly. "I've kept you at a distance. To be frank, I didn't know quite what to make of you. You're an unusual man, as you must realise. But Castor says you're invaluable, and twice now you have done me a personal service. I wanted to let you know that I'm grateful." I bit my lip. "And we will both be honoured to work more closely with you in the future."

Nebit smiled.

"That was a gracious little speech, Captain," he said, in his incongruously boyish voice. "You're a proud man and I'm sure it wasn't easy for you. But I believe what you are really trying to say is that, ever since you whipped that young fellow to death, you have found yourself rather short of friends. So all of a sudden, the friendship of a man like me seems worth having. When we first met, Captain, you laughed at me behind your hand. But now you fear you may need me. Is that not what you really mean to say?"

There seemed no point trying to deny it.

"Yes," I replied simply.

He stared at me with his bright green eyes. Then he nodded.

"Thank you for your honesty, Captain. I know I am unusual, as you put it. I have never had the gift of making myself likeable. Castration can have that effect. But please remember I am a proud man too, and only wish to be treated with respect. If you can just do that, then I would be honoured to call myself your friend. And yours also, Adjutant."

He adjusted his wig slightly.

"I think perhaps you are the gracious one, Secretary Nebit," said Castor smoothly. The Egyptian beamed.

"So," he said, clapping his knees happily, "now that we have made our compact, let us get down to business. But first, Captain, would you mind asking that handsome young slave to leave us?"

He gazed at Agbal and delicately moistened his bright red lips with the tip of his tongue.

I gestured to Agbal. For once, he couldn't leave the room fast enough. Nebit's eyes followed him out.

Castor was looking at the Egyptian in mild surprise. Nebit noticed his expression and tittered.

"The fact that I am a eunuch, my dear Adjutant, does not mean that I am entirely without impulses. Although I dare say you might find my appetites… unconventional." He giggled again.

It was an ill-judged comment. Nebit didn't seem to know quite how to behave in company. He had overdressed and now he was being overly intimate. However curious a man's personal proclivities may be, they are seldom a suitable dinner topic. I coughed lightly and smiled at him.

"Ah yes, to resume," Nebit said, wriggling on the couch to make himself more comfortable. "You have thrown your arms open to me because you are concerned about how you stand with His Majesty. But what you need to understand, Captain, is that His Majesty's mind is a labyrinth. It turns in every direction, and just when you think you might be close to the centre of it, all you find is another series of openings and corners. There are secretaries who have been with him for decades, and even they cannot fathom his intentions. So I am afraid I simply do not know where you stand. The truth is that one never really knows quite where one stands with him. But for what it's worth, I would imagine he is still weighing you up. I dare say that is why he has not yet made clear what he intends to do about Malmeides."

He took a sip of water. I rested my chin on my hands and stared forlornly at my feet.

"Dear me, Captain," Nebit said, widening his eyes. "There's no need to look so despondent. I have no doubt there is a way through this." He smiled.

"Really? So what would you advise me to do, Nebit?"

"If you will forgive me for being blunt, Captain," he replied, "you are a predictable man. His Majesty knows your methods are brutal. He could have simply cashiered those useless young lieutenants, but instead he has chosen to set you loose on them. Why? Well, perhaps he finds it convenient that they and their families should direct their resentment at you, rather than at him."

"I suppose that makes sense," said Castor. Nebit turned to him.

"Yes, Adjutant, but maybe not quite for the reasons that you imagine," he replied.

"What do you mean?" I asked.

Nebit couldn't resist a smug, know-all smile.

"You must remember that His Majesty is ninety years old," he replied. "Naturally, his mind dwells on Prince Gelon's succession.

But Syracuse is surrounded on all sides by a great war, and that makes everything uncertain. The king and the prince support Rome, but if we are honest, the Romans have made rather a mess of things so far. Many of the nobles believe we should be siding with Carthage instead. No doubt some are already in contact with the Carthaginians behind His Majesty's back. We watch them, of course, but we cannot know everything. So it is only natural that His Majesty should be taking precautions to ensure that, when the day comes, there are no difficulties in Prince Gelon's path."

"I don't understand. What on earth has all that got to do with me?" I asked.

"Well, Captain, you mustn't forget that you are the heir of King Dionysius. I am sure His Majesty doesn't. And the common people do like to chatter, don't they? Not that it much matters what they say, of course."

"Nebit, you can't possibly think… " I stammered.

He smiled and flapped his hand at me.

"No, no, of course not, Captain. You may rest assured that His Majesty knows you have neither the aptitude nor the desire to aspire above your present station. But even so, your mother might well have ambitions for you, might she not? And she is certainly not to be underestimated. How many ships has she acquired now? Thirty-six, isn't it? And another eight or so whose true ownership she has attempted to conceal, by purchasing them in the names of others? And her business affairs do bring her into contact with so many other interested parties, both inside and outside the kingdom…"

I closed my eyes. My mother's games would destroy us both yet, I thought.

"Fuck," I said.

"Fuck indeed, Captain," Nebit replied. "Fortunately for you, His Majesty's methods are subtle. Unlike your great ancestor, he prefers to bend the bough, rather than to break it. When he gave you the captaincy of the Guards, I am sure he realised that you would quickly earn the enmity of all those young lieutenants and their powerful fathers. I doubt he has been greatly displeased to watch you isolate yourself from your class. In fact, I imagine you have already exceeded his happiest expectations with this Malmeides affair. There is little danger of anyone wanting to raise your banner now, Captain, when His Majesty dies. And that is probably just as well, for both you and your mother."

Castor looked at me and burst out laughing.

"Over forty ships, Dion? And you still look miserable. Just how rich are you, for fuck's sake?"

"I don't know," I said bitterly. "It seems you'll have to ask Nebit that."

Nebit smiled.

"Oh, so your mother didn't tell you about the other eight ships, then? We wondered whether she would. The Lady Korinna does seem a most remarkable woman. It took us quite a while to work out what she was doing. It would be a great privilege to meet her one day." He smiled.

"You two would probably get along very well," I said. He pouted with pleasure, apparently taking it as a compliment.

I remembered General Lepides' yelling at me in frustration. 'No, Dion! Always look for the bigger picture. You cannot defeat the action until you understand the strategy. How many times must I tell you? There is always a bigger picture!' It had been his favourite speech.

I took a deep breath.

"So, what do I need to do, Nebit? You say the king is weighing me up. How do I tilt the scales in my favour?"

He crossed one podgy white foot over the other.

"Captain, allow me to offer you two pieces of advice. Firstly, you have said you think me unusual, but then you and I are both unusual creatures, in our different ways. That is why we are useful. I learnt many years ago that I best serve my masters, by being true to my nature. I would advise you also to be true to yours. Be the Bull."

"That's what seems to have got me into this mess," I said glumly.

"And it will help get you out of it," he replied.

"How?"

"Because when the time comes, it might be very convenient to have a man like you in command of the City Guard – a man who entertains no hopes for himself, but who also thinks nothing of whipping a fellow aristocrat to death. I dare say your presence by Prince Gelon's side would be quite enough to deter even the most ambitious nobles from trying to do anything silly when His Majesty dies."

"I see," I said, frowning. A phrase came to my mind. "You might say I am to be the foot on the city's throat?"

"If you wish to put it like that, Captain, yes, I suppose you are."

"So what's the second piece of advice?" I asked, although I had a feeling I wouldn't like it any better.

"Well, Captain, it strikes me that with all the chatter about you on the streets, a little demonstration of loyalty might help to clear the air. Prove to His Majesty that he can indeed place his trust in you. I'm sure it would smooth your way through this Malmeides business."

"But what can I do, Nebit, for pity's sake? What does the king want from me? I'll scale the walls of Carthage if he tells me to."

Nebit carefully moistened his lips again. Then he folded his white stubby hands in his lap, and looked me squarely in the eye.

"I don't think you need go quite that far," he said. "But it so happens that His Majesty has finally concluded the new grain agreement with Rome. And as I'm sure you appreciate, Captain, transportation is always a headache. Perhaps you might offer to make some of your family's own cargo ships available to His Majesty, as a patriotic gesture?"

There was a long silence.

"I see," I said.

And so we had come to it at last, I thought. It was all just another negotiation. I was expected to buy my way out of my disgrace.

"Do you suppose His Majesty might appreciate the loan of, say, five ships?" I asked.

"I am sure he would," replied Nebit politely. "But I imagine that ten would be even more welcome."

"But Nebit, there are contracts to honour. My family's ships are committed months in advance. I can't just hand over a quarter of our fleet at a moment's notice. That's ridiculous."

He stared at me.

"So break the contracts," he said.

The pretence at politeness had gone. His voice was as hard as flint.

Apparently, it was not a negotiation after all.

My mother had recently informed me that she would be visiting the villa at Acrae as soon as she could spare the time, to see for herself what was required to prepare the house for the Torquatus girl. I had assumed she would delegate the responsibility to someone else and wondered if her personal involvement might be a sign that she was trying to put our relationship on a better footing. But then it dawned on me that she probably just wanted to secure the moral ascendancy over my bride. I imagined that no future opportunity would be lost to remind the poor girl of how much trouble my mother had taken to welcome her into the family. The Lady Korinna did not bestow kindness; she wielded it.

I forced myself to visit her the morning after my conversation with Nebit. Scaling the walls of Carthage seemed a less daunting prospect than the interview I was anticipating.

When I arrived, I was alarmed to find several armed men at our gate, and others posted around the courtyard. They carried long, straight swords and oval shields of a type I vaguely recognised from one of Lepides' classes at Plymmerium. I found my mother in the garden, but when I asked her about them, she would only confirm that they were from Galatia, a backward nation known chiefly for the savagery of the mercenaries it exported. My mother was probably the only person in Syracuse who could speak their language: a grandmother of hers had been some sort of Galatian princess. One of our distant barbarian relatives must have provided the men for her.

"But what are they doing here?" I persisted.

"These are dangerous days," she replied with a shrug. "I'm just taking some precautions. And at least I can be certain of their loyalty. But the real question is, what are you doing here?"

We were sitting by the fishpond again, under the purple awning. I told her everything Nebit had said. She listened to me in stony silence.

To my surprise, she didn't berate me.

"Well, we are where we are," she said simply, after some thought. "For now, we have no choice but to play Hieron's game. Send this creature – what's his name? Nebit? – to me, and I shall arrange matters with him. Unfortunately, we will have to compensate our clients for breaking their contracts. I shall see what I can do to minimise the cost. Maybe Nebit will be reasonable. That is my part. As for your part, Dion, it seems Hieron wants nothing more from you than that you should continue behaving like a brute. So do it. If you are to be hated, then you must at least make sure that you are also feared. Now, leave me."

Nebit went to see my mother about the shipping arrangements two days later. He came round to my office immediately afterwards. He was still walking on a cloud. Being a eunuch, my mother had been able to entertain him as if he were a woman. She had shown him around the house herself, and afterwards they had dined together off gold plates that had been given to some obscure ancestor of mine by Alexander of Macedon himself. She had apparently been enchanted by Nebit's robe – he informed me he had worn his very best one – and had insisted he tell her who had made it, so that she could order one for herself. They had gossiped intimately about several nobles, none of whom he had ever met, but about whom my mother, of course, knew a very great deal.

It was obvious that Nebit understood perfectly well she had been flattering him, but the very fact that she had regarded him as worthy of her flattery seemed to have tickled his vanity. The lengths to which she had gone proved that the famous Lady Korinna viewed him as an adversary to be respected. She had tacitly acknowledged him as her equal. He was exultant.

My mother certainly had a gift for smelling out other people's weaknesses.

I asked Nebit how the discussion about the ships had gone. He replied that they had eventually agreed that she would make three available immediately, and the rest over the course of the coming year. He had brought the documents with him for me to seal in person.

"I am delighted to say that this timetable means you will only be required to break two contracts, Captain." Nebit beamed. "I imagine His Majesty may be a little displeased with me for having allowed you such gentle terms, but at least he should have no difficulty meeting his obligations to Rome, and that's the important thing."

"So, I assume the king will now dismiss this Malmeides petition?" I said, as I stamped my ring into the hot wax.

"Oh yes, I would imagine so," Nebit replied, rubbing his hands together in delight. "I am sure His Majesty will view such a generous public gesture as quite sufficient to expiate any possible offence you may have committed."

"I am pleased my family can be of service," I said with one of my grimace smiles, handing him back the documents.

"Thank you... You know, if I may say so, meeting the Lady Korinna was a most gratifying experience. What a remarkable mind she has! And such style and taste! I confess I have had little previous opportunity to mix socially with the nobility. I am greatly looking forward to maintaining the relationship that she and I managed to establish."

I nodded to him. I imagined that my mother would see things somewhat differently.

I waited for the promised exoneration from Hieron. Nothing happened. As the days passed, I began to grow a little apprehensive. I asked Gelon about it, but he brushed my anxiety aside.

"Stop being such an old woman, Dion. My father will get round to it. You are hardly the only matter on his mind, you know."

I ratcheted up the assault on my officers by introducing classes in hand-to-hand combat. I had Ajax give them wrestling lessons, while I took the sword practice myself. We trained them in groups of ten, each of us taking a different group every day. It is surprising quite how much pain and bruising you can inflict with a wooden sword, if you know what you are doing. Ajax was no fool and understood without being told what was expected of him. He relished it, of course. Our joint classes immediately became a popular spectacle among the men. They crammed their heads through the dormitory windows, to watch their delicate officers being smacked about by me, and then twisted and tossed around the exercise yard by Ajax.

The officers stood it for a couple weeks, and then gave in. For all Zoippos's efforts, nothing had yet come of the Malmeides affair, and staying in the Guards no longer seemed much fun. About fifty of my lieutenants handed me their letters of resignation on the same afternoon, citing my treatment of Malmeides as the reason. It was clearly a coordinated attempt to bring matters to a head and exact their revenge.

I couldn't believe my luck. I had their baggage thrown out into the street that same evening, to loud laughter and jeering from the men.

It was not till a few days later that a slave finally came looking for me, with instructions that I was to accompany him to the king's audience chamber. I had been drilling some of the men and had no time to clean up.

As we crossed the courtyard, I noticed Malmeides' timid, cross-eyed camp slave loitering in the colonnade. He shrank behind a column as I approached. I had sent him back to Malmeides' parents together with their son's body, so I guessed the father must be around too. But what was Malmeides' father doing here, I wondered?

The palace slave led me into the cavernous and gloomy audience chamber. At the far end stood an empty throne, raised on a broad

dais. Perched on stools below it to the right were both Malmeides'
parents and Zoippos. And then it struck me, like a knife in the liver.
Hieron wasn't going to exonerate me. He was going to try me.
I felt as though I were about to throw up.

I took a deep breath and tried to collect myself, before following
the slave down the room. My three accusers turned towards me as I
approached, glaring at me like angry ferrets. I knew the father only
in passing and had never before seen his wife, Zoippos's sister. I
vaguely remembered that they lived on a country estate somewhere
or other.

I was shown to a stool to the left of the dais, directly facing
the ferrets. I stared defiantly back at them. It occurred to me that
Zoippos and his sister must be twins: they had the same elongated
necks and small onion heads, with eyes set too closely together. The
only obvious difference in their features was his huge Adam's apple,
which seemed to have a life of its own, intermittently going into a
frenzy of valiant leaps as if trying to escape through his mouth.

We waited in silence. Eventually a scribe appeared from a side
door and settled himself at a desk in a corner. He was followed
by four black-plumed guards, who took up positions around the
throne. Soon afterwards, Hieron himself entered on the arm of a
slave and we all hurriedly stood and bowed.

Hunched, skinny and shrivelled, with only a few thin strands
of hair remaining on his head and chin, our decrepit king shuffled
slowly across the dais, seemingly oblivious to our presence. He was
dressed in a plain white tunic and wore no crown. The slave had to
help him onto his throne and he winced slightly as he wriggled to
make himself comfortable. Had I seen him in the street, I might
have thought him a beggar.

When he had finally settled himself, Hieron looked up and
gestured for us to sit.

"Well, you all know why you're here," he croaked weakly, "so
let's get on with it. Who speaks for Malmeides' family?"

"I do, my King," said Zoippos. Hieron nodded to him and he
sprang eagerly back to his feet.

Zoippos made a long, impassioned speech, full of rhetorical flourishes, accusing me of appalling cruelty and abuse of power. He clearly fancied himself a second Demosthenes. I was a monster to my men, he claimed. Morale among the Guards had never been so low, robbed as they now were of the brilliant young lieutenant in whom they had invested so much trust. Zoippos's Adam's apple bounced up and down excitedly as he got into his stride. No doubt it was for jealousy of Malmeides' military talents that I had singled him out and so callously murdered him. He waved a thick roll of papyrus at me. He had the testimonies of over fifty – fifty! – other officers in evidence of my incompetence and malice. These noble souls had since felt compelled to resign in disgust, gutting the City Guard of almost all its military expertise. The division had ceased to be an effective fighting force. They were rejoicing in the streets of Carthage.

Hieron leant his elbow on the arm of his chair and rested his head on his hand. His wrinkled face was expressionless. The flustered scribe was trying to keep a record of what was being said, but seemed to give up halfway through. Eventually, the frothy torrent of subordinate clauses exhausted itself and with a final exhortation to Dike, the goddess of justice, and a theatrical wave of his arm, Zoippos sat down. Malmeides' father clapped him warmly on the back.

"Well, what have you to say for yourself, Captain?" Hieron sighed.

I stood up.

"My King, Zoippos says I am a monster to my men," I answered. "But I have seen many men endure worse deaths because of the incompetence of officers like Malmeides. It was for the sake of my men that I acted as I did." Then I sat down again.

Gradually, the king's whole demeanour changed. He straightened himself, his mouth hardened and his face came alive. It was like watching some strange, dark moth emerge from its chrysalis. He turned to stare at me and our eyes briefly met. His were unblinking and the palest blue. I hastily bowed my head. His gaze seemed to fall on me for an eternity; it felt as though my skin were being slowly peeled away.

I think that may have been the moment when I first realised that Hieron was in a different category to any other man I have known.

Eventually he spoke.

"Dion, you have gone too far. The flogging of an officer is unprecedented. It was out of all proportion to his offence that Malmeides should have been subjected to a punishment that resulted in his death. You chose to make an example of him, and now I shall make one of you. Stand up."

I immediately rose. Out of the corner of my eye, I saw Malmeides' parents grinning expectantly. Zoippos's little head was wobbling happily on its stalk.

There was a silence, and then I heard Hieron pronounce my sentence.

"You will pay Malmeides' funeral expenses in full."

I kept my head bowed and waited for the rest of it. But Hieron was already in the process of painfully hoisting himself out of his throne. I glanced over at Malmeides' family. As the king stood, the three of them hastily jumped up too. The parents looked aghast. Zoippos had turned white. The mighty Adam's apple seemed stunned into near-immobility, and could do no more than quiver weakly in mid-throat.

Helped by his slave, Hieron shambled slowly out of the room.

That same night, Prince Gelon came to visit me in my apartment.

I was having dinner with Castor, who had been away for a few days, touring the smaller garrisons for which he was responsible. We were celebrating the humiliation of Zoippos.

Alpha and Omega were busy serving us our food as Agbal let the prince in. Castor and I immediately stood and bowed. I noticed there were at least three bodyguards in the corridor outside.

"Relax, both of you, relax," Gelon said easily, as Agbal closed the door behind him. "I hope you don't mind me coming round uninvited, Dion. I'm sailing to Rome tomorrow and wanted to see you before I left. I've some news for you."

"Would you care to join us for dinner, sir?" I asked, gesturing to a couch.

"No, I'm afraid I've eaten already."

"If you'll excuse me then, sir," said Castor, "I'll leave you two to talk alone."

"That's very considerate, thank you, Castor," replied Gelon. "Sorry to interrupt your meal. But before you go, you might like to know that my father has decided to cashier any remaining Guards officers who you think aren't up to the job." He turned to me. "Give Nebit your list tomorrow, Dion."

Castor grinned. There were still over twenty lieutenants whom we wanted to get rid of. They had not yet completed the minimum two years' military service, so they had not been free to resign with the others. They would now be drafted into the army like everyone else, and would be put through the training that they had gone to such great expense to evade. The thought of the little darlings pulling on the oars made me smile.

As Castor left, Gelon settled himself comfortably on one of the couches. Omega poured out a cup of water and deferentially handed it to him.

"Lose the slaves, would you Dion?" the prince said. "I'm sure we can look after ourselves."

I tilted my head towards the door to the anteroom.

"All of you, go to your room," I said. "Stay there till I call you."

I had not seen Gelon as much as I would have liked since leaving Plymmerium, and I didn't really understand what sort of a relationship we had been forming on those occasions when we had been alone together. Whatever else it may have been, it was certainly not a relationship of equals.

"Well," he said when the slaves had left, "I'm sorry we had to keep you dangling for a while, Dion, but everything seems to have worked out nicely in the end. I told you that my father would protect you."

"You didn't tell me his protection would cost me ten ships," I replied a little sourly. He laughed.

"You can afford it. Don't grumble. Anyway, you'll get them back when the war's over. Sorry about putting you through that business with the trial, but my father was annoyed with Zoippos for having made such a nuisance of himself and wanted to give him something to think about."

I took a sip of water.

"In any event, that's not why I'm here," Gelon continued. "I've good news for you. The terms of your marriage have finally been agreed. I imagine you've already heard that your wife is to be Vita of the Manlii, my cousin Seema's daughter? I confess I haven't seen her since she was five or six, but if she looks anything like her mother, you won't be disappointed. And you'll be pleased to hear my father has insisted on a rather substantial dowry for you. Torquatus is a bit of an old skinflint, but he's settled two large estates on the girl, nearly a thousand acres of timber and farmland altogether. You see, my friend, what my father takes with one hand, he returns with the other."

He smiled at me benignly.

"I'm very grateful, I'm sure," I replied. "May I ask, where are these estates?"

"Oh, in Italy somewhere," Gelon replied with a wave of his hand. "Now, we are going to have to get a move on with the wedding. The Romans are planning to march against Hannibal in a few months. They are assembling the largest army they have ever fielded, Dion. We've been asked to contribute some of our own men. That's why I'm off to Rome, to make the arrangements. You never know: if Hannibal decides to stand and fight, you may just get your ships back much sooner that you'd imagined."

"That would certainly be good news," I said.

"Well, yes, but I wouldn't get your hopes up quite yet. Hannibal's no fool; I doubt he'll offer battle. I imagine he'll just lead the Romans on a merry dance round Italy for a couple more years. Anyway, Torquatus wants his daughter safely out of Rome before the army marches, so I'll be bringing her back to Syracuse with me. She'll stay here at the palace until the wedding. The priests have selected a date for the ceremony in the autumn. I assume you have no objections?"

"No, not at all. Thank you very much." It made little difference to me.

"Excellent. I'm delighted for you," he said. "We'll send the details to your lawyer. My father will announce the engagement as soon as you've sealed the marriage contract."

He took a sip of water. I sat in silence, waiting for him to resume. He gazed around the room, taking in all the ostentatious clutter, and raised his eyebrows.

"You know, none of my family's rooms looks anything like this. I'd never have thought you such a show-off, Dion. My father must be losing his touch: he should have squeezed you for twenty ships."

"Blame the slaves," I replied morosely. "I only use it for company. I stay in my bedroom when I'm alone."

'Well, if that's where you'd feel more comfortable," he said with his boyish grin, "perhaps we should take our cups through there?"

When I went through the marriage contract with my lawyer two days later, I was unsurprised to discover that my future wife's two estates were both in Apulia, an area of Italy famous for the fertility of its soil. They would certainly have been extremely valuable properties, were it not for the fact that Hannibal had made Apulia his base of operations, and had been ravaging the region for months. Senator Torquatus had probably bought the deeds for a pittance from some refugees. No doubt it was his revenge on me for having humiliated his son.

I sealed the contract anyway, to my lawyer's dismay and my mother's undisguised scorn. Our betrothal was proclaimed the following morning in the agora, the large public gathering space in the centre of the city.

The portents could hardly have been worse: the announcement was followed by a violent thunderstorm. And it was on that very same night that we learnt the Carthaginians had landed at Pachynus, about five days' march away, on the southern tip of our kingdom.

VI

TWO OLD MEN

Sitting directly across the table from him, I could see the droplets of sweat forming on Thraso's pig-like face. He fiddled nervously with his gold ring. He was my cousin, but I had never greatly cared for him: like most lawyers, he had always seemed too clever by half. Even so, I had to admit that he was proving braver than I had expected.

"Would you care to repeat that, Thraso?" Hieron wheezed from the head of the table. I glanced down at my lap. It was the first time I had worn my blue tunic outside my rooms and I felt awkwardly self-conscious.

"My King," Thraso replied, "with respect, Hieronymus is only fourteen. Is this really a risk worth taking?"

Out of the corner of my eye, I thought I saw several heads nodding in cautious agreement.

"And whom would you choose instead, Thraso?" Hieron asked mildly.

Thraso swallowed. He knew he was on dangerous ground, but the fool pressed on anyway.

"I would advise giving the command to Dion," he said boldly, waving a puffy hand at me.

I rolled my tongue slowly around my cheek, tracing the inside ridge of the scar. Outside, the gulls were squawking, and the breeze coming through the windows carried with it the rank smell of seaweed. In my mind, I pictured the little fishing smacks bobbing across the wide bay, and wished I were on one of them.

Hieron stared silently at Thraso. Under that gaze, Thraso's courage collapsed. His head retreated into the folds of his neck like a snail's antennae.

Hieron snorted and looked down the table at the fifteen of us. We had all been woken in the middle of the night, to be told the council would convene at dawn. Several of my colleagues appeared pretty dishevelled and most seemed frightened. Hieron alone wore a simple white gown, and he alone appeared quite untroubled by the crisis that we faced.

The only information we had received so far from Pachynus was confused, but thousands were said to be fleeing up the coastal road to Syracuse. Our standing forces were small: between them, the Shield divisions and the City Guard numbered fewer than eight thousand men. Hieron had already ordered the mobilisation of citizens under the age of thirty, our first reservists. The city was sweaty with rumours.

"Does anyone else have any military advice to offer me?" the king asked, almost in amusement. Thraso winced and turned red. If I hadn't been so angry with him for dragging me into this, I might have felt sorry for him.

The chair next to the king, where Gelon should have sat, was empty: he had set sail for Rome three days earlier. As the most senior officer after Gelon, I was the obvious choice to lead our men; and yet the king apparently intended to give the command to his grandson instead. As far as I was concerned, Hieronymus was welcome to whatever glory awaited the army at Pachynus.

Zoippos was the first to hoist his sail before the prevailing wind. No doubt he thought he was doing me an ill turn.

"My King, I must disagree with our dear colleague, Thraso. It is six months now since he joined this council as our senior magistrate and he has impressed us all with his knowledge of the law. But I do not think he will object when I suggest that his expertise does not necessarily extend to matters of war. I would say that Hieronymus shows every sign of being a quite remarkable young man, well ahead of his years. By all means, send more experienced men to advise him, but let Hieronymus have his first taste of leadership. Let him crush our enemies for you, my King, like a young Alexander. After all, he is Gelon's son and your grandson: generalship is in his blood."

Hieron remained expressionless. Some of those who had appeared to agree with my cousin now started murmuring in agreement with Zoippos. The Adam's apple lurched up and down a couple of times, as if taking a bow.

An inconsequential man known as Woodpecker raised his hand.

"You have something to add, Themistos?" Hieron sighed.

"Yes, my King," Woodpecker replied eagerly. "Might the council perhaps prevail on you to lead the army yourself? It would certainly terrify those barbarians if they knew you were marching against them in person. They'd probably run for their ships as soon as they heard of it."

Woodpecker had a habit, when speaking, of constantly nodding his head, as if to emphasise how strongly he approved of his own opinions. He looked around the table, smiling smugly and stabbing at us with his spear-like nose.

Was this all that councillors did, I asked myself: try to out-toady each other? I sat silently, wondering what on earth I was doing there. For all its superficial complexity, soldiering is a simple business. If I sensed opportunity, I attacked; if I smelled danger, I retreated. But in this council, my instincts were useless. I didn't know what my objective was, and almost every man at the table seemed to be my enemy. I smelled danger, but had nowhere to retreat. It was a type of warfare of which I had no understanding.

Several other councillors spoke in turn, falling over themselves to urge the king to take the field himself. It was ridiculous. He could barely even walk without a slave to hold his arm.

Eventually Andranodoros, the king's younger son-in-law, intervened.

"Forgive me for being candid," Andranodoros said, his voice all honey and olive oil, "but to ask our king to assume this burden, at his time of life, would seem somewhat unreasonable. Should His Majesty seek our guidance between the other two candidates who have so far been mentioned, then I must of course agree with my dear brother-in-law, Zoippos. Better a younger man, of whose good judgement we are perhaps not yet certain, than a more experienced one, of whose poor judgement we have recently had tragic proof. But there is another candidate I think we must consider. Surely the obvious person to lead our army in Gelon's absence is Zoippos himself? After all, he is the next most senior member of our family."

Andranodoros smoothed down his hair, which he wore slicked back in an oriental style, and looked across at Zoippos with a triumphant leer. I had punched Andranodoros in the face once when we were children. The sight of the gap in his front teeth still gave me pleasure.

Zoippos tried to force a polite smile, but his expression was venomous. His enthusiasm for a battle with the Carthaginians seemed to be directly proportionate to his own remoteness from it.

The king's desiccated face remained blank, but he had apparently heard enough.

"Very well," he said, "my thanks for your attendance at such short notice. I shall consider your suggestions. Thraso and Dion are to remain behind. The rest of you may leave. Andranodoros, please wait outside. I have a task for you."

He signalled weakly with his hand and two thickly muscled slaves moved to open the heavy doors of the council chamber.

I shot my cousin a furious look. "I'm sorry," he mouthed silently to me across the table. But it wasn't for fear of me that the blood had drained from Thraso's flabby face.

The other councillors rose and bowed and started to make their way out. Andranodoros bestowed a patronising smirk on me as he left. Zoippos, Leatherskin, Woodpecker and the rest pointedly ignored me. Apart from Thraso, the king and myself, only my great-uncle Archimedes remained in his chair, at the opposite end of the table to Hieron. His hands were folded on his lap and his chin rested on his chest. He had tried to tutor me for a while when I was a child, but I had seen little of him since. He had passed the meeting either dozing or vacantly chewing the ends of his beard. My mother had always said that he was not quite right in the head.

As the other councillors filed out, I stood up and moved towards the old man, intending to wake him gently, but the king interrupted me sharply.

"Leave him alone, Dion. Come and sit by me. You too, Thraso."

I didn't know which of the two of us was more apprehensive. We meekly seated ourselves on either side of the king, who turned to stare at Thraso.

"My King," Thraso blurted out, before Hieron could speak, "I apologise for questioning you, but please don't blame Dion for my mistake."

Hieron raised his long white eyebrows. The moment dragged on.

"There is nothing to apologise for," he said at last. "I trust my councillors to give me honest advice, at least occasionally. I believe that is what you did. But now let me give you some advice in turn, young man. Some snakes are harmless, some have a painful bite, and a few can be deadly. Until you have learnt to tell them apart, it would be wise to tread lightly when walking among them. You are a lawyer, so I suggest you confine your advice to matters of law, at least for the time being."

Then Hieron leant forward, smiled, and patted Thraso affectionately on the arm.

"That's all I have to say to you. Off you go."

My clever cousin seemed at a loss for words.

"It's alright," said the king. "Now, go away and do something useful."

Thraso hesitated, then stood up and bowed in his usual clumsy manner. He was about to turn away when Hieron held up a finger to stop him.

"Just one more thing, Thraso. Those new guidelines you sent the courts, about how to weigh the testimony of slaves… Very sensible… Well done."

And with that, the king waved his hand in dismissal.

Thraso blushed deeply, his expression a mixture of bewilderment and pleasure. I was no less astonished than he was that the king should take such a close interest in his work.

To ruthless men, benevolence is a form of coinage, to be dispensed as carefully as gold. A good slave is expensive, but it seemed Hieron had just bought my cousin with a compliment.

When Thraso had waddled off, Hieron ordered the slaves to leave us and close the doors behind them. At the far end of the table, my great-uncle still hadn't stirred.

I looked up and met the king's hard eyes gazing intently at me. I immediately looked down again. I heard Hieron chuckle softly.

"You don't much care for your cousin, do you?" he said.

I didn't know if it was a question or a statement, so I remained silent.

"You misjudge him," Hieron said simply. "Men like you, Dion, have kept this city safe for five hundred years, but it was men like Thraso who built it... Well, now, let's get down to business. What are your thoughts, Archimedes?"

I turned to look at my great-uncle in confusion. Archimedes didn't open his eyes.

"My thoughts on what, Hieron?" he replied casually from the far end of the table. I wondered how long he had been awake.

"You know perfectly well. Should I send Hieronymus to deal with this Pachynus business? You're his tutor. Is he ready?"

Archimedes slowly raised his huge head, blinked and snorted.

"The boy's an idiot. He'll probably get himself killed. So, yes, please send him to Pachynus. I dare say you'd be doing Syracuse a favour. You'd certainly be doing me one."

My mother had obviously been right about my great-uncle.

Hieron tapped the table with his forefinger.

"Careful, Cousin," he said. "Hieronymus will be king one day."

"Then I suggest you just get it over with, and burn down the city now."

The king's face remained impassive.

"You know, Archimedes, if you weren't almost a corpse already, I'd probably have you crucified for talking to me like that," he said evenly.

"So crucify me, then, Hieron. It could hardly be more painful than trying to tutor your grandson."

Archimedes pushed back his chair, stood up and strode down the table towards us. I had thought nothing more could surprise me, but that did: in recent years, I had only ever seen him shuffling slowly along with his cane, like a man at the end of his life. He settled himself comfortably beside the king, in the same place that Thraso had just occupied, folded his arms and stretched out his long, bony legs contentedly.

Hieron looked at me and chuckled.

"You seem startled, Captain," he said.

"Like a gawping fish," said Archimedes. "For pity's sake, close your mouth, Dion."

There was a silence as I tried to think of what to say.

"Perhaps you are wondering how Archimedes dares to be so familiar with me?" Hieron asked helpfully. "So, let me explain. He was like a little brother to me before I became king, and he has been my only friend since. For over half a century, he and I have been harnessed to the same purpose: the survival of this kingdom."

I stared at my great-uncle. He had been in charge of public works for as long as I could remember. He was forever replacing old buildings with ugly new ones, or digging up the streets to extend the city's sewerage system. It seemed one could barely turn a corner any more, without getting stuck behind queues of carts and throngs of angry people, trying to find a way round his road closures.

"Forgive me, my King, but I'm a little confused," I said slowly. "I mean no disrespect, Great-uncle. I know your work is important, but I don't quite see what it has to do with the survival of Syracuse."

"Your great-uncle is not just a mathematician and engineer, Dion," said Hieron. "He serves me in other ways, too. But he prefers to stay behind the curtain, as it were."

My great-uncle smiled at me for the first time. He had a large mouth and few teeth. The effect was neither pleasant nor reassuring.

"So, young man," said Archimedes, "let's see what's going on inside that skull of yours these days... Tell us, what should we do about Pachynus?"

"Pachynus...?" I said. I looked from one white-bearded old man to the other. I remembered their mothers had been sisters, and I noticed for the first time they had the same eyes. And those two pairs of eyes were both trained on me.

I shuffled uncomfortably in my chair.

"Well, Great-uncle," I said hesitantly, "as you ask, I don't think we should do anything. There is no threat from Pachynus. Hannibal isn't done in Italy yet. He's hardly going to divide his forces now. This isn't an invasion: it's just a raid. So there's no point in sending the army to meet the Carthaginians because they will be gone again before we even arrive."

"Indeed?" said Hieron. "So, tell me, Dion, why would the mighty Carthaginians bother raiding Pachynus? There's nothing much down there, as far as I remember, apart from a few fishermen and goats."

"Perhaps to send you a message, my King?"

"Go on," said Archimedes.

I paused to gather my thoughts.

"Hannibal has been marching around Italy for two years," I replied after a moment, "destroying every Roman army he meets. The Romans increasingly rely on us for their grain. I think this raid is Hannibal's way of warning you to stop helping them, my King. He may be tied up in Italy, but he wants you to know he can still bite."

The king tapped his fingers together and exchanged a glance with my great-uncle.

"Well now," Hieron said, "that's quite good, Dion, at least as far as it goes... You're right, of course, that there is no real threat from Pachynus, but, you see, I cannot simply do nothing. We must restore confidence in the region, or else the people will not return to their homes and we will have too many mouths to feed here in Syracuse. So I'm sending a thousand men down there. Hieronymus will lead them and will stay there for a while as my governor. I can't say I'll miss him; he's not a very pleasant child. No doubt the people will see him as a hero for frightening off the Carthaginians and saving the kingdom. But I suppose life is full of little ironies."

Archimedes made a gurgling noise. The king ignored him.

"Anyway, Dion," Hieron continued, "in a short space of time, maybe a week or two, the people's fear will evaporate, and then they will grow oh-so-brave and angry instead. They will start demanding their revenge, and I shall have to give it to them. If I don't, the Carthaginians will think us weak. But ours is a small kingdom, and the empire of Carthage is vast. So what revenge can we realistically take? Tell me, what would you suggest?"

I could only reach for the obvious answer.

"Perhaps we could raid one of their own towns on the African coast, my King?"

"A mosquito biting an elephant," Archimedes snorted.

He was right, of course. The Carthaginians would barely notice.

"Well, let's try looking at it from a different angle, shall we?" Hieron said patiently. "I would imagine that these raiders were reinforcements on their way to join Hannibal from Africa, whom he merely needed to divert for a few days, in order, as you put it, to deliver his message. And if that's the case, they will probably have fully-laden supply and transport ships sailing with them, which means they will not be travelling very fast…"

I suddenly grasped what he planned.

My heart sank.

"You intend to attack them at sea?" I asked.

"Yes, Dion," Hieron replied drily. "I believe that is where one usually attacks ships… We have just over thirty quinqueremes available. They are preparing to sail as we speak. Archimedes estimates that if we move quickly, we have maybe six or seven chances in ten of catching Hannibal's convoy."

I stared in dismay at my great-uncle, who was scraping the dirt from under his long fingernails. Whatever nonsense had he been whispering in the king's ear? We might as well go hunting for a sparrow in a forest. I did my best to be tactful.

"Forgive me, my King," I said tentatively, "but I'm not sure my great-uncle fully appreciates the difficulty of trying to find an enemy in open waters... It's, well, it's a very big sea..."

My voice trailed off.

Archimedes gazed at me pityingly.

"We know where the Carthaginians are heading," he snapped. "We know where they are sailing from. We know that in this wind, their cargo ships will be travelling at about two leagues an hour; and we can make an educated guess that, having staged their raid, they left again yesterday, or perhaps the day before, at first light. We may reasonably assume they will travel due east for three or four days, to get well clear of our coast, and will then turn north. So we need merely estimate the size and angles of a quadrilateral... Tell me, Dion, what's to understand?"

So that would explain why the reservists had been mobilised, I thought. They weren't going to march south: Hieron needed them to row his ships. It would take fifteen thousand men to crew thirty quinqueremes.

"Of course, nothing is certain," the king continued. "The gods will decide the matter. But if we do catch them, well now..." He licked his upper lip with the tip of his tongue. "What I wouldn't give to see Hannibal's face when he hears of it."

I looked at Archimedes again and scratched my cheek. I didn't quite know what to make of it. The whole plan sounded like little more than speculation piled upon conjecture. More like one chance in ten, I thought. And yet... Perhaps... I turned it over in my mind.

"My King," I said after a moment, choosing my words carefully, "may I ask, what part am I to play in this? Am I to sail with the fleet?"

This must be why he wasn't sending me to Pachynus, I told myself. He needed a man like me for the real bloodwork.

But it was Archimedes who answered.

"No," he said indifferently. "Andranodoros will command the fleet. You are to stay here."

Down I crashed like Icarus. I visualised the king's younger son-in-law, with his oily, gap-toothed leer, and bit my lip.

Well, fuck it, I thought. Fuck it all. What a fucking joke.

"My King, is this because of Malmeides?" I asked, trying to keep the resentment out of my voice. "Am I still in disgrace?"

"I couldn't care less about Malmeides," Hieron said. "And no, you're certainly not in disgrace. You never were."

"Though it may be helpful if the world thinks otherwise," interjected Archimedes quietly.

The king smiled.

"I can see you're disappointed, Dion, but I have other work for you. And you must learn to take a wider view. You see, when all's said and done, it doesn't really matter how many Carthaginian ships we manage to sink or capture. If it did, I would certainly give you the command. But attacking Hannibal's convoy is merely a gesture. Hannibal sends me a message, and I send him one back. We are simply having our first conversation."

Hieron paused and lifted his head to gaze at the ceiling.

"No, Captain, you will not sail with the fleet," he said. "I am afraid Hannibal is not the only threat we face. If we aren't careful, we may find ourselves with even more dangerous enemies than him. And that is why I have decided to keep you here."

Archimedes looked at me.

"There are a few things I'll need to explain to you, Dion," he said. "I've too much to do today before the fleet sails, but come to my home tomorrow three hours after dawn. Now, do you have any questions that cannot wait till then?"

I was lost. I had no idea what they were talking about. What other threat? What enemies? I turned to Hieron again.

"My King, you said I must try to take a wider view. What is it that I've missed?"

"Ah, that's the first intelligent question you've asked," said Archimedes.

Hieron smiled thinly. His eyes glinted like the winter sea.

"What have you missed? Why, that Rome will eventually win this war, of course," he said.

It was the end of the interview. Hieron silently gestured to me to leave. The two old men nodded to each other in some wordless communication to which I wasn't party. I stood, bowed and walked over to the doors, banging on the thick wood to alert the slaves outside.

Archimedes appeared by my side.

"You are to say nothing of this to anyone, Dion," he whispered. "Do you understand?"

I nodded. That much at least was clear, even to me. Then my great-uncle handed me his cane and took my arm in his. He had never shown any particular interest in me before and I admit I was rather touched by the gesture.

Archimedes was tall, nearly as tall as me, but as the doors began to swing open, he stooped forwards, hunching his back. He tucked a thick strand of beard into his mouth and began chewing on it. As we walked out together, his footsteps were irritatingly slow and he kept his eyes fixed on the ground, like a man frightened of falling over.

Andranodoros was waiting outside in the anteroom, pacing up and down. He ignored me, but nodded politely to Archimedes. Archimedes twisted his face up and beamed at him, spitting his beard from his mouth.

"Ah, Andranodoros, my dear fellow, how are you? You do look well. You know, I still remember when you used to come to me for a little extra tuition. Such a clever boy. You had a lovely way with geometry. I always thought it a great pity you didn't persevere with your mathematics. Tell me, what are you up to these days?"

Andranodoros looked at my great-uncle condescendingly and batted his long eyelashes.

"I manage the city granaries, Archimedes," he replied, in that slightly exasperated manner we all use when someone old has forgotten something we expect them to know.

"Oh yes, of course you do. I remember now. Such a waste of your talents." Archimedes tilted his head at me. "Even this idiot could do that. Oh, for pity's sake, Dion, do stop squeezing my arm like that! Do you want to break it? I'll walk by myself, thank you. It's clearly safer."

My great-uncle shoved me weakly with his free hand and pulled his arm irritably from under mine.

"Give me back that cane... Well, good day to you, Andranodoros. Drop by my house some time. Perhaps we could do some mathematics together."

As Archimedes shuffled away, a slave hurried up to Andranodoros and gestured for him to follow. Andranodoros turned from me without a word and strolled back into the council chamber, patting his hair.

Of all the men in the kingdom, why Hieron should have chosen him to command the fleet was beyond me. What on earth did Andranodoros know of keeping your balance on a rolling deck made slippery by blood, while frantic men tried to kill you?

Well, perhaps he would find out soon enough, I thought. With a bit of luck, someone might even knock out the rest of his teeth for him.

After a few moments, I followed my great-uncle out into the wide, stone colonnade that ringed the central courtyard of the palace. There were several courtyards in the complex but this was the most impressive, giving access to the state apartments and public offices.

The Carthaginians may have been spreading panic in the south, but here in the palace, the business of government seemed to be continuing much as usual. In the shade of the colonnade, slaves and secretaries hurried about their work, darting in and out between ambassadors and courtiers and palace guards. Rich merchants seeking concessions and poor petitioners seeking justice sat patiently side by side, on the stone benches that lined the walls. Everywhere men huddled earnestly together, exchanging gossip, making deals and hatching their own elaborate schemes in whispers. The courtyard was like a giant cauldron, in which ambition, calculation and duplicity all gently simmered in the late morning heat.

I caught up with Archimedes. My thoughts were still tripping over each other in confusion.

"Great-uncle," I said, "I wanted to ask you…"

"Go away!" he barked, waving his cane at me irritably. Two or three curious faces turned to look at us. I immediately understood my mistake and strode past him without another word, leaving him to hobble along at his own pace.

The council meeting had clearly been a sham: Archimedes and the king had set their own plans in motion before the council had even met. I had wanted to ask my great-uncle why Hieron bothered with a council, but the answer eventually came to me of its own accord. To help the old king cobra keep an eye on his nest of snakes, of course, and to allow all the little snakes to bask in the illusion of their own importance. I suppose men who imagine they have power are less likely to trouble those who really do.

As I walked over to the exercise yard, I wondered if I should have stayed at Plymmerium.

Ever since I had attained my manhood, almost all men had called me 'Sir' or 'Master'. I had not yet turned thirty, but there were probably only a hundred or so people in the kingdom who could address me by name as an equal, and fewer than half a dozen to whom I was expected to defer. We are all puffed-up creatures, eager to believe in our own special significance on this earth. But it was slowly beginning to dawn on me that I might actually be of very little consequence at all. It seemed I was just another small bead on the king's abacus, to be flicked casually backwards and forwards on his whim.

A few dozen men were practising with wooden swords in the midday sun. It was still early spring, but the kingdom had been afflicted by a muggy heatwave for the last few days and their naked bodies were wet with perspiration. The only officer I could see among them was the handsome young man Leander, whom I had recently transferred to the palace from the citadel on Ortygia.

I felt the cloying fog that had enveloped me ever since I had sat down at the council table start to lift. I was back in a world I understood. I walked over to the men, who stopped practising and stood to attention. I nodded to them.

"Leander," I said with a smile, "may I borrow that sword? Thank you." I slipped off my blue tunic and undergarment, dropping them in the dust. The harsh sun beat down on my torso, but I welcomed it: it felt like the heat was scouring me clean. I turned contentedly to the men.

"Now then, ladies, let's see what you can do…"

VII

SEA AND STONE

As the sun slowly set that day, I stood at the window of my anteroom, watching our quinqueremes being made ready to sail in the Little Harbour. I bitterly envied Andranodoros his command. I was still doubtful whether he could catch the ships that had raided Pachynus, and I half hoped he wouldn't. If he returned triumphant, his smugness would be insufferable. And to see a man like him steal my chance… Well, fuck it. Fuck it all.

Our quinqueremes spent most of their lives out of the water. A third of our fleet was laid up in smaller ports along the coast and we rotated the rest, only keeping about a dozen at sea at any given moment. After nine months or so in service, they would be hauled back up into their sheds, where they were scraped clean and re-caulked with horsehair and pitch, to reduce the fouling of their hulls when they next went on patrol.

In the old days, it must have taken hundreds of slaves to drag a quinquereme out of the water, but now it required fewer than fifty. Thick ropes attached to the ships coiled backwards and forwards around wooden wheels of differing sizes, which somehow made titans of the men who pulled on them. The mechanism had been invented by Archimedes, and we used a similar system for lifting the ships' masts and lowering them back into place again. To this day, I have never understood the magic in those wheels: they looked perfectly ordinary to me.

Dozens of carts stood along the wharf in the twilight. Some were laden with food that had probably been commandeered from the shops, but most carried water barrels. I counted thirty-four re-masted quinqueremes at their berths in the harbour. Relays of slaves were loading the supplies, while others fitted the riggings. No doubt they would be working by torchlight through the night: the fleet was due to sail at dawn.

The giant ships were about fifty paces long and had ninety oars on each side, arranged in three serried banks. The shorter oars at the lowest level only needed one man to pull them; the longer oars in the higher banks required two. As a young man, I had done my time on the rowing benches like everybody else. I can still recall the noise of grinding wood and groaning men, but not as vividly as I recall the smell. It was like living in a sewer.

It was the Carthaginians' own quinqueremes that would be our quarry, not their cargo vessels. If they had been at sea for any length of time, I thought to myself, Andranodoros might just have a chance: the fouling of their hulls would make them sluggish. And we had a further advantage. All modern quinqueremes had hulls that were partitioned below the water line into three bilges, to reduce the risk of sinking. Even so, they all leaked and periodically required bailing – just a foot or so of water sloshing around below was enough to make a difference to a warship's speed and handling. But the bilges of our ships had all been fitted with another of Archimedes' clever devices: a screw contained within an angled cylinder. When turned by a handle on the rowing deck, the screw raised the water from the compartment below and channelled it overboard through a gutter. Teams of slaves continuously working the three drainage screws could keep a ship dry in all but the roughest seas. It was enough to ensure our own quinqueremes were significantly faster and more manoeuvrable than anybody else's. If Andranodoros managed to sight Hannibal's convoy, he should be able to close the distance on it within a few hours. But everything would depend on whether there was enough daylight left to overtake the Carthaginian warships, before they scattered and escaped into the night.

Still cursing Andranodoros, I eventually went to bed, but could only doze intermittently. I kept waking up and turning over in my head my interview with Hieron and Archimedes. The noise of all the preparations going on in the Little Harbour seemed to be amplified by the darkness and made falling asleep even more difficult. A few hours before dawn, I gave up, got out of my cot and dressed. Agbal was snoring gently on his paillasse in the anteroom. I stepped around him and let myself out of the apartment.

The wide, open space in the centre of the courtyard was jammed with men from the White Shields and Yellow Shields, who must have marched from Plymmerium in the night. They sat silently in the moonlight on their haunches, their arms around their knees, looking tired and waiting for orders. In addition to their crews, each quinquereme carried a company of a hundred soldiers from the standing army, who acted as marines and did all the actual fighting. I guessed they would be the last to embark. I couldn't see Theodotus or Eryx: they were probably both down at the harbour.

With little else to distract me, I toured the palace checking on the sentries. They were all at their posts and eager to ask me about Pachynus. Word had already spread that Prince Hieronymus had left the city that afternoon and was leading several companies of the Gold Shields down the coastal road. The sentries assumed our ships would be sailing south too, to destroy the invaders' fleet and seize the Carthaginian army in some sort of trap. I didn't tell them there was no Carthaginian army at Pachynus.

At least, I hoped there wasn't. It was all just guesswork; we knew nothing for certain. The first refugees had begun to arrive during the day, in groups of steadily increasing size. Hieron was making them wait outside the gates while he decided what to do with them, and I had put Castor in charge of collecting any useful information they might have to offer. Their stories had proved so confused and contradictory as to be entirely worthless. One man claimed that exactly seventeen ships had come to Pachynus; another said he had counted over two hundred. Some people believed that only infantry had come ashore; others, that large contingents of cavalry were ravaging the countryside. One woman, no doubt inspired by stories of Hannibal's exploits in Italy, even swore that she had seen a herd of elephants. Every family wanted to tell us something that they hoped might earn them admission to the city, but the more eyewitnesses we interviewed, the blinder we became.

If the Carthaginians really had landed in force, then Hieron was about to gift them his kingdom, by sending most of the army and all our best reservists far out to sea on a fool's errand. It struck me that only a man with complete confidence in his own judgement would take such a risk, for a reward of little real significance. I doubted whether I would have had the nerve to play as bold a game as our king. But perhaps that's why he was a king, I thought to myself, and I would never be more than a captain.

I decided to go down to the Little Harbour to see how the preparations were coming along. The sentries let me out of a postern gate and I walked down a ramp to the thoroughfare that ran between the palace's two circuits of walls. Queues of reservists were slowly shuffling along the cobbled channel, all carrying small sacks over their shoulders. It was impossible to tell how long the lines were; they stretched around the corners of the walls in both directions.

I followed the road round to a double tower in the perimeter wall, which gave access to the Little Harbour. Four long tables had been set up in front of its gates, behind each of which sat a dozen palace officials. Working by the light of oil lamps, they were taking the names of the men as they filed past, and checking them off against the reserve lists. My cousin Thraso and his magistrates were going to have a busy few weeks, I thought grimly. The gates of the city had been closed the previous morning to prevent the faint-hearted from absconding, but quite a few would still be missing and their excuses would have to be investigated. Any man who evaded his duty as a citizen risked being condemned to slavery instead. I suppose it was the logical punishment, though had it been up to me, I'd have crucified them.

The guards at the gate were my own men and saluted as I passed. I'd put on one of my blue tunics, so none of the officials who were strutting around gave me any trouble.

The wharf was dimly lit by torches, which had been placed in stands at regular intervals along its entire length. I noticed several had gone out and others were now beginning to fail. The reservists were being counted off as they came through the outer gate and allocated to their ships. They boarded silently in single file along narrow gangplanks, under the eyes of the army lieutenants who would act as the ships' captains. It took four hundred oarsmen and twenty deckhands to crew a quinquereme, with a hundred of the oarsmen at rest in the hammocks at any given moment. The reserve lists identified those who made their living as sailors or fishermen, and these men were used as the deck crews. They had been given ribbons to wear around their wrists to mark them out. The work was easier, but unlike the oarsmen, they would be fully exposed to the missiles of our enemies.

Thanks to their shallow drafts and three separate bilges, quinqueremes were almost unsinkable, except by the most violent storms. For the most part, we fought by boarding our enemies' warships, or by trying to set them alight with projectiles. Ramming another quinquereme was a difficult and dangerous manoeuvre, which seldom accomplished much. As a result, we tended to reserve our rams for merchant ships or the smaller triremes which, when holed, would disappear beneath the waves with a satisfying alacrity.

It was my ancestor King Dionysius who had invented the quinquereme, and for a while they had made him the master of the seas, smashing aside the flimsy triremes of his enemies as if they were fishing smacks. Eventually, the Carthaginians had worked out how to construct their own. Then the Romans, who had little knowledge of shipbuilding, had salvaged a Carthaginian quinquereme that had run aground, and they had copied that. Now everybody had them.

Even if I couldn't have the command, I yearned to be on one of our ships. The prestige of our kingdom rested on its fleet. The days when King Dionysius had terrorised the Mediterranean were long gone, but Syracuse retained its reputation as a sea power to be feared. The truth was that to keep even a dozen quinqueremes continuously patrolling our trade routes was an effort for us. We simply didn't have enough men. There were only about three hundred full-time sailors in our navy, barely sufficient to provide deck crews for the handful of ships on duty at any given moment. A third of the oarsmen on our patrol ships were draftees doing their training; the rest were reservists under the age of thirty, who were recalled for six weeks' service every other year.

If maintaining adequate peacetime patrols was a strain, to mobilise our entire fleet of eighty warships was an undertaking that sucked the lifeblood out of the city. I had only seen it happen once, five years previously, when the Romans had asked us to help them clear the coast of Gaul of pirates. Hieron had decided to put on a show of force, perhaps more with a view to making an impression on his Roman friends than to impressing the pirates. It had taken some forty thousand men to crew all our ships. In the city, shops and market stalls had been shut up; there was little traffic on the roads; and all across the Great Harbour, abandoned merchant vessels and fishing boats lay idle at anchor.

That campaign had lasted five months, under Lepides' command. Dozens of pirate ports were assaulted, and their populations systematically massacred or sold into slavery. I was still only a lieutenant back then and had not enjoyed the work: I have never found it easy to harden myself to the task of killing those too young to be enslaved. But Hieron had wanted to make a point, and I suppose it was kinder than just leaving the children to starve. Unfortunately, the squeamishness of some of my men had resulted in several botched and protracted incidents. In the end, I had instructed everyone in my company to bring any infants and youngsters they found to me. It was easier on both my men and the children that way. As far as I can remember, that was the only action I ever took for which Lepides openly praised me.

Of course, the campaign had eventually proved a waste of time, as Hieron had probably known all along that it would: within three years, the pirates were back. One might as well have tried to rid a field of worms.

I made my way through the throngs of men on the wharf, and eventually spotted Theodotus. I hadn't seen him since leaving Plymmerium. He was talking to three of his junior officers, whom I knew only in passing. The three lieutenants saluted me as I approached and I nodded in acknowledgement.

"Dion!" Theodotus shouted with a smile. "Or should I call you 'sir' now?" he added.

"'Captain Cowbrains' will still do," I replied sourly as we embraced. It was his own nickname for me.

Theodotus laughed.

"Yes, it didn't take you long to start killing your own lieutenants, did it? I thought we were supposed to leave that to the Carthaginians. But it's an interesting idea." He waved in the direction of the ships. "It would save us going to all this bother to thin out the population. Did you know Malmeides was my wife's cousin, by the way? She seems to think you should be crucified."

Out of the corner of my eye, I saw Theodotus's lieutenants grinning to each other. If only battles were fought with quips instead of spears, Theodotus might have conquered the world.

"I'm sorry," I replied, feeling awkward and not knowing quite what to say.

"There's really nothing to apologise for, my friend," Theodotus replied cheerfully. "Malmeides was a fart in a tent, and everyone knows my wife's a rancid old turbot. I should never have married her, but I needed the money, of course. Which reminds me, I hear you're to be congratulated? Let's hope your future wife turns out to have more sense than you, or I fear for your children."

"Thank you, I think," I said with a grin.

"So, has Hieron sent you here to sail with us?" Theodotus asked. "We could do with a few more men like you on the oars."

"I'm afraid not. I'm to stay in Syracuse. It seems someone has to keep the kingdom safe. We can't all go on holiday at once."

Theodotus snorted and smiled at me sadly.

"It's no holiday, I'm afraid, my friend. It seems the king's blood is up. We've been given very particular instructions what to do with any prisoners. To be honest, Dion, I don't know whether I want to find the Carthaginians or not. If we do, there'll be no turning back from this. Hannibal won't be likely to forget it."

"We've seen off worse than Hannibal before," I said. "Look, I can see you're busy. I just wanted to wish you luck. May the gods protect you, Theodotus. And try not to let Andranodoros sink the fleet before our enemies get a chance to do it for him."

Theodotus raised an eyebrow, then turned to his officers.

"You have your orders," he said to them with a nod. "You're dismissed; return to your ships now. And good hunting, my friends."

His lieutenants saluted us both. They had a boyish eagerness about them; but then, they had probably never seen a real fight at sea before. Destroying little pirate ships is as easy as swatting insects: the only difficult part is catching them. Taking on another quinquereme is a very different matter. I nodded to them and rather enviously wished them well. When they had gone, Theodotus clapped me on the arm.

"You should be a little more careful what you say, Dion. That comment will likely get back to Andranodoros. One of those young men was a relative of his."

I shrugged my shoulders indifferently. It was not that Andranodoros and I had ever openly quarrelled, at least, not since the morning I had sent him running off with blood streaming down his chin. It was just that our animosity had survived undimmed ever since.

"He already knows what I think of him," I said. "Anyway, he's a joke."

"No, he's not, Dion," Theodotus replied. "I don't much care for him either, but he's been up all night seeing to it that the ships are properly prepared and provisioned. He thinks of everything, and I have to say it's extraordinary how much information he can hold in his head. Have you any idea what it takes to get more than thirty ships out of their sheds and ready to sail in just a day and a night? I don't think either you or I could have done it. He might be a vain prick, but he's certainly no joke."

"But can he fight, my friend? That's the question," I replied, trying to keep the sourness out of my voice.

"I don't know. But we'll see soon enough, won't we? In any event, he's asked Eryx to sail on his flagship with him. He says that if it comes to a fight, he wants someone experienced on hand to advise him. That sounds to me like a man who cares more about winning than about personal glory, which only makes him more dangerous... I assume you already know we aren't heading to Pachynus?"

I nodded.

"Andranodoros has taken Eryx and me through the plan," Theodotus continued. "He says the king came up with it himself. It's a pretty remarkable idea, Dion. Intercepting an enemy in open waters? It's like trying to hit one arrow in the air with another. We're sailing in two squadrons. I'm to lead one. Andranodoros is going to try to get ahead of Hannibal's ships, while my squadron drives them towards him. Even if I can't find them, he should still have a chance of netting a few. I don't think anyone has ever attempted anything quite like this before, my friend, and if we pull it off, well, it really will be quite something. They'll still be talking about it in a hundred years' time."

It stuck in my gullet, but I had to admit Theodotus had a point about getting the fleet ready. I hadn't even considered what powers of organisation that must have required. The whole scheme depended on putting our ships to sea as quickly as possible; the expedition might well have failed before it had even begun, had I been in charge. Perhaps that was the real reason why Hieron had passed me over, in favour of his son-in-law. If I had felt resentful before, believing the command had gone to a lesser man, the realisation that it may have gone to a better one did nothing to comfort me.

I was about to say something ungracious, when we were interrupted by a slave, who came running up to Theodotus.

"Excuse me, Master, but I have a message from the admiral for you. He draws your attention to the fact that seven ships still have no tar barrels. We have already taken what we can find from the city, so he requests that you apply to the palace to see if they can help."

Theodotus nodded.

"Tell the admiral I'll attend to it."

The rank of admiral was only ever a temporary one, but I wasn't surprised to hear that Andranodoros was making full use of it.

"No, Theodotus," I said on an impulse, putting my hand on his shoulder. "Let me do something, at least. Please. You're busy enough. I can deal with this."

I turned to the slave.

"My name is Captain Dion. Give my compliments to... to the admiral, and tell him I'll see what I can find for him."

The slave looked at Theodotus, who shrugged and nodded.

"Yes, Masters," he said.

"Is there anything else you need?" I asked. The slave thought for a moment, and then smiled.

"Yes, Master. Everything. But we are especially short of victuals. We have emptied all the shops already. The admiral calculates the men will have to be on three-quarter rations on the outward journey, and just one-third rations returning."

"Very well. I'll see what I can do. And please tell the admiral..." I took a breath. The slave looked up at me. "Please tell the admiral that I wish him every success. May the gods bring him home victorious."

Although the position was now reversed, Andranodoros must have been a head taller than me when I had punched him in the face. I had caught him throwing stones at Titan, my father's half-blind and lame old hunting dog, making the poor creature cringe and yelp. It had been one of the few occasions on which my mother had displayed a sufficient interest in my welfare to administer my punishment with her own arm, not trusting even my malevolent governess to apply the willow switch with adequate vigour. Even so, it would have been worth the thrashing, had my mother not also ordered the dog to be killed, as an additional lesson for my benefit.

I had never really forgiven Andranodoros for the death of that dog, and he had never forgiven me for the gap in his teeth. But with Andranodoros struggling to ready our ships for sea, our old enmity seemed a petty, unbecoming thing.

I knew why Andranodoros needed the tar barrels. Our warships were equipped with two ballistae, one near the prow and the other at the stern. They looked like large crossbows, mounted on swivelling platforms, and they could be adapted to throw either rounded stones or five-foot long bolts. Both types of projectile were dunked in hot tar and set alight before being shot. The stones, which were about the size of a man's head, were heavy enough to smash through a ship's planks, providing they struck their target squarely; unfortunately, in all but the calmest seas, and at anything other than point blank range, they usually only landed glancing blows, or else missed completely. The bolts were more accurate, but less dangerous. Only old or poorly maintained warships, whose timbers had started to decay in the salt air, were at any real risk of being set alight by a bolt. At close quarters, of course, the stones and the bolts could both have a shattering impact on a tightly packed formation of marines. A fight to the finish between two quinqueremes is an unusually gruesome affair.

I returned to the palace and had a company of the City Guards rousted from their beds. We found a sufficient quantity of tar barrels for Andranodoros's needs in the storerooms, and we also emptied the palace larders of half their contents. Everything was loaded onto five carts. The food we had collected looked a pitiful contribution. I doubted there was enough to satisfy a single ship's crew for more than a few days. All our quinqueremes had nets, which they trailed in their wake, but they seldom caught anything; the oars probably scared off the fish. Andranodoros would just have to hope that one of the Greek cities along the southern coast of Italy would agree to re-provision the fleet. Some of them were friendly towards us, although with Hannibal roaming so close to their walls, it seemed unlikely that any would have the courage to help. We had already heard that several of our fair-weather allies were considering switching their support to Carthage.

The night was starting to lighten as the laden carts trundled through the gates of the exercise yard. It would be at least another hour before the fleet could sail, so I decided to go back to my rooms to get something to eat, before returning to the Little Harbour. I strolled through the passageway to the great courtyard, where the men of the White Shields and Yellow Shields still sat patiently, waiting to be embarked, and followed the colonnaded walkway around the perimeter.

I had nearly reached the staircase when I heard a solitary shout. It was immediately followed by another, and then more, and suddenly all the men in the courtyard were rising to their feet and cheering. I looked around, but at first I couldn't identify the cause. And then I saw the king.

Some thirty paces away from me, there was a small podium, maybe four feet high, which must have been erected during the night. I hadn't even noticed it. A slave now mounted it holding a torch. Two other slaves followed, carrying Hieron carefully up a flight of steps that had been fixed to the platform's side. They had made a cradle for him with their hands and he had his arms around their necks. Eryx, the captain of the Yellow Shields, followed behind them. Once the slaves had safely reached the top, they gently lowered Hieron's legs. One of them held the king's elbow to steady him and the whooping grew louder.

The king seldom left the palace any more. Many of those in the courtyard had probably not set eyes on him before that night, and knew they might never again. They pressed excitedly around the platform, standing on their toes to try to get a better glimpse of him in the torchlight. As usual, Hieron was dressed in a simple white robe and wore no crown, but then, he had no need of one. Even Eryx, standing deferentially at the king's back, seemed in awe of the old man.

I imagine most people might smile and wave when greeted by a cheering crowd, but Hieron just stared down at us without expression. Slowly, he turned his head from side to side to scan the faces of his men. It felt strangely as though he were bestowing a gift on everyone, the gift of merely being noticed by him.

Eventually, the king gestured for silence. As the cheering died away, he turned and beckoned Eryx forward, who stepped up to Hieron's side. Eryx held a small roll of papyrus in his hand. He probably had the loudest voice in the army, but he waited until the courtyard was completely still before he spoke.

"His Majesty has asked me to read you this message."

He paused as he unrolled the papyrus. The king put his hand on Eryx's shoulder and I felt my skin begin to tingle. I believe every man in the courtyard sensed that this was an event that would be branded on his memory, a moment when the small trajectory of his own life briefly intersected with something of significance. The atmosphere was as taut as a bowstring. The king nodded and Eryx held up the scroll, cleared his throat, and started to read.

"Men of Syracuse, I am old, and my voice is weak, so you must forgive me for borrowing the voice of another. In five hundred years, your forefathers never failed this city. Soon, we will see if you are worthy to call yourselves their sons. The uncertain and the spineless fall, and all that they love disappears with them. Only those willing to die for what they love can keep what they love. For your city and your king, for your wives and your whores, for the friend standing beside you, for the brats you have already spawned and for the generations as yet unborn, I command you now to fight, and if needs be to die, as your ancestors fought and died for you. My body may be a guttering lamp, but my soul still burns like flaming pitch. Take that fire and make it yours. For while I have a breath left in me, I will shout defiance at my enemies. I will see them crushed and broken. I will not suffer this kingdom to be insulted by barbarians."

We stood, mute and rigid, as Hieron's words pulsed through the courtyard. Eryx inhaled deeply and turned again to the papyrus; the king's hand still rested on his shoulder.

"My friends, you are about to embark on a long voyage. May the gods bring you safely home. For my part, I ask only one thing of you. Should you meet any Carthaginians on your journey, tell them that Hieron, King of Syracuse, sends his compliments. And then feed the bastards to the fish for me."

We held our breath for a moment, and then someone started slowly stamping his foot. The bowstring snapped. An instant later, over three thousand men had taken up the pounding rhythm.

"Hier-on, Hier-on," they began to chant, louder and louder.

"Will you fight for your king?" roared Eryx over our heads. "Will you die for him? Will you?"

The response must have been audible across half the city. I think I was shouting too.

For those who never knew his rule, it is impossible to explain what Hieron meant to his subjects. He was already our king when most of us were born and we could not imagine anything ever changing. To us, he was as eternal as the smouldering volcano of Etna on our northern borders, and just as unfathomable. He seemed quite indifferent towards his people, even as he dedicated himself to their safety. In the pursuit of peace, he was merciless to the point of cruelty. He hoarded power like a miser hoards gold, and yet he lived a life of complete simplicity, disdaining all the luxury that power has to offer. To this day, I have no idea whether Hieron cared nothing for himself, or only for himself. But it didn't matter. While that magnificent, terrible old man still breathed, we knew that all would be well.

The cheering and stamping must have continued for several minutes. With his back bent and shoulders stooped, Hieron remained motionless on the platform, gazing down impassively at his troops. I wondered what was going on in that mind of his. Did it trouble him that he might be sending men to die? Probably not.

Eventually, the king spread his arms for silence, and the noise abated. Hieron turned and nodded to Eryx again.

"Soldiers of Syracuse!" Eryx bellowed. "In a moment, I will give the order to assemble in company lines. The White Shields will form up on my left, and the Yellow Shields on my right. I am an understanding man, but do try not to fuck this up completely in front of His Majesty. Now, form company lines!"

The miraculous reconfiguration of chaos into order began. With so many men crowded together, the exercise took several minutes to complete.

When the company sergeants had finally finished straightening up their blocks of men, a litter was brought round to the foot of the platform. Eryx stayed on the podium as the king was carried back down the steps and helped into the seat. Four slaves smoothly hefted the poles onto their shoulders and began bearing the king towards the main gate, led by a fifth who held a torch.

"The Yellow Shields will follow His Majesty to the harbour in company order," Eryx boomed from the podium. "The White Shields will bring up the rear."

My height makes me noticeable. As Hieron was carried past, he spotted me standing in the colonnade and beckoned me over. I ran across and fell in alongside the litter.

"I hear you've been rifling my storerooms, young man, and stealing my tar barrels," Hieron said. "First a murderer, now a thief. Is there no end to your wickedness?"

"I thought you might judge it was in a good cause, my King," I replied. I had to twist my neck uncomfortably to look up at him. "And I am afraid I have another confession to make – I also rifled your larders."

"Did you, now? I hope you asked the cooks first. You certainly don't want to make enemies of them. They can do far worse things to you than Zoippos."

"Yes, my King." Hieron seemed to be in a good mood. "If I may say so, your speech to the men… It was…" I struggled to find the right words.

"No need to wipe my arse for me, Dion," the king interrupted. "I've quite enough people to do that already. But yes, I suppose it did work quite well, didn't it?" We had nearly reached the main gate. He looked down and smiled coldly at me. "If I remember rightly, the last time I used that particular speech, it was the Spartans I was urging our men to drown… Now, Captain, I believe you're seeing Archimedes in a few hours. No doubt you'll want to shave and wash before you call on him, so I shall leave you here."

It was a dismissal. I bowed and moved aside as Hieron was carried slowly through the gate. One after another, the companies of troops filed past behind him. Our king was leading out his army one last time, and it was a moment he apparently had no wish to share with me.

As the men marched past, I heard some muffled cheering coming from the direction of the harbour. I guessed the lieutenants who had been assigned to captain our ships had also been reading out Hieron's speech to their crews.

I returned to the apartment, intending to snatch a little sleep. Alpha, Omega and Agbal were already up, presumably having been woken by all the cheering. They pressed me for information, but I would tell them only that the fleet was sailing at dawn, which was hardly a secret.

"But why aren't you sailing with them, Master?" asked Agbal. "Or going to Pachynus with the prince?"

I glowered at him.

"Shush, Agbal," said Alpha hurriedly, "that's no concern of yours. Now, go and boil some eggs for the master… I imagine you do want some breakfast, Master?"

I nodded.

"Bring it to my room."

While I waited for the food, I sat at the table in my bedroom, staring at the withered circlet of olive twigs that hung above my cot.

It looked a sorry thing, although for a while it had put my name on the lips of Greeks the world over. I forlornly wondered if I would ever accomplish anything worthwhile again.

*

At the agreed time, I knocked on the gate of Archimedes' villa. Unusually for a noble, he lived in Achradina, the largest of the city's districts.

We have a saying in Syracuse: the sea brings wealth, and stone keeps it. Achradina had been the first quarter to take root on the mainland. In times of trouble, its early residents used to seek refuge on the well-fortified island of Ortygia, but eventually the population reached such a size that this became impractical. An impressive new circuit of walls was constructed, which sliced off several square miles of the mainland, before looping back down along the coast to join up with the sea walls of the Little Harbour.

The population continued to grow, and new settlements for the poor began to sprout up on the cheap, undefended land beyond Achradina. The poor have an unfortunate proclivity to multiply fast, and before long, nearly as many people were once again living outside the gates as within them. Thanks to one of our intermittent experiments with democracy, additional lines of fortifications were eventually thrown up. As is only to be expected of works commissioned by those who proclaim themselves servants of the people, these later walls were constructed at tremendous expense and were barely adequate to keep out the wild dogs.

It took the determination of a ruthless king, my ancestor Dionysius, to sort out the city's defences once and for all. His invention of the quinquereme had freed him to pursue a policy of voracious and indiscriminate piracy, and he put the enormous wealth this generated to good use. Like many coastal cities, Syracuse was most vulnerable to attack from the high ground immediately behind it, so Dionysius constructed two massive new walls, which run inland for mile after mile, rising into the hills in the shape of a giant triangle. They finally converge on the commanding plateau of Epipolae. At the highest point of Epipolae, where the walls form their apex, Dionysius built the citadel of Euryalus. The citadel is protected by a series of deep ditches, as well as by the contours of the plateau, and is all but impregnable.

With no prospect of capturing the high ground, an attacking army must choose between assaulting the city from either the north or the south, along the axis of the coastal road that runs through our gates. Neither is an appealing option. Dionysius's north wall follows the line of a steep ridge, which more than doubles its height. A second huge citadel, called the Hexapylon on account of its six menacing towers, straddles the road into Syracuse from this side. The land on the other side of the city is comparatively flat, but an enemy approaching from that direction, around the edge of the Great Harbour, must deal with a wide, fetid marsh instead, which extends nearly to the foot of our south wall. Any sensible general would take one look at our defences, and elect to blockade the city rather than attempt to assault it. But the malicious and irritable spirits who inhabit the marsh present him with yet another problem: his army would be liable to be destroyed by disease, long before we could be starved into submission. Those marsh spirits had broken more than one enemy for us in the past, and we took great care to propitiate them.

Two hundred years after they were built, my ancestor's walls still have no equal in the known world. It takes the best part of a day to walk their length. Our wealth is kept by stone.

All Syracuse knew where to find my great-uncle's house, but perhaps oddly, I had never been inside it before. His sister had died giving birth prematurely to my mother, my mother's indifference to the convenience of others being manifest from the first, and so beyond the legal necessities, there had never been much of a bond between Archimedes and my immediate family. It was, however, principally on account of his domestic arrangements that we kept our distance, for shortly before I was born, Archimedes had sent his first wife and her dowry back to her incensed family, and had married a slave woman instead.

Such things happened from time to time, of course: one of the uncles of my friend Theodotus had even married a famous society prostitute. But he was a well-liked man and had managed to laugh it off by claiming that his straitened circumstances had obliged him to make economies. What was so peculiar about Archimedes' behaviour, and what made it so much more difficult for his fellow nobles to excuse, was that the slave woman had apparently not even been young or pretty.

Naturally, there was no possibility that my mother would ever acknowledge such a woman, and so my great-aunt had always been a complete stranger to me. As I stood waiting for the gate to be opened, it struck me that I had never even seen her face.

I was admitted by a heavily muscled man with a small scar on his forehead, whom I thought I recognised, although I couldn't remember at first from where.

"Good morning, sir," he said politely. "Your great-uncle is expecting you. If you'd care to follow me, I'll show you the way."

I tried to place him as we crossed the broad but weed-infested courtyard. He was clearly not a slave. He had a military manner, but wore civilian clothes.

"Forgive me," I said after a moment, "but I'm sure I know you. Weren't you in the White Shields? A sergeant, I think?"

"That's quite right, sir," he replied, obviously gratified. "But I chucked the army in a few years back to join the Royal Watch. Always wanted to wear the black plume. Thought it would have the girls falling over themselves – more fool me. My name's Kleitos by the way, sir."

"But I see you're a civilian now. What happened? Why did you leave the Watch?"

"Bless you, sir, I haven't left them. It's just that those of us on your great-uncle's detail don't wear uniform. We've been told to make ourselves as inconspicuous as possible. He doesn't want to draw attention to himself, apparently, although I doubt there's a man in Syracuse who doesn't know who he is. Now then, here we are, sir. You'll find your great-uncle in his study on the left, at the top of the stairs."

We had reached a doorway, to which he gestured. He saluted and left me to go on alone. On the face of it, Archimedes was not an important enough member of the royal family to merit his own bodyguards. Their presence only confirmed how little I knew about him.

I found the study easily enough. The door was open. My great-uncle sat behind a desk, facing the door, under a large window that looked over the city wall to the sea. He was scratching furiously at a piece of papyrus. I don't think I'd ever seen anyone write so fast. Scrolls and wax tablets lay scattered all over the floor and further scrolls had been jammed messily into shelving around the walls. Someone whom I took to be a secretary sat at a second table in a corner, with his back to me. They were both working in silence. I tapped politely on the wall to announce my arrival. Archimedes looked up.

"Ah, Dion," he said, without standing. "Come in. I don't believe you've met my wife, Chrysanthe?"

The person at the other table stood and turned towards me with a smile. She must have been about sixty and was as plump as Archimedes was skinny. I had no idea what to say. I felt myself blushing.

She giggled.

"Oh dear," she said, with a faint accent that I couldn't place. "It seems the fearsome Bull of Syracuse has been quite confounded by the presence of a little old lady. I'm afraid we are not in the least formal in this house, Great-nephew. We set our own rules here. And it is a pleasure to meet you at last."

"Madam, I meant no offence. I just, well, I just wasn't expecting… But I'm… I'm honoured to make your acquaintance."

She smiled warmly. She wore her hair short, like a man's, and it was grey. She had made no attempt to conceal her age with a wig. I wondered what her history was; she seemed far too self-assured and well-spoken to have been born into slavery.

"Call me Chrysanthe. I look forward to getting to know you, Dion. Archimedes says you are an interesting man."

"As interesting as a fool can be," Archimedes interjected. "Now, sit there, Dion." He gestured to a stool, which I awkwardly took. Instead of leaving the room, Chrysanthe turned her chair round to face me and settled herself back down. Archimedes saw the look of consternation on my face.

"Oh, for pity's sake, do stop being such a prig, boy. Chrysanthe has the best brain in Syracuse, after my own, of course. Why do you think I married her? This was all her idea anyway."

I came to know Archimedes' study well in the three remaining years of his life. I remember that to one side of his desk, he used to keep a neat row of what, at first glance, appeared to be small wooden balls of equal size. I think there were thirteen of them altogether. When he spoke, he would sometimes pick one up and roll it between his hands. Those balls used to fascinate me, because when you looked more closely, you could see they weren't really spheres at all, but polyhedrons. Their surfaces were made up of complex, interlocking patterns of triangles, squares, pentagons and what have you. Each was slightly different to the others, and each must have had dozens of different facets.

On that first occasion that I visited his house, the three of us spoke for about an hour. I can still recall the morning as if it were yesterday.

"Let me explain why you are here, my dear," Chrysanthe began. "In my own modest way, I also serve the king. I am one of those whom Hieron uses to help him keep an eye on things here in the city."

"How do you mean, Great-aunt? What things?"

"Oh, people really. Various nobles, for the most part. A few merchants and officials. One or two of our sillier priests. The sort of men whom kings need to keep an eye on."

"Do you mean to say, you spy for him, Great-aunt?"

"Goodness, Dion," she giggled, "you do look astonished. We women may not be much use with a sword, but I would have thought you might have learnt from your mother's example that we are perfectly capable of a little intrigue. And we are rather better than men at understanding the workings of the human heart, are we not? In any event, I am sure our king does not rely on me alone. There are probably more informants in the city than there are slaves. But he likes to keep those whom he entrusts with this sort of work in ignorance of each other. We see our own threads, but only he sees the weave."

"And are you involved in this too, Great-uncle?"

"No, not really, Dion," Archimedes replied. "Chrysanthe sometimes consults me, but I leave the tedious mysteries of the soul to her. I deal in calculations."

"So, what do you both want of me?"

"Ah, well now," said Chrysanthe, "let me explain. It's to do with all that unfortunate Apollonius business... Ask yourself this, Dion, why should the Carthaginians have wanted to kill our prince, unless they were trying to prepare the way for someone else? Whom might they have, hiding in the shadows, ready to step forward when Hieron dies?"

"I've no idea, Great-aunt. And I don't see how I can help you answer that. Maybe they just wanted to cause trouble."

"Perhaps so, Dion. But nations are not like men. They are cold and deliberate. They do not lash out on a mere impulse. So let us assume for a moment that such a traitor does exist, working with Carthage to take the throne eventually. His first attempt on Gelon failed, and as an unexpected consequence of that failure, he now finds himself with a new obstacle to overcome. You. After all, under poor old Apollonius, the City Guard was hardly much of a consideration, was it? Its officers would not have had the nerve or nous to oppose a new regime, and many may even have welcomed it. But that is no longer the case, is it? In no time at all, you seem to have got the Guards firmly in hand. It really is a most impressive achievement." She turned to reach for a cup on her desk and took a sip from it. "Anyway, that is our hypothetical man's headache. The Guards control the city and you control the Guards. I would say that no conspiracy could now hope to succeed, unless you could also be recruited to it."

I bridled.

"I find that suggestion rather offensive, Chrysanthe. Have you only brought me here to question my loyalty? I am not my father."

"Goodness gracious, Dion. You are a prickly young chap, aren't you? And you misunderstand me entirely. If I doubted you, I would hardly be telling you all this, would I?"

"So, let me repeat my question. What is it you want of me?" Chrysanthe folded her hands in her lap and smiled. She had the manner of a kindly matriarch. She discussed plots and counter-plots as casually as she might review the day's menu with her cooks.

"I want you to be the worm on my hook, dear."

"I'm sorry?"

"It shouldn't be too difcult," she continued serenely. "Just don't bother to disguise your disappointment about being passed over for the command of the fleet. Be unhappy about the agricultural tithes on your estates as well, if you like... And keep your ears open. That's all you need do."

"You mean, you want me to spy on my friends for you?"

"If any of them is a traitor, Dion, he is hardly your friend. Nor do I ask you to spy on them. It is only if you are given grounds for suspicion that you need report anything to me. And just to be clear, I am not the one who requires this of you. If you would rather not help, I am afraid you will have to explain your reasons to our king."

"I see," I said quietly.

"Good... Now, a word of advice, young man. You'll need to be subtle about it. If we do have enemies within our walls, they will eventually have to approach you. So don't go looking for them, will you? Let them expose themselves in their own good time. And if anyone does approach you, don't appear too eager. The trick will be to make them think you might be open to persuasion, but only reluctantly so."

"But why on earth does Hieron need my help with this? Why doesn't he just kill anyone whose loyalty he doubts?"

"Oh, for two reasons, poppet," Chrysanthe replied lightly. "Firstly, we don't know quite what we are dealing with yet. There may be no real plot at all, but even if there is, we don't know who is involved or how. When we strike, we need to be sure that we are striking at the head of the snake and not its tail."

"Alright. So what's the second reason?"

Chrysanthe pursed her lips and met my gaze. Her eyes were dark brown, like those muddy street puddles whose depth you can never properly judge, until you make the mistake of stepping into one.

"Well, Dion," she said, "as a general rule, Hieron believes that excessive violence tends to recoil on the heads of kings who indulge in it. He says it almost always results in unforeseen consequences. You begin by killing a single man, and then you find you have to kill his friends and sons, and then you find you have to kill their friends and sons. You merely encourage real conspiracies, where perhaps none existed before. And so our king prefers to pull men's strings, rather than to cut them. Of course, your own father was something of a special case, but even then, Hieron took no further action against your family. Few other rulers would have been so merciful, I imagine... But don't mistake his subtlety for squeamishness, Dion. Dear me, no; whatever you do, never make that mistake. If he thought it necessary, Hieron wouldn't hesitate to slaughter every noble in Syracuse to keep his throne. His moderation is a studied policy, not a moral posture... But for the time being, at any rate, he has instructed us merely to watch and listen and wait. Do you understand? Good. Clever boy. And now I think that's probably quite enough scheming for one morning, wouldn't you say?"

She turned her head towards her husband.

"I don't believe there's anything else we need trouble the poor man with, is there, Archimedes?"

"No, dearest, I think you've covered everything," replied my great-uncle. "Although perhaps you might point out to Dion that if there is indeed a plot, the conspirators may decide it would be much simpler just to kill him too."

"Yes, there is that… So do take care, Dion, won't you? Now, would you like to stay for some lunch? I should warn you, Archimedes and I always eat together. It's very scandalous of us, I know, but then, we do so enjoy discussing mathematics over our meals. And if you'd care to stay, perhaps you can help him with his ostomachion problem while we eat."

She smiled at her husband teasingly.

He snorted.

"Ostomachion?" I asked. "He needs help playing ostomachion?"

My day seemed to be descending from the unsettling to the comical. Ostomachion is a child's game, consisting of a square tray that holds fourteen flat wooden pieces. The pieces are a mix of irregular triangles and quadrilaterals and no two are the same. The challenge is simply to empty the tray and then to fit all the pieces neatly back in.

"Oh no, he's not playing it, my dear," Chrysanthe replied with a laugh. "He's trying to calculate how many different solutions there are. It's a problem I set him a while ago. The silly old goat has been telling me he's on the verge of cracking it every day for the last four months."

She turned to Archimedes.

"Only a few weeks left to go, my darling, and then you lose our little wager." She giggled.

My great-uncle and his wife were well matched, I thought to myself. They were quite as peculiar as each other.

I politely made my excuses.

Archimedes accompanied me downstairs and across the courtyard. As we walked, I noticed two other men lurking in the shadows of the colonnade. More guards, I guessed. We were halfway to the gate when he abruptly stopped and turned to face me. He put his hand on my shoulder and looked me in the eyes.

"There is something I need to say to you, Dion. Listen to me carefully, now. I cannot foresee how all this will end, but you must rein in your mother. It's time for Korinna to stop playing her games. Can I trust you to do that? Hieron tolerated her business antics in the past for my sake, but if she starts trying to meddle in politics, I won't be able to protect her."

I stared at him.

"What...? Oh no... Don't tell me that she's done something stupid?"

"No, not yet, I think. But she does have a lot of dealings with the Carthaginian merchants in the city. And with things the way they are, this is certainly no time to be doing anything that might attract Hieron's attention. You need to get her under control."

"Yes, alright. I'll see to it," I replied. I looked down at my feet.

My great-uncle nodded.

"You know, I always assumed you had no interest in us," I said.

Archimedes pursed his lips and gazed at me for a few moments, as though I were a problem he was trying to unravel.

"I loved my sister very much, Dion," he said eventually, with a slight shrug. "I cannot be entirely indifferent to her children and grandchildren. I have watched you all from a distance. Now, I'm going to let you into a little secret, so that you will understand how serious this is: there are people in your mother's household in Hieron's pay. We know about every grubby deal Korinna has ever negotiated: I've had to persuade the king to stay his hand on more than one occasion. Did you know she's been bribing the agricultural inspectors?"

"Everyone bribes the inspectors, Great-uncle. No one pays the full tithes."

"That doesn't mean it's a safe thing to do, Dion. It's only because her activities provide so much interesting information about what other people are up to that Hieron tolerates her. She's a difficult woman, and too clever for her own good... Anyway, when you see her, don't mention me, or anything I've told you. Tell her you overheard something in the palace, if you like. But however you do it, make sure your mother starts behaving herself. For both your sakes. Do you understand?"

I nodded.

"Very well, then. Now, I'll see you out," he said. He threaded his arm through mine and we continued on towards the gate.

"I obviously should have taken Apollonius more seriously," I said. "You know, he tried to warn me about Mother, too."

"Did he?" replied Archimedes, in apparent surprise. "What did he say?"

"Oh, nothing really. It was the night he died. In fact, it was the last thing the poor fellow ever said to me. He just asked after my family, in a cryptic sort of way. He was obviously referring to her."

"How odd," my great-uncle said with a slight grunt.

We found the same man still on duty at the gate. He saluted me again and smiled warmly at Archimedes.

"Good morning, sir. A beautiful day," the guard said.

"Yes indeed, Kleitos," my great-uncle replied. "I think your boy is coming over later, isn't he?"

"Yes sir. He's been spending every evening working on the problems you set him last week. You've no idea how grateful his mother and I are to you."

"Believe me, my friend, it is you who is doing me a favour. There is no greater pleasure in life than teaching a child who wants to learn. He's a bright little thing. Not like this oaf here. But alas, one can't choose one's family."

"I'd have said you've been pretty lucky in that regard, sir. Captain Dion is probably the most famous soldier in the kingdom. After all, he brought us home an olive-leaf crown, didn't he?"

Archimedes chuckled.

"Well, you may have a point, Kleitos. We need our oxen as well as our stallions, I suppose... Dion, I'll leave you here. Oh, just before you go, there's something I forgot to mention: Hieron has asked me to cast an eye over the city's defences. Meet me here at noon in two days' time and we will make a start with the Hexapylon Gate. And bring Nebit with you."

I started to say goodbye, but he had already turned his back on me and was striding away on his long, thin legs.

I headed back towards the palace through a sequence of narrow and oppressive lanes. The walk did nothing to relieve my mood. I reckoned I could deal with my mother, although it would no doubt prove an ugly business. But everything I had always taken for granted suddenly seemed precarious. Our king was elderly and frail; in the city, his smiling enemies had apparently started whispering to each other behind their hands; and all the while, the poisonous tide of war was inexorably rising. At Pachynus, it had already begun to lap our beaches.

VIII

THE SECOND FRAGMENT

"So, my dear," I said, "what do you make of my great-nephew? He's not exactly the fastest fish in the river, is he?"

"I rather liked him," Chrysanthe replied. "And gosh, what muscles! Although I will admit, I am a little relieved that he didn't stay for lunch." She smiled.

"Yes, it's strange to think that he could be my flesh and blood, isn't it? Or Korinna's, for that matter." I settled myself back down behind my desk and stretched out my legs. "Who knows? Perhaps you'll get to meet her too one day… I wonder what you'd make of her."

"I think Dion is a perfectly sufficient quantity of your relatives for the time being, Husband."

I smiled sadly.

"I wish you could have seen Korinna when she was a child, Chrysanthe. Such a pretty little thing. She was only five when her father died. And of course, she never had a chance to know her mother… Maybe it's my fault. When she came to live with me, I had no idea what to do with her. Well, what do I know of children? The poor girl always seemed so sad. Now I wish I'd taken more of an interest; maybe tried to teach her some mathematics, at least. I certainly shouldn't have let my wife be so hard on her." I sighed. "Perhaps it's no surprise she's so full of anger… I suppose she and Dion have that much in common, at any rate."

"I'm sure you're right, Husband. Sadness and anger: such a tricky combination. Happy people are always so much easier to manage… Now, shall we eat? As we'll be alone, I thought we'd have lunch under the apple tree. I've sent word to the girls to set it up."

We made our way downstairs and crossed the courtyard arm in arm. Our little garden lay to the side of the house, its narrower end bounded by Achradina's sea wall. It was rather overgrown and wild, but I liked it that way. I find it a useful reminder that chaos is always prowling just beneath the surface of things, peering up at us and looking for any opportunity to escape. The wonderful thing about mathematics is that it is the only reality with which even our capricious gods cannot interfere. The child who learns his times tables has made a good start on freeing himself from their power.

I caught the scent of the sea breeze and wondered how the fleet would fare. Hieron had certainly handled my great-nephew very cleverly. I was fairly certain the real reason Dion had been passed over was because our king had no desire to see him win any more of a reputation for himself. Some dogs you feed well; others are best kept hungry.

In the garden, a platter of simple food had been set out on a table beside a jug of water, and we served ourselves as usual, sitting on a blanket on the grass.

"So, my dear," I said, as I helped Chrysanthe lower herself down, "I saw you had a letter from Alexandria this morning. Anything interesting?"

She sighed.

"Yes, I'm afraid I need to talk to you about that."

I raised my eyebrows as I settled myself beside her.

"It's this Apollonius business," she continued. "I didn't want to mention it in front of Dion, of course, but there's something about it that doesn't seem quite right."

"Oh yes?"

"Yes. You see, it's the poison that's been troubling me."

"How so, my dear?"

"Well, as you know, Archimedes, I am not entirely ignorant of the science of poisons. But I must confess, I have never heard of one so potent that it can be administered with a pin. Let alone one that might produce such a satisfactory result within a mere few minutes, in so miniscule a dose."

"How curious," I said.

"Yes, isn't it? So I wrote to our friends in Egypt, who of course know more about poisons than anyone else on earth. It was their reply that I received today. They send you their regards, by the way. Anyway, it would seem that they too have never heard of such a thing."

"And what do you conclude from that, my dear?"

"Isn't it obvious, Husband? Whatever killed Apollonius wasn't on those pins. So I imagine it must have been served up in his food. There are certainly several poisons that can kill a man that quickly, if they are eaten or drunk. Although you have to conceal them in something with a fairly strong flavour. Kidneys always tend to work quite well. Fish soup too, at a pinch."

I scratched my chin.

"How interesting," I said. "And do you happen to know what they were eating that night?"

"No, but I suppose you could enquire, if you think it worth the trouble... You do see the implications, don't you?"

"Oh yes, of course."

"Indeed. Because if the poison was put in his meal, then that would suggest that Apollonius was the intended victim all along."

I began to peel an egg.

"So you believe the whole business with the cushion was just a trick, to fool everyone into thinking that Gelon was the target? Whereas you suspect that Gelon was actually the culprit?"

"Does that not seem the most likely explanation, Husband? After all, it was Gelon who apparently insisted on all that curious swapping of places, to make everyone think the cushion was meant for him."

"And do you happen to have a theory as to why Gelon may have wished to kill his uncle?"

"Well, no, I have to admit I am rather perplexed by that. Of course, getting rid of poor Apollonius obviously cleared the way for Dion. Gelon would certainly have wanted to get a grip on the City Guard before his father dies. After all, successions can be quite awkward things, can't they? Although I have to say, Dion does seem rather a strange choice to replace Apollonius. Such a volatile young man… I'd say our prince is taking something of a gamble in him."

I frowned.

"Well, maybe rather less of a gamble than you might imagine," I said. "There is a rumour going round… I didn't want to mention it before."

"What rumour, my dear?"

"Well, just a bit of gossip within the Royal Watch. Kleitos thought he ought to pass it on. A story to the effect that Gelon may have gone to somewhat unusual lengths to make sure of Dion's personal devotion…"

She raised her eyebrows.

"Ahh," she said.

"Yes. Poor Dion…" I smiled sadly. "Ever the blinkered ox, drawing the farmer's plough without even realising it."

"And that may well be for the best, dear. A man like Dion needs blinkers and a harness. It's much safer for everyone that way. As I say, sadness and anger are such a tricky combination."

"Yes, you may be right…" I sighed. "So I assume you think Hieron had a hand in this Apollonius business as well?"

"Oh yes, I would imagine so," she replied, as she nibbled on a piece of cheese. "But what puzzles me is that it all seems so elaborate. I mean, there was also that Carthaginian family to deal with, the ones who took the blame. They had to be scared into running away… Unless, of course, they were simply murdered too, and quietly disposed of… Yes, such a lot of bother, just to get rid of silly Apollonius. I mean, if this was only about the City Guard, Hieron could simply have found some other job for his brother-in-law."

"So you think there must have been something else behind it?"

"Wouldn't you say so, dear? Some embarrassing family matter, perhaps, that Hieron wished to deal with discreetly…? In any event, I don't suppose we need trouble ourselves about it unduly. I imagine our king is just tidying a few things up, before passing on the reins to his son. And I dare say that's why he still wants me to dangle Dion at the end of my line. Hieron may know there was no real attempt on Gelon's life, but he's probably just trying to make sure there's nothing else he needs to tidy up as well."

"Yes, I imagine you're right," I said, and took a bite of the egg.

That set me wondering.

An egg is such an interesting shape.

"Tell me, my love," I said after a few moments, "do you think it might be possible to formulate the volume of an ellipsoidal solid?"

IX

THE CAMP

I visited Archimedes' grave recently, for the first time in many years. The site is marked by a modest memorial, which Archimedes designed himself. On a plinth stands a single column, surmounted by a little marble cylinder and, perched above that, a sphere. My great-uncle had been very particular about the proportions: the height and diameter of the cylinder are exactly the same as the diameter of the sphere, so that if the cylinder were hollow, the sphere would exactly fit inside it. There is an inscription on the plinth, claiming that the volume and the surface area of the sphere are precisely two thirds of the volume and surface area of the cylinder – something my great-uncle had apparently devoted an entire treatise to proving. This was a man who, in advanced old age, had humiliated an empire and sent its army reeling, and yet the achievement of which he had apparently been most proud was a formula that is of no use to anyone. I suppose I should not have been surprised to find that his monument is already half-obscured by a tangle of brambles and nettles. But then, perhaps it is only fitting that, in death, my great-uncle should be crowned with garlands of plants that sting and scratch.

I am an old man myself now, and almost all those of whom I write are dead. The kingdom I served is dead too, its institutions dissolved, its traditions and values derided. Only our great buildings endure, but they survive as embalmed corpses do, devoid of the spirit that was moved to build them and imbued them with life.

I wait out my time in a small house in a poor district of the city. My family's great limestone villa, our home for eleven generations, is owned by a Carthaginian merchant now. I occasionally see him being carried in his litter on his way down to the harbour. These days, the docks only serve merchant ships; our majestic quinqueremes were taken from us long ago. Sometimes, in the half-light of the evening, I sense the shadows of my forefathers turning their backs on me in shame.

The young are too busy making their own way to listen to my stories. Perhaps they are right: I am a relic of an age that failed. But I write for those who are not yet born. I am using what little savings I have left to buy the very best papyrus, in the hope that these scrolls may survive long enough for our voices to be heard again one day. It is the last service I can offer my king.

And so I must resume my account.

As soon as I had returned to my rooms from Archimedes' house, I sent Agbal over to our villa, to inform my mother that I would be visiting her that evening. I picked at a simple lunch, and contemplated the small pile of documents that Nebit had left for me. They were just lists of expenditure that required my attention. I had made an effort to stay more on top of such matters since my transfer to the City Guard, but my mind was still in a tumult over the series of surprises that had been sprung on me that morning. I found I couldn't concentrate on the work. I attached my seal to the documents without bothering to read them.

When Agbal retuned, it was to tell me that my mother had left the city for the estate at Acrae. She had already sent ahead a dozen newly purchased slaves, under the escort of some of her Galatians.

How typical of her, I thought, to have turned a promise to me to her own advantage. She must have left as soon as she got wind that the Carthaginians had landed at Pachynus. While everyone else was trying to get into Syracuse, she had immediately understood that it would be far safer to get out. I guessed she would not return until it became clear there was no real threat to the city. But at least, I told myself, she wouldn't be able to get up to any mischief while she was at Acrae, and her absence would give me time to make my preparations for my coming confrontation with her.

With nothing in the apartment to distract me from my own thoughts, I decided to head off to the exercise yard to watch the afternoon drills.

When I got there, the space was already bustling with men. Most were sparring with wooden swords; others were practising their javelin throw against a row of straw targets. Officers shouted encouragement and sergeants shouted abuse. There could be no doubting that the City Guard was gradually coalescing into a proud and fierce family.

One company stood apart from the others, by the stable block gates. They wore their breastplates and greaves but no helmets: they were clearly about to go on a run. Running in armour in the afternoon sun, even without helmets, is little short of torture and it was a widely resented exercise, but one upon which I insisted. One of the first lessons Lepides had drummed into his officers was that, in war, speed is almost always of greater importance than numbers.

I find that vigorous exercise helps me think through my problems and so, on an impulse, I sent a soldier to my rooms to collect my own armour from my slaves. As I stood in the yard strapping on my breastplate, I noticed that several of the men practising their swordplay were grinning to each other, while those by the gates were staring at me miserably. There would be no slacking of the pace today. I smiled grimly back at them.

The new lieutenant of the men on whom I was about to inflict my company was the eager young officer Leander. He, at least, greeted me with his usual enthusiasm. He had already outswum me, and without armour he could probably have outrun me too; but over a distance and carrying the extra weight, we both knew it was an altogether different matter.

"Another wager perhaps, Lieutenant?" I asked as I approached him.

"And have you judge me a fool, sir?" he replied with a grin.

Our usual run was halfway to Plymmerium and back, a round trip of about five miles, but the refugees fleeing the Carthaginians at Pachynus made that impossible. They had begun arriving the previous night, in ever-increasing numbers. As they were not being admitted to the city, the south gate was now completely blocked by the human mudslide piling up against our walls.

I chose to leave by the much smaller and less-used west gate instead, which lay in the shadow of the citadel of Euryalus. It gave access to a road that wove through our high, barren hinterlands and eventually to Acrae. Once outside, I led the company through the hills at a good trot, with Leander matching the pace beside me. It was a warm day, and so every half hour or so, I called a halt for a few moments to let everyone drink from their flasks.

When we had reached the furthest extent of our run, at the summit of a desolate mound known as Hunchback's Shoulder, I allowed the men a longer rest. They happily collapsed to the ground. I sat myself on a rock beside Leander, and wiped the sweat from my face. Some miles away, the indifferent sea stretched out before us. I scanned the horizon eagerly, but the fleet was already out of sight.

One day, when I was seven, my father finally gave in to my incessant pleading and took me down to the shore to gawp at *The Syracusia*, the largest ship ever built. Archimedes had designed it, but the project was beyond the capabilities of our own boatyards, so Hieron had commissioned the Corinthians to construct it for him. It had just made its maiden voyage to Syracuse and was lying at anchor a little way out, in the middle of the Great Harbour.

"Isn't she wonderful, Father?" I said eagerly.

"No, son, she isn't," he had snorted. "She's useless. She's too big for any of our docks and they say she's almost impossible to handle. This is what comes of giving someone like your great-uncle his head. Only a very clever man could have been so stupid. But if our king wants to waste his money indulging his own vanity, I suppose that's his affair."

To me, *The Syracusia* had still looked wonderful, a gigantic, lazy turtle, oblivious to the shoal of minnows darting about around it. I have been entranced by the miracle of ships ever since.

I remained lost in my own memories until Leander lifted his arm to point to a distant ridge to the south.

"Who do you think they are, sir?" he asked.

I squinted in the direction he was indicating but could at first see nothing. Then a movement caught my eye, and a small plume of dust appeared, signalling horses on the trot.

They were far from any road and few people lived up in these hills. The soil was thin and stony, and as unsuitable for farming as it was for riding.

"How many of them are there, do you think?" I asked.

"I'd say maybe a dozen," Leander replied. His sight was clearly better than mine.

I scratched my cheek, feeling the scar. Whoever they were, they were heading inland.

No bandits would have dared venture this close to the city, and even if they had, we would have been alerted to their arrival by the long trail of looted farmhouses and dead families that they always leave in their wake.

"I imagine it's just a cavalry patrol from Plymmerium," I told Leander casually.

With the other two captains at sea, and Prince Gelon in Rome, Sosis would be the ranking officer at Plymmerium. My former adjutant knew his business and would have sent out scouting parties, just in case the Carthaginians really had landed in strength at Pachynus and were marching on us even now. It would certainly have occurred to Sosis that an advancing army might try to find an inland passage through the hills, in order to bypass any force that we may have sent down the coastal road to block them. Dispatching riders to scour the remote countryside was a sensible precaution.

Even so, there was something about that distant puff of dust that didn't seem right. I couldn't put my finger on it.

"That's a long enough rest. Let's head back," I announced, provoking a chorus of ill-suppressed groans.

*

Leander tired noticeably on the return journey. Running downhill is harder on the legs than running uphill. He managed to keep ahead of his men, but towards the end I decided to slow the pace a little, so as not to show him up too badly.

It was not until we were inside the city walls again and the men were staggering back towards the palace that I suddenly understood what had been troubling me about the riders in the hills. It was not what I had seen, but what I hadn't seen. Our own cavalry wore simple armour, and even at that distance we should have been able to spot the glint of their breastplates in the sun. But there had been only dust.

When we got back to the barracks, I dismissed the company and turned to Leander.

"I'm afraid your day isn't over yet, Lieutenant," I told him. "Get yourself cleaned up and come to my rooms in half an hour. I have an errand for you."

I returned to my apartment and immediately settled myself at my table to compose a letter. I knew I was tired and probably overreacting, but then, no city was ever lost because its defenders were too circumspect.

The sun was already low in the sky when Leander came to my door. Alpha and Omega immediately started cooing over him excitedly. No doubt he received a lot of that sort of attention: he must have been one of the best looking young men in Syracuse. I dismissed the two slaves irritably.

When they had left the room, I handed Leander my letter.

"Take the barge to Plymmerium," I told him. "Find Captain Sosis and put this in his hands. Answer any questions he may have of you, then bring me back his reply without delay."

I washed, changed and ate while I waited for Leander to get back, but it was not until the moon had fully risen that he returned, his eyes now dark with exhaustion. He handed me Sosis's reply, which was sealed with the insignia of the Gold Shields.

My dear Dion, it read,

I did send patrols into the hills yesterday morning, but they should be well inland by now, so the men you saw are unlikely to have been our own. I agree we cannot exclude the possibility that they may have been Carthaginian scouts. If that is the explanation, then their presence would certainly suggest that a large force might be advancing on us, although as yet I have had no intelligence to this effect. We must also assume that any scouting party would have seen the fleet sail and would know that our own strength is significantly depleted.

As you requested, I have sent out trackers to try to pick up the trail of the men you saw, and have dispatched additional cavalry patrols to the south and west. On my own initiative, I have also sent a message to Prince Hieronymus, advising him to halt his march until we know it is safe for him to continue. If this all turns out to be nothing, then nothing will be lost by delaying him.

I will take your advice and ensure that our remaining troops at Plymmerium are ready to withdraw into the city at short notice, should the need arise. We have ten companies of the Gold Shields still here, as well as three companies of the White Shields. It goes without saying that, in the general's absence, I would be happy to combine our forces under your command.

If we are assaulted in strength at Plymmerium, my assessment is that we could hold the camp for two or three days at most.
Sosis.

"Leander, you are to tell no one where you have been," I said. "Now, get yourself to bed. I shall see you in the morning." I didn't show him the letter.

When he had gone, I lay on one of my plush gilt couches for a little while, thinking things through. Finally, I let myself out of the apartment, went downstairs, and crossed the great courtyard to the plain wooden gate in the far corner. The narrow shutter slid open at my knock and I found a suspicious pair of eyes staring back at me in the moonlight.

"It's Captain Dion," I said. "I wish to see the king, if he is still up. If not, I can return in the morning."

I was admitted without question by a soldier in a black-plumed helmet and invited to wait in the garden. After a few minutes, a slave with a lantern came to fetch me. He led me through maybe half a dozen rooms of steadily diminishing grandeur. It felt as though I was being drawn ever deeper into a gloomy network of caves. The final room was both the smallest and plainest. It contained almost no furniture, apart from a pair of simple wooden stools and a desk, behind which sat the king, working by the light of a lamp. The slave bowed and left and I stood to attention, waiting to be acknowledged.

"Well, Dion?" Hieron croaked finally.

"I am sorry to disturb you at this time of night, Your Majesty, especially as it is probably for nothing."

"At my age, Dion, I barely sleep anyway. As soon as I lie down, I feel the need to piss. So, what is this nothing of yours?"

I told him about the horsemen, and of the measures Sosis had taken on my advice.

Hieron nodded.

"Very well. I approve your actions. Anything else?" He seemed quite unperturbed.

"My King, I agree this is probably a false alarm, but might it not be wise to bring the troops at Plymmerium into the city anyway? It can do no harm, and it might help to reassure the people until the fleet returns."

"It could do a great deal of harm, Dion, because it would have precisely the opposite effect. The army has not entered the city for over forty years. If it did, the people would conclude the barbarians were about to fall upon us, and would panic. Have you ever seen a city in the grip of a panic, Captain? I have. The first thing the mob would probably do would be to rampage through the Carthaginian quarter, and I squeeze far too much tax out of all those fat old merchants to want to see them massacred to no good purpose. So I most certainly will not bring the army into the city until we have something rather more conclusive to go on. You are right to be cautious, but the chances are that some other explanation for your horsemen will present itself soon enough. In the meanwhile, you and Sosis will keep your concerns to yourselves. Alright?"

"Yes, my King." I bowed.

"Good. Now tell me, how did it go with Archimedes today?"

"I understand what is required of me, my King. But I must confess, the morning was not without its surprises."

"I imagine not," Hieron replied indifferently. Then he dismissed me with a wave of his hand, and returned to his documents.

I was eating breakfast in my room the following morning when I was interrupted by Alpha.

"What is it?" I grunted through a mouthful of egg.

"There is a slave at the door, Master. The king requests that you come to the council chamber immediately."

"At this time?" The sun had not yet fully cleared the sea. "Very well. Tell the slave I'm on my way. And you'd better fetch me a blue tunic."

I had assumed the king had called another emergency meeting of his council, but when I arrived, the only two people sitting at the long table were Hieron himself and Thraso, my chubby cousin. Hieron gestured to the guards and the heavy doors closed behind me. It appeared no one else was expected. Thraso had also put on a blue tunic and looked as dishevelled as I must have done. The king, by contrast, appeared quite refreshed. The Carthaginian landing at Pachynus seemed only to have rejuvenated him.

"Have a seat, Dion," he said, gesturing to the chair next to his. He waited for me to settle myself.

"I wish to discuss the problem of the refugees with you both," he began without ceremony. "It seems we have three bad choices. We can let them in, we can leave them on the road to rot, or we can drive them away at the point of our spears. The first will exacerbate our own food shortage and risks unrest within the city. The second is liable to result in an outbreak of disease on our doorstep, which could eventually spread to the city itself. And the third is unlikely to work: before long, hunger would bring them all back, and in the meanwhile, the surrounding countryside would probably become lawless. Dion, what are your thoughts?"

I hesitated for a moment before replying.

"My King, I'd say the important thing is to ensure the coastal road is passable. I gather it's now blocked for several miles by the refugees' carts. The easiest way to clear it would be to let them in."

The horsemen I had seen were still playing on my mind. The reason I wanted the road cleared was so that we could bring the troops at Plymmerium into the city at short notice, if the need arose. But having been told to keep my concerns to myself, I didn't elaborate in front of Thraso.

"And what is your view, Thraso?" the king asked.

My cousin puckered his fleshy lips.

"Your Majesty," he said, "I also believe you should allow them in. To maintain order, we need to maintain confidence. If the inhabitants of Syracuse see their fellow citizens left on the road to starve or, worse still, driven off by our own troops, it may create the impression of desperation. And, my King, I fear it might also undermine the people's faith in your benevolence."

Hieron gazed at Thraso without expression. My cousin gulped and hurriedly looked down at his lap, his face blanching.

The king smiled icily.

"Well now, we can't have the people doubting my benevolence, can we?" he said. "Very well. We will let them in, but I want this properly managed. Dion, you are to take personal charge of the situation. Once admitted, the refugees are to be directed to the plateau of Epipolae. They can make a camp for themselves up there."

I nodded.

"You will see to it that the camp is well regulated," Hieron continued. "The gods punish filthiness, so you will arrange for a sufficient quantity of latrines to be dug and for the disposal of bodies. I want no outbreaks of disease. I want men of the City Guard on duty on Epipolae at all times. Within the camp, martial law will be in force and a strict curfew will be imposed. The refugees are to be confined to Epipolae. The rest of the city will be off limits to them, and the camp will be off limits to everybody else. I'm giving you a free hand to do whatever you think necessary to maintain order, Dion. Spill a little blood, if that's what it takes. Understand?"

"Yes, my King," I said.

Hieron turned to my cousin.

"Thraso, you will arrange for the camp to be supplied from the city. I want the refugees to be adequately fed, but not generously so. I do not wish to encourage them to stay any longer than necessary. Have some food stalls erected on Epipolae, add a tax of one tenth to everything they sell, and see to it that there is never quite enough to go round."

"Yes, my King," my cousin muttered.

"One more thing occurs to me," Hieron said thoughtfully. "Many of these refugees will have been stupid enough to bring their slaves with them. We have quite enough people to deal with already, and I dare say things will only get worse over the coming days. The slaves will have to be disposed of. I don't care how you do it, Thraso. Arrange for them to be sold, if you like, or send them to the quarries. Throw them into the sea, if you prefer."

Thraso coughed nervously.

"What is it?" asked Hieron.

"And the animals, Your Majesty?"

Hieron pursed his lips.

"A good point. They'll need to keep their horses and mules and oxen, I suppose, otherwise we'll never get rid of them again. So make whatever arrangements you think appropriate for the draught animals. They can keep their chickens with them. Send any other farm animals to the temples to be slaughtered. And have your men kill all the dogs, Dion."

"Yes, my King," I said.

"Now, let me make myself clear," Hieron said. "I want no trouble from these people, and I will hold you two accountable if there is any. Off you go. I expect you to be ready to open the gates by midday, so you'd better get on with it."

Thraso accompanied me to my office in the barracks yard, to discuss what had to be done.

"Tell me, how on earth did you manage to get to the council chamber before me?" I asked him, as he waddled along beside me. "You're still living at home, aren't you?"

He laughed.

"I'd already been in there for about an hour before you arrived. The old man wanted to talk to me about the city granaries. He's told me to manage them while Andranodoros is away."

I whistled admiringly.

"You've obviously impressed him, Thraso. Good for you."

It was a significant responsibility. The Royal Council had its own peculiar hierarchy: only the general of the army and the Royal Treasurer were seen as more important positions than the Supervisor of the Granaries. As captain of the City Guard, I was almost at the bottom of the pile.

"Well, I imagine the king took one look at me and thought, 'There's a man who understands food'," Thraso replied with a chuckle. "Anyway, it's only till Andranodoros gets back, which is just as well for me. If there are any bread shortages, the people will probably assume I ate it all. And in answer to your second question, Dion, I've been given an apartment here in the palace as well, so it seems we're to be neighbours."

We had reached the staircase to my office. Thraso eyed the climb forlornly. He was already out of breath.

"You know, Dion," he wheezed, as he began hauling himself up the stairs, "feeding a city is a lot more complicated than I'd realised. I suppose I'd never bothered thinking about it before. I'll help you as much as I can with this refugee business, but after today, I'm afraid I won't have too much time to spare."

I sent word to the duty officer to cancel the morning drills, and when Thraso and I had made our plans, we briefed the palace officers on what we intended to do. I gave my adjutant Castor two full companies and sent him to supervise the establishment of the camp on Epipolae, with orders to call in more men from the Euryalus and Hexapylon garrisons if he needed them. I took charge at the south gate myself, taking Leander's company with me.

By midday, we were ready to open the gates. Imposing the king's benevolence on his subjects proved a predictably depressing task. There was a great deal of cursing and wailing, as people were forced to part with the slaves who provided them with their livelihoods and probably constituted the greater part of their wealth. Thraso was determined that the refugees should be compensated as fairly as possible for the loss of their property, so he set about arranging a series of auctions; in the meanwhile, the slaves would be held in the city pens. Their owners were all given receipts, but with so much stock to be sold, they had little hope of obtaining fair prices. Many tried to slip their slaves through to Epipolae by claiming that they were relatives, but it was usually easy enough to spot the lie: a blue-eyed and well-fed family seldom produces an undernourished and brown-eyed son. When they understood what was happening, a few slaves even disclosed their own status, in the hope of improving their lot.

Only those who wore the purple of the nobility were permitted to take up residence in the built-up area of the city, and they alone were also allowed to keep their slaves. But there were few such families on the road: the soil in the south was poor and my class had never found much worth appropriating for itself down there. Perhaps inevitably, every moderately successful merchant and minor official who passed through the south gate demanded the same preferential treatment. My officers listened politely to their outraged protests, and then sent them to join the files of the bewildered and the dispossessed heading up to the plateau.

At least we were able to do a good turn for one unfortunate young woman, who presented herself at the gate still wearing her mourning robes. She told us that ever since her husband had died, their only slave had proved ungovernable. He did no work and she was growing increasingly frightened for her safety. The wretch lay sprawled out in the back of her cart, drunk and insensible. She could not hold back a few quiet tears of relief as, shouting and mumbling incoherently, he was dragged away by my men. Her gratitude made a welcome change from the abuse to which we were more routinely subjected.

A week later, the woman's brother-in-law turned up. It transpired that it was her father for whom she had been mourning, and that the drunkard we had taken to the slave pens was in fact her husband. By then, it was too late and he was never traced. As the refugee camp was under martial law, the case eventually came before me. I should have had her executed, as her brother-in-law loudly demanded, but I was so entertained by the story that I settled for sending her to the slave pens too. I remember how she thanked me proudly for my mercy, and told me that whatever life awaited her, it could hardly be worse than marriage. I admired her spirit, so on a whim, I sent word to my steward to buy her when she came up for sale and to send her to one of my own estates.

Some hours after we had opened the gates, I rode over to Epipolae to see how Castor was managing. I was not surprised to find that he had organised everything well. A rough square had been marked out on some relatively flat ground, near a small spring, on which a number of food stalls had already been erected. A series of concentric squares had been pegged out around this, subdivided into tiny individual plots, to accommodate the refugees. The three squares closest to the centre had nearly filled up: I guessed there were maybe a thousand people already in the camp. Some families had rigged makeshift tents for themselves; others just sat on the ground by their carts, looking lost. Small groups of guardsmen carrying spears patrolled the lines of tents and carts. Their presence made it clear that Epipolae was as much a prison as a refuge.

I found Castor with a spade in his hand, working alongside a detachment of my men at a little distance from the camp. They were digging rows of trenches, a foot or so deep, to serve as latrines. He greeted me with a wave and a sad smile.

"Hello sir," he said as I dismounted. "You know, I never imagined my duties would include the digging of shitholes. I suppose I have finally risen to the level of my talents."

I laughed.

"I fear, my friend, that this may be as good as it gets for the next few days. You seem to have everything in hand here. Do you need anything from me?"

He shook his head. He looked tired.

"I don't think so. Did you see your cousin in the camp?"

"Thraso's here? Whatever for?"

"No idea, I'm afraid. I think he's just walking around talking to people."

I rode back into the camp and eventually found Thraso, sitting on a stool, chatting to a crowd of refugees. Somewhat absurdly, he had a small, grubby-looking boy on his podgy knee. The men and women who thronged around him seemed to be mixing freely with each other, so I guessed they were just simple peasants, although to be fair, their new circumstances precluded a decent separation of the sexes anyway.

"Ah-ha, my friends," said Thraso cheerfully as I rode up, "allow me to introduce you to my cousin, the famous Captain Dion. He is the man who is going to keep you safe." Their haggard faces all turned to stare at me. "You only have to take one look at him to know those barbarians don't stand a chance," Thraso went on. "Who in their right minds would want to fight *him*? He's going to kick the Carthaginians up their backsides for you, and then we'll have you all back in your homes in no time. Isn't that right, Dion?"

I grunted.

The boy on Thraso's lap gawped at me.

"Sir, are you the Bull of Syracuse, sir?" he asked.

I grunted again and nodded.

"Do you really become a bull when you get angry, sir? My father says you do. He says your eyes turn red and you grow huge horns and that he once saw you charge a whole phalanx of men and kill them all by yourself. He used to be a soldier too. He says he fought with you in a big battle against the Spartans. But he doesn't turn into a bull when he gets angry. He just spanks me."

Thraso burst out laughing and even I couldn't help smiling.

"Where is your father, lad?" I asked. "If we served together, I'd like to say hello to him."

"I don't know, sir. He didn't come with us. He told my mother to take us away and said he was going to stay and fight the barbarians."

"What's your name, boy?"

"Alexander, sir. The same as my father."

"I remember your father well," I lied. "He's a very brave man." That, at least, seemed to be true.

I got down from my horse and the small crowd nervously parted to make way for me.

"Tell me, son, do you want to be a soldier too, like your father?"

"Oh yes, sir. More than anything."

"Well, perhaps you'll grow up to be another King Alexander," I said. "But for now, I think I shall call you Alexander the Brave. So, Alexander the Brave, how would you like to be able to tell your friends that you once rode the ugly old Bull of Syracuse?" I opened my arms to him.

He looked at me in terror.

"Are you going to turn into a bull, sir?"

I laughed.

"No, not today. I only do that when I have to fight people."

"It's alright," Thraso said to the child. "He won't hurt you."

The boy grinned, jumped off Thraso's knee and ran up to me. I swung him, giggling with delight, onto my shoulders. He felt as light as a satchel. Within a few moments, I found myself surrounded by a crowd of children with dirty faces, all screaming excitedly for a turn as they plucked at my tunic with their thin, outstretched arms.

*

As the sun dimmed, Thraso and I left the camp together to find the cart that had brought him up to the plateau. I was leading my horse by the reins.

"Dion, I hope you won't mind me making a suggestion," he said, "but I really think you should try to find a way of occupying these people. Otherwise, I fear you may need a lot more men up here to keep order before long. At the moment they're all just frightened, but they'll soon grow restless and angry. We aren't exactly treating them kindly."

I nodded.

"Do you have something in mind?"

"As it happens, yes, I do have an idea. They're all reservists, I imagine. Perhaps you could get the king to recall them? Get them to march around a bit and hit each other over the heads with swords, or whatever it is that you military types do all day. If the Carthaginians come, I dare say you could find a use for some extra men, and if not, well, at least it might keep them out of trouble." He shot me a sly glance. "And of course, if they are recalled, they'd be entitled to reservists' pay. Most of these people are dirt poor, Dion. I'm sure they've all brought a few coins with them, but when those run out, how will they buy themselves food?"

It was one of those ideas that seem so obvious that you cannot understand why you didn't think of it yourself. I promised to speak to the king in the morning and left my cousin by his cart.

As I rode carefully back down the long, stony slope to the south gate, I thought about Thraso. Our families lived almost next door to each other on the Avenue of Athena, but were barely on speaking terms. His mother, my kindly but slightly dull Aunt Maia, was my father's eldest sister, and she and my own mother had fallen out long ago. I suppose it was no surprise that Thraso and I had never been close as children. Later, my cousin had been one of those who had avoided the usual military training by taking advantage of Apollonius's soft-heartedness, and I had despised him for it. I had thought soldiering was the only life worthy of a man, and all my army friends naturally believed the same. We celebrated our own physical prowess and openly mocked the likes of my plump cousin. But even though I had never shown him any kindness, Thraso was the only councillor who had stood up for me at my first council meeting, and the only one who had dared to question the king.

We build our misjudgements like walls, and only abandon them with reluctance. I had always known my cousin was a clever and capable man, but then, Syracuse was full of clever and capable men. What marked Thraso out, I had come to realise, was that he was also an honest one.

When the south gate was finally closed for the night, I returned to my rooms, ate a large meal and collapsed onto my cot. My blue tunic felt thoroughly soiled, but I was too tired to bother undressing. I immediately fell into a deep and dreamless sleep.

Dawn had already broken when Alpha woke me.

"An officer from Plymmerium is here, Master," he said. "He brought you this letter. He is waiting outside to see if there is any reply."

I swung my legs out of the cot, grabbed the scroll from Alpha's hand and hurriedly broke the seal.

My Dear Dion, it read,

During the night I received the first reports from the patrols I sent out. You will be relieved to learn that, as yet, none has sighted any Carthaginian troops. The patrols will press further south and west today and I shall of course keep you informed. I have also had word from Prince Hieronymus, whose own scouts report that the coastal road appears to be clear of any enemy forces, at least as far as the village of Helorus, which lies only about fifteen miles north of Pachynus. The prince has therefore decided to resume his march today. He informs me that the flow of refugee traffic, which has significantly impeded his progress to date, appears to be thinning. This may be a further indication that the Carthaginians have not advanced beyond Pachynus, if indeed they are even still there. I have sent a separate letter to His Majesty with the same information.

I believe I now have an explanation for the riders you saw. The tracking party I sent out returned in the early hours of this morning, with twelve bodies that they had recovered from a remote ravine. I examined the corpses myself. They were all killed with swords or long knives, and the nature of their wounds suggests that their killers were experienced. The killers appear to have headed inland, taking the dead men's horses with them, but having discovered the bodies, my men decided not to pursue the trail any further.

The only clue to the identity of the dead men is that one of them had a punishment brand on his cheek. It would therefore seem quite likely that all twelve men were merely runaway slaves, who absconded on stolen horses, perhaps hoping to take advantage of the present situation by passing themselves off as refugees from the south. I dare say that they were hunted down on the orders of their owner, who no doubt wished to retrieve his horses and administer his own justice.

Whatever the explanation, we can at least be certain that your riders pose no threat now, if they ever did. I therefore propose to take no further action.

Sosis.

My first response was to breathe a sigh of relief, and my second was to wonder why on earth I had been jumping at shadows. I am hardly the nervous type. All military logic had told me that there could never have been a serious threat from Pachynus, and yet a handful of runaways had been enough to make me doubt myself, and send men scuttling around the countryside in search of phantom armies. My instincts had always served me well in the past, but this time, they had only made a fool of me. I grunted and stood up.

"Alpha, it seems I am turning into an old woman."

"I'm afraid I cannot picture you weaving, Master," he replied drily. "There is a bowl and sponge on the table, and Omega is preparing your breakfast. Will you be wearing the blue again today?"

I nodded. At least the tunic helped to cow the refugees at the gate.

Alpha smiled happily and went over to one of the trunks to fetch me some clean clothes, while I sat myself at the table to write a short note to Sosis. I thanked him and apologised for having wasted his time.

When Alpha had left the room with the note, I stripped off and began to sponge myself down with the cold water. The explanation Sosis had suggested for the horsemen seemed convincing. Almost all the larger country estates employed retired soldiers or mercenaries to deter bandits and chase down runaways. And yet... and yet... I still could not fully muffle the alarm bell in my head.

Lepides once told me that no general is ever in possession of enough information to act on reason alone. The most important decisions, he said, always come down to instinct. As it turned out, the old grouch was right. If I had only paid more heed to my misgivings about those horsemen, I might have changed history.

Once I had dressed and eaten, I made my way over to the royal apartments. After the guards had admitted me through the gate, a slave escorted me into a modest anteroom and invited me to take a stool. He took up a position by the door and for some time we both waited in silence. After maybe half an hour, I kicked back the stool and started walking listlessly around the walls with my hands behind my back, examining the frescoes. I don't pretend to know anything about art, but they didn't seem very good. They appeared garish and lifeless at the same time, and I couldn't even work out what they were supposed to be about. Fawns and satyrs pranced aimlessly around a forest, while some nymphs stood by gormlessly, like a party of bored prostitutes.

In the Temple of Athena, there is a famous series of paintings celebrating the exploits of mad King Agathocles, which all visitors to Syracuse make a point of seeing. Those, at least, have an obvious vigour to them. They tell the story for which Agathocles is best remembered. The Carthaginians, having been provoked by him beyond all endurance, finally invaded the kingdom and besieged him in his city. The situation was desperate. Agathocles responded by slipping out of Syracuse with most of his men and sailing to Africa, where he devastated several Carthaginian towns and slaughtered anyone he came across, which was something of a habit of his.

In their panic, the Carthaginian nobles burnt three hundred of their own children to placate their gods. Their army was forced to abandon its siege of Syracuse and hurried home to retrieve the situation.

Agathocles' adventure eventually ended in disaster: his army was annihilated, although characteristically, he managed to save his own skin by deserting his troops. But at least he had also saved Syracuse. And as no one had ever managed to invade the Carthaginian homelands before, he immediately became a hero to Greeks across the entire Mediterranean – except, perhaps, to those within his own kingdom, who found they still had to live with him. As Hieron might have said, life is full of little ironies.

I was eventually shown into a modest chamber, where Hieron was sitting at a table with Archimedes and Philocrates, the elderly secretary who had brought me my box of blue tunics. They were scrutinising a very long roll of papyrus together. Philocrates' equally decrepit slave stood against the far wall. Archimedes seemed engrossed in the document and entirely ignored me, but the secretary looked up and smiled.

"Captain Dion, it is a pleasure to see you again," he wheezed.

I nodded politely to him.

"You are right, Philocrates," Hieron said, also ignoring me. "The wording is too vague here as well. We will have to specify the number of ships they can bring into the harbour. No more than thirty quinqueremes, I think. No, make that twenty."

"Yes, Your Majesty," Philocrates replied. "I shall draw up the amendments."

"Well, that is all for now, I suppose. Come back with your revisions this afternoon. Thank you, Philocrates."

Philocrates beckoned his slave who stepped forward to help him out of his chair. When he was finally on his feet, the secretary nodded to me.

"Do forgive me for not staying to chat, Captain," he said amiably, "but I must dash."

Together, Philocrates and his slave began to shuffle slowly towards the door.

Hieron waved me forward but didn't invite me to sit down.

"So, what do you want, Captain?" he asked.

"My King, as you may know already, all our patrols report that there appears to be no threat to the city. Everything suggests that the incursion at Pachynus really is nothing more than a raid. The horsemen I saw appear to have been a dozen runaway slaves. I can only apologise if I caused any unnecessary alarm. I fear I was rather stupid."

Archimedes finally looked up.

"What horsemen, Dion?" he asked. I briefly explained to my great-uncle what had happened, feeling increasingly embarrassed as I did so. When I had finished, Archimedes merely grunted and turned back to the document, but Hieron continued to scrutinise me impassively.

"No need to apologise, Dion," the king said eventually. "There's no harm done, and keeping one's mind open to all possibilities is hardly stupid. Besides, you have a reputation for impulsiveness. I find it reassuring to discover that you are also capable of prudence. Now, is that all you have come to say?"

"No, my King. I have come to ask you to call up the refugees."

Hieron narrowed his eyes.

"Have you, now?" he said. I could almost hear his mind turning, as he considered the proposal from who knows how many perspectives that I hadn't thought of.

"No," he said after a moment or two. "It's a good idea, but I won't call them up as reservists. That would require them to rejoin their old Shield divisions and I don't think Sosis would welcome the additional responsibility at the moment. They are your burden, Dion. But I'll tell you what you can do, if you wish: you can conscript them into the City Guard instead. Will that answer?"

"Yes, my King. Of course. Thank you."

Hieron dismissed me with a wave and I bowed and left. I had to admit Hieron's suggestion was much neater. Captains were entitled to conscript anyone not already under arms into their divisions with no notice, although it was meant to be an emergency power and I could not remember the last time it had ever been used. But it would keep the refugees directly under my own command.

I went straight to Nebit's office and found him hard at work, as usual. I told him of my conversation with the king.

He looked at me and raised his eyebrows.

"So, Captain, His Majesty does not wish to recall the men, but invites you to use your powers of conscription instead?"

"Yes," I replied testily. "I've already explained that. It's just a technicality."

Nebit began tittering.

"What's so funny?" I demanded.

"My dear friend," he said, "you really are a lamb among wolves, aren't you? Allow me to explain. When a citizen is recalled for duty as a reservist, his weekly pay is charged to the Royal Treasury. He is paid by the state, because he is fulfilling an obligation to the state. But if a captain directly conscripts a man, that is another matter.

The man is deemed to be answering a divisional need, and so the division must pay him. I suppose the intention is to deter captains from abusing their power over the citizenry, although if you will forgive me for saying so, only the Greeks would bother themselves with such fine distinctions. Rather like poor old Aristotle fretting about the difference between fog and mist… In any event, the long and the short of it is that the cost of conscripting all these poor people will now be added to our own divisional deficit, which by custom will eventually have to be made good by you personally… A technicality, as you say, but one of which I imagine our famously thrifty king is fully aware."

I stared at him.

"You mean, I'm going to have to pay them all out of my own pocket?"

He smiled and nodded.

"Fuck," I said eventually.

"And for this, I am afraid I can provide no unfuck," replied Nebit, not very sympathetically. "Do you still wish to proceed, Captain? If so, there are various administrative matters I will need to put in motion."

"Sod it," I growled. I could see no way out of it now without losing face. I bit my lip. "Yes, I suppose so. Alright, go ahead, Nebit."

It was only money, after all. I imagined we would be able to start sending the refugees home again after a few days or so, and to put the men on the payroll for such a short time was hardly beyond my means. What rankled was that for the second time that morning, I felt I had made a fool of myself.

"In that case, Captain, if I may suggest a slight modification, perhaps it would be sufficient for your purposes only to conscript those under the age of thirty? I would imagine that might halve the final cost."

"No, Nebit," I said after a moment. "The old have to eat too. We'll conscript all the able-bodied men up to the age of fifty."

"I admire your public spirit, Captain. Very well. I should have everything ready for you to proceed by this afternoon. Now," Nebit continued, "to turn our conversation to a happier subject, you will recall that you and I are expected at your illustrious great-uncle's house at midday to inspect the city's defences. Should I meet you there?"

I had forgotten about that.

"Yes, I suppose so," I replied, without any enthusiasm.

"You know, I had the honour of working closely with the noble Archimedes on a previous occasion," Nebit twittered. "I must confess it is a source of great satisfaction to me that he should request my services again. I do not exaggerate when I say that he is widely acknowledged to be the world's greatest living mathematician, and quite possibly the greatest ever."

"Oh, did he rope you into helping with one of his sewerage projects?" I asked. I was feeling sour and it was meant to be a put-down, but I should have known better.

"Goodness, no, nothing like that," replied Nebit, in a rather wounded tone.

I knew I had been graceless. Nebit was an annoying man, but he had been guilty of nothing more than a little vanity. I immediately regretted my words.

"I'm sorry, Nebit. I'm not having a good day," I said. "You know I'd be lost without you. I am not in the least surprised my great-uncle values your abilities. I dare say it takes a mind like his fully to appreciate one like yours."

The Egyptian almost purred with pleasure.

"My dear Captain," he said, "I realise you must be under a dreadful strain at the moment, what with the military situation and all those wretched refugees. If there is anything I can do to be of assistance, please do not hesitate to ask."

I had learnt to manage him well enough, I suppose, but I had started to despise myself for it. It seemed palace life was turning me into a first-class hypocrite.

I left him and went to my own office to write a short letter to my adjutant Castor, explaining the conscription arrangements. I asked him to start drawing up a list of all the eligible men in the camp. When I had finished, I had one of my men deliver the note to Epipolae, and then I hurried off to the south gate to resume my dispiriting duties there.

X

RETURNING HEROES

It took us four days to clear the backlog of carts and animals on the coastal road. By then, the rate at which new refugees were continuing to arrive had slowed considerably, which was just as well. In the end, there must have been getting on for ten thousand people crammed onto Epipolae, and I had over three thousand unwanted conscripts under my command. We didn't have enough weapons in our armoury for them all, but Sosis sent over some cartloads of sarissas from Plymmerium to help out. We occupied the refugees for most of the day by marching them around the plain to the north of the city in different phalanx formations. By the time they got back to the camp, they were too tired to cause any trouble.

I brought Xeno over from the South Citadel to supervise the training. He may have only had one hand, but as an army veteran, he knew how to manage large blocks of infantry. He had great fun playing at being a general, although the whole thing was a farce. A phalanx depends on a core of professional soldiers to steady the lines and hold them together, especially when there is a turn of any sort to be negotiated. The refugees spent most of their time falling over each other. If the Carthaginians ever came, Xeno told me drily, we would just have to hope that they would laugh themselves to death.

As soon as Thraso found out that I had managed to land myself with the bill for all the conscripts, he offered to pay half the cost himself. It had been his idea, he insisted, and now he felt hugely embarrassed. His own family was not nearly as well off as my own, and I dare say the expense would have been quite painful for him, which only made the gesture more remarkable. Naturally, I refused.

My cousin did his best to keep the camp adequately supplied, but food was scarce throughout the city and the people of Syracuse were growing restless. The burden of provisioning the fleet had left most of the shops empty and, every day, the reserves in our granaries were depleted further. The summer harvests had not yet been gathered. We had the sea, but most of our fishermen were with the fleet, and even fish prices had soared. Women were taking out their husbands' boats. You could sense an ugly atmosphere on the streets.

Nine days after we first opened the gates to the refugees, Hieron summoned me to the council chamber.

"Ah, Dion," he said perfunctorily as I was shown in, "this letter has just arrived. I thought you might like to read it yourself. Come and sit down." He held up a roll of papyrus with which he beckoned me forward.

I took it from him and settled myself in a chair. The seal, which had already been broken, looked unusually large and unnecessarily elaborate, but I didn't recognise it.

Esteemed Grandfather, the letter began,

I am pleased to report that our forces have been triumphant and that I have now completed the re-conquest of our southern territories.

The strategy I devised took the Carthaginians entirely by surprise, forcing them to flee our shores in confusion without even offering battle, despite their superior numbers. Although I was disappointed not to have been able to engage them directly, I console myself with the thought that the humiliation I have inflicted upon them has fully avenged the insult they offered you by attempting to invade us.

I shall be returning to Syracuse presently. Although unimaginative, the officers under my command are, in my judgement, perfectly capable of administering the district without my supervision, so I see little point in remaining here myself.

I trust that my conduct of this difficult campaign has earned me your confidence and that you will agree I am now ready to undertake a more prominent role in the affairs of the kingdom. I therefore hope that you will see fit to appoint me to the Royal Council upon my return to Syracuse. I believe such recognition is no less than my birth demands, and my talents deserve, although of course I understand that I should perhaps assume only a relatively junior position, at least initially. In the light of my recent military experience, I would suggest that I be given the captaincy of the City Guards. As everyone knows, your present captain has wasted no opportunity to display his brutish incompetence, and it is a post for which Uncle Zoippos tells me that I am particularly well suited. He spoke to most of the other councillors before I left, and he says they all feel the same.

Having heard of our victory at Pachynus, the Roman governor of Agrigento, just across the border from here, was most anxious that I should visit his little province for a few days. The dreary fellow probably hopes to add some glitter to his reputation. He certainly sounds a dreadful bore (he proposes a tour of their local temples!), but having now established something of a military reputation for myself, I hope also to prove to you that I have a similar flair for diplomacy. I leave for Agrigento tomorrow and expect to be home in about two weeks' time.

Hieronymus.

When I had finished reading it, I handed the letter back to Hieron without comment. There had obviously been much slithering in the snake pit. Zoippos and the other nobles had timed their revenge carefully: my most powerful friend on the council, Prince Gelon, was away. It was clever of them to use Hieronymus.

"So, Dion, what have you to say?" the king asked drily. "Should I replace you with Hieronymus? It would certainly make my life considerably easier. Both my sons-in-law hate you, my daughters hate you, my grandson hates you, his mother hates you, most of my councillors hate you, and almost the entire nobility hates you. And then there's your future brother-in-law, who also hates you, as I imagine does his father, my friend Senator Torquatus – and he hasn't even met you yet... I am beginning to suspect you may be lacking in social skills. By all accounts, even your own mother doesn't like you very much."

I felt myself blushing.

"I have disappointed you, my King. I am sorry for all the difficulty I seem to be causing. It seems I am not suited to palace life. If it is your wish, I will of course retire to my estates."

Hieron gazed at me without expression for a few moments.

"No, I think not, Dion," he said quietly. "You still have your uses, I suppose. I am not done with you yet."

He smiled thinly at me.

"In any event," he continued, "it would appear that the refugees can return to their homes now. Start clearing the camp. The sooner we can get rid of them, the better. And one more thing: I suppose we ought to arrange a suitable welcome home for my all-conquering grandson. A parade of the City Guard, I think. Have Nebit come and see me. I'll arrange it with him. That is all; you may leave now."

As I stood and bowed, Hieron picked up the letter again, glanced at it and sighed.

Emptying the camp proved more complicated than filling it, and took a week. We cleared it section by section. Only those slaves we had collected in the first two or three days had so far been auctioned off; the rest had to be washed down and returned to their owners, once the bills for keeping them had been settled. They had only been provided with subsistence rations and, towards the end, the pens had been packed tight. Some of the older ones had already died and those who had been confined for more than a few days looked severely weakened, so I imagine quite a few more were lost on the long walk home. There were similar problems with the draught animals, which had also been kept in increasingly dreadful conditions in the city's livery yards. Those that looked like they could not make the journey south were sold for their meat. Their owners had to abandon their carts on Epipolae, and return to their homes with whatever possessions they could carry on their own backs.

Between us, Thraso, Castor and I had done what we could for them, but the people we sent back to Pachynus made a forlorn spectacle. I went down to the south gate to see the last of them off, and found Leander on duty there. Though he tried to hide it from me, there were tears in his eyes as he watched the seemingly endless procession of hollow, blank faces trudge silently past. I silently clapped the handsome young lieutenant on the back. There was nothing shaming in his tears. He had simply reached the moment through which every soldier must pass sooner or later, the moment when he comes to realise that a belief in our innate dignity is the most foolish of all man's delusions.

And yet, so far, the kingdom had suffered nothing worse than a minor raid on a remote and sparsely populated province. Although thousands of lives had already been blighted, I knew Pachynus was just a small foretaste of what might soon be to come.

Hieronymus returned a few days after we had finished clearing the camp. The City Guard was commanded to fall out on honour parade early the next morning. Nebit told me that the king had instructed him to make the arrangements directly with Castor; Hieron appreciated that I would probably prefer not to be involved. I was surprised by the king's thoughtfulness, and grateful for it. There was to be a full meeting of the Royal Council immediately after the parade, which Hieronymus had apparently been invited to attend. That made me a little apprehensive, but I put it out of my mind. I didn't want to start jumping at shadows again.

Castor must have reduced all the garrisons around the city to skeleton watches, because when I came downstairs that morning in my blue tunic to attend the parade, I found over a thousand of my men already standing to attention in the great courtyard. They were dressed in full battle armour and all carried their spears and shields. They had formed up in company order, facing a platform that had been erected during the night and along which a row of stools had been placed.

Some of my fellow councillors had already taken their seats on the platform, and were chatting happily to each other. Zoippos occupied the central position. Sitting either side of him were two of his friends, Leatherskin and Ision, who seemed to be hanging on Zoippos's every word. As far as I knew, Zoippos had never said a witty thing in his life, but as I watched, his companions burst into apparently uncontrollable laughter. Leatherskin bent forwards and clapped his hands to his knees, while Ision threw his head back and patted Zoippos warmly on the shoulder. Zoippos's little head wobbled happily, as he held up his finger to make some new point.

I walked round the colonnade, determined to get through the whole nonsense with as much grace as I could muster. Quite a few palace officials had turned out to watch the show. I had to weave my way through them to reach the short flight of steps at the side of the platform, beside which stood two men of the Royal Watch. As I approached them, one of them stepped forward to speak to me.

"I'm very sorry, sir," he said with evident embarrassment, "but I am afraid I have been told there is no seat for you on the platform. His Majesty requests that you go directly to the council chamber instead."

He gestured with his hand to the nearest door.

"I see," I said.

I looked up and saw Zoippos smirking down at me from his stool. Ision was sneering and Leatherskin pouted mockingly.

Their expressions told me all I needed to know.

The cacophony of voices surrounding the king must have finally persuaded him that I was more trouble than I was worth. True to character, Hieron had decided to work with the grain.

So, this is how it ends, I thought. I should have known. There had been enough warning signals, if only I'd bothered to think about them: the parade, my exclusion from the preparations for it, Hieronymus's invitation to the council meeting. My mother had always said I was a fool.

I wondered how many men would be waiting for me in the anteroom, and whether they would be wearing their black-plumed helmets. Even though I wasn't armed, I guessed there would be at least four of them. I am not an easy man to kill.

How stupid it had been of me to imagine that withdrawing to my estates was ever a possibility. I was the heir of King Dionysius, after all, and my father's son into the bargain. It would give him no pleasure, but how else was a man like Hieron going to dispense with a man like me? It was obvious, really.

I snorted, took a moment to compose myself, and walked through the door into the anteroom.

It was empty.

The large cedar doors to the council chamber were wide open, and I could hear indistinct voices coming from inside. I went on through.

Hieron was sitting at the head of the long table, with Thraso next to him. Archimedes lay slouched in his usual place at the opposite end, his head on his chest, apparently asleep.

I took a few slow, deep breaths.

Not today, it seemed. Tomorrow maybe, or perhaps the day after, but at least it would not be today. And maybe not at all. I remembered Nebit's words: no one ever really knew how they stood with the king. If Archimedes was as complex as one of his little wooden polyhedrons, then Hieron was as inscrutable as a polished sphere.

The king had turned to look at me as I entered.

"Dion," he said, "come and sit down. Is everything alright? You seem rather tense."

"I'm fine, thank you, Your Majesty."

"I hope you won't mind, but I thought it best if you and I didn't join the others on the platform. This is Hieronymus's little moment of glory. He wants to play at being a soldier, and if you were on show out there, I'm afraid the comparison would not be entirely to the poor child's advantage."

I pulled out a chair and exhaled heavily one last time. Thraso smiled and nodded to me across the table. I was still fixed on my own thoughts, but forced myself to return the smile as casually as I could.

"Besides," Hieron continued jovially, "I'm really doing you quite a favour: Zoippos is going to be giving one of his speeches… Now, we have some business to discuss."

He coughed and cleared his throat.

"A year ago, I finally concluded some rather complicated negotiations with King Ptolemy of Egypt. He's a strange man. Did you know he married his own sister? The Ptolemys do that quite a lot. I believe his own mother was also his aunt, although of course his father probably wasn't really his father… Anyway, after much dithering, Ptolemy finally agreed to supply us with a limited quantity of grain. I have been stockpiling it in warehouses along our coast ever since… Please don't look so surprised, Thraso. Do you really believe I could have kept my throne for fifty years if I had no care for the city's stomach?"

"No. Of course not, Your Majesty," Thraso mumbled, clearly astonished.

"Ptolemy's own kingdom, of course, directly borders the territories of Carthage," Hieron went on, "and he is anxious not to provoke them. So we agreed that everything would be routed quietly through Crete. The Egyptians sell their grain to our friends in the city of Rhodes, from whom we purchase it in turn. Ah, is that Zoippos I hear? It would seem your men's ordeal has begun, Dion."

We all turned to listen to what was being said outside. The disembodied voice coming through the doors was unmistakable.

"… as the gallant Orpheus descended into the tar-black caverns of the underworld, to retrieve his love, the ravishing Eurydice, from the icy embrace of death, so too…"

Hieron cupped a hand to his ear.

"What on earth is he talking about?"

"I'm afraid I really couldn't say, my King," I replied.

Hieron shrugged.

"Well, to resume, it is of the greatest importance that these arrangements remain confidential. Do you understand? Outside this room, only Gelon and Andranodoros know of them, and a handful of my secretaries. I have been defrauding my own treasury, under poor Zoippos's nose, to hide the fact we are sending gold to Crete. Andranodoros has been using a variety of foreign merchants from around the Mediterranean to ship the grain here from Rhodes, always in relatively small consignments. As far as the merchants are aware, they are simply making deliveries on behalf of private grain traders."

"My King," I asked, "I don't understand. Why don't we just ship the grain straight from Rhodes to Rome, and keep our own?"

Hieron smiled and turned to my cousin.

"Can you answer Dion's question, Thraso?"

"I would imagine it is because you don't want the Romans to know about these arrangements either, my King."

"Clever boy. Exactly so. It is very useful for me to be able to point out how dependent the Romans have become on us to feed their own people, and to remind them of the great sacrifice that Syracuse is making on their behalf. The last thing I want is for them to start thinking that they could negotiate their own deal with Rhodes or Egypt, and dispense with my friendship. It is a delicate balance. I wish above all else to stay out of this war, at least as far as I can; but at the same time, I must put the Romans in our debt. They can have no excuse to turn on us, once Hannibal is beaten. And so our own people must go hungry, so that I can say to Rome, see how we suffer alongside you! Of course, I also sprinkle gold around their senate, and make sure my friends there waste no opportunity to remind their colleagues of our steadfast loyalty. But I take precautions too. What I ostentatiously give to Rome with one hand, I quietly put back in my pocket with the other."

My cousin coughed politely.

"My King, may I ask, just how much grain have you stored away?"

"Oh, quite a lot, Thraso, quite a lot. In any event, the food situation is becoming somewhat desperate, so it seems I now have little choice but to start dipping into my reserves. I require you two to make the arrangements to start bringing some grain into the city. It must be done without arousing suspicion. The Romans and the Carthaginians have their own eyes in Syracuse. I do not want our enemies, our allies, and most especially our own people to start wondering how much I may have been holding back, or where it came from. Bring in just enough to make sure there are no riots. Don't let the people starve, Thraso, but keep them a little hungry. Secretary Philocrates can tell you the locations of all the warehouses… Tell me, is Zoippos still talking?"

We turned to listen to the distant voice again. It seemed to be building to some sort of crescendo.

"… the prowess of Achilles… the wisdom of Odysseus… the courage of Jason…"

"Has he mentioned Alexander yet?" asked Hieron.

"I don't think so, my King, not yet," I replied.

"No? Well, that's all I wanted to tell you. So, unless you have any questions, I'd quite like to see what's happening outside. I think the worst should be over by now. We'll watch from the anteroom. Help me up, would you, Dion? Join us, Thraso."

When he was out of his chair, Thraso and I helped the king walk slowly through to a window in the adjoining room, which looked out onto the courtyard. Hieron was stick-thin and age had shrunk his frame. In his day, it was said he had cut a fine figure; now, I could have carried him under my arm.

We got to the window just in time to see Zoippos conclude his oration. Our Royal Treasurer stood on the platform with one hand on his hip and the other held aloft, his onion head thrown proudly back, as if to display to best effect the magnificent protuberance in his throat.

"... with the precocity of a young Alexander, who first gave proof of his promise at the immortal battle of Chaeronea, so our own glorious son of Syracuse, favoured of Ares, returns victorious to us. Brave men of the City Guard, behold the saviour of the kingdom, Prince Hieronymus!"

I do not know what effect Zoippos had been hoping for, but there was only silence. Someone coughed.

"Do you go to the theatre much, Dion?" Hieron asked quietly as he leant his elbows on the window ledge. "I have always enjoyed it greatly myself. As I get older, I find my taste turns increasingly to comedy. Comedies seem so much more true to life than the tragic plays."

Zoippos eyed the men nervously. He bit his lip, then leant forward and waved his arm in the direction of an archway, beckoning whoever was waiting on the other side. There was an abrupt clattering on the cobbles and a white chariot emerged from the shadows, drawn by a handsome pair of white stallions. The reins were held by a half-naked African slave, and next to him stood Hieronymus, gripping the rails with both hands. He was wearing a sword, but his only armour was a golden helmet, which seemed to be too big for him. As the wheels bumped over the cobbles, the helmet tilted forward and slid down over his forehead, almost covering his eyes.

"They say that helmet used to belong to King Agathocles," Hieron whispered to me. "I thought it would be a nice touch."

The chariot bounced forwards in front of the ranks of men, turning a half-circle at the end of the line to return and draw up before the platform. When it had stopped, Hieronymus let go of the handrails and adjusted the helmet. Then he drew his sword and raised it in the air.

"Men of the City Guard," he shouted in his strangulated voice, "I return from Pachynus with news that will gladden your hearts!"

The men in the courtyard remained silent.

"I have hurled the barbarians into the sea!" The last word turned into a shrill squeak.

The uncomfortable silence continued for a few moments.

And then someone made the sound of a squawking chicken.

There was a ripple of suppressed laughter. Hieronymus's sword wobbled over his head.

"Who made that noise?" he shouted nervously.

He was answered by a second squawk, and then several more, now coming from different directions. The men started laughing openly.

Zoippos was still on his feet.

"Be silent!" he thundered.

"Oh, fuck off, you windy cunt," someone shouted back. It sounded like Leander, except that it couldn't possibly have been. Leander was an officer; it was inconceivable. The men began jeering as well as laughing.

I was horrified. I turned to make for the door, but Hieron grasped my arm.

"Where are you going, Dion?" he asked.

"I've got to stop this," I said.

"Stay here."

I gawped at him.

"But, my King..."

"I said, *stay here*."

Outside, the men continued to jeer and laugh.

"Be quiet!" screamed Hieronymus.

"Piss off, pus face," a voice called back.

"Where's Dion?" another shouted. "Why isn't our captain sitting up there with you lot?"

"Who are all you wankers anyway?"

"What a bunch of fucking tossers. Who the fuck do you think you all are?"

"Where's our captain?"

"We want our captain."

"Dion! Dion!"

Suddenly, a thousand men were chanting my name and banging their spears against their shields in time. Hieronymus looked up at Zoippos in terror. Zoippos seemed to have no idea what to do. He swallowed hard and tried frantically waving his arms for silence, but it had no effect. The other councillors sat frozen on their stools. They stared at my men with wide, disbelieving eyes.

Hieron still held my arm. After a few moments, he bent his head towards me. He had to shout a little to make himself audible.

"In comedy, Dion, timing is everything. You can go and shut them up now, but don't dismiss them. I want them to stay in the courtyard. And you'd better tell my grandson and those other idiots to come inside."

He smiled and released my arm. I ran out.

As I emerged into the sunlight, a huge cheer went up.

I strode over to the chariot and turned to face the men. Hieronymus cringed behind me.

"Siiiilence!" I thundered.

The men obeyed at once.

"Attention!"

They snapped smartly to position.

"Castor!" I shouted.

My adjutant came running forward and saluted me. I glowered at him.

"We will talk about this later."

"Yes, sir."

"The men are to remain here until I return to dismiss them."

"Yes, sir."

I turned to look up at Hieronymus. He tried to put on a dignified expression, but he was trembling and his helmet had slipped again. I felt a little sorry for him.

"Get down, lad," I said. "Your grandfather wants you inside. Don't worry, you're quite safe. Hurry along now. And you'd better take off that helmet."

He removed it and, not knowing what else to do, stiffly handed it to me. It wasn't nearly heavy enough to be solid gold; I guessed it was just painted bronze. As he climbed down, I looked up at the platform behind him. Zoippos was still standing and glared at me murderously. I gestured with my thumb for him and the others to move indoors. One after another, they stood and sheepishly began shuffling along the platform. Zoippos wordlessly went with them. They had suffered nothing worse than a blow to their vanity, but most of them looked more traumatised than the refugees from Pachynus had been.

I followed them all into the council chamber, still carrying the helmet. Hieron was already in his chair at the head of the table, with Thraso next to him, in the seat that Zoippos usually occupied. My cousin fidgeted uncomfortably. The king had obviously told him to sit there. There was no formal seating plan that I knew of, but for some reason, we always arranged ourselves in the same places. Archimedes was still where we had left him, although at least he was now awake. The other councillors stood in an embarrassed and guilty huddle just inside the door, uncertain what to do. My great-uncle smiled and nodded amiably to them, seemingly oblivious to all that had just happened. I walked on past my colleagues and took my usual chair close to Archimedes, putting the helmet down on the table in front of me.

"Sit down, everyone," Hieron said coolly.

They silently took their places. Only Hieronymus and Zoippos remained standing. Zoippos, with more dignity than I would have expected from him, put his arm supportively around the prince's shoulder.

"Fuck off, Uncle," Hieronymus said viciously, shaking him off.

From the expression on his face, you would have thought Zoippos had been stabbed in the belly.

The prince raised his arm and pointed at me.

"You did this, you cunt," he snarled. His fear had apparently evaporated. I had no idea what to say, so I just gazed back at him.

"You insolent fucking pig," the prince shouted. "You're going to suffer for this. Grandfather, I want this bastard crucified."

"Dion had nothing to do with it, Hieronymus," replied Hieron calmly.

"Of course it was him," yelled the prince.

"No, Hieronymus. You managed to make a fool of yourself without any help from Dion, and fools get laughed at. You also disobeyed me. I told you to stay in Pachynus, but you ignored me. For your father's sake, I shall overlook your disobedience on this one occasion, and on this occasion only, but I warn you not to try my patience further."

"What?" Hieronymus said, dumbfounded.

"I want you outside the city walls within the hour, young man. You will return directly to Pachynus and you will remain there until I tell you that you may come back. And while you are there, you will endeavour to make yourself useful. If you fail to do so, you will find yourself staying in Pachynus for a very long time. Now, leave us. There is no seat at this table for you."

The prince stared at his grandfather in outrage.

"You can't do this," he squawked. "I'm your grandson. I won't go. I demand that you punish this fucking animal!"

Hieron raised his eyebrows.

"Punish him!" shrieked the boy, pointing at me again. Tears were running down his cheeks now.

There was a long silence.

The king eventually pursed his lips and turned to me.

"Dion," he said, "I was told that the first time you met my grandson, you warned him that if he insulted you again, you would put him over your knee and spank him. Apparently, he did not take you seriously... So do it."

I stared uncertainly at Hieron's wrinkled, impassive face.

"Well, get on with it," he said.

I hesitantly pushed back my chair and stood.

"But not here, Dion," the king continued coldly. "I want you to take the prince outside, and bend him over the back of that ridiculous chariot in front of all your men. Use your sandal, please. Ten firm strokes, I think: five for you and five for me. Then put him in a cart and have some of your men escort him down to Pachynus. I will have his baggage sent behind. Hurry up, now."

I reflected that I had been ordered to do far worse to children before. I began to walk round the table.

Hieronymus stared at me with bulging eyes, then turned to his grandfather and screamed. It was a long scream, a poisonous and uncontrolled outpouring of rage, fear and humiliation. Before I reached him, he ran sobbing from the room, as fast as his spindly legs could carry him.

I had no intention of chasing him round the palace, so I returned to my place. The only sound in the room was the noise of my sandals on the marble floor.

Hieron leant back in his chair.

"To think he has my blood in him," he sighed. "Now, sit down, Zoippos, or leave if you prefer, but don't just stand there."

Zoippos gazed at the king for a moment, then silently moved to the last empty place, which was opposite my own.

"So, that was your Achilles, Odysseus and Jason, all rolled into one?" Hieron continued, as his son-in-law settled himself. "A boy who runs away sobbing, for fear of being spanked?"

"You arranged it all, didn't you, Hieron?" Zoippos replied bitterly. There was hatred in his eyes. "You ordered those men to humiliate us."

Hieron smiled.

"I did no such thing, Zoippos. I merely let it be known that you wished to replace Dion with Hieronymus. Naturally, before reaching a decision, I wanted to see how the men felt about the idea. I think we have our answer. It would seem, my dear son-in-law, that even your own remarkable powers of oratory failed to persuade the Guards of my grandson's superior merits. But I certainly wouldn't want anyone to think me a tyrant, so if you like, we can put the matter to a vote of this council. And if the decision is to replace Dion, then I would be delighted to give you, Zoippos, the honour of going back outside and making the announcement to those men. I wonder how they would react. It would certainly be a tremendous display of bravery on your part. In fact, I think it would be an act every bit as worthy of a great speech as my grandson's heroics in Pachynus. So, shall we put it to the vote? No...? No. I thought not."

One by one, Hieron slowly turned his gaze round the other councillors. If my men's catcalls had frightened them, the king's icy stare was worse.

"We are all family here," Hieron said mildly, "and every one of you is dear to me, so I hope you will forgive me for being candid with you. We are in danger of being drawn into a terrible war, which could very easily destroy this kingdom. We teeter on the edge of a crumbling cliff. And what do my councillors do? They pursue their own petty feuds, and scheme to put our city's defences in the hands of a child."

He coughed.

"I must confess that I am a little disappointed in you all. I know you believe that Dion is an unthinking savage, and perhaps you are right, but when our enemies come for us, I imagine you may be very grateful to have him standing on our walls... Now, does anyone wish to debate this further? No? Very well, then. I shall assume that we are all in agreement. Dion will retain the command of the City Guard. So, let us now move on to other business. Although Dion will not be replaced, I have decided to rearrange some other people's roles on this council."

The king looked round the table happily. I saw several hands tighten on the sides of their chairs. Zoippos was staring up at the ceiling with clenched teeth.

"As you know," Hieron went on, "Thraso has been managing the granaries while Andranodoros is away. I am making his appointment permanent. He will combine the position of Supervisor of the Granaries with his existing responsibilities as senior magistrate. Zoippos, you have been my Royal Treasurer for six years now, and a most excellent one too, I might add. But I think the time has come to broaden your experience of government."

Zoippos looked at Hieron through narrowed eyes. The king smiled benignly.

"A man of your ambition and talents shouldn't have to waste his life poring over ledgers. So I am creating a new position, especially for you. The recent food shortages have brought home to me how dependent our people are on the sea. When all else fails, it is to the abundance of our coastal waters that Syracuse must turn to feed herself. So I am making you responsible for the regulation of the city's fish markets. Assuming he returns safely, Andranodoros will replace you as our new Royal Treasurer."

Hieron paused and rolled his thin lips, like a man delicately savouring a mouthful of food.

"I suppose all families have their little upsets," he continued after a few moments, in the tone of an indulgent father. "But I am sure all of you will take to heart the lesson of today... You know, there are many things in life that can bestow power on a man: wealth, birth, knowledge, even love. But at the end of the day, there is only one sort of power that really counts, and that is the power that comes at the point of a spear. And I command every spear in Syracuse. You would do well to remember this, because if you forget it again, I may have to ask Dion to give all of you a spanking too... Well, I think that is quite enough drama for one day. You may dismiss your men, Dion. And thank you all for your attendance."

The king might have made a little joke of it, but the menace was clear enough. He wanted the council to know that I was his dog, and that he was quite prepared to take off my muzzle. Everything was working out exactly as my mother had predicted. But now that Hieron had finally made my true purpose clear to everyone, I found I really didn't mind. As I looked round the pale, silent faces of my colleagues, I realised that apart from Thraso and my great-uncle, I had come to despise them all.

*

I dismissed the men, but told the officers to go directly to my apartment. I had Nebit fetched as well: he had obviously had a hand in the whole appalling fiasco in the courtyard. I made the officers stand to attention and bawled them all out furiously, but when I saw Castor grinning at me, I found I couldn't keep it up. After much determined clenching of my jaw, I finally abandoned the struggle and just burst out laughing. I ended up warmly thanking everyone instead.

Nebit was the hero of the hour. The king had shown him the letter from Hieronymus and had of course made clear what he wanted to happen, but it was Nebit who had overcome my officers' reservations and had insisted they have a quiet word with their sergeants. The Egyptian had never been a popular figure in the division: my officers had treated him with suspicion and had avoided him. But now he found himself being clapped on the back and congratulated by one after another of them. It was a brief, happy moment in a life that had probably known scant warmth. Nebit's chin quivered and his eyes kept moistening. Leander went down on one knee and presented him with a sword in a little mock ceremony, in which there was no mockery at all. Nebit had become one of us. He was, without a doubt, the most unlikely recruit ever to be welcomed into the brotherhood of the City Guard.

The following two weeks were busy ones for me. Secretary Philocrates gave us the locations of Hieron's secret grain stores and we began trickling food into the city, by both sea and land. Several of my family's ships lay idle at anchor in the Great Harbour, their crews having been recalled for service with the fleet. I found enough experienced sailors among the City Guard to man two of them. We put them under the command of two ship's captains on my family's payroll, who had been too old to be recalled. The story we put about was that Hieron had discovered that several merchants had been stockpiling quantities of grain, intending to profiteer from the city's shortages, and that the king had been so incensed he had confiscated it all. I also commandeered the carts that had been abandoned on Epipolae, and used those to collect supplies from the nearest of Hieron's warehouses. The city's own grain reserves continued to be depleted, but at a significantly slower rate. Thraso calculated we should have just enough to see us through till the harvests.

I finally received word that my mother had returned to Syracuse. I had taken my great-uncle's warning to heart and had prepared for our confrontation, but now that the moment had arrived, I found myself dreading it. As I set off down the Avenue of Athena, I rehearsed over and over again in my head what I intended to say. I kept hoping that I might alight on some formula of words that would enable her to forgive me for what I intended to do, or at least to understand the necessity of it. At one point, I suddenly became conscious that the people standing aside to make way for me were looking at me oddly. My lips must have been moving. The idea that a man like me might be frightened of his own mother was something that even those closest to me could never have understood. But I *was* frightened of her. Or, to be more accurate, while I yearned to be rid of her, I was frightened of losing her. They say that the cruellest thing you can do to a man born into slavery is to set him free.

A slave escorted me round the courtyard with its outsized statue of the irritable-looking goddess, and into a small but elaborately decorated room that had once been my father's study. It had been refurnished with four couches and tables, to serve as my mother's private sitting room. She kept me waiting for over quarter of an hour before making her entrance.

"You were a long time at Acrae," I said neutrally, standing to give her the obligatory embrace from which we both recoiled slightly.

"I only spent one night there," she replied with a forced smile. "I'm afraid it's in a worse state than I'd imagined. I had to throw the caretaker out and sleep in his apartment." She shuddered at the memory. "Anyway, I went on to Leontini afterwards. I thought I'd better make sure things are in order there, as you seem to have no interest in the place."

"Thank you," I muttered, with an effort.

Unlike Acrae, our landholdings at Leontini were extensive. The estate lay in the wide plain to the north of Syracuse and consisted of a number of contiguous farms that my family had acquired over the centuries. The soil there was the most fertile on the island, probably on account of having been so extensively irrigated, during the course of countless wars, by the blood of men. But the landscape was dull and featureless, and the house was just a sprawling, ugly monster that had been expanded by my ancestors in fits and starts, to keep pace with the growing size and importance of the surrounding estate. To have installed the Torquatus girl at Leontini would have been too cruel; at least Acrae was a fashionable resort where she could make suitable friends. Many of the nobles had villas in the hills around Acrae; Hieron's own summer palace lay only a few miles away.

"So, Dion," my mother said as she settled herself down, "I gather you've given Hieron the use of another two of my ships. No doubt I shall wake up one day soon, to find him eating breakfast on my couch."

"It's not like that, Mother. And can we try not to quarrel, please? I'm not here about ships. There's something else I must talk to you about."

"Oh yes?" she said indifferently.

"Yes. I'm worried. Hieron is watching you. It seems he has spies everywhere. I don't know what you've been up to, or to whom you've been speaking, but it's all going to have to stop now."

She narrowed her eyes and gazed at me.

"Of course he's watching me," she said after a few moments. "He watches everyone. He's the king. What else do you think kings do all day? But you seem scared, Dion. That's most unlike you. You don't usually have the imagination to be scared. What have you heard?"

"Nothing specific, really. Only that you've been keeping bad company. Also, something about bribing the agricultural inspectors.

And Nebit let slip a little while ago that you've been buying ships in other people's names. I don't know why on earth you'd want to do that, but if you thought you were keeping them secret, you were wrong. Anyway, the point is that whatever it is that you've been up to, Hieron seems to know all about it."

She raised her eyebrows in surprise, but stayed silent. Something I had said must have struck a target.

"Mother, I don't know exactly what Hieron's intending, but I think he's preparing to do something. It's not just about us. You heard about Hieronymus's parade?"

She snorted.

"Of course. It's all that everyone's talking about. It seems our king intends to promote you to the position of palace governess. What title will he give you now, I wonder? Master of the Royal Sandal, perhaps?"

I dug my nails into my palm.

"Well, Hieron was behind the whole thing, of course," I went on, choosing to ignore her. "But it wasn't just about putting Hieronymus in his place. At the council meeting afterwards, it seemed like the old man was going out of his way to humiliate and frighten everyone. Zoippos especially. As though he was poking them all with his stick to see how they'll react. Thraso and I are the only ones he seems to have any time for, and Andranodoros I suppose, but I still don't feel safe. I don't think anyone's safe. Anyway, you won't like it, but I'm afraid I've come to a decision."

"You've come to decision?" she said sarcastically.

"Yes, I'm afraid I have, Mother. You're going to have to leave the city. You can go to Leontini, or any of the other estates, if you'd rather. I've hired a new lawyer, and I'm putting our business affairs in his hands, at least until I can find someone else to run them. Someone I can trust not to overreach himself. I've already sealed the authority for the lawyer to start managing everything. He's my agent now, so I'll be wanting my ring back. I'll give you a week to pack up here. You can take whatever you want."

Her eyes widened in disbelief.

"I'm sorry to have to do this, Mother," I said gently. "Who knows, when Gelon's king, perhaps you can return. We'll just have to see how things play out. If you'd like me to, I could even start looking for another husband for you. You could make an entirely new life for yourself: it's not too late. Think about it, at least. I'd provide you with the largest dowry Syracuse has ever seen. But given what happened with father, I can't take any risks. I'm afraid I've just got too much to deal with, without worrying about what you're getting up to behind my back."

I watched her incredulity gradually turn to icy fury. For a few moments, she just glared at me. Then she stood up, smoothed down her robe, and walked haughtily from the room without a word. A slave closed the door behind her.

She left Syracuse five days later with her retinue of Galatian bodyguards and a cavalcade of carts, laden with most of my best furniture. She chose to set up home at a vineyard I owned near Catana, further up the coast. I went to say goodbye but she refused to see me.

Was I really so naïve as to think that a woman like my mother could be tamed, just by sending her away? If I was, she made sure to leave me a farewell gift to disabuse me of the idea. On the morning of her departure, my duplicate signet ring was found. It was still on the finger of our elderly steward, whose broken and twisted body had been left in the courtyard, like some grotesque offering, at the foot of the statue of Athena. I guessed my mother had decided he must have been one of those in Hieron's pay; or perhaps she merely had no intention of letting him help with the handover of our affairs to my lawyer. Whatever the explanation, like my father's old dog Titan, it seemed our steward was of no further use to her.

My new lawyer's name was Linus. Thraso had recommended him as an astute and honest man and he dutifully set about trying to make sense of the piles of leases and contracts that he found stored in my mother's study cupboards. Linus had her well-drilled regiment of business clerks to help him – there were twenty or so of them, working out of a converted slaves' dormitory in the villa – but each was familiar with only a single thread of my mother's cobweb of dealings, none having sight of the full extent or design of it. Linus soon discovered that tweaking one thread was liable to send unforeseen tremors down another. Such-and-such a tenant, for example, might turn out to be the brother-in-law of such-and-such a merchant; the rent paid by the one had quietly been waived to secure the shipping contract of the other – but this would only come to light after Linus had tried to have the tenant evicted.

On top of my regular duties, I had the grain deliveries to organise, but now I also found myself obliged to try to help Linus out of the various traps into which he quickly stumbled. My own role usually consisted of calling on people in the suburbs, to present them with gifts of wine from one of my estates and to plead forgiveness for whatever blunder had occasioned my visit. Fortunately, for the most part, they seemed sufficiently flattered by my presence in their homes to forget the whole affair.

It was therefore a considerable nuisance to have to waste several afternoons with Archimedes and Nebit, touring the city's defences. Everything involving my great-uncle recently seemed to have acquired a certain unreality about it, as though I were entering a dislocated dream world whenever I was in his company. On our inspections of the walls, Archimedes and Nebit would walk in front, followed by four of my great-uncle's slaves. One had a long line of measuring twine, two carried pots of whitewash, and the fourth a satchel full of wax tablets, on which he took notes at Archimedes' dictation.

Every so often, my angular, long-legged great-uncle would stoop to whisper something in the ear of the gelatinous eunuch, who floated alongside him, trailing tentacles of clothing. Nebit would nod earnestly and whisper something back; then Archimedes would stop to have a stretch of wall measured, and would order apparently meaningless marks to be painted on the stonework, in the form of numbers or single letters or sometimes combinations of the two.

While Archimedes and Nebit entertained themselves in this way, I generally dawdled at the rear of our strange little column with Kleitos, Archimedes' bodyguard, making small talk about soldiering. On one of our excursions, I tried to find out more about the Royal Watch from him. It was said the Watch had no officers, and if they had a commander, even I didn't know his identity. But when I asked Kleitos to whom he reported, he told me he wasn't allowed to discuss it. He wouldn't even tell me how many men there were in the unit. "Oh, enough for the work, I dare say, sir," was all that I could get out of him. I took the hint, and changed the subject.

Occasionally, Archimedes would interrupt us to fire a question at me. How far could most of our reservists throw a javelin from the ramparts? How might we expect men carrying a battering ram to be shielded from our missiles? If I were assaulting Syracuse from the sea, where would I focus my attack? I answered him patiently, but it was all quite pointless. You can breach a wall, or undermine it, or scale it, and that's all there is to say on the subject. Ever since walls were first invented, they have been attacked in the same simple ways and defended in the same simple ways. Our city had never fallen; we hardly needed my great-uncle to teach us how to repel our enemies.

It was on our fourth such excursion, while we were touring the most northerly section of Achradina's long sea-facing fortifications, that I spotted the sails of our first returning quinquereme, rounding the corner of the coast.

Our ships came back to us individually or in small groups. The first to find their way home had all been under the command of my friend Theodotus; it was not till many days later that those that had been part of Andranodoros's squadron began to return. Each of Theodotus's captains could only provide an account of his own experiences; their ships had ended up scattered over a wide expanse of sea and they had no knowledge of how the rest of the fleet had fared. They could all tell us how the battle had begun;

but none could tell us how it had ended. In those first few days, we did not even know for certain whether we had met with success or failure. Almost everyone had a relative who had sailed with the fleet, and the whole city held its breath while we waited for news. We counted our quinqueremes in, but the news they brought came in small, seemingly unrelated pieces, like the individual shapes of the ostomachion.

Theodotus himself was not among those to disembark in the first days. I learnt that he was safe, but that he had no sooner docked than he had been required to sail on to Pachynus on the king's business. Andranodoros's own flagship finally arrived two weeks after the first of our emaciated crews had gratefully stumbled off their gangplank onto the wharf of the Little Harbour. I was supervising the drills in the exercise yard, when a slave came running up to inform me that the council would be meeting the following morning, to hear the admiral's report. By then, of course, we already knew most of the story, but I was curious to hear what Andranodoros would have to say. Simple facts can be fitted together in all manner of different ways, to create very different impressions.

Most of the other councillors had already taken their chairs by the time I got to the council chamber an hour after dawn. Instead of pointedly ignoring me as usual, three or four of them nodded and smiled nervously at me. Hieronymus's parade had apparently elevated me from an object of loathing to an object of fear. I suppose it was a promotion of a sort. I snorted in amusement and smiled back in my deformed way as I took my own place. The chair to my left was still empty.

Leatherskin and Ision, Zoippos's cronies, arrived together a moment later, deep in conversation. Ision looked up and, noticing the vacant space beside me, promptly left his companion's side and started walking casually round the table. Finding himself abandoned in mid-sentence, Leatherskin stared at his friend in consternation. As Ision strolled straight past his customary seat, the light of understanding flashed in Leatherskin's face. His expression immediately hardened and he began walking around the table in the opposite direction, sliding his sandals over the floor in a series of quick, short steps, like a woman hurrying to answer a call of nature. Ision had clearly not anticipated this, and accelerated by increasing the length of his stride. Unfortunately for him, he had made the fatal error of taking the longer way round, and was still two or three paces away from me as Leatherskin gleefully grabbed the back of the empty chair next to my own and pulled it out for himself.

"My dear Captain, I do trust you are well," Leatherskin said as he slid in beside me, throwing Ision a triumphant glance over my shoulder.

Archimedes and Thraso arrived together, but when the king finally shuffled in on Andranodoros's arm, one place remained conspicuously unoccupied. The great Adam's apple was nowhere to be seen.

Andranodoros helped the king settle down and then walked round the table to seat himself. We all stared at him in shock.

"My dear Andranodoros," said Archimedes after a moment, "you look quite dreadful. Are you unwell?"

It was no less than the truth. Andranodoros's cheeks were hollow and his eyes appeared to bulge. The long, elaborately styled hair that he had been so fond of petting had been cropped short, which only accentuated the gauntness of his face. There was an ugly blister on his forehead, which I guessed had been caused by sunburn. Andranodoros had been away for less than two months, but he looked several years older.

"I'm afraid you must blame your great-nephew for my appearance, Archimedes," he replied with a faint smile.

I raised my eyebrows.

"What on earth do you mean?" Hieron asked sharply.

"My King," Andranodoros said, "no one would call me a born warrior, so I thought I should at least study the example of someone who is. Before we sailed, Eryx told me that Dion always makes a point of sharing his men's hardships. So I decided to put myself and the officers on the same rations as the men." He spread his arms.

"And as you can see, in consequence, I return to you a fraction of my former self."

The king and Archimedes chuckled. Andranodoros nodded to me across the table.

"I appreciated the message you sent me, Dion, wishing me luck."

He eyed me coolly, waiting to see how I might respond to the surprising compliment he had paid me. We would never like each other, but I realised he was tacitly offering me some sort of accommodation. Unlike the other councillors, he had no fear of me at all – he was, after all, married to one of Hieron's daughters – but I had risen above my animosity before he sailed, and he was apparently prepared to do the same. As I gazed at him across the table, I recognised something in his bright eyes that had not been there before. It told me Andranodoros was now blooded too. Driving a blade into another human being's flesh for the first time has a curiously maturing effect: it makes a man's demeanour at once more solemn and more confident.

I politely nodded back to him.

"Does anyone know where Zoippos is?" asked Hieron.

"Probably counting fish," Leatherskin sniggered to me behind his hand.

"Well, no matter," said the king. "Now, Andranodoros, let us hear your report."

"Thank you, my King," Andranodoros replied, and cleared his throat.

XI

THE BITER BIT

" A nd that concludes my report, my King," Andranodoros said. His account had been sober and measured. He had gone out of his way to praise his captains and Theodotus, but to my surprise, he had claimed little credit for himself. Andranodoros was just as much of a snake as Zoippos; the only difference was that he was a far cleverer one. I suspected that having heard of Hieronymus's vainglorious antics, he had calculated that his own reputation would be better served by understatement.

The king's eyes were glinting. He broke into a wide smile and began lightly clapping the table with the palm of his hand. One by one, the other councillors started to do the same, including me. For a brief moment, all our venomous rivalries and resentments were forgotten. Andranodoros's triumph was also ours. The clapping turned into pounding and I found myself chuckling with pride in my city. Hannibal was the world's most feared general, and yet our ninety-year-old king had just clipped him round the ears like a child.

Andranodoros nodded modestly in acknowledgement, but there could be no doubting the scale of his achievement.

In the weeks that followed their return, I spoke to many friends who had served with the fleet, all of whom had their different versions of events. And shortly before he died, I discussed it with Archimedes too. So I shall set down here what happened as I came to understand it, because as far as I am aware, even Andranodoros never learnt of my great-uncle's involvement from behind the curtain.

In truth, our success was as much the fruit of Archimedes' mind as of Andranodoros's own aptitude for organisation. Without Archimedes' systems of pulleys, our ships may never have been re-masted and launched in time; without his drainage screws, they may not have been fast enough to catch the convoy; without his calculations, they would not even have known where to hunt for it; and without his battle plan, we might never have visited such destruction upon it. Although perhaps only Hieron appreciated the fact at the time, Archimedes' mind was the most formidable weapon our kingdom had ever possessed. Muscular men like me may have prided ourselves on our skills with a sword or a javelin; but on the night we learnt of the Pachynus landings, my geriatric great-uncle had merely sat behind his desk for several hours, chewing on his beard. And then he had leant forward, and had swept Hannibal's ships from the sea with the back of his hand.

It was to prove the last sea battle that our proud kingdom ever fought, but for some reason, it has never acquired a name. Nor, I dare say, will you be likely to find any mention of it in whatever histories our new masters eventually commission. It will hardly suit them to acknowledge it. Yet it happened, all the same.

The ships under Theodotus's command had been tasked with intercepting and breaking up the Carthaginian convoy before it could reach the Italian coast. Over a distance, our quinqueremes could cruise at more than twice the speed of oarless merchant ships. Unless my great-uncle had missed his guess, it seemed Theodotus might be clawing at the convoy's heels within three or four days. There was only one problem: while navigating by the stars is easy enough, using the sun to chart a course is a fairly haphazard business. Even if Archimedes had anticipated the Carthaginians' intended route correctly, there was no certainty that either they or Theodotus would manage to follow it.

Warships almost always sail in a column. It is a little easier on the oarsmen to row in the wake of another ship, and it makes it much harder for an enemy to estimate the numbers of an approaching fleet. Theodotus formed ten of his quinqueremes into a central column, but on either side of this he placed three outriders, spaced three or four miles apart from each other in a long line. The ships at the far ends of the line could not see each other, but the formation provided his squadron with eyes over a front of more than twenty miles altogether. If any crew sighted the sails of a large convoy, they were to set a fire of tarred logs in their ship's brazier.

For three days, the squadron followed its designated course as best it could. At dusk, the outriders drew in closer to the central column, to avoid drifting apart during the night, and at dawn they fanned out again.

Fortunately, the sailors of Carthage and Syracuse know their business equally well. Both nations have lived off the sea for so many centuries that salt water practically runs through their veins. At noon on the fourth day, the ship at the most northerly point of Theodotus's line finally lit its brazier. The squadron adjusted its course to the north-east.

Theodotus had a difficult decision to make. If he picked up the pace, he might catch the Carthaginians before nightfall, but his oarsmen would be tired and there would be little time to do much damage before the convoy scattered into the night. He decided to lower his sails instead. It was a signal to the outriders to return to the main column. Theodotus would keep his squadron below the horizon for the remainder of the day, halving his speed and resting his men, by hauling in alternating banks of oars. The convoy must have noticed the plume of smoke, and would have seen the distant sails of one or maybe two of his outriders, but those outriders would now fall back out of sight. The Carthaginians would probably just shrug their shoulders and think no more about it.

That night, Theodotus ordered lanterns to be lit in the stern of his ships. The lanterns were shuttered on three sides, so that they were only visible from aft. He raised his sails and picked up the pace again, each of his quinqueremes following the light of the one immediately in front. All sixteen warships in his squadron now rowed under the half-moon in a single column. Theodotus risked losing the Carthaginians again in the darkness, but Hannibal's captains were complacent. As merchantmen usually do, they hung their own unblinkered night lanterns from the tops of their masts, to avoid colliding with each other. At some point in the early hours, a lookout on Theodotus's lead ship spotted a host of lights glimmering and bobbing in the distance. He thought there were fifty or sixty of them altogether. Theodotus adjusted his course again, and continued to close the gap on his unsuspecting quarry.

When dawn broke, the vessels to the rear of the Carthaginian convoy were finally able to see our sails, now no more than three or four miles behind them. But at that distance, they would still not have been able to identify what types of ships were trailing them, or how many of them there were. They probably reasoned that the convoy's lanterns must have attracted some pirate vessels in the darkness, which were now dogging them in the hope of picking off any stragglers.

Two Carthaginian quinqueremes broke away from the convoy and turned to investigate. No pirates possessed anything larger than a trireme, and they seldom hunted in packs of more than three or four ships. But even half a dozen triremes would not choose to pick a fight with a pair of quinqueremes, and the realisation that the convoy was well protected would probably be enough to send any pirates scuttling off in search of easier prey.

As the Carthaginians closed the distance, Theodotus gave the signal for his column to fan out into our standard battle formation. His ships began to pull away obliquely, with one moving to port and the next to starboard so as to form a crescent, with Theodotus's own ship in the most forward position at the centre. With no more than a mile now between them and the deploying squadron, the two

Carthaginian captains realised their mistake. One turned east, the other west, their crews rowing for all they were worth in an attempt to get out of the way of Theodotus's squadron. Behind them, some merchant vessels saw the danger too, and started to peel away from the rear of the convoy.

Theodotus had ordered his ships to hunt in teams. Two pairs of his quinqueremes broke off, sailing in opposite directions to pursue the two fleeing Carthaginian warships. The chase would be touch and go. Our ships were cleaner and drier, but the Carthaginian oarsmen were better rested, having rowed through the night at the leisurely pace of the merchantmen.

The rest of Theodotus's warships ploughed on towards the convoy. Within a few hours, they had begun to overtake the hindmost of the cargo vessels. They ignored those: it was the quinqueremes that Theodotus was after. The convoy was now disintegrating, with individual ships trying to escape in different directions, like a slowly scattering flock of sheep. The cleverest of their captains tried to double back, intending to sail around or even through the crescent of our quinqueremes, but cargo ships are fat, ungainly things, with high freeboards and wide beams, and several of them collided and became entangled with each other.

One clumsy monster of a merchantman managed to smash into the side of a Carthaginian quinquereme, snapping dozens of its oars and no doubt causing gruesome mayhem on the rowing decks. The hobbled warship tried to limp away, but before long, two of Theodotus's ships had fallen upon it. They pummelled it from both sides with flaming ballistae shot. The sails and rigging caught fire and the flames quickly spread to the gunwales and then the deck timbers, which must have been rotten. Parties of oarsmen rushed up from below to try to douse the blaze, only to be mown down by the arrows and javelins of our marines. The fire took hold and soon all that could be heard were the screams of the men still trapped below. The smell of roasting flesh began to seep from the oarlocks, and Theodotus's two ships moved on.

By late afternoon, Theodotus's squadron had dispersed far

and wide, chasing fleeing quinqueremes. A second of Hannibal's warships was sunk and a third boarded and captured. It was an old ship but still a prize worth taking back to Syracuse. Its marines, both the living and the dead, were thrown overboard and the surviving oarsmen enslaved. They did not have to endure a long captivity. The quinquereme's planks must have been shaken loose by the barrage of ballistae stones to which the ship had been subjected, and it slowly sank the following day. Our boarding party was rescued; the oarsmen were left to contemplate their fate as the ship gradually went down, inch by cruel inch.

Once darkness had fallen, those quinqueremes that had managed to stay ahead of their pursuers had the best part of seven hours in which to make good their escape, in whatever direction they chose. There was little hope of running down any more of them, and so that night Theodotus's crews rested. One of his ships had been de-masted, but was still serviceable. Only about a hundred of his men had been killed or seriously injured.

When the sun rose, Theodotus's squadron turned its attention to sweeping the sea for Hannibal's merchantmen. Eight were chased down and meekly surrendered. Some were laden with arms and armour of various kinds; others carried tents and blankets or had been converted to hold horses. But the greatest prizes by far were two huge transport ships, in each of which were crammed nearly a thousand frightened mercenaries. A few of the mercenaries were Numidians, but most came from various shards of Alexander's former empire in the East. Faced with the prospect of being rammed and sunk, they readily agreed to change sides and be escorted back to Sicily.

Most of the quinqueremes and cargo ships that had escaped eventually resumed their course north, now sailing individually or in small groups; their captains had mistakenly judged it safer than trying to double back through Theodotus's hunting packs. Once they sighted the coast of Italy, they followed it, intending to round the heel of the Italian boot into the Adriatic and the safety of the Apulian coast. And it was in a cove a few miles inside the Adriatic, just south of the little town of Hydrus, that Andranodoros awaited them. His own squadron had taken the most direct route, sailing along the coasts of Sicily and southern Italy, which run north-east in an almost straight line. Theodotus's ships had done their work: they had torn Hannibal's convoy into digestible mouthfuls. It was up to the admiral's squadron to do the fine chewing.

The ships of Carthage are easily distinguishable from those of other nations by the cut of their sails and the length of their prows. Andranodoros had to wait three days before the first Carthaginian quinquereme finally rounded the coast. Four more followed over the days that ensued. They arrived singly and their oarsmen were worn out, having rowed almost nonstop to try to put as much distance as possible between themselves and Theodotus. With insufficient time to turn about, none managed to give Andranodoros the slip. Guessing the fate that awaited them, they fought to the end. One was destroyed and the others boarded. It was butcher's work.

It was not till the seventh day that some of the Carthaginian cargo ships finally began appearing. They were ransacked for food and anything worth taking, then rammed and sunk.

The slaughter continued for a further four days. Two more transports carrying mercenaries went to the bottom. But although Andranodoros had sent raiding parties ashore to forage what they could, his provisions continued to dwindle. Eventually, he calculated he could stay in the Adriatic no longer, and reluctantly gave the order to set sail back to Syracuse.

The squadron sailed home in a line rather a column, each ship a mile or so apart from those alongside it. No further quinqueremes came their way, but as the squadron swept across the Gulf of Tarentum and along the Italian coast, they sank a few more merchant stragglers.

Altogether, eight quinqueremes and over thirty merchantmen had been captured or destroyed, and we had lost not a single ship. We learnt later that of the sixty or so ships Hannibal had been expecting, only half a dozen eventually arrived. They had been lucky enough to sail past Andranodoros in the night. All told, we had suffered fewer than a thousand dead or seriously injured, a small fraction of the numbers that must have been lost to the Carthaginians.

One of the quinqueremes that Andranodoros captured had been so badly damaged that he judged it not worth bringing back with him. He left it anchored in the cove, with its captain's headless torso strapped to his chair on the deck. Below, the crew had been neatly arranged along their benches, with their arms draped over the oars. They had all been decapitated too. On the shattered stump of the ship's mast, Andranodoros nailed a note.

To the illustrious General Hannibal Barca, greetings from Hieron, King of Syracuse. His Majesty is pleased to return this ship after its recent visit to his kingdom. He trusts that one day he will be able to extend his hospitality to the general in person.

"Well now, Andranodoros," said Hieron, when the clapping had finally died down, "we must give thanks to Athena for your victory. We shall arrange a ceremony so the people can see their new hero. But," he added drily, "no chariots this time, I think."

"My King," said Andranodoros, "Theodotus deserves an equal share of any honour."

The show of modesty was becoming rather cloying, but Hieron nodded.

"Of course. I shall consult the High Priestess about dates, although I doubt I'll get much sense out of the poor old thing. The last time I saw her, she seemed to think I was her husband. Now, unless anyone has any questions, I suggest that we let my son-in-law go home and get some well-earned rest."

The meeting broke up. I was heading to the door when I heard Andranodoros's voice behind me.

"Dion, a moment of your time, if I may."

I turned and looked into his thin, tired face.

"Of course, Andranodoros. And I must congratulate you. What you did… well, it was extraordinary."

"Thank you," he said simply. "Look, I want to say I realise it must have been a disappointment for you when Hieron gave me the command. I don't know why he did; you were the obvious choice. Anyway, I appreciate the way you behaved about it."

"It's kind of you to say so, Andranodoros, but I think it's pretty clear he chose the right man. No one could have done better. I certainly couldn't have."

We walked through to the anteroom together and stood by a window as the other councillors filed past. Archimedes shuffled by with his cane and gave Andranodoros a wide smile but didn't stop.

"There was something you left out of your report, wasn't there?" I said.

"What do you mean?" he asked sharply.

"The quinqueremes your squadron captured. You boarded them yourself, didn't you?"

He looked at me in surprise.

"Only the first, Dion. I thought I had to, if the men were to respect me. But to be honest, I'll be happy if I never have to lift a sword again. Eryx saved my life, you know. It wasn't exactly a glorious moment. I slipped and fell flat on my arse. If he hadn't been beside me, well… Anyway, from now on, I think I'll leave the soldiering to the soldiers." He smiled sadly. "How did you know? Did Eryx tell you?"

"No, just a guess. These things seem to leave their mark on a man." I smiled back and shrugged. "Anyway, what can I do for you, Andranodoros?"

He pursed his lips.

"I don't know quite how to put this, Dion. Let me be frank. We've always disliked each other." He smiled wryly to display the gap where his front tooth should have been. "And I admit I would have been happy to see you broken over Malmeides. He was a good friend of mine, you know."

I gazed at him evenly but stayed silent.

"Anyway, things have changed, I suppose," he continued. "From what I've heard, it looks like it's going to be the four of us from now on: Gelon, Thraso, you and me. It seems we're the ones the king intends to rely upon. I think you love him as I do, and we won't serve him well if we are enemies to each other."

I nodded. There was also a fifth, I thought, but Andranodoros seemed unaware of my great-uncle's work in the shadows.

"So, peace then?" I said.

"Yes, peace. You will find that I will deal fairly by you, Dion, if you will do the same by me. I'm sure there will be time for us to be enemies again in the future, but not now. I fear for our kingdom, I really do. The old man took a big risk, you know, sending us after Hannibal's ships."

"You mean, when there might have been an army marching on us from Pachynus?"

He laughed.

"No, not that, Dion. You know as well as I do that there was never any threat from Pachynus. You don't honestly think I'd have suggested sending Zoippos down there, if there was a real possibility there'd be a battle, do you? I may not be a soldier, but even I could work that much out."

I gazed at him. My friend Theodotus had been right about him: he was certainly no joke.

"No," he continued, "what I mean is that Hieron took the risk that the fleet would actually succeed as it has done. The king has bitten the Carthaginians as hard as he can, and he is gambling that the effect will be to deter Hannibal from coming after us, rather than provoking him into doing so. But who knows how Hannibal thinks? Carthage may no longer have the ships to threaten us from Africa, but Hannibal isn't in Africa. He's in Italy. And between Italy and Sicily, there are just two miles of water."

I considered my words carefully before replying.

"Whatever you and I may think, Andranodoros, we have to trust the king's judgement," I said eventually. "I suppose we'll just have to hope the Romans finally learn how to fight. Anyway, I want you to know, you've won my respect, after what you've just done. I mean it. And you're right, of course: we have quite enough enemies outside our walls, without looking for more within them."

He smiled thinly at me and we formally clasped each other's arms. His own must have been less than half the thickness of mine. I forced myself to smile back.

I stayed at the window and watched him saunter off, trying to work out his game. It was always possible he was being sincere, I thought. Time would tell.

As he walked through the door into the courtyard, I noticed him lift his hand to his head as if to pat his hair, but then he must have remembered that his elegant curls had all been shorn off, and he dropped his arm to his side again.

Ever since I had turned eighteen, I had made a point of going to the Temple of Ares on the winter solstice, to sacrifice to the god of war. I always gave the priests a bag of silver to clear the temple for me. And after making a sacrifice, I would strip naked and prostrate myself before the gaunt, dark statue to pray out loud. All I ever asked for was that the god might bestow on me a chance to prove myself. A chance to redeem the past once and for all and bring some peace to my father's anguished ghost. But Ares had chosen to shower the glory that should have been mine on Andranodoros instead. It felt as though the god was mocking me.

Prince Gelon finally returned from Rome the following day. He sent me a brief note, informing me that he had brought the Torquatus girl back with him. He apologised for not having time to see me, but explained that he had only just learnt of the raid on Pachynus and the attack on Hannibal's convoy, and wanted to return to Plymmerium immediately.

I understood. The casualties we had suffered at sea had been overwhelmingly among the men of the White and Yellow Shields, who had acted as the fleet's marines. They were the ones who had been exposed to the Carthaginians' missiles, and who had formed the boarding parties, while most of the reservists stayed safely below decks at their oars. It was natural that Gelon should want to go straight to his men. He would certainly have his work cut out at Plymmerium over the coming months, reorganising the companies and trying to fill the gaps in their ranks. I imagined – wrongly, as it turned out – that I would probably have to wait till the next council meeting before I saw him again. It seemed I would also have to wait to meet my future wife, who had presumably been closeted away somewhere in the palace until our wedding day. But that was altogether of less consequence to me.

By coincidence, Theodotus finally returned to Syracuse on the same day as Gelon and he, at least, found time to call on me that evening, before taking the barge to Plymmerium. I was in my office talking to Nebit when he put his face round the door.

"So, I hear you tried to thrash the king's grandson," he said cheerfully. "Well done, my dear Cowbrains. That's even better than beating up his great-nephew."

Nebit respectfully stood up as Theodotus strolled in.

"It's good to see you safe, my friend," I replied with a grin. I got to my feet as well and embraced him. He looked in much better shape than Andranodoros had been.

"Have you met Secretary Nebit?" I asked.

The two men nodded to each other.

"My warmest congratulations, Captain," Nebit said. "You have burnished the prestige of the whole kingdom. I hear your squadron performed most valiantly."

"To tell the truth," Theodotus replied, flopping into a chair and languidly stretching out his legs, "I hardly saw any of the fighting myself. The ship I was chasing got away in the night, so I had to make do with a little merchantman the next day. And all the blasted thing was carrying were some cloaks and tents. But at least I suppose I'll be able to claim the credit, if Hannibal dies of a sneezing fit."

"And now it seems there's a chance you'll be off to Italy next," I said.

"Really? What do you mean?" he asked, raising his eyebrows.

"Haven't you heard? Gelon got back from Rome this morning. Nebit was just telling me that our Roman friends want us to send them one of the Shield divisions, to join the army they're marching against Hannibal."

"Sounds fun," said Theodotus.

"Alas, Captain," Nebit said, "as I was just about to explain to Captain Dion before you so happily joined us, I suspect on this occasion, His Majesty may decide not to oblige our allies. Or at least, not quite as fully as they hope."

"Why ever not?" Theodotus asked. "We've already wounded the beast for them. Surely the old man wants us in at the kill?"

Nebit pouted self-importantly.

"I dare say that after our fleet's heroic performance, His Majesty may feel that he has done quite enough to assist already. And I understand that he considers bringing Hannibal to battle an unnecessary risk. After all, the Romans have already tried that on more than one occasion, with what one might perhaps describe as mixed results."

Theodotus grunted in amusement. There was nothing mixed about Hannibal's victories. At Tricia, the Romans had been routed. That was our allies' best result. A short while later, at Trebia, they had been encircled and had lost more than half their men. But if Tricia was a disaster, and Trebia a catastrophe, even we Greeks had no word to describe what had happened at Lake Trasimene. On their third encounter with Hannibal, an entire Roman army had been ambushed and virtually annihilated.

Lake Trasimene had left the Roman senate reeling. Their only consolation was that Flaminius, the birdbrained consul who had marched his troops straight into Hannibal's maws, was among those who failed to survive the experience. For the last year, the Romans had stayed behind their walls and tried waiting Hannibal out, perhaps hoping he would grow bored and go home of his own accord. Unfortunately, that didn't seem to be working very well either. Like a burglar presented with an open door, the general had gratefully seized control of Apulia, the richest of Rome's agricultural provinces. While Rome went hungry, the Carthaginian army now feasted on Roman bread and milk. Hannibal was proving as adroit at waging war with grain as with iron.

"Of course, I cannot pretend that His Majesty confides his intentions in me," Nebit continued breezily, "so I am only guessing what his response may be… In any event, I regret you will both have to excuse me now. It has been an honour meeting you, Captain, but I am afraid I have an appointment I must keep."

He stood up and gave Theodotus a polite bow.

"That sounds very mysterious, Nebit," said Theodotus, not bothering to stand. "Are you running off to see some secret girlfriend?"

It was a crass and cruel joke. Nebit blinked in surprise as he took it in. His cheeks started to flush in humiliation and for once he seemed lost for words. He nodded to me and turned silently to the door.

"Nebit," I called after him, "thank you for your time. I'll see you tomorrow."

"What a comical creature," Theodotus remarked, after the Egyptian had left. "You should put him on display in the marketplace."

"I know he's odd, Theodotus, but he's alright," I replied. "There's more to him than you might imagine."

"Really? From the sound of his voice, I'd have thought there was rather less to him than I might imagine."

"Drop it, please. I said he's alright."

"As you wish, Dion."

"Thank you. I don't want to quarrel. Now, my friend, what are you doing this evening? Would you allow me to bask in the radiance of your glory by having dinner with me?"

"No, I'm afraid I can't," he replied with a smile. "I've got to get back to Plymmerium. I only stopped by to congratulate you on not murdering any more of your own officers while I was away. But why don't you walk to the barge with me?"

I accompanied him only as far as my family's villa, where I had decided to spend a night or two every week to keep the household in order, now that my mother was no longer around. One of Theodotus's slaves followed silently behind us, carrying a heavy-looking sack over his shoulder. From the clanking it made, I guessed it contained his master's armour.

"You know, what you did with your squadron was really quite something," I said, as we crossed the bridge onto the Avenue of Athena. "But I've been meaning to ask you, why did you sail on to Pachynus afterwards? You'd no sooner got back than you left again."

"Oh, don't you know?" he replied. "I was delivering a little present from the king to the people there. One of the mercenary transports we captured."

"I see," I said.

A group of men was blocking the end of the bridge. They seemed to be arguing about something. I barked at them to get out of the way and they fell silent and grudgingly parted to let us through.

"So tell me, what did you do with it? The transport, I mean?" I asked the question, even though I could already half-guess the answer.

Theodotus shrugged.

"We sailed it to within half a mile of the coast, and then we rammed it. I don't know how many of the poor bastards managed to swim ashore. Most, I imagine. Anyway, we'd arranged for young Hieronymus and his men to meet them on the beach. We didn't stay to watch what he did with them, but I'm sure he had fun."

It was not till sometime later that I heard that Hieronymus had been obliged to improvise, a mass crucifixion being too impractical. As the mercenaries crawled out of the sea, he had them trussed up instead, with their legs bent double and their wrists strapped to their ankles. He had left them writhing on the beach for days, while the locals came and mocked them. Most lost their eyes to the gulls before they died of thirst. Later, the prince was able to decorate the cliffs of Pachynus with over eight hundred heads, mounted on poles. After a week or two of being cured in the sun, they apparently came to resemble a crop of black, rotting melons.

To me, it seemed a waste of a perfectly good ship, but I dare say the spectacle provided some consolation for all the returning refugees. I wondered if Alexander, the boy who had ridden on my shoulders, had been among those who went down to the beach to crow at the dying men.

✳

Our quinqueremes were de-masted again and hauled back up into their sheds to be cleaned and caulked. The reservists returned to their families and their trades, each one walking a little taller than he ever had before, and all of them now the owners of a story to share with wide-eyed children. The army's work, however, was not quite done.

Through Nebit, I learnt that Hieron had decided to send just five companies of the Gold Shields to Rome. Half of my old division was still in Pachynus with Hieronymus; the other ten companies had been left kicking their heels at Plymmerium when the fleet had put to sea. They would now have their own chance to earn a little glory. Gelon apparently arranged for the ten senior company lieutenants to draw lots, to see which of them would be joining the army the Romans were assembling.

One of the quinqueremes that Andranodoros had captured had been patched up and given new sails and rigging. It was to be a present from Hieron to the Romans. When the ship was ready, the five lucky lieutenants boarded it with their companies. They would crew it themselves.

Although it was only a small command, I would have jumped at it, but of course I was passed over again, this time in favour of Sosis. I suppose he had the better claim: after all, he was the captain of the Gold Shields now. I went down to the Little Harbour to embrace him and wish him luck.

"Have you seen the state of this fucking thing, Dion?" he called out to me cheerfully, as he mounted the gangplank. "We'd be safer in a boat made of straw."

He was right. Hieron must have selected the oldest and most rotten of the captured warships to give the Romans. In my father's day, Carthage had been the greatest sea power on earth, but judging by the ships we had taken, whatever remained of their fleet seemed barely fit for kindling.

Sosis took the second Carthaginian transport ship with him. It had lain at anchor in the Great Harbour for a week, with the defecting mercenaries still on board. We had sent them food, but only their commander had been allowed ashore. He had been given a little silver for himself and his men, with the promise of more when they returned from fighting Hannibal. Our king was famously contemptuous of mercenaries, and they were fortunate not to have shared the fate of their comrades at Pachynus, but Hieron was thrifty, even in his vengeance. It was typical of the elegance of his methods that he should answer an unwelcome demand from Rome with an unwanted windfall from Carthage.

Sosis and his men sailed without much fanfare. The king stayed in his palace and only a small crowd of relatives gathered on the wharf to wave them off. As the quinquereme slipped through the narrow mouth of our sea walls, I wished for the hundredth time that I had never left the army. It seemed as though every man in Syracuse was getting the chance to fight, except for me. My battle sword of Seric iron lay on my bedroom table like some chained animal, its patterns of whorls twisting and turning impatiently for release.

The date for the celebration of the fleet's victory had been set for a few days after Sosis sailed. On the eve of the festivities, I was eating dinner alone in my bedroom, when Alpha came gliding in to tell me that a slave had arrived, with a message that I was wanted in the council chamber. To Alpha's visible dismay, I left my food unfinished and hurried downstairs. When I got there, I found Prince Gelon, Andranodoros and my cousin Thraso already seated at the table with the king. It seemed I was joining the tail end of their meeting. I bowed to Hieron and nodded politely to the others. It was the first time I had seen Gelon since he had returned from Rome. He stood up, smiled warmly and embraced me. As he did so, Archimedes also came shuffling in with his cane.

"Pull up a chair, Archimedes. You too, Dion," Hieron said amiably. "I've asked you to join us because I wish to discuss the city's defences," he went on, as we settled ourselves down. "As Dion knows, a little while ago I asked Archimedes to inspect the walls. So tell us, Archimedes, what have you concluded? Do you have any suggestions to make?"

My great-uncle grinned, favouring us all with a glimpse of his nearly toothless gums.

"I do have some ideas, as it happens," he replied. "But there are a few things I'm afraid I'm going to need. I've got a list somewhere here." He began rummaging through his tunic. "Perhaps, Andranodoros, as our new Royal Treasurer, you might be kind enough to arrange some purchases for me? Now, where did I put it? Ah yes, here it is." He produced a crumpled scrap of papyrus.

"Just let me know how I can be of help, Archimedes," Andranodoros replied smoothly. "I'm afraid I'm not quite on top of things yet at the treasury, but I'll pass on your requests to my secretaries."

"My dear boy, that's very kind of you. Tell me, do you still practise your mathematics? I remember you used to be terribly good at algebra. Or are you too busy nowadays?"

"You'll be pleased to hear, Archimedes, that mathematics is all I seem to have been doing since I got back. Perhaps His Majesty should have put you in charge of the treasury instead. So tell me, what is it you need?"

"Oh yes, let me see. Shall I read it out? Yes, that might be easiest." My great-uncle coughed and flattened out the papyrus on the table with the palms of his hands. "To start with, then, a large workshop, at least twice the size of a quinquereme shed. It would probably be best if it were outside the city, away from prying eyes. The use of a foundry. Twenty stonemasons, forty blacksmiths, a hundred carpenters and ten wheelwrights. Eight thousand feet of horsehair rope; two thousand feet of heavy chain; two thousand ingots of iron, and fifty sheets of beaten copper. Five hundred trunks of seasoned hardwood and a similar quantity of seasoned softwood. Also five hundred low-grade limestone blocks of four tons each. I'll need a separate workshop for the stonemasons, by the way, but that can be smaller. Two hundred hides of leather. Three hundred male slaves in good health. Twenty oxen and ten large carts. And lastly, if my great-nephew can spare him, I should also like to borrow Secretary Nebit for a little while."

He looked up and smiled.

"I may need more chain later."

There was a long silence. Finally, Andranodoros cleared his throat.

"I take it this is a joke, Archimedes?"

Archimedes raised his thick white eyebrows.

"Certainly not, my dear fellow."

"Archimedes, have you any idea what all that would *cost*?"

"Not a clue," replied Archimedes blithely. "As our Royal Treasurer, I rather thought I might leave that side of things to you."

"But what on earth is it all for?" Andranodoros asked.

"Oh, artillery, mostly. Catapults and so on." Archimedes smiled and spread his arms wide. "*Big* ones."

Andranodoros stared at my great-uncle incredulously.

The king coughed.

"So what does everyone else think? What's your view, Thraso?" he asked.

My cousin frowned thoughtfully.

"Your Majesty, I know nothing of warfare, but it seems an extraordinary stroke of luck that the world's most famous engineer happens to live in Syracuse. I think it would be very strange if we failed to take advantage of the fact. And in any case, what is our gold for, if not to make the city as safe as possible?"

Hieron turned to me. His face, as usual, gave no hint of his own thoughts.

"Do you have an opinion, Dion?"

"My King, my great-uncle is right to point out that we lack artillery, but then so does Hannibal. He has no siege engines. If he comes to Syracuse, he will almost certainly try to starve us out, rather than assault the walls. That's the greatest danger. So our first priority should be to fill the city granaries. If there is still gold to spare after that, then by all means, build artillery as well."

Hieron nodded.

"Your Majesty," said Andranodoros, "Dion makes a good point. And we mustn't forget that the Romans are preparing to march on Hannibal as we speak. In a few weeks' time, he may be hanging from a cross. Shouldn't we at least wait to see how things turn out, before committing to all this expenditure?"

Hieron scratched the corner of his mouth.

"Andranodoros," he said eventually, "do you know what happens if you try to lance a boil before it's ripe?"

"It gets worse, Your Majesty."

"Exactly so. I rather fear our Roman friends may find that Hannibal is a boil not yet ripe for lancing. In any event, Hannibal is not my only concern."

The king looked at Gelon and raised his eyebrows. The prince pursed his lips and nodded silently to his father. It seemed the two of them were in agreement.

"You are right to question the expense, Andranodoros," Hieron resumed, "but as I recall, Dion's famous ancestor became master of the seas because he was the first man to build a quinquereme. No doubt his treasurer also baulked at the cost. Who knows? Perhaps Archimedes' catapults will give us a similar advantage. So this is what I should like you to do. Get a good night's rest. You still look exhausted. Tomorrow we are due to celebrate your splendid victory, but when you return to the treasury the day after tomorrow, your first task should be to calculate how much all these things that Archimedes has asked for will cost. And your second can be to start buying them for him."

"Father," said Gelon, "there's an old granary at Plymmerium that we don't use any more. It must be more than twice the size of a quinquereme shed. It's not in very good shape, but perhaps that might serve as a workshop. What do you think, Archimedes?"

My great-uncle gave the prince a wide grin.

"My dear boy, it sounds like it might do very well indeed," he replied.

Andranodoros shrugged and sighed.

"It seems I'm to be remembered as the man who ruined the kingdom in his first month as treasurer," he said. "Well, I suppose you'd better give me that list, Archimedes."

"Good," said Hieron. "That's that, then. I shall see you all tomorrow at the celebrations. Andranodoros, help me up, will you?"

The two of them left by a door that must have led to the royal family's private quarters by some round-about route. The king was leaning on his son-in-law's arm.

"I think you're going to make an excellent treasurer," I heard him say as they walked slowly off together. "I like a treasurer who enjoys collecting my money more than spending it."

The rest of us headed out into the great courtyard. Thraso and Archimedes said goodnight and I found myself standing alone with Gelon in the warm evening air. He looked up at the rising moon.

"How was Rome?" I asked.

"Interesting, Dion, interesting. I met their two new consuls. They're going to divide the command again. They never learn. Paullus seems a competent fellow, but Varro is a typical Roman prick. Another glory-hungry idiot, just like Flaminius. But at least they should outnumber Hannibal nearly two to one when they finally get round to marching on him. So who knows? Maybe they'll even manage to win this time, although if there's a way to fuck it up, Varro strikes me as the sort of man who can find it."

I laughed.

"May I offer you some wine?" I said.

The prince looked me in the eyes and smiled sadly.

"No, not tonight I'm afraid, Dion, but thank you. I've got to get to bed. I've had a long day."

The Temple of Zeus lies a mile or so inland, halfway between the city and the camp at Plymmerium, on a gently rising slope that faces out across the blue expanse of the Great Harbour. The house of the Father of the Gods is exactly aligned with the mouth of the bay. Nearby stands the long stone altar of his daughter Athena, who, the priests tell us, was born from Zeus's head after he had seduced and then eaten her mother. An enviable approach to maternity, I have often thought. Athena has another, smaller altar outside her own temple on Ortygia, but the space there is too confined for a great public ceremony.

At dawn, our gates were thrown open and a trickle of families began heading out of the city, eager to find themselves choice spots near the altar. It would be a warm day and they carried their own water flasks: the only slaves permitted to attend were those who had official work to do. Children skipped beside their parents as they made their way along the road through the marshes. Religious ceremonies were among the few occasions on which men and women could mix openly with each other, although the women would stay close by their husbands' or fathers' sides, and would not speak directly to the men of other families.

When they arrived at the broad meadow where the altar lies, the families made themselves comfortable on the grass. By midday, maybe a hundred thousand people had gathered on the slope in their brightly coloured robes and tunics. To any fisherman casting his nets in the bay, the distant spectacle must have resembled a rippling mass of wild flowers.

Several rows of stools had been set up in a wide semicircle around the altar for the nobility. My class was willing to fight and die alongside the common people, but we preferred not to sit with them. I arrived late in the morning, by which time men and women in purple robes had taken most of the stools. Seeing my blue tunic, a soldier directed me to a place in the front row near the centre. Archimedes hadn't bothered showing up, but a dozen or so other councillors were already there with their wives and children, seated in a line. They all put on a great show of smiling and nodding to me as I walked past them, as if my arrival had made their day. Fortunately, I found myself with Thraso to my right, while to my left were the cushioned chairs reserved for the royal party.

As the sun approached the apex of its arc, the king arrived. Hieron rode on a simple, horse-drawn cart, on which a chair had been fastened, with the rest of his family following on foot. As if of one mind, the people stood and began cheering when they saw their king. He smiled and waved weakly to them. The cart skirted the edge of the crowd and pulled up in front of the long stone altar. Two slaves carefully lifted Hieron down and helped him to his place in the centre of the front row. Gelon took a seat next to his father, giving me a friendly nod as he did so, and the other members of the royal family settled down around them.

The chair immediately beside mine remained empty, but somewhat awkwardly, Nereis, Prince Gelon's narrow-eyed wife, ended up taking the next place along. She descended from a celebrated line of royal lunatics. Her great-great-grandfather was none other than the murderous Agathocles, whose helmet Hieronymus had worn. Agathocles had married off his only daughter to King Pyrrhus of Epirus, a man almost as unremittingly violent as himself. Nereis and her children, the acne-riddled Hieronymus and his sister, Harmonia, were the last living descendants of that ominous union. Hieronymus was still kicking his heels in Pachynus, but Harmonia and Woodpecker, her husband, were both with the royal party and had seated themselves between Nereis and Gelon.

Nereis gazed at me malevolently. I dare say she blamed me for the humiliation my men had inflicted on her darling son at his parade. After a moment, she leant over to her son-in-law and whispered something to him. They stood up and swapped places.

I sighed as Woodpecker sat down. I would rather have endured the hostility of Nereis than the tedium of his company. In despair, I looked at Thraso but he was already chatting politely to the councillor on his other side.

"Hello, Dion," Woodpecker said loudly, forcing me to turn back round to greet him.

"Hello, Themistos," I said.

He leant across the empty chair between us, stabbing at me with his nose.

"So, how's business going, Dion? I'll let you into a little secret. I've been investing in bronze myself. Done very nicely out of it, too. The price just keeps on going up and up." He brayed happily at his own good fortune.

"Congratulations," I said.

"It's not too late to get in, you know. I could let you have some of my own holdings if you want... By the way, did you know I have over two thousand slaves in the quarries now? That's nearly twice as many as I started with three years ago. You must come and have a look round. Managing the place can really get quite exhausting at times, but I soldier on."

"Good for you," I said.

"You know, when I took over the quarries from my father, the average lifetime yield of a slave was only about a hundred tons of limestone. I've managed to get it up to over a hundred and twenty tons now." He brayed gaily again. "I'll tell you how I did it..."

As Woodpecker jabbed and jabbered away, I glanced along the row of chairs. Harmonia was watching her husband as he talked to me. Her expression was disdainful, although I couldn't tell whether her contempt was directed at Woodpecker, or me, or both of us. She was a plain and scrawny girl, but her sneer exuded a ferocity that would have made her mother's swivel-eyed ancestors proud. We had never spoken, of course, and probably never would, and as soon as she noticed I was looking at her, she turned away. No wonder Gelon spent so little time with his family, I thought.

Zoippos and his wife Heraclia, the elder of Hieron's two daughters, were seated a few places further along, on the far side of the king, with three girls between them. Two of the girls were small and fair-haired, so I assumed they were Zoippos's own children, but the third was wearing a veil. I guessed this must be Vita, my wife-to-be. She was facing away from me. Zoippos's daughters leant forward, shot me a furtive glance and began giggling. Their mother turned to see what they were tittering about. Heraclia had the face of a buzzard. Our eyes met and I nodded courteously to her. She snorted in disgust, then turned back to hiss something angrily at her children.

A few moments later, a trumpet sounded three long blasts and the vast crowd gradually fell silent. I put Vita out of my mind.

"... So managing our public works when Archimedes steps down would be an obvious move for me," Woodpecker was saying. "Perhaps you could put in a word on my behalf with the king, Dion? I hear he rather likes you. Naturally, I'd make it worth your while..."

Prince Gelon leant forward.

"Shut up, Themistos," he whispered irritably to his son-in-law.

The gossip was that Gelon had been forced to accept the match by the king, who had wanted to bring the quarries under the royal family's control. As Themistos seemed to have nothing much else to commend him, I imagine that was probably true.

A large tent had been erected to the side of the altar and from this a procession now started to emerge. Andranodoros and my friend Theodotus walked in front, dressed in simple white tunics. My tiny and wizened great-aunt Delia, the High Priestess of Athena, tottered between them, her arms threaded through theirs. Next came Eryx with my Aunt Maia, Thraso's mother, who looked terrified. She and my mother were the two most senior priestesses after Delia, and given my great-aunt's incapacity, took it in turns to perform Delia's duties on her behalf. Today Maia would have to preside over the ceremonies, as I had refused to let my mother return to Syracuse for the occasion. I was still annoyed with her for having had our steward beaten to death.

The thirty-four army lieutenants who had captained our ships followed in single file. The procession slowly made its way down the path that ran along the front of the long, low altar. Forced to walk at my great-aunt's pace, it took a while for Andranodoros and Theodotus to reach the king. When they had drawn level with him, they turned to face him and bowed. My great-aunt didn't seem to understand quite what was going on. She looked at Hieron, smiled happily and winked at him. Andranodoros and Theodotus escorted her towards the empty chair next to mine. Theodotus grinned at me, clearly amused by my discomfort.

I stood to greet them.

"Great-aunt Delia, you are looking very well," I whispered awkwardly, as I helped her into her seat.

"I have no idea who you are, young man," she replied, "but you have an interesting face. Honey and salt, kind and cruel, that's how the goddess likes her gruel."

"I'm Dion, your great-nephew," I said gently.

"Oh, are you Korinna's boy, then? Goodness, you've certainly grown since I last saw you. What a titan you've become. How is your father these days, Dion? He should never have married that bitch, you know."

"He's very well, thank you," I said, not knowing how else to respond.

She turned to Woodpecker.

"You're not my husband."

"No indeed, Lady Delia," he replied condescendingly. "I am Themistos, Prince Gelon's son-in-law. You may remember we met last year, at the Festival of Eleutheria."

My great-aunt furrowed her brow.

"No, I don't remember," she replied after a moment. "But I am afraid my memory isn't what it used to be. And you don't seem a very memorable sort of person. Now do stop trying to talk to me. It isn't becoming."

The ceremonies began. My Aunt Maia stepped forward and mumbled her way through a lengthy prayer to the goddess. When she had finished, she and all the men in the procession mounted the short flight of steps to the altar. A slave led the first cow up onto the stone platform from the field behind. Bright ribbons had been tied to its legs and tail. Maia took her place on one side of the animal, while the slave handed Andranodoros the short length of rope that had been fastened round its neck. My aunt lifted up a silver jug and poured some water over the cow's head. It lowed and nodded as she did so, signalling its assent to the sacrifice. Theodotus and Eryx threw handfuls of barley seeds over the animal while the slave tied its legs together to prevent it thrashing out, and then Andranodoros quickly slit its throat.

Altogether thirty-four cows were sacrificed, one for every ship that had safely returned to us. Each ship's captain slaughtered his own animal, which he was supposed to have paid for himself, although I learnt later that Andranodoros had donated the whole herd, a remarkably generous gesture. One by one, the livers of the animals were brought on a silver tray to my great-aunt for inspection, who prodded and poked them with a bent finger, before declaring the sacrifice acceptable to the goddess.

When the last cow had been killed, fires were lit at the back of the altar along its entire length. Teams of slaves set about butchering the carcasses, while other slaves began cooking the cuts. Only the long bones would be left in the flames, for the gods to enjoy. Everything else had to be consumed before sunset and it would probably be the first meat that many of our citizens had tasted in weeks. Behind me, families began to stand up to stretch their legs or go looking for friends. People clustered around in groups, chatting and laughing with each other as children scampered around their legs.

My great-aunt had dozed off, so my cousin Thraso and I detached ourselves from our fellow councillors and went to eat with some of my officers and their families. Nebit was there too. At some point shortly after nightfall, Prince Gelon strolled over to join us.

"Dion, there you are," he said. "I've been looking for you. Your great-aunt is asking for you. At least, I think it's you she's asking for," he added with a chuckle. "She's still sitting with my family. By the way, I'm sorry if I've seemed rather remote recently. My father has been keeping me pretty busy. I'll try to drop by your rooms one evening this week."

He looked me in the eyes and smiled sadly, but a face over my shoulder suddenly caught his attention. He broke into a wide grin.

"Xeno, is that you, you one-handed old bastard?" he shouted out happily. "Hasn't anyone done us the kindness of killing you yet?"

I left them to it and went to find my great-aunt. She was where I had left her, sucking on a rib and talking to a dark-skinned old man with an extremely long beard who had taken my stool. My Aunt Maia was sitting on Delia's other side, watching on with an expression of affectionate amusement. I noticed Hieron was also still in his place, a few paces further along the row, chatting to Andranodoros and my friend Theodotus.

"Hello, Dion," Maia said with a kindly smile as I approached. She stood up and embraced me. "How are you? I hear you and my son have finally become firm friends. I'm so pleased."

"I am too, Aunt. Although why a clever man like Thraso should choose to befriend me is a mystery."

She laughed lightly. We both knew I had been the one who used to disdain Thraso's company.

"I shall leave you with Aunt Delia. I don't know what she wants to talk to you about, Nephew, but if you'll take my advice, you'll listen carefully to whatever she has to say. Don't waste this moment. You may never get another."

I inclined my head politely.

"Of course, Aunt," I said. "By the way, Thraso's just over there with some of my men, if you'd care to join us?"

"No, thank you, Dion. I must be getting home. But do call round to see me some time. Thraso tries to come home at least once a week. Have him bring you along, if you can bear the company of a dull old widow."

"Thank you," I said. She smiled at me again, then turned and walked away, leaving me alone with the High Priestess and the old man.

"You wanted to see me, Great-aunt?" I said politely.

"Did I? And who are you?" she replied, continuing to gum at the rib. The prohibition on eating sacrificed meat after nightfall did not appear to apply to her.

"I'm Dion, your great-nephew," I replied. "Korinna's son."

"Are you indeed? Goodness, you've certainly shot up since I last saw you."

"Yes, it's been a while," I said tactfully.

"Sit down here next to me, Dion." She scrutinised the bone to see if she had missed anything, and having satisfied herself, dropped it onto the grass.

"Have you met my great-nephew, Tabnit?" she said, turning to her companion. "Such a naughty child. I imagine his mother wishes she'd handed him over to you when he was born."

The old man raised his long white eyebrows and began chuckling.

"Now who's being naughty, Lady Delia?" he replied, with a slight accent. He had a sly face. From his Phoenician name, I guessed he was one of our Carthaginian citizens, which only made it even more peculiar that my great-aunt should be talking to him.

"Are you a tutor then, Tabnit?" I asked, leaning forward to face him. "I'm afraid my tutors never had much joy with me."

"Don't be silly, Dion," interrupted Delia with a titter. "Tabnit is the priest of Ba'al here in the city. He doesn't teach children; he burns them. It pleases his god, apparently. I've never tried it myself. I wonder if the goddess would appreciate it."

She smiled at me.

"Pay no attention to your great-aunt, Captain," Tabnit said with a grin. "It's been many years since we've sacrificed any children here. Unfortunately, the king forbids it. Perhaps that is why none of my people ever wants to go home to Carthage. But if you will excuse me, I think I should leave you two to talk alone... Lady Delia, as always, it has been a joy to see you. Captain, I am honoured to have made your acquaintance."

He stood and nodded politely to me. My great-aunt watched him walk away.

"What a charming man," she said, with obvious sincerity.

"Yes, indeed," I replied, with rather less confidence.

"I'm so pleased you were able to be of such help to his people."

"I'm sorry?"

She looked at me in surprise.

"Oh dear. You don't know what I'm talking about, do you? Hasn't that happened yet?"

"Hasn't what happened, Great-aunt?"

She frowned and pursed her lips, as if trying to remember something.

"How silly of me... You must forgive me. I'm afraid I sometimes get my yesterdays and tomorrows a little muddled up."

Her mind appeared to have slipped again. She seemed to be confusing me with someone else entirely.

"Delia, I'm Dion, your great-nephew," I said gently.

"Yes, who else would you be...? You know, your mother's been waiting to succeed me for years." She cackled. "I only stay alive to spite her."

"I'm sure that's not true, Great-aunt."

She stared into my eyes for a long moment. Her own sparkled in the dark like distant stars. Then, to my surprise, she softly patted my cheek.

"A titan perhaps, but still a sad little boy, eh?"

I didn't know what to say. The dancing shadows cast by the fires on the altar exaggerated the lines on her small, wrinkled face. She must have been as old as Hieron.

"Well now, Dion," she continued, wiping the grease from her lips and licking the tips of her bent fingers, "I have a message for you from the goddess. She still comes to me sometimes in my dreams, you know. Anyway, she wants me to tell you that the way to her is dangerous."

I am not a pious man, but only a fool would dismiss the words of a High Priestess out of hand, especially one who lived in the mists between sanity and madness, where the gods are said to play.

I scratched my cheek thoughtfully.

"I'm grateful to you for telling me, Great-aunt," I said. "But I'm afraid I don't quite understand. If you'll forgive me for asking, what does it mean?"

She shrugged her tiny, rounded shoulders and smiled.

"How on earth should I know? She just asked me to tell you that the way to her is dangerous. Make of it what you will. But at least one thing seems obvious, Dion. The goddess has taken an interest in you. She is watching you."

"Thank you," I said again.

"Well, that's all I have to say to you. Now, would you do me a kindness? Please go and tell my husband that I'm tired and would like to go home. That's him sitting over there, playing with the spiders."

She nodded towards the king.

Hieron was still talking to the two heroes of the day, Andranodoros and Theodotus.

XII

CANNAE

Delia died in her sleep three weeks later.

My Aunt Maia supervised the preparation and laying out of the body in the pretty little courtyard of Delia's villa. My father had provided the house for her use, and had staffed it with slave women for her. When he had died, my mother had begrudgingly allowed the arrangement to continue. No doubt my lawyer would want to rent it out now, and would try to sell the slaves – although most of them looked nearly as old as Delia had been. I made a mental note to see to it that they were cared for instead. I thought my great-aunt would like that.

The following morning, the doors of the villa were thrown open, to allow the citizens of Syracuse to pay their respects. Thousands must have filed past over the course of the day, while Maia, my sisters and the relays of mourners whom I had hired sang the customary dirges. I stood beside the little crinkle-faced corpse, silently nodding and being nodded to, till my neck ached.

Shortly before sunset, just as I was on the point of ordering the gates closed again, I heard the clattering of a cart in the street outside. A few moments later, to my astonishment, the king himself shuffled slowly in, on the arms of two men of the Royal Watch. I immediately left my place and went to greet him.

"Dion, my boy," he wheezed, "I wonder if I might ask a favour of you. Would you be so kind as to clear the courtyard for me?

I should very much like a few moments alone with your great-aunt."

I did as he asked, and had a chair brought out for him and placed by the body.

To this day, I have no idea what may have passed between my great-aunt and the king in life, or what drew him to her side upon her death. I suppose I might have asked Archimedes, but I never did. The old have their secrets too. I know only that Hieron sat by Delia's corpse for maybe half an hour, and when he left, his cold blue eyes seemed emptier than ever.

My great-aunt was buried the following day. By custom, the High Priestess was accorded the honour of a public funeral. Hieron stayed in his palace, but everyone else whom I knew came, and a great many more whom I didn't. My friends and enemies, the highborn and the poor, the young and the old all crushed into the cemetery to participate in the occasion. I think it was not so much grief that impelled them to attend, as foreboding. My great-aunt had presided over the temple for almost as long as Hieron had been our king, and her death felt strangely ominous, like a loosening of the kingdom's planks.

Apart from the king, the only conspicuous absentee was my mother. I had felt obliged to send her my permission to return to Syracuse. There would be rites to observe at the temple and at the grave over the next few weeks, and I had no wish to prevent her from performing her sacred duties. She managed to get back to the city two days after my great-aunt was buried. She had left the estate in Catana within a few hours of receiving my message, even though there was no prospect of arriving in time for the funeral. But it was not to honour Delia that she had hurried home.

Only a woman whose father or husband had been the head of my family, and who was already an initiate of the goddess, was eligible to become the High Priestess. That meant there were just three candidates to replace Delia: my Aunt Maia, my elder sister, Dionysia, whom I seldom saw and whose only interest in life seemed to be the unceasing production of children, and my mother. My mother was so far the most prominent of the three, and so obviously the most capable, that her succession seemed a foregone conclusion. The matter required only the formal assent of the senate.

The senate, I should explain, was an institutional vestige of the republic that had preceded Hieron's reign. When he had taken the throne, Hieron had chosen to preserve it, presumably in order to avoid the appearance of tyranny. Ever since, its main purpose had been to approve whatever laws the Royal Council proposed, which, after exhaustive debate, it invariably did. The only other function it performed, to the best of my memory, was the appointment of various civic officials and the high priests of the temples.

Twenty seats in the senate were reserved for the heads of the oldest families in the city, although we never bothered attending, unless there was an appointment to be made that touched upon our interests. The other eighty members were chosen by popular vote. These men seemed to hold in common a strange belief that the principal purpose of language was to communicate the importance of their own existence to anyone within earshot. For the most part, the membership comprised of prosperous merchants and lawyers, although every now and again, our citizens would delight in electing an illiterate fishmonger or grocer, just to annoy all the other senators.

The king had retained for himself the privilege of appointing the senate speaker, who was the man tasked with arranging and presiding over its dreary deliberations. Fittingly enough, Hieron had chosen Leatherskin, the thrusting arriviste, for the post. Leatherskin duly announced that the senate would convene to elect the city's next High Priestess as soon as the period of mourning for Delia had officially concluded, thirty-one days after her funeral.

✷

One evening, a few days after Delia was buried, Nebit called on me in my apartment at the palace. He now only worked one day a week in his office in the barracks yard; the rest of the time, he spent with Archimedes at Plymmerium, organising the construction of the mysterious contraptions my great-uncle was designing.

Alpha opened the door to him and he glided in, wearing one of his oversized and garish gowns.

I put down my work and stood to greet him. He bowed politely to me. As he did so, I noticed Agbal slip out through the door to the anteroom.

"My dear Captain, I do hope you will forgive the intrusion," he said unctuously.

"You are always welcome, my friend," I replied. "Will you take a seat?"

To call him a friend was an exaggeration of course, and a cynical one. I dare say he knew it, but it was enough for him that I should treat him with courtesy. To be the object of anyone's genuine affection was, for Nebit, a dream of which he had probably been disabused in childhood.

He settled himself on a couch as Omega entered the room with an ugly silver jug. Omega poured out two cups of water and silently brought them to us. He bowed to each of us in turn before handing them over, and then took up the position in the corner that Agbal should have occupied.

"I am afraid I am here on a slightly delicate matter," the Egyptian said, puckering his lips and taking a small sip from the cup. "As you know, my dear Captain, in a little while, the senate will be choosing a new High Priestess, to succeed your august and universally lamented great-aunt."

I grunted unhappily. My mother's election filled me with apprehension. Once she was installed in the office, I could hardly send her back to Catana. Nebit smiled.

"It has been made known to me that His Majesty believes your Aunt Maia would make an excellent High Priestess."

I stared at him.

"I couldn't agree more, Nebit," I said cautiously.

"I am sure the king will be pleased to hear it. You will understand, of course, that His Majesty feels it would be quite improper for him to try to exert any direct influence over the senate in this matter."

I raised my eyebrows.

"However," Nebit went on, "there is nothing to prevent you from making your own feelings known to your senatorial colleagues."

So that was it.

"I shall be sure to do so," I replied, and smiled back.

"I knew you would understand," he purred. We chatted politely for a while about his work with Archimedes, before he made his excuses and left me to my thoughts.

The following morning, I supervised the drills in the exercise yard as usual, then left the palace and headed down the Avenue of Athena to the villa. I had not visited my mother since her return from the country. I still hadn't forgiven her for the murder of our steward.

The suggestion that our king might be too squeamish to interfere directly in the business of the senate was laughable. If Hieron wished to prevent my mother becoming High Priestess, he would only have to summon Leatherskin and make his feelings plain. No one in the senate would dare defy him. But I had seen how Hieron operated. It was because he was playing another, more subtle game that he had chosen to use me as his cat's paw instead. I was certain he had sensed an opportunity to drive my mother and me further apart. He wanted her to blame me for wrecking her ambitions, not him. She was the brains and I the brawn of the House of Dionysius. The more fractious our relationship, the happier he would be.

I didn't mind. If she never spoke to me again, it would be a relief.

It may sound strange, given that I am hardly the pious type, but I would never have presumed to meddle in the affairs of the temple, just for the sake of my own convenience. But now that Hieron had asked me to intervene, I felt justified in doing so. I reasoned that he could not have ruled for fifty years without the blessing of Athena; in serving his ends, I was probably serving Hers too. At least, that's what I told myself.

All the same, to scheme behind my mother's back with the little windbags of the senate was beneath my dignity, and nor did I have any wish to subject her to the humiliation of being publicly passed over. I had decided to take a more direct approach.

When I arrived at my villa, I sent one of the slaves on duty at the gate to find my mother and bring her to me in the garden.

"And tell her not to keep me waiting," I shouted at him as he ambled off. I walked through to the garden and sat down on the bench by the pond.

She timed her appearance perfectly, of course, keeping me waiting just long enough to needle me, but not quite long enough to justify a scene.

"Hello, Mother," I said coldly as she approached. "Have a seat." I didn't stand to embrace her.

She settled herself in a chair facing me and looked me silently in the eyes. Her expression was unreadable.

"I need to tell you about a conversation I had with Nebit last night," I began, not bothering with any small talk.

I had already cut off her right hand, by depriving her of control of our family affairs; and now I proceeded to cut off her left hand too, by sinking her hopes of succeeding Delia. It was a brutal encounter, but she had overreached herself. Minor phenomenon or not, I told myself, she needed to learn her place once and for all.

The following afternoon, I had a proclamation read out in my mother's name in the agora and from the steps of all the temples in the city. It announced that she did not wish the senate to consider her for the position of High Priestess. She preferred to withdraw from public life and spend her remaining time quietly in the bosom of her family. She prayed that the goddess would continue to extend her protection over the city and the king.

Once the official mourning for Delia was over, I would send her back to Catana.

The remaining high weeks of the summer passed uneventfully for me. Each of the twelve Guards companies was now under the command of two designated lieutenants, one senior and one junior, but I had retained Castor's practice of rotating the companies around the city garrisons every four months. It gave me the opportunity to scrutinise and train them myself when they were assigned to palace duty. I was beginning to enjoy the settled routine of my palace life.

And then, everything changed.

As if from nowhere, the series of disasters that was to reshape my world started to crash down upon our kingdom.

I had just returned from a run in the hills with one of the palace companies when I received the first inkling that all was not well. As usual, I was the first back to the exercise yard, although for once, a sergeant had stayed stubbornly on my heels all the way and had very nearly managed to overtake me at the last. As soon as I was back through the gates, I ripped open the fastenings of my breastplate, gratefully threw it off and fell to my knees. A few moments later, the sergeant collapsed beside me. He groaned and rolled over onto his back.

Agbal was waiting for me. He sprinted over with a grin, picked up the breastplate and handed me a flask of water. I took a few gulps and passed it to the sergeant with a nod.

"Maybe next time, Leon," I said consolingly. He groaned again. Still panting, I struggled to my feet.

"Before I forget, Master, there's an urgent message for you," Agbal said, fishing a small scroll out of his tunic. I recognised the seal at once: it was the king's own. I immediately broke it open.

Captain Dion, the note read,
    His Majesty requires your attendance in his audience chamber this afternoon, at the eighth hour.

I glanced up at the sundial above the gates. I had precious little time to clean up.

"Fetch me a blue tunic, Agbal," I said. "I'll be in the bathhouse."

Why should Hieron want to see me in the audience chamber, I wondered nervously, as I dragged my exhausted legs across the yard. The last time I had been summoned there, it had been to answer for the death of Malmeides.

Two men of the Royal Watch in full armour and carrying spears stood outside the high doors of the chamber and opened them for me as I approached. Hieron was already in his throne on the dais at the far end, looking small and fragile, with two further bodyguards standing close behind him. Prince Gelon sat next to the king with a face of granite, tapping his knee with a scroll of papyrus. Below the dais, two rows of stools had been set out facing each other across the room. All but two were already occupied by other councillors; whatever was going on, it seemed it was not about me, at least. With a weak wave of his hand, the king silently gestured for me to take a seat as well. I found myself between Andranodoros and the last vacant stool.

"Do you know what this is about?" I whispered to Andranodoros.

"Not a clue," he replied. He also seemed ill at ease.

We all waited in silence for several minutes. Finally, the doors were opened again and Archimedes shuffled in with a cane and his usual expression of benign bewilderment.

"Oh dear," he said. "I'm so terribly sorry if I've kept you all. I'm afraid I lost track of time."

"Well, at least you're here now," said Gelon a little irritably. "Please take a seat." He pointed to the empty place beside me.

Archimedes shambled over.

"Do make a little room, Dion," he said testily. I turned my shoulder to accommodate him.

When Archimedes had finally settled himself down, with much clattering of his cane and further half-whispered apologies to the man on his other side, the prince cleared his throat.

"Thank you all for coming," he began. "None of you is to repeat a word of anything that you are about to hear. Is that understood?"

He gazed slowly round the room and we all nodded dutifully.

"Very well," he continued. "I am afraid I have bad news. Late last night, a merchantman put in to the Great Harbour, with a letter for my father. I'll read it to you."

He unrolled the scroll he had been holding.

"'To Hieron, King of Syracuse, greetings from Hannibal, son of Hamilcar. I write to you from my tent on the day after battle. I am tired and shall be brief. The army of Rome no longer exists. Its remains lie in the dirt in the Aufidus valley, near a small town named Cannae. The bearer of this letter speaks for me. I ask you to hear what he has to say, great King, and to accept the gift that he brings you as a token of my respect.'"

Gelon carefully rolled the papyrus up again and pursed his lips.

"We sent five companies of the Gold Shields to Rome," he resumed in a low voice. "Hannibal has sent us back the survivors; it would seem that is his gift to my father. There were forty-two of them on the ship, most of them injured. We've had them all discreetly ferried to Plymmerium. Another twenty-six of our men were apparently too badly wounded to make the journey. Hannibal's ambassador has promised that any who recover will also be free to return. Just sixty-eight survivors, out of five hundred men."

We all stared at Gelon in shock.

Those five companies had all been under my own command a little over a year previously. I probably knew almost every man who had died by name. I would have counted their officers among my friends.

I swallowed and raised my hand. The prince nodded to me.

"And Sosis, sir? Is there any news of him?"

"The gods were merciful in his case, at least, Dion. He was on the ship. He's lost an eye, but he'll live. I spoke to him and some of the other survivors this morning. They've confirmed what Hannibal says. He managed to surround the entire Roman army. The Romans had nearly twice his numbers, and somehow he encircled them. It beggars belief. At best, a few thousand men may have managed to escape. I would never have thought it possible, but it sounds like this was an even bigger fuck-up than Lake Trasimene."

Hieron straightened himself in his chair.

"We will release the news in the city in due course," he croaked. "But I wanted you to hear for yourselves what Hannibal's man has to say."

"Where is this ambassador, my King?" asked Andranodoros.

"Sitting in an anteroom, waiting to be called in," Gelon replied, answering for his father.

"Now, my friends," Hieron said, "I know this is shocking news, but collect yourselves, please. You are not to betray your thoughts to this man. Leave all the talking to Gelon and me."

He raised his hand and gestured to one of the bodyguards standing behind him. The soldier stepped off the dais and let himself out through a side door. He returned a few moments later, followed by Hannibal's ambassador.

He wore his beard differently now, but I still recognised him at once.

The ambassador was Nico, the lieutenant whom Gelon had forced me to cashier.

He smiled and nodded to me as he entered.

The greeting could hardly have been more misjudged. The thought that one of my own former officers had helped butcher my friends started to burn the inside of my brain. I clenched my fists, digging my nails into my palms, but the flames only grew more fierce. An instant later, I kicked my stool back and rose snarling to my feet. Nico stared at me incredulously. His smile evaporated and he froze.

"Dion!" barked Gelon, jumping to his feet as well. "Sit down! Now!"

I narrowed my eyes. The guard who had escorted Nico into the room rather bravely stepped in front of him and lowered his spear protectively. His comrade jumped off the dais to join him, and the two other members of the Royal Watch who had been standing by the main doors also started sprinting down the room towards us.

"Sit down, Dion! I won't tell you again!" shouted Gelon furiously.

My nostrils flared, I clenched my fists and leant forward menacingly. The other councillors were gawping at me in horror.

From his stool, I felt Archimedes clasp my wrist and gently pull on it. I looked down at him and he smiled and shook his head. I turned to Gelon who was staring at me coldly. Beside him, Hieron was also watching me. The king's eyebrows were raised. His expression seemed to be flickering somewhere between amusement and curiosity.

I growled and rolled my head around my shoulders two or three times. I felt the fire in my brain begin to subside a little. I took a deep breath and gazed malevolently at Nico.

The four men of the Royal Watch had formed a line between the ambassador and me. They looked nervous.

Reluctantly, I did as my prince had commanded. As I sat back down, I heard Andranodoros exhale quietly in relief. Archimedes patted me gently on the back.

"Alright, stand easy," Gelon said to the guards. "But you'd better stay close." He shot me another angry glance.

Two of the guards took up a position a few feet behind Nico while the other pair returned to the dais. Nico turned to the king and bowed low.

"Thank you for your protection, Your Majesty," he said, clearly still shaken. It was Gelon who answered him.

"And what sort of a welcome did you expect?" he demanded, not hiding his irritation. "Hannibal sends us a traitor and asks us to accept him as an ambassador. Is this meant to be an insult?"

I could see Nico bristle, as if he had been slapped across the face.

"I am no traitor, Prince," he snapped back. "I have only ever wanted to serve your father. I would have bled for Syracuse, and been proud to do so. But all my life in this city, I was sneered at and despised, just because my hair is black. My comrades mocked me to my face. And then you became my general, Prince, and you had me thrown out of the army, for no fault of my own. But even now, I only wish to serve this kingdom. In fact, I am here to save it. So would you like to hear what I have to say, or do you only wish to insult me?"

Gelon snorted but I saw the king smile.

"That was well answered," Hieron said mildly. "Sit down, Gelon, and let us listen to what the ambassador has to say. What's your name, young man?"

"Nico, Your Majesty."

"Ah, yes, I think I've heard of you. You have spirit, Nico. So, what is it you have come all this way to tell me?"

Gelon returned to his chair beside the king while Nico took a breath and composed himself.

"Thank you, Your Majesty, and I apologise for my outburst. It was unseemly. I am afraid I was a little shaken. But my message is a simple one: Hannibal offers you his hand in friendship. And if you take it, he promises to give you what every king of Syracuse has always dreamt of."

"And what might that be?" Hieron asked.

"Peace, Your Majesty, and the crown of all Sicily. He offers you the whole island. He further offers you a trade treaty with Carthage that will make you richer than Midas. He offers you a niece of his own as a bride for your grandson, Hieronymus. And finally, he offers to take a girl of your own family as a bride for himself. As you may know, he was recently widowed. He leaves the choice of his wife to you."

"How very kind of him," said Hieron drily. "Although I was not aware that Sicily was in Hannibal's gift... So tell me, what does your general want in return? That I join him in his war on Rome, I suppose? No doubt my ships would be quite useful, given how few Carthage has these days. Or maybe he wants my army instead, seeing how his own gets smaller every year?"

Nico smiled.

"No, Your Majesty. He knows you will never openly turn on Rome. Nor does he need you to. Rome is all but finished anyway.

Hannibal does not want you to do anything. In fact, he requests that you do precisely nothing. Just stop sending Rome your grain, and when Rome falls, all Sicily will be yours."

"And that is all Hannibal requires of me?" Hieron asked.

Nico met the king's gaze.

"Not quite, Your Majesty. He does have one modest further request. As I say, he does not need your fleet, or your divisions. He asks only that you send him a single man, and only for a single year at that."

"Really?" said Hieron, raising an eyebrow. "Who?"

"Archimedes, Your Majesty."

My great-uncle spluttered and spat his beard out of his mouth. Hieron looked over at him and chuckled.

"I think that might please my grandson," he said. "But tell me, Nico, what does Hannibal want with my cousin? I'd have thought the general is a little old for tutoring."

The ambassador laughed.

"No, Your Majesty. Hannibal does not ask your cousin to play Aristotle to his Alexander, although it is a charming thought. He would like Archimedes to build some machines for him. Siege engines, to be precise. Ones powerful enough to breach the walls of Rome."

"But what on earth do I know of such things?" interrupted Archimedes, in apparent consternation.

Nico turned to face my great-uncle.

"You are too modest, Archimedes," he replied smoothly. "I wouldn't be surprised if you know more than any man alive. Let me be candid. Why waste your genius at Plymmerium, building weapons for your walls that will never be used, when you can build weapons in Italy instead, that will deliver the whole of Sicily into your king's hands?"

"You seem very well informed, Nico," said Hieron.

"Your Majesty, why play games? I dare say you are just as well informed of everything that goes on in Carthage."

"And what if my father declines Hannibal's offer?" Gelon asked.

Nico shrugged.

"Then perhaps, Prince, when his business in Italy is concluded, the general will accept the invitation your father's admiral left him, to visit Syracuse in person. But he would far rather have your father as a friend than an enemy. Who would not? The general compliments you on the remarkable achievement of your fleet, by the way, Your Majesty. He hopes that one day, he will have the opportunity to share a jug of wine with you, and learn how you did it."

"And why should I trust your general to leave me in peace, Nico?" Hieron asked. "He started this war. Do you really expect me to believe that all he wants now is to lay down his sword and play the doting husband to a Greek girl? You compared Hannibal to Alexander yourself. I think perhaps you're right. Even if he conquered the whole earth, I suspect he would still not be satisfied, and would immediately turn his eyes on the moon."

"No, Your Majesty, his quarrel is only with the Romans, and he fights them for only one reason. If Carthage does not break Rome, Rome will one day break Carthage. You know this is true. But between you and Carthage there can be peace. Syracuse does not menace us, as Rome does. And you will find Hannibal a better friend to you than the Romans. What do they give you in return for your loyalty? They drag you into a war that you are anxious to avoid. They take your grain, while your own people starve. They demand you send them your soldiers, and then they march them to their deaths. I urge you, do not burn with Rome, great King, when you could prosper with Carthage."

The king gazed at Nico thoughtfully.

"And Hannibal sends me back my men, as proof of his good intentions?"

"He does, Your Majesty."

"And what did he do with all the other prisoners he took, if I may ask? The men who were sent against him by Rome's other allies? Or does his mercy only extend to Syracuse?"

"I understand he is returning them to their homes too, Your Majesty, also without conditions. He is generous."

"Really? Surely he's going to sell all his Roman prisoners into slavery, at least?"

"Your Majesty, Hannibal is not the monster the Romans would have you believe. I gather that even the Roman prisoners will be freed, although Rome will have to ransom them. The only captives who will be sold into slavery are the mercenaries you sent, although I believe only a few dozen survived. But given their treachery, I think you would agree even that is remarkably lenient."

"Thank you, Nico. That is all I needed to know. Now, unless you have anything else to add, I wonder if you would be kind enough to excuse us, while we discuss Hannibal's proposals among ourselves? I shall give you my answer tomorrow. Tonight, you will be my guest here at the palace. I regret that for your own safety, you will have to remain within the palace walls, although perhaps it would be prudent to keep your distance from Dion. Your crew will also need to be confined to their ship, but we will see they are sent provisions for your return journey."

Hieron nodded to one of the guards standing behind Nico. The ambassador bowed and then followed the guard out by the same door through which he had entered. He walked with a straight back and his head high.

"He spoke well," said Hieron thoughtfully, once Nico had left. "So, let us discuss Hannibal's proposal. My dear son-in-law, I wonder if I might turn to you first. What advice would you offer me?"

Andranodoros cleared his throat.

"Well, my King…" he began, but Hieron held up a hand to silence him.

"Not you, Andranodoros. I mean my other son-in-law," he said. "Zoippos, what are your thoughts?"

Zoippos and Andranodoros both stared at the king in surprise. Hieron smiled benevolently at Zoippos.

"Come, come," he said. "We may have disagreed about my grandson's readiness for responsibility, but let us put all that behind us. You are a clever man, Zoippos, and I have always valued your advice. And I certainly need it now, in the face of this calamity."

Gelon nodded in agreement.

"Zoippos, as you know, I am in your debt for everything you have done for Hieronymus," the prince said, picking up from his father. "His failings are his own, not yours. And I should also like to hear what you have to say."

Zoippos looked suspiciously from Hieron to Gelon and back again. But vanity conquers all. The opportunity to parade his indispensable wisdom was clearly too tempting to pass up. He pursed his lips and the huge Adam's apple bobbed up and down two or three times as he gathered his thoughts.

"Here we go," I heard Andranodoros sigh quietly beside me.

"Thank you, my King, for your kind words," Zoippos said after a moment, "and for yours also, my brother Gelon, for although you and I are only brothers by marriage, is not every man here a brother in the most profound sense, as Ares and Apollo are brothers, one the fierce god of war, the other, the gentle god of music, and yet forever bonded together, despite their divergent temperaments, by the common paternity of Zeus, their all-powerful father, just as we here are all united in fraternity by the father figure of our resplendent king?"

Hieron nodded and smiled graciously.

"My King, you seek my counsel on these grave matters," Zoippos resumed, leaning back and tapping his fingertips together in the manner of a sage contemplating some profundity. "Hannibal offers you peace and prosperity and the crown of all Sicily. Let us seize this unparalleled opportunity with both hands. Let us write a new page in the sad annals of our history with Carthage. Where once there was only the discord of enmity, let the harmonious music of amity play instead, like the sweet harp of Orpheus. For nothing is more terrible than war, and even the greatest of cities can fall. And to those here who believe our walls are impregnable and proof against

Hannibal, I say, so said King Priam too, from the walls of Troy, as he scorned the might of Agamemnon; so also believed the barbarians of Tyre, when they defied the will of Alexander. Trust not to stone, my King; the only true security lies in friendship."

"Thank you for those wise words, Zoippos," said Gelon. Zoippos could not suppress a satisfied smirk. He evidently believed he had managed to restore himself to favour, although I had my doubts about that.

What had struck me was how naturally Gelon seemed to be picking up his father's methods.

Hieron turned to Andranodoros.

"And what is the view of my Royal Treasurer?"

"My King," Andranodoros replied carefully, "I imagine Rome's other allies are already scrambling to change sides. If you are thinking of abandoning the Romans too, I would advise you to do so quickly. Hannibal will not make you such a generous offer again. And if the Romans capitulate before we make peace with him, he will certainly turn on us afterwards. If Rome falls, we fall. So if we don't come to terms with Hannibal now, then I fear our only alternative will be to send everything we have to try to save Rome: the fleet, the army, everything. And who knows if that would even be of any use? It sounds as though the war may already be lost. Agreeing to Hannibal's proposal seems to me the safest option; and on top of this, to gain all Sicily, at no cost to us in gold or blood, well, what more could we ask of him? It is an outcome of which Syracuse has dreamt for centuries."

"Does anyone else have anything to add?" asked Gelon. Several other councillors spoke in turn, all in favour of accepting Hannibal's terms. The prize of the whole island had them drooling. Most were probably already picturing the estates and slaves and villas that would drop into their laps. Having already drawn too much attention to myself, I said nothing as usual, and nor did Archimedes, but eventually Thraso put his hand up.

"Yes, Thraso?" said Gelon.

My cousin fidgeted uncomfortably.

"It seems I am the only person here who thinks you should reject Hannibal's proposal, my King," he said awkwardly.

Hieron gazed at him.

"Why?" he snapped.

Thraso wriggled on his stool some more, but pressed on.

"My King, I'm no general, so I don't know if Rome can be saved, but I do know that if we abandon them, all her other allies will follow, and Rome will almost certainly be lost. And then Carthage will control the coasts of Africa, Spain and Italy. Sicily will be like a grape in her mouth. Even if Hannibal could be trusted not to bite down, in ten years' time, or twenty years, when Hannibal is dead and Carthage has rebuilt its fleet, what then will stop them swallowing us too? If we accept these terms, I believe we would be trading our kingdom's only chance of survival, however slight that may be, for inevitable destruction in the future. I would call that cowardice. We would be betraying our children for the sake of our own comfort. At the very least, my King, I urge you not to send Archimedes to Hannibal. I think it would be utter folly to give Hannibal the means to breach our own walls."

Thraso looked down meekly at his lap. Perhaps he realised he had gone too far. Hieron stared at him with his cold, dead eyes.

"So, Thraso," the king said, "if I decide to accept Hannibal's offer, you would judge me both a coward and a fool?"

Thraso's jaw dropped slightly and his flabby cheeks turned red. He started to mumble something but Hieron silenced him with a wave. Beside me, I heard Andranodoros chuckle quietly at my cousin's discomfort.

"Well, Thraso, at least we know where you stand," said Gelon with a smile. "Thank you all for your advice. My father and I will consider what you have said. We will meet here again at midday tomorrow, when my father will give Nico his answer."

As I made my way out, I noticed that Ision, Leatherskin and three or four other councillors had lingered behind. They clustered around Zoippos, who remained seated, and who was smiling and nodding earnestly at whatever they were saying to him.

That evening, I sent Sosis a note, thanking the gods for his return and promising to visit him at Plymmerium as soon as I was able. I ate little and spent a restless night in my cot. I wondered how Hieron and Gelon were sleeping. Whatever decision the king reached, it would probably prove the most momentous of his long reign. I didn't envy Hieron the burden of his crown. For my own part, I couldn't make up my mind whether I agreed with Andranodoros or Thraso. Only one thing seemed clear to me: Hieron's gamble in attacking Hannibal's convoy had paid off handsomely. The general was offering us far better terms than we could ever have expected, had our king not shown what a dangerous enemy he could be. But what puzzled me was why Hieron had been so interested in what Hannibal was doing with all his prisoners.

I joined my men for their drills in the morning. Their mood of good-natured resignation was much the same as always. It seemed that no word of Hannibal's victory or the return of our survivors had yet reached their ears. As usual, I led the sword practice, sparring with two volunteers at once, but my mind was elsewhere, and one of them, the vicious little scrapper known as Needle, managed to get under my guard and bruise me on my thigh with a hard cut of his wooden blade. My two opponents both broke off immediately to look at me aghast, and several other pairs of men who had been practising nearby stopped to stare as well. I was a little shocked myself.

The whispers began to ripple out from where we were standing.

"Fuck me, I think the captain just lost."

"He *lost?*"

Soon the whole courtyard had fallen silent. I laughed.

"Well done, both of you," I said, and gave the two men an approving nod. "Your company's next run is cancelled."

They grinned at me.

"Right, back to your drills, everyone," I bellowed.

An hour or two later, I left my men, to have a bath and change into my blue tunic. I arrived at the audience chamber in good time. About half the councillors were already there, including Archimedes, and before long the rest had also filed in. For some reason, we all went to the same places we had occupied the day before. We nodded to each other, but other than a few whispered greetings, no one spoke. We were all tense.

Hieron was the last to arrive, walking in on Gelon's arm from a door at the back of the dais. The prince helped his father onto his throne and sat down beside him. Two bodyguards in their black-plumed helmets took up their positions behind the king.

Hieron looked down at me.

"Are you planning any more theatrics today, Dion?" he said.

"No, my King. I'm sorry for yesterday."

"Well, no harm done, I suppose. But you do seem to be making quite a habit of frightening my guests. First you attack the son of one of Rome's leading senators, and then you nearly assault the Carthaginian ambassador. If you keep this up, Dion, Rome and Carthage will soon be putting aside their differences to form an alliance against me... Now, if we are all here, we'd better get this Nico fellow back in."

He raised his hand and one of the guards stepped off the dais and let himself out through the side door. He returned a few moments later with Nico behind him.

The ambassador bowed deeply to the king and prince.

"So Nico, I hope you had a good night's rest?" asked Hieron politely.

"The bed was most comfortable, Your Majesty, but I am afraid I could take little advantage of it. As I'm sure you will understand, I am eager to be able to return to my general with good news."

"Oh, I'm sorry to hear that. I had an excellent night's sleep myself. Over six hours without even wetting myself. That's quite an achievement at my age."

"And I am certain you will have many more such nights, Your Majesty," replied Nico with an easy smile, "once we have managed to overcome all the anxieties that this war must occasion you."

Hieron chuckled.

"If Hannibal could offer me the gift of sleep, Nico, it would be worth even more to me than the crown of Sicily."

Nico laughed lightly and inclined his head.

"So, may I ask Your Majesty if you have arrived at your decision yet?"

"Ah yes, you want your answer. Well, I have given your offer the consideration it deserves." The king put his hand over his mouth and coughed lightly. "Please thank Hannibal on my behalf for returning my men. It was a thoughtful gesture. And tell him my invitation to visit Syracuse still stands. I can assure him of a most warm welcome."

Nico looked at Hieron uncertainly.

"Do you mean, Your Majesty, that I should tell the general that you accept his proposal?"

Hieron smiled, and then, slowly, the awful metamorphosis that I had witnessed once before in that same room took hold of him again. His pale eyes glinted and came alive; his lips twitched slightly and something indefinable altered in his expression. For a long moment, the king gazed down coldly on Nico from the dais, but now his smile exuded only menace.

"No, that is not what I mean at all," he said, his words slow and wet with venom. "Now, get out of my sight, you little barbarian monkey. And if you ever dare come back, I will have you crucified for the traitor that you are."

Nico stared at the king. Then he turned on his heel and strode out of the room without a word. The bodyguard hurried after him. No one else moved.

"Well, I think that concludes our negotiations with Hannibal, at least for the time being," said Gelon coolly. "Thank you all for coming. I'm afraid I've got to get back to Plymmerium, but we will reconvene at the next council meeting in twenty days' time. Dion, stay behind please. My father would like a word with you."

"Well, that's a relief," said Archimedes after a moment, standing up shakily with the help of his cane. "I'm far too old to go gallivanting around Italy."

He began to shuffle towards the door. The other councillors seemed as shocked as Nico had been. Andranodoros turned to look at me, pursed his lips and shook his head sadly.

"Well, I doubt Hannibal will send us back the rest of our men now. He'll probably crucify them instead. I'm sorry, Dion. I know they were your comrades."

Then he stood too and followed Archimedes. One by one, the other councillors got up and silently made their way out. Zoippos looked completely bewildered.

Gelon left through the door at the back of the dais, and Hieron beckoned me to join him.

"Help me up, Dion, would you? Thank you." He put his arm through mine. "I'd be grateful if you'd walk me back to my apartments. This way."

The door Gelon had used opened into a long, gloomy corridor. The two guards followed us out.

We had only gone a few paces when I felt Hieron wobble beside me. He clutched at my arm and all at once, his legs began to buckle. I spun round in front of him as fast as I could and wrapped my other arm around him to hold him up. The guards immediately dropped their spears and jumped forward to support him from behind.

As we sorted out the tangle of our arms, I caught a momentary glimpse of the king's face. It was the face of a frightened old man.

The guards expertly slid their necks under the king's armpits and formed a cradle with their hands, and then they lifted him gently off his feet.

"It's alright, sir, no need to worry," one of them said to me as they manouevred sideways past me. "This happens sometimes."

"My fucking legs," hissed Hieron. "Pick up those spears, would you, Dion?"

I followed them down the corridor and through a maze of sparsely furnished and apparently unused rooms of various sizes.

Eventually we reached a small, plain sitting room, with a view out to the open sea, where Hieron told the guards to lay him on a couch.

"Thank you, boys," he said as they set him carefully down and made him comfortable. "I hope I wasn't too much of a weight for you. Wait outside, please. And have a slave bring us some water. Make yourself comfortable, Dion."

I handed the guards back their spears and settled myself on another couch. The king closed his eyes and almost immediately started snoring softly.

A slave came in, carrying a tray with two plain cups and a jug. He bowed and set the tray down quietly on a small table beside me, before pouring out a cup and silently handing it to me.

When he had left again, I sipped at my water, lost in my own confused thoughts and waiting for Hieron to wake. The king dozed for maybe a quarter of an hour.

Eventually, he stirred and rubbed his eyes.

"Ah, Dion," he said, "I'm sorry, I must have nodded off. An old man's vice. Bring me over some of that water, would you?"

I did as I was told and, as I handed him the cup, he eyed me shrewdly.

"So, do you think it was a mistake to send Hannibal's man packing?" he asked as I sat back down.

"I really don't know, my King. You once told me that Rome would eventually win this war. If that's true, then you obviously made the right decision."

"But you don't believe the Romans will win, do you?"

I shrugged and smiled.

"They certainly seem to be taking the long road round to victory," I said.

He chuckled.

"Do you know why I asked Nico about Hannibal's prisoners, Dion?"

"No, my King, I'd been wondering about that."

"Because it tells me what Hannibal is intending. He hasn't sold the Romans into slavery because he wants to negotiate a peace with the senate. And that means he knows he cannot win. Do you think a man confident of victory would have offered me all Sicily?" Hieron snorted contemptuously. "He must have been exhausted when he sent Nico to me with those terms. I imagine he is already regretting it. Hannibal may be a great general, but he'd make a poor king. He let me see into his mind, Dion, and it is the mind of an anxious man. He knows he can never take Rome."

"But if we cut off Rome's grain, or help Hannibal build siege engines, surely he could?"

"Even then, I doubt it. It is not the strength of a city's walls that matter, but the strength of the men inside them. The Carthaginians are like us, Dion. They have grown fat and rich and cynical. They no longer believe in anything much, other than money. They wage war merely to protect the wealth they already enjoy, or to gain more of it. They don't even fight their own battles any more. They hire their mercenary armies, and then they calculate the profit or loss of using them. They make reasonable, sensible, predictable decisions."

He took a sip of water.

"But the Romans are not like us, or the Carthaginians," he resumed, cradling his cup. "They don't fight for money. They are children, who still lap up every silly story their nursemaids tell them. They believe with all their hearts in their own destiny. They really do. Of course they want wealth too, but they are fanatics, Dion. They think the world will only be perfect once they rule every last acre of it. They will never give in, no matter how reasonable Hannibal's terms may be. If they had no grain, they would eat their own children, rather than open their gates to him. You'll see. Just wait till you meet your future father-in-law. He's the maddest of them all. Hannibal can destroy as many Roman armies as he likes, but it will do him no good. The Romans will just keep raising new ones. And eventually, Hannibal's squabbling paymasters in Carthage will get frustrated, and their people will start grumbling about their taxes, and little by little, the money he needs to replace his mercenaries will start to dry up. It may take years, Dion, but eventually Carthage will lose this war, for the simple reason that they do not have the will to win it. But the Romans do. Remember this when I'm dead. Reasonable people lose wars. It is unreasonable people who win them."

"It sounds like you are more frightened of your allies than you are of your enemies, my King," I said with a smile.

He didn't smile back.

"I am, Dion, I am. Hannibal is one man, a man of extraordinary talent, I grant you, but without him, Carthage is just an irritable, toothless old woman. Syracuse has always known how to deal with Carthage. But the Romans, well, they are something else. They are the world's true barbarians. Everything I do, I do to protect us from Rome."

"Thank you for explaining that to me, my King," I said politely, although I remained unconvinced.

"Anyway, Dion, keep your ears open. I know Archimedes spoke to you about this a while ago. If any of the councillors start sounding you out about this business with Hannibal, be coy. Let them seduce you. If there is a plot against Gelon and me, you can be certain that the person who approaches you first will not be the most important. Be patient, and let my enemies expose themselves in their own time."

XIII

MONSTERS

It so happened I had invited Nebit, Castor and a handful of my other officers round to my rooms for dinner that same evening. The news of the defeat at Cannae and of the return of our survivors had not been released, and I was hardly at liberty to discuss the brutal dismissal of Hannibal's ambassador. Nebit probably knew all about it, but secrets were the bricks and timbers of his life and he would certainly say nothing. His sense of social propriety, however, was dull, and he could not resist broaching the one subject that everyone else was too well bred to ask me about. The lamps had already been lit and we had almost finished our food when he brought it up.

"I gather His Majesty was taken by surprise by your mother's announcement," he said, as he lounged awkwardly on a couch, with one short, chubby leg dangling over the side like a dead fish. "I must say, it does seem rather a shame for her to choose to closet herself away. She has always been such a prominent and forceful figure. I for one shall greatly miss the colour she added to the life of the city."

He was trying to be tactful about it, but he was trawling for information. He wanted to know what had happened; he had expected me to work through the senate.

"I shall be sure to pass your kind words on to her, Nebit," I replied. "Coming from you, I am certain she will be touched by them."

The Egyptian beamed.

"But, as you may have already guessed," I continued a little smugly, "I'm afraid I am to blame for her withdrawal. In fact, I insisted upon it. How should I put this? Let us just say my mother has an unfortunate tendency to stray beyond the proper boundaries of her sex on occasion. I'd be grateful if you all kept this between yourselves, but I was worried she might get a little above herself if she were elected High Priestess."

"How very wise of you, my friend," Nebit simpered. "It must have been terribly difficult for you to disappoint her, but I am sure it was the right decision."

Our rather nauseating exchange was interrupted by Castor.

"Do you hear that? What's that noise?" he asked.

We fell silent. In the distance, a bell was ringing. As we listened, two or three others joined in the faint clangour. And then, to our horror, the palace bell began to sound too.

I stood up and the other officers immediately rose to their feet also.

"Agbal," I said calmly, "fetch my army sword. Nebit, I'm afraid we must leave you. I suggest you stay here till we know what's going on. Castor, you and Leander run ahead. Seal the palace. I'll meet you in the exercise yard. The rest of you, join your companies and wait for me. Alpha, bolt the door behind us."

Castor and the others hurried from the room. Nebit hadn't moved. He looked terrified.

"What is it, Captain? Is the city under attack?"

"I doubt it. This must be something else, but I've no idea what," I replied.

A moment later Agbal came running out of the anteroom with my sword. He handed it to me and I belted it on.

"You'd better come with me, Agbal," I said to him, and strode through the door.

Downstairs in the courtyard, a few frightened-looking palace slaves were scuttling back to their quarters. A small group of officials had gathered in a corner.

I jogged over to the main gate with Agbal at my heels.

"You, up there in tower," I bellowed. "What can you see?"

A sentry put his head over the parapet.

"Fire, sir," he shouted down. "In the Tyche district, by the looks of it."

"Which way is the wind?" I called up to him. It was impossible to tell from the shelter of the courtyard. The sentry paused as he tried to judge it.

"From the north-east, I think, sir."

I swore under my breath.

"Are you sure?"

He briefly disappeared from sight, then re-emerged and threw a piece of cloth as high as he could into the air. The breeze caught it and it fluttered down towards me, landing a few yards from my feet. I couldn't resist a grim smile. It was the man's undergarment.

"Stay at your post," I shouted up. "Come on, Agbal."

We ran through to the exercise yard, where the four palace companies were already forming up under the eyes of my officers. Their sergeants were barking orders.

"Agbal, go to the stables and have them saddle up all the officers' horses. Hurry up. Find a horse for yourself, too."

He darted off and I marched up to the lines of men. A few stragglers were still falling in. I waited for them, using the time to collect my thoughts. Fires were a rare but occasional fact of city life, and every district had its own measures in place to deal with them. They seldom damaged more than a few buildings. In my entire lifetime, there had never been a fire dangerous enough to cause the general alarm to be rung.

"It seems a fire has broken out in Tyche," I announced in my parade-ground voice. "Sergeants, I want you to lead your companies over there as fast as they can run. Head for the Temple of Tyche. The men are to take their swords but to leave their armour here. Only the duty sentries are to stay behind."

I paused for a moment, while I decided which officers to send on the various tasks I had been listing in my head.

"Timon, go to the king's apartments and tell the Royal Watch that I'm going to have to leave the palace undefended. Then ride to the city slave pens and fetch all the slaves they have. Leander, ride round the livery yards and commandeer every horse you can find. Bring the grooms too. Memnon and Xanthos, go to the quarries and collect the slaves from there. They should bring their pickaxes and I want them unshackled; they're no good to me in chains. If the overseers object, show them the sharp end of your swords. All other officers will ride to Tyche with me immediately. Now, do you all understand your orders? Good. I'll see you all at the temple. Get moving."

A few moments later, I was galloping out of the palace with Agbal, Castor and four of my lieutenants. The bells were still ringing. It was not till we had passed through the gate that straddled the landward end of the isthmus that I got a glimpse of the faint orange glow on the northern horizon. We raced across the open agora, where the slaves who should have been sweeping up the rubbish from the day's market huddled dumbly together, not knowing how they were required to respond to the alarm. I noticed that a small group of people had climbed the steps of the senate house to gather under its portico. They stood as still and silent as statues, gawping to the north.

Our route took us through the large, elegant suburb of Neapolis. A few torches had already been lit in the main streets. The bells had brought small groups of frightened people out of their homes to try to discover what was going on. They had to press their backs to the walls to avoid being ridden underfoot as we cantered past.

There could be no worse place for a fire to break out, I thought bleakly as I rode. Tyche was the most northerly of the city's districts, and also the poorest and most densely populated. Its houses were packed tight. The summer had barely started to fade into autumn; the quarter would be tinder.

It was the theatre season. The evening's play must have ended an hour or two earlier, but at the foot of the hill below the amphitheatre, the taverns of Neapolis had been enjoying a busy night. We were forced to slow down several times by parties of bewildered drunkards, who were stumbling around in terror trying to find their way home.

We finally reached the Labdalum Road, which marked the boundary of Neapolis. As we crossed it into Tyche, the streets grew noticeably narrower. We passed several frightened families, laden with sacks and coarse wooden boxes, into which they must have hurriedly crammed whatever they most valued. Babies cried and women called out anxiously for their children to stay close. They seemed to have no idea where they should go; they were just running from the fire.

We pressed on through the dark, winding roads towards the Temple of Tyche, the goddess of fortune, after whom the district had been named, presumably by someone with a sense of humour. The temple stood on a small, squat hill. I led the way up the stony path to the summit and brought my horse to a halt at the foot of the temple steps. My officers pulled up behind me.

"Fuck," I heard one of them gasp under his breath.

For a few moments, we all gazed in silence at the tips of the flames twisting over the low rooftops in the distance. It looked as though the fire had taken hold of the warehouse district, at the northernmost edge of the city, about two or three miles away from us.

Back at the palace, my vague plan had been to contain the blaze, by demolishing whatever buildings were closest to it and letting it burn itself out. I had no idea how large it might be, so I had decided to collect a small army of slaves to help. Better too many hands than too few, I had reasoned. But one look was sufficient to tell me I had not nearly enough. The fire already sprawled across a front of two or three hundred yards.

Castor brought his horse up alongside mine.

"It's a fucking monster, Castor," I said quietly.

"Should we try to evacuate the area, sir?" he asked. "We could direct the people up to Epipolae."

I took a deep breath and tried to survey the scene as my old general, Lepides, had trained me to do. Without fear or pity. As coldly as an Olympian god.

A low mound of rubble, the remnants of one of the feeble democratic walls that predated my ancestor's fortifications, curled around the foot of the hill below us. It still ran right across Tyche, cutting the district in half and serving as an unofficial boundary. Our side of the wall was known as Lower Tyche or Temenites. The poorest of our citizens now lived on the far side of the wall, in Upper Tyche, and the most wretched of all lived in Upper Tyche's shanty town, an area of maybe fifteen or twenty acres mockingly called Little Athens. Little Athens directly adjoined the burning warehouse district. I guessed its shacks would be reduced to ashes within a matter of hours.

And then what? To the west lay the barren slope of the Epipolae plateau; to the east, the high, sturdy walls of Achradina. The fire was trapped in the wide channel between them. But to the south, it faced no impediment. After it had consumed Little Athens, there was nothing to stop it sweeping through the rest of Upper Tyche, and then across the useless boundary wall into Temenites, and then, perhaps, even into Neapolis. With a shudder, it dawned on me that half the city lay at its feet. And the breeze was in my face. The inferno was coming our way.

Castor was probably right. Unless I learnt to command the wind, nothing I could do seemed likely to make much difference. Houses can be rebuilt. My men would be best employed in helping get the people to safety. Tyche's fate was in the hands of the gods.

Somewhere inside me, I felt the beast begin to stir. I sensed it toss its heavy head and roll its small red eyes.

I ran my tongue around the inside of my cheek.

Fuck it, I thought. The gods help those who help themselves.

"No, Castor," I replied. "We'll stop the fire at the boundary wall."

I turned my horse around to face the others.

"I'm going on ahead to take a closer look. Castor, when the men get here, spread them out and have them start taking apart the buildings along the far side of the wall. Put the slaves to work as well. I want anything that can burn moved a safe distance inside Temenites – roof timbers, doors, furniture, whatever… Agbal, I want you to ride to Plymmerium as fast as you can. Here, take my ring. You'll need it to get out of the city. Have them give you a fresh horse at the gates. Find Prince Gelon, and tell him we need him here." I smiled. "And I'd be greatly obliged if he'd bring the army with him. Do you understand?"

Agbal nodded.

"Good lad," I said, and turned to one of my junior lieutenants.

"Eleon, go back to the palace. Ask the king to call out the reservists. We'll need every man we can get."

Eleon and the other officers stared at me incredulously. I knew what they were thinking: what I intended must have seemed insane. I was going to try to cut a firebreak right across the belly of the city. If the wind didn't change, I probably didn't have enough time; and if it did change, I might well end up doing more damage than the fire itself.

"You have your orders, Eleon," I said icily. "Now get going."

He knew better than to argue. He turned his horse without a word and began to canter back down the hill, with Agbal following immediately behind him.

"And Upper Tyche, sir?" asked Castor. "What about the people over there?"

"Those who can't run will die," I said. "Now, you know what you have to do, my friend. Can I trust you to do it?" I rested my hand on his shoulder and he nodded unhappily.

"Very well, then," I said. "I'll see you all later."

I put my heels to the stallion's flanks and rode down the slope alone, into Upper Tyche's claustrophobic maze of alleyways.

It seemed most of the inhabitants had either already fled or were hiding indoors. Those few I saw cowered in the shadows and looked meekly down at their feet as I spurred the horse on past them.

"Get to the boundary wall," I shouted out in each street I rode through, but they just cringed and ignored me. To the poor, a man on horseback was seldom a friend.

The crush of tiny brick-built houses finally ended at a rubbish-strewn storm drain. Beyond it lay the squalor of Little Athens, where families lived in shacks cobbled together out of discarded rotten planks and odd patches of sailcloth salvaged from around the city. Nothing here could even be called a street. The shacks had just been thrown up haphazardly in any space available. I spurred my horse on across the drain. There was smoke in my nostrils now, mixing with the smell of sewage. The horse whinnied and tossed its head skittishly, but I patted its neck and it continued to obey me.

I pressed on, threading my way through the narrow gaps between the ramshackle sheds. The thin sickle of the moon threw off almost no light. Whatever around me wasn't obscured in darkness was lit by a sinister red glow. Every now and then, a piece of cloth would twitch and I might spot a grimy, expressionless face staring at me through a gap in the planks.

"Get out," I shouted at them. "Get to Temenites." But they just ducked out of sight again or gazed back at me blankly.

I turned a series of bends and, suddenly, there it was. Less than five hundred yards ahead, I could see what looked like an unbroken tidal wave of flame. It billowed and rippled across my horizon. An entire row of warehouses must have been ablaze. Closer by, a few smaller and apparently disconnected spumes of fire had already started to spit through the roofs of some shacks.

I stood in my stirrups, trying to understand what it was that I faced. It may have been my imagination, but even at that distance, I thought I could feel the heat in the breeze. I noticed there were some stubby fingers of flame far over to my left as well. The blaze seemed to be coiling around the western perimeter of Little Athens. I had thought the fire would be a stupid thing, which knew only how to advance in a straight line along the axis of the wind, like a phalanx. I swore at my own foolishness. Even if the wind didn't change, I saw now that it would move fastest wherever it met buildings most to its liking, jabbing and testing its way forwards in veering, unpredictable directions. As I looked at the flames to my left, it dawned on me how easily they could get behind me. At the palace, I had planned to trap the fire, but the fire seemed to be trying to trap me instead.

I turned and wove my way back through the hovels as fast as I could, navigating by the dim silhouette of the Temple of Tyche. I could see no one, but I shouted as I went all the same. My voice was hoarse and the sooty air felt like sand in my throat. I had no idea how many families were still cowering silently in the darkness of their shacks. They seemed to think like rabbits. I suppose trying to become invisible was the only way the residents of Little Athens knew how to protect themselves.

I finally reached the storm drain and drove my horse back over it. More than anything, I felt anger.

A hundred yards to my right, a small crowd stood staring across the slums. A tall fellow at the front appeared to be giving orders. He turned and pointed towards the mouth of an alley behind them, and three men broke away and disappeared into the rat runs of Upper Tyche.

On an instinct, I turned the horse's head and cantered towards them along the weed-infested path that ran by the side of the drain. They fell silent as I approached.

"You there," I shouted, pulling up the horse. "Yes, you. The big man. What's your name?" He was an ugly brute, snub-nosed and heavy-set, of about my age. He pushed his way towards me, forcing his companions to squeeze together to let him through.

"What's it to you?" he demanded. He furrowed his brows as he approached and stared at me oddly for a moment. He seemed surprised by my presence.

"I'm Captain Dion," I said calmly. "And I asked you a question. What's your name?"

The big man took hold of my horse's bridle, keeping his eyes on me all the while.

"Never mind what my fucking name is," he growled. "What do you want here? Come to see how poor people burn, have you?"

I leant down from my saddle, bringing my face close to his.

"Mind your manners," I said softly.

He snorted contemptuously, then tilted his head in the direction of the men behind him.

"Or what?" he said. "You'll teach us all a lesson, will you?"

I smiled coldly and kept staring at him.

Upper Tyche was ruled by three or four criminal gangs. No doubt the big man was a somebody in one of them. He gazed back at me evenly. There was no fear in his eyes, only curiosity. He seemed as unused to being defied as I was. I imagine he was calculating whether he could make good use of the knife he probably had hidden in his tunic before my sword split his skull in half.

He was a thug, but not a fool. After a few moments, he shrugged, then gave me a curt nod and wisely let go of the bridle.

"So, I guess it's true what they say about you, then," he said with an amused grunt. "Balls of iron. Brains of wool though, coming here alone." He cleared his throat and spat. "Lads, it seems this is the famous Bull of Syracuse. I hope he's not here to collect his rents."

I straightened up again. I knew I owned some streets in Upper Tyche, but I'd never visited them and they couldn't have been worth much. I imagined they would soon be worth even less.

"So how may we be of service, Captain?" the big man asked with mock civility. "If you're looking for your boys, they're over that way." He pointed down the path towards the west.

I nodded. I wasn't surprised to hear some of my men were already in Upper Tyche. The commanders of the various garrisons around the city knew better than to sit on their hands while the bells rang.

"What are you all still doing here?" I asked.

"Just out for a quiet stroll, Captain. Thought we'd take in the view."

Behind him, I noticed some of his companions grinning to each other. They'd obviously only stayed behind to help themselves to anything of value that had been abandoned in the panic.

"Will the people over there do what you tell them?" I asked the big man, nodding towards Little Athens.

"I reckon so," he replied with a modest shrug.

"Then take your men and spread the word that everyone should clear out as fast as they can. There isn't much time: the fire's coming round the side. When you've done that, get yourselves to the boundary wall. We're going to try to make a firebreak in front of it. I need all the men I can get."

"Oh, so you want us to help you save Temenites, do you? And let Upper Tyche burn? But then, I suppose your houses over there are worth a lot more than our shitholes."

I leant forward in my saddle again.

"Listen to me, whatever your fucking name is," I said quietly, so his men couldn't hear me. "Unless the wind changes, everything this side of the wall is charcoal anyway. And if you and your scum don't make yourselves useful, when this is over, I swear I'll put an end to the Tyche gangs, once and for all. I'll crucify the lot of you."

Hieron and the nobles had tended to tolerate the gangs, provided they kept a low profile and stayed on their side of the Temenites boundary. They helped to maintain order, of a sort. They had even proved useful to my class on occasion, when it came to collecting unpaid rents around the city, or clearing out difficult tenants to make way for some new development. But if I took it into my head to suppress them, no one would greatly object.

The big man looked at me thoughtfully for a few moments, trying to read me.

"I think you would too, wouldn't you?" he replied eventually. "If you ever want a job, Captain, let me know. I'm sure I could find a use for a bastard like you."

"I'll keep it in mind. Now move your arse," I said.

The big man sent an urchin with me, to guide me to my men. The boy led me silently through a warren of tiny side lanes, zigzagging his way across Upper Tyche. We eventually reached an open space that must have served as a market, to judge by the amount of rubbish and rotting vegetable waste lying around. Xeno was standing by the well in the centre of the square, talking to two sergeants.

"Thank you, lad," I said to the boy. "Better get yourself into Temenites now. Here, this is for you."

I fished into my tunic pocket and threw him a small coin. He bowed timidly and scampered off.

I rode up to the men. Xeno's company had recently rotated to the Hexapylon fortress, on the north wall. It was a far more important position than the South Citadel, and happened to be the nearest garrison to the fire.

His sergeants snapped to attention as I approached and Xeno saluted me as best he could with the stump of his arm.

"Hello sir," he said, clearly relieved to see me.

"Draw up some water for my horse, would you?" I said to one of the sergeants. "So, what have you to report, Xeno?"

"It looks pretty hopeless, sir. We're just trying to get the people out. But a lot of them don't want to leave. They're frightened the gangs will loot their homes, so they're waiting till the last minute, hoping the fire will just burn itself out or pass them by."

As he spoke, I noticed Ajax, the man who had challenged me to a wrestling match, hurry into the square from a side lane. He was holding the hand of a young child and carrying an old man on his back. Two other children and a woman clutching a baby ran behind him.

"Well done, Ajax," Xeno shouted after him.

"How many men have you got here, Xeno?" I asked. The sergeant placed a bucket in front of my horse and it began to drink noisily.

"I only left ten at the gate, sir. I brought all the rest. The Labdalum garrison is here too and the Euryalus men are on their way. About four hundred of us altogether."

"Very well. This is what I need you to do. We're going to try to stop the fire at the boundary wall. I want you to buy us as much time as you can. Just try to slow it down. Make as many small firebreaks as you can. Concentrate on the streets that run north-south, and pull down whatever buildings look likely to come apart most easily. Tell the Euryalus and Labdalum commanders to do the same. When it gets too hot, fall back a safe distance and begin again. But if the fire starts to outflank you, run for the wall. Alright?"

"But what about the people, sir?"

"Do as I say, Xeno."

"Yes, sir," he replied. He looked unhappy, but then he stiffened himself and nodded.

"By the way, sir, there's something you should probably know," he added. "When we arrived, there must have been half a dozen warehouses already on fire."

"What of it?"

"Well sir, we were pretty quick off the mark getting here. So how does a fire spread so fast? And how does a warehouse catch fire at night anyway?"

I grunted.

"We'll worry about that later. Now, you have your orders. I'll see you later, Lieutenant."

I turned my horse's head and set off back towards Temenites. But Xeno's question was a good one. I had asked myself much the same thing when I had first seen the distant flames from the summit of the hill. The answer had not been difficult to guess.

Hannibal.

The Carthaginians were taking their revenge for the destruction of their convoy, and the rejection of their peace terms. Hannibal might not yet be able to strike us with his army, but he certainly knew how to make good use of his agents in the city. Before he sailed, Nico must have somehow got word to them.

I swore that if I ever met him again, I would gut Nico like a fish.

When I got back to the wall, Castor had already organised the palace companies and the slaves from the pens and quarries, and set them to work. There must have been about three thousand of them altogether. Less than two hours had passed since the palace bell had first rung. There seemed nothing else I could usefully do, so I tethered my horse to a tree near the temple and joined one of the work parties.

The flimsy houses of Upper Tyche came apart easily enough. We left the shells standing, but we took their roofs and doors off, ripped up the floorboards and emptied them of their furniture. We used the horses that Leander had brought from the livery yards to drag away the heaviest timbers. But the wall was over two miles long, and even with so many of us, it felt as though we were trying to empty the sea with a spoon.

Gradually our numbers swelled. The reservists began to arrive, at first in a hesitant trickle, and then as the hours wore on, at a slightly faster rate. But those who came were almost all from Temenites and Upper Tyche. The men from Achradina, Neapolis and Ortygia either stayed at home, or else put in a short appearance only to slip off again in the night. They realised there was no one to take their names, which meant there would probably be no pay for those who answered the call, and no penalty for those who didn't. They were the heroes who had recently destroyed Hannibal's convoy. I imagine they told themselves someone else could do the work this time, and that even if the fire didn't blow itself out, it would probably never reach their own homes.

Sometime in the middle of the night, the army's cavalry division arrived, with Prince Gelon himself at their head. He had seen the glow on the horizon from Plymmerium and had understood the danger at once. By the time Agbal met him on the road, he was already halfway to the city.

I was struggling to carry a thick wooden beam on my shoulder when Agbal came to find me. It probably amused the men around me to see a royal councillor labouring like a mule, while my young slave rode up on a fine-looking stallion.

Agbal hurriedly dismounted and told me the prince was waiting for me at the Temple of Tyche. I let the beam thud to the ground and took my horse.

At the summit of the hill, a dozen cavalry officers were gazing in stupefied silence across Upper Tyche. In the distance, Little Athens was already a lake of flames.

"Where's the prince?" I asked one of them.

He looked at me dumbly, then pointed towards the temple. In the dim light of the fire, its limestone blocks glowed pink. Gelon was surveying the scene from the portico. He stood between two of the temple's giant columns, with Eulus, the cavalry commander, beside him. Hannon, the prince's African slave, and two royal bodyguards waited at the foot of the steps. Their horses were tethered along a railing nearby. I tied up my own alongside and ran up to Gelon; it was a relief to be handing over the command.

Gelon looked me up and down and raised an eyebrow in dry amusement. I was filthy.

"Well, make your report, Captain," he said coolly.

I briefed him. The fire was now only about two miles away. It was moving south but fanning out as well. The brick-built houses of Upper Tyche would burn more slowly than the shacks of Little Athens, but the larger and hotter the fire grew, the more quickly it would probably start to jump the streets. Assuming the wind didn't change, my best guess was that we had maybe two days to make our preparations.

Gelon pursed his lips.

"So, it's going to be tight, then," he said. "Why aren't there more men here, Dion? Hasn't my father called out the reservists?"

"He did, sir, but most of them must have better things to do," I replied, not bothering to hide my bitterness.

"I see," he said. "Well, leave the reservists to me. You'll be pleased to hear the Shield divisions are on their way. They should be at the gates soon. The cavalry are already here with me. Where do you want me to post them?"

"We need more horses everywhere, sir."

"Very well. You heard him, Eulus. Leave me fifty of your men and spread the rest out along the length of the wall. And send a rider back to Plymmerium. I want all the remaining horses there brought over immediately. Off you go."

"Yes, sir." Eulus saluted us both and ran down the temple steps.

Gelon leant his shoulder against a column and stared at the flames.

"Arson?" he asked quietly.

"Almost certainly, sir."

He pursed his lips. After a few moments, he straightened himself up and walked down the steps. I followed him silently. When he reached the bottom, he went over to Hannon and spoke to him quietly. I respectfully kept my distance. Hannon nodded and ran over to the railing to untie a horse for himself. Eulus and his officers were already filing off the summit and as soon as he had mounted up, the slave cantered off behind them.

Gelon turned to me.

"You've done well, Dion," he said. "Now, I suppose you'd better get back down there. You're dismissed."

※

Gelon used the fifty cavalrymen whom he had held back to summon the reservists from Achradina and Neapolis. They rode through the streets, announcing that the city gates would remain closed until the fire was out. Any man caught evading his duty would be crucified.

It did the trick. By dawn, the trickle of reservists arriving at the wall had turned into a flood.

We worked on through the following day and night. There must have been fifty thousand of us by then: citizens, slaves, criminals, soldiers and cavalrymen, all sweating side by side. Women and children brought us drinking water and food while we tore down the houses of the poor. I sent word to Xeno to abandon Upper Tyche and bring his men into Temenites. The fire by now was far too strong for anything they could do to be of any use. It was jumping streets easily and unpredictably, and they were in danger of being cut off. As the smoke began to thicken around us, I was sure I saw Gelon himself helping to rip up the roof of a shop, in the company of a group of slaves. He was probably enjoying himself.

The fire gorged itself on Upper Tyche, like a mindless glutton. Building by building, it crawled relentlessly towards us. It finally burst upon us in the early hours of the third day, in flames as tall as siege towers. A vast hand of grey-black smoke curled out over our heads, as if readying itself to snatch us off the ground. By then, we had cleared a strip maybe a hundred feet wide along the entire length of the wall. The air quickly became too hot and acrid to breathe and we retreated into Temenites, uncertain whether we had done enough. Gelon immediately ordered us to start dismantling the buildings closest to the wall on our side as well.

The fire had consumed two thirds or more of Upper Tyche. Hundreds must have been killed, maybe thousands – the weak, the greedy and the stupid. We never bothered counting them: they were not important people. But the gods were merciful. Our firebreak held.

By the end of the fourth day, there was nothing left within its grasp for the fire to devour. It spat and hissed and flared sporadically in rage, but it grew weaker every hour, and finally it fell into a smouldering sulk. The crisis was over.

The northern district of our city had been transformed into a charred, smoking wasteland. The streets and market squares of Temenites were cluttered with newly homeless families, sleeping rough among stacks of planks and tall, unstable piles of cheap furniture. We all looked like Numidians. A dark canopy of smoke still hung over us, and the streets and roofs were filthy with soot. The warm ash got everywhere: nothing was clean, indoors or out.

Once the danger had abated, Gelon wasted no time in ordering the cavalry and Shield divisions back to Plymmerium. He seemed to share his father's reluctance to have them in the city. The prince, Castor and I had remained in Temenites throughout, sleeping in shifts in a modest house near the wall. But now Gelon decided to return to the palace, and ordered me to follow as soon as I felt I could.

Before the prince left, he had all the slaves from the quarries and pens gather in front of the Temple of Tyche. He stood on the temple steps and thanked them for their service. Then he freed every tenth one. They drew lots for their liberty. The gesture seemed to give him a great deal of satisfaction, mainly, I suspect, because all those from the quarries belonged to Woodpecker, his odious son-in-law.

I still had some work to do. The prince had reluctantly agreed to my request to put Temenites and Neapolis under martial law. I was worried that the criminal gangs that had come across from Upper Tyche might start making trouble. Before sending the Guards back to their garrisons, I thinned out every company, so as to leave four hundred men behind to patrol the streets.

I left Castor in command and told him to be ruthless with the gangs. General Lepides used to say that the sooner you make a start on the crucifixions, the fewer crosses you need. But then, Lepides always liked to take an energetic approach to executions. Few things probably saddened the old man more than the reflection that so many perfectly serviceable wooden posts had to be wasted on housing.

It was not till late in the afternoon of the fifth day that Agbal and I mounted our horses and wearily set off back to the palace under the smog-diminished sun. Most of my men had already left that same morning.

"You did well, Agbal," I told him, as we trotted through the grimy streets. I rummaged inside my ruined tunic and managed to find a silver piece. "Here, catch."

He caught it gracefully and gawped at it.

"Thank you, Master," he said, grinning from ear to ear, although I think the praise probably pleased him even more than the coin. While the fire had raged, I had used him to run messages. It may sound a simple enough task, but it is one that requires a degree of intelligence and a cool head. I dare say many a soldier has died needlessly, because some dim-witted camp slave forgot or mistook part of an officer's message.

We were just about to cross the Labdalum Road into Neapolis when I heard a vaguely familiar voice call out to me.

"Leaving us already, Captain?"

It was the big man from Upper Tyche. I pulled up my horse as he detached himself from a small huddle of unpleasant-looking hangers-on and sauntered over. I hadn't seen him at the wall, but he was as filthy as me and one of his hands was crudely bandaged with a rag. It seemed as though he had done his part. He smiled at me insolently and nodded at my torn and grimy tunic.

"You look like one of us now," he said. "Maybe you should move to Little Athens, Captain. I hear there are some properties going cheap there these days."

Perhaps it was because I was exhausted, but for some reason, I just laughed. The world seemed to have turned upside-down: great nobles kissed my backside, while common criminals were openly impertinent to me.

He started chuckling too. He had a deep, rather pleasant laugh.

"You're an ugly turd," I said, "and you'll end up on a cross."

"You're hardly an Adonis yourself," he replied cheerfully. "And they'll have to catch me first."

I put my hands on my thighs and gazed down at him.

"So, what will you do now?" I asked. "You know there's nothing for a man like you this side of the wall? I hope you understand that. You'll not live long if you start to make trouble over here."

He shrugged.

"There's not much for me on the other side of the wall now either," he replied. "And in my line of work, Captain, you don't expect to live too long."

What a waste of a man, I thought. If he wasn't so full of vinegar, he might have made a decent life for himself. I scratched my cheek.

"You could try signing on for the City Guards," I said on an impulse. "You've done your training, haven't you? Perhaps I could find a use for a bastard like you."

He looked at me in surprise.

"Yes, I've done my time in the army. But somehow, I don't think joining your gang would work out very well for me, Captain. I'm not much of a one for regulations, and I hear you've a nasty way with a whip."

I grunted.

"Well, think about it. Better to be whipped than crucified. You know where to find us if you change your mind."

I put my heels to the horse but it had only taken a couple of strides when I reined it to a halt again. I turned in the saddle.

"By the way," I called out to him, "you never told me your name."

He walked back to my side and looked up at me coolly.

"Dionysius," he said.

I smiled again. After Alexander, it was probably the most popular name in Syracuse among the common people, but it was an amusing coincidence all the same. The head of my family was always called either Dion or Dionysius. It alternated between the generations: my own first-born son, if I had one, would be named Dionysius.

"Would you like to know how I came by it, Captain?" he asked. "You may find the story amusing."

I shrugged and nodded.

"Well, you see, my mother was a washerwoman, but every now and then, she did a bit of whoring on the side. She was a classy one, mind you, not like those foreign skanks. She used to charge her customers in silver when she still had her looks. Anyway, one day the silly cow got herself in the family way, thanks to some fancy soldier boy. She didn't know his name, of course. But then, a few months later, when her belly was all fat and swollen and the customers were harder to come by, she waddles off to the Temple of Athena. She was always going there with a little offering of something or other. And suddenly she sees this same officer riding past on a great big black horse. A bit like yours, I imagine. So out of curiosity, she asked the people standing on the steps if anyone knew his name. And as luck would have it, someone did. And not knowing who her own father was, and with nothing else suggesting itself to her, when I popped out a few weeks later, she decided to call me after him."

He paused for a few moments to let what he had just said sink in.

"So you see, Captain," he went on as I stared down at him, "I'm grateful for the offer. I have to say, it's big of you, given that I haven't exactly shown you the respect I probably should have. But I don't imagine it would work out very well for either of us if I joined the Guards, now, would it?"

I blinked at him but could think of nothing to say.

He met my gaze evenly, then gave me another nod and turned away. My eyes followed him as he strode back towards his companions and the small, dark corners of his own world. After a moment, I put my heels to the horse again and Agbal and I rode on in silence.

Perhaps I should not have been as taken aback as I was. I dare say most of the blue-blooded nobles of Ortygia had bastard half-siblings scattered around the city. I had just never expected to meet one of my own.

When we got back to the palace, I dismounted and handed Agbal my sword. I told him to take our horses to the stables, and then to find Alpha and send him to me at the bathhouse with a change of clothes and a razor. I hadn't shaved or washed for five days.

I found the bathhouse crowded with my exhausted men, who had only returned from Tyche themselves a few hours earlier. I stripped off, tossing my ruined clothes under a bench.

Mounted high on an adjacent wall was a row of half a dozen stone animal heads. I stood under the face of a boar and called up to the slave on the platform above. A moment later, a stream of warm water began to flow from the boar's mouth. I immersed myself in the shower, relishing the cascade over my hair and upturned face as I scrubbed myself with a flannel.

"Again," I called, when the flow eventually stopped.

Finally feeling clean, I walked stiffly over to the large stone tub in the centre of the room, in which half a dozen of my men were already lounging. They looked at me nervously and fell silent as I approached. I climbed into the cold water, leant my head against the lip of the bath and closed my eyes.

Every muscle in my body seemed to ache. I had allowed the men and slaves to rest for a short while every three hours, while I had toiled on like a plough ox, prising planks free with my sword or hauling timbers on my shoulders. I had paused only occasionally to drink some water or snatch a few mouthfuls of food, and then to sleep for a short while before starting again. I am blessed with unusual stamina and strength, but I was paying the price now.

"Sir?"

I recognised the voice. I didn't open my eyes.

"What is it, Phylas?"

"I just wanted to say, well, I wanted to say 'thank you', sir."

"For what? Not taking you on any runs these last few days?"

The other men in the bath laughed.

"No sir," he continued awkwardly. "Forgive me, sir, I'm not very good with my words. But if it weren't for you, half the city would have gone up in flames. Everybody knows it."

I grunted.

"It's Prince Gelon you should be thanking then, Phylas. If he hadn't come, we'd all be roast chestnuts now."

"No, sir. It's you. No one would have known what to do without you. And you've made the Guards strong, sir, not like we was before, so we could do the things what you told us to. And…" he mumbled, "and, well, my woman and kids are in Temenites, sir. They live with my old man. He's got a little barber's shop there. I just wanted you to know that."

I opened my eyes, but Phylas was already climbing out of the bath. As he walked over to the benches to dress, I gazed at the white criss-cross of scars and welts on his back.

He was one of the men I had whipped in my first week as his captain.

He was overstating it, of course, but I was gratified anyway. I had thought only battle and blood could finally bind the Guards together, but perhaps a fire would do.

Out of the corner of my eye, I saw Alpha walk in with a pile of towelling and clothes in his arms. After I'd soaked for few minutes longer, I climbed out as well and went over to where he stood waiting for me.

"It's good to have you safely back, Master," he said happily.

After I had dried myself off, he shaved me and then I lay on the bench while he rubbed oil into my back and shoulders.

"What a terrible business, Master," he twittered gaily. "You know, I was in the butcher's just this morning, and he was saying the fire must be a sign. A sign as clear as day is what it was, he said. And everyone in the shop agreed."

"A sign of what, Alpha?" I said drowsily.

"That the goddess is displeased, Master."

"And what does the butcher think she is displeased about, Alpha? The scarcity of pork?"

"No, bless you, Master," he said with a giggle. "She's displeased about your mother, of course. The goddess wants your mother for her High Priestess, doesn't she? Well, it's obvious when you think about it, isn't it? Lady Korinna announces she won't be our High Priestess, and sure enough, just a few days later, the city has the worst fire anyone can remember. A right proper visitation is what it was, the butcher said. And it's not just the goddess who's displeased, I might add. The people all want your mother too, don't they? Such an elegant woman. A pity you never inherited her dress sense. And she's just as famous for her brains, of course. I mean, no one really knows who the other two ladies are, do they? Not that I mean any disrespect to your sister and auntie, Master. There, that's your back done, you can turn over now… Yes, the people certainly love your mother, especially with everything she's been doing for all those poor families in Temenites."

I rolled over and stared up at him incredulously as he began to rub the oil into my chest.

"What exactly has she been doing in Temenites, Alpha?" I asked quietly.

"Goodness, haven't you heard, Master? Every day since the fire started, she's been sending over those women who live in your stables with baskets of bread. They hand it out as a gift from her to the people sleeping in the streets. And what with her son having just saved us all from the cooking pot, well, it's hardly surprising feelings are running high, is it? There must be four or five hundred people on the street outside your house. They've been there for two days now. They say they won't leave till your dear mama changes her mind about becoming our High Priestess."

My good mood had been short-lived. It didn't require the brains of Archimedes to work out where the stories of the goddess's displeasure had originated. My mother's opportunism was shocking, but I was too tired to start worrying about her antics. I told myself I would deal with her the following day. But at least I had finally understood why she kept the old women in my stables. They had probably earned their keep many times over, spreading profitable rumours and gossip among the lower orders. By the time I returned to my rooms, I could hardly keep my eyes open. Omega was waiting for us inside the door.

"Welcome home, Master," he said with a wide smile. "I hope you won't mind, but I told Agbal to go to bed as soon as he had cleaned himself up. The poor child was fit to drop."

"That's fine," I said. "So am I."

"I've put some food out on the table in your room, Master," Omega continued. I nodded.

"Good. Run over to the barracks for me, would you, Omega, and tell the duty officer there'll be no drills tomorrow. The men can stay in bed as long as they like. Then you can both turn in as well."

I walked through to the anteroom, where Agbal was snoring lightly on his paillasse. As usual, the two ivory-handled throwing knives were laid out neatly on the floor by his side. I smiled to myself and stepped quietly around him.

Once in my bedroom, with the door closed behind me, I sat down at the table and fell on my meal. My shoulders and back still ached.

Omega had lit half a dozen small lamps around the room. As I chewed on my food, their feeble flames seemed to assume a sinister, almost menacing character. It was as if the fire were still quietly watching me.

"Fuck off," I snarled at the nearest lamp.

It was an absurd thing to do, but it cheered me up anyway.

I wolfed down the last of my meal in the flickering light, and then undressed and went round the room carefully extinguishing every lamp. When I finally collapsed onto my cot, I fell at once into a deep, untroubled sleep.

I was awoken sometime after dawn by Alpha and Omega. They were both leaning over me and shaking me for all they were worth.

XIV

THE HELL GATE

"Wake up, Master," they squealed.

"What is it?" I demanded, blinking and confused.

"Something terrible has happened," said Alpha.

"At your house, Master," said Omega.

"You're needed, Master. A slave came to say you should go there at once."

I swung my legs out of the cot, shook my head and ran my hands through my hair.

"Where's the slave? Bring him in."

"He's already left, Master," said Alpha. "He would only say there's been bloodshed. And that you should hurry."

"Agbal has already gone to the stables to prepare your horse, Master."

Fifteen minutes later, I was galloping down the Avenue of Athena. Several men who didn't recognise me hurled angry obscenities as I careered past them, forcing them to jump out of the way.

Alpha had said that there were four or five hundred people outside my house, but there must have been well over a thousand by the time I arrived, thronging around the main gate and entirely blocking the street. It seemed word had already spread that something had happened. A few faces turned and saw me and began shouting and waving, but I veered off down an almost deserted alley and followed the way round to the back of the villa.

Two of my mother's Galatian mercenaries stood guard outside the stable gates. They looked at me with sheepish, guilty expressions. Despite the expense, I had let her keep them, as the estate at Catana required protection if it was to be her new home, but I hadn't realised they had accompanied her back to Syracuse.

The men let me in. A slave took my horse and one of the guards beckoned me to follow him across the yard. He led me into a small side hall that the slaves used to get in and out of the family apartments.

Once inside, the guard opened the door of a storeroom and gestured to me to follow him. A few pieces of broken furniture were stacked against one wall. Slumped incongruously under a small window lay the body of a dark-haired young man. His arms, legs and tunic were plastered with congealed blood.

"So, who is he?" I demanded.

The Galatian meekly shrugged his shoulders. He didn't seem to speak Greek but he was clearly frightened.

"Who?" I repeated, pointing to the body.

The mercenary nodded.

"Yes. Kill," he said, with an almost impenetrably thick accent. "Mother."

I stared at him, uncertain whether I had understood him correctly.

"Lady Korinna?" I asked.

He nodded at me with wide eyes.

"Yes. Kill," he repeated. "Korinna."

I bolted out of the little room and turned up the narrow flight of stairs that adjoined it. I took the steps three at a time and crashed through the door on the first floor into a long, high corridor. At the far end, a score of household slaves had gathered outside my mother's old bedroom. As I ran towards them, they turned to look at me with white faces. None of them dared speak.

I pushed my way through them.

My mother's gilded bed stood in the centre of the room.

She lay on her side under the sheet, facing away from me. I could see only her hair, which was cut short. It was entirely grey, almost silver, and so thin that a few patches of her scalp were visible. She had worn wigs ever since my father had died. As I gazed numbly at her, I wondered if that had been when it had changed colour.

The sheets should have been white, but they were crimson. The marble floor should have been white too. I walked round the side of the bed in a daze. A hand dangled over the edge, the tips of the fingers resting in an expansive red puddle. Several long streaks of blood had splattered some distance across the floor. Those must have been the first to spurt from her severed throat, I realised, while her pulse was still strong. The spray would have subsided quite quickly after that.

I stared blankly at the unrecognisable, blood-caked face, which had assumed a strangely crooked angle, trying to comprehend what I saw. Her jaw and cheeks seemed distorted and her eyes gazed vacantly at the wall. The enormity of the outrage overwhelmed me. For perhaps the first time in my adult life, I felt completely at a loss. I had no idea what to do.

I became dimly conscious of a rustling of robes behind me. A moment later, a crisp, disdainful voice cut through my thoughts like a razor.

"Well, you certainly took your time getting here," my mother said.

I spun on my heels and stared at her. She stood with her hands folded together, as self-possessed as ever.

She gazed back at me coldly.

"You're alive," I gasped.

"Perhaps, Dion, you might refrain from stating the obvious. It makes for very dull conversation. Now, I think you and I should have a little talk. Have you had breakfast yet? Let's go to my dining room." She turned to the slaves who still crowded around the door.

"Get out of my way. And for pity's sake, stop gawping and get this mess cleaned up… Come on, Dion, don't dawdle."

'Her' dining room turned out to be one of half a dozen rather grand upstairs rooms that she had evidently appropriated for her private use after returning from Catana. She had already taken most of my best furniture with her to the country, and now it seemed she had picked over whatever remained to furnish her new apartment in the house. Alexander of Macedon's set of gold plates was ostentatiously laid out on a serving table, like the war booty of a victorious army, alongside a large, antique silver bowl piled high with fruit.

She invited me to make myself comfortable on one of my couches, and clapped her hands. Two slaves came hurrying in.

"Now, what will you have to eat, Dion?" she asked, settling herself down opposite me. I drew a deep breath.

"Nothing, thank you, Mother."

She turned to the slaves.

"Give him some figs and apricots. I shall have the same."

The slaves went to the side table and began spooning fruit onto a pair of the heavy plates, which she had apparently adopted for her everyday use.

"Can we please dispense with this nonsense?" I said irritably. "Tell me what happened here. Who was that woman in your room?"

One of the slaves came over and placed a generously loaded dish on the small table beside me.

"Take it away," I snarled, and he bowed and picked it up again.

"Don't be silly, Dion. Do you want your bowels to become congested? Leave the plate there, whatever your name is. The master can pick at his fruit later. Now, leave us, both of you."

The slave bowed again and put the plate back down. Then he and his equally nervous companion disappeared through a side door as fast as they could.

I let it go.

"So, who was that woman, Mother?"

"Agatha, my chamber slave. It's a tragedy. She was my dresser for over twenty years, you know." She picked up an apricot and began nibbling on it. "I've no idea where I'll find the time to train up someone else."

"Are you going to tell me what she was doing in your bed?"

My mother raised her eyebrows.

"Isn't it obvious? Agatha has been taking my place at night for months. I sleep in a different room every night. Anyway," she continued, "you'll be pleased to hear my bodyguards caught the man before he could escape. One of your new gardeners, apparently. I ordered two for you, by the way. They were only delivered the day before yesterday. He was hired to do it, of course; in fact, he probably wasn't a gardener at all. Unfortunately, the idiots killed him before he could be questioned – not that he could have told me anything I don't already know. I suppose you may want to make your own enquiries, but you'll find the threads lead straight to Carthage."

I was more bewildered than ever.

"But why on earth should the Carthaginians try to kill you, Mother?"

"You really are quite obtuse, aren't you, Dion?" she sighed. "The Carthaginians didn't try to kill me. Hieron did. But he's hardly going to announce it in the agora, is he? He'd have made quite sure the blame falls somewhere convenient."

She discarded the clean apricot stone on her plate and turned her attention to a fig.

I stared at her in shock for a few moments, then put my head in my hands. A hailstorm of confused, inchoate thoughts began clattering around inside me.

"And why would Hieron want to kill you, Mother? What have you been up to? Tell me the truth, please."

"Nothing, my dear. But he's obviously desperate to stop me becoming High Priestess."

"But that makes no sense," I said eventually, struggling to keep my voice even. "You're not going to be High Priestess. I've already announced your withdrawal."

"Yes, Dion, I know." She smiled. "But I wouldn't be surprised if the senate refuses to accept it."

I burst out laughing.

"You're deluded, Mother. The senate would never go against Hieron. I only made you withdraw to spare you the humiliation of losing to Maia. Hieron hardly needs to kill you. He can stop you with a click of his fingers."

She looked at me contemptuously.

"Can he, now? I wouldn't be quite so certain of that, if I were you, Dion. Hieron clearly isn't, or else he wouldn't have had your gardener try to murder me, would he?"

"Mother, you're arguing in circles… Someone else must be behind this."

She sighed.

"Dion, while you were happily demolishing all our property in Tyche, there was an announcement. It was very short. All it said was that the Romans had attacked Hannibal in Apulia but failed to defeat him. Everyone else was too busy with the fire to pay much attention to the news, but I did. It made me suspicious, so I called in on the wife of your friend Captain Sosis. It so happens I lent her father some money a few years ago, on the security of their family home. I don't normally lend money, but he had served under your own father and I felt obliged to help… Anyway, she had been sworn to secrecy, of course, but she told me everything all the same. It seems our imbecile allies managed to get themselves annihilated again, and now there's nothing standing between Hannibal and Rome itself… You look surprised, Dion, but I see you don't deny it…"

"Mother, you've lost me. What has all this got to do with anything?"

Her eyes flashed with malice.

"Don't you see, Dion? It changes everything. Hieron is vulnerable. I can smell it. He's been starving the city for nearly two years to keep the barbarians fed, and when the truth of this disaster sinks in, the people won't be happy. They could even start turning against him. He knows it. He certainly won't want to provoke them needlessly, by denying them their choice of High Priestess. It will stick in his shrivelled old gizzard like a fish bone, and naturally he'll exact a price, but at the end of the day, he will instruct the senate to choose me, because he will calculate that keeping the people sweet matters more than keeping me out of the temple. He will have no choice now, given that he's missed his chance to kill me."

I stared at her.

"Mother, Hieron's hardly going to murder you just to stop you becoming High Priestess. It's not as though it really matters who succeeds Delia. Why on earth would he care that much?"

"As usual, my poor darling, you miss the point. The High Priestess is inviolate. *That's* the point. No one, in the entire history of the Greek people, has ever dared to interfere with a High Priestess. Hieron would become an outcast in his own kingdom if he tried it. He would be cursed by every priest in the Greek world. Once I am chosen, he will never be able to get rid of me. And nor, for that matter, will you. Why do you think I want the position? Do you imagine I enjoy fiddling around with chicken entrails like some common cook? I want it, because it will make me safe, and it will set me free. I shall be High Priestess, Dion. And no man will ever command me again."

She dropped the half-eaten fig on her plate and calmly dipped her fingers in the little bowl of water beside it.

"You're quite mad, Mother. And if Hieron really is behind this, all I can say is that you've brought it on your own head. I warned you. For fuck's sake, stop playing these games. You'll lose. If you want to be safe, just go back to Catana."

"Go back to Catana? I'd rather die," she replied coolly. "And besides, I wouldn't be safe there either. I didn't create this danger, Dion. *You* did. It's entirely your fault that poor Agatha is dead. None of this would have happened if you hadn't been such a fool. You have no idea how much inconvenience you've caused me. I've had to surround myself with bodyguards. My meals always arrive cold, because they have to be tasted before I dare touch them. I can't even sleep in my own bed. But how very like you, only to think of yourself."

"What's it to do with me?" I exploded. "Fuck it. I should never have let you come back… I should have married you off years ago. Well, just you watch me do it now. I'm going to find some poor bastard with a little estate in the country who needs the money, and you can go and rot."

"You still can't see it, can you?" she hissed. "All you had to do was bide your time quietly in the army. But, oh no, you had to let Hieron make you his creature instead. It's pathetic. He only needed to dangle a little blue tunic in front of you, and off you went, running to him with open arms. And now you'd do anything to please the new daddy you think you've found for yourself, wouldn't you? And how very happy you must have made him. He already has the nobles exactly where he wants them, thanks to you. He needs you; but while I'm around, he can never be entirely sure of you, can he? In his mind, you are still a sword that could cut two ways. That's why he wants me dead, Dion. Because with me standing behind you, you are still the heir of King Dionysius. But without me, you are just a dim-witted child with big muscles, for Hieron to use as he pleases. It was your willingness to sell yourself for a pat on the head and a seat at his table that has put me in danger, and I won't be safe again until I've succeeded Delia. And as to marrying me off, well, I think you'll find it's a little too late for that. Why don't you go to the window and see for yourself?"

"What do you mean?" I muttered. "See what?"

She stood, smoothed her robe and gazed down scornfully at me.

"I'm putting on a little show for the crowd," she replied. "It should be starting any moment now. I'll leave you to watch it from here. I'm going to take a nap: I barely got a wink's sleep last night. Think about what I've said, Dion. You've always been a disappointment to me, but I loved your father, and I know my duty to his children. Hieron cares nothing for you. I'm all you have."

She bent to pick up her plate of fruit, then swept majestically from the room, without giving me another glance.

I sat motionless, trying to take everything in. Could it really have been Hieron? Could it?

I remembered the night the Royal Watch came for my father. I was woken by the sudden commotion in the courtyard, by men shouting furiously at each other and slave women screaming and the muffled clanking of armour. Terrified, I ran down the corridor to my parents' room. My father was already out of bed, pulling his blue tunic over his head. Cerberus, our porter, was standing trembling near the door.

"What's going on, Father? What's happening?"

My mother was still in the gilded bed.

"Shut up, Dion," she said.

My father looked at me and bit his lip. There were tears in his eyes. I had never seen him cry before.

"Come here, son," he said. He folded his arms around me and lowered his head to kiss the top of mine. "I'm sorry, Dion. I'm so sorry. When you are a man, perhaps you will understand. Then try to forgive me."

"If he lives that long," my mother said.

My father released me and took my hand. His eyes slowly widened as my mother's words sank in. After a moment he turned to the slave.

"Try to slip out the back, Cerberus. If you can, get to my Aunt Delia's house and ask her to speak to the king. Maybe she can persuade him to spare the children, at least. Go on. Hurry now."

When Cerberus had scurried from the room, he turned back to my mother.

"Shouldn't we try to hide the boy?" he asked.

"What's the point?" she replied. "If they've come for him too, they'll find him. No. We will not meet this like rats."

A minute or two later, a slave woman opened the door and a middle-aged man wearing a black-plumed helmet sauntered in. Four younger men followed behind him, almost as casually.

Somehow, it was more frightening than if they had burst in on us with drawn swords. It was as if they owned the house.

The older man nodded to my father, who was still holding my hand.

"Sorry to intrude, General," he said, smiling coldly.

My father forced a grim smile in response.

"I understand," he said.

And then my mother did something I shall never forget.

She rose from their bed, completely naked, and with her head held high walked over to take my other hand. She made no attempt to hide her body from the men. She looked down at me and gave me a slight nod.

"Good boy," she said. Then she turned her unblinking gaze on the soldiers.

The middle-aged one eyed her over slowly and raised his eyebrows in amusement. Beside me, I sensed my father bristle.

My mother tossed her head slightly and with her free hand pulled back her long golden hair so that it hung down over her shoulder.

"Very well, then," she said. "Let's get this over with."

The senior man clicked his fingers at the slave woman who had led them to the room.

"You there. Fetch your mistress a robe… Well, go on, woman, get a move on… No, we're not here for you, Lady Korinna. Or the children. At least, not tonight. But none of you is to leave the house till the king has decided what to do with you. You'll be kept under guard here. But I'm afraid you're to come with us, General."

My father nodded, released my hand and stepped forwards. My mother gasped almost inaudibly and stretched out to touch his shoulder blade with her fingertips. He turned to smile at her.

As he strode out of the door, there were tears on her cheeks too. Before that night, I had never seen her cry either.

Rather than sit in judgement on them himself, Hieron sent my father and his fellow conspirators to the courts to be tried. The trial was held publicly, in the agora, but we were not allowed to go.

Incriminating letters were produced. Inevitably, the magistrates found them guilty. My father, two of his captains and a dozen lieutenants were all sentenced to crucifixion. That was the most severe punishment the court could impose, so the frightened magistrates had to make do with urging the king to substitute some less gentle alternative. Instead, Hieron allowed all the other officers to go into exile, and commuted my father's punishment to beheading behind closed doors. His body, with the head carefully sewn back on, was delivered to our house, so that we could see he had not been tortured. We were permitted to bury him properly, in a ceremony that no one else dared attend, apart from Archimedes. And then Hieron withdrew our guards, and let it be known that no further action would be taken against my family. He didn't even confiscate any of our property. The city marvelled at his mercy. Whatever popularity or reputation my father may once have commanded evaporated faster than dew. Hieron had played it perfectly.

Had the king finally come to regret his leniency towards the House of Dionysius, I wondered? I sat on the couch, asking myself if the man I served might have turned on us. I could feel my heart pounding and, for an instant, I even thought I could hear it, till I became conscious that what I was listening to was the dull sound of tramping feet. Still giddy, I stood and went over to the window.

The room faced across the courtyard to the statue of Athena and, beyond it, the villa's main entrance gate. A dozen Galatian mercenaries carrying spears were marching towards the gate in two short lines. Between them walked a tall and thin middle-aged man, whom I didn't recognise. A slave followed behind him carrying a wooden crate. The wide gates began to swing open and the Galatians formed a cordon under the archway, so as to prevent anyone from entering the compound. The slave put the crate down a few feet behind them and the man climbed onto it, with his back to me. I could see a small section of the crowd on the street outside. They began to jostle and heave to try to get a better view of what was happening in the courtyard.

The man produced a scroll from his tunic. He unrolled it with a flourish, threw back his head, paused for effect, and began to read. I recognised his deep, honeyed voice immediately. Everyone within earshot probably did. His name was Aristo, and he was the most famous tragic actor in Syracuse. It was the first time I had seen him without his theatrical mask.

"The Lady Korinna wishes to address the rumours now circulating, regarding the terrible events that occurred last night in her son's house," he intoned.

A man in the front row of the crowd turned and shouted angrily to the people behind him to be quiet.

Aristo cleared his throat, and resumed.

"Two nights ago, the Lady Korinna was blessed with a vision – a vision such as she has never previously experienced. A tall and beauteous woman, wearing a golden helmet and clasping a golden spear and shield, appeared to her as she slept."

"Was it the goddess?" a voice shouted. "It was, wasn't it?"

"Tell us, what did she say?" another called out.

"Shut up and let the man speak," yelled someone else.

Aristo raised his hand for silence.

"In a voice like a silver trumpet, the radiant apparition spoke. 'Child, you have ever been my faithful handmaiden, and beloved are you in my eyes. Heed well what I now tell you. Command your slave Agatha to lie in your chamber tonight, and do not enter it yourself, for Death will stalk you when the moon is high.' And with that, the lustrous vision melted into the mists, and the Lady Korinna awoke."

From the window, I could see faces in the crowd gawping at the actor with wide eyes and open mouths.

I gripped the window ledge with both hands.

"The Lady Korinna did as the vision bade her," Aristo continued. "And last night, as had been foretold, a man of swarthy complexion, with eyes as black as his jet-black hair, stole into the room where Agatha the slave woman slept. With the cry of a wild animal, he threw himself onto the bed, slashing and stabbing with his long, curved blade. In terror, Agatha cried out, and at once, Lady Korinna's bodyguards, who had concealed themselves in an adjoining chamber, ran in. Long and dreadful was the fight. Again and again, the assassin was struck and wounded, till, exhausted at last, he finally collapsed to the floor in a lake of his own black blood. And there the dog died, with a vile curse on his lips."

Aristo paused again. The crowd was completely still and silent.

"Alas, my friends," he eventually resumed, his voice dropping to an even lower register, "I have more to tell, though it grieves me greatly so to do. Not a moment later, the Lady Korinna herself entered the chamber. Immediately, she ran to the side of her faithful slave, and let out a fearful cry. For in the attack, Agatha had received a mortal blow, and she too now lay dying. 'Shed no tears for me, Mistress,' said the good woman, as the Lady Korinna clasped her small, cold hand, 'for I die content, knowing I have served you well.' And then, with a face as serene as a sleeping child's, Agatha exhaled her final breath."

Aristo let the hand in which he held the scroll drop to his side, and hung his head in sorrow.

"Who was the bastard?" a voice demanded. "Was it a Carthaginian?"

"My friends," Aristo shouted back, "I cannot say. I know only that he was no Greek, for what Greek could be so vile? But you may be sure of this at least: such an outrage will not go unanswered. For no sooner had he received the news, than the noble Dion came hurrying to his dear mother's side. As each of you well knows, these last days and nights, our young hero has not slept, while he wrestled like a Hercules reborn with the flames of Tyche. But no sooner was the fire overcome, and all your homes made safe, than he was summoned here, where under his own roof, he found this scene of bloody sacrilege. How tenderly he comforted his weeping mother in those colossal arms! And when he learnt of how the gentle Agatha had died, straight away he ordered that her two daughters should be freed – for both were born his slaves. And, more than this, for each of them he has pledged a dowry – a dowry of golden coins. But when the noble Dion was shown the body of the faithful woman, lying in his own mother's bed, his rage was more terrible than any one of you could possibly imagine. No man has dared go near him since, for his anger flows like molten lava."

Aristo slowly spread his arms and leant slightly forwards. I imagine the gesture was intended to convey what a very nasty thing molten lava can be. He held the pose for a moment, then dropped his arms again and resumed.

"My friends, you ask me if the assassin was a Carthaginian. As yet, I cannot say from what hot, sandy shores this dark-skinned, black-haired villain came. But enquiries are being made, and in his wisdom, you may be certain that our king will soon discover all. Nothing can remain concealed from him. And when the truth of this is finally exposed, who here would wish to face the wrath of Hieron, mighty King of Syracuse, or the dreadful vengeance of The Bull?"

Had his bony backside only been within reach of my foot, Aristo would have been the first to feel my dreadful vengeance.

"And that, my friends, is all the information that I have to give," the great actor concluded. "When there is more to tell, you shall be told. The concern you have shown by gathering here has touched the Lady Korinna beyond the competence of words. As always, she prays that the goddess will continue to extend her protection over our king and our city, and over each and every one of you."

Aristo carefully rolled up and put away the parchment, climbed down from the crate and began to make his way back across the courtyard. The slave picked up the crate again and followed him. But the gates did not close at once, and the mercenaries remained motionless under the archway. My mother's modest contribution to the canon of Greek drama had not quite concluded yet.

As Aristo disappeared through one door, a woman in a flowing white gown emerged from another. Her face was veiled, in the old-fashioned manner that ladies of rank occasionally still adopted when appearing in public. She walked with a straight back and her head held high, and in her hand she carried a small spray of olive twigs.

Had I not known better, even I might have been fooled by the impersonation. The woman was of much the same build as my mother and had captured her walk perfectly. I learnt later she was Aristo's wife, and she clearly shared something of her husband's theatrical talent. She ignored the people at the gate; it was as if, to her, they did not exist. Instead, she directed her steps to the statue of Athena in the centre of the courtyard, her pace measured but purposeful. She bowed low and laid the twigs at the statue's feet. And then she knelt and silently prostrated herself before the goddess.

After a few moments, the gates of the villa finally closed, leaving the hushed and awed crowd outside with an unforgettable image of the Lady Korinna's piety, a piety that somehow combined dignity and humility in equal measure.

The inference that the crowd had been invited to draw from Aristo's and his wife's performance could hardly have been plainer. Lady Korinna's relationship with the goddess was a peculiarly intimate one. No doubt Athena would be dropping by for supper at my house any day now. Who else could possibly succeed Delia?

I was a little surprised that my mother had preferred not to appear before the crowd in person; but then, I suppose public prostration was never really her style. Having had no qualms about getting poor Agatha to do the dying for her, she was hardly going to baulk at getting someone else to do the kneeling.

I turned from the window and walked over to the gilded couch on which I had recently been sitting. I contemplated it for a moment or two, then gripped its headboard with both hands and, coiling my hips and shoulders, flung it against the nearest wall. In the process, I knocked over the little side table. The gold plate crashed noisily onto the marble tiles at much the same moment as the couch hit the wall. The couch splintered into several pieces and a large section of the frescoed plasterwork detached itself and crumbled to the ground, sending up a thick cloud of white dust.

I watched the dust begin to settle, then walked over to my mother's couch and hurled that against a wall as well, with much the same effect.

Out of the corner of my eye, I saw a door open. A slave peaked round the edge of it to stare at me in horror. I picked up my mother's side table by the leg and threw it at his head. He yelped and ducked back just in time. The table smashed into the wooden door and shattered.

I rolled my shoulders a few times, took a breath and surveyed the wreckage. Only the serving table still required my attention. I strolled over, put my hand behind it and flipped it violently forwards. The stack of gold plates and the silver fruit bowl made a tremendous din as they hit the stone tiles. It sounded as though all the bells in the kingdom were being rung at once. Pieces of fruit bounced and scattered across the floor.

Finally satisfied, I strode over to the door and let myself out.

I encountered no one as I made my way back through the house and out into the slaves' yard. The slaves and bodyguards all seemed to have gone into hiding.

"Someone bring me my fucking horse," I shouted across the deserted yard as I marched towards the stables. After a few moments, a dirty and skinny boy, maybe ten years old, jogged out leading the stallion. His hair was dark and greasy. He kept his head bowed and, as he offered me the reins, I saw his hand was shaking.

"Look at me," I growled.

He raised his head a little but kept his eyes lowered, as if I were Medusa herself.

I cupped his chin in my hand and forced his head up. He had a large black bruise on his cheek.

"Are you afraid of me, boy?" I asked.

He gulped and nodded.

"Good. Were you born in my household?"

He nodded again.

"Did you water the horse?"

"Yes, Master," he said in a whisper, "and I brushed him down too."

I grunted and let go of his chin.

"Who beat you?"

His eyes widened and he shook his head in fear.

"Was it another slave?" I demanded.

He nodded timidly.

I turned towards the slaves' dormitories, which ran at right angles to the stable block. Two or three faces that had been watching us from the upper windows hurriedly ducked back out of sight.

"This boy is my property," I bellowed up at the windows. "If anyone lays a hand on him again, I'll fucking kill them."

I turned back to the child and took the reins from his still trembling hand.

"You seem to be the only person round here who knows his job," I muttered, as I mounted up. I found a small copper coin in my tunic and flicked it to him. The boy caught it and stared up at me, apparently frozen to the spot.

"Now, get those useless Galatian cunts to open the gates for me," I said, and winked at him.

I rode round the side alleys again to avoid the crowd at the front gate. When I got back to the palace stables, I handed the horse over to a groom and returned directly to my rooms. Alpha brought me a cup of water, and I lay on a couch sipping it and trying to think. I began to make a list in my head of all the people who might have ordered the attack on my mother. My family was hardly short of enemies; but the more I turned it over, the more confused I grew. I felt I was drowning in a sea of irreconcilable and unreciprocated loyalties.

An hour later, my hopelessly tangled chain of thought was interrupted by a knock at the door. Alpha went to answer it. I heard someone in the corridor outside say something indistinct, and a moment later Alpha came back over and silently handed me a small roll of papyrus bearing the king's seal.

I broke it open nervously.

Captain Dion, it began,

His Majesty was distressed to hear of the events at your home. He gives thanks that the Lady Korinna was unharmed. As a token of his concern, he has ordered that your house be placed under the protection of the Royal Watch. A detachment of men will remain close by your mother, until this matter has been investigated and her safety is assured.

His Majesty requires that you and your mother wait on him in his audience chamber tomorrow morning, an hour after dawn.

His Majesty further informs you that the Royal Council will meet this afternoon at the seventh hour, to discuss arrangements for the population of Upper Tyche.

One never really knew where one stood with the king, Nebit had told me. Hieron was obviously playing to popular sentiment by posting his own bodyguards ostentatiously around my home. And yet it also looked very much as though he was putting my mother under something close to house arrest again. I could hardly blame him: even if he wasn't behind the attack, the king must have been infuriated when he heard of the little show she had staged.

I ran my hands through my hair and sighed. At least she wouldn't be able to get up to any more mischief, I told myself, while she had the Royal Watch breathing down her neck. As to what Hieron intended to do with her now, I would just have to wait till tomorrow to find out.

I tried to put my mother and the king out of my mind and turned my thoughts to the City Guard. There was something I needed to take care of. I went over to my table and wrote a short note to Castor, then called Agbal in and sent him over to Temenites to deliver it. I told Alpha to take the note from the king to my mother.

✳

I headed over to the barracks yard. Having cancelled the day's drills, I wasn't surprised to find several dozen of my men lounging around the yard in small groups, gossiping or playing dice. Fifty or sixty others sat in a semicircle on the ground, shouting and swearing at two thickly muscled men who were arm wrestling across a camp table. I imagined it was some sort of tournament between the palace companies. In a far corner, four men were practising their swordplay: I still occasionally received challenges from those hoping to win a silver coin off me, no doubt encouraged by their sergeants, who apparently took bets on how long the contests would last.

The first men to notice me immediately started climbing to their feet and coming to attention.

"As you were," I shouted over to them. I forced a smile and gestured with my hands for them to sit down again. Their manner seemed much the same as always, so I guessed word of the attack at my house had not yet reached them. They had earned their leisure, I thought. It was a shame it would only last a short while longer.

I climbed the staircase to the offices, where I found Leander in the duty officer's room, working at a table under the small window. He jumped up as I entered and saluted.

"Is everything alright, sir?" he asked. "My slave came to find me just a minute ago, to say there's a story flying around that some Carthaginian spy tried to kill your mother last night."

"I don't know if he was a Carthaginian spy, Lieutenant, but yes, someone tried to kill her. Anyway, she's fine. Thank you."

"The gods are merciful, sir."

I grunted. I wasn't wholly convinced that my mother's survival was proof of the gods' mercy. At any rate, I was fairly certain that poor Agatha hadn't seen it that way.

"Sit down, Leander," I said, settling myself into a battered old chair. "So, what are you working on?"

"New sentry rosters, sir," he replied. "With so many of the men having to stay in Temenites, they needed redoing. Castor asked me to take care of it. In fact, he gave me quite a list of jobs." He smiled.

"Well, that'll all have to wait, I'm afraid. I have something else for you. What with this business with my mother, I'm worried there may be trouble in the Carthaginian quarter. I want you to take two of the palace companies over to North Achradina, and have the garrison commanders at Labdalum and Euryalus send you some of their men too. Let's put on a show of force before the mob gets any stupid ideas. We've just watched Tyche burn. The last thing we need is a fire in Achradina. Alright?"

"Very good, sir." He tried to suppress a grin. It was more responsibility than I had ever given him before. "Should I get going immediately?"

"Yes. And stay there till I recall you. It may be a while before things settle down. Make your base at the arsenal. You'll have to sort out your own supplies."

Leander nodded. The arsenal was the defensive complex that surrounded the naval boatsheds of the Little Harbour.

"And just so that we are completely clear on this, Leander," I continued, "I expect the City Guard to protect our Carthaginian people as if they were Greeks. If I hear that there was trouble, and that any of our men chose to look the other way, I'll flog them myself. And you'll answer for it too. Understood?"

"Yes, sir, of course. And thank you for trusting me with this."

"I wouldn't be too grateful, Lieutenant. It's a shitty job. Now, I've got a council meeting this afternoon, but I'll try to ride over afterwards to see how you're getting on. Good luck. And I suppose you'd better give me those sentry rosters."

"Yes, sir," he said. He picked up a sheet of papyrus and two wax tablets and handed them to me.

"I've nearly finished them, sir. The last part is on that tablet. I just haven't copied it out yet. The other tablet is the list of the other things Castor asked me to take care of."

I glanced at the papyrus on which Leander had drawn out an intricate chart of times and duties. In contrast to my own clumsy, jagged scrawl, his handwriting was fluid and graceful, much like the man himself. I nodded to him, stood up and turned to leave. I was halfway through the door when he called out after me.

"By the way, sir, have you heard about the prisoners?"

I stopped and looked back at him in surprise.

"No. What prisoners?"

"In the palace cells, sir. Here in the barracks yard."

"Really? Who are they?"

"I've no idea, I'm afraid, sir. Apparently the Royal Watch started making arrests around the city the night the fire broke out. They've taken over the cells. No one seems to know how many people they're holding down there. I only heard about it this morning, but when I went over to ask what was going on, I was told to clear off and mind my own business."

I had some time to spare before the council meeting, so I went to my own office and settled down to some administrative work. After a little while, I heard the sergeants begin to form up the men in the courtyard outside. I went to the window to listen to Leander address them. He gave them a good, quick summary of what they would be doing in North Achradina. It sounded as though he had already worked out in his head how he intended to deploy them around the district. But it wasn't Leander's capacity for planning that I was testing. Although I liked him, I worried about his tender-heartedness. I was fairly certain there would be trouble that evening, once the taverns began to empty, and I wanted to see if Leander had the stomach to deal with it. But I wasn't taking any chances. In the note I had sent Castor, I had asked him to keep his eyes on Achradina and to be ready to step in if the young lieutenant got out of his depth.

With so many men now posted to Achradina and Tyche, the palace contingent was reduced to a quarter of its usual numbers. I sent word to the commander of the South Citadel to leave just a skeleton garrison behind and to bring the remainder of his company over to the palace. I sent a further note to the king, informing him of the precautions I was taking to protect the Carthaginian district. When that was done, I started drawing up new sentry rosters. The ones Leander had devised were of course already useless. I struggled to wrap my head around the problem. Just when I thought I had finally worked it all out, I noticed I had allocated one group of men to different places simultaneously. I swore violently, threw the wax tablet at a wall, and then started laughing. I had wasted over an hour on a task that Castor could have completed in twenty minutes, and Nebit probably in five. For all my skill with a sword, without men like them behind me, I was a sorry excuse for a captain.

A camp slave brought me some bread and sausage for lunch, which I ate at my desk while I attacked the rosters again. But I was careful to leave in good time for the council meeting.

As I emerged into the sunlight, I noticed two men in conversation by the entrance to the cells, on the far side of the exercise yard. One was a member of the Royal Watch, whom I recognised as Dinomenes, the man who had sewn up my face years earlier; the other was Hannon, Prince Gelon's slave, who was wiping his hands vigorously on a piece of cloth as he talked.

I headed over towards them.

When he saw me approaching, Hannon said something quietly to Dinomenes and handed him the cloth. He bowed formally towards me and then turned and jogged off towards the main courtyard before I could reach them.

Dinomenes stared after the slave. There was no mistaking the expression of distaste on his face.

As I strode up, he turned to salute me and tried to force a cheerful smile.

"Good afternoon, sir."

I nodded to him.

"Dinomenes, I just wanted to ask you if your son is alright? Did he go to Italy with the Gold Shields?"

He looked at me in surprise.

"Bless you for remembering him, sir. Yes, he went with his company. He couldn't wait to sign on after he'd finished his training. We're still waiting for word of him, but I know in my heart the little bastard's alright. I can feel it."

I put my hand on Dinomenes' shoulder.

"I'm sure you're right."

"You know, sir, the last thing he said to me before he left was that he's going to try to transfer to the Guards when he gets back. Fancy that: a proper soldier wanting to join the City Guard. But it seems he's set on serving under you again."

I smiled.

"He's a good lad. When he gets back, tell him I'd be delighted to have him, if Sosis can spare him."

He bit his lip and swallowed.

"Thank you, sir."

"You know, you were one of the best sergeants I ever had, Dinomenes," I said. "Be sure to let me know when he's home."

Dinomenes looked me squarely in the eye. He was a tough man. In our time, we had both seen and done things we wished we could undo.

"I hope I'm not speaking out of turn, sir," he said carefully, "but sometimes I miss our days together in the Gold Shields. It was proper soldiering back then, under old General Lepides. Perhaps I should try to transfer to the Guards, too." He smiled grimly and nodded towards the door to the cells. "I'm not sure I've the stomach for this sort of work."

"Well, I can always find a place for you as well," I replied sadly.

He didn't need to explain. The blood-smeared cloth he was holding told its own story.

*

I went back to my rooms to change into a blue tunic and then headed straight to the council chamber. When I got there, I found Thraso waiting by himself just inside the door. Hieron and Gelon were already seated at the head of the table. The slave Hannon was bending forwards between them, whispering something.

"Dion, is Aunt Korinna alright?" Thraso asked me quietly.

"Yes, thank you, Cousin. She's fine." I smiled at him. His concern was evidently sincere, which made it all the more touching, given that my mother had never shown any concern for him.

Thraso and I waited together in silence, keeping respectfully out of earshot of the king. After a moment, Gelon asked Hannon a question. The slave whispered something further. When he had finished, the king nodded silently and Gelon dismissed Hannon with a wave of his hand. The other councillors began filing in and joined us by the door, while Hieron and the prince continued talking privately.

I heard the familiar tapping of Archimedes' cane behind me and turned to greet him. He looked at me anxiously and raised his eyebrows in enquiry.

"She's fine," I whispered, anticipating his question. "Let's talk outside."

Archimedes nodded and I followed him back out into the antechamber. He shuffled over to the window where we wouldn't be overheard.

"There's something I need to ask you, Great-uncle."

He fixed me with his glittering eyes.

"I think I can guess what it is," he said softly.

"I'm sure you can. Who tried to kill my mother, Archimedes? Was it Hieron? She thinks it was."

He pursed his lips and shrugged his shoulders.

"I'm afraid I honestly don't know, Dion, but I doubt it. If this was Hieron's doing, I'd like to believe he would have spoken to me first – but he doesn't tell me everything, so I can't be sure. She has certainly annoyed him enough over the years, and what with all these stories she's been spreading about the will of the goddess... He must have been furious. But this attack... well, it's just not his way of doing things. He likes to control events, and the consequences of killing Korinna would be quite unpredictable. For one thing, he couldn't tell how you might react, if you decided he was to blame. Given all his other headaches, I'd have to assume he judges it more important to keep you close, than to be rid of her. I suppose we'll just have to see what he does next. But my instinct is that someone else is behind this. I'm sorry I can't be more reassuring... Now, I think we should probably go back in, don't you?"

I was none the wiser. My mother thought Hieron had wanted to kill her, to gain more control over me. My great-uncle thought Hieron would not have wanted to kill her, in case he lost control over me. I wondered if both of them had simply chosen to believe whatever suited each of them best.

Hieron and Gelon were still talking when we returned, but after a moment they seemed to reach some agreement, and Gelon finally beckoned us forward to take our places at the table.

XV

COMPROMISES

When we had all settled down, Gelon looked at me and nodded.

"Before we begin, I should like to express my thanks to Dion," he said. "The fire would certainly have been a great deal worse, had it not been for his leadership."

"Hear, hear," said Leatherskin, and began drumming the table with the palm of his hand. A moment later, all the other councillors joined in. I nodded in embarrassed acknowledgement. Directly opposite me, I saw Thraso smiling. He winked at me.

After a few moments, the king held up his hand for silence.

"Well, I'm delighted to see that everyone finally shares my own high opinion of Dion," he croaked. "So, let us get down to the business in hand. There are two main topics to discuss: the reconstruction of the district, and the relief of those who have been made homeless. I have asked Archimedes to prepare some thoughts on rebuilding Upper Tyche, and I have asked Andranodoros to propose a plan for dealing with the homeless. I should like to hear from Archimedes first."

My great-uncle, who had been scraping the inside of his ear with his little finger, sat up with a start.

"What was that? Oh yes, Upper Tyche," he said, and scratched his head. "Well now, it seems we have a most interesting opportunity…"

For what must have been nearly half an hour, Archimedes droned on without interruption about construction materials, and the two-way circulation of carts around concentric squares of streets, and aqueducts and refuse collection and sewerage systems and communal gardens and underground food stores.

I stopped listening after a while and by the time he had finished, so had most of my colleagues. Only the king, Thraso and Andranodoros seemed to pay close attention to him throughout.

"Wonderful," said Hieron, with evident sincerity, when Archimedes eventually fell silent. "What a remarkable vision. You really must work up some drawings for me as soon as you can, Cousin."

Archimedes beamed with delight.

"So," continued Hieron, "let us turn now to the rather more dreary issue of the homeless. Andranodoros, what have you to propose?"

Andranodoros had largely recovered his good looks in the weeks since his return with the fleet. His cheeks and eye sockets were no longer hollow, but he had kept his hair cut short in the military fashion. I had no idea whether this was an attempt to master his vanity, or a new way of indulging it.

"My King," he began, "having examined the census records of Upper Tyche, we estimate that some sixty thousand people are probably living in the streets. I propose dividing them into a number of categories, for each of which different provisions should be made. Firstly, we have citizen families of good character, by which I mean those with no record of any sort of delinquency. We believe roughly half the homeless are likely to fall into this group. I suggest that they are billeted around the city, on the following basis: homeowners with three slaves or more would be required to take in one homeless family; homeowners with six slaves or more would take in two families; and so on."

Several of my fellow councillors started to shuffle uncomfortably in their chairs and two or three put their hands up.

"No, hear me out, please," Andranodoros said, a little irritably.

"I will deal with any questions you may have when I am finished…
So, moving on. In the second category are ten thousand or so
people whom I would classify as belonging to citizen families of
poor character, that is to say, those that include someone who
has a criminal record, or who is a registered prostitute, or who
has defaulted on their rent or a debt. I certainly do not pretend
that these families are as deserving of our charity as those in the
first category, but nor do I believe it would be prudent to leave
them on the streets, if only for considerations of public order and
decency. I therefore propose that we re-establish the camp on
Epipolae that was set up for the Pachynus refugees, and put them
there. It would be helpful if Prince Gelon could make available a
sufficient number of the army's campaign tents to provide them
with some shelter."

Andranodoros put his hand to his mouth and coughed lightly.

"Many of the men in these first two categories will have lost
their livelihoods as a result of the fire," he resumed. "I suggest that
those who are unable to demonstrate that they still have work, and
who are under the age of thirty, should be recalled for military
service and sent to Plymmerium. I have discussed this with Prince
Gelon already. Our preliminary estimates are that this will result in
an increase in our standing forces of around three to five thousand
men. The Shield divisions will all be expanded and we will also be
increasing our naval patrols."

"By the way, Dion, what about the City Guard?" interrupted
Gelon. "Do you happen to need any more men?"

"I could certainly use another five hundred or so, sir," I replied.

"Very well, we'll see what we can do. Sorry, Andranodoros,
please carry on."

"Thank you, my Prince. As to the remainder of able-bodied
individuals in these first two categories, I propose that they should
all be put to work on the reconstruction of Upper Tyche, including
the women and any children over the age of ten. It so happens that
almost all of Upper Tyche is owned by a relatively small number of
families, my own included. As we will be the beneficiaries of their

labour, I believe it is only reasonable that the cost of this workforce should fall on us, rather than on the Royal Treasury. I propose that we pay them in food, rather than coin, and that we also provide sufficient food for those who have been billeted in the city or sent to Epipolae, but who are too old, too young or otherwise too feeble to work. I have drawn up a schedule showing how this cost might be apportioned between us, based on the extent of our individual landholdings in Upper Tyche."

I noticed that several of my more quick-witted colleagues, who had previously been fidgeting uncomfortably, now began to nod and murmur in approval. It had obviously dawned on them that Andranodoros had found a clever way to provide us with a small army of labourers, who would be our slaves in all but name, without putting us to the expense of having to purchase them.

"Thirdly," Andranodoros continued, "there are maybe some two or three thousand slaves whose owners lost their homes in the fire. The relatively small number of slaves among the homeless is of course explained by the poverty of the districts affected. Given the need to rebuild Upper Tyche, it would seem sensible to increase the output of the quarries, so I suggest we requisition any male slaves and send them there. As the quarries will not be put to the expense of having to buy them, Themistos has agreed that, in exchange, all stone purchased specifically for the reconstruction of Upper Tyche will be marked down in price by a fifth. Any female and child slaves will of course be sold at auction."

Andranodoros looked round the table but now no one seemed inclined to interrupt him.

"Very well… My final category consists of those who are free but who do not have citizenship. Altogether, we believe there are maybe fifteen thousand such people, the majority being former slaves, with the remainder being immigrants of one sort or another. It goes without saying they have no claim on our charity either. I suggest that those capable of working should also be sent to Epipolae and used in the reconstruction of Upper Tyche. However, we need to consider how best to deal with any former slaves who were freed precisely because they are no longer able to work, and who drifted into Upper Tyche when their owners discarded them. Our best guess is that there may be four or five thousand such people, most of whom were probably living in Little Athens. If we leave them to their own devices, I dare say they will simply rebuild their shacks elsewhere and create a new fire hazard for us. I therefore propose we expel all our superannuated former slaves from the city. They seem to live by begging in the streets, so they are just a public nuisance anyway. Of course, I appreciate this might create some disruption in the countryside; however, I believe the problem should resolve itself quite quickly. Given their age and general condition, they are unlikely to last long outside our walls. I would expect few to survive the winter."

Andranodoros looked round the table.

"And that is the gist of my recommendations. A policy document setting out these proposals in more detail is presently being copied, and will be circulated to all councillors in the next day or two."

"A most thoughtful plan, Andranodoros," said Hieron. "So, does anyone have any questions?"

Thraso tentatively raised his hand.

"If you will forgive me, Andranodoros, I'm afraid I do have one or two concerns," he said, blushing self-consciously.

"My dear fellow, naturally I welcome your thoughts," replied Andranodoros with a smile, which failed to extend to his eyes.

"Thank you, that's most kind of you," said Thraso. "You see, my worry is that the mood among the common people seems rather volatile at present, what with the food shortages and now the fire. I think we should be careful to avoid stirring up any unnecessary resentment. We certainly wouldn't want the people to think that the nobles were trying to exploit the misfortune of Upper Tyche. So, I would like to propose that we soften your plan just a little, Andranodoros, in two ways. Firstly, I think we should pay reasonable wages to any men employed in the rebuilding of Upper Tyche, or at least, to those who are citizens. And, secondly, I fear that driving a large number of elderly former slaves out of the city might also reflect a little unfavourably on this council. So I would recommend that, instead, we assign a parcel of land outside the walls to these poor men and women, on which they might be allowed to live rent-free and rebuild their shelters. Perhaps Prince Gelon could even find some old army tents for them as well? It so happens I own some land immediately beyond the Hexapylon Gate, which I would be happy to make available for the purpose. I suggest we present this as a gift from all of us on the council."

Thraso's proposals were discussed at great length. Andranodoros didn't say anything more, but predictably, almost everyone else who spoke found some reason or other to object to my cousin's first idea, which seemed likely to cost us all a fair amount of money, although they were happy enough to endorse the second, and share in the credit for his generosity.

Eventually, the king turned to me.

"And what is your opinion, Dion?" he asked archly.

I immediately understood why the king wanted me to speak. He must have known I would feel obliged to side with my cousin, but whether Thraso won the argument or not was probably of little concern to him; he was merely curious to see how I would deal with my fellow nobles. After the attempt on my mother's life, he wanted to know if he could still rely on me to be the whip in his hand. I glanced over at Gelon, who smiled at me and nodded encouragingly.

And so that was how I came to offer the first of the only two contributions I ever made to a council debate.

I scratched my cheek and looked slowly around the table.

"Over the next few nights," I said, "there may well be riots in North Achradina, and quite possibly also in Temenites and Neapolis. I have already had to take half my men off their regular duties to try to keep a lid on things. If you ignore Thraso's advice, you will risk turning the mob against our own families, and I don't have enough men to start protecting all your homes as well... So my opinion is that you should all stop being so fucking stupid."

My colleagues stared at me like startled rabbits. After a long moment, Gelon began chuckling. And as I looked from one end of the table to the other, I thought I saw Hieron and Archimedes exchanging a smile.

＊

"Well," said Hieron drily, "that is not quite how I would have put it myself, but Dion's point does seem rather compelling. So, do I take it that we are all now in agreement that Andranodoros's admirable plan should be adopted, but that it should incorporate Thraso's two modest amendments? Yes? Good. Now, it so happens I have a little idea of my own to propose. But first, Gelon has some information to share with you."

"Thank you, Father," said Gelon. He coughed lightly. "I can now confirm that the fire was the result of arson. And given that it started within a few hours of the departure of Hannibal's ambassador, it is not difficult to guess who was behind it.

"My father has been aware for many years of the presence of a network of Carthaginian spies in Syracuse. Indeed, from time to time, it has been useful to us to be able to feed them misleading information about our activities. On the night the fire broke out, I ordered their arrest and interrogation. It was perhaps fortunate that I did so, as they had apparently intended to take advantage of the confusion to flee the city on the morning tide. Only one suspect has so far evaded capture. The rest have confessed to their guilt and they have implicated several other members of the Carthaginian community as well, in addition to a number of our own officials who were in their pay. These people have also now been arrested and are being interrogated in turn."

So that would explain the prisoners in the palace cells, I thought, and Hannon's bloody piece of cloth.

"From what we have discovered so far," Gelon continued, "it would appear the preparations for the fire were made four years ago, before Hannibal had even embarked on his present war with Rome. A number of old warehouses that had been put up for sale were purchased in different names to avoid suspicion. These were then filled with dry straw bales, which had been coated in tar, and the warehouses sealed up again.

"It is my view that, even as he was making his preparations for the invasion of Italy, Hannibal already envisaged a day when he might besiege Syracuse. I believe the fire was designed to play some part in that eventual siege, possibly as a diversion; however, the destruction of his convoy appears to have tempted him into taking an early revenge on us instead. Hannibal must have told Nico what he wanted done, if his peace terms were rejected. Before he sailed home, Nico had a man swim ashore to pass word to Hannibal's agents here. He is in the cells now too. I would only add that all this merely underscores what an extremely dangerous enemy Hannibal is, capable of laying the groundwork for his plans years in advance."

"You know, I met Hannibal's father once," said Hieron thoughtfully. "He commanded the Carthaginian army here in Sicily during the last war. He was a clever man, albeit in a rather conventional sort of way. But I must admit, Hannibal is something else entirely. In fifty years, he is the only fox who has ever managed to slip inside my henhouse... Anyway, I certainly have no intention of letting such an outrage go unanswered."

"How do you intend to respond, my King?" Andranodoros asked.

Hieron looked at him and smiled. His eyelids flickered.

"I am going to expel everyone of Carthaginian descent from the kingdom."

We gawped at him.

"What, *all* of them, my King?" asked Thraso.

"Well, not those who are slaves, obviously," replied Hieron with a snort. "Otherwise, only families who have been granted citizenship will be allowed to remain, and I shall tax them into penury. As to the rest, I shall confiscate everything they own: they can leave with just the clothes on their backs. All their land holdings will be transferred to the Royal Treasury. Andranodoros can use their houses to billet some of our own citizens. Everything else that the barbarians possess – their gold, their ships, their slaves, their goods

– will be distributed among the landowners of Upper Tyche, as compensation for the destruction of their property. This, however, will be on condition that the landowners agree to implement Archimedes' plans for the reconstruction of the district... We will have the last laugh, my friends. Hannibal's own people will pay to replace the slums he has destroyed with avenues of stone."

Archimedes didn't join in the gleeful pounding of the table that greeted Hieron's announcement – my great-uncle had apparently fallen back into the sinkhole of his own mind and had reverted to chewing absently on his beard. I must admit my own contribution to the applause was rather half-hearted as well: it is a failing of mine that I have never been able to derive as much pleasure as most men from profit or vindictiveness. I also realised it would be the Guards who would have to implement the expulsions, and I was worried it could prove a messy affair. But that apart, it seemed to me that Hieron had come up with a characteristically clever way to keep the nobles happy, please the common people, enrich the treasury and advance my great-uncle's reconstruction plans, all at once. He might even be doing our Carthaginians a favour. My men could hardly protect them forever, and with the kingdom sliding into open war, the mob would probably end up massacring them eventually.

But then I glanced across the table at Thraso, and my heart sank. He was looking at me despairingly. I shook my head very slightly to warn him to keep quiet. He bit his lip and nodded.

Unfortunately, Zoippos had also noticed my cousin's discomfort.

"Forgive me, my King," Zoippos said, when the applause had died away, "but our young friend Thraso seems lost in reflection. His insights never fail to illuminate our discussions. I wonder if we might press him to share his thoughts?"

Zoippos looked at me and smirked, his little onion head wobbling with pleasure. I dare say he resented Thraso's rapid rise within the council, but I was the real target of his malice. If he could cause me some pain by injuring my cousin, he would go home a happy man. I glowered back at him.

"I have no thoughts to offer, I'm afraid," replied Thraso wisely.

"But my dear fellow, you're a lawyer," chipped in Andranodoros with an easy grin. "I thought lawyers always had something to say."

A ripple of laughter went round the table.

"Only when we're paid," replied Thraso, his cheeks reddening again, although now perhaps more in irritation than embarrassment.

I looked at Hieron, who was gazing at my cousin without expression. After a moment, the king scratched his face and leant back in his chair.

"Come now, Thraso," Hieron said finally. "Don't be coy. What do you have to say?"

My cousin was cornered.

"Well, Your Majesty," he replied awkwardly, "I was only thinking of the Greek families in Carthage. I believe there are nearly three times more Greeks there, than there are Carthaginians here, to say nothing of the Greek families in all the other cities of their empire. Those families have their roots all over the Greek world, not just Syracuse. I gather the largest element originally derives from Rhodes. It occurs to me that Rhodes and perhaps several of our other allies might well blame us, if their kinsmen end up being expelled in turn."

"So what are you suggesting, Thraso?" asked Hieron, with his usual blank face.

"My King, I would recommend that we allow the Carthaginians to leave with at least enough money to start new lives for themselves, and that we present their expulsion as being for their own safety. Perhaps we might even arrange for some ships to take them to the African coast. If we are seen to have acted generously, our allies will be more likely to direct their anger at Carthage, rather than at us, should Carthage retaliate in kind."

The king put his elbows on the table and began tapping his fingertips together. There was a long silence as he stared at my cousin. Thraso looked down nervously at his lap.

"Well now," the king rasped finally, "you make a good case for moderation, young man, although I suspect you do so more out of soft-heartedness, than out of calculation. In time, Thraso, you will discover that squeamishness is the cruellest vice in which powerful men can indulge. But on this occasion, whatever your motivation, I cannot fault your reasoning. What you propose is a small enough cost to keep our allies happy. We shall do as you suggest."

"Thank you, my King," said Thraso in obvious relief and perhaps surprise.

"However," Hieron continued, running his tongue slowly over his dry upper lip, "if we are to present this as being for the barbarians' own safety, then first they need to be persuaded that they are in danger. Dion, withdraw your men from North Achradina. And tomorrow we shall announce in the agora that Carthaginian agents were behind the fire. That should do the trick, I think."

I stared at Hieron incredulously.

"My King…" I stammered.

"You have something to say, Dion?"

"But my King, if the mob are allowed into the Carthaginian quarter… they could start another fire."

"No, I don't believe they will," replied Hieron complacently. "Now then, I think that is enough debate for one day. Thank you all for attending at such short notice. Andranodoros, put your plan for the homeless into motion immediately. Thraso, I should like you to help Andranodoros re-establish the Epipolae camp. Gelon, please send over some army tents for Epipolae. But no tents for the beggars on Thraso's land. We must draw the line somewhere… And you, Dion, will start making preparations for the deportation of the Carthaginians. That is all."

We all stood respectfully as Gelon helped his father up. Andranodoros seemed mildly amused; Zoippos was grinning from ear to ear, and my cousin looked like a man condemned to the quarries.

Thraso and I walked out together.

"What have I done, Dion?" he whispered angrily. "I just wanted to help those poor people, but I've only made it worse. Now he's going to set the mob on them. Do you know, I think the old bastard just wanted to teach me a lesson for having dared to question him. It's monstrous."

I stopped in my tracks and took hold of my cousin's arm.

"Listen to me carefully, Thraso," I said, staring down into his round, pink face. "Maybe he was punishing you; maybe he wasn't. I don't know, I can't read his mind. But for pity's sake, learn to keep your thoughts to yourself, will you? Hieron has been scaring the wolves away for fifty years. He couldn't have done it if he wasn't a bastard. That's his nature. And with Hannibal on the rampage, just be grateful we've got a bastard like him on the throne."

Of course, events were presently to overwhelm us all, so in the end, nothing ever came of Archimedes' great vision for Upper Tyche. The drawings that he made for Hieron have long since been lost, and it took nearly thirty years for the district to recover fully from the fire. It regrew haphazardly, a handful of buildings at a time, which sprouted up like clumps of thistles in a neglected field, until eventually they colonised it completely. The streets are owned by new landlords now, with black hair and brown eyes, but little else has changed. I live in Upper Tyche myself these days, and it is still a shithole.

Thraso and I parted company in the courtyard. I headed off to my rooms to change and put on my armour, and then I rode over to North Achradina to find Leander.

Our Carthaginians had always been an enterprising community, owning most of the city's jewellery and textile businesses, but with one or two ostentatious exceptions, the houses in which they lived were relatively modest. The only evidence of the huge wealth they were rumoured to enjoy lay in the proud manner in which their streets were maintained, with doors and shutters conscientiously repainted every year and no litter anywhere in sight. North Achradina was certainly one of the prettiest quarters of the city: its residents had a tradition of suspending densely planted baskets of flowers from their windows, so that what struck one first upon entering the district was its heavy fragrance. It might have been one of the most tranquil quarters too, were it not for the strange laxity with which the local children were allowed to play freely in the streets.

Before long, I had attracted a noisy following of small, olive-skinned boys, who ran after my horse, imploring me to show them my captain's sword. The only thing that differentiated it from any other army sword was its silver pommel. But the boys were fascinated, nonetheless. Whatever other treasures lay hidden within their homes, family armour and weapons were probably not among them: without citizenship, their fathers would have been excluded from military service. I eventually brought the horse to a halt and tried to buy the boys off by holding out a bronze coin to the largest, a lad of maybe eight or nine years. He thanked me politely, but declined, and then produced two bronze coins of his own, which he cheekily promised to give me if I would let him hold the weapon. I laughed, but I felt uncomfortable. For some reason, I couldn't bring myself to show them the blade. Instead, I put my heels to the horse's flanks and cantered off with a wave, feeling like a coward abandoning the field and leaving the boys staring forlornly after me.

Leander proved difficult to track down, as he was moving about the district himself, conscientiously checking on his men. I eventually found him at the Achradina wall, by an ancient gate tower that gave access to the charred remains of Upper Tyche.

"Anything to report, Lieutenant?" I asked, without dismounting.

"Nothing really so far, sir. Half a dozen drunks from Neapolis were already wandering around the streets when we arrived, shouting abuse at everyone and looking for a fight, but one of the locals told me that's nothing unusual. We chased them away, and there's been no trouble since. But the people seem pretty grateful we're here, sir. They keep sending their slaves out with funny little cakes for the men. Rather tasty, actually."

I nodded grimly.

"That's good. You've done well, Leander. But I'm afraid I have new orders for you. Keep the men here tonight, then return to the palace. You're to withdraw everyone from North Achradina at dawn."

He looked at me uncertainly.

"But sir, are you sure? Just because there hasn't been any trouble yet..."

"Shut up, Lieutenant, and do as you're told. I'll see you back at the palace tomorrow. Understood?"

"Yes, sir," he said, and instinctively snapped out a salute. He tried to keep his expression blank, but he couldn't stop his face turning white. The rebuke had stung him, coming on top of the disappointment of losing his first command within just a few hours of receiving it.

I had no sympathy for him; he needed to grow up. The whole kingdom seemed to be swirling around the lip of the whirlpool, and I was in no mood to worry about his bruised feelings.

Several of my men were standing nearby. I beckoned Leander to come closer and leant down in the saddle to whisper to him.

"Find their priest, Lieutenant. He's called Tabnit. Tell him I sent you. Warn him there's going to be trouble tomorrow. His people need to keep their children indoors, and their doors bolted. But he didn't hear it from you. Tell him to say he had a vision or something."

"Yes sir," he replied. He looked up at me and seemed about to ask a question, then sensibly changed his mind.

I nodded curtly to him and turned the horse around. As I headed back towards the palace, I told myself that I had done what I could. But I still felt like a coward.

❋

When I got back to my rooms, I found Agbal waiting for me alone. He helped me out of my armour, and then I sent him over to the treasury, to ask if they could prepare me a summary of the North Achradina census. The treasury occupied an entire range of the great courtyard and seemed to be run primarily for the convenience of those who worked within it. I gave Agbal my ring to ensure that he wasn't ignored. When he had gone, I settled myself down at the large table in the sitting room, and started drawing up a plan for the deportation of the Carthaginians.

I had not been at my miserable task for more than a few minutes when Alpha and Omega returned, laden with shopping and the gossip of the streets. They could barely stop gabbling in their excitement, but nothing they had to say lightened my mood. The people were apparently lapping up the slop that Aristo and his wife had fed them on my mother's behalf. Whoever was behind the attempt on her life, had only succeeded in elevating her from a minor phenomenon into an object of near veneration. In the fish market, Alpha happily told me, they were already calling her the People's Priestess. If the king had been mildly irritated by my mother in the past, she probably felt like a boil on his neck now. She certainly felt like a boil on mine.

I made an effort to put her out of my mind. I would find out soon enough what Hieron intended to do with her.

Agbal eventually returned, to tell me someone at the treasury had promised him that the census information would be ready to collect by the end of the following day.

About an hour after dawn, I presented myself at the audience chamber. Two men of the Royal Watch, whom I had come to recognise, but whose names I didn't know, admitted me into the gloomy room. I was the first to arrive. A pair of stools had been placed directly in front of the dais, facing Hieron's throne.

I had been kicking my heels for about five minutes when

the doors were opened again and my mother walked in. With appropriate if insincere modesty, she had dressed in black from head to foot and wore a veil. Two large men in black-plumed helmets of about my age accompanied her into the room.

"Ah, Dion, there you are," she said, without any obvious enthusiasm. She lifted her veil to embrace me. "Let me introduce you to my new bodyguards. This one is Medon and this is Phidias. Boys, this is my son, Dion."

The two men saluted me and I nodded in acknowledgement. I could see at once they were hard, experienced men.

"Aren't they strapping fellows?" my mother continued. "I cannot tell you, Dion, what a relief it is to have them around. I don't think I've ever felt safer in my life."

She turned and beamed at them.

"What a credit you both are to your parents. Your mothers must be so proud of you."

The one called Medon smiled nervously and Phidias began to blush.

"Dion, Medon's parents live in one of our houses in Temenites. Apparently the roof leaks. Tell your lawyer to sort it out, would you? I'll have my secretary send him the address. And seeing how their son is risking his life to protect me, I really think you should waive the rent."

"Lady Korinna," Medon stammered, "you promised you wouldn't say anything…"

"Oh, don't be so silly," my mother gushed. "It's the least we can do."

"I'm sorry, sir," Medon said, turning to me, "but please understand I couldn't accept anything like that. It wouldn't look right. Not that I'm ungrateful to the Lady Korinna for asking you."

He looked at her sheepishly.

"I understand," I said.

"Oh well," my mother said with a warm smile, "perhaps we can find some other way to show our appreciation to you both. I'm sure I'll think of something."

I was sure she would. Medon and Phidias exchanged an embarrassed glance. Hard and experienced they may have been, but they were no match for my mother.

"Sir," said Phidias, nodding towards the dais. I turned and saw that the door behind Hieron's chair had been opened by a slave.

"Come on, Mother," I said.

She lowered her veil again and followed me to the two stools. We stood silently in front of them waiting for the king to appear. I was certainly nervous, but if my mother shared my apprehensions, nothing in her manner betrayed the fact. I hoped she wasn't trusting in her kinship to Hieron to win him over. Her own mother, Archimedes' sister, had been one of the king's many cousins. It was at best a remote connection, and all the more tenuous for depending on an entirely female line.

The king finally shuffled in on the arms of two other guards, who helped him slowly into his throne. We respectfully bowed.

Hieron gazed down at us with his usual blank expression.

"Sit," he said finally. "Now, leave us, everyone, and close the doors behind you."

When the three of us were alone, the king leant his elbows on the arms of his chair, pressed his fingertips together and smiled thinly.

"It's been many years, Korinna," he said. "I'm delighted to see you escaped your recent ordeal unharmed. I don't know what the city would do without you."

"I am touched by your concern, Your Majesty," my mother replied.

"Tell me, would you mind lifting your veil, please? Ah yes… Thank you. It is indeed you. Forgive me, but from what I hear, one can't be too careful… If I may say so, my dear, you've barely aged a day. Dion is clearly neglecting his responsibilities. Surely he could have found you a suitable new husband by now? You'd still make a splendid catch for some lucky fellow, you know."

"You are too kind, my King. But if Your Majesty has summoned us here to express an interest in marriage, I think you really must address yourself to my son."

Hieron raised his eyebrows, and then he grinned.

"Well, that's certainly an idea. What a pair we'd make, eh?"

My mother bowed her head.

"So, shall we get down to business?" Hieron said.

"I am at your disposal, Your Majesty."

"Yes. Indeed you are, Korinna... Now, I have asked you here because I wish to consult you about the will of the goddess. I gather that this is a subject on which you are remarkably well informed."

"I serve the goddess as best I can, my King," she replied.

"I am sure you do. So tell me, Korinna, do you believe that Athena approves of my alliance with Rome?"

"Your Majesty, you have ruled here for over fifty years, and have brought the kingdom peace and prosperity. What could be more proof of the goddess's favour?"

"So you believe that my policies reflect the will of Athena?"

"I am sure of it, Your Majesty. You have always been most respectful of the temple. The goddess knows you serve her, and so I imagine whatever policies you pursue must serve her too."

"And tell me, Korinna, do you believe that it is also the goddess's wish that Gelon should succeed to the throne when I am dead?"

"Undoubtedly, my King. Indeed, I myself was recently blessed by a visit from the goddess in a dream, when she as much as told me so... And I pray that she will bless our next High Priestess with visions of equal clarity."

"I see. But even if the goddess favours my house today, how can I be certain that she will not change her mind tomorrow?"

My mother smiled.

"Athena is steadfast in her love, my King. She is not fickle like some other Olympians. That is why I have devoted myself to her service. Steadfastness is the virtue I prize above all others. Once I have given my word, I never break it. Ask anyone who knows me."

"And I believe you, my dear. Indeed I do. You are famous for your many remarkable qualities. In fact, I was rather hoping you might succeed poor Delia yourself. It would make the people so very happy, and I do like to see my people happy. I gather they're even calling you 'the People's Priestess' these days... I wonder who coined that phrase... It's such a pity you have decided to rule yourself out of consideration. I don't suppose there's any way I might persuade you to change your mind?"

"If it is Your Majesty's wish that I allow my name to go forward, then of course, I must put my duty to you and the people above my own comfort."

She inclined her head again, but I noticed she could not resist a little smirk of triumph. And it seemed all her victory had cost her was a worthless undertaking not to cause the king any headaches.

"That is terribly noble of you, Korinna. I am so pleased."

The king smiled down at her. And then his eyelids flickered, and he licked his lip, and I felt something inside my stomach turn.

"Unfortunately, my dear," he continued, "I am afraid there is just one small problem."

"Is there, Your Majesty?" my mother replied cautiously.

"Yes, I am afraid so. I am rather worried that your past may prove to be something of an embarrassment to you."

"How so, Your Majesty?"

"Well, though I blush to admit it, it appears that the secretary of my agricultural inspectorate was corrupt. Of course, every little farmer in the kingdom probably bribes his local inspector: I doubt anyone really pays the full tithes. But you can imagine my disappointment to discover that the man I had trusted to oversee the entire system was taking bribes himself. Although in his case, it would appear that the only people from whom he took them was your family... But then, I suppose few other families own – what is it? – seven estates, I believe? How very sensible to strike a deal directly with the man at the top, instead of trying to negotiate with seven local officials separately. I'm surprised none of the other nobles thought of it... In any event, it seems that this secretary of mine bought a tenement block from you early last year, at a fraction of its true value. I have to say, that sounds like an awful lot of neglected tithes to me, Korinna. And this occurred while, as we all know, you were running your family's business affairs yourself."

My mother looked at Hieron warily, but she didn't seem to be thrown.

"Your Majesty, I am shocked, but I am afraid I have no knowledge of this at all. We employed a steward to manage our affairs. It is true that he often asked my advice, but he certainly didn't consult me about everything. I am merely a woman, after all. He always struck me as an honest man, but I suppose it is possible I was deceived. Maybe our steward had some arrangement of his own with this secretary? I only wish we could ask him for an explanation. Unfortunately, he recently died."

"And alas, Korinna, by a strange coincidence, the secretary of my agricultural inspectorate recently died too."

"That is most unfortunate, Your Majesty. So perhaps we will never know the truth of this?"

"Perhaps not. But I suppose at least my man got the punishment he deserved. Some ruffians knifed him to death in the street. A slave girl by an open window overheard his attackers talking. She says they spoke a language that she didn't recognise. I wonder if it might have been Galatian… Of course, were you to become High Priestess, you would in any event be inviolate. No court could touch you."

"And being quite innocent of any wrongdoing, Your Majesty, I am sure no court would condemn me anyway. It seems I may have made the mistake of trusting a dishonest man, but did Your Majesty not make the same mistake himself, in trusting your secretary? Of course, if our family steward was guilty of any impropriety, it goes without saying that the House of Dionysius would wish to compensate the Royal Treasury for whatever tithes may have been lost. I imagine my son would regard it as a matter of family honour. Perhaps Your Majesty could arrange for an estimate of the amount to be sent to Dion's lawyer?"

The king nodded.

"Your integrity is a credit to your family, Korinna. I shall be sure to do that. But perhaps I have not explained our little problem quite as clearly as I should have. You see, there must have been a deed transferring the ownership of that building to my official. And that deed must have had a seal on it. And as you obviously do not have a seal of your own, I fear we must assume it was Dion's."

I turned to stare at my mother. She bit her lip.

"You do see the problem, don't you, Korinna?" Hieron said sadly.

My mother stayed silent.

"Of course," Hieron continued, "were you to become High Priestess, it would be a huge relief to me to know that you would always be protected from any unjust accusations by your office. But Dion wouldn't be, would he? And he has so many enemies. I would hate to think what might happen, if that deed ever fell into the hands of a man like Zoippos, for instance. You may not be aware of this, Korinna, but the penalty for the corruption of a public official is the forfeiture of all one's personal property. Every house, every ship, every slave. Down to the very last gold plate. I have to say, it does sound quite excessive, but that, alas, is the law. As you know, I have come to hold Dion in the highest regard. It would break my heart if such a calamity were ever to be visited on his head, as a consequence of the past or future misjudgements of others."

My mother glared at him. She was thinking hard.

"My King," I said, "I don't understand. I had no part in any of this. What on earth am I guilty of?"

"My dear boy," he replied benevolently, "in the eyes of the gods, you are guilty of absolutely nothing. Apart, perhaps, from having been neglectful of your duties as head of your family. Unfortunately, in the eyes of the law, if your seal is on that document, then you are responsible for it. But maybe on this occasion, it would be best if you let your mother do the talking?"

"Your Majesty," she said carefully after a moment, "you say you 'assume' the seal was Dion's. Do I take it that this document, if it even exists, cannot be produced?"

"There you are, you see, Dion, your mother has asked exactly the right question… And to answer it, Korinna, apparently all records of the sale went missing from the public notary's office some time ago. An administrative error of some sort, I imagine. No one seems to know what happened to them. I doubt they will ever turn up again, so perhaps we have nothing to worry about. What do you think?"

I noticed my mother's hands were trembling slightly. She looked down at them and clasped them together.

"Your Majesty," she said quietly, "my son is devoted to you. He has just saved the city from being burnt to the ground. Surely you would seek to protect him…?"

Hieron smiled.

"No man is above the law," he replied. "Not even Dion. I do not interfere with the business of the courts."

And then he dropped the mask. He leant forward in his chair and stared at her.

"Look into my face, Korinna."

She slowly raised her head and met his gaze.

"You presumptuous woman," he sneered. "Who do you think you are, to try to play games with me?"

My mother's eyes widened.

"I am Hieron of Syracuse," he hissed. "Do you think you can defy me, and hide behind your son? Do you really believe that I am so sentimental, that I would stay my hand for his sake?"

"I would never defy you, my King," she replied quietly.

Hieron leant back in his chair again and snorted.

I gazed up at him. All I understood was that my world seemed to be hanging by a single horsehair again.

"Well, Korinna, today you have been lucky. Because of Dion's recent service, I will take no action for now. But from today, I will be holding Dion accountable for your behaviour. One more misstep from you, my dear, and he will answer for it. I spared your family once; I shall not do so again. You are a woman who believes in nothing, but you had better believe that."

My mother swallowed.

"So do you have anything clever to say to me now?" Hieron wheezed.

"Your Majesty is generous and merciful."

The king's lip curled.

"No, I am not. I certainly wouldn't make the mistake of thinking that, if I were you, Korinna. I am merely expedient... Very well, then. It seems we finally understand each other. You will succeed Delia. But when you become High Priestess, you will confine yourself to the affairs of the temple. You will cease to have any communication with men outside your own family or household, unless it is a requirement of your temple duties. I expect you to become an exemplar to your sex, rather than an exception to it."

"Yes, Your Majesty, of course. As you command," my mother mumbled, meekly bowing her head.

"I am not finished yet," Hieron snapped. "You will remain under the protection of the Royal Watch indefinitely, Korinna. Get rid of those Galatians of yours, or I'll do it for you. Of course, it is for Dion to decide whether or not you should remarry, but perhaps he will now conclude that it would be for the best... And to express his gratitude to the goddess for his mother's deliverance from the assassin's knife, Dion will present the kingdom with a suitably magnificent gift. I think the twelve ships presently on loan to me should be sufficient compensation for the loss of my tithes. Have your lawyer transfer their ownership to the treasury, Dion. And throw in three more for good measure. And as for you, Captain, you would be wise to take this warning to heart. If you cannot control your house, you will lose it... Well, that is all. You may both leave now... Korinna, it has been a pleasure to see you again after so many years."

My mother and I mutely stood and bowed.

Her wine had turned to vinegar in her mouth. She had only wanted the office because she had believed it would make her safe and set her free. Perhaps it would make her safe, but it certainly didn't look as though it was going to set her free. How characteristic of Hieron to menace us with the courts, I thought. He had wanted me to know my popularity with our common citizens was no protection. He could destroy me on a whim and still keep his hands clean in their eyes.

I had spent my adult life trying to find my way across the desert of my father's disgrace. I wondered if I had been stumbling around in circles.

My head was still reeling as I walked towards the high doors. It seemed to me there was only one small nugget of comfort to be salvaged from our audience. Whoever had tried to murder my mother, it wasn't Hieron. She had been wrong about that too. It was obvious there had never been any reason for him to have her killed; she was no impediment to him at all.

I was already halfway down the room when my mother caught up with me.

"Dion," she whispered, "we must talk about how we're going to deal with this."

"Fuck off, you stupid bitch," I said, and strode away from her.

XVI

THE THIRD FRAGMENT

So far, I had only managed to devise a method for calculating the area enclosed by a parabola drawn over a straight line. Unfortunately, it had proved impossible to expand this work into a solution for any associated solids, forcing me to seek an altogether different approach to try to solve my egg troubles. But I had recently been struck by the idea that it might be possible to apply some theoretical mechanics to the problem, using the principles of the fulcrum and lever that I had developed many years previously.

I was happily chewing on my beard as I pursued this train of thought, when Hieron finally returned from the audience chamber on the arm of a slave. I stood and helped the slave to make him comfortable on a couch.

"So, Cousin, how did it go?" I asked a little nervously.

"Oh, it was quite entertaining, really," he replied. "Don't worry, what did you think I would do? I've taken some of Dion's ships, but I had the use of most of them anyway, so it won't really cost him much. Gelon is going to give them back to him when I'm dead, as a pat on the head for his loyalty. Do you want something to eat?"

I shook my head.

"No," he said with a sigh, "at our time of life, all the appetites seem to disappear. Although I gather the first Ptolemy was humping the boys right till the end, and he must have been nearly my age when he died…" He turned to the slave. "Pour us some water, would you?"

When the slave had handed us our cups, Hieron dismissed him.

"Yes, Korinna's certainly an interesting character," he resumed. "I wonder what on earth the gods were thinking when they made her. It's a mystery to me why they should have wasted a brain like that on a woman. Perhaps she was a mistake."

He chuckled and laid back on the couch, stretching out his legs. His ankles were densely hatched in thin blue veins and there was a black bruise on one of his calves.

"Oh, she's not that bad really, Hieron. I think she's probably just angry that she wasn't born a man… So, are you going to let her become High Priestess?"

"Oh yes, of course. That was always the plan. Who else is there? I just needed her a little better house-trained. Unfortunately, Dion is the only stick I have to beat her with… But I dare say Korinna will be careful to behave herself now."

A thought occurred to me. I turned it over in my head for a moment or two.

"Hieron, may I ask you a question?" I said eventually. "Was that agricultural secretary of yours working on your instructions all along?"

He smiled at me slyly and shrugged his shoulders.

"What do you think?" he replied. "In any event, I imagine once your niece has settled down, that brain of hers will prove very useful to Gelon when he's king… Although, of course, she'll never be in Delia's league."

"Yes, Delia was certainly one of a kind," I said sadly.

"By the way, Archimedes, speaking of Delia, here's a little story that may interest you. Did I ever tell you that she came to see me the day that Dion was born? She made me swear an oath to protect the child. She said that if Dion ever falls, so too will my crown. Strange prophesy, eh? But I think you'll agree I've kept my word, although his father hardly made it easy for me… Anyway, when that whole pigfuck of a crisis broke, Delia sent me a note reminding me of my oath. She actually threatened to curse me from the steps of the temple if I laid a hand on the boy. Can you believe it? You were urging moderation too, of course, but she was the one who really decided it." He grunted in amusement. "People of absolute integrity are quite impossible to manage. I've still got that note in my desk. I keep it as a reminder of the limits of my power... What a woman."

"How curious," I replied politely. "I must admit I've never set much store by prophesies myself." I laid back on the couch and sighed. "Anyway, I do hope Gelon eventually manages to find a use for Korinna. My niece needs an outlet for her talents."

"I see you still feel guilty about her, Cousin. You really shouldn't. It was all so long ago. And it's hardly your fault she's a widow."

"No, I suppose not," I muttered, and took a sip of water. "You know, Hieron, I thought I'd done the right thing to let Dionysius marry her... Of all the people who wanted her, that I should have chosen him..."

"Well, we all make mistakes, my friend. Even you." The king winced and shuffled uncomfortably on his couch. "I'm growing tired of this game, Archimedes. I can't keep playing it much longer. Every day, it seems to get a little harder to keep my grip. As I shuffle slowly towards my grave, all I sense is hungry insects crawling out from beneath the bark."

"Perhaps that's only to be expected, Hieron... Incidentally, that reminds me. I've been meaning to ask you: was Apollonius something of a hungry insect, by any chance?"

He grinned.

"Oh, so you worked it out, did you? I thought you probably would."

"Well, yes. Although it was actually Chrysanthe who guessed it first."

"Chrysanthe, eh? You're certainly lucky there. I still miss Philistis, you know. Anyway, sorry I didn't take you into my confidence at the time, but I hardly needed your help to deal with him, and you were busy enough already."

"That was considerate… Thank you. So, what was it Apollonius had done, if I may ask? The usual, I suppose?"

"Of course… What else? Another fool snatching at clouds. He'd realised that if Gelon could be disposed of, he'd be the most senior member of the family once I was dead. So he spent a fortune greasing the nobles to make certain they'd choose him to act as regent, till my grandson came of age. Which obviously the poor boy was never destined to do. And then he reckoned the crown would just drop onto his head. So my dear brother-in-law offered Carthage a deal. If they would get rid of Gelon for him, he would abandon the alliance with Rome after my death."

Hieron and I looked at each other for a moment, and then we both began chuckling.

"Oh dear. King Apollonius," I said. "What a thought."

"Indeed," said Hieron.

"So how did you get wind of it?"

"Ah, well, obviously he needed a go-between with the Carthaginians. And of all people, the idiot tried to use Tabnit. I mean, for pity's sake, what on earth was he thinking? Did he seriously imagine that I wouldn't have their people's priest here in my own city in my pocket?"

"You're joking?"

"No, honestly. Tabnit. Apollonius spent nearly two years exchanging earnest messages with the nobles of Carthage, without a clue that it was really me he was corresponding with all along. I only kept it going because it amused me so much."

I couldn't suppress a guffaw. He joined in and a moment later there were tears of laughter in both our eyes.

"I see," I said eventually. "So, may I ask, why did you decide to kill him? I mean, it's not the way you usually handle these sort of things."

"Ah well, to tell the truth, Cousin, I would have been happy to ignore the whole ridiculous affair, maybe pack Apollonius off as an ambassador somewhere unpleasant at some point. But Gelon told Nereis about it, and she insisted. What a harpy *that* woman is. I should never have arranged for Gelon to marry her... She made a terrific fuss about it. And of course, we had to do something about the City Guard anyway. So in the end, we decided we may as well just be done with him, to shut her up as much as anything. It was actually Gelon's idea to make it all look as though it had been an attempt on his own life, and to blame the Carthaginians for it. He thought it might help put an end to the food riots. Clever. He's going to make a good king, I think."

"Yes, I think you're right about that, Hieron."

The king smiled and took another drink.

"In any case," he resumed after a moment, "we still have our great prize before us, Archimedes. You and I must stay focused on that. Everything is almost in place for our final scene, my old friend. Our little comedy is nearly over. The nobles are too terrified of Dion to make any trouble. The army and the City Guard are ready; the treasury is full of gold, and we have plenty of grain hidden away. And everything continues to move in our favour in Italy. That last battle of Hannibal's... Quite remarkable. Better than I had ever dreamt possible... The time to strike is very nearly at hand... I only wish Lepides were here to see it. When I think of the hours we three spent planning this. Just imagine, Cousin, if we can pull it off, how very different the world may look in a few months' time."

I grinned.

"It would certainly be quite something, Hieron. What a way to bow out that would be."

"Yes, it would, wouldn't it? Well, I suppose it's in the hands of the gods now. We'll just have to see how things play out." He took a sip of water. "Anyway, it looks like that only leaves my charming sons-in-law to deal with. I'm rather surprised they haven't tried to cozy up to Dion yet. What on earth should I do with the pair of them, I wonder?" He pursed his lips. "The scorpion and the frog..."

"Leave them to Gelon, Cousin. Let him decide what he wants to do with them, once he's king. You can't solve every headache for him."

"Yes, perhaps you're right, Archimedes. Perhaps you're right… But enough of politics. Politics always come down to the same old story, endlessly repeated… So tell me, what are you working on these days?"

"The volume of an egg," I replied.

"Goodness," he said, "how fascinating. How on earth do you propose to calculate that? I'd have thought immersion was the only way."

As I headed home for lunch, I found my thoughts turning to Korinna and Dion again. Hieron had said I shouldn't feel guilty, but what else was I supposed to feel?

It was Dion's governness who had hurried to my house to bring us the letters she had found. She had been Chrysanthe's creature for years. Chrysanthe had handed the letters to me and told me I must decide what to do with them.

I suppose some of the officers who were eventually exiled may have been innocent, but Hieron judged it best to make a clean sweep of all those he doubted.

And my niece had become a widow.

XVII

TOADS

Leander was waiting for me outside the audience chamber. He looked as though he hadn't slept.

"Good morning, sir," he said, saluting me as I emerged into the crowded colonnade. I don't know if it was tiredness, but his greeting seemed devoid of its usual warmth. I didn't mind; I was in no mood for civility either.

"Are all the men out of North Achradina?" I asked curtly.

"Yes, sir."

"Good. Well, what do you want, Lieutenant?"

"I thought you should know, sir: apparently there was an announcement in the agora an hour ago, blaming the Carthaginians for the fire and the attack on your mother."

"Did you find Tabnit?"

"Yes sir, I passed on your message... But is that all we're going to do? Just warn them to stay indoors?"

"Yes. Anything else, Leander?"

"But you do know what's going to happen, don't you, sir? Surely we're not just going to stand by and watch?"

I glared at him.

"Go to your room and get some sleep, Lieutenant, before you make the mistake of opening your mouth again. You're dismissed."

"Yes, sir." He saluted, but he clenched his jaw as he did so.

A movement just over my shoulder caught my attention and I turned to see my mother walking out between her two new bodyguards. She had lowered her veil again, so I couldn't see her expression. I snorted and she ignored me. She whispered something to Medon, then held up her hand and clicked her fingers. Two slaves, who had been waiting nearby in the open courtyard, immediately picked up the litter by which they had been standing and hurried over to her. Once she had settled herself down, they hoisted the poles smoothly onto their shoulders. Medon and Phidias took the lead, and the little procession began to make its way back towards the palace gates. They went around the colonnade, instead of cutting across the courtyard, forcing the groups of officials and palace visitors who had gathered in its shade to break apart and step out of their way. My mother ignored their curious, upturned faces as she was carried past in silence.

The riots started that evening. Two or three hundred hooligans rampaged through the streets of North Achradina, looking for any men foolish enough still to be out. Finding few victims, the mob resorted to breaking into some of the larger houses, beating up the male inhabitants and throwing pieces of furniture out into the streets, where they were gleefully smashed up. Two old men died and no doubt any girls who were discovered met the usual fate of girls who are discovered by men freed from all governance.

In the morning, the residents emerged and silently cleared the streets of the debris, then went back inside and barricaded their doors again.

I asked to see the king and was refused, so I tried to see Gelon instead, and was told that he had left for Plymmerium.

The mob returned to North Achradina every evening for the next three days, always behaving in the same way. At least there were no fires: to my surprise, the king was proved right about that. Every morning, I went to his private quarters and applied to see him, but it was not until the fourth day that I was finally admitted and shown into his plain little study, where he grilled me about my preparations for the deportation. By then, I had commandeered and provisioned nearly a hundred merchant ships, all owned by local Carthaginian merchants. I still needed about forty more, but ships were returning to Syracuse every day from their journeys around the Mediterranean, and I expected to have enough to transport everyone within the week.

"And where do you propose to send them?" Hieron asked. "I want those ships back, Dion."

"My King, I thought we should split them up, and send three or four to each of the smaller ports along the Carthaginian coast. Hopefully, they'll be able to leave again, before the local authorities understand what's happening and try to seize them."

"Very well, Dion," Hieron croaked. "I think by now our meat should be tender enough for the plate. Send your men back into North Achradina. Seal up the district. You can begin the deportations tomorrow."

"What should I tell the Carthaginians, my King?"

"Whatever you like." He waved his hand in dismissal.

I briefed my horrified officers. Within two hours, I had over three hundred men back in North Achradina. I sent Leander to see Tabnit again, to warn him privately what was going to happen the following day. The young lieutenant looked at me accusingly, but said nothing.

The mob stayed away that night, deterred by the presence of my men, and in the morning, we began clearing the district, street by street. The Carthaginians boarded their ships meekly enough. It seemed the food situation had become quite desperate, with market traders not daring to enter the quarter, and families not daring to leave it. The realisation that they were neither going to starve nor be murdered was sufficient to ensure the pathetically grateful compliance of most of the residents.

There were a few ugly scenes, of course, mainly over slaves to whom their owners had formed an attachment. We explained that there was insufficient space for everyone on the ships, but told the families that their slaves would be sent on later. With a bit of luck, we said, they would all be able to come back to Syracuse soon, when things had calmed down. I set a limit of one sack for each adult, but I forbade my men to search the sacks. Hieron had told me to make sure no family left with more than ten silver pieces, but I trusted Tabnit to have spread the word, and I dare say that as the ships sailed away, one after the other, they all sat just a little lower in the water than they should have done.

They left from the Trogilus Port to the north of the city, which directly adjoined the warehouse district where the fire had started. I had put Xeno in charge of the embarkations, while I supervised the evictions, but at some point in the afternoon, he sent word that I was needed at Trogilus. It seemed news of the expulsions had spread across the city, and a large crowd had gathered along the wharf to jeer and spit at the Carthaginians as they boarded their ships. Xeno was worried.

The fierce old lieutenant was not a man to ask for help if he didn't need it, so I rode over as fast as I could and ordered a company of my men to come running after me.

Two hundred or so Carthaginians had formed a queue just inside the gate tower that gave access to the wharf from north Achradina. Small children were crying and clinging to their parents' legs. It seemed that Xeno had been escorting the families from the gate to their ships in batches. Beyond them, a dozen of my men had formed a line across the gateway. But it wasn't the Carthaginians they were blocking; they were facing out towards the port.

"Make way," I ordered as I rode up behind them. "What's going on?"

A young sergeant turned to look up at me with obvious relief.

"Out there, sir. Looks like Lieutenant Xeno's got into a bit of trouble. What should we do?"

I rode past the men onto the wharf. About a hundred yards from me, I could see a group of maybe eighty Carthaginians. They were surrounded by a thin cordon of my men, who had lowered their spears to try to hold back the baying mob. I guessed there must have been a thousand people or more pressing in around them. Xeno stood in the centre of the line, clutching his sword in his only hand. The families had their backs to the sea and could neither reach their ship nor retreat into Achradina. Xeno was shouting something but he was drowned out by the catcalls of the surrounding throng.

Five days' worth of fermenting frustration welled up inside me. It seemed to cascade through every vein and muscle in my body. I didn't even try to control it.

I snarled and dug my heels into the horse's side, jerking back hard on the reins at the same time. It was a well-trained animal and obediently reared up, pawing at the air with its front legs and neighing loudly. That got the attention of several men at the back of the crowd.

"You fucking *turds*," I roared at the top of my voice.

I forced the horse to rear up a second time. Its whinnying shrieks scythed across the wharf. I am a heavy man and need a strong mount, but that black stallion was a monster. As its iron-shod hooves crashed back down onto the cobbles, its eyes bulged and swivelled like a crazy thing and it began shaking its head and snapping its teeth. Two or three hundred members of the mob now seemed to have transferred their attention to me. They were gawping.

I drew my sword and transferred it to my left hand.

"Fuck you all!" I bellowed at them.

And then I charged them.

At first they just stared at me incredulously, but as I closed the distance, those in my direct line started to shout and throw their weight against their neighbours to try to get out of my path. Two or three of them stumbled and fell over. Within a matter of seconds, their fear had rippled out and men began to break away and scatter.

I was still thirty feet from them but now a space was opening up in front of me. The crowd seemed to be dissolving like mist. The horse careered into the gap, craning its neck forward as it tried to bite the people scrambling to avoid it. Suddenly, there was no one between Xeno's men and me. I turned the horse's head to gallop along the line of their spears, swinging my sword out and forcing the mob to recoil and push back on itself. One man was too slow to evade my reach and I managed to slash him across the face before racing past. A moment later, I reached the far end of the line and made the horse rear once more. Its front legs flailed wildly and the terror-struck faces in front of me cringed, turned and fled, pushing each other over and tripping themselves up in the chaos.

"Two paces forwards!" I heard Xeno shout behind me. I turned in the saddle to see his little line advance with their spears levelled. There were only about fifty of them, but that was the end of it. The central mass of the crowd broke. Gripped in an unthinking collective panic, they ran, scrambling through the charred remains of the warehouse district like a plague of rats.

I patted the horse's sweating neck and whispered my thanks in its ear, then sheathed my sword and dismounted.

"Hold him," I said, handing the reins to one of Xeno's soldiers. He was staring at me as though I had two heads.

A dazed-looking ruffian nearby was on all fours and trying to stand. I took a running kick at him, catching him in the ribcage with my iron-tipped sandal. He spun through the air to land on his back a few feet further away. He curled into a ball, clutching at his side, and began wailing.

Another man was coming unsteadily to his feet close by. He watched me dumbly as I strode over to him, unsure whether to run or not. He should have run. I punched him hard in the stomach and he fell to his knees and vomited violently. He groaned feebly and wiped his mouth with the back of his hand, not daring to look up at me as he tried to catch his breath. I grasped the collar of his tunic in my left hand and dragged him, flailing and wriggling, across the cobbles towards the sea.

"Let go," he squealed. "I'm sorry, noble sir. Please let go. I'm begging you, please..."

I ignored him and tossed him over the edge of the wharf. He screamed briefly as he somersaulted the twenty feet through the air to splash headlong into the water.

Xeno came up and stood by my side, and for a few moments we watched together in silence as the man flapped around desperately below us.

"Do you think he can swim?" I asked indifferently.

Xeno shrugged.

"Not very well, by the looks of it, sir."

"A Greek who can't swim. Who'd have thought it?"

"It's a disgrace, sir."

We turned and headed back towards the families. Apart from the whimpering of some small children, they had fallen silent. I rested my hand on Xeno's shoulder as we walked.

"I'm sorry, old friend," I said. "I should have given you more men. My mistake. There's a company on the way."

Xeno chuckled.

"Oh, I've been in worse scrapes, sir." He held up the stump of his forearm and smiled grimly. "Besides, I doubt I'll be needing them now. Those arseholes won't be back... And thank you for what you did. It'll certainly be something to tell my grandson."

I grunted.

"This is a shitty business, Xeno."

"It is indeed, sir."

His men had gathered together in a loose group beside the Carthaginians. Most were grinning and, as we approached, they parted to make way for us and started pounding the ground with the butts of their spears.

"Alright, alright," I said, gesturing with my hand for them to quieten down. "That's enough..." I took the reins of my horse back from the man who had been holding him for me.

"What shall we do with this one, sir?"

Two of Xeno's troops were supporting the man whose face I had slashed. He sagged between them. His eyelids were flickering and he was making a faint, wet hissing noise as he tried to breathe. Part of his shattered cheekbone had been laid bare and nothing much remained of his nose. The cavity was bubbling and oozing blood over his lips and chin.

"Kill him," I said. "Mount his head over there." I nodded towards the piles of rubble.

The man's feet trailed limply behind him as they dragged him off. It was probably a mercy.

"Xeno, I'll see you later. I suppose you'd better get these families onto their ship now. I imagine they've had their fill of Syracuse."

I led my horse back towards Achradina. The line of men blocking the gate hadn't moved.

"That was unbelievable, sir," said the young sergeant breathlessly as I drew up in front of him.

"And you just stood by and watched, while our men got cut off?" I said.

"But, sir, Lieutenant Xeno told us to stay here."

"You're stripped of your rank. Now get of my way."

It took a week to complete the embarkations, but there were no more incidents. Although he had citizenship, I heard Tabnit chose to sail with his people on the last ship to leave. I suppose the prospect of being free to start burning children again was too strong a lure to resist.

My men's work was not yet done. We still had to clear the houses of all the slaves who had been left behind. They were in a sorry state, having had little food for several days. They were escorted in batches to the agora, where the stewards of the noble families haggled and struck deals with each other as they divided them up between our households. Andranodoros had provided a schedule as to how the windfall should be apportioned, based on our individual landholdings in Upper Tyche, and I eventually found myself with forty more mouths to feed. Once they had been restored to a saleable condition, I had them all auctioned off.

When North Achradina was finally empty, we began repopulating it with the families of homeless citizens from the streets of Temenites and Neapolis. We crammed them in, allocating just one room to each family. To everyone's relief, we found that there would be no need to billet anyone in our own villas. Within a matter of months, North Achradina was transformed from one of the city's prettiest districts into the new slum quarter. Its replacement residents seemed feral. They threw their rubbish out of their windows, leaving it to rot on the streets, and undertook no maintenance of the buildings in which they had been resettled. Before long, the Tyche gangs had become the North Achradina gangs.

Gelon ended up allocating the City Guard three hundred men who had been made homeless by the fire. They were a rough and ill-disciplined crowd, even though all were citizens who had completed their military training. They had all been recalled to serve with the fleet and at first they tended to swagger around a little, pretending to be heroes, much to the irritation of my men. My criminal half-brother, Dionysius, was not among those who were assigned to my command. I felt I ought to try to do something for him or his family, if he had one, and so I sent a message to the army clerks at Plymmerium, asking if he was with any of the Shield divisions. When they replied to say they had no record of him, I entrusted Agbal with a bag of coins and sent him to the makeshift camp on Epipolae to ask around there. He returned to tell me that no one appeared to want my money. Whenever he mentioned my half-brother's name, people lost their tongues. It seemed Dionysius had disappeared. I wasn't entirely surprised.

Castor and I formed our new men into two additional companies, to which I transferred some of my tougher sergeants. We garrisoned them all in the large and ancient Labdalum fortress. Labdalum predates my ancestor's great triangle of walls, but fortuitously sits almost exactly at the centre of them, being more or less equidistant from the city's north and south gates and from the Euryalus citadel. Its own walls were low and weak and, as a stronghold, it was next to useless, but it was the obvious place to station a contingent of reserves. More to the point, the new camp on Epipolae lay only a few hundred yards away, and I wanted to make sure that I had enough men close by to maintain order there.

I put Xeno in command of Labdalum, with instructions to start getting the new companies into shape. When he had softened them up a little, I intended to swap them over with two of the palace companies and take over their training myself. I moved Leander to Labdalum too, to command one of the new companies. The lad had sent me a handsome letter of apology for his all-too-obvious disapproval of my handling of the Carthaginian expulsions. I had a soft spot for Leander, but I was still unsure whether he had the stomach for soldiering. Decency is the virtue of losers.

It was not till two weeks after the deportations that I was finally able to make time to take the barge across to Plymmerium to visit Sosis. I got there shortly after sunrise to find the parade ground already bustling with companies of the Shield divisions going through a variety of exercises. The army had taken on some three thousand men from Upper Tyche and Gelon was clearly trying to integrate them as quickly as possible. As I threaded my way across the parade ground, I was met with salutes and smiles and, to my embarrassment, even some cheering. I felt a fraud. When the fleet had sailed, I had stayed safely at home. When my friends had marched to their deaths in Italy, I had stayed safely at home. And yet it seemed I was being greeted as some sort of hero. I jogged most of the way to try to escape the attention.

There were a hundred cots ranged against the long walls of the infirmary, and I never thought I would have wished to see them all filled, but only about a quarter were occupied and that was an even grimmer reminder of the scale of the slaughter at Cannae. Some of the men were sleeping but most were sitting up, gazing silently across the aisle at each other with empty eyes. Half a dozen slaves were quietly changing dressings or feeding those too weak to eat their breakfasts by themselves. Two others supported a man by the arms as he squatted over a bucket.

Sosis wasn't there. A sergeant who had lost both his feet told me that the captain had recovered sufficiently to return to the cottage that had been my home before it became his. I spent about an hour with the wounded men, moving from one bed to another. Although there were a few new trainees whom I didn't recognise, the rest had all previously served under me and I knew them by name. I asked after Dinomenes' son, but they could only tell me that he had not been among Hannibal's prisoners. Two of the men who remained unconscious were groaning intermittently. Their wounds smelt, so I imagined they were not long for this world.

By the looks of their injuries, fewer than half a dozen of the men in the infirmary would be able to return to duty with the Gold Shields. When they had recuperated, the rest would be discharged with five silver coins as a token of the kingdom's gratitude. Those who were too broken to find employment for themselves would probably be given light work on the estates or in the family businesses of the division's officers. The sight of crippled veterans begging in the streets was something the army preferred to avoid.

I promised to visit them all again when I could, and headed towards the door. When I reached it, I turned, stood to attention and saluted them. Before the injured men could recover from their surprise at the gesture, I had ducked out of the room and was striding away, my sense of shame more acute than ever.

I found Sosis sitting on a comfortable chair on the porch of the cottage. A thick bandage smeared with honey and herbs covered half his face. I don't know if it was helping the wound to heal, but it certainly seemed to be attracting the flies. Half a dozen buzzed around his head unrelentingly.

"I'll be as ugly as you now, Dion," he said weakly, trying to smile, as I grasped his hand in greeting.

His elderly camp slave brought me out a stool and we started to talk about what had happened in Italy. Sosis was a cool-headed man, the sort of person whose brain works in precise and deliberate clicks. Perhaps it was the wound that was agitating him, but when he spoke of Hannibal, his poise dissolved.

"We threw everything at the centre of his line, Dion," he whispered, his remaining eye wide with apparent awe. "That was where Hannibal was himself. We thought they were breaking, but he was just drawing us into his trap. They fell back, step by step, and as we pressed forward, they slowly wrapped themselves around us, and then from nowhere their cavalry suddenly appeared behind us. It was like nothing in any of the books. The plan, the discipline… We were crushed in on ourselves. I couldn't breathe or move my arms. There was no space to move, and no direction to move in. He drowned us in our own numbers, Dion… Pray that he never comes to Sicily. We're lost if he does."

I leant forward, patted Sosis on the knee and smiled.

"I wouldn't be too sure of that, my friend," I said, trying to sound confident. "We still have our walls, after all. Unless he can fly, even Hannibal won't find it easy to get past those."

Sosis sighed sadly and waved his hand feebly to drive the flies from his face.

"Well, maybe you're right, Dion. I hope so. You know, he came to see me himself before he sent us back. He had his own physician dress my wound. He's only a little fellow and he speaks softly and smiles a lot. You'd never guess he was so dangerous, at least, not until he looks at you. I can't really explain it, but he's like some sort of wizard. If he told you to jump off a cliff, you'd want to do it, just to please him."

I was intrigued.

"What did you talk about?" I asked.

"I congratulated him on his victory and he just laughed and said he was lucky in his enemies. Of all things, the only question he asked me was if I knew Archimedes. I told him the old boy used to be my tutor when I was a child, but that I hadn't seen him in years, and then Hannibal said something odd. I was in a pretty bad way and Hannibal's Greek isn't that good, so I may have misunderstood him. But I think he said that if the Romans had any sense, they'd ask Hieron for tutorials with Archimedes rather than shipments of grain. Or something like that. I suppose it was a joke. Anyway, when he realised I couldn't tell him very much about your great-uncle, he lost interest and walked off."

We talked for a few minutes more, but then Sosis's remaining eyelid began to flicker and he drifted off into a heavy sleep.

I sat beside him for a while in silence, lost in my own thoughts, before I got to my feet and walked as quietly as I could along the porch. His camp slave was sitting at a table at the far end, spreading honey on a fresh length of bandage with a brush. I told him I would try to return in a week or two, and stepped out into the sunshine.

I didn't have to be back at the palace until lunchtime, so I decided that while I was there, I might as well see how Archimedes was getting on with his new weapons.

The disused granary that Gelon had made available to him as a workshop was a mile away, at the end of a track that ran through a coppice of pine trees. I emerged from the treeline to find that the entire southern tip of the camp, an area of some three or four acres, had been fenced off. The palisade looked flimsy so I imagine its main purpose was to conceal whatever was happening inside. A rough gate straddled the path, one side of which was open. Beyond it, I could see several long, neat lines of army tents, which I guessed had been put up for the slaves Archimedes had requested. Six sentries were standing guard in front of the gates, blocking the way. The white circle on their shields identified them as Theodotus's men. I was only wearing a plain white tunic but they recognised me and snapped to attention as I approached.

"Is my great-uncle here?" I asked a ruddy-faced sergeant, who stepped forward to greet me.

"I'm afraid I can't say, sir," he replied awkwardly, but it was unclear whether he meant that he didn't know or wasn't allowed to tell.

"Alright. I'll find him myself. Make way."

"Yes, sir, of course, but if it's not too much trouble, would you mind showing me your pass?"

"My pass?"

"Yes, sir. I'm afraid we're not allowed to let in any visitors without a pass sealed by your great-uncle or by the general himself. No exceptions… I'm sorry, sir."

We were interrupted by a loud, shrieking noise from somewhere behind the palisade. It sounded like two large pieces of metal being violently scraped together. I winced.

"What the…" I began, but before I could finish the question, I felt a slight tremor beneath my feet and an instant later I was silenced by a deep, distant crash, as something immensely heavy smashed into something else.

The sergeant smiled and shrugged.

"They're just starting the day's tests, I'm afraid, sir. Would you like me to send a man to the general's office to see if we can arrange a pass for you?"

Out of sight, someone began shouting. I couldn't make out the words, but it sounded like a warning.

"Just send someone to tell my great-uncle I'm here, would you?" I said irritably, but the sergeant wasn't listening. He had clapped his hands to his ears. I was at a loss for words. I had never seen such impertinence. Behind him, the sentries had dropped their spears and were doing the same. I stared at them, wondering if my friend Theodotus had somehow managed to arrange a joke at my expense. The sergeant pulled a face and nodded anxiously at me. Suddenly there was a stupendous clatter and a whoosh, as some awful mechanism that I could not begin to picture was released, and my eardrums were assaulted by a shrill whizzing sound. The effect was terrifying. I instinctively wrapped my hands around my head as well. As the whizzing faded, its pitch grew lower, but it was immediately followed by a further clatter, whoosh and whizz, and then half a dozen more in rapid succession. A chorus of screeching harpies could not have made a worse racket.

"I'm very sorry, sir," said the sergeant, when the din had finally died away. "That's the worst of them. No offence intended. I hope you understand."

"Fuck," I said simply. "Don't worry about that pass, Sergeant."

I turned and headed back towards the coppice. As I reached the treeline, I was startled by yet another noise at my back. I couldn't help flinching and ducking my head. This one sounded as though a thousand giant hailstones were striking the rocky ground almost at once. I straightened myself up and remembered Sosis's ruined, frightened face. Let Hannibal come, I thought grimly to myself. I wondered how the little general would enjoy the greeting my great-uncle was preparing for him.

On the way back to the ferry, I stopped by the administration block, where Gelon had his office. The prince was out conducting inspections, I was told, and they had no idea when he would be back. I decided not to wait. Plymmerium, once my home, now only made me feel uncomfortable.

Almost no one comes to call on me any more in my little house in Upper Tyche. By and large, I am a forgotten man, and when I reflect on the unspeakable things that I have done, believe me, that seems a mercy. But just this morning, out of the blue, I found a young stranger waiting for me on my doorstep. I was returning from the market with a pair of fish heads for my soup. The fishmonger gives them to me, for old times' sake. His name is Piso, and he is the son of Dinomenes, the man who had sewn up my face after the Battle of Sellasia. His father's intuition had been right: Piso hadn't died at Cannae, although he had been obliged to play dead for three days, till Hannibal's army finally moved on. It took him nearly two months to make his way back to Syracuse. He was always a good soldier, but we have an understanding never to talk about those days. I suppose we both have too many bad memories. I gather he hasn't even told his own children about his adventures. Dinomenes himself choked to death on a fishbone twenty years ago, and he is now a forgotten man too, although he doesn't deserve to be, given the role he was eventually to play in our kingdom's history. But I am getting ahead of myself.

The man waiting for me outside my house today was a puny little fellow with a large, bobbing head, greasy hair and eyes set too closely together. He greeted me excitedly and with the pretence of great pleasure, as though I were some ancient uncle from whom he was hoping to inherit something. He told me his name is Polybius and that he is researching a book he intends to write. Apparently, it is going to be a history of everything. I was the last, he said, bowing and rubbing his hands together, who had known Hieron and who had stood on the walls with Archimedes during that long, terrible siege. He had so many questions he wanted to ask me. He had sailed to Syracuse because he had heard a rumour I was still alive, and he had spent the last three days tracking me down.

He shouldn't have bothered. I've known enough toads in my life to recognise the species. After listening to him gabble on for a few minutes, I let myself in and slammed the door in his face. If he ever gets round to writing his silly book, no doubt it will be full of nonsense about how noble and righteous our new masters are. Their shocking treachery will be buried among lots of windy speeches that no one ever gave and valiant deeds that no one ever performed, and Polybius will probably get an approving little pat on the head for his efforts and a pocketful of silver. Well, fuck Polybius and fuck his history. I may no longer have the strength to take a sword to my enemies, but at least I am still man enough to hate them.

Day by day, the date fixed for my wedding was marching closer, like the slow but inexorable advance of an enemy phalanx. I had put Alpha and Omega in charge of the preparations months before, with instructions to bother me as infrequently as possible with the details. They had been making the arrangements with my new steward, a kindly and intelligent old household slave whom I had known since childhood and whom I trusted, although not so much as to give him a duplicate of my signet ring. I had granted him his freedom when I gave him the job. It would probably make little difference to his life, the remainder of which would continue to be spent in my service, but I suppose the fact that he was now a freedman set him apart from the rest of the household. With only three weeks left before the big day, Alpha and Omega moved back into the family villa to supervise the final preparations, leaving Agbal and me to fend for ourselves in the palace.

The senate had, of course, sent a deputation to my mother, beseeching her to accept the office of High Priestess, and after an appropriate display of reluctance, she had graciously accepted. The common people were ecstatic and celebrated her acquiescence in the usual way, with a drunken riot. She was the queen bee of society once more. Among the women of the city, only Nereis, Gelon's wife, would be able to claim precedence over her, but not until Hieron was dead and Nereis had her own throne beside her husband's. That Hieron had his leash fastened around my mother's neck was a secret of which the world remained ignorant.

I had decided to delay choosing a new husband for her until after my own wedding. I refused to talk to her, but given her new position, I could hardly send her back to Catana. I had to content myself with evicting her from our family home and installing her in Delia's old villa instead, with a more modest household of her own. I guessed that Alpha and Omega had been consulting her about the wedding arrangements all along and that she had probably taken charge of everything behind my back. I didn't really care, providing she kept out of my way. Between the three of them, at least I could be confident everything would be done properly.

I was working in my office one morning when Leatherskin put his pockmarked face round the door.

"Dion, am I disturbing you?" he asked, nervously rubbing his hands together. "I can come back another time, if you wish?"

I suppressed a sigh.

"No, Polyaenus, it's alright. What can I do for you?"

"Oh good… May I sit down? Thank you so much… I know you're a busy fellow, so I'll come straight to the point. I wanted to ask you if I might have your permission to correspond with a certain relative of yours? As you know, one of my responsibilities as speaker of the senate is to sort out the practical arrangements for all our religious festivals. So, now that your relative is to be installed as High Priestess – and, I may add, no one is more delighted than I – our duties will to some degree overlap. Naturally, I shall route any correspondence through you."

"No need for that," I replied brusquely. "Just deal with her directly. And by the way, feel free to refer to her by name. She's a public figure now."

What a prissy little worm, I thought. I was half-tempted to throw him out of the window. I doubted whether anyone would greatly care if I did.

"That is most gracious of you, my friend. Thank you. Now, I would like to send the Lady Korinna a little gift, as a token of my desire to achieve the most cordial cooperation with her in the future. I hope you will not judge such a gesture too bold or impertinent. I have brought the present with me, to ensure it meets with your approval. May I have it brought in?"

He was sweating. Most of the less important councillors had taken to fawning and cringing in my company, but Leatherskin was being even more obsequious than the rest. I dare say his previous efforts to arrange a boycott of my ships had come to weigh quite heavily on his mind.

I snorted and smiled.

"That's most kind," I said.

He grinned and clapped his hands and a slave entered the room with a cage. Inside, lying on a folded blanket, was a tiny white puppy; I didn't recognise the breed but it looked like some sort of exotic lap dog.

"How very thoughtful," I said. "I'm sure my mother will be delighted."

"Oh, good. You're sure she'll like it? It's terribly rare, you know. It comes from the Orient, apparently. I'll have it taken round to her today… You're certain it will please her? I can't tell you how gratified I am. Well, thank you so much for your time, Dion. I won't keep you any longer."

I have no idea what eventually happened to the puppy; I never saw it again. My mother never had much time for dogs.

The wedding promised to be the grandest society event for years. Every noble family in the city had to be invited, and they would all feel obliged to come. Then there were all the common citizens who worked for us, whom I was apparently expected to invite too, along with a host of merchants with whom we did business, to say nothing of my Guards officers and most of the army's officer corps. There were probably two thousand people on the guest list. I made sure Nebit was included. At least he would be happy to be there, however much I might wish I wasn't. In the event, I only had two refusals. The first was from Zoippos, who sent me a stiffly phrased note citing a prior engagement. The second was from Hieronymus, who had finally been allowed to leave Pachynus. He merely returned the invitation, torn in half.

The main banquet was to be held in the courtyard and garden of my house. I ordered half the slaves from my various country estates to be brought to Syracuse to help, about a hundred and fifty of them altogether. Most were simple agricultural labourers and would have to be trained to serve at table. The steward arranged for them to be accommodated by various tenants of mine around the city, who were apparently only too delighted to help, in exchange for receiving invitations themselves. Even so, it looked as though we would still be short-handed, until Gelon offered to lend me a contingent of fifty palace slaves, including thirty from the palace kitchens, which solved another headache. My stables were cleaned up and converted into additional kitchens. I had toyed with the idea of simply throwing the old women back out onto the street, but in the end had them moved out to the estate at Leontini instead, where there were some disused slave quarters they could occupy. They cried fearfully as the carts took them away, perhaps not trusting my steward's assurances. But at least my mother made no objection to the women's removal: she had finally been installed as High Priestess, and was doubtless relieved to be able to abandon her charitable pose.

I could hardly exclude the ordinary ranks of the City Guard from the festivities, so I ordered feasts to be laid on for each of the companies in their various garrisons around the city, over the course of the week leading up to the wedding. And I arranged a second little treat for my men as well. The largest and most celebrated brothel in Syracuse was called The Mercy of the Gods. It had operated out of the same somewhat dilapidated but still elegant building in Neapolis for over a century. Whatever her other failings, my mother could never be accused of priggishness, at least not when it came to making money. She had snapped up the building for a pittance several years earlier, with its colourful and energetic tenants *in situ*. The rent was probably double what any other occupants might have paid for the use of the premises. I had my lawyer approach The Mercy's manager, who agreed to provide every man in the City Guards with an hour's free entertainment, in exchange for the waiver of a month's rent. The sergeants were given special copper tokens to distribute, which would secure admission at The Mercy's doors. My only stipulation was that Cleopatra, a doe-eyed Egyptian girl who was a particular favourite of mine, should not be among those made available to my men.

Old Senator Torquatus sent me rather a curt letter to say he would be bringing three hundred friends and relations from Rome with him, whom I was apparently expected to accommodate for the better part of a week. Fortunately, Hieron himself came to the rescue and offered to make the guest wing of the palace available for the Torquatus locusts, although he made clear I would be expected to foot the bill for their food.

My lawyer Linus, overwhelmed by the range and scale of my financial interests, had gleefully given up all his other clients and was now working for me alone. Altogether, he calculated that my wedding day would cost me nearly three months' income, which meant that I would have to visit the vault in the cellar of my house. The vault was usually only opened once a year, and only my mother and I knew its secrets. We had smaller hiding places at our country estates as well, each with a few boxes of silver in case of emergency, but it was in the great villa on the Avenue of Athena that we stored most of our ready money.

Three weeks before the wedding, on one of my regular sleepovers at the villa, I rose in the dead of the night and, taking the flickering lamp from my bedside table, walked through to the small antechamber that adjoined my room. A dozen nondescript clothes chests had been arranged around its walls. The chests had lain there for so long that, when I moved one aside by its handle, the pale boards immediately beneath looked as though they had been cut from a different type of wood to the rest of the floor. I lifted up one of the boards on which the chest had rested and retrieved what I sought from the shallow cavity below. It was an old, iron key, about two-foot long and fashioned to resemble a snake, with opposing curves along its shaft and two long teeth protruding from its head.

I let myself out of the chamber. The house was still and noiseless as I made my way along the corridor and down the stairs to my mother's former study. On the wall behind her desk hung a large tapestry, which concealed a squat, heavy door. I put my lamp and the key down on the desk and removed the dusty hanging from its hooks. The door had no lock and swung open smoothly and silently, to reveal a short, steep flight of steps. At their foot I lit another lamp that had been suspended from a hook in the ceiling. Its light was barely sufficient to illuminate the claustrophobic room. The walls were entirely lined with shelving, onto which had been crammed all manner of scrolls and bundles of papyrus and parchment. Some of the documents were so ancient they looked liable to crumble to dust if they were disturbed. Anyone who discovered the room might think it contained all manner of precious secrets. The truth was that none of these documents was of any continuing value to my family. They were just old, fulfilled contracts and letters and records, whose only remaining function was to deceive.

I put the key and my lamp down on the floor and pulled on a set of shelves in the centre of one of the walls. The section was hinged and swung forwards with a faint creak to reveal a second door, lower than the first. It had been so extensively reinforced with strips of metal that one could barely see the wood beneath. It took three full revolutions of the key to retract the bolt on the far side, and I had to put my shoulder to it to get it open.

The vault beyond was about six paces square, with a low ceiling and damp brick walls. I placed my lamp on a bracket just inside the entrance. Dozens of boxes of coins, many of them more than a century old, had been neatly arranged in stacks at the back of the room. In the dim, flickering light, the tall stacks looked like rows of ghostly sentinels. Almost all the coins they held were silver, but two of the boxes contained gold. There was nothing in their appearance to differentiate those two from any of the others, but they were probably worth as much as all the rest put together. Each had been carefully positioned at the very bottom of a stack, and had been bolted into the floor. The House of Dionysius had always been circumspect with its treasure.

I brought up twelve boxes of silver to the study, carrying two at a time. I returned to the vault for the last time to retrieve the lamp and was about to seal the room again when, on an impulse, I decided also to retrieve a small, silk-wrapped package from its hiding place behind a loose brick near the bracket. There were over a dozen loose bricks around the walls of the vault, and each concealed something. I put the package carefully inside my pocket. When I had locked up again and put all our elaborate precautions back in place, I began carrying the boxes of silver up to my mother's former bedroom. I didn't mind the exercise – in fact, I welcomed it – and besides, I didn't want to give any members of my household a clue as to where the silver had really been stored. If my slaves concluded that my family had a hiding place somewhere in my mother's old suite of rooms, all the better. I left the little package under the floorboard beside the key.

In the morning, I would have the boxes loaded onto a cart and taken to the Royal Treasury, where Hieron allowed the nobles to keep their money in exchange for a handling fee. It was a useful service. My steward would write out bills of payment for the wedding expenses, and once I had put my seal on them, the recipients could take the bills to the treasury to collect the specified sum. Most of the nobles probably kept all their silver at the palace. My family used the facility for our business dealings, but at the end of the year, we withdrew any profits that had not already been reinvested in further property or ships. We preferred to keep our money close.

At least my mother should have fun with the seating plan, I reflected, as I laboured breathlessly up the stairs for the final time that night, my face and torso glistening with sweat. No doubt she would make sure that I was far from the only person at the banquet with a long face.

With the additional boxes of silver, I reckoned I should have sufficient funds at the treasury to meet all the costs of the wedding. The expense was an irritation, of course, but only in the way a mosquito bite might be. It would require a fairly observant eye to notice that the vault was now any less full than it had been, and in any event, its contents represented merely a fraction of my wealth.

As a rule, we find rich people much more pleasant than poor people, unless they start talking about their money, when the reverse rule applies. For this reason, I have avoided going into any great detail about my interests till now; but as there is nothing left to be gained for me or mine by discretion, I may as well set down everything.

For all the precautions that we took to protect its contents, the vault was not my family's most closely guarded secret. There was something we were even more anxious to keep concealed from the eyes of the world, buried on the far side of the Mediterranean, beneath the stables of an isolated farm a few miles outside Corinth.

It was not till I came of age that my mother eventually told me the story, having first solemnly sworn me to silence. When she had finished, she showed me the drawer in her bedroom cabinet, where she kept the dirty and faded deed to the property among an innocuous bundle of private letters.

It so happens I had the opportunity to visit that farmhouse five years later, when I was sent by my king to help the men of Corinth fight the Spartans. It was a fairly unremarkable building. In any event, the deed is long since lost, along with my city, my home and whatever appetite I may once have had for wealth and power. I am clearly fashioned from much softer clay than my ancestor, the second King Dionysius, who never lost his own hunger for such things.

This Dionysius devoted his reign to terrorising the forebears of most of my noble friends, executing some and confiscating their wealth, while obliging others to hand over huge sums to avoid a similar end. The nobles finally combined against him to drive him from Syracuse. Dionysius was, by all accounts, quite content to abandon his wife to her fate, but at least he had possessed sufficient decency to send the contents of his treasury safely on ahead, before fleeing himself. And it was to Corinth that he went, where he spent the remainder of his life implausibly feigning poverty. After his death, the deed to his farmhouse was quietly passed down from one generation of my family to the next, until I eventually contrived to lose it. Even my mother had no idea how much gold and silver my grasping ancestor had concealed beneath the flagstones of his stables.

When all else was finally lost to me, I tried to retrieve the hoard. I came out of hiding and made my way to Corinth, working my passage on a merchant ship. I tramped the roads for two days, sleeping under hedges, until I managed to find the place again. But the farmhouse and its stable block had disappeared, and where they had once stood, a magnificent new villa was under construction. I dare say that villa is still there. No doubt the gods enjoyed a hearty chuckle.

A week before the wedding ceremony, my officers threw a predictably rowdy party for me in our mess at the palace. It ended up with everyone walking over to The Mercy for an orgy, of which I still retain the most delightful memories, not least because of the series of complex combinations in which Cleopatra, my little Egyptian doxy, and the no less beautiful Leander enthusiastically indulged me.

Two days later, my best friend Theodotus held a much smaller dinner on my behalf, in the modest villa that his father-in-law had made available for him in Neapolis. Theodotus's ancestral home was even older and almost as large as my own, but it had long since been subdivided into a number of apartments, which were let out to puffed-up merchants who wished to boast of an address on the Avenue of Athena.

I should perhaps explain that it was my friend's misfortune to have had a grandfather who was not only recklessly extravagant, but also tragically long-lived. Theodotus's father had attempted to repair the damage by arranging for Theodotus to marry an only child, the absence of any siblings being a virtue of such precious rarity that it comfortably outweighed the girl's notorious defects of appearance, intellect and temper. It even outweighed the fact that her father was none other than Leatherskin, who was of course exultant at being able to buy his daughter such a blue-blooded husband. Although Theodotus was obliged to live on Leatherskin's charity, his own son would one day inherit several thousand acres of high-quality timber and the largest herd of cattle in the kingdom. Having overcome his revulsion sufficiently to perpetuate the family line and ensure its future solvency, Theodotus now lived apart from his wife and their child, to the general satisfaction of everyone concerned.

There were only seven of us at the dinner, which was nearly as many as Theodotus could accommodate comfortably. Sosis was still too weak to attend, but Prince Gelon came, along with my adjutant Castor, my cousin Thraso and Eryx, the captain of the Yellow

Shields. Andranodoros was the seventh. I had asked Theodotus to include him, to the surprise of both. Andranodoros had never been popular among my military circle, but recently it seemed he had struck up something of a friendship with Theodotus, perhaps as a result of the generosity with which he had shared the credit for the fleet's victory. Cleopatra told me the two of them were frequently at The Mercy together.

To much laughter, Theodotus announced that in my honour, the main course would be boiled cows' brains, with a side dish of fried bulls' testicles. Neither is a delicacy of which I am overly fond. Most cooks seem to boil the brains for too long, with the effect that they disintegrate in your mouth like jelly, whereas they usually don't fry the testicles for long enough, so that you have to chew on the spongy meat for a tediously long time before daring to swallow it. Fortunately, in those days I still had excellent teeth.

Two slaves began to serve us. One of them, a surly man with an ugly red birthmark that covered most of his cheek, looked familiar, although it was not till he stumbled and sent a copper plate clattering across the floor that I remembered him.

"You idiot," sighed Theodotus sadly. "Get that cleared up."

The man hurried from the room.

"Well," I said with a laugh, "if you will have your grooms serve at dinner, what do you expect, Theodotus?"

"Oh, is he a groom?"

"Didn't you know? He used to work in the palace stables. We sold all the grooms when we got rid of the officers' horses."

"So that's where Leatherskin must have found him. I'm afraid he's just on loan to me for the night. I might have guessed the old man would send me someone useless."

"How are things with your father-in-law?" asked Eryx mischievously.

Theodotus pulled a sour face.

"The fool spoilt his daughter, and now he's spoiling my son. Says he's destined for greatness, although the child seems a complete dunce to me. He keeps stuffing the lad's head with all sorts of goosecrap about my family history. He seems to know more about my ancestors than I do. It's 'King Gelon this' and 'King Gelon that' from dawn till dusk at Leatherskin's house. The old sod's been dead nearly three centuries, for fuck's sake. But so long as I let Leatherskin keep the boy, I get my captain's bills paid. And at least I only had to hump the ghastly old sow a couple of times, so I suppose I mustn't complain."

"You must be the most expensive whore in the kingdom," laughed Gelon, who had himself been named after Theodotus's ancestor, although Hieron's own claim to descend from the famous king was highly questionable.

"Perhaps we should put you to work for the treasury, Theodotus," said Andranodoros drily.

The conversation flowed easily, with Andranodoros going out of his way to be charming and telling several funny stories. It is a gift I have always envied: sadly, I seem even more proficient at killing jokes than I am at killing people.

When the meal was finished and the wine had been prepared, Gelon stood to perform the libations and propose a toast to me. He was very sad, he said, to have to disclose that his father was considering offering my seat on the Royal Council to my now-famous horse. Although the horse seemed to be just as mad as I was, Gelon continued, the king hoped that it might have more to say.

We began drinking but, after a little while, Gelon made his apologies and announced that he had to return to the palace. I did my best to conceal my disappointment. We all stood and the prince wished me well for my wedding night and embraced me. Perhaps I clung to him for a moment too long, because as Gelon left the room and the rest of us settled ourselves back down on the couches, I noticed Thraso observing me with an expression of mild surprise. He smiled gently and raised his eyebrows. I quickly turned my head and pretended to cough to hide my confusion.

With Gelon gone, the talk inevitably turned to the war. The disaster at Cannae had left the road to Rome wide open and the whole Mediterranean seemed to be holding its breath as it waited to see if Hannibal would march on the city before the winter came. Most of the Greek colonies along the southern coast of Italy had fallen over themselves to switch their allegiance to Carthage and had closed their harbours to our ships. The powerful kingdom of Macedonia had just declared war on Rome. Shorn of its most productive provinces, deserted by almost all its allies and with its army annihilated, Rome seemed as good as finished.

But Hieron had been right about the Romans. As a gesture of goodwill, Hannibal had allowed a few of their captured officers to return to the city, taking with them a message for the senate. Hannibal offered to ransom all his Roman prisoners, they reported. A Carthaginian ambassador had travelled with them and was waiting outside the walls to begin peace negotiations. The general had promised his terms would be mild.

It had been my future father-in-law who had put paid to any chance of peace. Word had soon reached us in Syracuse of the blood-curdling speech old Torquatus had given in the Roman senate. The thousands of soldiers who had been taken prisoner by Hannibal were a disgrace to their ancestors, he had thundered. How dare they be captured alive? They should have fallen on their own swords in shame at their defeat. On no account should they be ransomed. Let Hannibal sell them into slavery, and good riddance to the lot of them. As to the ten thousand or so men who had managed to flee the carnage, they were also a disgrace, apparently. Why had they not been honourably slaughtered too? His own son, Felix, was among those who had escaped. The senator publicly disowned him, and urged the fathers of any other returning officers to do the same. The survivors should all be banished. Who cared that they were virtually the only battle-ready troops that Rome now had left? The city's women would probably make a better job of defending its walls than those miserable apologies for Roman manhood.

Any normal body of men would have greeted this demented rant by shaking their heads sadly, and summoning a priest and a doctor to lead Torquatus quietly home to bed. Instead, his fellow senators had stood and cheered him to the rafters. The gates of the city were slammed in the face of Hannibal's astonished ambassador, and the captives were abandoned to their fate. The senate decreed that those who had escaped the massacre would be sent to garrison western Sicily in punishment for their survival, where they would be denied the opportunity to fight Hannibal again. All things considered, I could imagine worse punishments.

A new army was already being raised and the Roman nobles were donating vast sums to the public coffers to pay for it. Slaves were being offered their freedom if they enlisted. In the temples, the priests cursed all things Carthaginian, and to seal their curses, a young man and woman had been ritually sacrificed and buried in the forum. Rome would burn before it bent the knee to Carthage.

"Poor old Captain Cowbrains," said Theodotus sadly. "It seems you're to be married to the daughter of Senator Pighead. What strange children you'll make."

"I suppose we're completely fucked, then," said Eryx cheerfully. Few things seemed to make Eryx happier than the prospect of an imminent catastrophe.

The wine flowed freely, and we talked on till the early hours, even though no one had much to add to Eryx's succinct assessment. Strangely, none of my friends suggested that Hieron should change sides. It was as if they all wanted someone else to say it first. If any of them was entertaining thoughts of disloyalty, this was his opportunity gently to sound me out. And yet no one came close to broaching the subject, even obliquely.

Andranodoros alone said almost nothing more. He just smiled and watched and listened. Like me, he pretended to get quite drunk, but his eyes were as bright as ever, so I knew he wasn't. But then, perhaps he just didn't like the rather cheap wine that Theodotus had served.

XVIII

THE WEDDING

It was just as well that I stayed sober that night, because I had not been in my bed in the palace for more than three hours before Agbal entered my room to rouse me. Dawn was just breaking.

"Master, a slave has come to say that the king wishes you to join him for breakfast in his apartments."

"Fuck."

"There's a bowl of water on the table, Master, and I've put out a clean tunic for you."

I groaned, swung my legs out of the cot and rolled my head around my shoulders three or four times.

"Alright, Agbal. You can leave me."

I decided it would be better to arrive unshaven than to keep Hieron waiting. I washed and dressed hurriedly and, once outside, jogged around the colonnade to the plain wooden gate. Three men in togas were standing in the centre of the courtyard, in the first rays of the sun, chatting and gazing up at some architectural feature or other. It seemed that my guests from Rome had started to arrive during the night.

Once admitted by the guards, I found a slave already waiting inside the passageway to escort me to the king. He led me around the small garden, up a flight of stairs and through a succession of loudly painted but sparsely furnished chambers that I had never previously seen. Although I have a soldier's brain for topography,

I could never quite understand the internal layout of Hieron's apartments. They contained more rooms than seemed possible, and if you looked out of a window, you were likely to find that you were not at all where you expected to be in relation to the external world.

The room into which I was finally shown was cavernous. Five couches had been arranged in a circle at its centre. Hieron and Gelon occupied two of them. Two men in togas, both in their mid-fifties, lay on two of the others. No one stood as I entered, but at least Gelon gave me a broad smile and a nod. I bowed to the king.

"Ah, Dion," rasped Hieron. "At last. Come on over here. Torquatus, my dear fellow, allow me to introduce you to your future son-in-law."

One of the Romans got up. He had a red, heavy face and small, sharp eyes. His grey hair was cropped very short. He was broad and seemed surprisingly fit and powerful for a man of his age. I bowed courteously. He looked me up and down without expression and then, to my surprise, came to stand so close to me that our chests were almost touching. He must have been more than a head shorter than me but he tilted his face back and gazed up aggressively.

"So," he said, speaking Greek with a near perfect accent, "you're the man who draws his sword against his fellow citizens to defend Carthaginian scum?"

I looked down at him evenly and shrugged.

"No, Senator," I replied. "I draw my sword to serve my king. Greeks, Carthaginians, Romans: I don't really care whom I fight. Their blood all looks the same to me."

"So you think all races are just the same, do you?" he demanded.

I rolled my tongue around my cheek.

"They're the same to me if they're my king's enemies," I replied. "I'm honoured that you are to be my father-in-law, Senator, but if my king told me to take that noble head of yours off your shoulders, I wouldn't think twice about it."

Torquatus stared at me for a moment longer. And then, to my surprise, he put his hands on his hips and burst out laughing. Behind him, I saw the other Roman grinning too.

"You were quite right, King Hieron," Torquatus boomed. "I *do* like him. I like him very much. I think he's going to make me fine grandsons."

He clapped his hands to the sides of my shoulders, smiled up at me and gave me a friendly shake. I met his gaze warily.

"Now, listen to me, lad," he said, lowering his voice so the others couldn't hear. "Promise me you'll look after Vita. You don't have to love her, but treat her with respect and protect her for me. That's all I ask of you. Just do that, and I shall always be your friend."

He stared up at me with his intense brown eyes. I fancied I could see fire smoldering there.

"Do we understand each other?" he asked.

I nodded.

"I promise, Senator," I replied. "And I look forward finally to meeting her."

"Good man," he said, and gave me another hearty shake. "Now, come and meet my friend Marcellus."

Torquatus put his hand on my back and led me over to where the other Roman had risen to his feet. He was taller than I had first realised. I bowed again.

"Dion, of the House of Dionysius," I said formally.

"And I'm Marcus Claudius Marcellus," the man replied with a thin smile. His Greek was not nearly as polished as the senator's and his accent was thick. "I'm pleased to meet you, Captain."

I raised my eyebrows.

"You're General Marcellus? It's a privilege to meet the hero of the Gallic War, sir. My old general, Lepides, made us all study your campaign."

He made a dismissive gesture with his hand.

Marcellus's thin face was brown and deeply lined, like crumpled papyrus. He was half-bald with a broken nose and broad shoulders. There was no fat on him at all. At first glance, you might have taken him for a farmer, who had spent his life toiling in the sun, but the way he moved was sharp and fast. It was the only clue that he was Rome's most decorated soldier.

"I'm honoured that you're to be a guest at my wedding, General," I said, with what must have been obvious sincerity. "I'm afraid I had no idea you were coming."

"Sadly, I can't stay for your celebrations, Captain, much as I would wish to. I sail back to Italy this evening. I'm here to discuss other matters."

"Matters that concern you too, Dion," Torquatus interjected.

"So, Dion," Marcellus said, eyeing me coldly, "Prince Gelon was just entertaining us with a story of how you recently charged a thousand men by yourself. You sound quite the warrior."

I laughed in embarrassment.

"Sadly, General, I'm not in your league. You rode out in front of your army and killed the king of the Gauls in single combat. And apparently he was twenty years younger than you. I just charged an unarmed mob. It's hardly the same thing."

"I suspect it is exactly the same thing, Captain," said Marcellus, without smiling. "You and I both enjoy killing people, I think, but it is only by putting ourselves in danger that we can justify indulging our appetites."

I looked at him more closely.

"It is not the killing I enjoy, General, it is the thrill of surviving."

"Perhaps so, Captain. Although that thrill wears off soon enough, does it not? And then the yearning to kill or be killed takes hold of us again. I find it is like fucking. One can only be satisfied for a day or two, before one yearns to fuck again."

I laughed once more, but this time more awkwardly.

I had always assumed that the beast I kept penned up inside me was unique. I wondered if I might have been wrong about that.

"Well, if that really is your nature, gentlemen," interrupted Hieron, "you are certainly fortunate to be living in the time of Hannibal. I suspect he will provide you both with all the fucking a man could ever want, before we are done with him... So, shall we get down to it? Please make yourselves comfortable." The king gestured towards the couches with his hand. It seemed I had been invited to a breakfast without food.

When we had settled ourselves, Torquatus began.

"Dion, allow me to fill you in. Marcellus now has under his command a force of some fifteen thousand men, consisting principally of those who escaped from Cannae. In the event that Hannibal remains in the south of Italy for the winter, so too will Marcellus, to try and protect our remaining allies and interests there. However, we believe it more likely that Hannibal will march on Rome. If Rome is besieged, a more radical strategy will be required…"

He folded his arms and stretched out his legs.

"The senate has of course been preparing for just such an eventuality for some time – in fact, ever since Hannibal crossed the Alps two years ago. Your king and Prince Gelon have been closely involved with those preparations from the outset. As it happens, it was King Hieron who first proposed the plan that we may now be forced to implement."

Torquatus paused and nodded respectfully towards Hieron, who smiled thinly in acknowledgement. I waited for the senator to resume, but it was Marcellus who picked up from his friend.

"Captain, if Hannibal marches on Rome, my men and I will cross into Sicily. Torquatus has already laid the groundwork for that in the senate. Hopefully, Hannibal will believe that the legions really have been sent here in punishment and will not guess our true intentions. King Hieron has agreed to make available his fleet and an additional thirty thousand men. Our forces will sail with yours, and together we will surprise the Carthaginians and force them to raise the siege."

For several moments I didn't know what to say. I glanced at Hieron in dismay but his wizened face was blank.

"Do you have a question, Dion?" Gelon asked, looking rather amused.

"It is certainly a bold plan, my Prince," I replied cautiously. "But if I may make the obvious point: Rome has just failed to defeat Hannibal with an army nearly twice the size of his. What makes you believe you can defeat him with one much smaller than his own?"

Marcellus smiled.

"I am sorry, Captain, I have not explained myself well. I'm afraid my Greek is not very good."

"You nitwit, Dion," Hieron interrupted irritably. "The army won't be sailing to Italy to fight Hannibal. It will be sailing to Africa. We are going to sack Carthage."

✳

My jaw probably dropped open, as I tried to comprehend the plan. It sounded no less suicidal than going up against Hannibal himself. It was much the same tactic that Agathocles had pursued a century earlier, resulting in the glorious loss of all his men. And, mad as he was, even Agathocles hadn't been mad enough to try to assault Carthage itself. Sited on a rocky promontory, and surrounded on three sides by the sea, the only approach to the city is blocked by no fewer than three lines of gigantic walls. There were drawings of them in my office.

"Forgive me, my King, but how exactly do you intend to sack Carthage?" I asked.

It was Gelon who answered for his father.

"Just as Alexander sacked Tyre," the prince replied, almost casually. "We shall attack them from the sea."

I raised my eyebrows.

"But, sir, Alexander controlled the whole coast, and he had to have equipment specially built for the purpose, and even then it took him seven months. I don't see how that could work."

"No one is saying it will be easy, Dion," Gelon replied. "The obvious difficulty is that the sea wall of Carthage is almost impossible to scale. For most of its length, the water is too shallow to bring our ships directly alongside it, but it is also too deep to disembark our men. You must have still been a baby, Dion, when my father first asked Archimedes to consider the problem. And of course, being the man he is, your great-uncle proposed a solution."

I stared at Hieron.

"Just how long have you been planning this, Your Majesty?"

"What sort of a king do you take me for, Dion?" he snapped. "The Carthaginians have been trying to prise us off our rock for five centuries. Do you really imagine I have not anticipated a day when we might try to prise them off theirs instead? Every man who has ever worn my crown must have asked himself how we could rid ourselves of this menace once and for all... Archimedes, Lepides and I spent years planning how it might be done."

"And if I may ask, my King, exactly what was my great-uncle's solution?"

"He designed a ship for me, Dion," Hieron wheezed. "The largest ship in the world, in fact. It took over two years to build."

"*The Syracusia?*" I asked incredulously.

"Yes Dion, *The Syracusia*," said Gelon gently. "Although apparently it's known as *The Alexandria* now."

"*Hieron's Folly* is what they used to call it behind my back," chuckled the king. "Not surprising, really. It's a complete pig, unbelievably hard to handle by all accounts. Did you ever see it, Dion? It's more than double the length and breadth of a quinquereme, and three times the height. At a pinch, it can carry three thousand men. There are two towers on each side, towers that rise nearly forty feet above the water. The sea wall of Carthage rises thirty-four feet above the water at its highest point. What a surprise that will be for the Carthaginians, eh? When they see our men looking down on them, instead of the other way round... And those towers have hinged gangplanks fitted to their sides, which can be lifted high into the air and then dropped onto a wall..."

He widened his eyes, as if showing a child a trick, then raised his forearm and let it flop down again.

I was bewildered.

"But you sent *The Syracusia* to Egypt, Your Majesty," I said.

"Of course I did," the king snorted. "I couldn't just leave the blasted thing sitting here in our own harbour, could I? The Carthaginians would have wondered what on earth it was for, and sooner or later they would have worked it out. So I fitted it out as a pleasure boat, and filled its hold with grain, and sent it over to old King Ptolemy as a present, on the understanding that I could have it back whenever I wanted. Even he had no idea why I really built it. It's so useless for any normal purpose that it hasn't left its berth in Alexandria for twenty years. I gather the present Ptolemy uses it as a royal brothel. But at least he keeps it seaworthy."

"All we lack," said Gelon, "is some artillery powerful enough to send the Carthaginians scurrying from their walls."

"And do you have a solution for that, too, sir?"

"Tell me, Dion," interjected Torquatus mildly, "what exactly do you think your great-uncle has been working on these past few months?"

I blinked and Hieron gave me a toothless smirk.

"Ah yes, Dion. All those ostentatious tours of our walls that you and Archimedes undertook… Hannibal's fool of an ambassador just couldn't resist showing off how much they know about Plymmerium, could he? But all he accomplished was to reassure me how little they really know."

"And not just machines for *The Syracusia*," Gelon added. "Archimedes has some ideas to convert a dozen of our quinqueremes into floating platforms for artillery. Instead of masts, they will have huge catapults of some sort. The problem is stability, of course, but your great-uncle believes he's cracked that."

"I don't suppose you've ever read his treatise on the stable equilibrium positions of floating paraboloids, have you, Dion?" asked Hieron. "No…? No, I can't say I blame you: I have to confess most of it went completely over my head. But he tells me it was really all about ships… Anyway, Archimedes reckons everything should be ready in just two or three more weeks, although we won't be fitting out the fleet till the last minute."

"Naturally, we will be taking steps to soften Carthage up beforehand," Gelon continued. "Ptolemy has agreed to assemble his army on the border when the time comes. With Hannibal in Italy, the Carthaginians will fear an attack and will have to send a force to meet it. There shouldn't be too many men left to defend their walls. And my father has a few other little surprises in store for them, too."

Hieron smiled malevolently.

"Carthage is ruled by its nobles, Dion, and they are even more fractious than our own. I shall have two or three of the leading ones murdered. That should be enough to set them all at each other's throats before the fleet sails."

"You can do that?"

"Oh yes, Dion. I can do that. And more besides."

"May I ask, why you are telling me all this, my King?" I asked eventually.

"Because you will have your own part to play in this enterprise, Dion," Hieron replied. "Gelon will command the fleet, and Marcellus the army. You will be Marcellus's second-in-command."

My heart must have skipped a beat as I bowed towards the Roman. Perhaps my time had come at last, I thought.

"It would be an honour to serve under you, General," I said.

"We have agreed that you will lead the attack from *The Syracusia*, Captain," Marcellus said. "There is a point near the harbour where the ship can be brought directly alongside the wall. Your task will be to create a bridgehead by capturing the harbour. That is where we will disembark the rest of the army, and from there we will advance through the city."

I began to experience a sensation in the back of my mind, almost like a rustling of leaves. For all its promise of glory, the plan was obviously fraught with danger: even the largest ship can be burnt or sunk. But that wasn't it. There was something else missing… Why had they waited till now, I wondered? Why had they not attempted to destroy Carthage as soon as Hannibal crossed the Alps?

And then it dawned on me. Because Hieron had a price, of course, and not until Hannibal was at their gates would the Romans agree to pay it.

All four of them were watching me.

I knew I was on dangerous ground, so I chose my words carefully.

"My King, perhaps it is not my place to ask, but if I may, exactly what does Syracuse stand to gain from this? We are being asked to risk our entire fleet and thirty thousand men to help save Rome. Is it for friendship alone?"

"You were right, King Hieron," said Torquatus with apparent satisfaction. "He's no fool."

"And you are quite right too, Dion: it is not your place to ask," replied Hieron coldly. "But on this occasion, I shall answer you. In exchange for my help in sacking Carthage, Gelon will be king of all Sicily when I am dead. He will continue to pay a tribute to Rome of course, and my idiot grandson will be found a Roman wife, but our island will have peace at last. My people will finally be safe, Dion. Safe."

"And of course, my dear boy," the senator added happily, "when Prince Gelon is crowned king, my daughter will find herself married to the new general of his army. The army of the Kingdom of Sicily."

I felt myself blushing.

Hieron rubbed his bony hands together and cackled.

"Does Hannibal really believe he can burn my city with impunity?" he rasped. "Well, just wait till he sees what I am going to do to his."

The king's eyes glinted with joy.

Marcellus turned to gaze at Hieron with raised eyebrows. Perhaps he was a little shocked that someone so old could still be capable of such ferocity. But then, Hieron was not at all like other men.

"Well now, Torquatus my friend," the king continued, "I am sure our three soldiers have much to discuss. Why don't you and I go and have some breakfast? Perhaps you would be so kind as to help me up."

After the king had shuffled out of the room on the senator's arm, Gelon, Marcellus and I spent two hours considering the various logistical problems that the expedition would face. My stomach gurgled periodically, but I was too excited to mind. The smiling face of the sailor that I had appropriated for my father kept appearing before me. I contributed relatively little to the conversation. Like Gelon, Marcellus had a head for details. It was apparent the two of them had been friends for many years, although the prince had never mentioned Marcellus to me. I cared for Gelon more than any other man, but much of his life had always been hidden from me, and probably always would be.

When there was nothing else useful to be said, Marcellus and I bade each other good fortune, and he went off to find Torquatus while Gelon accompanied me back to the gate.

"So, what do you really think?" the prince asked, when we were out of earshot of anyone else.

"It sounds a pretty desperate gamble, sir. But of course, it could change everything."

"If Hannibal marches on Rome, Dion, things are likely to become pretty desperate."

"And if he doesn't, he may well march on us instead. Have we really done all we can to prepare for that?"

Gelon looked at me and snorted.

"Don't be stupid, Dion," he said. "Do you really think my father is a man to neglect our own defences? There are warehouses all over Syracuse with pieces of war machines in them, just waiting to be assembled. Even the Romans don't know about those, by the way, although they've probably guessed we have a few toys hidden away. Archimedes has been building them quietly for years. He's the only one who understands how most of them work."

"You seem to have a lot of faith in my great-uncle's machines."

"So does my father, Dion. And it seems he has faith in you, too." He smiled. "And so do I. Just pray the Carthaginians take the bait and go for Rome. My father won't risk letting us sail until he knows Hannibal is tied up elsewhere. And of course, the Romans won't agree our terms till then anyway. But if he does go for Rome... Well, Syracuse will write her own history, Dion. Men will still remember you and me and the sack of Carthage, long after Hannibal and Cannae are forgotten."

When I eventually returned to my apartment, I told Agbal to prepare me a plate of food. He looked at me in surprise, but said nothing.

I sat at the table in my bedroom, chewing happily on a piece of bread and marvelling at the labyrinthine mind of my king. At last, I thought. It seemed Ares had heard my prayers after all.

*

My wedding was finally upon me. Greek marriage ceremonies are tedious affairs, sprawling over three days. On the first day, my bride was expected to stay in her father's house in the company of women and go through various rites marking the end of her childhood, such as cutting off a bit of hair and burning her toys. As her own home was in Rome, Hieron had allowed the family the use of the palace instead, so I had to move back to the villa.

My own duties that day were limited to making a sacrifice at one of the appropriate temples and mumbling my way through a few prayers. Theodotus and I had an enjoyable lunch together at my house, before strolling out to perform the rituals. To spite my mother, I had chosen to use the Temple of Artemis, which lay directly alongside Athena's. Obliged to occupy the less impressive of the two buildings, its priestesses naturally resented my mother and her colleagues, and made a terrific fuss over me. Theodotus and I arrived an hour late and a little drunk, to find two dozen devotees of Artemis lined up on the temple steps, patiently waiting to greet us. They were dressed up in long white robes and wore garlands of white flowers. Their obese High Priestess bowed and scraped to me for a while and then presented me with a deer she had set aside for the occasion. While I slit its throat on the small altar at the foot of the steps, the devotees gleefully shrieked their way through the accompanying hymns at the tops of their voices, to make quite sure that everyone next door in Athena's house could hear them. I slipped the High Priestess a handful of silver coins for their trouble.

The main affair took place on the following day. There were some more rites to go through in the morning, of which I now recall little, except for the fact that my bride and I were supposed to have a bath together. Torquatus had agreed to a Greek wedding ceremony, but somewhat to my disappointment, he had drawn the line at letting me leer at his daughter in a wet, half-transparent shift before she was legally mine. Vita consequently took her bath at the palace, while I bathed at the villa.

That evening, Torquatus hosted the first banquet in the main courtyard of the palace. Its purpose was to introduce the groom to the bride's family and friends, so while my immediate relatives were invited, my own friends were not. The rows of tables had already been set up when I arrived, with those for the men on one side of the courtyard, separated from the women's tables by a central aisle some twenty feet wide. This, however, was very much a Roman affair, and the sexes were allowed to mix relatively freely under the surrounding colonnade before the meal was served. For all their affectations of refinement, the Romans still have one foot in the farmyard.

As custom required, I had put on a white tunic and was wearing a crown of myrtle. I have always been a little self-conscious because of my size, and the ridiculous foliage on my head did nothing to help. As I entered the courtyard, I passed a group of squat Roman women clustered around my mother, who stood half a head taller than all of them. To my irritation, I noticed she was wearing a string of large pearls, which should have been safely tucked away behind one of the loose bricks in our vault. I wondered when she had decided to help herself to them. I pointedly ignored her, not that she seemed to mind the snub. She was clearly having too much fun, trampling the matriarchs of Rome underfoot.

"What an interesting gold bracelet, my dear. It must be the thickest I've ever seen... I'm surprised you have the strength to lift your arm... What, these? Oh, they're nothing really. Just some old pearls my late husband's family was given by the King of Persia a few centuries ago..."

My sisters were there too, with their dull husbands and several squealing nephews and nieces whose names I could never remember, but who seemed terrified of me and happily kept their distance. Three impoverished country cousins whom I was obliged to support also showed up, and spent the entire evening competing with each other to try to catch my eye. They nodded and grinned at me with such unrelenting enthusiasm that their face muscles must have ached for weeks afterwards. Unfortunately, Archimedes and Chrysanthe didn't bother coming, although I had insisted that both should be invited.

I saw Hieron sitting on a stone bench near the gate to his apartments, talking to Andranodoros and Zoippos and a Roman who had his back to me. The king beckoned me over. As I made my way towards them, Zoippos sidled off, and the Roman turned. It was Felix, the senator's son.

I bowed formally to Hieron and nodded to the other two. Felix flushed as our eyes met, although whether out of ill will or embarrassment I couldn't tell.

"Now, no fighting, you two," said Hieron drily.

"Of course not, Great-uncle," replied Felix stiffly. "Dion had the decency to apologise for his behaviour when we first met and I have no further quarrel with him."

I had no intention of letting that pass.

"Nor I with you," I replied easily. "I hear you were at Cannae, Felix. Many of my friends died there. I am relieved to see that you at least managed to escape entirely unhurt."

I saw Andranodoros raise a hand to his face to conceal a smirk. Felix stared at me. This time, there was no mistaking the hatred in his face. His fists clenched.

"If you will excuse me, Great-uncle, there are some matters I must attend to," he hissed. Hieron lightly waved his hand and the Roman turned his back on me and marched off.

"What an extraordinary gift for making enemies you seem to have, Dion," Hieron sighed.

"I apologise if I spoke out of turn, my King," I said.

The king grunted.

"Felix is a turd. He's of no consequence. But you'd better make his sister happy, Captain, or you'll answer to me for it. Torquatus adores the girl, and the senator's friendship is valuable to me."

"I shall certainly try, my King."

He glared at me.

"Try, Dion? Try? I'm hardly asking you to undertake the labours of Hercules, for pity's sake. Just hump the girl every now and again, put a smile on her face, and give her father grandsons. How difficult is that?"

I bowed.

"No matter the peril, Your Majesty, know that I am always ready to draw my sword in your service."

He stared at me for a moment and then he snorted.

"You're an impertinent brute, aren't you, Dion? Well, let's just hope that famous sword of yours lives up to its reputation."

As the sun began to wane, a bell was rung and we made our way to our places. Hieron excused himself and disappeared back inside his apartments. I was seated at the centre of the head table near Gelon, with an empty space between us for Torquatus, whom I had not yet seen. Felix sat glowering at the far end, but apart from him, I only knew one of the others, a man named Otacilius, who commanded the Roman fleet in Sicily. Two years previously, when I had still been with the Gold Shields, we had cooperated in trapping and destroying some Sardinian pirate ships, and he had proved himself highly capable. Otacilius leant across the table to clasp my arm and offer me his congratulations.

"So, I hear you met our great General Marcellus?" he said with a faint smile, as he sat back down again.

"Yes, indeed. Do you know him?"

"Oh, yes, quite well, as it happens… He's actually my half-brother."

He looked me hard in the eye for a moment, as if to communicate something, but didn't elaborate. Instead he turned to the man beside him.

"Claudius, would you be so kind as to pass that jug of water, please," he said.

It struck me that it must be hard to live in the shadow of a famous brother. There was clearly some bad blood between the two of them, so I judged it best not to pursue the conversation.

"Now, tell me, Dion," Otacilius resumed, "how can we beat Hannibal most quickly, do you think?"

"Just find a dozen more men like yourself and your brother," I replied. "That should be quite sufficient." Everyone apart from Felix laughed. That Rome might be teetering on the brink of final defeat did not seem to have occurred to any of them.

The bell rang again and we all fell silent. After a moment, Torquatus appeared from an archway with a dignified, middle-aged woman on his arm who was evidently his wife, Hieron's niece. She had an attractive expression, but it was somewhat spoilt by the hooked nose that seemed to be a recurring feature within the king's family. I unhappily wondered if my future children would exhibit the same characteristic. My bride followed behind her parents, wearing a long, flowing purple robe, braided with gold, and her own myrtle garland. She walked well, with her shoulders back and her head high, but I still could not see her face. It was concealed by a yellow bridal veil.

Torquatus led the two women around to my table and as they approached, I stood.

"Dion," the senator said, "allow me to present my wife, Seema."

"Lady Seema, it is a pleasure to meet you," I replied. She inclined her head in acknowledgement.

"And this, Dion, is Vita," said Torquatus.

The senator and his wife parted and the girl stepped forward. All that was visible through the slit in her headgear were two large, almond-shaped brown eyes, beneath a pair of black eyebrows that had been plucked in the slightly arched fashion of Roman women.

"It is a joyous, to be husband, my Lord," she said haltingly, in a voice so quiet that I was uncertain whether her Greek really was as appalling as it seemed, or whether I had perhaps misheard her. "I am in learning your speak, so we is talked at you."

I smiled at her. She blinked as I did so and I thought I saw her small frame stiffen and recoil a little.

"Vita," I said, "I want you to call me Dion. I know my scar makes me ugly and that when I smile, it can look frightening. But you must never be afraid of me. I want you to know that I am smiling now because I am very happy. And I hope I will be able to make you happy too."

She turned to her father.

"What is he saying, Father?" she asked in Latin.

Torquatus translated what I had said.

"Tell him I do not mind his scar, Father, I just wasn't expecting it. And he is not ugly. I think he is very handsome. He has kind eyes."

The senator started to translate again but I interrupted him.

"I think you are the kind one, to say so," I replied in Latin.

She giggled. It was a lovely sound.

"Dion," she said in her own language, "your Latin is nearly as bad as my Greek. What interesting arguments we are going to have."

"Don't be rude, child," snapped her mother. "Tonight this man will become your husband. Be respectful."

"I have a little present for you, Vita," I said, and took the small, silk-wrapped package out of my pocket. I held it out to her and, as she took it from me, her long painted nails brushed the palm of my hand.

"How sweet of you. Thank you, Dion," she said. "May I open it now?"

"Perhaps wait till you are at your own table," I replied, feeling myself blush.

She was watching me closely and, behind the veil, I think she may have been smiling at my embarrassment.

"Come along, child," said her mother. "You two will have a lifetime to chatter. You must come and meet the Lady Korinna now."

I bowed to them and Seema led Vita across the aisle to their own table, where my mother was waiting to greet her future daughter-in-law with all the warmth of a coiled asp.

I was still blushing and smiling as Torquatus and I took our seats.

"I hope she didn't offend you, Dion," he said.

"Not in the least, Senator. She has spirit. I like her."

"So do I, Dion, so do I… Now, there's something I need to talk to you about."

He leant in towards me and lowered his voice so the others wouldn't hear.

"I owe you an apology. I was angry with you over that business with Felix, so I'm afraid I was a bit of an arsehole about the marriage contract. It was very dignified of you not to make a fuss about it at the time. Anyway, I wish to put things right. My family is not as old or as wealthy as yours, Dion, but we are honourable, and I don't want Vita's marriage to get off to a bad start. So I have transferred some further property into her dowry. That funny little Egyptian secretary of Hieron's has the details. I hope you will be satisfied."

I raised my eyebrows in surprise.

"That's very decent of you, Senator. You know, if I may say so, you are not at all what I expected."

"And if I may say so, Dion, neither are you."

I grinned.

"It's an old man's prerogative to lecture the young on their wedding day," Torquatus continued. "You'll probably be relieved to hear I have only one piece of advice for you, my boy. It's this: spend as much time as you can with your children, and if you have sons, don't expect too much of them. That way, they'll never disappoint you."

We were interrupted by a little shriek from Vita's table. The women surrounding her were all craning forwards on their stools, cooing and gasping as they leant in to inspect something Vita was showing them in her outstretched hand. It seemed my bride had opened her present.

A moment later, Seema leant back, and nodded approvingly to me. Then Vita herself stood, turned to face me, and held up her hand to display the ring that she was now wearing. I imagined she was smiling. To my surprise, I found the thought of that gave me considerable pleasure. Almost as much pleasure, in fact, as the sight of my mother sitting directly opposite her, trying to choke back her fury.

Torquatus beckoned his daughter over and she almost skipped back across the aisle to our table. She held out her hand to show him her finger but her eyes didn't leave my face.

"Is that what I think it is, Dion?" he asked softly, as he stared at the ice-clear diamond. There were probably no more than two or three such gems in the whole of Sicily. The stone, which was roughly the shape of a triangle, was nearly half the size of my thumbnail.

"Yes, Senator," I replied, but it was Vita at whom I was looking as I spoke. "No one knows where diamonds come from. Some say they are the tears of gods; others, that they are splinters of the stars. But they are the only things on this earth that can never be altered in the slightest way. They cannot be broken or divided or even scratched. An officer of Alexander's came into the possession of this one at the far edge of the world. He went on to serve the first King Ptolemy and took the stone with him to Egypt. When my father was born, my grandfather acquired it from the man's descendants as a gift for my grandmother. And now it is my wedding gift to your daughter."

Perhaps it was my imagination, but as I finished speaking, I thought I saw small tears forming in Vita's eyes.

"You can go back to your place now, Daughter," said Torquatus gently. She dropped her head. As she turned and walked away, Torquatus held his hand over his mouth and coughed awkwardly two or three times. He bent towards Gelon.

"It is some consolation, I suppose, to know that I have served at least one of my children well," I heard him say in a slightly strained voice.

"Knowing Dion as I do, Senator," Gelon answered smoothly, "I have no doubt Vita will come to think herself even better served than you realise." Then the prince leant forward and smiled at me. I felt myself blushing again.

The musicians and singers appeared and took up their positions in the open aisle between the men and the women. As they began their caterwauling, the food was brought out. Instead of waiting for the men to finish, the women ate alongside us.

✳

Dusk was falling as the musicians finally ran out of songs to inflict upon us and the banquet came to an end. It was time for the marriage procession. Torquatus and I walked out of the palace gates side by side, with Vita and her mother immediately behind us. All the other guests silently followed. A dozen of my slaves stood on the bridge with lit torches. Agbal was waiting for us, holding the bridle of a mule, which had been harnessed to a simple cart. Beyond the bridge, many thousands of people had lined up along the Avenue of Athena. The more my fellow nobles loathed me, the more the masses seemed to love me.

Vita stepped forward and Torquatus took his daughter's hand and offered it to me. I took her by the wrist. Vita turned to face me, her dark eyes fixing on mine.

"In front of these witnesses," Torquatus intoned in his deep, powerful voice, "I give this girl to you for the creation of children."

I could feel Vita's wrist trembling slightly in my grip. I gently lowered it to her side and let go. For a moment, we stood facing each other in silence. I felt a bewildering mix of emotions flowing through me, feelings I had never imagined my wedding would occasion: anxiety, fear, hope, excitement. I raised my hands and, taking the corners of her veil in my fingers, raised it up over her head and let it drop over the top of her garland.

As I did so, the wedding guests began clapping and cheering, and a moment later, their cheers were being echoed along the entire length of the avenue. As I gazed into my bride's face for the first time, the noise seemed to become disconnected from the two us, as though everyone else in the world was shut out on the far side of an invisible wall.

"Do I please you, Husband?" she asked nervously.

I gulped.

"Yes," I said simply.

Her rose lips parted in a wide smile.

"That makes me good joy," she said in Greek.

"It makes me good joy too," I replied softly. "Shall we go?"

"Yes, Husband," she said. "Up my new takes home."

I put my hands on her hips and lifted her, giggling, high into the air and swung her around onto the back of the cart. I vaulted up to stand beside her, and took her hand in mine again.

Agbal was grinning up at us.

"Vita, this is my slave, Agbal. He's a cheeky fellow, but I like him. Take us home, Agbal... You know, Vita, you are supposed to be looking sad at leaving your family."

She laughed and her eyes sparkled.

"What? Sad at leaving my mother's household?" she replied in Latin. "You must be joking."

It was my turn to laugh.

"I know what you mean," I said.

The procession was probably the largest that Syracuse had seen since Gelon's wedding, and was predictably raucous. When we got to the villa, there were more tedious rituals to perform. But that night, as a choir sang outside my bedroom door, Vita and I finally became man and wife.

I awoke as the first rays of the sun began to shine through the windows. My room had been hung with saffron-coloured fabrics for our wedding night. Vita's bridal girdle lay discarded on the floor, along with the rest of our clothes. She was still wrapped around me, her knee resting on my stomach and her arm stretched out across my torso. Her curls spread over my giant chest like blackbird wings and I could feel her soft breath on my nipple. I didn't want to move for fear of waking her. I looked down the length of her back to her tight, round buttocks and bit my lip.

I have always been a vigorous lover, but on that first occasion with Vita, I had moved as tenderly as I could. I had seen the look of surprise and pain in her face, her eyes widening as she had gasped and gripped my shoulders. Afterwards, she had cuddled up to me, tracing her fingers over my scars and muscles, and we talked about ourselves and our families, she in Latin and I in Greek, understanding each other well enough. After a little while, I had felt her hand beginning to explore me. She giggled as my body responded.

"Dion, I have seen naked men at the slave markets, and of course my mother told me what to expect... But I definitely wasn't expecting anything like this..." She giggled again as she stared down at me in the flickering light of the bedside lamps. "Are all men like you?"

I smiled awkwardly, feeling embarrassed.

"No... I am sorry if I hurt you."

"Only to begin with. You were very sweet and gentle... Look: I can barely get my hand all the way around it. How should I hold it?"

"A little higher up. Yes, that's it."

I swallowed and took a deep breath.

And so we started again. But this time, she was curious and wanted me to show her everything. At first there was a lot of laughter, but her giggling soon gave way to gasps.

When we had done at last, I collapsed happily onto my back, my body glistening with sweat, and lifted my arm to my forehead.

She lay on her front beside me, resting her chin on her hands and watching me mischievously. Her slender body was shimmering too. Without dropping her gaze, she touched the tip of her tongue to her upper lip.

"I like this," she said with a smile. "Again."

It was nearly midday when we emerged from my bedchamber – or our bedchamber, as it had now become. The musicians had left but the villa was busy with houseguests from around the kingdom and beyond, who seemed to be making themselves at home. They wandered about freely, letting themselves into rooms and eyeing up the various curiosities and treasures my family had acquired over the centuries. Vita and I took breakfast alone in the small dining room downstairs, which I had reserved for our private use, and where Alpha and Omega waited on us. To my complete surprise, I found they both spoke much better Latin than I and, encouraged by my bride's informality, they soon had her in stitches with stories at my expense. I tolerated it: I found my wife's laughter gave me more pleasure than any musicians ever could. After we had eaten, one of my slave women escorted Vita to the women's bathroom, while I went to wash in the larger bath to the side of the main courtyard. Five of my guests were lounging in the water when I arrived and greeted me warmly, although I couldn't remember the names of two of them and one of the others I didn't recognise at all.

The courtyard had been transformed for the banquet that I was to host later that afternoon. Every column had been wrapped in strands of brightly dyed wool and decorated with wreaths of supposedly auspicious plants and garlands of autumn flowers. Dozens of long trestle tables had been set up. Alpha appeared and the other slaves started scampering around under his supervision. He clucked and fussed and sporadically threw tantrums as I watched on in amusement from the water.

The men would be eating in the courtyard and the women in the garden, where Omega was in charge. Once I had dried off and dressed, I wandered through to see how things were getting along there, only for Omega to shoo me impatiently away again. I retreated into the villa to find Vita. I had promised to give her a tour of the compound.

When I had walked into the palace the day before, with my myrtle crown on my head, it had still been my intention to pack her off to the countryside after a week or two. I had pictured myself visiting her occasionally at my own convenience to fulfill my marital obligations, before returning alone to the city and my already settled life. But quite inexplicably, all that had changed overnight. It was as if a sorcerer had cast a spell on me. I wanted Vita to be the new mistress of this house. I wanted it, perhaps more than I had ever wanted anything. My children would be born in my ancestral home, and I would run around the garden with them on my shoulders, while she looked on and laughed. She would be carried through the streets in a litter and my bed would be the envy of Syracuse. In time, our grandchildren would be brought into the garden to play around our feet. And perhaps by then, I reflected with a chuckle, my wife might even be able to talk to me in Greek.

I eventually found Vita in the kitchen, of all places, tasting the food that was being prepared and chatting to one of the old kitchen slaves as though he were a long-lost friend. I doubt I had exchanged more than two or three sentences with the man in my entire life: the kitchen slaves were not allowed in the rest of the house. I had no idea what his story was or how he came to speak Vita's language. I called her away but I didn't chastise her. She would learn how to behave in time.

XIX

THE BANQUET

I was showing Vita around the house when we were ambushed by a potbellied layabout called Pelion. I groaned as he emerged, grinning stupidly, from behind a bronze statue in the sculpture gallery, followed by his embarrassed-looking wife. He had written to me some months earlier to ask for a large loan. His wife, Sophia, was a second cousin of mine, and he seemed to think this placed me under some sort of obligation to help him out. I had gently refused. Having squandered most of his own inheritance, I saw no reason why Pelion should now be entitled to live off mine. He knew he was not a close enough relative to be seated at my own table, and so he had probably been lurking around the house all morning, hoping for an opportunity to corner me and press me on the matter. I talked politely with him for a few minutes, carefully denying him any opening to broach the subject, while Vita and Sophia chatted in Latin. Fortunately, before long, Agbal came hurrying into the gallery in search of me, although my sense of relief at seeing the boy evaporated as soon as I heard what he had to say.

"Master, the Lady Korinna has arrived. She wishes to speak to you."

"What about, Agbal?" I sighed.

"Master, she had not expected the Lady Vita's brother to be coming to the banquet, but last night she was informed that he will now be attending. She wants to know if you would like him to be seated at your table. If so, she asks which of your own relatives you wish to offend, by moving them elsewhere."

Pelion, my mother, Felix – it was one irritation after another. I growled.

"Tell my mother to leave our family just where they are. She can seat Felix wherever she likes. She can put him in the kitchens, for all I care."

I felt a tug at my sleeve.

Vita was staring up at me anxiously with her wide brown eyes. She had obviously caught the gist of the exchange.

"I'm so sorry, Dion, this is all my fault," she said in Latin. "Please don't be angry. I begged Felix to come, for my sake. I didn't realise it would cause a problem. I'm so stupid… But can't you find a way to put him on your own table? He'll be so upset if it looks like you're snubbing him and I'm sure your other brothers-in-law will be up there with you. And he's a soldier too, you know; you've got so much in common. I'm sure you'll get to like him when you know him better."

Agbal clearly didn't understand what Vita had said, but Pelion did. He raised his eyebrows in surprise, coughed and looked discreetly away. It was hardly Vita's place to tell me where to seat my dinner guests. Besides, she belonged to me now: it was quite improper for her to favour her own relatives over mine.

And then I saw the tear in her eye. I checked myself.

"Vita," I said gently after a moment, "you don't seem to understand quite how we do things here in Syracuse. That's not your fault of course, but just so that you know for the future, it is not a wife's place to contradict her husband in front of other people, even relatives."

For a moment she looked at me as though I had slapped her across the face. Her lower lip began to quiver, and then she burst into tears.

"Oh no, now I've only made things worse," she sobbed. "I've ruined everything. You'll never forgive me." And with that, she turned and ran down the long room to disappear through the double doors at the far end.

I stared after her, completely at a loss.

"I wouldn't worry about it, old boy," said Pelion cheerfully. "Just give that pretty bottom of hers a spanking every now and again and she'll soon learn her place. That's what I do."

I glared at him.

"Piss off," I snarled, and he recoiled in shock. He turned red and started to mumble some fawning apology but I cut him short. Sophia hurriedly looked down at her feet but I thought I saw a smile on her face. She didn't seem to care much for her husband either.

"Come on, Agbal," I muttered. "Let's get this fucking nonsense sorted out."

We found my mother in the main courtyard. She was walking slowly around the tables scrutinising the settings. Alpha and Omega followed a few paces behind, looking nervous.

"Ah Dion, there you are," she said casually as I approached. "You seem a little upset. Did things not go well in the bedroom last night?"

"Don't provoke me, Mother, or you'll regret it," I replied coldly. "Now, about this business with Felix. Put the little prick on my table, but seat him as far away from me as possible. I don't care whom you get rid of instead, providing it's not Thraso or Archimedes. I'm sure there must be some relative of ours you'd like to spite."

She raised her eyebrows in obvious amusement.

"I see, Dion. So that's how it is, is it...? Very well, leave it to me. I'm sure I can work something out."

"Thank you," I said formally, and turned to walk away.

"Alpha," I heard my mother say behind me, "I suppose we'll just have to move Uncle Alexander elsewhere. His wife eats with her mouth open, you know. Dreadfully vulgar woman."

A slave knocked on our bedroom door an hour or so later, to announce that the first of my guests had arrived. He had the good sense to do so from the corridor. My wife was still expressing her apparently inexhaustible gratitude towards me for my kindness to Felix, hanging in the air from my neck with her legs locked around my thighs. A valuable antique table lay upturned near my feet, having been somewhat thanklessly cast aside after its recent service. Vita giggled and bit my ear as I shouted to the slave to clear off.

✳

I stood at the main entrance to the villa, greeting my guests with Vita beside me. The women were escorted into the garden as soon as they arrived, while their husbands were shown directly to their places by relays of slaves. Archimedes was among the last to arrive, but to my disappointment, Chrysanthe was not with him.

The bell eventually sounded, the gates were closed, and Vita headed off to the garden while I took my own place.

A low platform had been constructed for my table slightly to the side of the entrance archway. Below us, nearly a hundred other tables had been crammed into the courtyard. At least my guests seemed to be enjoying themselves, I reflected, even if the goddess was not. Her statue scowled down disapprovingly at the rippling rainbow sea of brightly coloured tunics that lapped impertinently at her feet.

Gelon was seated next to me. The slave Hannon hovered menacingly in the shadows behind us, tasting his master's food before it was served. The various relatives on my table, most of whom I seldom saw, were too apprehensive to say much, perhaps because of the presence of the prince, although I probably had something to do with it as well. I suppose it is on account of my physique that men instinctively draw back from me, even when I wish to be friendly. Strangely, I seem to have almost exactly the opposite effect on women. In mixed company, while the men shuffle about nervously and avoid my eye, I have frequently caught their wives and daughters stealing furtive, sidelong glances in my direction and tittering to each other behind their hands. I am not sure which response makes me feel more awkward.

Perhaps, I thought to myself as I chewed on a duck leg, Pelion was right after all. Maybe I should give my wife a light spanking after my guests had gone to instil the proper degree of respect in her. Better that she learn her place quickly. A few moments later, I found myself obliged to pull my stool forward, to try to conceal under the table the effect that the prospect of spanking Vita's bottom had all too obviously had on me.

Between them, Thraso and Gelon kept the talk going, drawing in the others as best they could. Torquatus tried to engage my great-uncle in conversation several times, but Archimedes seemed lost in a world of his own, tracing intricate but invisible shapes on the tablecloth with his finger. The senator's only success with my great-uncle was to prevail upon him to explain the mathematical relationship between the distance over which an object can be thrown, and the length of the arm that is employed to throw it. Archimedes proceeded to demonstrate the theory by using a spoon to flick a piece of sesame cake down the table, scoring a direct hit on Felix's face.

"You clumsy old fool," spluttered Felix, and an embarrassing silence immediately descended on us. Felix looked as though he was about to give his do-you-know-who-I-am speech, but unfortunately for him, and rather to my surprise, my great-uncle evidently knew exactly who he was.

"My dear boy, I am so terribly sorry," Archimedes replied in apparent consternation. "I do hope I didn't hurt you. What a tragic irony that would be, to have escaped the horrors of Cannae entirely without injury, only to be felled by a morsel of sesame cake."

The senator glowered down the table at his son, who had turned the colour of a tomato. I had yet to see the two of them exchange a single word. I might have felt a little sorry for Felix, if I hadn't been too busy trying not to choke on my food. Opposite me, Thraso seemed to be suffering from a similar difficulty.

"If you will excuse me, Dion," Felix said, rising to his feet, "I am afraid I don't feel very well. I must have eaten something that disagrees with me. I think I had better return to the palace."

I stood as well.

"I'm sorry to hear that, Felix," I said, suddenly feeling rather guilty. "Look," I added on an impulse, "if you feel better tomorrow, why don't you and I go riding together in the afternoon? I've got a wonderful stallion I could lend you that I imagine would suit you very well."

"Thank you for the offer," he replied stiffly, "but I feel certain I shall not have recovered sufficiently by then to join you."

"Well, maybe another time," I said, and smiled.

Felix bowed to Gelon, then he and I also exchanged an awkward nod, and he stalked off.

"I must apologise for my son's behaviour, Dion," Torquatus said quietly. I noticed he was gripping the edge of the table.

"There's nothing to apologise for, Senator," I replied easily. "He's just proud. If that's a failing, then it's one from which I'm afraid I also suffer."

"At least you have something to be proud about," Torquatus muttered.

After we had eaten, the wine was served. The courtyard fell silent as Gelon stood to perform the ceremonies, before wishing me many sons and toasting my health. Everyone cheered.

As the drinking began, I left my place and began circulating around some of the other tables. I was talking politely to a group of merchants when, out of the corner of my eye, I spotted Nebit. As usual, he was wearing one of his absurd gowns. For some reason, my mother had placed him at the end of Theodotus's table, in the company of Andranodoros and some of my most aristocratic army friends, where Nebit could hardly have been more out of place. Perhaps she thought she was being considerate, by providing an amusing spectacle for my friends' entertainment; if so, by the time I got near their table, they must have already had their sport, because they were now merely ignoring him. It made me wish I had taken more of an interest in the arrangements.

"Cowbrains!" Theodotus shouted out happily when he saw me. "What are you doing talking to all those boring old farts? Come on over here!"

He stood to greet me and we hugged each other.

"Many congratulations, Dion," he said with a warm grin. "At least your wife doesn't look anything like the hairy old hag I had to marry. You should hear my wife snore. It's like listening to a pig snuffling for acorns."

He wrinkled his nose and made a series of grunting noises and we both laughed.

"Mind you," he said, "there's a rumour going around that you're actually quite smitten…" He looked at me archly and I felt myself blushing.

"Ah, so it's true then." He laughed again and, putting his arm round my shoulders, turned me slightly to face the other men on his table. "Gentlemen, gentlemen, your attention please! I have some most tragic news. Behold! This fellow was once the mighty Bull of Syracuse, but as you can see for yourselves, he is now reduced to a wide-eyed little calf. Yes, my friends, I can confirm that everything we have heard is true. Our hero has fallen. Poor Dion is completely cuntstruck."

Everyone burst into uproarious laughter, except Nebit, who was gazing at Theodotus with open distaste.

It seemed Pelion's tongue had been wagging. I rolled my shoulders to dislodge Theodotus's arm, but I forced as close an approximation to a smile as I could manage.

"Unfortunately, I've been cuntstruck for years," I said. "It seems all my dearest friends are cunts."

"Ooooh!" gasped Theodotus, widening his eyes and clutching his hand to his heart as though he had been stabbed. The laughing continued.

I strolled down to the far end of table where Nebit was sitting, stopped in front of him and held open my arms.

He looked up at me uncertainly, not understanding why I should be singling him out for my attention.

"Nebit," I said, "aren't you going to embrace the groom?"

His expression turned to one of surprise.

"Why, yes, my dear Captain, but of course…"

He hurriedly got to his feet and rather awkwardly put his arms around me. The sight must have amused my friends further: the top of Nebit's head barely came up to my chest.

"I'm so pleased you were able to come," I said as I released him. "Look, I wonder if I might ask you a favour? I'm stuck on a table with a lot of unbelievably dull relatives. It so happens we've got a spare seat now. Would you mind coming over and joining us? I could really use some help with the conversation."

He gawped up at me.

"Captain, I hardly know how to respond," he stammered. "What an honour! Just to be invited to your magnificent home today was… well, it was… but I never dreamt… I mean, to be so singularly favoured…"

"Shut up, Nebit," I said, putting my arm round his tiny shoulders.

I gave Theodotus and the others a nod.

"I'll try to catch up with you fellows later," I said cheerfully, and led Nebit away, leaving them staring in astonishment at our backs.

"My dear Captain," the little Egyptian wheezed as he waddled alongside me between the rows of tables, "you must forgive me for forgetting my manners. This is all so very overwhelming. But allow me now to offer you my most sincere felicitations on this, the happiest of days. Oh dear. Oh dear me. Won't the prince be offended by my presence at your table? I am merely one of his father's servants, after all."

"Don't be stupid, Nebit, of course he won't be offended. Besides, this is my house. I'll sit with whom I want… Now, here we are… Listen up, everyone. For those of you who don't already know him, allow me to introduce you to Secretary Nebit. The king asked him to babysit me when I first joined the Guards, and he has already saved my neck on more than one occasion." I smiled at one of my dull brothers-in-law. "Maro, why don't you go and sit over there, where Felix was? Then we can put Nebit next to Archimedes and the two of them can chat about equations or something."

✳

Half an hour or so later, as the afternoon's shadows began to lengthen, Gelon leant in towards me and whispered that he would have to be leaving.

"Will you walk me out?" he asked.

"Of course," I replied.

"Let's try to do this discreetly," he said.

He and I started to get to our feet, but as soon as he rose, everyone else at the table respectfully did so too. Within a few moments, the entire courtyard had fallen silent and was standing.

"Please sit down, everyone," Gelon shouted amiably, waving them down with the palm of his hand. He and I stepped off the platform and turned under the archway, where his four black-plumed bodyguards waited for him.

"I'm sorry, Dion," the prince said. "I'm afraid I can't even take a piss without everyone making a fuss about it."

I laughed.

"Thank you for having made the time to join us today," I said, and signalled to Cerberus to open the gates.

"What did you think, Dion? That I would miss your marriage feast?"

His eyes fixed on mine and I blushed and looked down at my sandals. I was confused. Overnight, the ground beneath me seemed to have shifted slightly. There was no reason why my marriage should have changed anything, but it had, even if I couldn't articulate how. All I knew was that I felt as though I were betraying him in some way.

Gelon was silent for a moment, then he smiled.

"I understand," he said. "You don't have to explain. Now, let me embrace you."

He put his arms around me, and I clasped his back.

"I am happy for you, Dion," he said, as we separated.

"Thank you," I replied simply.

"Well, don't exhaust yourself too much with your new bride, Captain. My father expects you back on duty the day after tomorrow."

"Yes, of course, sir." I bowed.

He turned and marched briskly out into the street, followed by Hannon and his bodyguards.

I craned my head back to gaze absently at the underbelly of the high arch. After a few moments, I became conscious of Cerberus standing at my side.

"Yes?" I asked indifferently, my thoughts still elsewhere.

"Master, I hope you won't think it out of place, but I just wanted to offer you my congratulations. May you have many sons, Master. Although for your wife's sake, I shall pray that they are not as naughty as you were."

I laughed.

"Indeed, Cerberus... Alright, I suppose you'd better close the gates again."

I was heading back into the courtyard, still smiling, when I heard some muffled shouting coming from the avenue. Probably drunks, I thought. And then a woman screamed. I turned on my heels.

Cerberus was in the process of swinging the gate closed. He stopped and took a step outside, a look of puzzlement on his face. The shouting and screaming intensified and I saw people starting to run past in the street beyond.

"Master!" Cerberus screeched, turning towards me and flapping his arms wildly. "Master!"

I launched myself forwards, hurtling full tilt past him onto the street.

It was chaos. Over a thousand slaves, who had been loitering outside the house waiting for their owners to reappear, were now scattering in blind panic. The litters in which they had carried their mistresses to the banquet lay abandoned in neat rows down the middle of the avenue. Some men were trying to clamber over them and others lay sprawling on the cobbles. Two or three horses were rearing wildly over the heads of the crowd.

In the frenzied blur of movement I couldn't make out what had caused the panic.

"Where's the prince?" I yelled at Cerberus.

"There, over there, Master," he shouted back, pointing in the direction of the palace. "I think I saw men... men with knives..."

I began running down the street, but the crowd was coming in the opposite direction and slowed me down. People careered into me. I bellowed and shoved them aside, forcing myself forwards. Gradually the wave of people thinned out and then suddenly they were all behind me.

I could finally see Gelon, fifty paces or so away. He was on one knee, struggling to get to his feet. Hannon and three of Gelon's bodyguards had formed a protective square around him.

They were entirely encircled by a pack of ten or eleven crouching men with long, glinting knives, who were repeatedly darting forwards and jumping back again, trying to get under the swing of the bodyguards' swords. The bodyguards seemed to have abandoned their spears for the close-quarters fighting. A man wearing a black-plumed helmet lay motionless on his back between Gelon's attackers and me. Two other men were writhing on the ground nearby. One seemed to be trying to crawl away, dragging his purple, snaking intestines along the cobbles behind him.

I charged towards the prince, and as I ran, I saw a man lunge at Hannon, who alone seemed to be unarmed. Instead of recoiling, the slave sprang forwards as well, his hands extended like a cuttlefish. Their arms intertwined in a wriggling knot. Another man leant in to slash at Hannon, and seemed to catch him across the shoulder, but an instant later, the slave had skipped back again. His first attacker stood stock still for a moment, then took a single tottering step sideways and crumpled to the ground. His own knife had been driven so deeply into the underside of his chin that only the hilt protruded.

As I closed the distance, one of the attackers noticed me.

He shouted something to his companions. Two of them turned and ran forwards to keep me away from the melee; both held their knives in their right hands. The one to my left took up a position maybe five paces to the side of his companion but two paces ahead of him. I immediately realised they knew their business, expecting me to swing right, to try to avoid the reach of their knife arms. If I did, the one to my right would attempt to block me and slow me down, to allow the other to come at me from the side.

So I went left instead.

At the last second, I sidestepped across the front of the nearer man. I saw a flicker of surprise in his swarthy face as he stabbed at me. He was slender-hipped and quite fast, but not nearly fast enough. I turned on the balls of my feet, leaving his knife to jab harmlessly through the air in front of my stomach. I seized the wrist of his extended arm with one hand and continued to pivot, dragging him forwards on his feet and forcing him to swing around me in a stumbling arc. I clamped my other hand onto his bicep and accelerated into the turn. His feet were off the ground now. A moment later, I hurled him like a discus straight at his companion. He spun through the air and crashed sideways into the second man's chest, knocking that one clean off his legs as well. They hit the ground a few paces away from me, with the second man's face and shoulders buried under his comrade's sprawling torso. As he wriggled to free himself from the weight, I ran over and kicked him as hard as I could in the groin.

The man I had used as a projectile was now pushing himself up onto all fours. I straddled him and wrapped one hand around his forehead, pulling back sharply, while pushing down between his shoulder blades with the other. I heard a sound I recognised, somewhere between a crunch and a snap, and let him flop forward again over the contorted face of his companion.

Dealing with the pair of them had forced me to waste a few precious seconds. I turned back towards Gelon, sprinting for all I was worth across the final yards between us. He still hadn't managed to climb to his feet. The left side of his tunic seemed to have turned black and clung wetly to his body.

The pack was making a last desperate attempt to get to him and finish him off. As they surged in, I saw one of the prince's bodyguards step forward and swing his sword backhanded across an attacker's throat, opening a pumping geyser of blood. It was the cut of an artist, precise and elegant, but before he could drop his blade again to protect himself, a rat-faced little man darted under his sword-arm and drove a dagger into the bodyguard's side. I reached them a second later and slammed my fist down like a hammer on the knifeman's head. His legs buckled and he collapsed to his knees.

Someone else came at me from nowhere. Out of the corner of my eye I saw his arm beginning to lunge and he would have had me, had not something shiny and spinning suddenly hurtled between our faces, making him blink. It gave me the split second I needed to start twisting. His knife sliced through my tunic but only struck me obliquely and glanced off a rib. I grabbed his forearm as it shot past me and, turning my back to him, lifted his arm high and jerked it down over my shoulder, snapping it like a twig at the elbow. He screamed once and then I turned back and gripped his head between my hands, driving my thumbs deep into his eyeballs. They burst, spraying my face in salty little globules of jelly, and his screams became continuous. He tried to stumble away, but only managed three or four paces before he tripped over a corpse and crashed to the ground.

The injured bodyguard was clutching his side and swaying slightly on his feet.

"You little shit," he spat, and rammed his sword angrily into the open mouth of the rat-faced man who was kneeling in a daze beside him.

I turned to see Agbal standing thirty feet away, trembling. He still held one of the throwing knives I had given him. Well, at least he had managed to miss me too, I thought.

Behind him, dozens of men, led by Theodotus and Andranodoros, were now sprinting towards us from the villa. It was nearly over.

Agbal's eyes suddenly went wide.

"Master!" he yelled desperately, pointing behind me.

I spun round, but I was too late.

Someone with a shock of black hair had managed to slip through the cordon and stood behind the prince. I glimpsed the flash of the blade as it was raised over Gelon's head. He seemed to sense the danger and, from his kneeling position, tried to throw himself backwards to knock his attacker off balance. But he was too weak for it to do any good, and the knife swung down over his shoulder and slammed into the centre of his chest, just below his sternum. I was already vaulting towards him, but Hannon got there first. He seized the knifeman by the throat and, crooking a leg behind the assassin's knees, effortlessly threw him backwards.

A moment later I was standing over the man. He was only about twenty, I guessed, a handsome-looking lad with full lips and olive skin. He could almost have been Agbal's elder brother.

The last of his comrades still on their feet had already abandoned the fight and were running away for all they were worth. Their work was done. I watched them swerve into an alleyway and disappear into the maze of Ortygia's dark passageways.

The young man looked up at me. He seemed perplexed. "You must be the Bull of Syracuse," he said in Greek, with a strong Carthaginian accent. "I wasn't expecting you... More fool me, I suppose. Well, I hope you appreciate your wedding present."

I slowly lifted my knee. He didn't try to protect himself. He just continued to meet my gaze, and then he coolly tilted back his head to expose his throat.

I stamped down on it. His pretty green eyes bulged and his tongue went rigid and started flapping around between his teeth. I didn't bother watching him die.

Hannon was kneeling on the ground cradling Gelon in his lap. The prince was spluttering quietly and his arms and legs were twitching. One of his bodyguards sat cross-legged on the cobbles nearby, clutching his helmet to his chest and weeping. Another now lay on his back a few yards away, in a widening puddle of blood. The third, his leg red from the wound in his side, looked at me grimly. A moment later, his sword clattered to the ground and with a wince of pain, he fell to his knees.

I sat beside Gelon and held his hand as my guests gathered around us in a packed, silent circle. Before he died, the prince turned his face towards me, but I saw no recognition in his eyes, only fear.

*

Andranodoros alone seemed to retain his presence of mind.

"Dion, are you injured?"

I looked down at my tunic. It was thickly spattered with blood, but I could see only the one cut in it where I had been nicked. I turned to Andranodoros and shook my head.

"Good. Then pull yourself together. I need you."

I hauled myself slowly to my feet. Hannon gently laid Gelon's head on the ground and stood as well. The slave surveyed the scene with his bulbous, expressionless eyes, then turned away and started walking slowly around the bodies of the assassins. His coarse tunic seemed to have become stuck to his shoulder blade, where a large bloodstain had begun to congeal.

"We have to get the city gates closed," Andranodoros continued. He turned to Agbal. "You, boy. Run to the palace as fast as you can and have them sound the bell. Dion, give him your ring. Go on, get going! Dion, how many of them got away, do you think? I saw three."

"Yes, three," I replied numbly.

I handed Agbal my ring and he sprinted off, swerving and stooping on the way to pick up the knife he had thrown. Andranodoros turned to my guests.

"All officers of the City Guard are to return to their garrisons now. Send out as many men as you can to patrol the streets. You army men, get after the fugitives. It looks like the bastards were all dressed as slaves. Theodotus, take charge of the search. They may be trying to reach the harbour; send some men ahead to block their way. Keep an eye out for any trails of blood, or doors that may have been kicked in. And, Theodotus, I want them alive…"

Theodotus and thirty or so younger men started running towards the alleyway, but my own officers didn't move. Castor looked at me enquiringly.

"Captain?" he said.

"Do as Andranodoros says," I replied in a daze. Castor nodded, and he and my own officers immediately took off towards the palace on Agbal's heels, leaving most of my middle-aged guests standing around stupidly.

Something behind me caught Andranodoros's attention.

"No! Stop!" he shouted out, and I turned in the direction of his stare. Hannon was bent over the whimpering man whom I had blinded. I saw the slave flick his wrist almost imperceptibly and another jet of blood sprayed out over the cobbles. The eyeless man's legs started thrashing around.

"You fucking idiot!" Andranodoros yelled. "Didn't you hear me? I said I want them alive!" The slave straightened and turned to face us. He shrugged.

"I don't," he said in his strange accent, and contemptuously tossed away the knife he must have picked up.

"You two," Andranodoros barked, addressing a pair of white-faced merchants, "see if any of these men is still breathing. The rest of you had better get back inside. Send some slaves out to bring in the bodies. Perhaps someone will recognise them. And fetch a doctor."

He walked over to me and rested his hand on my shoulder.

"Dion, listen to me," he said quietly, looking up into my face. "I've no idea what's happening. Someone may be trying to seize the throne. You need to get yourself to the palace and take charge there. Make sure the king and Hieronymus are safe. Can I rely on you?"

I nodded. My heart had frozen but at least my mind seemed to have started functioning again. I didn't bother trying to conceal the tears dripping down my cheeks.

"You may not be safe either, Andranodoros," I replied stiffly. "Perhaps you'd better come with me."

"No," he said. "I'm going to stay here for a while."

"Why?"

"Because almost every noble in Syracuse is here. I want to work out which ones aren't... Now, you'd better tell the Royal Watch to send some men over to escort the rest of the family back to the palace. I'll break the news to Nereis and Harmonia. I'm afraid I'm going to have to leave it to you to tell Hieron and Hieronymus. Alright?"

"Alright."

Andranodoros was staring behind me again. "For pity's sake, what's that fucking man doing now?"

Hannon had hauled Gelon's limp corpse up off the street by the armpits and was hoisting it over his shoulder.

"Stay where you are!" barked Andranodoros, but the slave ignored him. He walked over to an abandoned cart and gently lowered the body onto it. The mule that stood in harness turned its head indifferently to observe what was going on behind it.

"The impertinence!" muttered Andranodoros. "I'll have him flogged for this. Stop him, Dion. He doesn't seem to listen to me."

"Leave him be," I said softly.

Hannon returned to help the wounded bodyguard to his feet. The man put his arm round Hannon's neck and together they walked awkwardly back to the cart, where Hannon scooped the injured man's legs off the ground and lifted him up beside Gelon. Then he took the mule by its harness and began leading it down the centre of the wide, deserted avenue towards the palace. The other surviving bodyguard slowly got to his feet and wordlessly fell in behind them, his helmet dangling in his hand by his side.

"Stop!" barked Andranodoros at the guard's back. "I didn't give you permission to leave."

But the guard walked on, without so much as a backward glance. The men of the Royal Watch seemed no more inclined to take their orders from Andranodoros than Hannon or Castor.

"I'd better get going too," I said. I nodded in the direction of the pair of men who had first run forward to try to block me. "By the way, one of those two should still be alive."

Except he wasn't.

Someone had cut his throat. He couldn't have done it himself; his knife lay on the ground beyond his reach. Someone must have killed him while the rest of us were watching Gelon die.

Altogether, nine of the assassins lay stretched out on the street around us, and those that weren't dying were already dead.

I jogged past the cart, following my officers, and was nearly at the palace when the bell started ringing. It was not dusk yet, but my men would close all the gates around the city as soon as they heard the sound. Andranodoros was probably right: if the assassins had any sense, they would have planned to escape by ship. No doubt there was an anonymous merchantman somewhere in the Great Harbour waiting for them, and there would be nothing we could do to catch it. By the time we had got a quinquereme manned and in the water, they would have slipped away into the night.

Something must have gone wrong with their ambush, I realised as I ran. They should have been able to surprise and overwhelm Gelon's bodyguards in a matter of moments, but someone in the prince's party must have noticed a drawn knife, or a suspicious movement, in time for the men of the Royal Watch to react and make a fight of it. Those bodyguards were good, I thought, as I remembered the elegant backhanded slice that had half severed one of the assassin's necks.

But the assassins had been good too. They had been prepared to die, rather than break off before they could be certain their job was done. I recalled the triumphant sneer of the young man whose windpipe I had crushed. They were more than just hired knives. Somebody had handpicked them.

This could only be Hannibal's doing. But someone else must have helped. Someone powerful in Syracuse had hidden and sheltered the assassins, someone who knew all about my wedding and who had the brains to plan the attack.

As I jogged over the bridge, I swore to myself I would find the traitor. I would have my vengeance, even if I had to cut the throats of half the nobles in Syracuse to get it.

Most of my officers had been at my house for the banquet, but I had brought Xeno back from Labdalum to command the palace garrison for the night. After Castor, the one-handed old warhorse was probably my most competent lieutenant. He and Castor were both waiting for me at the top of the steps to the inner wall. By the look of shock on Xeno's white face, Castor had already told him the news.

I didn't waste time.

"Xeno, is Hieronymus in the palace?"

"No, sir. He went out about an hour ago with his bodyguards. He's gone to Neapolis, apparently. But they'll have heard the bell, so I imagine they're already on the way back. I've sent a company of men out anyway, to find them and keep the little turd safe."

"Well done."

I paused.

"So, has anyone told the king yet?" I asked quietly.

"Sir," replied Xeno, "I sent a man to tell the Royal Watch that the prince had been attacked. I left it at that. Your young slave was in a bit of a state and I couldn't be sure he'd got his facts straight... So, is it true? Is he really dead?"

"Yes," I replied flatly. "He's dead, Xeno. They're bringing him back now, in a cart. Put him somewhere out of sight for the time being."

"Perhaps we should take him to the bathhouse?" said Castor. "I can have some men wash the body there, before the family sees him."

"Yes," I said, "do that."

The bell was still ringing.

"Sir," asked Xeno, "what the fuck's happening?"

"I don't know," I replied.

"Dion," said Castor gently, putting his hand on my shoulder, "I think you'd better go and speak to the king."

✻

The shutter slid back at my knock and a pair of eyes scrutinised me. A moment later the little wooden gate opened and I was greeted by Dinomenes, wearing full armour. He inspected my blood-splattered tunic as I stepped past him into the passageway.

"You're hurt, Captain."

"No. A scratch. I need to see the king."

He looked at me searchingly, but after a moment's hesitation, he bit his lip, restraining the impulse to ask any questions. Perhaps my face already told him all he needed to know.

"Gelon's dead, Dinomenes. Listen, you need to send men to my home to bring back Nereis and Harmonia. And you'd better assign bodyguards to Andranodoros and Zoippos. Andranodoros is at my house. I've no idea where Zoippos is, but I think you should get him and his family here too."

"Don't worry, I'll take care of it, sir."

He nodded and clicked his fingers. A slave appeared at the far end of the passageway.

A few minutes later I was shown into the king's plain little study. The sun was setting now but the lamps had not yet been lit. Hieron sat motionless behind his desk, his hands clasping its edge. The weak light seemed to exaggerate the countless lines that criss-crossed his face.

I bowed and stood to attention before him.

"Well?" he snapped. "Is he alive?"

I clenched my jaw as I felt my eyes watering. I didn't trust myself to speak. I looked down at the floor and shook my head silently.

I heard a sharp gasp but didn't look up at first. When I did, Hieron was staring at me expressionlessly. After a moment, he pushed himself to his feet and turned his back to me. He lifted a hand to his forehead, rubbing his temples between his thumb and long, bony fingers. He groaned almost inaudibly. Then he dismissed me with a backhanded wave, and as he did, I saw his hunched shoulders heave.

XX

CHOICES

I sat on a stone bench in the great courtyard, as the last flickers of the day died around me. The bell had finally stopped ringing. Agbal came to find me to give me back my ring. He had also brought me a clean tunic, which I changed into there and then. I gave him the bloody one and told him to go and ready my rooms in the palace for the night.

Soon after, Castor ran up to ask for orders, but I had none for him. I saw Nereis, Harmonia and her husband, Woodpecker, arrive in the company of half a dozen men of the Royal Watch but they didn't notice me in the shadows and I had no wish to talk to them. They disappeared silently through the little gate to the royal apartments.

I must have been sitting on the bench for about half an hour before I heard the tramp of feet and a whole company of my men marched in from the exercise yard. Hieronymus walked in the middle of the column, flanked by his two bodyguards.

I heaved a sigh of relief, rose to my feet and went to meet the lieutenant of the company.

"Any problems?" I asked.

"No, sir, apart from His Royal Arsehole himself."

"That's enough of that, Lieutenant. Take your men back to the yard and report to Castor."

Hieronymus had seen me and was already scuttling over towards us. He looked frightened.

"What's going on, Dion?" he demanded. "Why did you send all these men for me? Why was the bell ringing? No one has told me anything."

I hadn't seen him since his disastrous parade. His limbs were still spindly and his face riddled with red and yellow spots, but at least his voice seemed to have stopped squeaking.

I lifted my arm and he cringed, perhaps thinking I was going to strike him. When I put it around his shoulders instead, he flushed and looked up at me in perplexity.

"We need to talk, lad," I said gently. "Come on over here and let's sit down."

I led him to the bench while a sergeant marched my men off again. His bodyguards discreetly positioned themselves a little distance away from us.

"Well?" he demanded impatiently. "Has my grandfather died?"

"No," I said, and then I told him about Gelon.

He didn't interrupt me. He just stared down at his feet and fidgeted awkwardly.

When I had finished, he was silent for a while. Finally he looked up.

"So, does that mean I'm going to be king now?" he asked calmly.

"Not while your grandfather is still alive, no," I replied.

"And when he dies?"

"Well, probably. But we'll have to see what your grandfather wants to happen," I said.

"What do you mean?"

"Hieronymus, you haven't even reached manhood yet. You can't expect to go from being a boy to being a king in just one step."

"I see. So that's what you think, is it…? Is my mother here?"

"Yes, she's inside."

He nodded.

"Good. I want to go and see her now."

"Alright, son. And I'm really very sorry about your father."

He looked at me coolly.

"Dion, my grandfather won't be around to protect you forever. Sooner or later I will be your king. I told you once before to address me as 'Your Royal Highness'. You had better start doing it."

I raised my eyebrows but said nothing, and he turned his back on me.

"Come on," he barked at his two guards and walked off.

After a little while, I went up to my rooms, where Agbal had already lit the lamps. I badly needed to wash and would have gone to the bathhouse, but Gelon was there, and I couldn't face seeing him. Instead, I stripped off and stood on a bronze tray in the centre of my bedroom while Agbal sponged me down.

"I owe you my thanks," I said, as he dabbed carefully around the cut I had taken. It was only about four inches long and had already scabbed over, but it was quite sore.

"How so, Master?"

"You probably saved my life today. Although you very nearly killed me in the process."

"Forgive me, Master," he said, smiling nervously. "I have been practising my throw every day like you said, but I have never practised with a moving target."

He peered closely at the cut.

"I think we had better put some stitches in this, Master. It will only keep opening up again if we don't."

He passed me a towel and went to fetch a needle and thread. When I had dried myself off, I lay on the cot and he knelt beside me and sewed me up. I couldn't help wincing but he was surprisingly skilful and swift.

"You must have done this before, Agbal," I muttered through gritted teeth.

"Yes, Master. When I was a child, I worked in the infirmary at Plymmerium. The doctors made me practise on dead animals. There, all done, now."

He deftly tied off the end of the thread and left me to dress myself. When I emerged into the sitting room a short while later, he had already set out a plate of ham, bread and fruit, and had taken up his position by the front door. I fell on the food mindlessly. Win or lose, most men only want to fuck after a fight, but for some reason I find that killing people usually makes me hungry instead.

I had nearly finished when there was a loud knock at the door. I nodded to Agbal. He opened it and Torquatus strode in. He might have been in his fifties, but he exuded the vigour of a man twenty years younger. I stood to greet him, still chewing on a mouthful of bread.

"Dion, I've been looking for you. I'm sorry to interrupt you at such a time. I was wondering if you could spare me a few minutes? There are some things we need to discuss." He shot a glance at Agbal. "In private," he added.

"Of course, Senator. Take a couch. Do you want some wine or anything?"

"Thank you, but no."

"Agbal, fetch the senator a cup of water and then make yourself scarce."

I took my own cup from the table and sat down opposite him, waiting for him to speak.

"Does my daughter please you, Dion?" he asked after a moment.

"Yes, very much." I ran my hand through my hair. "But everything suddenly seems to have turned to shit, doesn't it...? If it's news you're after, I'm afraid I have none."

"No, it's not that." He fixed me with a stare. "I'm here to remind you of your promise to keep her safe, Dion, and to ask you a simple question... What are you going to do now?"

I shrugged.

"Well, the king and Hieronymus are being well guarded. We've got patrols out on the streets and everything seems quiet. If those bastards haven't managed to get out of the city yet, they've probably missed their chance and we should find them soon enough."

"That's not what I meant, Dion," he said calmly. "What are you going to do... when Hieron dies?"

I stared at him, not knowing how to respond.

"I haven't thought that far ahead, Senator. With a bit of luck, that won't be for years yet."

He snorted.

"And it may be tomorrow. Hieron's shut himself away and he's not seeing anyone at the moment. He's the strongest-willed man I know, but this could break him. So, for the third time, Dion, let me ask you, what do you intend to do?"

I blinked in surprise at his directness. But having entrusted his daughter to my safekeeping, perhaps he had a right to ask. I thought about it for a moment.

"Well, Hieronymus certainly has no love for me," I said eventually. "I suppose I'll have to make myself scarce, maybe move out to one of my estates. Would Vita mind living in the countryside, do you think?"

He waved a hand dismissively.

"Don't be stupid, Dion. You know that's not an option. As soon as he gets the chance, Hieronymus will have you killed. You're too dangerous to leave alive. And then my daughter will be a widow."

I smiled grimly.

"You're not suggesting we should move to Rome, are you, Senator? It hardly looks as though we'd be any safer there."

"Well, you'd be very welcome, Dion, and I'm sure we could find a use for a man like you. But no, that's not what I'm suggesting."

I gazed at him, saying nothing.

"Very well, Dion, let me spell it out for you, then. If Hannibal doesn't march on Rome, he will probably turn on Sicily instead. Your army has no general. Your king may be a broken man. And any day now, the future of your kingdom could be placed in the hands of a squealing brat who can barely wipe his own arse. That is not in your own or your people's interests, and it is certainly not in Rome's interests either."

"What are you saying, Senator?"

He took a sip of water.

"Isn't it obvious? When Hieron dies, you must cut the little bastard's throat, before he cuts yours. And then you must take the crown yourself… Don't look so shocked, Dion. If you haven't already considered the idea, you are probably the only person in the palace tonight who hasn't. What do you suppose Andranodoros and Zoippos are thinking about at this very moment? Or that bitch Nereis? They're all thinking about you, Dion. And I've come here to tell you that Rome will support you, assuming you are committed to our alliance. No one wants Hieronymus to be king. But the army, the Guards, the common people – well, they all love you, don't they? And, more to the point, they will have need of a man like you when Hieron dies. You are the heir of Dionysius. Accept your duty to your city."

"And then, of course, your daughter would be a queen," I said coldly.

He bridled visibly at that.

"If you think I'm motivated by family ambition, Dion, you do not understand me at all. I wouldn't hesitate for one instant to sacrifice myself and my entire family for the good of Rome."

He met my stare evenly, and I believed him. Maybe Hieron had been right about him after all: perhaps he was a little mad.

"Well, I'm sorry to have to disappoint you, Senator, but I'm afraid I don't much enjoy cutting the throats of children."

He shrugged.

"If that's all that's bothering you, my people can take care of that side of things for you… Children die every day, Dion. And a lot more will die, if Hieronymus becomes king."

"Then it seems you don't understand me very well either, Senator. I don't want to be king. I serve Hieron and I loved Gelon. How could I possibly murder Gelon's son?"

He stared at me thoughtfully for a long moment.

"Well, think about it, Dion," he said eventually. "To stand aside and do nothing, when you can prevent a disaster, would be a far more shameful crime. Anyway, that is all I came to say."

He stood, and I stood too.

"I must leave tomorrow, Dion. I have no power here; I cannot sort out this mess for you. Only you can do that now… Anyway,

I hope my daughter will bring you as much joy as she has brought me."

"Thank you, Senator." I forced a smile to try to conceal my fury and walked him to the door. I opened it for him and he stepped outside, but then he turned to face me again.

"Just one last word of advice, Dion," he said very quietly. "Many important people in Syracuse will want you out of the way now, some because they fear you, others because they will soon come to perceive you as an obstacle to their own schemes. The palace is not safe for you any more. Sleep in your own house from now on, and make sure you always have your own men around you… Well now, I hope we will meet again, perhaps when you have some grandchildren to show me. Let me embrace you. I wish you a long life, young man."

The corpses of the assassins were taken from my house and put on display in the agora, in the hope that someone might recognise them. No one came forward with any information, and nor had the surviving fugitives been found by the time we came to bury Gelon three days after his murder.

The prince's body had been laid out in the palace courtyard, and the queue to view it stretched all the way through the gate into Neapolis. Gelon's widow, Nereis, led the chanting of the dirges as the people shuffled past. Hieronymus sat by his father's corpse, fidgeting and looking nervous, with a dozen men of the Royal Watch surrounding him. It was not until the moment arrived for Gelon to be taken to the cemetery that the king himself finally appeared, to lead the procession. He was carried silently on a litter and seemed so inert and devoid of expression that he might have been an effigy.

I walked to the cemetery beside Archimedes, a little way behind the bier bearing the prince's body. Hieronymus, Andranodoros, Zoippos and Woodpecker flanked the bier. Vita and my mother were with the other women at the back of the procession. For once,

Hieron had allowed the army into the city and the men of the three Shield divisions silently lined the funeral route. Many of them seemed to have tears in their eyes.

After we had walked a little way, Archimedes threaded his arm through mine.

"So, are you enjoying married life, my boy?" he whispered.

"Yes, Great-uncle. I don't know quite how to explain it. I suppose she gives me some hope for the future, despite all this…"

"She's certainly a pretty little thing."

"Yes, clever too, I think. Cleverer than me, at any rate… You know, I'd been planning to move Vita into the old villa at Acrae. Mother's been renovating the place for her. I doubt anyone's been in it for twenty years, apart from the caretaker. But I'm going to keep her here with me now instead."

"I'm pleased to hear that, Dion," he said. "Although Korinna won't be." He chuckled.

"I imagine not," I said, smiling thinly.

We walked on in silence.

After the funeral, I returned to my rooms in the palace, intending to try to snatch half an hour's sleep before returning to my duties. Twice since Gelon's death, I had frightened Vita by waking up in the middle of the night, drenched in sweat and shouting incoherently.

I found Alpha and Omega in the sitting room, dusting and sweeping. They must have come back for a few hours to clean the apartment.

"I think you'd better have everything valuable taken back to the house," I told them. "I'm not going to be here very much now… Alright, I'm going to lie down for a while."

"I'm afraid I've just stripped your cot, Master," said Alpha apologetically. "We'll put some clean sheets on it."

I nodded and flopped onto a couch, and they disappeared through the anteroom door. I was exhausted and confused. I thought of Gelon, and of Vita, and of the face I had borrowed for my father, and began to cry.

I was still quietly crying when the slaves returned. Without saying a word, Omega sat himself beside me on the couch and began rubbing my back, while Alpha knelt in front of me and silently put his hand on my knee. I remembered it was almost exactly how they had comforted me after my mother had ordered Titan, our old dog, to be killed.

For a month, the kingdom appeared to be frozen. The king stayed in his apartments, seeing no one. Everyone was on edge as we waited for something to happen. The nobles eyed each other nervously. I received invitations at short notice to three or four dinner parties but declined them all. It seemed the men of my class were already making pacts and forming little factions, to try to advance their own ambitions or thwart those of their rivals.

I was spending my nights at home, not because my father-in-law had advised me to avoid sleeping at the palace, but simply because I wanted to be with Vita. On two occasions, as I was walking back to the villa at dusk, I had a sensation that someone was following me, but when I turned, all I glimpsed was a dark shape disappearing into a side alley.

After the second time it happened, I grew a little unsettled. Perhaps Torquatus had been right, I thought. Whoever had arranged Gelon's murder might only just be starting to carve his path to the throne. But whoever it was, he had not yet revealed himself.

That evening, I suggested casually to Vita that perhaps she should move to Acrae for a few weeks. We were having dinner alone in the little dining room, lying on couches that had been positioned head to toe a few feet apart.

"Why?" she asked.

Alpha and Omega were waiting on us. I gestured to them to leave the room.

"It's beautiful up there," I replied when the door had closed. "I think you'd like it. My mother has had the house redecorated specially for you. Why not go and see it, at least?"

"Where will you be?"

"I'm afraid I have to stay here. But I'd come to visit you as often as I could."

"No," she said.

"I really think it would be for the best, Vita… Look, I'm not sure the city is entirely safe. I promised your father I'd keep you out of danger."

"Are you in danger?"

"I don't think so, but after what happened to Gelon, who knows?"

"No," she said again, this time in Greek.

"Well, I'm afraid I've made my decision."

"Have you now?" Her eyes flashed. "Then you'd better think again, Dion. I am a daughter of the Manlii: we don't leave our men. If you send me away, I'll just come back again."

"And I'm your husband. You'll do as I tell you."

She pouted, and then she smiled wickedly.

"Is that what you think, Dion…? That I'll do as you tell me? No, you'll do as I tell *you*, you big brute… Stay exactly where you are. I want you to watch me."

She slowly raised a hand to her breast and began to caress it, pinching and tweaking the nipple through the thin blue cotton. After a moment, she slid her other hand down between her legs, her almond eyes never leaving mine. She bit the corner of her lower lip and took in a sharp little breath.

"Do you like this?" she asked softly. "Do you like watching me?" She gasped and bit her lip again. "Do you?"

The following morning, I had Castor arrange for two dozen of my men to move in with us. It seemed a reasonable compromise.

✻

The new moon finally arrived, the day on which the Royal Council regularly met. I had received no confirmation as to whether the meeting would even go ahead, but I put on my blue tunic all the same and arrived at the council chamber at the usual time.

Several of my colleagues were already in their seats, whispering earnestly to each other. They fell silent when I entered, looking sheepish and nervously nodding and smiling at me as I took my customary place. We sat in silence as one by one the other chairs filled up. Thraso arrived and I beckoned him over to sit beside me. Archimedes appeared, folded his hands across his chest and stared up at the ceiling. Eventually only Hieron's and Gelon's chairs remained empty.

We must have all been waiting for nearly ten minutes when the door to the king's apartments was finally opened by an attendant and two slaves walked in carrying a desk, followed by a third carrying a stool and a box of writing materials. They arranged the furniture in a corner and withdrew. Five minutes later, the door was opened again, but instead of the king, Nebit entered, looking quite flustered. I had heard that Archimedes' workshop at Plymmerium was winding down and that the king had recently recalled Nebit to the secretariat.

The little Egyptian bowed to us.

"I am so sorry that you have been kept waiting," he said in his girlish voice. "His Majesty regrets that he will not be joining you today. However, he has asked me to make some announcements on his behalf…"

I looked over at Andranodoros but he seemed as surprised as I was.

Nebit coughed and continued.

"Firstly, His Majesty feels that, without his son by his side, he can no longer shoulder the burden that he has been carrying for more than fifty years. He therefore proposes to transfer most of his duties to this council. He will confine himself to determining broad issues of policy. He will also retain control of all military matters. However, he now looks to this council to assume responsibility for the day-to-day running of the kingdom.

"Secondly, His Majesty informs you that he has amended his will to name Prince Hieronymus the heir to his throne. In the event that His Majesty dies while the prince is still a minor, the council will act as the prince's guardians, ruling in his name, until Hieronymus attains his majority. The prince will be joining the council from next month.

"Thirdly, it is the king's wish that you should now appoint one of your own number to act as the First Man of the Council, whose task it will be to preside over your meetings. It will be for the First Man to decide how to allocate responsibilities between council members.

"Fourthly, His Majesty has appointed me to act as the council's secretary. My function will be to prepare the agendas for your meetings and to circulate whatever information you may require to arrive at your decisions. I will not, however, have a vote: I am merely your servant."

Nebit turned to me.

"Captain, His Majesty requests that you should go to him in his apartments once today's meeting has concluded... That is all I have to say, gentlemen. May I suggest that you proceed to the selection of the First Man."

Nebit bowed again and then walked over to the desk in the corner and settled himself down.

I looked round the table. Everyone else was doing the same, apart from Archimedes, who was chewing his beard and scraping dirt from under his fingernails. One could almost hear their brains clicking.

Many of the offices held by councillors brought with them considerable opportunity for self-enrichment, in the form of bribes from merchants. If a builder wanted his stone delivered promptly from the quarries, he had to keep Woodpecker happy. If a slave dealer wished to avoid a shipment of slaves being quarantined for weeks, and becoming so emaciated in the process that no one would buy them, he would be wise to befriend Ision, the councillor responsible for regulating our slave population. The allocation of council duties was one of the mechanisms by which Hieron had kept the nobles sweet, rotating the offices between them every few years, so that each leading family got its chance at the trough. If the

First Man was now going to be making those decisions instead, he would enjoy enormous powers of patronage, in addition, no doubt, to a rake-off from everyone.

My colleagues' brains continued to work through the calculus of self-interest. Whom should they support? Whom should they risk opposing? Who would dare to declare his position first?

One by one the faces began to turn nervously in my direction, until eventually they all seemed to be looking at me. It was Andranodoros who broke the silence.

"Well, Dion," he said with a little smile, "you would seem to be the obvious choice to be our First Man."

"Hear, hear!" said one of the toads, and several others quickly began clapping the table with the palms of their hands, not wanting to be seen as laggards.

"No," I replied emphatically, and the toads fell silent.

"No?" replied Andranodoros, raising an eyebrow.

"No," I growled. "I'd be no good at it, and I don't want it. Choose someone else."

I was angry, and I suppose it showed. My colleagues stared at me nervously, but I knew my king's methods well enough by now to suspect that Hieron was playing some game with us. There was a reason he hadn't named a First Man himself, and whatever it might be, I smelled mischief.

"I mean it," I snarled.

"Very well," said Andranodoros. "We must respect Dion's decision, much as I am sure we all regret it. So, does anyone else wish to nominate a colleague, or to put themselves forward?"

Zoippos looked up at the ceiling and cleared his throat, his Adam's apple bobbing energetically up and down as it limbered up for the occasion.

"My dear friends," he intoned solemnly, opening up his arms as if to embrace us all, "I am sure we all share in our king's grief at the loss of my dear brother-in-law, although how much worse must his grief be even than our own. Let us hope that in time his pain will abate and that he will be able to resume his place at the head of our table. But for now, it is our clear duty to ease His Majesty's burden in whatever way we can. The position of First Man will be an onerous one, and it is one that I no more covet than the captain. However, poor Gelon's death would now seem to place me in the invidious position of being the most senior member of the royal family at this table. With considerable reluctance, I therefore feel obliged to offer myself for the position."

There was a brief silence.

"Does anyone else wish to propose someone?" asked Andranodoros.

"Yes, I do," said Woodpecker. "It is certainly selfless of you to put yourself forward, Zoippos. But perhaps this is a burden that you can be spared." He smiled maliciously. "You mention that you are the most senior member of the royal family here but, like me, you are only a member by marriage. What should guide us is surely our seniority as members of this council. The most senior position is that of Royal Treasurer. Should we not choose Andranodoros?"

Zoippos glowered and I saw Andranodoros try to repress a smirk. Woodpecker looked round the table, stabbing at us with his sharp nose.

"Actually, if seniority is the issue," piped up Ision, "then surely we must choose Archimedes. After all, he is our longest-serving councillor."

I doubt Ision meant it seriously; he just wanted to contradict Woodpecker. The two of them had been fighting a turf war over the supply of slaves for the quarries that had begun long before my arrival on the council.

"So, what do you say, Archimedes?" Andranodoros asked.

My great-uncle spat out his beard and blinked in bewilderment. "Say to what, dear boy?"

"To Ision's suggestion. That you should be our First Man."

"Oh... Who's Ision?"

There was an embarrassed silence.

"Perhaps," Leatherskin said, "a younger man might be better suited to the task... What about Thraso?"

Leatherskin smiled slyly at me, as if to convey that he had managed to divine what I secretly wished to happen. There were some murmurs of approval from the quicker-witted toads. Thraso blushed.

"I only joined the council a little over a year ago," he said awkwardly. "I'm afraid I'm far too inexperienced. I must rule myself out."

The bickering went on for half an hour, and gradually became more fractious. All our old rivalries and animosities rose to the surface. People took sides on the basis of family quarrels stretching back generations. Thraso and I said nothing more, but eventually he leant in to whisper to me despairingly.

"Dion," he said, "you need to settle this."

I sighed.

"Are you sure you don't want it?" I whispered back. "You're the only honest man here."

"It stinks, Dion. You know it does. Nothing good will come of it."

"Very well," I said.

Zoippos was in the middle of another flowery speech about public duty or virtue or something.

"... were I but free to do so, I myself would choose to emulate the sage Diogenes, and take up residence in a humble barrel, asking no more of my fellow man than that he should not obstruct the sunshine on my face. But, alas, the responsibilities of my noble birth preclude..."

I slammed both my fists down on the table. The crash reverberated around the room like a crack of thunder and the table jumped slightly. Zoippos froze in mid-sentence, his mouth open. Everyone stared at me.

"I vote for Andranodoros," I said. "Does anyone vote against?" I gazed slowly around their frightened faces. "No? Good. That's decided then. I'll tell the king."

I pushed back my chair and strode out of the room, having now made my second and, as things were to turn out, final contribution to a council debate.

I found Hieron sitting in his little garden in the weak autumn sun. He seemed to have shrunk even further since Gelon's murder. His white tunic hung loosely around his skinny frame and his shoulders sagged.

A table had been set out in front of him with a jug of water and two plain clay cups. Beside them lay two scrolls, tied with ribbons. I bowed and he gestured to me to take the empty chair beside him.

"Pour yourself a cup of water, Captain," Hieron croaked weakly. "Pour me one too."

He took the cup in both hands, as though unsure of his grip.

I sat and waited for him to speak, but his mind seemed elsewhere. Eventually he turned his eyes on me.

"So, Dion, I wasn't expecting you to be here so soon. I thought they would be squabbling till nightfall," he said.

"There was some discussion, Your Majesty, but in the end everyone agreed that Andranodoros should be First Man."

"I see. Everyone? I take it you intervened, then?"

"Yes, my King."

He chuckled.

"Yes, I suppose that would explain it… So, why not Thraso?"

"Thraso refused to do it, my King."

"He is a clever boy, isn't he? Honest, too. If it is possible to be clever and honest at the same time, that is. He's quite right not to want it, of course. I imagine our new First Man will not find the position altogether what he expects… Let me tell you what will happen, Dion: it will begin with all his colleagues fawning over him, and it will end with half of them conspiring to murder him. Happily, I will not be here to see it. But I like to think that they will all be too busy scheming against their First Man to scheme against my grandson… Anyway, that is my hope. So, why did you choose Andranodoros, Dion? Tell me the truth."

"It had to be either him or Zoippos, Your Majesty. And I don't much enjoy listening to Zoippos."

"Who does? Maybe I should have his speeches read out in the dungeons. But why do you say it had to be one of those two?"

He was looking at me intently. I took a sip of water.

"Because it is in their interests to make sure Hieronymus becomes king, Your Majesty. Their own positions become stronger when he does."

"But it certainly wouldn't seem to be in your interests, Dion."

"No, perhaps not, Your Majesty."

"My grandson will probably want to kill you, in fact, just as soon as he's got my crown on his head."

"Maybe, my King. But I hope he will decide against it."

Hieron scratched the side of his face thoughtfully.

"So, why do you want to see Hieronymus become king, then?"

"Because there is no one else, Your Majesty. The nobles cannot even agree who should be First Man on your council. If Hieronymus does not succeed you, they will rip the kingdom apart, and Hannibal will swallow us up. Or perhaps Rome will."

"But there is always you, Dion. You could be king, couldn't you? They're all frightened enough of *you* to fall into line... Even Zoippos and Andranodoros wouldn't dare to pit themselves against you. Nereis has already started badgering me to have you killed now, to make sure Hieronymus succeeds me. Of course, she doesn't realise that the child won't last a year on the throne without you to protect him. That is my dilemma. It would seem you are both his greatest threat and his only hope... Come on, don't be coy, you must have thought about it."

I laughed awkwardly, not knowing quite what to say.

"I would make a very poor king, Your Majesty. I don't have your subtlety. I know my limits. As my mother never tires of reminding me, I am just a brute."

"So was your famous ancestor, Dion, and yet he proved to be rather a good king. Besides, what has all my subtlety achieved? Nothing. Every day, we get drawn deeper into this war. I twist and wriggle, but I cannot prevent it. There is a time for brutes, and it will soon be upon us."

I shrugged.

"You misjudge me, my King. I loved Gelon, more than any other man. How could I betray his son?"

He grunted.

"Yes, Torquatus told me that's what you'd said."

"He told you?" I asked in astonishment.

"Don't be naïve, Dion. Of course he did. He said you got quite angry with him when he suggested that you should cut my grandson's throat."

I stared at him.

"Did you put him up to it?" I asked quietly. "Were you testing me, Hieron?"

The king blinked.

"Was that a flash of temper, young man? You sounded quite menacing just then. How interesting… The world turns so quickly… I wonder, if I ordered your death, whether anyone would even obey me any more. Perhaps my power is already draining away. What do you think, Dion? Would my men be willing to kill their best hope for the future, out of loyalty to the past?"

"Did you put him up to it?"

"Of course not. Torquatus and I have been playing this game for years. We understand each other perfectly well. His only concern is to make sure our alliance survives after my death. In his eyes, the best way to secure that now would obviously be for you to succeed me… Anyway, he insisted on seeing me before he left, although I was in no mood to see anyone. He wanted to come to an understanding with me about your future."

"An understanding?"

"Yes, Dion. An understanding. Which we reached. I assured him that I would not have you killed, providing you give me your word that you will spare Hieronymus when I am dead. Take the crown, if you want. But don't kill the boy. Allow my line to continue, that is all I ask of you. Torquatus has agreed to give Hieronymus refuge in Rome if you decide to usurp him."

"I have already told you, I don't want your throne."

Hieron narrowed his eyes to scrutinise my face.

"Well, what a strange world this is," he said eventually. "The one man whom my crown might fit is the only one who doesn't seem to want it..." He looked up at the sky and pursed his thin lips. "I always knew my own destiny, of course. I don't think I was ever really driven by ambition, at least, not in the conventional sense. You might as well call an eaglet ambitious for hatching from its egg. I simply became what nature intended me to become."

I shrugged.

"Whatever I am meant to become, it isn't king," I said.

"Perhaps; perhaps not... But in any event, it seems I now have no choice but to place my grandson's future in your hands..." He sighed. "You do know, don't you," he said quietly, "that I have always regretted your father's death? I looked on him as a friend. I wish with all my heart he had not forced me to that. But I have tried my best to do right by you ever since."

"I have never blamed you, Hieron."

He suddenly drew in a sharp breath, as if he had been suffocating, and as he let it out again, he bit his lip.

"It's all turned to dross, Dion. It's all turned to dross. I thought I could fashion a new kingdom for us. I never wanted to be an Alexander, conquering the world. I just wanted to protect our own little corner of it. I have done terrible things to try to keep my people safe, things that no decent man would ever contemplate. And now my son is dead and men still envy and hate each other. We are diseased, Dion. It can't be stopped. It will never stop."

The tears were running down his cheeks. He made no attempt to hide them from me.

I pushed back my chair and rose to my feet. For a long moment, I stood there, towering over him, gazing down at the shipwreck of a great king. He looked up at me uncertainly, as helpless as a child.

And then I went down on my knee beside him, and silently bowed my head in homage.

I heard him choke back a sob.

"I swear two things to you, my King," I said softly. "I will protect Hieronymus. And I will find Gelon's murderer."

He rested his hand on my shoulder. After a few moments, I felt the pressure increase as he tried to lift himself to his feet. I rose, taking his arm to help him up.

"You can let go now," he wheezed.

Hieron peered up at my face and I awkwardly forced myself to meet his unblinking stare, as his pale blue eyes peeled me like a piece of fruit. Finally, his lips curled into the faintest of smiles and he nodded.

"By the way, those are for you," he said, gesturing to the two scrolls on the table.

I picked them up and bowed again as he turned his back on me and began to shuffle slowly away.

The king was halfway across the lawn when he stopped and tentatively stretched out a hand as if trying to balance himself. He tottered for an instant and took a small sideways step. And then he crumpled to the ground like a rag doll.

My desperate shouts brought slaves and guards running. Hieron lay on his side as they clustered round him helplessly. Within minutes a doctor appeared from somewhere inside his apartments. I stood apart, with my back to a column, grateful for the coldness of the stone as I tried to take in the enormity of what seemed to be happening.

"He's alive at least," I heard the doctor say. "Take him to his bed. Be careful now."

Two slaves gently hoisted Hieron off the grass by his armpits. A pair of guards formed a cradle with their hands behind his knees and the slaves draped the king's flaccid arms around the guards' necks.

As the guards lifted Hieron off his feet, his head lolled to one side and his tongue flopped out of the corner of his mouth. A long spool of saliva dangled from his lower lip. Only his eyes still seemed able to move of their own accord. As he was carried past, they swivelled towards me, fixing on mine in a silent scream of anguish.

XXI

THE ERASTOS

It was Andranodoros himself who brought me the news early the following morning. I was in my office overlooking the exercise yard when one of my men showed him in; I had spent the whole night there, considering my future. The two scrolls the king had given me lay on my desk. One seemed to be a legal document of some sort, transferring the ownership of a building that I had never known was mine to a man whose name I didn't recognise. But it had my seal on it.

The second document bore Hieron's seal. It was a military commission, appointing me general of the army. In addition to commanding the Shield divisions, I was to retain authority over the City Guard. Rolled up inside it I had found a further small scrap of papyrus, on which a few words had been scrawled in what I took to be Hieron's own shaky hand.

'*Keep my people safe. H.*'

Perhaps I should have felt more gratified. But the moment only tasted sour in my mouth.

I stood as Andranodoros entered.

"He's still alive, Dion, but he might as well be dead. He can't speak and he can only move a few fingers. The doctors say he may improve a little, but at his age… It's probably just a matter of time now."

I bit my lip and nodded, gesturing to a chair. We sat facing each other across the desk and I couldn't help noticing there were dark hollows under his eyes. He obviously hadn't slept either.

"I've sent word to the council," he said. "You know we're meeting later this morning? I've asked Hieronymus to join us."

"I got the message. I'll be there," I replied.

He stared at me for a long moment.

"Dion, why have you turned out your men? There must be nearly a hundred of them in the main courtyard alone. What are you up to?"

"I've decided to take some precautions."

"I hear you've also posted men outside the homes of every councillor."

I shrugged.

"I thought it might help them feel safe."

"No, Dion, it doesn't. It has exactly the opposite effect, as I'm sure you realise perfectly well. In fact, it looks very much like you might be planning to make the palace your permanent home when the old man dies. Maybe you are just your father's son, after all. Is that what you're intending? To take by force what isn't yours by right?"

"You've certainly got balls, Andranodoros," I said drily. "If I really were thinking of stealing the throne, that wouldn't seem a very prudent way to talk to me."

"If that's what you're really thinking, Dion, I doubt it would make any difference how I spoke to you."

I grunted.

"I'm sorry. I imagine neither of us has slept much… Look, I've no desire whatsoever to take the boy's place. Alright? And no one who's loyal to Syracuse has anything to fear from me."

He looked at me warily.

"So, what should I tell the prince? He's been hysterical ever since he saw your men in the courtyard. Given how they treated him, you can hardly blame him."

"Tell him I've sworn to protect him. Tell him I'm not his enemy."

He eyed me suspiciously.

"If you say so, Dion. But you have to stand your men down. The City Guard is not your private army. You must take your orders from the council now. We'll tell you when we want the Guards turned out."

"Do you mean, you'll tell me, Andranodoros?"

"No, I mean the council will."

"Fuck off."

"I beg your pardon?"

"I said 'fuck off'. Someone arranged Gelon's murder, and it was probably a councillor. So I'm going to do whatever it takes to keep the city safe and to make sure Hieronymus becomes king. When the boy turns eighteen, he can get rid of me if he likes. You and the rest of the council can run the kingdom till then. I won't interfere with you. But the only man I take orders from is Hieron."

"Dion, be reasonable. That's not going to work. The king is too sick to give anybody orders. The council has to act for him. That's what he wanted. He arranged for the council to rule in his place until Hieronymus comes of age. Not you. You can't hold a sword to our throats."

"That's exactly what I'm going to do, Andranodoros. Someone has to make sure you all behave yourselves."

He frowned.

"It sounds to me like perhaps you want to be king in all but name, Dion. Is that your game? To wear the council like a veil?"

"Actually, that isn't what I want at all. All I want to do is to go home to my wife. I've already told you, Andranodoros, I've no wish to meddle in the council's business. You do your job, and I'll do mine... By the way, you should probably see this."

I picked up the commission and tossed it across the desk to him.

He read it carefully and raised his eyebrows in surprise.

"So, he's given you both the army and the Guards...? My congratulations." He handed the parchment back to me. "Very well, Dion. I suppose we'll just have to see how this plays out. But

I'd tread carefully, if I were you. You may know how to frighten people, but when it comes to wielding power, you're no Hieron."

✳

Later, on my way to the council meeting, I came across Archimedes, sitting on a bench in the colonnade resting his chin on his cane.

He smiled sadly at me.

"I just tried to see him, Dion. They wouldn't let me in. Children and grandchildren only, apparently. I've been his friend for over sixty years, but it seems I'm not allowed to visit him."

"I'm sorry. Perhaps he'll recover enough to have visitors soon."

Archimedes shrugged and rose slowly to his feet.

"Well, let's hope so. Congratulations on your promotion, by the way."

"Oh, you know about that?"

"Of course. Hieron discussed it with me a few days ago. He said he had to decide whether to kill you or to promote you, and on balance, he preferred not to kill you... You know, there are so many things I would like to say to him. If I'd only known this was going to happen..."

He sighed. We began walking slowly towards the council chamber.

"So, Great-uncle, what now?" I asked.

"Who knows...? But it looks as though Hieronymus will be wearing the crown soon enough, doesn't it? Although I'd be surprised if he manages to keep it for as long as his grandfather... King Hieronymus. That beansprout. What a thought... Well, each generation must find its own way I suppose, and mine has had its day. No doubt our new First Man will waste no time elbowing the rest of us aside... I see you've turned your men out. Don't do anything hasty, Dion. Just let Andranodoros get on with it."

"I promised Hieron I'd find Gelon's killer, Great-uncle. One of these bastards was behind it. My men are going nowhere till I know who it was and he's hanging from a cross. And I expect you and Chrysanthe to help me find him."

"I dare say it will all come to light in time, Dion. But you must be patient. Alright?"

"Patience isn't one of my virtues, Archimedes."

"So you're still a fool, then... Well, let's just hope that poor old General Lepides turns out to have been right about you."

"Lepides? What on earth are you talking about?"

He snorted.

"Who do you think kept pushing you forwards? Lepides seemed to think quite highly of you, although I've no idea why... That temper of yours... But Lepides believed we could turn it to our advantage. He always said the kingdom would have need of a man like you one day. And so he nurtured you for us, like a little tomato plant, until Hieron judged the time had come to pick the fruit."

My confusion must have been apparent.

"I don't understand."

"You and Hieronymus..." he muttered to himself. "The tomato and the beansprout. It seems I'm doomed to die with the taste of idiot salad in my mouth."

"But I thought Lepides always hated me?"

"Don't you mean, you always hated him?"

"Perhaps. But I had good reason to."

"Did you, now? And I suppose all his other officers felt the same, didn't they? You poor dears. Did he make you all cry and feel sorry for yourselves...? What on earth did you all think? That the army was meant to be fun?"

"No, of course not, but... Well, Lepides was a pure bastard."

Archimedes stopped in his tracks and turned to face me. There was undisguised fury in his eyes. I had never seen him quite like that before.

"Let me tell you something about Lepides, Dion," he snapped. "He was probably one of the best generals this kingdom has ever had, and he didn't even want the job. It took Hieron a week to persuade him to take your father's place. All Lepides wanted was to go back to his vineyard and spend the rest of his life mourning his family. Did you know the Carthaginians killed them all, early on in the last war?

He was just a captain back then, but they still sent a raiding party to his villa, out of sheer spite, because they feared him. His wife, his three young sons… No, you probably didn't know, did you?"

He glared at me icily.

"No, I had no idea," I mumbled. "He never said anything…"

Archimedes flapped his hand irritably at me.

"No, of course he didn't. And do you understand why Lepides finally agreed to accept the job, Dion? Because he knew our enemies would eventually return. The thought terrified him. And in the end, he felt he had a duty to do whatever he could to try to prepare us for that day. You think he was a bastard? Who cares if he was a bastard? His one and only purpose was to help Hieron keep our people safe. So Lepides spent his last twenty years struggling to turn spoilt brats into men with a little iron in their spines. And I fear the time will soon be upon us, when even a fool like you may finally learn to appreciate everything Lepides did for this kingdom."

I looked down at my feet, uncertain how to respond.

"I'm sorry, Great-uncle," I said eventually. "It's just I never knew. About his family and everything."

He glowered at me.

"No. Well, why would you? It all happened years before you were even born. But you're supposed to be a general now. Stop thinking like a child, for pity's sake… You have many of your ancestor's gifts, boy. You have an instinct for leading men. You have the ruthlessness to win, and the heart to see the fight through to the end. In your own way, I suppose you are not entirely devoid of cunning. Lepides saw those qualities in you. He thought you were the best natural warrior he had ever trained. But those gifts are not enough. You lack balance, Dion. That is what Lepides was trying to teach you. Hieron too."

"You are not the first man today to remind me I'm no Hieron, Great-uncle. I hardly need to be told."

"No Dion, you certainly are not. Not even Gelon could have been that. But what exactly are you, I wonder? Another Dionysius? A second Agathocles? Or something else entirely? I cannot fathom it."

He tapped the ground with his cane a few times. Finally he sighed.

"Well, we are where we are, I suppose. For good or ill, it looks as though you are all we've got... But do try to acquire some patience, Dion... Power and mathematics are much the same thing, you know. Do you even realise why Hieron has been a truly great king? It is because he always understood that real power is not about commanding the most weight. It is about becoming the fulcrum and lever on which opposing weights can be balanced, even when they are of differing magnitudes. Can you grasp that? Few men have ever exercised power more elegantly and beautifully than Hieron. In his own way, he may even be as great a mathematician as I am. We have both devoted our lives to the pursuit of poise, to trying to discover perfect equilibriums, like a dancer standing motionless on a single toe. That is all that equations express, and that is how Hieron always tried to rule." He sighed. "A shame I never made more progress with you as a child... Anyway, come on, I suppose we'd better get this nonsense over with."

He threaded his arm through mine, and together we walked slowly over to the council chamber.

The council meeting was a subdued affair. Everyone apart from Thraso seemed even more than usually timid around me, although given my ostentatious display of spears in the courtyard outside, that was hardly surprising. My colleagues took their places in nervous silence. Zoippos glared at me but when I met his gaze, he quickly turned away.

We had all been in our seats and waiting a while when Hieronymus was finally escorted in by Andranodoros, followed by Nebit and six men of the Royal Watch in full battle dress. Our future king looked at me with wide eyes and I thought I saw his hands trembling.

As he approached, I rose to my feet, turned towards him and bowed my head.

The other councillors stared at me in confusion. There was a moment of silence, and then they all started scrambling to their feet too. Only Archimedes remained in his chair.

"I'm sorry, I'm afraid I must have dozed off," he said, clapping his hands on the table. "Have we finished already? Oh, good. I'm really quite ready for lunch."

Andranodoros showed the prince to his father's former place, then walked round to his own chair. He shot me a glance and nodded approvingly in acknowledgement of my gesture. Hieronymus self-consciously took his seat, but everyone else had their eyes on me and I remained standing. There was a scraping noise as my great-uncle pushed back his chair and ponderously started rising to his feet.

Hieronymus didn't seem to know what to do. He looked at Andranodoros, who gave him an encouraging smile.

"Oh, yes. Please sit down, everyone," the prince said, blushing, and so I sat again and the others sheepishly followed.

As we lowered ourselves into our chairs, my great-uncle finally managed to hoist himself out of his.

"Would anyone care to join me for lunch?" he said.

Beside me, I heard Thraso try to suppress a chuckle.

"The meeting isn't over yet, Archimedes," said Andranodoros, visibly irritated.

"Isn't it? Oh dear," replied my great-uncle sadly, as he lowered himself slowly back down. "We do seem to be taking an unusually long time today. You really should try to move things along a little faster, Andranodoros." And then he stuffed his beard into his mouth, folded his hands in his lap and closed his eyes again.

There was little to discuss, and I stayed silent throughout. Andranodoros read out a bleak assessment of Hieron's condition from his doctors. He suggested we all offer sacrifices for the king's recovery. The common people would have to be informed of his collapse, he said; the presence of so many additional soldiers around the palace was already starting to fuel all sorts of rumours. He would start writing daily bulletins himself. He wanted to lead the people by degrees to the realisation that Hieron's reign was drawing to its close.

Andranodoros went on to announce that he could not manage the duties of both Royal Treasurer and First Man, and so he had decided that his brother-in-law Zoippos should once more take over at the treasury. The post of Surveyor of the City Fish Markets was to be abolished. Zoippos, who seemed to have been in something of a sulk until that moment, immediately brightened up and would have embarked on one of his interminable speeches, had not Andranodoros held up his hand.

"Forgive me, my dear Zoippos," he said, "but there is really no need for you to express any gratitude. After all, the council is merely seeking to exploit your talents."

It struck me that Andranodoros already seemed to regard himself and the council as being much the same thing.

"Now, I have a further appointment to announce," he continued. "Before he fell ill, our king promoted Dion the new general of the army. The City Guard will remain under Dion's command as well. I am sure we will all rest easier, knowing he is watching over us."

I looked round the table. The expressions on my colleagues' faces did not suggest that they found the thought of being watched over by me particularly reassuring. Good, I thought.

"Hear, hear," said Leatherskin hurriedly and began clapping the table, beating his startled friend Ision to the mark. A moment later, Ision and the others all joined in with ostentatious enthusiasm.

I looked at Hieronymus, who was staring at Andranodoros in horror.

When the applause had died down, Ision put his hand up.

"I wonder, Andranodoros," he said, apparently anxious to make up lost ground, "if it might not be a good idea to announce Dion's promotion at the same time as the king's illness? I am sure the people would find it hugely comforting…"

Andranodoros turned to the war. The latest reports from Italy suggested Hannibal was attempting to consolidate his position in the south, he said. It remained unclear whether the Carthaginians intended to turn on Rome or on Sicily next. A small Roman force under Marcellus was dogging them. It appeared that Rome's tactic was to try to keep Hannibal tied down for the winter, while they rebuilt their army. Andranodoros invited me to add any comments of my own, but I shook my head. I could no more read Hannibal's mind than anybody else.

Finally, Andranodoros asked Thraso for a summary of the food situation. Without consulting any notes, my cousin ran through the crop estimates region by region. The barley and wheat had been harvested in the summer, but the vegetable and late fruit forecasts seemed promising. He hoped to be able to introduce a slightly more liberal rationing regime in the city within two months.

"And that is all for today, I think," Andranodoros concluded. "Unless anyone else has something they wish to raise? No? Good. Well, let's not keep poor Archimedes from his lunch any longer."

He turned towards my great-uncle and smiled, but there was no affection in his eyes.

Thraso and I started to make our way out of the room together. He had some questions for me about protecting the last of the year's grain shipments to Rome from pirates. As we talked, I noticed Andranodoros and Hieronymus heading to the far door, which led to the royal apartments. And then something peculiar happened. Andranodoros put his arm around the prince's shoulders, which was natural enough, but the prince responded by putting his own arm around Andranodoros's waist. I stopped in mid-sentence to stare at their backs and Thraso turned to look too. Andranodoros hurriedly dropped his own arm again and smoothly moved to disengage himself, by inviting the prince to walk through the door ahead of him. But I had seen enough.

It was apparent that Andranodoros was the prince's *erastos*, that is, his mentor and lover. Almost every noble-born adolescent boy had one, to help him transition to manhood, although now that Hieronymus was more man than boy, the relationship should have been ended. Perhaps, given his father's death, the prince had felt the need to rekindle it.

"Oh dear, Dion," said Thraso quietly. "I wonder if we might not have made a rather serious mistake."

He was clearly thinking the same as me. Our First Man's hold over the heir to the throne was obviously a great deal stronger than either of us had realised. Gelon's death seemed to be working out rather well for Andranodoros.

＊

Two days later, I arranged to see Andranodoros again to discuss two appointments I had decided to make within my new command. We both knew I could do whatever I wanted, but I wished to appear reasonable, although quite where my power should end and his own should begin was a question I had not really thought through.

The king had only collapsed three days previously, but our new First Man had already appropriated the council chamber and turned it into a private office for himself. The long table had been moved to one end of the room, and at the other he had installed the largest desk I had ever seen for his own use, which he had surrounded with a semicircle of lesser desks for assistants. Twenty or so additional assistants and secretaries, presumably of lower status, had been crammed into the anteroom.

Andranodoros and I sat facing each other across the council table as flustered-looking men scurried around us clutching wax tablets and scrolls, which they were wedging into tall stacks of shelves that had been positioned around the walls.

I raised my eyebrows in enquiry and Andranodoros shrugged.

"I'm reorganising the secretariat," he said. "Between you and me, I fear the king let his secretaries get a bit too powerful over the last few years. There seem to be armies of them scattered around the palace... Anyway, what can I do for you, Dion?"

I explained the two promotions I planned to make.

"I appreciate you consulting me about this," he said amiably. "That all sounds very sensible; yes, of course you have my support. But I understand Castor is not a particularly wealthy man. I imagine taking on the captaincy of the City Guard might be rather a burden for him. Would you perhaps like me to have a quiet word with Zoippos about increasing the treasury's contribution to the division…?"

He batted his long eyelashes at me. I had assumed I would simply have to continue making up the Guards' deficit myself. It was my own financial burden Andranodoros was offering to relieve; but of course, he had already realised that.

"Thank you," I replied with a nod, "I'm sure he'd appreciate it."

"Well, Dion, a little while ago, I promised I'd deal fairly by you, if you would do the same by me. I don't know quite how all this will play out between us, but I'll do my best to make it work. So I'll be happy to help with Castor. But I've a favour to ask you in return. I fear Archimedes is struggling a little these days to keep up with our discussions. The prince was rather annoyed to see that he slept through almost the entire meeting yesterday… I wonder if you'd mind having a quiet word with him? Perhaps suggest it's time for him to lay down the burden of his public duties? It would probably be better coming from you…"

I sighed sadly.

"I dare say you're right, Andranodoros. I'll speak to him," I said. "Although he won't like it."

I was fairly certain my great-uncle would be delighted to step away from the new administration that seemed to be emerging from the deformed womb of Hieron's council.

"By the way," I added, "I noticed you've moved Nebit into the anteroom. If you can spare him, I could quite use his help at Plymmerium…"

"Oh, I was rather hoping to hang on to him. He's such a clever little fellow. But I suppose if you really want him…" Andranodoros pursed his lips. "Very well, he's yours." He waved his hand in a gesture of largesse and smiled.

Nebit had dropped by to see me the previous evening to congratulate me on my promotion, and over a cup of wine had forlornly confided that Andranodoros had already shunted him into some bureaucratic backwater. It had been almost the first thing Andranodoros had done after Hieron's collapse. Nebit would have been perfectly happy to serve any master who valued him, but it seemed our new First Man didn't trust the little Egyptian; doubtless, he was too close to me for Andranodoros's comfort. I was delighted to rescue him. I collected him from his desk on the way out.

I had asked the three Shield captains to come over from Plymmerium later that evening. It would be our first meeting since the announcement of my appointment and I was a little apprehensive. Although I regarded them as among my closest friends, I had no idea how Eryx and Theodotos felt about being under my command.

We met in my rooms at the palace, together with Castor and Nebit. Sosis had finally recovered sufficiently from his injury to resume his captaincy of the Gold Shields. He wore a patch now to keep the dust out of his empty eye socket, and when he saw me he hugged me in undisguised delight. Eryx clapped me warmly on the back, and told me I shouldn't worry too much about being a useless girly arsewipe as we were clearly all doomed anyway. Theodotos clasped my arm and smiled.

"General Cowbrains, I salute you," he said. He was trying to put a brave face on it, but I could tell he was a little disappointed. We both knew he had been the only other possible candidate to succeed Gelon at Plymmerium. While I had been left kicking my heels in Syracuse, he had been covering himself in glory with the fleet.

When Alpha and Omega had served everyone a cup of water, I dismissed the pair of them and we settled down in a circle on the stools and couches.

I told Castor of his promotion first. He looked at me in horror.

"But I can't possibly afford it, sir," he said.

"In these rooms, Castor, you still call me Dion, and the treasury is going to help out with that side of things… Alright? But I'm afraid there's no seat on the Royal Council for you. Sorry. Anyway, start thinking about whom you want as your adjutant."

"I don't know what to say, Dion… It will be an honour. Thank you."

"Good. Secondly, I'm creating a new post of secretary of the army. That will be Nebit's job. He'll work with your adjutants and the quartermasters and will be responsible for all administration. I advise you to embrace him, my friends. You'll find him invaluable."

Nebit was beaming. Sosis gave him a friendly nod. Theodotus merely raised his eyebrows in mild surprise. Eryx eyed the Egyptian up and down and scowled.

"Well, I suppose we can always eat him," he muttered.

"Pay no attention, Nebit, he doesn't mean it. Now, I'll try to get over to Plymmerium whenever I can, but for the time being, I'm afraid I'm going to have to spend most of my time at the palace. I have some unfinished business here in the city. So, Theodotus my friend, if you are willing, I'd like to make you my second-in-command. I need you to run Plymmerium for me. Alright?"

"My dear fellow, I'd be delighted."

"Good… Oh, and perhaps I should say, the job comes with a blue tunic."

He blinked in surprise, and then he grinned from ear to ear.

I had not been surprised that Andranodoros had approved of my suggestion that my second-in-command should be given the council seat that had previously been the prerogative of the captain of the City Guard. After all, our First Man was much closer to Theodotus than to Castor. The arrangement suited him just as well as it suited me.

The winter months rolled by painfully slowly as the kingdom waited for its king to die. His doctors insisted that no one outside his immediate family should be permitted to see him, which may have been as much a kindness to us as it was to him.

As it became increasingly apparent that I had no intention of murdering him, Hieronymus began to grow in confidence. He took to riding around the city on a white horse, surrounded by a cordon of bodyguards, over whose heads he would throw handfuls of coins at the crowds. At least the silly child stayed well away from me.

Word came that Marcellus had managed to get the better of Hannibal's rear-guard at a small town called Nola. It was a minor battle of no consequence in itself, but in their hunger for hope, the people seized on it, just as they seized on every bulletin announcing that Hieron still breathed.

I was pleased too, but for different reasons. It seemed to me that Hannibal had missed his best chance of assaulting Rome. Even if he tried, *The Syracusia* would never now leave her berth in Alexandria. I had no desire to risk both our fleet and our army, merely to put the crown of all Sicily on Hieronymus's greasy head. So long as the Romans were fighting Hannibal, I was happy to keep sending them our grain; for the rest, they would just have to save themselves. Besides, I had already concluded that I preferred the prospect of a ruined Rome to that of a triumphant one. But as the possibility that Hannibal might march on Rome receded, so the possibility increased that he would turn on Sicily instead. I began preparing a plan to defend our kingdom, and the only men I enlisted to help me with it were Archimedes and Nebit.

If Hannibal came, he would come from the north. The Roman troops who garrisoned their Sicilian provinces would make their stand at Messana, just across the straits from the Italian mainland. I knew the Romans would ask me to send our ships to Messana as well, to help them try to block him there.

I had no intention of obliging. I wanted Hannibal to come. I didn't want to block him; I wanted to destroy him.

Once he had got past the Romans, he would turn south towards Syracuse and the large, fertile plain around Leontini on whose harvests our hopeless allies had come to rely. Naturally, he would expect us to withdraw behind our walls, as we had always done, and he would then invest the city in the hope of bringing us to terms. But to reach Syracuse, Hannibal had to march down the coastal road, and for twenty miles or so, before it emerges into the

Leontini plain, the road threads its way between the sea and the steep foothills that surround Mount Etna.

There were several pinch points along that stretch of road where we could hold an approaching army with a relatively small force. In a pitched battle, I knew I had no answer to Hannibal's cavalry, but his cavalry would be of no use to him on such a narrow front. And at some of those pinch points, the road was within range of our ships' ballistae. Hannibal would be trapped between the rocks and the sea, and the machines my great-uncle had been creating at Plymmerium would do the rest. I would use those twenty miles to rain down my kingdom's bloody vengeance on his head. I would make the barbarians squeal for Gelon's death.

XXII

THE OLIVE LEAF CROWN

One night, I was woken from my sleep by the cold. I couldn't remember what I had been dreaming about but the sheets were damp and clammy with sweat. I had left the shutters open. I felt the need to relieve myself and gently lifted Vita's arm from my chest. She mumbled something and rolled over. With my eyes still half-closed, I wearily swung my legs around and levered myself off the bed. An instant later, there was a muffled crack as something splintered beneath my weight and stabbed into the arch of my foot.

It was the brittle circlet of olive twigs. Alpha and Omega had retrieved it from the palace when I moved back home and had reverently hung it over my marital bed. I suppose I must have knocked it off its nail with my hand as I tossed in my sleep. It lay on the floor in the weak moonlight, snapped into pieces.

My bellow of anguish was so loud that it brought two guards running into the room with drawn swords, followed a few moments later by two or three slaves. Vita was staring at me with wide, startled eyes, clutching the sheet to her chin as if to protect herself from me.

Being an old man now, I have nothing better to do with whatever time remains to me than to set down my stories. I find I am already on my twentieth scroll, so if anybody happens to have discovered them and has persevered this far, I can only assume that he has nothing very useful to do with his time either. When I started writing, I had not intended to record the tale of how I first became something of a hero to my fellow citizens, as it has no bearing on the events that led to the final ruination of our kingdom. But as one idle man scratching out words that will only be read by other idle men, if they are ever to be read at all, I suppose I may as well tell it.

It was all so long ago. I was still a junior lieutenant when Lepides informed me that I was to represent Syracuse in the combat events at Olympia. We Greeks measure the passing of time by the four-year cycles of the festival; that was the last year of the 163rd Olympiad, and I had only just turned twenty.

I was not a popular young man: my fellow officers tended to avoid and exclude me. I don't know whether they were motivated more by antipathy or political prudence, but either way, it was understandable enough. I still had no reputation of my own; I was merely my father's son. I had responded by affecting an air of disdain, which of course only made matters worse. When Lepides told me of his decision, it felt as though my heart had stopped, but among my comrades, I feigned indifference.

All Olympic contestants are supposed to train for ten months before the games, but I didn't take the requirement too seriously. I confined myself to sparring with anyone at Plymmerium who was willing to earn a few coins by letting me practise on him. The army used to hold its own wrestling and boxing championships, both of which I had won for the previous two years, and so despite the offer of payment, there were few volunteers and nothing much they could usefully teach me. It was obvious I had an unusual talent; as to how far it might carry me, I assumed time would tell.

We had to be at Olympia a month before the festival got underway and I invited my fellow athletes to sail with me in one of my family's more comfortable merchant ships. My teammates were a pair of long-legged enlisted men from the slums of the city, who were hoping to qualify for the races. Once they had managed to set aside their understandable inhibitions, we got on rather well.

None of us had ever been to the festival before, so we didn't know quite what to expect. Leatherskin, ever hungry for status, had entered a team of his own for one of the chariot events, but his charioteer and horses had already been sent ahead, to give the animals more time to recover from the journey. He and Lepides would follow us later, although they would not travel together. The two men were known to dislike each other intensely, which I suppose was only natural, given how intensely unlikeable both men were.

Each athlete was required to bring his own trainer, so I took along the sergeant who had been the army's boxing champion before me. His real name was Jason, but everybody used to call him Etna, for reasons that were immediately apparent upon encountering him. We also had half a dozen slaves with us, whom Lepides had insisted on selecting himself from among the cooks and orderlies at Plymmerium.

I am told there are carpets of flowers in the deserts of Egypt, which only blossom for a day or two, having waited patiently for years for a few drops of rain to awaken them. Olympia is a little like that. The site briefly bursts into life to celebrate the festival of Zeus and is then all but abandoned, until it is revived two years later for a lesser festival in honour of Zeus's queen, the goddess Hera. The two of them seem to have a rather miserable marriage. The goddess is said to be jealous of the many pretty girls her husband has bedded and to have resented the half-human children they bore him. She had been so angry when Hercules was born that she even sent a pair of snakes to kill the baby in his cot. Fortunately for our poets, the infant strangled the snakes instead.

Olympia nestles at the foot of Mount Kronos, in the lush crook of the Alpheus River and one of its tributary streams. At the heart of the compound lies a walled sanctuary of about two or three acres, which over the centuries has become cluttered with temples, shrines and altars of various styles and sizes. They encircle an ancient grove of olive trees. All our Olympic crowns are fashioned from sprigs cut from the very oldest tree of all, which the priests claim was planted by Hercules himself. But then, you can hardly visit a village anywhere in the Greek homelands without the locals proudly pointing out some legacy or other of Hercules: a lake dug here, a hill raised there, and massive rocks cleft in two almost everywhere. The poor fellow seems to have been forever digging or hauling or clefting something, seldom to any obvious purpose. But when all's said and done, I think perhaps Hercules really did plant that olive tree; at any rate, it is impossible to gaze at it without being a little awestruck by its fame.

The facilities for the games lie outside the perimeter of the sacred enclosure. The site was already bustling with thousands of athletes and their hangers-on when we arrived. There are some fifteen hundred Greek cities and islands that are entitled to send competitors to the Olympics, and they are all eager to be represented in at least one event. The reason we had to arrive early was to allow the judges sufficient time to decide who should be allowed to compete, a problem they traditionally resolved through a complex process of observation, trials and bribes. There were no women around of course, although I was pleased to discover that several dozen enterprising prostitutes had set up a line of tents along the riverbank, which was as close as they dared venture.

My teammates and I were shown to the accommodation block where we were allocated our own little dormitory, which we were to share with our trainers. Our slaves had to camp in a nearby field. Their most important task would be to see to our meals: every time the games were held, a surprising number of athletes would mysteriously fall sick, and Syracuse certainly didn't lack for enemies at the festival.

Etna and I spent our first morning exploring the sights, visiting the Temple of Zeus to gawp at his famous statue. The immense effigy of the father of the gods sits impassively on a giant throne, which is just as well, because were he to stand, his head would smash through the temple roof. Hera, his wife, used to have a temple of her own nearby, but its columns had been toppled by an earthquake two hundred years before I was born. She must have had a particularly ferocious argument with Zeus on that day to provoke him to such fury. It has always been a mystery to me how men can be so foolish as to expect happy lives, as if by right, when even the gods cannot ordain a contented existence for themselves.

It was not till the early afternoon that Etna and I strolled over to the palaestra, the smaller of the two gymnasia, which is reserved for the use of the combat athletes. For half an hour or so, we sat silently on a bench in the colonnade, watching some of the other contestants practising in the courtyard with their trainers.

"I wouldn't worry too much, sir," said Etna eventually. "They can't all be as good as this."

I felt ill.

It was not that I was frightened of the pain that the other competitors were clearly all too capable of inflicting on me; what made my stomach churn was the humiliating realisation that I was unlikely to qualify for a single one of my events. I would be obliged to sail home without even having managed to set foot in the stadium.

Pride is an overseer's whip. For the next four weeks, Etna and I did the best we could to remedy my failure to prepare adequately. We studied the other athletes closely every morning, and afterwards we practised any moves that we had never previously seen and tried to devise ways to counter them. We concentrated on my wrestling, the only event for which I still retained some slight and desperate hope of qualifying. As the other contestants and I grappled with our trainers in the courtyard, the judges walked around making notes on wax tablets. Sometimes they would ask two of the athletes to spar with each other for a few minutes, but they barely gave me a glance.

When Lepides finally arrived, I decided I should warn him that I would probably not be chosen to compete in anything. He merely snorted contemptuously and stalked off without a word.

The list of athletes who had been selected to compete was posted two days before the festival began. To my astonishment, my name was included in all three combat events. I still don't know quite how Lepides arranged it, but I doubt he gave the judges any cause to welcome his intervention. He was a man who instinctively preferred menaces to bribes, and in Hieron's day, Syracuse was certainly not a kingdom to be needlessly antagonised.

The sporting events at Olympia must be squeezed into the intervals between seemingly endless religious ceremonies. I lost count of how many dreary hours I spent in the first three days of the festival, following one procession after another around the sacred enclosure. Every obscure little altar had to be visited in its turn, and at each one the priests would perform their libations and chant their dismal hymns and cut the throats of yet more animals. The father of the gods must have been bored out of his wits by our interminable grovelling.

The combat events finally took place on the fourth day. They are held in the stadium, a clay rectangle over two hundred paces in length, surrounded by grassy banks for the spectators. Over forty thousand men come to watch the games, many travelling great distances. Shortly after dawn, I walked out onto the clay for the first time, as naked as the day I was born, to their polite applause. I closed my eyes and silently prayed that I might avoid making a laughing stock of myself.

The first of my tournaments was the wrestling. There were sixteen contestants in all and we had already drawn lots to see whom we would be fighting. As things turned out, I acquitted myself better than I had feared. The first man to throw his opponent three times is declared the winner, and somehow I managed to throw my opponent once before losing the bout. As I crashed down heavily on my back for the final time, the jolting pain was quickly superseded by an overwhelming sense of relief. At least, I reflected happily, I had justified my appearance before the crowds.

The boxing tournament began at midday. Etna wrapped the leather strips around my hands for me and told me not to worry because it would all be over soon, an assessment that he seemed to think might comfort me.

Greatly to my own surprise, I made it through the first round, landing a lucky left-handed punch with considerably more force than my opponent had anticipated. I suppose that is one of the advantages of being ambidextrous. It unbalanced him sufficiently to allow me to knock him off his feet with a right-handed blow a second later, which probably fractured his eye socket. It certainly hurt my hand.

Unfortunately, my next fight was a very different affair. The man I found myself facing was lankier than most boxers and as close-eyed as a hawk. He must have been nearly forty, but he danced around me with ease, slowly wearing me down with lightning jabs that were not especially dangerous individually, but to which I had no answer. Although I am a fast man for my size, I barely managed to lay a hand on him. After twenty minutes, my left eye was so swollen I could no longer see out of it, and he finally put me out of my misery with a swipe to my temple that left me reeling, followed by a sharp upper cut to my chin. It was the most elegant display of the art I have ever seen, although I would have preferred to witness it from a different perspective.

When I managed to pick myself up off the dirt, I bowed to him somewhat unsteadily, while the crowd cheered at the tops of their voices. His name was Kleoxenos of Alexandria, and he had won the Olympic crown for boxing sixteen years earlier. Only later did it emerge that Lepides had played a part in persuading him to come out of retirement.

My final tournament was the pankration contest. Pankration is the most prestigious of the three combat events, and the most brutal. Anything is permitted, apart from biting and gouging. The match only ends when one of the contestants concedes defeat or is rendered unconscious. Lepides had always discouraged the sport at Plymmerium because it resulted in too many permanent injuries, which he found inconvenient.

Most combat athletes will enter either one or two of the three tournaments, but it is fairly unusual to compete in both the boxing and the pankration at the same games, and extremely rare to go in for all three events. Lepides obviously knew I stood no chance in any of them and had probably just wanted to test my mettle. Or perhaps he had simply wanted to teach me a lesson. In any event, I was already half-blinded and so battered that I failed to make it past the first round. The pankratiast to whom I lost was far more adept than me and gave me a fairly merciless walloping. He could have ended the fight at will, but it seemed to amuse him to protract my punishment. Eventually, he caught me in a chokehold and after thrashing around helplessly for a little while, I blacked out. One of my fellow athletes told me afterwards that I had so clearly been outmatched that the crowd barely bothered applauding the victor. I was lucky to escape without any broken bones and when I came to, I had to be helped off the stadium by Etna. My cumulative bruising from the three tournaments was so extensive that I looked like a Numidian.

Etna took me directly to the athletes' infirmary, and there I stayed for a week, until my bruises had subsided sufficiently to allow me to make the journey home. Etna kindly remained with me, perhaps out of a vague sense of guilt. But at least I had a good excuse to miss the fifth and final day of the festival, which was given over entirely to yet more ceremonies in the sacred enclosure, in honour of the twenty new Olympic champions. I think I would rather have endured another pankration bout than go through that.

Naturally, I was not expecting a hero's welcome on my return to Syracuse, but it was still something of a surprise to find myself being bawled out by Lepides for a performance that he assured me had shamed the entire kingdom.

Only one thing in life appeared to give the general any pleasure, and that was winning. Or perhaps it would be truer to say that Lepides only derived pleasure from making other people lose. In any event, he seemed sufficiently annoyed by my first Olympic appearance to inform me, via a curt message delivered on a wax tablet, that he had engaged a professional trainer for me.

The man Lepides selected for the task was none other than Kleoxenos, the boxer who had beaten me so convincingly. Quite remarkably for someone of his age, Kleoxenos had made it all the way to the finals of the tournament, although he had failed to win a second crown for himself. It so happened he was also a fine pankratiast, and had won some lesser tournaments in that sport too.

My famous new trainer arrived at Plymmerium two months after my own return. He was given the honorary rank of lieutenant and allocated an officer's cottage, although his sole duty was to prepare me for the next festival. His temperament proved to be almost as cold and sour as Lepides' own, so we never became friends; but for the better part of four years, when I wasn't busy killing bandits or Spartans, I devoted my spare time to learning everything I could from him about the seemingly limitless science of inflicting injury on the human body.

It was actually Theodotus who persuaded me to throw myself wholeheartedly into the training. He was my one real friend in those days. Although he was a few years older than me, our families had been intertwined for centuries and he seemed to be the only officer in the army blithely unconcerned about associating with me. I suppose I have loved him ever since. In any event, he was the one who convinced me that the Olympics could be my gateway to acceptance.

When the games finally came round again, Lepides consulted with Kleoxenos and decided that this time I should confine myself to the pankration contest, the sport for which I appeared to have developed the greatest aptitude. I protested, being eager to compete in the wrestling as well, but naturally Lepides got his way. I had no idea what my chances were, because Lepides and Kleoxenos had refused to let me fight in any of the other festivals that are held in the intervening years of the Olympic cycle. But I suppose Lepides was proved right in the end, because as things turned out, I managed to return to Syracuse from my second excursion to Olympia considerably less bruised, and wearing an olive leaf crown of my own.

Unfortunately, my last fight had turned out to be not only the shortest final in living memory, but also the most controversial. For a while, it seemed as though no two Greeks could meet anywhere in the world, without eventually falling into a ferocious argument about me.

I had made it through the preliminary rounds without any great difficulty. The crowd seemed to have developed quite an affection for me, mainly, I suppose, because I had made a point of bowing respectfully to my opponents when I had done with them, even though all three were by then unconscious.

I had already stripped naked again, and was about to walk out onto the stadium for the final, when Lepides found me. He was quite short and stringy, but that didn't deter him from tapping me menacingly on the chest as he stared up into my face.

"I want you to send this man's people a message, Lieutenant," he rasped. "Do you understand me?"

I frowned.

"I'm sorry, sir, I'm not sure I do... What people?"

"The Macedonians, you idiot. It is not enough that you should beat this fellow. I want you to break him in half. And I want the whole crowd to see it."

I nodded slowly. I could never really keep track of Greek politics, but I guessed that the Macedonians, who two years earlier had been among our allies at the Battle of Sellasia, were our allies no longer.

"Well, go on then, Lieutenant, what are you waiting for? Get out there."

My opponent, the Macedonian army champion, was a snarling braggart known for the power of his punch. I had noticed him use it a few days earlier on one of his slaves, who had presumably displeased him in some way. We had barely got going before he attempted an ill-judged swing at my head, allowing me to sidestep him and dislocate his ankle with a sharp, downward kick.

To his credit, the man had gamely soldiered on, until I also broke his arm. I can still recall the expression of bewilderment on his face, as he stared at the protruding, jagged bone. The crowd gasped and held its breath. Everyone knew my opponent must concede, just as soon as the injury had registered in his brain.

But I had set the beast free, so I didn't give him the chance.

I swung round behind him, bellowing like an animal, and drove my fist into his lower spine. All my rage exploded down my arm. I could feel his vertebrae crack and buckle beneath the punch.

The fight had probably taken less than a minute.

As I walked off the shocked and silent stadium, four orderlies ran out and awkwardly tried to get the Macedonian onto their stretcher. His legs flopped around limply; they reminded me of long strands of kelp. I doubted he would last more than a few days.

The furious judges came to see me straight afterwards. They admitted that I hadn't breached any rules, so they couldn't disqualify me, but it was hardly in the spirit of the games to deal a clearly beaten man a deathblow. They made it plain that I would never be allowed to fight at Olympia again. But at least Lepides had no cause for complaint: I had certainly broken the Macedonian in half for him.

Lepides departed that same evening, without troubling himself to say goodbye. Kleoxenos stayed for the final day of the festival, to see me crowned to a raucous mix of cheers and hisses. I gave him his share of my victor's purse, and then he sailed directly home to Alexandria. I heard he was killed by a bucking mule a few months later, a rather silly death for such a great boxer. He left his family comfortably off, at any rate: I had arrived at the games virtually unknown and entirely unfancied, and he and Lepides had both made small fortunes for themselves by backing me at long odds.

It was not till the morning of his departure that Kleoxenos smugly explained everything to me. Lepides, playing the long game as always, had been planning for my second appearance at Olympia before I had even sailed for my first. He had recognised my potential as soon as he saw me fight in the army championships, and had already written to Kleoxenos to invite him to train me. But first, the general believed, I should be allowed to fail, and so he intended to take no steps to prepare me for my initial games. I was complacent and proud, Lepides had written. A little humiliation should make me more malleable, and might also provide an opportunity for a tidy profit at a later date.

Kleoxenos was intrigued. He missed the adulation of the crowds and had already been toying with the idea of coming out of retirement. Lepides' letter decided the matter for him: between his own fights, he would watch my bouts and judge for himself whether the general was right about me. It was pure luck that Kleoxenos had ended up fighting me himself, but he had been taken aback by the speed and strength of my punch and my ability to attack with either hand. Apparently, no other virtual novice had ever obliged him to adopt such cautious tactics. He had met Lepides immediately after our encounter and had swiftly agreed the terms of his employment. And, of course, it was to ensure that I would return to Olympia as a long-odds outsider that the two of them had subsequently refused to let me compete in any of the lesser festivals.

Rather strangely, if mine was the Olympic victory that was most talked about overseas that year, at home I found my achievement eclipsed by that of one of my teammates. His name was Zopyros, and the day before I won the pankration, he had managed to win the sprint. The sprint is the oldest and by far the most prestigious of all the Olympic events; even the dramatic manner of my triumph could not compare to the glory of bringing home that particular title.

I didn't mind in the least. Zopyros was on the fringe of my own acquaintance and seemed a pleasant enough fellow. Naturally, the fact that the kingdom could now boast two Olympic champions sent the city into a frenzy of celebrations. The news of our success was brought to Syracuse by faster ships than our own, and we were greeted at the docks by cheering crowds. A four-horse chariot was waiting to drive us through the streets. Afterwards, Hieron himself hosted a banquet for us in the palace courtyard, while thousands drank and danced in the agora till the early hours.

When Zopyros and I finally returned to Plymmerium the following day, Lepides had the entire army turn out on parade in our honour. He greeted us on the podium, and as the old man stiffly clasped my arm, I believe I saw the flicker of a smile cross his face. I think that sight was worth almost as much to me as my crown.

And Theodotus was proved right, of course: my brother officers embraced me at last, with apparent sincerity. In the years that followed, I could still feel the weight of the stone that I carried on my back, but at least I no longer stooped under the burden.

Although I found the gesture embarrassing, Hieron ordered a pair of marble statues to be made in Zopyros's and my honour. It took the sculptor nearly two years to finish them and when they were ready, they were raised up on plinths, flanking the entrance to the theatre on the outskirts of Neapolis. For the sake of aesthetic balance, or perhaps out of political expediency, mine was made somewhat smaller than life, while that of Zopyros exaggerated his size. His statue still stands, with his name immortalised on its base, but my own was lost in the great siege that finally broke our kingdom. It probably sits in the faraway garden of some dark-haired merchant now.

All that remains to commemorate my victory is a painting, commissioned by my mother, which hangs in a gloomy corner of the Temple of Zeus outside the city. It is nearly sixty years old, and quite spuriously shows me gripping a very ugly and hairy-faced opponent in a headlock, with the olive tree of Olympia in the background. These days, everyone seems to mistake the painting's meaning. I am told that even the priests assume it is merely a rather poor depiction of Hercules slaying the Nemean lion.

XXIII

SNAKES

Removed from our sight, Hieron still clung to life within the little dungeon of his body.

I took to absenting myself from council meetings, relieved to let Theodotus deputise for me. Andranodoros was nothing if not a skilful administrator and things seemed to run smoothly enough. He soon hit upon a pet project of his own. He instructed Ision, the councillor responsible for our slave population, to buy up several thousand slaves from around the Mediterranean, who were put to work on improving the great coastal road that ran like a vein from one end of the kingdom to the other. I didn't mind; it would make it easier for me to fight Hannibal in the north. Archimedes had nothing to do with the scheme, as he had given up his seat on the council and, with it, his responsibility for public works. Rather than appoint a new councillor, Andranodoros had reassigned my great-uncle's duties to Woodpecker.

While it lasted, the road project must have made a lot of people very happy. The scale of the works ensured there was plenty of gold to go around. Theodotus's finances certainly appeared to improve quite quickly after taking his seat on the council. When I teased him about his new slaves and horses, he tried to explain them away, by claiming that Leatherskin had wanted to show his appreciation of the fact that his daughter could now strut about the city wearing the royal blue herself (although, as Theodotus put it, a pig in a blue dress is still a pig). I had my doubts, but I let it pass. It was really no concern of mine. Besides, my own finances had improved as well. Andranodoros had quietly given me back the ships that Hieron had extorted from me and was now paying me for their continuing use on the grain convoys to Rome. After fifty years of thrifty management by Hieron, the treasury had gold enough to spare, and Andranodoros certainly seemed willing to sprinkle it about generously.

Whenever I could find the time, I drilled with my men at Plymmerium or in the city. Every evening, I eagerly hurried home to Vita's arms, but I remained on edge. I imagine so too did my fellow councillors, albeit for different reasons. I still kept my men outside their villas, as a none-too-gentle reminder that I was watching them. I had no intention of lifting my heel from the council's throat. Not wishing to antagonise me, Andranodoros didn't raise the subject again, although he must have had to listen to a lot of whining about it from his colleagues.

As to who might have been behind Gelon's murder, I remained none the wiser. I frequently asked Archimedes if he and Chrysanthe had been able to discover anything yet, but he would always respond by urging me to be patient, and to be careful.

One day, the lawyer Linus came to see me. He also was trying to unravel a mystery. I had asked him to investigate the throwaway comment Nebit had made to me a year earlier, to the effect that my mother may have been buying ships in other people's names. Linus had been too busy to pursue it. My affairs were still in a rather chaotic state and several clients had finally taken their custom elsewhere. Linus was forever assuring me that he was slowly getting a grip on things, but I could see little evidence of it. Only the week before, I had been obliged to send some irate merchant a box of silver, in compensation for a consignment of wine that had somehow ended up being dispatched to Corsica instead of Corinth.

By chance, however, Linus had recently unearthed among my mother's documents a small scroll written in her own hand. It seemed to be a list of eight cargo vessels, each briefly described in the usual way by the number of its masts and the capacity of its hold. Alongside the description of each ship, my mother had recorded the name of a buyer and a seller, a purchase price and a date. Alert to the possible significance of the document, Linus had dutifully trawled the family ledgers, and had found eight corresponding withdrawals from our funds in the Royal Treasury.

His problem was that he could find no trace of the ships: they didn't seem to exist. Nor had he been able to track down a single one of the supposed buyers or sellers – they didn't seem to exist either. And yet the money had been withdrawn. He was at a loss to understand it.

I sent a note to Nebit at Plymmerium asking if he could provide any further information. Nebit replied apologetically, writing that I already appeared to know more than he did. The eight withdrawals from the treasury, which had been spread over a four-year period, had been sufficiently substantial to attract the interest of Hieron's secretariat, which monitored such things. At first, they had suspected my family was being blackmailed in some way, but then one of their sources among my mother's clerks overheard a conversation between her and our late steward, suggesting that she controlled a larger fleet than anyone had previously realised. The secretariat guessed my mother must have been buying ships on the sly, but knew no more than this. Nebit confessed that, when he had made his comment to me, he had to some extent been fishing.

It seemed that I had no option but to ask my mother to explain what she had been up to; but having cut her out of our affairs and being barely on speaking terms, I had no idea how I could persuade her to cooperate. Neither a menacing approach nor a conciliatory one seemed likely to be particularly effective: she would take too much delight in rubbing my nose in it. My only leverage in the past had been the threat to marry her off, but that had little force any more. Now that she was High Priestess, I could hardly harness her to someone glaringly unsuitable, and the only suitable candidates all seemed to be elderly and dim. Handing her over to any of them to try to manage would merely have been a waste of a dowry.

It was Vita who suggested how I might set about tackling her, without too much loss of face.

My mother, to my surprise, had made an effort to take Vita under her wing, going out of her way to introduce her to other society women. Vita proposed that she should now appear to return the favour. We had adopted Archimedes' novel idea of eating our meals together and so, ostensibly without consulting me, Vita invited my mother to join us for supper one evening. She had already laid the groundwork by telling my mother that she was anxious to try to reconcile the two of us. My mother, probably scenting blood, had agreed to come.

The Galatian mercenaries had all been sent packing months previously at Hieron's command, but she duly arrived with her two black-plumed bodyguards, Medon and Phidias, in tow. I had made a point of telling Dinomenes that I'd be grateful if the arrangement could continue, and presumably he'd passed the message on to whoever now made those decisions.

Naturally, I feigned surprise and indignation when my mother was shown into our sitting room. Vita gave a little speech about the need to put the past behind us and I scowled convincingly, before pretending to let Vita talk me into behaving myself for her sake.

The meal went better than I might have expected, with my mother managing to refrain from volunteering any unwanted advice or gratuitous criticism. She was now enjoying a near-complete social ascendancy, thanks to the fear that I inspired among the husbands of those in her circle. Even Hieron's two haughty daughters, the wives of Andranodoros and Zoippos, had finally been reduced to a satisfactorily cowed position at her feet, and so it seemed she was finally willing to accept that I must be doing something right. Only Nereis, Gelon's widow, continued to put up any resistance, waging unyielding guerrilla warfare from the social hinterlands to which my mother had contrived to expel her.

When we had finished eating, she recomposed herself on her couch and turned to me.

"So, Dion," she said, casually examining her fingernails, "what is it that you want from me?"

"I don't want anything," I replied disingenuously.

"Don't be silly. Do you really imagine I can't see through this little charade? Come on now, don't be coy. State what you want, and then I shall tell you my price for giving it to you."

I sighed, and wondered how painful she was going to make it.

"Very well, then, Mother. It seems you bought some ships in other people's names. I'd like to know where they are."

She laughed.

"Oh dear. Haven't you managed to find them yet?"

I glared at her.

She gazed back at me coolly and took a sip of water as she considered her response.

"Alright, Dion," she said eventually, "send that lawyer of yours round to see me tomorrow. I won't waste my breath trying to explain it to you: you would only get it all muddled up in your head. But I'll take him through everything and answer any questions he may have. Does that satisfy you?"

I frowned, thought about it for a moment and then nodded.

"Thank you… So, what is it you want in return?"

She smiled coldly.

"Nothing," she said. "I shall be pleased to help. I want you only to accept that you and I are stronger when we work together. Hieron succeeded in dividing us; but he is of no consequence now. I realise I have never been an affectionate mother, Dion, but that does not mean I am your enemy. So all I ask in exchange is that you should feel free to confide in me and seek my advice. You will find it is good advice."

Vita leant forwards to rest her hand on my mother's arm.

"Mother Korinna, I hope you understand I wasn't trying to trick you in any way. I really do just want us to be a happy family."

My mother snorted in amusement and lightly pulled her arm away.

"What's happiness got to do with anything, my dear? Is your father's family a happy one? I don't know of any myself. All that matters is loyalty. Families are like little armies. They must be careful to face in the same direction. And if you will take my advice, child, I wouldn't try to play games with me ever again. I've been doing this a great deal longer than you… Well, I think we all understand each other. Thank you for having invited me round: I am pleased we were able to clear the air. So if you will both excuse me now, it's quite late and I am a little tired. I shall be interested to meet your man tomorrow, Dion. From all I hear, he's not exactly the business genius you had hoped."

Linus went to see my mother the following day, and she was as good as her word. He couldn't help chuckling about it when he came round to the palace afterwards to report back to me.

It turned out the ships did indeed exist, but they had been lying idle at anchor in Alexandria for months. The reason Linus had been unable to find any trace of them was because they had always operated out of Egypt, where my mother had decided to establish a second fleet. The trade between Egypt and Syracuse was considerable, but in both kingdoms, foreign-owned ships were charged higher duties on whatever goods they brought in than those imposed on ships owned by their own citizens. My mother's ingenious idea had been for our ships from Syracuse to meet our ships from Egypt at the halfway point, in the harbour at Rhodes, and to swap cargoes there, before returning to their home ports. In this way, both consignments of goods would attract lower duties, significantly increasing our profits. But for the scheme to work, the Egyptian ships had to be owned by Egyptian citizens.

A lawyer in Alexandria acting on my mother's behalf identified eight low-born Egyptian families of Greek descent, whose ancestors had first come to Egypt as soldiers of Alexander. She lent them sufficient funds to buy the ships, with the ships themselves being pledged as security for the loans. Any profits the ships generated were to be made over to my family, by way of interest on the debt. Their nominal owners received nothing at all, apart from an annual bag of coins; but then, all they had to do to earn it was to put their seal on a few documents.

The genius of the scheme was that, as far as Linus could make out, there was nothing illegal about it. As it seemed safe enough, I instructed him to revive the operation.

The upshot of all this was perhaps predictable. Linus returned to my mother the following week, with further questions about Egypt; and then he started calling on her with questions about other aspects of my affairs that remained obscure. She encouraged him to do so and could not have been more helpful or friendly towards him. Before long, Linus found himself routinely seeking my mother's guidance on this tricky decision or that, and almost invariably deferring to her advice. She had him where she wanted him. I won't say that he was reduced to the same position that our former steward had previously occupied, because that would be a gross exaggeration; but then again, nor was it wholly dissimilar.

At least Linus was honest enough to inform me of their evolving relationship, perhaps because he had guessed that I was having him watched and knew all about it anyway. I had suborned some of my family's own business clerks to act as my eyes on the very same day that I had first sent him to see her. It had seemed a sensible precaution. I knew my mother well enough to realise immediately that Linus would be wet clay in her hands. But I made no objection to the new arrangements: with her standing behind him, things soon began to run more smoothly again, and before long the gold was once more flowing in.

Shortly after her election to the post of High Priestess, my mother had instigated a project to repair the temple roof, which had been leaking for many years and was apparently now rotting and in danger of becoming unsafe. I was expected to pay. Maintaining the temple was an obligation my family had accepted centuries earlier, in exchange for obtaining control over the position of High Priestess. I agreed to the works, stipulating only that they should be undertaken as a tribute to my Great-aunt Delia. As things were to turn out, that project very nearly cost me more than mere silver. In fact, it was almost the death of me.

I had just returned from a run in the hills with one of the palace companies, and was in the bathhouse towelling myself off, when Agbal came running in to find me. The winter equinox had been celebrated the previous week and we were in the midst of a cold snap, and so my bath had been the briefest of affairs. The company's senior lieutenant and one of his sergeants were still shivering miserably in the icy water, while other men stood around laughing and placing bets as to which of the two could endure it the longest. I had wagered a silver coin on the sergeant: I reasoned he needed the money more.

"Master," Agbal panted, "a slave woman has come to the palace with a message from your mother. The Lady Korinna requests that you meet her at the Temple of Athena this evening, after you have finished here."

"Did she say why?"

"The builders claim to have discovered some additional problems, Master. Your mother suspects a fraud, and she feels it would be helpful if you were present to hear their explanation. She has arranged a meeting at the temple tonight in the hope that might be convenient for you."

If there were a swindle, my mother certainly didn't need my help to identify it. It seemed more likely that she simply wished to renegotiate the terms of the contract, and judged that my presence might be useful for the purposes of general intimidation.

I thought about it for a moment. It had already been a year of one extraordinary expense after another. Reluctantly, I decided any saving on the temple project was probably worth the irritation.

"Very well. Tell the slave woman I'll be there."

Agbal bowed and disappeared, and I started to dress.

"Fuck it, you win," I heard the sergeant say behind me.

I sighed. I should have known better. The lieutenant was a proud young man, and one should never underestimate the power of pride.

After my day's work was done, I headed off towards the temple. It was only about quarter of an hour away on foot and although torches had already been lit along the Avenue of Athena, the side streets were impenetrably dark. I wore a cloak against the cold, intermittent drizzle. The avenue was normally still busy in the early evening, but the weather had apparently persuaded people to stay indoors, and those few who were out kept their heads bowed as they hurried to their destinations.

When I reached my villa, I stopped at the gate to let Cerberus know I had business at the temple and would be a little while yet. He promised to relay the message to Vita, and I pressed on.

Approaching the temple from the avenue, one sees it first from its long side, at a slightly oblique angle. The building looms so large that it entirely conceals the Temple of Artemis immediately behind it.

Athena's house is surrounded on all four sides by a vast colonnade, and the whole edifice is raised several feet above the ground on a stepped stone platform. One enters from the narrow end, where six ribbed columns, each twice the width of a man's shoulders, support the pediment with its glinting copper shield. Inside stands the enormous, helmeted statue of the goddess. She cradles her spear and wears a flowing gold dress, and her wide azure eyes stare into the distance over the heads of her worshippers with an expression that seems infinitely sad. The temple had been built by King Gelon, Theodotus's ancestor, to celebrate his triumph over a Carthaginian army, and the statue apparently depicts Athena resting after victory. In her sombre wisdom, it seems to me the goddess understands that no victory is ever final. Nearly three hundred years after King Gelon's exploits, we were still wrestling with the problem of Carthage. I suppose only defeat can be final.

The entrance front of the temple was cluttered by several tiers of ramshackle wooden scaffolding, which had been tied to the columns for support. I began to climb the steep steps that led up to the main doors. Chipped by weather and then worn smooth again by countless feet, the stone treads had become rather uneven and were slippery with the rain.

Perhaps it was the uncertainty of my footing that made me more than usually attentive, but I was halfway up when I heard a slight creak. I glanced up and saw a man, standing on the edge of the scaffolding thirty feet over my head, with his arms raised. In the gloom he was little more than a shadow, but then he moved and I knew he was bringing his arms down fast.

I instinctively jumped sideways, and slipped. I tottered and tried to catch my balance, but something extremely heavy crashed just inches from my feet and I fell, my shoulder catching the sharp edge of a step. I rolled and slid downwards in a tumble, to finish with my legs on the cobbled pavement and my back jammed against the lower treads. The block of stone that had been thrown at me had come to rest a few feet away.

I looked up. The man on the scaffolding had pulled back out of sight, but now two other men emerged from the darkness, sprinting towards me across the square. I caught the glint of metal in their hands. I pushed myself awkwardly to my feet as fast as I could. Concealed under my tunic, I had a short blade of my own strapped to my thigh, but the men were coming at me fast and I knew I didn't have time to start fumbling for it. One of them looked unusually tall, the other unusually short. I crouched to meet them, my right arm slightly extended. Only two, I thought. I wondered if they were good enough to kill me.

"Are you alright, sir?" the tall one shouted out.

It was Ajax.

He pulled up breathlessly a few steps away. Needle drew up alongside him a moment later.

I heaved a sigh of relief. I had no idea what they were doing there but that could wait till later.

"Yes, yes... Go on, Sergeant, get after him," I said. "I think he's trying to get over the roof. Take one side of the temple each. He's probably got a rope. I'll wait here. Don't worry, I'm fine."

They exchanged a glance and ran off, and I took a few limping paces backwards to crane up at the pediment. Its apex must have been fifty feet or more above my head. I hitched up my tunic and pulled out my own knife. The stubby blade was only as long as my index finger, but there are more than a dozen places where one can cut or stab a man with a small knife that are sure to kill him, and I knew them all.

A middle-aged man and two teenage boys who I assumed were his sons cautiously approached me. They stopped a safe distance away.

"Are you alright, mister?" the older man shouted out nervously.

"I'm General Dion," I barked at him. "Do you know that name?"

He nodded dumbly.

"Good. I need your eyes. I think there's a man somewhere on the temple roof. Get yourselves round the sides and back. If you see him trying to climb down, call my men. Leave the rest to them. Understand?"

"Yes, sir," he replied, with an evident lack of enthusiasm.

"Alright then. Get going. There's a silver piece in it for you all if you spot him."

As I watched and waited, it struck me there was something strangely amateurish about the attack. Throwing a block of stone at my head seemed a very haphazard way of trying to murder me. I had been lured here by a woman, so more than one person was involved, but whoever was behind the attempt certainly didn't seem to know much about the business of killing people.

My thoughts were interrupted by some distant shouts coming from the longer, south side of the temple.

I hurried round the corner, limping slightly. I seemed to have sprained my ankle when I took my tumble down the steps.

At the far end of the temple colonnade, I could just make out through the drizzle some figures in the street, dimly illuminated by the flickering light of a torch mounted on the wall of a building nearby. One of the figures, who must have been Ajax, stood nearly a head taller than the others, but even he looked tiny beside the temple's monstrous columns. As I approached, other people began to appear from the shadows to join the little group, till there were maybe a dozen of them altogether. They were all looking up and several were pointing.

It was not till I was just a few yards away that I realised they were also laughing. It was easy enough to see why. A man was dangling maybe twenty feet above their heads from a thin rope, which had been knotted at intervals to provide footholds. But the end of the rope was swaying through the air, a good fifteen feet short of the cobbles.

"If you don't mind me saying, sir," said Ajax, "he seems a bit of a fuckwit, doesn't he?"

I grunted.

"He certainly does, Sergeant. Very well, when you've got him down, bring him over to my house. I'll deal with him there. Have him tied to the whipping post in the slaves' yard. I'll send a couple of men over to give you a hand."

Ajax peered up at my would-be assassin.

There was a splashing noise as a thin trickle of urine hit the street from above.

"I don't think there's any need for that, sir. I reckon Needle and me can handle this fool easily enough," he said.

I nodded. I didn't doubt him. I opened my cloak, hoisted my tunic and put the little knife back in its sheath.

"Very well. By the way, what are you both doing here, Sergeant? Your company's over at Labdalum. And Needle's supposed to be at Euryalus, isn't he?"

Ajax looked at me sheepishly.

"Captain Castor's orders, sir. Ever since the prince was killed, he's had Needle and me following you around when you go out. He brought us both back to the palace for the job. Not that you really need much babysitting, of course, sir. The captain probably just wanted to make sure someone would be on hand to cheer you along, if you ever picked yourself another fight with a thousand men."

I grunted.

"I'll see you later, Sergeant," I said and turned away, wincing and trying not to limp as I walked off. I had only taken a few paces when a cold gust of wind caught me in the face and brought me to a halt. I heard my great-aunt's voice in my head.

"The way to me is dangerous," it chirruped.

Could this be what the goddess had meant? That I would be attacked outside her temple?

The priestess of Apollo at Delphi demands a large sum of gold for every prophecy she utters, but the true meaning of her words only ever becomes clear after the prophecy has been fulfilled. I was far from convinced that the idiot dangling from his rope was a serious enough threat to be worthy of a warning from the goddess. Whatever the danger that hung over me, I decided it had not passed yet.

Not fancying a second freezing bath, I had Agbal sponge me down in my bedroom. A large bruise had erupted on my left shoulder and upper arm, and there was another on my thigh, but apart from my swollen ankle, those were the extent of my injuries. Vita sat on the bed watching us and after a few minutes burst into tears.

"But who could possibly want to kill you?" she sobbed.

"It was probably the husband of one of your new friends," I replied offhandedly. "I don't know which one yet, but don't worry, I will before the evening's over." I smiled, but she didn't seem to find my answer very reassuring.

Omega knocked on the door as I was drying myself, to let me know Needle and Ajax had arrived with my prisoner, who was being made ready for me.

"See the two of them are given some supper, would you Omega?" I told him. "And they may as well sleep here. And have the steward find me a whip… Agbal, fetch me a plain tunic. I don't want to ruin another good one tonight."

Vita and I ate together in the small dining room, but all my efforts to lighten the mood seemed to fail. After a while, I gave up. My prisoner had probably been allowed to stew for long enough, I decided, so I excused myself and took the back stairs down to the slaves' yard.

The drizzle had finally stopped, at least. A dozen torches had already been lit and placed in brackets around the walls.

Ajax, Needle and five or six of the City Guards who were now quartered at my house were waiting for me outside, together with my steward. A dozen or more slaves were leaning silently out of the windows of their dormitories.

The steward stepped forward nervously, bowed and handed me a whip. It was a fairly tatty old thing that had started to come apart at the end. I couldn't remember the last time it had been used, but as I took it, a strange sensation ran down my spine, as if a cat were scratching the back of my neck.

My incompetent would-be murderer stood trembling in the far corner of the yard. His hands had been tied to the post.

"So you got him down eventually, I see," I said to Ajax. For some reason, my mouth had gone dry.

Ajax grunted.

"He's an annoying bastard, sir. Needle had to climb up onto the roof himself and threaten to cut the rope, before we could get the silly sod to jump… You'll never guess who it is, sir."

"I know him?" I asked in surprise.

I gave the whip a crack to loosen my arm. And, as I did so, something inside me seemed to crack as well.

I looked down at my hand, which was shaking.

The whip it held seemed to have been transformed into a long, thin black snake that I was grasping by the tail.

I felt a terror that I have never experienced before or since.

The hissing head slowly coiled round to stare at me and, as I watched, it began to rear and gather itself to strike at my face.

"I imagine you do, sir," Ajax was saying. "Why don't you come and take a... Sir? Are you alright, sir?"

The sweat was already breaking out across my forehead and my back. I gasped and threw the whip aside in a mix of horror and revulsion. For a moment I stood frozen, too scared to move; and then I bent down to clutch my knees and started throwing up.

"Fetch a doctor, someone, for fuck's sake!" Ajax yelled, putting one hand on my shoulder and the other round my back.

I held out my arm and waved my hand, still heaving spasmodically. I tried to catch my breath.

"No," I said eventually, shaking my head.

I took a few deep breaths and wiped my mouth with the back of my hand.

"It's alright, Ajax... I'm fine."

I turned my face up towards him and did my best to smile reassuringly.

"It's alright..." I exhaled. He took his arm off my back as I straightened myself.

"It must have just been something I ate... I'm fine now... Thank you."

"Are you sure, sir?"

"Yes, I'm fine. Just something I ate, I imagine. I'm better now..."

I wiped my brow with my forearm and turned to my frightened steward.

"Fetch me a cup of water, would you? And a bowl of water too."

He turned and hurried off. I glanced over at the whip. It was just an old whip. I looked down at my hand and was relieved to see it had stopped trembling.

"Don't worry, Ajax, I'm alright." I forced another smile.

He exhaled in relief.

"You gave me a fright there, sir."

"Nothing to worry about..." I was anxious to change the subject. I tried to remember what he had been saying before.

"So you say I know the man?"

He nodded. I took one last deep breath.

"Very well. Let's go and have a look at him, then."

I still felt a little shaky as we walked across the yard together, and my ankle wasn't helping. I was uncomfortably aware of my tunic clinging damply to my back.

My prisoner stared at me. Tears were streaming down his face and he was desperately trying to say something, but the rag in his mouth made him unintelligible.

Even by the dim light of the torches, I recognised him at once.

I gazed at him, as I considered what to do.

The steward came running over to hand me a cup of water; behind him, a slave was carrying a bowl. I rinsed and spat several times to clear the taste from my mouth, and then I washed my face and the back of my neck. I was finally starting to feel myself again. Maybe it really was just something I'd eaten, I thought, although it hadn't seemed like that. But I had no idea what else it could have been.

I pulled the rag from my prisoner's mouth, and he immediately began whimpering.

"Shut up," I said.

He gulped and went silent.

"What were you offered to kill me?" I demanded.

"Master, please be merciful, I swear I didn't…"

"I asked what you were offered to kill me. I won't ask you again."

"My freedom, Master. And the quarries if I refused."

"I take it this was all your master's clever plan?"

He nodded vigorously.

"Where is he now? He's not in the city, is he?"

"No, Master. He's at his estate in the country."

"Where's that?"

"About four hours' ride away, Master, just before the village of Cyros, off the road to Acrae."

I stared into his face.

"Has your master had any important visitors recently?" I asked. "Is there anyone he has been seeing more often than usual?"

"No, Master, I don't think so," he stammered.

I sighed. He seemed to have nothing useful to tell me.

"Cut him down, Ajax," I said.

Ajax looked at me in surprise, but took out his knife without question and walked behind the post. As he cut the knot binding the man's wrists, the slave collapsed to his knees. Ajax stooped down and freed the man's ankles, and the sorry creature rolled over onto his side and began to sob.

"Have a couple of men take him to the Euryalus gate and throw him out of the city," I said. "As for you, go home and tell your master I will be calling on him tomorrow. Tell him I intend him no harm. I only wish to talk to him."

I gave him a parting kick, but not a particularly hard one, and turned and limped away. My slaves were still staring down at the scene from their dormitory windows. I wondered what they had made at the sight of me retching like that; I wasn't sure what to make of it myself. I felt embarrassed.

"Get to work or get to bed," I bellowed up at them.

I still didn't know for certain who was behind Gelon's murder, but at least I was finally beginning to understand how the puzzle might fit together. The following day should bring confirmation of my suspicions. And if I was right, there was more than one traitor.

I could feel the red-eyed beast, tossing its head impatiently. After my strange turn in the yard, it was a relief to have him back.

The stables once more smelt as they should: I kept about a dozen horses at the villa now. Most were common geldings for the use of the household, but I had also stabled two of my own stallions there for the winter. The other two were at the palace. No one else was permitted to ride those black giants. They had been trained as warhorses, and in inexpert hands they were just as much a danger to their rider as to anyone within reach of their teeth or hooves.

I rode out at dawn. Ajax, Needle and Agbal followed behind on three of the geldings, although only Agbal seemed comfortable on horseback. Needle looked as though he had never even ridden before, so Agbal kept his own horse alongside Needle's until he got the hang of it.

We stopped at the palace on the way out of the city. I wanted to speak with Castor.

"Please take more men with you, Dion," Castor implored me, when I had explained where I was going and why. We were sitting in my office overlooking the exercise yard.

"No need, my friend," I replied. "What's the old fool going to do? He's hardly going to set his slaves on me. Besides, I don't want to scare him. Not unless I have to. But just in case something does happen, and I'm not back by tomorrow, you must finish this for me. Can I trust you to do that, Castor? For Gelon's sake?"

"But you still don't know for sure it was them, do you?" he said, looking at me uncertainly.

I shrugged.

"Perhaps not," I said. "But it all makes sense... So kill the three of them anyway."

He furrowed his brows and stroked his neat little beard thoughtfully.

"I'm sorry, but I won't do that, Dion," he said eventually.

I stared at him.

"What?" I said.

"Sorry, but I won't. We can't just start killing everyone we don't trust."

"What's got into you?" I demanded, more in surprise than anger. "You're a soldier, for fuck's sake. And you're supposed to be my friend."

"And you're supposed to be mine. What kind of friend would ask such a thing?"

"Then I'll make it a fucking order."

"That won't change my mind. But it would probably make me despise you."

That threw me. Castor had never spoken to me like that before; I don't think anyone had.

"How dare you?" I asked quietly.

"Oh, so do you want to add me to your list now?" he said.

"Of course I don't," I snarled.

"I'm pleased to hear it… But I still won't do it, Dion. Every noble in the city is shitting himself, trying to guess what's going on in your head. Where does this all end? With the murder of anyone you don't like? That's probably half the city. If that's the road you want to travel, I'm afraid you'll have to follow it without me. I'm honoured and more grateful than you can ever imagine for all you've done for me, but you ask too much. You'll have my resignation, of course."

"Don't be an idiot," I snapped.

"Then come to your senses, Dion. Hannibal could be at our gates in a few months. Just think about that, will you? Make yourself king when the old man dies, if that's what you want. Everyone is praying that you will. I'm certainly praying that you will. But do it to save the kingdom, for fuck's sake, not to rip it to pieces."

"They killed Gelon," I shouted.

"Maybe they did, maybe they didn't," he shouted back. "But I won't start murdering people for you, just in the hope they happen to deserve it."

We glared at each other.

"You're dismissed, Captain," I said finally.

He stood, saluted, and walked stiffly to the door.

"They all fucking deserve it," I muttered to myself, as he closed it behind him.

XXIV

THE OSTOMACHION

The gates by the Euryalus fortress open onto a dirt road, which twists its way through the hills towards Acrae, where our recently renovated summer home still awaited a visit from its new mistress. A few trees cling like broken-backed beggars to their precarious holds between the rocks, but otherwise only scrub relieves the landscape immediately behind the city. You must travel several miles inland before you round a high, jagged shoulder of stone, and abruptly find yourself on the edge of a dense forest. The highway skirts the treeline, but a little way beyond the stone shoulder, a spur road, barely wide enough for two carts to pass each other, splits off and leads into the gloom of the trees. We took the spur road. The trees closest to the edge of the forest are mostly pine, and of little value, but further in you come to the hardwoods, which are harvested to feed our shipyards. Rutted tracks run off the lane at erratic intervals, ending in distant clearings where choice trees have been felled. In the summer, the canopy is thick, but even though the branches overhanging our heads were now bare, the lane remained dark and oppressive under the winter sky.

Ajax, Needle and I had all put on our armour at the palace, and under my heavy woollen cloak I wore my captain's sword. Only Agbal appeared unarmed, although I imagine he had his knives hidden on him somewhere. Not that they seemed likely to be of much use in his hands.

Despite the precautions, I was not concerned for our safety. Absconding slaves sometimes sought refuge in this forest, but they would stay well clear of men in breastplates. Those who did not starve to death usually ended up slinking home to their owners after a few weeks. Providing they had not committed any other crime, returning slaves were almost always taken back in and commonly suffered no worse punishment than a facial branding. The key to making a success of slavery is not fear, but dependency. My slaves led far more comfortable lives than the freeborn poor of Syracuse, and were grateful for it. They had a roof over their heads, the certainty of regular meals, and even medical attention if they needed it. Only a fool would trade all that for the insecurities of freedom.

In any event, the only people we met in the woods that day were occasional wagon drivers, taking timber into the city. We had to follow the lane for two hours before we finally emerged from the tree line and saw the village of Cyros a couple of miles ahead of us. It was a place I had never previously had cause to visit, and it had nothing obvious to commend it. The village sat on the summit of a small hill, surrounded by an expanse of upland meadows. The road curled up round the hill and ended at the perimeter wall, which appeared to be fairly low and useless. The people here clearly relied for their security on the fact that they lived out of the way of anywhere, and on the way to nowhere.

About half a mile distant from us, between the woods and the village, stood a complex of farm buildings adjoining a fairly grand villa. It was probably the only substantial house for many miles in any direction; its owners must have led a very thin social life whenever they were in residence here.

We rode past the farm buildings to the main gates, which had been left open. I could see no porter on duty, which seemed curiously lax, but visitors here were probably few and far between. Half a dozen chickens wandered around the forecourt, pecking at whatever caught their eye. They squawked and scattered as our horses clattered across the cobbles.

We tethered the horses to a wooden railing that separated the forecourt from the adjoining meadows, and Ajax and I led the way up the short flight of steps to the main door. He hammered on it with his fist.

"Open up," he shouted. "Open up for General Dion."

We waited for a short while but there was no response.

I scanned the length of the villa's wall as Ajax banged on the door again. Like every other country house in the kingdom, its high, outward-facing windows were little more than slits, made too narrow for a man to climb through. I wondered if the slave had lied to me about his master's whereabouts. I decided I wasn't going to leave without finding out.

"Looks like you're up on the roof again, Needle," I said, and gestured with my thumb.

"Yes, sir," he sighed. He unfastened his sword belt and laid it on the ground.

Ajax braced his back against the wall and locked his fingers together. A moment later, Needle was standing on his shoulders, grasping the overhang. I put my hand under one of the little man's sandals and pushed it up, locking my elbow to give him a higher footing. I felt the pressure increase on my palm as he nimbly swung his other leg onto the tiles and then he was out of sight. Ajax picked up Needle's sword and we took a few steps back, to see him perching near the edge of the shallow-pitched roof like a cat. Ajax threw him up the sword. He drew it and tossed the scabbard and belt back down, then scampered up and disappeared over the ridge.

"Agile little bugger, isn't he, sir?" said Ajax.

"Rather him than me, Sergeant," I muttered. I've never been much good at climbing, and I have no head for heights.

I drew my own sword and Ajax did the same. Agbal looked at us both nervously.

"You'd better stay with the horses," I said, and smiled reassuringly. The boy would probably only get in the way if there were a fight, although I still doubted it would come to that. If our host intended to ambush us, the woods were the obvious place to have done it, not his own home: there could be no protesting his innocence if we were attacked here. But then it struck me that perhaps he no longer cared a fig for his own future, providing he ended mine, and I began to wonder whether I shouldn't have brought more men with me after all.

We waited silently for a minute or two until we heard the muffled clattering of the bolt being drawn back on the inside. The door swung open and I strode through into the entrance archway with Ajax a step behind. My ankle hurt, but I had no intention of letting it show.

Needle stood aside for me as I entered, his own sword in his hand.

"Seems safe enough, sir," he said. "The place looks deserted."

"Then who bolted the door?" I grunted, and he bit his lip.

"Alright, let's take a look round," I said. I strode through into the wide, silent courtyard, with my two men flanking me. An old olive tree stood at its centre, and I noticed a well in one corner.

We didn't have to search for long.

Malmeides' father was in the marble-tiled bathroom that opened onto the courtyard. He lay beside his wife in the red water. The knife they had used to open the veins of their wrists rested on the lip of the bath.

I sheathed my sword and sat down on a stone bench between the two little piles of neatly folded clothes. Their sandals had been left side by side in a tidy row just under the bench. I stretched my legs out, crossed my arms and sighed. This wasn't what I had wanted.

Ajax and Needle stood silently nearby, waiting for orders.

"The slaves may be hiding somewhere," I said eventually. "See if you can find them. Bring them to me."

The two of them ran off, and left me to my thoughts. I wondered if the couple in the bath deserved this end. They might have lived another twenty years in happiness, had their lives never intersected with my own. I don't know why the sight of their corpses troubled me. I have none of the refined sensibilities of men like Castor or Leander. I have sent many people to their graves with whom I had no particular quarrel, and it has never cost me any sleep. But although the dead man and woman were certainly my enemies, I would have spared their lives, for some reason that I still cannot entirely understand.

After a few minutes, I noticed Agbal had ventured into the courtyard. He stood near the olive tree peering around nervously. I called him over and he gawped at the bodies.

"What a fucking mess, Agbal," I said sadly.

He looked at me and seemed to understand.

"I'm sorry, Master," he replied.

"You'd better go and water the horses. There's probably a stable yard round the back. We'll be leaving soon."

Ajax and Needle reappeared a short while later, to report the house was empty. Perhaps the slaves had absconded in terror at the prospect of my arrival. Or maybe, I thought, their master had told them all to leave, when the cross-eyed former camp slave, who had once belonged to the family's only child, had returned to confess that I still lived.

I gazed sadly at the two bodies in the water. Malmeides' parents looked exactly the same in death as I remembered them in life. The wide, unblinking eyes in their angry ferret faces still seemed to be staring at me accusingly.

It was dark by the time we got back to Euryalus, and we had to wait at the foot of the citadel for the gates to be opened for us. Once inside the city walls, the road weaves across the rocky plateau of Epipolae, past the Labdalum fortress. Several hundred small fires had already been lit in the makeshift camp beside the fortress. There had been over fifteen thousand people in the camp in the immediate aftermath of the destruction of Upper Tyche but now only three or four thousand were left. The rest had been quickly reabsorbed by the city: its intestinal coils of alleyways and backstreets seemed to have a greater capacity to digest the poor than we had realised.

The lights of Syracuse twinkled in front of us as we reached the edge of the plateau and began to descend the long slope to Neapolis. To our left, where most of Upper Tyche should have been, there was only a pool of darkness. Little progress had been made on removing the deep carpet of charred debris that covered the district. By day, sooty-faced women and children picked through the wreckage, searching for anything that could be salvaged and sold, while the remaining men of the Epipolae camp loaded up carts with rubble. They worked despondently and without energy. It looked as though it would take years just to clear the area.

When we reached the isthmus, I sent Agbal into the palace to tell Castor what we had found at Cyros. Ajax, Needle and I continued on to the villa. We rode around the back of the compound to the stable block, where Ajax and Needle unsaddled their own horses, while the little groom tended to mine. The boy seemed to have no fear of the stallion. As I dismounted, he held out a handful of barley, and the huge beast nuzzled it gently off his palm.

"What's your name, boy?" I asked.

"Perdix, Master," he whispered timidly. "My mother was Callidora, the washerwoman."

I vaguely recalled her. She had died of a fever a few years previously.

"She was a good woman, Perdix... Do you like looking after my horses?"

He nodded enthusiastically. I smiled and ruffled his hair.

"Good lad... Alright, off you go now."

He grinned happily and led the stallion away by its bridle.

Perdix would probably grow old in my household, and he would continue to be fed and housed when he could no longer work. If he had children of his own, they would enjoy the same security in their turn. Many of my slaves could boast of several generations of forebears who had lived and died in my family's ownership. We had to be careful about inbreeding, of course, and so when Perdix reached puberty, my steward would probably move him to one of the country estates. If he grew into a vigorous young man, we might even arrange some suitable couplings for him. Most of the noble families aimed to breed at least a quarter of their slaves themselves, to maintain a core of high-quality stock, and notably strong and healthy male specimens were sometimes passed around our households, in exchange for stud fees.

I emerged from the stable block tired, stiff and saddle-sore. But at least my ankle seemed better: keeping the weight off it by spending most of the day on horseback had probably helped. Someone must have alerted Vita to my arrival, because she came running across the yard and tearfully threw her arms around my neck. I had only spent a day in the countryside, but from the warmth of her welcome, you might have thought I was a returning Argonaut. I lifted her off her feet and swung her happily through the air.

I rose early the following morning, disentangling myself from Vita's arms as gently as I could. Despite our lovemaking, I had slept poorly, waking intermittently to turn my choices over and over in my mind, before dozing off again with nothing resolved.

I dressed in the gloom of the dawn and went down to the study. For the sake of respectability, there used to be a lattice screen in the corner, behind which my mother had sat when conducting her business negotiations. I am told the effect was quite unsettling. I had ordered it to be burnt. I had brought my collection of weapons back from the palace and they now lay on display on a marble table in the centre of the huge room. I suppose it was an attempt to mark the space as my own, like an animal leaving its scent, but I felt a trespasser, nonetheless. The study had been strictly off limits when I was a child. It was decorated with frescoes of laughing men and boys, presumably celebrating something, although I had no idea what and had always found their faces a little sinister. To my sisters and me, the room had been a forbidden temple, where nervous strangers went to worship the cold, mysterious goddess who was apparently our mother.

I settled myself at the desk and wrote two short notes. The first was to Archimedes, inviting him and Chrysanthe to the villa the following afternoon. The second letter said much the same thing, and was addressed to Thraso.

I thought long and hard about the third note before I wrote it, but in the end, I swallowed my misgivings and my pride, and invited my mother too. Only a fool goes to a dogfight and leaves his meanest dog behind.

I had informed my unusual assortment of relatives that I wished to discuss a family matter, which was true up to a point, although each of them could hardly fail to intuit the real reason I had summoned them. The whole city had been holding its breath since Gelon's death, waiting to see what I might do, and in my mind, the attempt on my life had finally brought matters to a head. I was convinced that whoever had arranged Gelon's murder had also used Malmeides' parents to try to kill me. The same people were probably behind the attack on my mother as well, although I still couldn't understand why they should have needed her dead too.

There were three men I suspected above the rest, and they would be the first to die. But I would not stop there. Castor had been right about that, clever fellow that he was: this was about more than just avenging Gelon. I would keep my promise to Hieron and put Hieronymus on the throne, but I would see to it that he was my creature and no one else's. It had apparently fallen to me to try to save Syracuse from Hannibal, and I certainly didn't want to have to worry about my enemies scheming behind my back. I would start with a purge of the Royal Council, but I had not forgotten that petition with the seals of over fifty of my own former officers on it. Hercules had cleaned out the Augean stables by diverting a river. I would clean out our own stinking city with a torrent of noble blood.

After all, I was the heir of Dionysius. My family had never been known for its squeamishness.

*

I told Vita over breakfast that my relatives would be visiting us the following day.

"Maybe you'll finally get to meet Archimedes' wife," I said, as Alpha set out a plate of fruit beside me. "If she comes, you will be kind to her, won't you? My mother has always snubbed her. They've never even met, apparently."

"Of course, Husband," she replied with a smile. "I think it's a lovely idea that you are bringing us all together."

"We'll use the study, I think. You should be there to greet everyone, but there is no need for you to stay once they've all arrived."

"I beg your pardon?" she said.

"Vita, we will be discussing things of which you have no knowledge," I replied gently, "and which you would find very dull. These are not matters with which a sixteen-year-old girl should be troubling her pretty little head."

"What sort of matters are they, then?"

"Politics, mainly," I said.

She glared at me.

"I spent my entire childhood listening to my parents discuss politics," she snapped back. "I may not be as clever as your mother, Dion, but I am not a complete fool. I have ears and I hear what people are saying about you. This is about my future too, isn't it? And the future of our children? How can it be proper for you to discuss that with Archimedes' wife but not with me? Am I not part of your family?"

I sighed. I had to admit she had a point.

"But you are to say nothing unless I ask you a question directly," I told my wife sternly. "Understand?"

Vita pouted teasingly and blew me a kiss.

After breakfast, I dispatched slaves to deliver the letters and then returned to the palace as usual, accompanied once more by Ajax,

Needle and Agbal. In some ways, Agbal had become even closer to me than Alpha and Omega. He had recently started to develop a heavier musculature, as his arms and thighs thickened in the final transformation from boyhood to manhood. But despite his shapely body and handsome features, I continued to resist the temptation to sodomise him. Unless habituated to the purpose from childhood, treating a slave as a catamite tends to diminish his usefulness, making him either presumptuous or resentful. It can even lead to a reversal of the proper dependencies: many a moonstruck owner has been reduced to a social laughing stock by a pretty houseboy. But although I exercised restraint, I had fallen into the habit of taking Agbal with me wherever I went. He had come to understand my moods and if I had a complicated message to send, I could trust him to relay it accurately. With Needle and Ajax also in tow as my bodyguards, it seemed I had inadvertently acquired my own little princely entourage.

Xeno, who was now the division's adjutant, had recently sent Castor one of the new Guards companies that we had formed from reservists made homeless by the fire. Xeno had been knocking the rougher edges off them at Labdalum, and had judged they were now ready to be put through their paces at the palace. After Gelon's death, I hadn't wanted to dilute the palace garrison with unproven men, so rather than rotate out one of the experienced companies, I had retained all four of those and had converted the hayloft above the stables into a makeshift dormitory for the new recruits. They had only been at the palace for a week and Castor didn't yet know them well enough to risk putting them on duty. They spent all day training instead, as their physical fitness and weapon skills still fell short of the standards of the rest of the division.

When I got to the exercise yard, I found them setting out bales of straw for javelin practice under the direction of Leander, to whom Castor had given their command when the company was formed. They all came to attention and saluted as I approached.

"Good morning, sir," said Leander with a smile. "Will you be joining us?"

I rubbed my cheek thoughtfully. I needed to do something to try to clear the night's sticky cobwebs from my mind, and all that awaited me in my office was administrative work.

"I'll tell you what, Leander," I replied, "I'll take the drill myself, if you don't mind."

I made Ajax and Needle join in the practice. Ajax had a good arm, but Needle could never get the hang of it. Had he not been disadvantaged by his short reach, he might have been as dangerous as me with a sword or knife, but half the women of the city could probably have put a javelin to better use than him.

I sighed and clapped him sadly on the back as his first throw fell predictably short and wide.

"You're still releasing too early," I said.

"Sorry, sir," he replied miserably. "When Hannibal comes, perhaps I should just spit at him." He was a taciturn little fellow and that was about as long a speech as I had ever heard him give.

"Don't worry, Needle," I laughed. "If he comes, I'm sure we'll find a use for you."

I always enjoyed spending time with the men. Although those in the newly formed Guards companies were still strangers to me, I knew most of the rest by name and they seemed to regard me with a mix of awe and affection. I was the wellspring of the Guards' revived self-esteem and the subject of their drunken tavern stories. I might be a pitiless savage, but I was *their* pitiless savage. I had no doubt that when the time came, they would do whatever I asked of them without hesitation.

I was less sure of the Guards' officer corps. Jeering at the Royal Council during Hieronymus's parade had been one thing; it would be quite another to start cutting the throats of fellow citizens. Several of the lieutenants might feel constrained by friendships and family connections, but those, at least, were scruples that I could understand. I was more perplexed by Castor, who seemed to believe that killing a few corrupt and untrustworthy nobles was an immoral thing to do. Even if it was, that he should care more about the pursuit of virtue than about the preservation of our friendship was incomprehensible to me. Why on earth would such a sensible man chase after virtue, that most slippery and useless of rainbows? Are the gods virtuous when they visit plagues and famines upon us? Does virtue save anyone from plagues and famines? I blame the Athenians myself. As if democracy wasn't a bad enough idea, they had to corrupt us with their ethics too. These notions are like maggots, hollowing us out from within. Wolves eat sheep, and as far as I'm concerned, that's all there is to say on the subject of ethics. I suppose it might be some comfort for the sheep to reflect on the moral value of its sacrifice, but frankly, I'd rather be the wolf.

Leander's men threw in groups of ten, helping themselves to javelins from two heavily stacked handcarts that had been positioned at opposite ends of the throwing line. Every company of the City Guard was divided into three squads of forty men and I drilled each squad in turn, while their sergeants looked on in embarrassment.

Four lines of straw bales had been set up in the exercise yard at different distances, the furthest being eighty paces away. Those in the front row were for target practice; the other three rows were for ranging exercises. In battle, ranging a throw properly is far more important than getting the line right, because that is the skill that enables hundreds of individual weapons to be melded into a single, terrible one. A phalanx's roof of overlapping shields will withstand any number of arrows raining down from overhead; but those shields can sometimes be hammered in by concentrated salvos of javelins, reducing the entire phalanx to a chaotic, stumbling mass of vulnerable flesh. Arrows will not stop a cavalry charge either, but a well-timed javelin volley, thrown at the horizontal by men who know their business, will bring down most of the horses in the front rank of a charge and turn them into wildly thrashing obstacles for the riders behind.

"Prepare... Throw!" the squad sergeant bellowed. Ten javelins flew through the air towards the first row of targets, more than half landing ineffectually at seemingly random distances.

"You there," I barked. "The third man along. What's your name?"

"Demeter, sir." He seemed terrified. He had obviously heard some of the stories about me.

"Just look at how you're standing, Demeter. Your feet are all over the fucking place. Where should your left foot be pointing?"

"Straight at my target, sir." He sounded uncertain.

"Is it?"

"No, sir."

The sergeant clipped him round the ear and Demeter and the other nine men scuttled off to rejoin the rest of their squad. The next group stepped up to the line.

As I watched the men throw, I decided I would hold a dinner party at my villa, to which I would invite all those Guards officers of whom I was uncertain. And while we ate and drank and laughed together, their men would fall upon my enemies around the city. I would probably put Xeno in charge of the killing; I could certainly trust that old warhorse not to baulk at the task. By the time my dinner guests left the house, it would all be over. The ruse might well cost me Castor's friendship, but that would be up to him, and the others would fall back into line quickly enough. In their hearts, they would know a cull had been inevitable. New reigns always start off with a little spring-cleaning. In any event, everything would quickly be forgotten, once Hannibal came knocking on our door.

"Why don't you show us how it's done, sir?" shouted out a voice from somewhere behind me. All of Leander's men had thrown once already, and were now queuing up for their second attempt.

"Yes, sir, go on," said Ajax mischievously.

I shrugged.

"Very well," I said. "Distance or target, Ajax?"

"Shall we say target, General? But I reckon that front row is a bit too easy for you, sir. How about one in the second row instead? Say, the fourth from the left?"

I grunted. To hit a man-sized target at sixty paces is quite a challenge.

"Alright," I said.

"But if it's not too much to ask, sir, would you mind holding on for just a couple of moments, while Needle and I have a quick word with the sergeants?"

I couldn't help but be amused by his brazenness. I gazed at him as I considered it.

"You're a shameless turd, Ajax," I said eventually. "But if you must…"

I began to exercise my shoulders and neck, while Ajax, Needle and the three sergeants huddled round whispering to each other. They seemed to come to some agreement, and then the sergeants broke away to speak to their squads. One by one, they gave Ajax a nod or a wave and then he and Needle returned to my side.

"So, what odds are you offering, Ajax?" I demanded under my breath.

He grinned.

"Evens, sir, though I reckon they'd have been happy with two to one. It seems the new boys are all in for a bronze coin each. The greedy bastards just can't wait to take our money. And here's poor Needle with a wife and three kids to feed… I trust you won't let him down, sir."

"Can you even cover that bet, Sergeant?"

"Unfortunately, the other sergeants insisted on pooling it with us, sir."

I grunted again and walked over to the handcart.

Throwing a javelin properly requires a degree of expertise. The thrower loops a leather thong over the first two fingers of his hand, the other end of which is wrapped around the shaft of the weapon, close to its centre. He takes three running strides, landing with his left foot forward, and releases his hold of the shaft near the apex of the throwing arc, so that the last part of the throw is made using only the thong. The leather increases the length of his throwing arm by nearly a foot and, as it unravels, it makes the javelin spin. The device almost doubles the range over which the weapon can be used effectively, but every thrower must decide how best to wrap the thong to suit his own arm. Accuracy is greatest when it is wound around the exact centre of the shaft in a short pattern; but by using a longer pattern and wrapping the thong a little way behind the centre, one can increase the distance of the throw instead. The thrower must obviously also judge the angle of the javelin's trajectory. The flatter the angle, the greater the accuracy, but the price is a corresponding reduction in range. The art lies in striking the right balance for each throw between the power of one's arm, the angle of the trajectory and the manner in which the leather is wrapped.

The javelin hissed as it flew away from me, a sound they only make when they are spinning unusually fast. It struck its target a little high and to the left, about a foot off centre, and with sufficient force to leave only half the shaft protruding from the straw.

Behind me, I heard Ajax chuckling.

"Fuck me," muttered one of the new men quietly.

We had gathered in the study, seated in a circle. There was a long, embarrassed silence. Thraso shuffled awkwardly on his stool.

"But how can you be certain it was them, Dion?" he asked eventually.

Although I had just revealed my suspicions, I had not yet disclosed my intentions. We would get to those later. Even so, Thraso was clearly uncomfortable. He knew I was not a man to forego my revenge. He had a good idea of what I was planning; they all did.

I had dismissed the slaves so that we could talk freely, but no one seemed to want to say anything. Archimedes stared at the ceiling and chewed his beard. Chrysanthe perched on her stool with her hands calmly folded in her lap, eyeing me thoughtfully. She had taken the place next to Vita's. My wife had been as good as her word and had welcomed Chrysanthe warmly when she and Archimedes were shown into the room. They had chatted together like old friends while we waited for my mother to make her appearance. Naturally, she had been the last to arrive. She had embraced each of us in turn but had merely nodded haughtily to Chrysanthe, before sitting down in frosty silence. Chrysanthe seemed to have been neither surprised nor unsettled by my mother's behaviour. If anything, she appeared to find it mildly amusing.

"Can one ever be entirely certain of anything in this life, Thraso?" I replied. "They've been clever. And now that Malmeides' parents are dead, I admit I can't prove it. But it certainly explains everything, doesn't it?"

"Maybe it does," said Thraso. "But I'm not wholly convinced. Anyway, I don't see how we can solve this for you. But you probably knew that already. So why have you invited us all here, Dion? What is it you want from us?"

I considered my words carefully. I wished to appear reasonable. I wanted to carry them with me; I would need my family's help in the months ahead.

"It is intolerable," I said eventually, "to think that Gelon's murderers could escape justice. And you have to admit, don't you Thraso, that those three stink like rotting fish? I agree it's just about possible it may only have been two of them working together, but I'm pretty certain they were all in on it. So my intention is to kill them all… As to what I want from all of you, I will need your help and guidance. Yours especially, Thraso. When I have cleared the way, you must become First Man on the council. Between us, we have to make sure the kingdom is ready to face Hannibal."

"It doesn't sound like there will be much of a council left," replied Thraso coolly. "And what do you have in store for Hieronymus, if I may ask?"

"I promised Hieron I would protect him, and I shall. He can ride around in his chariot and play with his whores, but you and I will rule for him." At least for the time being, I thought to myself. Time would tell what should be done with Hieronymus.

Archimedes finally looked up. He spat his beard out of his mouth and snorted.

"536," he snapped.

"What? I'm sorry, I don't understand you, Great-uncle."

"536, Dion. There are 536 pure ways to solve the ostomachion. Or 17,152, if you include rotations, reflections and reversals. And you have not even begun to consider them all. Have you learnt nothing from Hieron?"

Chrysanthe put her hand on his knee.

"Calm yourself, Husband," she said mildly.

"Very well," I said. "So give me your 536 solutions, Archimedes, if it makes you feel any better. And if that is how many possible traitors there are, then I suppose I will just have to kill 536 people."

Archimedes pointed a bony finger at me.

"Kill, kill, kill! Is that your only answer to everything, you fool?"

"It is not something I particularly wish to do," I said calmly. "But it must be done, all the same. You say there are many possible solutions to Gelon's murder. I dare say there are. Perhaps the assassins were really evil spirits, sent up from the underworld. But can you actually give me any explanation that fits the facts better than mine? Can you?"

He glared at me, but he was clearly at a loss.

"No...? No, of course not," I continued. So much for all his brains, I thought. "I have never known a man as clever as you, Great-uncle, but you are over-complicating matters. Hieron himself told me that the time for being subtle is over, and that the time has come when we must be ruthless instead. That is why he gave me the army. I think you are simply trying to hide behind abstractions, because you would rather not confront realities. I asked you months ago to find me the killers. I've given you long enough. So, either explain why I am wrong, or admit that I am probably right."

Archimedes seemed about to say something, but then thought better of it.

"Bah!" he spat, and stuffed his beard back into his mouth.

I looked round their faces.

"You all want me to save you from Hannibal. Very well, I shall try. But this is the hard truth of it: those three very likely murdered Gelon. And whoever killed Gelon was working with Carthage. When Hannibal comes for us, I cannot risk being betrayed by men within our own walls. So if you want me to try to save the kingdom, I must first kill those men." I turned back towards my great-uncle. "How else do you expect me to protect you all, Archimedes? It seems to me you want me to serve you up a steak, without killing a cow."

"So, my dear," Chrysanthe said calmly, looking straight at me, "once you've killed those three, will that be the end of it?"

I hesitated. I had my list, and it was not a short one. I had already decided it would be much better to get everything over and done with in a single night.

It seemed my hesitation was answer enough.

"I see," said Chrysanthe.

"This is completely monstrous, Dion," Thraso exploded. His face had turned red. "You're doing Hannibal's work for him. You can't just murder everyone you've ever quarrelled with! I beg you, don't do this. You mustn't do it."

I smiled sadly.

"I'm sorry, but I'm afraid it must be done, Thraso. Don't you see? I have to break the nobles. You know what they're like. They only think of themselves. I must teach them to fear me more than the Carthaginians. It's the only way we'll be able to control them when the war comes to us... Look, I realise this is hard for you to swallow. You're a decent man. But I need you, Thraso. I can fight, but I cannot govern. I will see to our enemies, but you must see to the people."

"If I remember rightly, Dion," Thraso replied icily, "the second King Dionysius tried to break the nobles too. So tell me, how did that work out for him?"

"I am afraid Thraso is quite right," interjected Chrysanthe. "Once you start down this path, my dear, you will never be able to turn back. Have your little massacre, if you must: none of us can stop you. But do not delude yourself that you will be making either the kingdom or your own position any more secure. All you will accomplish is to set men against you who were previously your friends. It will be unending. Those whom you do not kill will unite against you, for fear they may be next. Your enemies will become like the heads of the hydra. Two more will appear for every one you cut off. You will merely find yourself fighting two wars instead of one." She smiled at me sweetly and then, to my surprise, she turned to Vita.

"Tell me, child, I'm curious, what is your opinion?"

Vita looked shyly at me and I nodded curtly.

"Husband," she said timidly after a moment, "perhaps it isn't necessary to kill anyone immediately? Why not wait to see how things work out when Hieron dies? You can always kill them later, if you still think it for the best. It seems to me that the trouble with killing people is that, if you ever come to regret it, you can never make them alive again."

"What a clever girl you've married, Cousin," said Thraso quietly. "You should listen to her."

This wasn't going at all as I had hoped. I sighed.

"So, what do you think, Mother?" I asked finally, relieved that I had decided to invite her to join us. Perhaps she would be able to talk some sense into them all.

She didn't answer at first. Instead she turned to look coldly at Archimedes and then at Chrysanthe. Chrysanthe met her gaze evenly, without blinking.

My mother's jaw hardened. Having finally deigned to be in the same room as my great-aunt, she no doubt felt entitled to a rather more ostentatious display of grovelling than Chrysanthe seemed willing to provide. But to my surprise, she decided to let it go. She merely turned her head away, and directed her gaze at me instead.

There was a moment of silence as she considered her response.

"Frankly, Dion," she said finally, "I am far from certain that you have the clarity of purpose to follow the path of your ancestors. The mere fact that you seem to require our approval suggests you may not... By all means make yourself king, or king in all but name, if you believe you are man enough. But the crown is not some weapon, to help you take revenge for the past. If you want it, you must put all that aside. Forget Gelon. Everything you do must serve the future alone. You must either play this game cleverly, or not play it at all."

"And what exactly do you mean by that, Mother?"

"Very well, then. It seems I must spell it out, as usual… Let the people eventually thrust power upon you, instead of seizing it for yourself. You should seem reluctant, not eager. That will make it much harder for others to oppose you. If you wish, I can help with that; I dare say the goddess would be happy to provide the kingdom with a useful hint or two. Let the council flap and flounder for a while, till the people are quite sick of it. Bide your time for now, and build your position. Make certain of your friends, and kill no one, at least not yet. That is always a last resort. The slave woman is right about that much, at least."

She cast a disdainful glance at Chrysanthe.

"So," she resumed after a moment, "if you believe these three men are traitors, then force yourself to smile, and use them to your own ends. Turn Hannibal's own weapons against him. As to the other nobles, the skill in managing those in your power, Dion, is always to leave them with rather more to lose than you have already taken from them. That way, they become inclined to appease you, instead of trying to resist you… That is how Hieron did it, at least. You, of all people, should appreciate that… Anyway, that is all I have to say."

She rose to her feet and smoothed down her dress.

"But now I am afraid I have some matters at the temple that require my attention… Thank you for your hospitality, Vita, my dear. It is such a pleasure to see how you have made yourself at home in this house."

Perhaps Hieron should have made her our general, I thought, as I watched her glide imperiously from the room.

That night, my sleep was troubled. I dreamt I was standing alone, wearing my helmet and clutching my battle sword of Seric iron, at the exact centre of a circular garden. Everything was grey: the bushes, the grass, the flowers, all were shades of grey. It was night and the garden seemed to be floating in the sky. I could see the stars above, but around the edges of the circle, there was only darkness. Every time I tried to move from my position, the entire garden began to tilt alarmingly, threatening to send me tumbling and sliding off the edge. No matter in what direction I moved, I was always forced to skip back hurriedly, to try to level the swaying ground again. I awoke to find my sheets damp with sweat, and Vita shaking my shoulder.

I didn't leave the house for several days. I practised my swordplay with Needle and Ajax, chopped firewood that we didn't need for the kitchens, and bellowed at the slaves. In the end, I just stayed in bed, contemplating my future. Ever since Gelon's death, something had been slowly changing within me. The beast was becoming hungrier and darker. I could no longer even be certain that he was my friend.

Castor and Theodotus both called by, but I refused to see them, so Vita told them I had a fever. On the fifth day, Vita sent a slave to fetch Thraso over. I was lying naked on the bed, staring at the ceiling, when she brought him into our room.

"Dion, look, you have a visitor," she said gaily. "I'm afraid I have my Greek lesson, so if you don't mind, I'll leave you two boys alone... See if you can get him to eat something, Thraso."

As she closed the door behind her, Thraso waddled over and perched awkwardly by my side.

"So, Cousin, I see you're growing a beard," he said. "I'm afraid it really doesn't suit you."

"It's my metamorphosis," I grunted.

"Goodness. So what are you turning into? A sulking teenager?"

I snorted and smiled at him.

"Into myself."

"What a wondrous transformation. Although I'm sorry to have to say that you still look just as ugly as you did when you were someone else."

"All my adult life, Thraso, I've felt like some monster in a labyrinth, charging around in a rage, searching for the daylight. But now that I've finally found a way out, I'm not sure I should leave. I don't think people would like what they see."

"Ah! Now I understand this metamorphosis of yours, Dion. You're changing into a philospher. That's it, isn't it? It's a miracle! I shall sacrifice in the temples. The gods have transformed you from an occasional fool into a professional idiot."

"What a loving cousin you are."

"Well, let me give you some help. Your way out is just over there." He nodded towards the bedroom door. "No one's seen you in days. The city's already getting nervous. We need you, Dion. So once you've finished anguishing over your soul, kindly rejoin the world."

I narrowed my eyes to look at him closely. I had every intention of rejoining the world. But I wondered if my soft-hearted cousin might not come to regret it.

"Tell me, Thraso," I said, "do you ever wonder what the point of it is? In the end, we all just turn to dust and most of us are quickly forgotten. Will I be remembered, do you think?"

"Oh, my. A poet now, as well as a philosopher... The point, Dion? Why must there be a point to anything? We work, we eat, we make love, we sleep, over and over again, until we die. And then our children do the same. If we're lucky, maybe we can make the gods laugh a little in the process. And perhaps sometimes we can even get them to sit up and pay attention. That's the point. Now, get your backside out of bed, will you? Have a bath and a shave... And then why don't you go over to the palace and try to see him?"

He was right, of course. And so that is what I did.

It was Dinomenes who opened the plain little gate to the king's apartments. He smiled and saluted me and then nodded to Ajax and Needle who had accompanied me as usual; they seemed to know each other.

"I'm here to see the king," I said.

"I'm very sorry, sir," he replied awkwardly, "but I'm afraid that's not possible. Family only. Prince Hieronymus's orders, sir."

"I am family."

"Immediate family, I mean, sir."

"Listen to me carefully, my friend. I said I want to see him."

"I'm sorry, General, I really can't... But if you'd like, I can send a runner to Andranodoros or the prince to ask for permission, if you don't mind waiting, sir?"

"Let him in, Dinomenes. I'll take him."

It was Hannon, Gelon's slave. He stepped out into the passageway from one of the side rooms.

Dinomenes looked at him with poorly concealed distaste.

"Very well. As you wish," Dinomenes said. "Come on in, sir. But I'm afraid these two rogues will have to wait outside."

"Please follow me, General," said Hannon, and turned away. I wondered what sort of a slave could command men who refused to obey me.

"So I suppose you belong to Hieronymus now?" I said to him as we crossed the little garden.

"Not yet," he replied flatly. "I have always belonged to the king."

"Oh, I didn't realise... By the way, Hannon, there's something I've been meaning to ask you. The day the prince died... Why did you kill the man I'd blinded? He could have been questioned."

He stopped abruptly in his tracks in the middle of the lawn and turned to face me, fixing me with his strange, bulging eyes.

"I wonder, General," he said quietly, "if you fully appreciate quite what questioning a man involves? As it happens, I am the one they usually send for, when they want to be certain someone will answer a question truthfully. It took many years of training to acquire such skills. I was just a boy when I started working in the dungeons of Babylon... Pray that no one you care for is destined to spend his final hours in my company, General."

I had no idea how to respond. I wondered if he was trying to menace me in some way.

"I imagine it is difficult work," I replied, narrowing my eyes.

"Yes... Difficult... But it was obvious there was no need for any great expertise in this instance. The man you blinded was already in great pain. I told him I would end it quickly, if he gave me a name."

"And did he? Give you a name?"

"Of course he did, General. He whispered it in my ear, and then I killed him, as I had promised. I have been thinking about that name ever since, because it makes no sense to me."

I raised my eyebrows but said nothing.

"It was your name he gave me, General. He just said 'Dion'. Nothing more. Do you have any idea what he may have meant by that?"

I stared at him, at a loss.

"What? Surely not...? But... I don't understand. Why would he give you my name? You can't possibly think...?"

"No, I don't think that," Hannon replied in his strange, flat voice. "I saw you weep." He pursed his lips and gazed back at me in silence for a moment. "Anyway, despite your fearsome reputation, General, I hear you are a kind master. Alpha and Omega certainly love you... Oh yes, we've spent many hours talking about you, first at Plymmerium and then here at the palace. Prince Gelon ordered me to befriend them. He wanted me to keep my eyes on you... And little Agbal practically worships you, of course. He says the weaker someone is, the kinder you are to them. That's unusual."

He looked around the courtyard and shrugged.

"Your slaves are lucky, General. I have no love for any of these people. But then, I suppose I know better than most men how far kings and princes will go to keep their crowns... In any event, I think that Carthaginian assassin was probably just trying to make trouble for us, right to the very end. I am glad I did not let him live to be questioned further... Now, I had better take you to the king."

I was too shaken to say anything more. Hannon led me silently through several rooms and down a dark corridor. Two men of the Royal Watch flanked a door at its far end. As we approached, the door opened and Andranodoros and Hieronymus walked out. Andranodoros's arm was round the boy's shoulders.

The prince glared at me.

"What's he doing here?" he demanded.

"The general wants to see the king, Your Royal Highness," replied Hannon. "He insisted. I did not think it wise to refuse."

Andranodoros looked at me and smiled sadly.

"I'm very sorry, Dion, I'm afraid you can't. You're too late... I'm sorry to say the king died a few minutes ago."

I lay on a couch in my rooms in the palace, with my arm resting on my forehead, listening to the city bells toll for Hieron. Agbal stood silently by the door; I had left Ajax and Needle in the corridor outside.

In the council chamber, Andranodoros was drafting a proclamation, announcing the accession of Hieronymus to the throne of Syracuse. I had agreed to let him issue it in both our names; he thought it might help to calm the people if any speculation about my intentions could be laid to rest at once.

I doubted anything would allay their fears. After all, what hope could the people have, without Hieron to stand guard over them? Hieron the Wise, Hieron the Pitiless. It made little difference who would hold the reins of power now. Andranodoros, Thraso, me... We were all inconsequential men by comparison.

I still did not know for certain what I would have said to him, had I seen him one last time. I had pictured him lying withered and helpless on his bed, his tongue lolling out of the corner of his mouth; and I had imagined his icy blue eyes swivelling round to meet my face. I knew why Thraso had urged me to see him. He wanted me to take Hieron as my model. He must have hoped a final sentimental parting would tip my judgement in favour of moderation. He need not have worried. I had already resolved to keep my sword sheathed, at least for the time being.

I would go back to Plymmerium, I decided, and leave the city to Andranodoros and the toads. Let them scheme and plot against each other while the world turned black; I would not interfere. I had to prepare the army for war, even if I no longer knew quite what we would be fighting for. But I could not afford to wait too long. I would certainly have to act before Hannibal came calling.

Hannon was right: that assassin had obviously just been trying to make trouble. All the assassins must have been told to give my name if they were caught. In fact, they had probably been tricked into believing I really was behind the attack. Yes, that would have been the way to do it.

But for all their cleverness, I had still found the traitors out.

They would be the first to die, I told myself, as I lay on my couch. Andranodoros, of course. Naturally, I had suspected him from the first, but one question had continued to nag away at me and make me doubt my own instincts. If Andranodoros was guilty, I had kept asking myself, why had he been so insistent that the assassins should be captured alive?

Well, I knew the reason now. What a snake… He had already known whose name the assassins would give. To murder Gelon and pin the blame for it on me… I had to admire the neatness of it. The twist was worthy of Hieron himself.

Andranodoros must have realised that I was a threat to his ambitions as soon as I moved to the palace. That was why he had helped Zoippos try to break me over Malmeides. And at some point, he must have lured Zoippos into his plot, although Zoippos had probably been easy enough to persuade. For the sake of appearances, the two of them would no doubt make a big show of ruling together in their nephew's name, playing the part of concerned and loyal guardians.

But their hopes of implicating me in Gelon's murder had come to nothing, and while I lived, they would only enjoy as much power as I allowed them. So, at the temple, they had tried to get rid of me a second time. And they had hoped to throw everyone off the scent again, this time by using Malmeides' parents to do their killing for them. Zoippos must have been the one who had put his sister and brother-in-law up to that. That was how I knew he was in on it as well.

I wondered when they would try to kill me again, and how.

No doubt, once I had been disposed of, Andranodoros did not intend to wait too long before arranging for the great Adam's apple to cross the River Styx as well. At least I could sympathise with him there. Listening to Zoippos every day must drive anyone to murder or suicide eventually. But presumably silly little Hieronymus would never get to celebrate his eighteenth birthday either.

The guilt of Hieron's two sons-in-law had been easy enough to spot: I had known it as soon as that block of stone had crashed down on the temple steps. No one else stood to benefit sufficiently from my death to take the risk of attacking me. When you looked at it from that angle, it seemed obvious enough that it had to have been them all along. But I was rather proud of myself for having identified the third conspirator.

It had been the manner of Gelon's murder that had first set me thinking. Gelon's killers had been disguised as slaves. That was hardly a surprise; there was no other way for a dozen unknown Carthaginians to avoid attracting attention, especially when all our own freeborn Carthaginians had been expelled from the city. But where had they been hiding, until the moment came for them to strike? It's not as though they could have simply walked into someone's house. And if a conspirator had tried to pass them off as members of his own household, someone would certainly have noticed they had gone missing again, or might even have recognised their bodies.

It had taken me a while, but I had worked it out in the end. There is only one place in Syracuse where no one would question the arrival of a dozen new slaves, and where they could be concealed from sight so effectively that none of our own citizens would ever be likely to encounter them. The quarries. And the quarries were run by Woodpecker, Gelon's son-in-law, a man whom Gelon openly despised and who had probably hated him in return. Money was all that Themistos cared about; being given control of our public works in Archimedes' place must have been his pay-off from

Andranodoros. Archimedes would never have taken a bite of the apple, but after a few years in that job, Woodpecker would probably be as wealthy as me.

Andranodoros, Zoippos and Themistos: all three of them had married royal women. Like woodworm, they had burrowed their separate ways into Hieron's family, and together, they had devoured it from within. But they would all receive my answer soon enough. My family may have persuaded me to stay my hand a while, but they had not persuaded me to change my course. I owed Gelon that much, at least…

My thoughts were interrupted by a knock on the door. I turned my head to watch Agbal open it slightly and exchange some words with whoever was outside.

"No. I don't want to see anyone," I shouted over to him.

He turned towards me, a look of complete bewilderment on his face.

"Master, I think you will want to admit this man."

"Really?" I grunted sceptically.

"Yes, Master, I really think you should see him."

"Very well," I sighed.

Agbal opened the door wide. The man who strode confidently into the room was tall and burly. He wore a sword and breastplate and a long black cloak, and in the crook of his arm he held a black-plumed helmet.

"Hello there, General," he said with a grin. "How have you been keeping, then?"

I sat up and stared at him in astonishment.

"What the fuck?" I said. "Dionysius?"

"Actually, General," replied my half-brother, "it's Lieutenant Dionysius, if you care… Nice crib you've got here… Anyway, sorry to be disturbing you, but I reckoned it's probably time you and me had a little chat…"

This concludes the first bundle of Dion's scrolls.

EPILOGUE

THE FOURTH FRAGMENT

*L*ogon didonai is what our tragedians call it, this compunction to explain, which accompanies the final blood-soaked expiation of our sins. But I fear my city's expiation is very far from complete. Gelon's death will not be the end of it. The consequences of my actions twenty years ago continue to cascade through time, and now seem to be accelerating and gathering force. I dare not think how many lives the landslide may yet come to claim, before its power is eventually exhausted. My own perhaps will be among them. And so, while I still can, I must explain: *logon didonai*.

The day after Gelon's funeral, the king summoned me to the palace. Though it was midday when I arrived, the room into which I was shown had been shuttered up and was poorly lit by lamps. The only other person present was Hannon, the slave.

Hieron was in a pitiable state, his mind unfocused and his mood uncertain, swinging wildly between despair and rage. He brushed aside my words of sympathy. The only comfort I could offer him, he shouted, would be to find him the traitor. Hannon would do the rest. Of course, I knew enough of Hannon to understand that whatever justice the king intended to dispense, it would be neither swift nor merciful. All the same, I swore that I would do as my cousin commanded. And so, as things have turned out, I have finally contrived to betray Hieron, too.

The knot proved surprisingly easy to unravel. Over dinner that evening, Chrysanthe and I recalled various nuggets of information, each insignificant in itself, but which, when taken together, appeared extremely curious. It was the numbers that tipped me off. I have always had an eye for patterns of numbers: a dozen assassins; a dozen dead runaways; a dozen horsemen. Although it seemed something of a long shot, I went to the slave pens myself the following morning, and had them show me their accounts.

I returned home in a daze.

When I had recovered myself, I dispatched my bodyguard Kleitos to the countryside, and I sent other men to all the city gates.

Unaccompanied slaves are not allowed either to enter or to leave the city without a permit, in the form of a wax tablet stating the purpose of their journey and bearing their master's seal. These tablets must be left with the sentries at the gates to prevent others using them; I suppose they are eventually wiped clean and recycled. My men brought back a dozen crates of wax tablets from around the walls, and I put my entire household to work searching through them. We soon found the ones that I had expected to find and, sure enough, we failed to find the ones that I had expected not to find.

It was not till the following day that Kleitos returned to report what he had discovered in the countryside.

Chrysanthe and I now knew more or less how it had been done, and that in turn told us who had done it. We even thought we understood why – although, in the event, it transpired we were quite wrong about that.

I was at a loss to know what to do; I could not sleep for two nights. In the end, it was Chrysanthe who suggested I should speak to Korinna.

And so, exactly a week after Gelon's death, I called on my niece at Delia's former house, where she was now living. I was shown into a bright and airy room overlooking the courtyard, which Korinna had evidently adopted as her study. She was working behind her desk at the window when I was shown in.

"This is a pleasant surprise, Uncle," she said, standing and forcing a smile. There were crow's feet round her eyes now, but to my mind, they only augmented her beauty, a tiny imperfection that made her look a little less like some marble idealisation of womanhood. We embraced stiffly and she led me over to a pair of couches where we made ourselves comfortable. A slave girl silently handed both of us cups of water, before Korinna dismissed her from the room with a casual flick of her hand.

"I hope I'm not disturbing you," I said.

"No, not really. I was just composing an announcement. The people do seem so very frightened. Well, I suppose we all are now. Anyway, I thought it might be helpful to let the city know the goddess came to me in a dream, with words of reassurance... All will be well, she is still watching over us, Gelon will be avenged, and so on and so forth." She smiled thinly. "So, what can I do for you, Archimedes?"

"Well, I'm afraid Gelon is the reason I'm here. But I don't know quite where to begin... You see, Korinna, I think I know what happened. But I don't know what to do about it. That's why I thought I must speak to you."

"I'm flattered, Uncle. You've never asked my advice about anything before. It goes without saying I'll help in any way I can."

"Thank you." I sighed. "So, let me explain. You probably don't know this, my dear, but at the time of the Pachynus raid, Dion caused a bit of a stir when he saw some horsemen riding in the hills outside the city. At the time, the fear was they might have been a scouting party for a Carthaginian army. But of course they weren't, because there was no army. I think they were the assassins. I think the whole raid was just a smokescreen to land those men, and to create so much chaos that they would be able to travel north safely. After all, with so many people fleeing the area, who was going to bother about a dozen men riding through the hills?"

"Goodness," she said, "that's quite a smokescreen, Uncle. If you're right, our enemies are certainly bold."

"Yes. But of course, getting the men ashore wasn't their only problem. After all, the assassins could hardly just knock on the palace gates. They had to identify an opportunity to strike, and they had to lie low somewhere until that time came. If I'm right about Pachynus, they were in hiding for nearly six months. So someone must have been helping them."

"Do you know who?"

"Yes, I believe I do. But our enemies aren't just bold, Korinna; they are also clever. You see, thanks to Dion, we sent men in search of those riders, and our scouts eventually found the bodies of a dozen slaves in a remote valley. Naturally, we put two and two together and thought no more about it. But I fear the equation was rather more complex than we realised…"

"What do you mean?"

"Well, I think whoever was helping the assassins bought themselves a dozen slaves on some pretext or other, making sure that at least one of them had a punishment brand. Then they had them escorted to that valley. The traitor probably also had someone already waiting at Pachynus, to meet the assassins and guide them to the same spot. When the assassins got there, they killed the slaves and assumed their identities. Or maybe the slaves had already been killed by their escorts. I don't know. But in any event, should anyone decide to follow the trail of the horsemen, they would eventually discover a dozen bodies, one of them immediately identifiable as a slave with a history of absconding. That end of the thread would be neatly tied off. Meanwhile, a dozen slaves would eventually arrive wherever they were expected, for whom a bill of sale could be produced if necessary."

Korinna raised her eyebrows.

"Yes, that's undeniably clever, if that's what happened." She folded her hands in her lap and pursed her lips as she thought it over.

"So, how can I be of help?" she asked after a moment. "Would you like me to make some discreet enquiries as to whose husband might have bought a dozen new slaves at around the time of the Pachynus raid?"

"No, my dear, that isn't necessary. I've already been to the city pens myself and looked through their records. And that is why I am here. Because their accounts show a job lot sale of a dozen slaves a few days before we learnt of the raid. One of them had a punishment brand..." I took a deep breath and bit my lip. "And it was to Dion that they were sold."

Korinna stared at me, her mouth slightly open.

"I don't understand, Archimedes... What are you suggesting? Surely that must be some sort of coincidence?"

"I fear not. But let me continue. You see, at Gelon's funeral, Dion told me that he had been renovating the house at Acrae. I imagine that is what those slaves were supposedly for. It was at Acrae that the assassins must have been hiding all that time."

"But that's preposterous, Uncle. You can't possibly imagine that Dion had anything to do with it?"

I smiled sadly.

"No, of course not. Not for a moment. After all, he tried to save Gelon's life, at quite some risk to his own. To suspect Dion would require crediting him with great subtlety of mind, and I think you and I can agree that is a quality of which he has never displayed any particularly compelling evidence."

"So, who then?"

"Why, you of course, my dear. You. It was you who arranged Gelon's murder, wasn't it?"

Her eyes widened, but she managed to retain her composure. I took a sip of water. I noticed my hand was trembling slightly.

"Yes," I continued, "the clerk at the slave pens remembered you arriving with your old steward and picking out your victims yourself. You made quite an impression... To kill a prince is no easy matter, but when you learnt of Dion's wedding, you finally knew where Gelon was likely to be on a particular day in the future. And, quite fortuitously, you also had a perfect hiding place for the killers, because it was you whom Dion entrusted with the renovation of the house at Acrae. So you sent word to Carthage, and in due course they sent you a team of assassins. No doubt the Carthaginians were already preparing a convoy for Hannibal when someone had the bright idea of diverting it to Pachynus… Tell me, Korinna, when exactly did you decide to betray us all?"

"Do you know how deranged you sound, Uncle? You look exhausted. Perhaps a lack of sleep has muddled your wits. No one could possibly take such an absurd accusation seriously."

"You think not?"

She drew her eyebrows together.

"Look, it's true that I bought some slaves for Acrae. But unless Dion has sold them on or moved them elsewhere, they should still be there."

"No, they are not, I'm afraid. I had a man go to the estate to take a look around. He says the house seems to have been repainted recently and the gardens put into good order, so the Carthaginians obviously made themselves useful, presumably to avoid arousing any suspicion among the locals. But the place seems to be deserted again. There was no sign even of a caretaker. I imagine that when the assassins arrived at the villa, they murdered him and his family as well."

"Go home and get some sleep, Archimedes. In the morning you will realise what a fool you are making of yourself. If those slaves are really missing, then I would imagine they have simply run off. Slaves do that sometimes, you know. I suppose it's possible they killed the caretaker. Perhaps they killed him in some quarrel and then panicked."

"But they didn't run off, did they, Korinna? Because I found their permits, granting them access to the city on the day of Dion's wedding. He was bringing in slaves from all his estates, so I suppose it was easy enough for you to make sure the new men at Acrae were summoned too… But I could find no permits to record their departure. They entered the city, but it seems they have not yet left it. So what has become of them? Can you explain that? Incidentally, is that the real reason your old steward had to die before Dion's wedding day? Because of the risk he might notice that the men from Acrae were not who they were supposed to be…? Anyway, do you wish me to ask Dion's new steward if he can produce these mysterious vanishing slaves? Or will you now abandon this pointless pretence?"

Korinna's eyes didn't leave mine. Behind the sculpted façade, that wonderful, athletic mind of hers must have been sprinting for all it was worth. Eventually she snorted lightly.

"So, what do you intend to do with this theory of yours, Uncle?" she asked me coolly. "Are you going to run to Hieron with it? How very typical of you that would be."

The effort to suppress my emotions had drained the last of my reserves. My eyes began to water and suddenly I found myself choking for air. Korinna watched me impassively.

I took a few deep breaths. I had come to her home in the hope that confronting her might help me decide what to do. I cradled my head in my hands and pictured my sweet, dead sister's face. How poorly I had served her child. I wondered if the gods were visiting some sort of justice on me, for my neglect of my niece. When all is said and done, I suppose I am a weakling. I knew there was no chance that her office might preserve her from Hieron's vengeance. My cousin wouldn't hesitate to pull down the whole temple to get to her, if that's what it took. And in that moment, I realised that the prospect of subjecting her to the ingenuities of Hannon was simply too much for me.

"No," I muttered after a while. "You are Dion's responsibility. He'll have to decide what to do with you now… But I just don't understand. How could you have done this, Korinna? You do realise it's all been for nothing, don't you? Dion doesn't even want the crown. This will break him when he hears of it. You've probably destroyed the kingdom and it was for absolutely nothing."

She smiled at me contemptuously.

"Is that what you think? That I did it for *him*? You old fool. Maybe Dion will take the crown, maybe he won't. Either way, it's poor consolation for me. I've never really been able to control him."

She took a sip of water. "No, I did it for Dionysius, of course. And for Apollonius too, I suppose… For the husband I had, and for the one I never had."

I gawped at her.

"Oh yes, that's right, Archimedes," she jeered. "Not so clever now, are you? Two men wanted to make me their queen. And Hieron killed them both… So I killed his boy."

And then she tilted back her head and spat at me. She actually spat.

"You're all contemptible. You've all sold yourselves to Hieron. Even my own son. And now you come here and presume to sit in judgement on me? How dare you? Anyway, you just go ahead and tell Dion whatever you like. Go on, Archimedes. Let's see if you've got the nerve… After all, I'm sure he would be fascinated to learn how you were the one who betrayed his father."

An hour later, I found myself stumbling back towards my own house. At one point, I had to ask a baker if I could make use of the chair on which he was sitting outside his shop. The sight of me slumping down onto it unnerved Kleitos sufficiently for him and one of his men to break from the crowd and come running up to ask if I was alright.

"No," I said, looking up with unfocused eyes. "Could you kindly find me a litter or something? I don't think I can walk any further."

When I eventually arrived home, I found Chrysanthe in the garden. I lay down on the grass and rested my head on her lap and she stroked my hair while we talked.

I told Chrysanthe everything Korinna had eventually confessed to me. I described how my niece had gazed at me triumphantly. How she had been unable to resist explaining every twist and turn of her plot. How she had positively gloated about it.

"Unfortunately," Korinna had said, "I only found out quite recently that it was you, Archimedes, whom I have to thank for being a widow."

"Who told you?" I asked numbly.

"Apollonius, of course. Hieron used to tell his wife everything. And the stupid woman passed on most of it to her brother. I don't know how you managed to steal those letters from our house, Archimedes, but Apollonius told me you were the one who went running to Hieron with them." She sneered. "You had no idea about Apollonius and me, did you?"

"You were... intimate?"

"What do you take me for? A common whore? Of course not. But he was certainly infatuated with me. Even a woman my age can be quite alluring, you know, especially when she has the glow of wealth behind her. At first, all he wanted from me was a loan. The poor man was never very good with money. But I saw my chance. I had him at my feet in no time, like some silly moonstruck teenager. I think perhaps he really did fall in love with me, as much as with my silver. Either way, it was quite comical. I took to dropping a few coins in his pocket, just enough to keep him afloat for a month or two, so that he would have to keep coming back. I wanted him in my power, not free from it. But as to everything else, I told him no, not until Gelon was dead. He would have to wait till then. He had to prove that he was offering me more than just a childish fantasy. I was hardly going to jump into his bed until I knew it might be worthwhile."

I groaned.

I should have seen it.

Apollonius hadn't waited. He had approached Dion and tried to hint at his interest in a marriage. He had probably grown desperate for the dowry. Only Dion had entirely mistaken his meaning and, less than half an hour later, Apollonius was dead. My niece was right: I was a fool.

"How on earth did you become such a monster, Korinna?"

"A monster? A *monster*...? Hieron steals a crown to which he has no right, and you adore him. I try to take it, and you call me a *monster*?

Why? Because I'm a woman? I might have ruled Syracuse through either Dionysius or Apollonius. And I would have ruled just as well as Hieron. I am every inch that creature's equal. After all, in the end, I outwitted him, didn't I? And what does my own uncle conclude? You call my ambition monstrous, and Hieron's noble. You hypocrite."

"So was it you who put them up to it then, Korinna? Was it you who made traitors of both Dionysius and Apollonius?"

She stared at me icily.

"Was Hieron any less of a traitor when *he* took the crown? The House of Dionysius had more right to it than he ever did… But since you ask, no, I was responsible for neither of them. Dionysius hardly needed any encouragement from me. And Apollonius was already in contact with Carthage when he first came my way. But I made him swear to tell the Carthaginians nothing about our understanding. There was always a danger that someone in Carthage might betray him… It seems I was right about that, at any rate. I had an uneasy few days, I can tell you, when Hieron killed him. Of course, I could see exactly what had happened. I knew the Carthaginians certainly weren't behind it. All that nonsense with the cushion. Was that your idea, by the way, Archimedes? Do I have you to thank for Apollonius, as well as for Dionysius?"

"I had nothing to do with it."

She snorted.

"Well, anyway, I wasn't going to let matters rest there, was I? When Dionysius was killed, I had been obliged to let it go. The family was too weak; I was impotent. The children were shackles around my ankles. But circumstances are rather different now, aren't they? It has taken me twenty years, but I am not weak now. My tendrils sprout and coil everywhere. And when Hieron also killed Apollonius…" Her lip curled in a bitter smile. "Twice that man cheated me of my dreams. Well, I was hardly going to stand by and watch his own come to fruition."

And so Korinna told me the rest of it.

*

An attempt on Hieron's own life my niece ruled out as being an altogether hopeless project. Given his age, the Carthaginians would gain nothing from the king's death that they were not anticipating imminently anyway. If they were to be enticed into helping her, the target must be Gelon. In any case, the murder of the prince would be a far more cruel and satisfactory revenge on Hieron. And she needed the Carthaginians to help her exact it. There was little hope of recruiting local men for the task, whose families would be within reach of Hieron's retribution.

My niece was shrewder in her choice of a Carthaginian go-between than Apollonius had been. She had been doing business with Nico's family for years, and after Nico had been driven out of the army by Gelon, she had little difficulty recruiting him to be her envoy.

Through Nico, Korinna informed the Carthaginians that she was contacting them on Dion's instructions. She told them that her son was prepared to usurp the throne himself on Hieron's death, and repudiate the alliance with Rome. That was her bait. It was seemingly of little consequence to her that this deceit would have put Dion himself in peril, had her plot been discovered. Her sole concern was to manipulate the Carthaginians into helping her take her revenge, and she was quite prepared to risk her son's destruction in the process. Nico enthusiastically testified to his own experience of Dion's goodwill towards their people, and the Carthaginians swallowed it all. The chance of making Syracuse their ally was too tempting to pass up. I have no idea what Nico must have made of Dion's furious reaction upon seeing him again; he probably concluded it was just a little bit of theatre for Hieron's benefit.

"I imagine it would amuse your great-nephew," interrupted Chrysanthe with a faint smile, "to know that the Carthaginians, no less than the Romans, are now hoping he will make himself our king."

"Perhaps so, my dear," I sighed. "And perhaps there's some comfort in the thought that the Carthaginians may soon be eating their own poison. They will find that all they have accomplished by killing our prince is to replace a cool and clever adversary with a murderous and feral one. Dion will not forgive them for Gelon's death, and I doubt Hannibal has ever had to fight anyone quite like Dion before."

"Yes, Husband," she chuckled. "I suppose it is some consolation to think that Hannibal himself may soon be joining that long and sheepish line of men, who have come to lament the day they ever agreed to do business with your niece… In any event, we certainly need a man like Dion now, to protect us from our enemies. But who, I wonder, will protect us from Dion? Anyway, please do continue. What else did Korinna tell you?"

But, by then, there was little more to recount. Although Hieron had ordered her to dispense with her bodyguards, Korinna had kept them on hand somewhere in the city. On the day of Dion's wedding, the Galatians were apparently mixing with the crowd on the street, disguised as slaves themselves. Their only task was to ensure that if any of the assassins were left behind, they would not live to be interrogated. In the event, they only had to cut one man's throat, which proved easy enough in all the confusion.

Three of the assassins managed to flee the scene, and as they were never found, it was assumed they had made good their escape by sea. In fact, they were led to a vacant house nearby, where Korinna's bodyguards killed them too. The corpses of the missing Carthaginians are apparently rotting in one of my sewers now. The only murderers who finally sailed home were the Galatians.

"Goodness, what a frightful mess," said Chrysanthe when I had finished. "You do realise, don't you, that you cannot tell Dion any of this?"

"You think we must protect Korinna?"

"We have a hold over her now, Husband, and she may prove of great use to us. When Hieron dies, it seems our kingdom's future will come to rest in Dion's clumsy hands. Perhaps Korinna will be able to help us control him. Besides, what choice do we have? Who knows what Dion might do if he discovers that his mother murdered his lover? We can hardly risk him putting the head of Athena's own servant on a spike. What on earth would the people think? I must say, it does all sound rather like one of those awful Sophocles plays, doesn't it? Anyway, you and I must try to stop this wheel of retribution from turning any further, or we may all eventually be broken beneath it."

"Hieron and Dion will both want a name soon, Chrysanthe. I don't know how long I can put them off."

"Play for time, Husband, play for time. But if we must eventually give them a name, then we will just have to think of one." She pursed her lips as she considered the possibilities. "Andranodoros is far too valuable, of course: we can't do without him. But I suppose we could always serve them up Zoippos? He's certainly dispensable... Anyway, let's hope it doesn't come to that..." She sighed. "All this killing, Archimedes. So very pointless. It achieves nothing in the end, except more killing."

"Yes, I suppose you're right."

"Of course I am. Now, leave everything to me. I shall ensure that there is enough evidence to incriminate Zoippos, should that eventually prove necessary. And I'd better go and see Korinna myself and arrange matters with her. Send her a note, would you, to let her know that it would be wise to receive me."

And so that is how we came to make our squalid pact with the killer of our prince. Chrysanthe returned from her first encounter with Korinna to report that my niece had once more threatened to inform Dion of my part in his father's death, if we disclosed her part in Gelon's. But Chrysanthe had laughed that off. As Dion had never even blamed Hieron for his father's execution, it seemed unlikely he would turn on me. In any case, my wife had asked Korinna, why should either of them want to break open this hornet's nest? An alliance to try to manage Dion was clearly now in Korinna's best interests, as much as our own. My niece could recognise a cheap deal when she saw one, and had sullenly agreed to cooperate.

So it seems there will be no reckoning for Korinna. She will probably die a rich old woman, still revered within the city she betrayed.

*

I put off Hieron as best I could, but he had also set his secretariat on the hunt and I had no means of controlling them. I was particularly concerned about Nebit. If any of the secretaries managed to sniff out the truth, I guessed it would be him. Who knows? Maybe he did. He was certainly on the right track. I heard he went to the Euryalus gate a few days after my own men, asking to see all the slave permits the sentries had recently collected. Perhaps the discovery that I had already taken them was sufficient to confirm his suspicions; in any event, for whatever reason, Nebit chose to drop his own investigations there. He never so much as mentioned the permits to me. I can only assume that his love for Dion persuaded him that it might be best to dig no further.

Hieron collapsed a few weeks after Gelon's murder, still none the wiser. I have been unable to see him since, which has at least relieved me of the burden of having to keep lying to him. In the isolated confines of his mind, he must be tormented by questions and suspicions. It is a cruel irony that a man who wielded power with such exquisite skill should finally be reduced to a state of total impotence. Men say the gods are merciful, but I say they are vicious.

Although Hieron can no longer press me for answers, Dion has continued to do so. My great-nephew now commands every spear in the kingdom and, what is more, those spears would willingly follow him into the crater of Etna if he called on them to do so. I fear I will be unable to prevaricate much longer. Only yesterday, Dion summoned his closest relatives to his house for a conference, and held my feet to the fire.

The incident that had prompted him to gather us together was an attempt on his own life by the parents of Malmeides. Dion seems to believe that this was connected to Gelon's murder and, by some peculiar logic of his own, has concluded that Andranodoros, Zoippos and Themistos must have been behind everything. But that was not the worst of it. It quickly became apparent that my great-nephew is disinclined to confine his bloodlust to those three, and is considering a general massacre of the nobles.

To my relief, Korinna upheld her part of our bargain, and joined with the rest of us in our efforts to dissuade him. Not for the first time in my life, I found myself giving thanks for my wife's wisdom. As yet, I do not know whether we have succeeded in talking Dion out of it, but I think Korinna may just have tipped the balance in his mind. I suppose we will have to throw him Zoippos soon, in the somewhat desperate hope that a single head may be sufficient to appease him. But then, one way or another, it looks like Zoippos is a dead man anyway.

The truth, of course, is much more straightforward than Dion imagines. The attempt on his own life was merely the final act of two decent and despairing people, trying to obtain some justice for their only child. I am quite certain that Andranodoros knew nothing of their scheme: he would never have permitted it. He may have no love for my great-nephew, but he is shrewd enough to have foreseen the likely outcome of such a reckless move. Had the attack succeeded, Dion's devoted men in the City Guard would almost certainly have leapt to the conclusion that Andranodoros and the Royal Council were behind it, and quite possibly Hieronymus too. All of them would have been lucky to outlive Dion by more than a few hours.

Zoippos, on the other hand, who was the uncle of Malmeides, may well have been involved in the nonsense at the temple. I doubt that nincompoop would have grasped the probable consequences for himself of Dion's death. But whether he was involved or not is of no particular importance, because neither is he. Far more troubling is the possibility that Dion's great friend Theodotos may have had foreknowledge of the attack: his wife was also related to Malmeides. I used to tutor Theodotus when he was a child, and always thought him a slippery little fellow. Chrysanthe and I will have to keep our eyes on him.

It only remains to explain the notorious attack on Korinna at Dion's house. This was, of course, a sham, arranged by Korinna herself, a fact she also proudly confessed to me – although that much Chrysanthe and I had already worked out for ourselves. She had seen how Gelon had faked an attempt on his own life, and had borrowed the idea. My niece apparently believed that, by stirring up the mob, she could force Hieron to let her succeed Delia. In this, I believe Korinna entirely mistook her man. Hieron may frequently have made use of the mob himself, but he couldn't have cared less for its opinion. He let her have the temple, because that is what he had always intended. In any event, the Tyche gangs were all firmly under Hieron's control, and they in turn controlled the mob. My cousin always saw to it that his men were well placed in the gangs.

All in all, the death of Korinna's poor slave woman appears to have served no purpose whatsoever.

Will Dion prove our salvation or our destruction? I cannot say. Between them – and with the help of Lepides – Hieron and Gelon trained my great-nephew to be their personal attack dog; but he is now a dog with no master, and whom he might choose to savage as he roams unchained through our city is anybody's guess.

The events that I have set down here are known only to three people: Korinna, my wife and myself, and we all have good reasons to take these secrets to our graves. I record them by way of a confession. *Logon didonai*. I failed in my duty to protect our kingdom, and now I find myself refusing my dying king and Gelon's angry ghost the justice they demand. Should some future generation find this history, let them know my shame.

HISTORICAL NOTES

I
EXTRACT FROM *THE HISTORIES*, BY POLYBIUS

... Hieron gained the sovereignty of Syracuse and her allies by his own unaided abilities, without inheriting wealth, or reputation, or any other advantage of fortune. And he was established king without putting to death, banishing, or harassing any one of the citizens. During a reign of fifty-four years he preserved peace for the country, maintained his own power free from all hostile plots, and entirely escaped the envy which generally follows greatness... And though he passed his life in the midst of the greatest wealth, luxury, and abundance, he survived for more than ninety years, in full possession of his senses...

II
THE LEGACY OF ARCHIMEDES

Nine of Archimedes' treatises survive, and they continue to astonish. Wherever he turns his attention, he seems to lay the foundations for entirely new fields of study.

In terms of technique, Archimedes made frequent use of infinitesimals (quantities that are not quite zero, but are smaller than any finite quantity). He did not invent the concept, but he extended it in a manner that anticipates the calculus by two millennia. No one was able to improve on the precision of his methods of discovery till the age of Leibniz and Newton. And at the extreme opposite end of the spectrum, he was also the first person in the western tradition to devise a notation system for immense values. Although Vedic mathematicians in India were dealing in large numbers much earlier, it was Archimedes who conceived and proved the elegant law of exponents ($a^n \, a^m = a^{n+m}$), which remains the essential building block of large-scale calculations. In effect, he created the mathematics of astronomy.

Archimedes himself made the first recorded attempt at a scientific astronomical measurement, by trying to compute the diameter of the sun. Given that he was dealing in miniscule differences between the tiniest of observed angles, without so much as a pair of sunglasses to help him, perhaps he can be forgiven for having got the answer wrong. Even so, his approach was remarkably sophisticated, allowing for the effects of solar parallax, and even taking into account the size of the human eye. It is consequently also the first known instance of psychophysics, the study of how our biology affects our grasp of reality.

In the field of geometry, he was the first person to compute π to a high degree of accuracy. The famous 22/7 approximation was in fact only the upper bound established by Archimedes: he proves that π is less than 3 1/7 but greater than 3 10/71. He went on to investigate numerous geometric quantities, from parabolic segments to the spiral named after him. Along the way, he dreamt up thirteen complex and yet regular polyhedrons, known as the Archimedean solids, each of which is so visually satisfying that it could arguably be said to jump the border between mathematics and art.

Archimedes' methods are as dazzling as his conclusions. To give a flavour of his ingenuity, in one treatise he turns to the principles of a fulcrum and lever to establish the ratio between the volume of a cone and the volume of its associated sphere. This application of theoretical mechanics to a problem that appears to be purely geometric is quite mind-bending.

It also happens to lead to a discovery of miraculous beauty. Take a sphere with a diameter of x. Now imagine a cone with a height of x and a diameter of x at its base. And now picture a cylinder, also with a height and diameter of x. These are the three most regular solids that can be derived from a circle. Archimedes shows that the cone has exactly half the volume of the sphere, while the sphere has two thirds of the volume of the cylinder, making the combined volumes of the cone and sphere equal to that of the cylinder. In other words, this family of solids is a three-dimensional expression of the sequence 1, 2, 3. It is almost enough to make an atheist believe in God.

Elsewhere, Archimedes deploys geometry to arrive at arithmetical solutions. Indeed, it may well have been through some geometric method that he became the first person to provide a precise estimate of the square root of 3, although no one knows for certain quite how he did it. Equally tantalisingly, the surviving fragment of his treatise on the ostomachion puzzle suggests that he had started to develop some fairly advanced combinatorics, a branch of mathematics of which Christian civilisation was to remain wholly ignorant until the Renaissance.

Archimedes created the concept of a centre of mass, and demonstrated how to discover it in various figures and solids. But he goes a step further, and also proves that fluids will form a sphere around a centre of gravity. His interest here was in the behaviour of the fluid rather than in the nature of gravitational fields, and he did not realise that gravity is a function of mass itself: Archimedes perceived his centre of gravity as being distinct from the fluid. Even so, the notion implies that he conceived of gravity as a force like any other, rather than as some sort of property unique to the surface of the earth. In this, he was again far ahead of his time, and we can once more draw a fairly straight line from Archimedes to Newton, with only Galileo contributing ideas of any real consequence in the middle.

It was Archimedes who first formulated the law of the lever ('magnitudes balance at distances from the fulcrum in inverse ratio to their weight'). He did not invent levers, but he did invent the compound block-and-tackle pulley. Every time we pass by a building site, or step into an elevator, we can still hear him whispering to us. By the same token, crops across the developing world continue to be irrigated by the water screw attributed to him. If he deserves the credit for that, he must have saved more people from starvation than all the NGOs and rock musicians of the world combined.[1]

Perhaps most extraordinary of all, there is reasonable evidence to suggest that Archimedes' interest in force multiplication may have led him to the invention of differential gearing. Cicero records that Archimedes constructed two orreries, which supposedly replicated the rotations of the earth and five known planets around the sun, as well as the rotation of the moon around the earth and the earth's own axial rotation – all on the turn of a single dial. Because such devices would have required intricate differential gears, Cicero's claim was, until quite recently, dismissed out of hand. It was self-evidently ridiculous to imagine that the Ancient Greeks might have designed machinery of such complexity, or were capable of the precision engineering necessary to manufacture it. One might as well believe that they were flying around in aeroplanes.

And then, in 1901, the Antikythera mechanism was retrieved from the seabed of the Aegean. The apparatus had rusted and congealed into lumps, so that at first no one could understand quite what they were looking at. Decades of painstaking analysis and reconstruction followed. Even today, the mechanism may not have surrendered all its secrets, but we now know that it dates from the first century BCE, between one and two hundred years after Archimedes' death, and was an even more sophisticated orrery than Cicero describes. Originally, it had no fewer than thirty-seven

---

1   *He originally created the device to drain* The Syracusia, *the colossal ship he designed for Hieron. However, a type of water screw was being used to irrigate the Hanging Gardens of Babylon from a much earlier date. It is not known whether Archimedes borrowed the idea or came up with it independently.*

intermeshing bronze gearwheels of differing sizes. To put that in perspective, a modern wind-up wristwatch will typically have five or six. Among its many functions, the device could track the nineteen-year-long Metonic cycle (an elaborate lunar calendar), predict solar and lunar eclipses and the future positions of the planets, and fix the dates of important Greek religious festivals. The mechanism may, quite simply, be the single most stunning archaeological find of all time. It appears the Ancient Greeks possessed technology so advanced that it took nearly two thousand years for later civilisations to develop anything remotely comparable.

Unfortunately, as with so many of the other discoveries of the Ancient Greeks, the astronomical knowledge necessary to construct an orrery disappeared under the Christian hegemony.[2] And the world had to wait until the eighteenth century before differential gears were reinvented. They are, of course, now the basis of almost all engines and tools with multiple moving parts: our modern prosperity was created as much as anything by gearwheels. One could push the envelope even further. An orrery is essentially a mechanical calculator, a form of analogue computer. If Archimedes was indeed the first person to construct one, which now seems quite plausible, then he would appear to have a stronger claim to be the originator of computer technology than either Babbage or Pascal.

As if all this were not enough, in a two-part study Archimedes also created the science of hydrostatics. The first volume establishes the fundamental law of buoyancy. ('Any body wholly or partially immersed in a fluid experiences an upthrust equal to, but opposite in sense to, the weight of the fluid displaced.') This is the famous 'eureka' principle, by which Archimedes was able to determine whether Hieron's crown was made from pure gold without damaging it. It seems unlikely that he really jumped out of his bath and ran

---

2   *Formally, at least, the one true Church continued to insist that the earth was the immobile centre of the universe until 1822. The Ancient Greeks knew better: they even managed to calculate the degree of the earth's axial tilt relative to its orbit. Progress is far from inevitable. For roughly two thirds of the Christian era, scientific knowledge was lost to Europe at a faster rate than it was gained.*

naked through the streets, but the rest of the story is probably true. Apparently, Hieron suspected that the goldsmith whom he had commissioned to make a new crown had cheated him. The exact test that Archimedes devised is unknown, but the simplest method would have been as follows: balance the crown on a pair of scales against the same weight in pure gold. Now immerse everything in water. If the gold used to make the crown had been alloyed with a less dense material, then in order to be of equal weight, it must be of slightly greater volume than the pure gold. It will consequently displace a little more water and experience correspondingly more upthrust. Once submerged, it will rise on the scales while the pure gold sinks.

The second part of the treatise on buoyancy has never fired the popular imagination, for reasons that become humiliatingly obvious within the first few lines. It consists of an analysis of 'floating paraboloids of right rotation', and is quite beyond the grasp of this author. It may or may not be about ships. And yet it is this recondite tract, above all his other works, which has come to be regarded as Archimedes' supreme achievement. Among professional mathematicians, it is acknowledged as a volcanic explosion of mathematical genius, of a magnitude that perhaps only Newton and Gauss ever managed to equal. Today, the most prestigious prize in mathematics by some way is the Fields Medal, which is only awarded once every four years. Not for nothing is the medal embossed with the head of Archimedes on its front, and a depiction of his tomb on the reverse.

Finally, a word about Archimedes' war machines, the designs of which have all been lost. We can be fairly confident that he built catapults and ballistae of exceptional effectiveness (the original invention of the catapult is traditionally credited to Dion's ancestor, Dionysius I). Of these, and of some extraordinary other weapons attributed to Archimedes, more anon. However, myths abound and one must tread cautiously. No one, for example, has ever convincingly reproduced the 'burning mirror' or 'death ray' that Archimedes reputedly created to set enemy ships on fire. That particular story is almost certainly apocryphal, however appealing it may be to imagine that he contrived a means to weaponise the sun.

In any event, Archimedes hardly needs to be credited with death rays: the list of his inventions is quite impressive enough without them. But more even than his inventions, it is his mathematics that sing. The nine treatises rank among the milestones of civilisation. Mathematicians still approach them with a mixture of reverence and awe, almost as if they were religious relics. In a way, perhaps they are, because they offer us hope of salvation. Written in an age of great turbulence and savagery, they continue to testify to the god-like potential of the human mind.

III

THE MINOTAUR MYTH

The Minotaur legend is many thousands of years old and probably derives from the rituals of a prehistoric Minoan fertility cult.

The story goes that King Minos of Crete is sent a white bull by Poseidon, as a sign of the sea god's favour. Minos is supposed to sacrifice the animal, but substitutes an ordinary bull instead. When Poseidon finds out, he is infuriated and causes Minos's wife, the priestess Pasiphae, to fall in love with the white bull.

Pasiphae orders the engineer Daedalus to build her a wooden cow, in which she conceals herself to entice the animal to mate with her. She subsequently gives birth to the Minotaur, a monster with the body of a man and the head of a bull. In disgust, King Minos orders Daedalus to construct a labyrinth, in which the Minotaur is imprisoned.

The white bull is taken to Athens for the Panathenaic games, where it kills Minos's son. For this, Minos blames the Athenians. To punish them, he demands that every nine years the Athenians send him seven young men and seven young women. On arrival, the fourteen victims are forced into the labyrinth, to be eaten by the Minotaur.

Eventually, Theseus, the son of the king of Athens, insists on being among those sent to Crete. He is greeted with respect by the Cretans, and Ariadne, Minos's daughter, falls in love with him. She gives him a ball of wool, which he unravels as he enters the labyrinth. Theseus manages to kill the Minotaur and uses the wool to find his way back out. He then flees Crete, taking Ariadne with him, only to abandon her on the island of Naxos.

The myth can be interpreted in numerous ways. For example, it can be seen as a story about the replacement of the ancient Minoan civilisation of Crete by the emerging Classical civilisation of mainland Greece. Or it can be taken as a reassuring illustration of the triumph of intellect over impulse. Or it could be read in the opposite way, as a warning about humankind's fundamental depravity – the half-human monster in the maze being a reminder, as Archimedes puts it, that 'chaos is always prowling just beneath the surface of things'. Make of it what you will.

IV

DION'S MANUSCRIPT

It remains a mystery how Dion's scrolls came into the possession of the early twentieth-century sinologist Sir Edmund Backhouse, who included them (quite possibly by accident) in his extensive gifts to Oxford University. The subsequent demolition of Backhouse's moral and scholarly reputation may explain why the journals lay neglected in the stacks of the Bodleian Library for so long. It is indeed fortuitous that the library's present curator of papyri and palimpsests, Dr Peregrine Weevil, happened across the scrolls while undertaking some light dusting duties, and immediately appreciated the necessity of drawing them to the world's attention.

The present volume represents roughly the first half of the journals. I am indebted to Professor John Yardley of the University of Ottawa for his help in deciphering some of the more problematic passages in Dion's text. The Doric Greek of ancient Syracuse is a complex and frequently ambiguous regional dialect, which in this instance is rendered even more than usually opaque by the author's lamentable style. For the sake of intelligibility, I have taken the liberty of substituting contemporary units of time and distance for the Ancient Greek methods of measurement, although I appreciate this decision is liable to provoke a degree of controversy.

Whether or not Dion is to be accepted as a reliable witness I leave to academic debate. Any readers who wish to enter into a correspondence about the numerous historical difficulties raised by his account may find it more profitable to direct their enquiries to Dr Weevil.

T.R.

EXTRACT FROM
THE BEAST ON THE LOOSE

TO BE PUBLISHED IN 2024

I stood alone in the middle of the road, leaning on a spear. The day was only an hour old. Some fifty feet below me, to my left, the sea lapped the foot of the cliff. To my right, the upper reaches of the cliff continued to rise up for perhaps another forty feet. It was steep on the landward side, but not sheer. Needle could probably have scaled it, but I doubted I could. Certainly not today, not wearing full armour and with my shield slung over my back.

Through the eye slits of the helmet, I patiently watched the column approach, snaking its way along the winding road. It was led by a man on horseback. When he was about fifty yards away, he raised his hand for the column to halt and came on with just two men.

He cautiously drew up some thirty feet ahead of me. He stayed in the saddle, but his two men took up positions on either side and slightly ahead of him. They were both large and wore battle dress, but they were only there as bodyguards. Brick glanced at the spear in my hand, reassuring himself that it wasn't a javelin.

"You must be rather hot in that helmet, General," he said with a friendly smile. "Why don't you take it off?"

"Hello, Hippocrates," I replied, but I didn't take off the helmet.

"So, if you don't mind me asking, Dion, what are you doing here? Are you intending to march with us to Messana? Or did you just lose your way?"

"No. I'm simply returning a favour. Hannibal spared our men after Cannae, so I thought it only civil to offer to spare his. If you want, you and your brother can both go back to him."

Brick chuckled.

"I guessed I might be bumping into you again, Dion, when Catana refused to open its gates to us. So tell me, out of curiosity, what are you intending to do with my twelve thousand men? Are you and your three thousand comrades willing to spare them, too?"

"No. Sorry. I'm afraid I don't greatly care for mercenaries. I'm going to kill all of them."

He grunted in amusement.

"Well, it's a pity you feel like that, Dion. I assume the Gold Shields are waiting for me somewhere up ahead?" He peered up at the cliff and then down at the sea and sighed. "I suppose I'll just have to push my way through you. What a nuisance. But if it's a glorious death you're after, so be it. I regret that the deaths of your family and slaves will not be so glorious, but don't worry, I'll do my best to make them equally memorable, in their own way."

"I doubt that, Hippocrates. You won't be returning to Syracuse."

"I suppose we'll just have to see about that… You know, I really must thank you for turning traitor, Dion. We were rather hoping you would. It makes everything so much simpler. And it seems that all it took was a taste of Roman cunt… I'll have to remember to have a little taste myself, before I cut that child out of your wife's belly." He smiled again. "What? Did you think we didn't know about that? How naïve you are… Anyway, you're an interesting man, General. I've enjoyed our brief acquaintance. Good day to you."

Brick turned his horse about. I stared at his back for a few moments as he trotted away, with his two bodyguards jogging after him. Then I returned to my men, who were waiting around the bend in the road behind me. When I reached them, I silently signalled for the beacon on the clifftop to be lit. I didn't trust myself to speak.